The Complete Escapades of The Scarlet Pimpernel

Volume 2

The Complete Escapades of
The Scarlet Pimpernel
Volume 2

The Elusive Pimpernel

and

Eldorado

Baroness Orczy

LEONAUR

The Complete Escapades of The Scarlet Pimpernel
Volume 2
The Elusive Pimpernel
and
Eldorado
by Baroness Orczy

FIRST EDITION

First published under the titles
The Elusive Pimpernel
and
Eldorado

Leonaur is an imprint of Oakpast Ltd

ISBN: 978-1-78282-732-0 (hardcover)
ISBN: 978-1-78282-733-7 (softcover)

http://www.leonaur.com

Publisher's Notes

The views expressed in this book are not necessarily
those of the publisher.

Contents

The Elusive Pimpernel

Contents

CHAPTER 1

Paris: 1793

There was not even a reaction.

On! ever on! in that wild, surging torrent; sowing the wind of anarchy, of terrorism, of lust of blood and hate, and reaping a hurricane of destruction and of horror.

On! ever on! France, with Paris and all her children still rushes blindly, madly on; defies the powerful coalition,—Austria, England, Spain, Prussia, all joined together to stem the flow of carnage,—defies the Universe and defies God!

Paris this September 1793!—or shall we call it *Vendèmiaire*, Year 1 of the Republic?—call it what we will! Paris! a city of bloodshed, of humanity in its lowest, most degraded aspect. France herself a gigantic self-devouring monster, her fairest cities destroyed, Lyons razed to the ground, Toulon, Marseilles, masses of blackened ruins, her bravest sons turned to lustful brutes or to abject cowards seeking safety at the cost of any humiliation.

That is thy reward, oh mighty, holy Revolution! apotheosis of equality and fraternity! grand rival of decadent Christianity.

Five weeks now since Marat, the bloodthirsty Friend of the People, succumbed beneath the sheath-knife of a virgin patriot, a month since his murderess walked proudly, even enthusiastically, to the guillotine! There has been no reaction—only a great sigh!—Not of content or satisfied lust, but a sigh such as the man-eating tiger might heave after his first taste of long-coveted blood.

A sigh for more!

A king on the scaffold; a queen degraded and abased, awaiting death, which lingers on the threshold of her infamous prison; eight hundred scions of ancient houses that have made the history of France; brave generals, Custine, Blanchelande, Houchard, Beauharnais; worthy patriots, noble-hearted women, misguided enthusiasts, all by the score and by the hundred, up the few wooden steps which lead to the guillotine.

An achievement of truth!

And still that sigh for more!

But for the moment,—a few seconds only,—Paris looked round her mighty self, and thought things over!

The man-eating tiger for the space of a sigh licked his powerful jaws and pondered!

Something new!—something wonderful!

We have had a new Constitution, a new Justice, new Laws, a new Almanack!

What next?

Why, obviously!—How comes it that great, intellectual, aesthetic Paris never thought of such a wonderful thing before?

A new religion!

Christianity is old and obsolete, priests are aristocrats, wealthy oppressors of the People, the Church but another form of wanton tyranny.

Let us by all means have a new religion.

Already something has been done to destroy the old! To destroy! always to destroy! Churches have been ransacked, altars spoliated, tombs desecrated, priests and curates murdered; but that is not enough.

There must be a new religion; and to attain that there must be a new God.

"Man is a born idol-worshipper."

Very well then! let the People have a new religion and a new God.

Stay!—Not a God this time!—for God means Majesty, Power, Kingship! everything in fact which the mighty hand of the people of France has struggled and fought to destroy.

Not a God, but a goddess.

A goddess! an idol! a toy! since even the man-eating tiger must play sometimes.

Paris wanted a new religion, and a new toy, and grave men, ardent patriots, mad enthusiasts, sat in the Assembly of the Convention and seriously discussed the means of providing her with both these things which she asked for.

Chaumette, I think it was, who first solved the difficulty;—Procureur Chaumette, head of the Paris Municipality, he who had ordered that the cart which bore the dethroned queen to the squalid prison of the *Conciergerie* should be led slowly past her own late palace of the Tuileries, and should be stopped there just long enough for her to see and to feel in one grand mental vision all that she had been when she

12

dwelt there, and all that she now was by the will of the People.

Chaumette, as you see, was refined, artistic;—the torture of the fallen queen's heart meant more to him than a blow of the guillotine on her neck.

No wonder, therefore, that it was Procureur Chaumette who first discovered exactly what type of new religion Paris wanted just now.

"Let us have a Goddess of Reason," he said, "typified if you will by the most beautiful woman in Paris. Let us have a feast of the Goddess of Reason, let there be a pyre of all the gew-gaws which for centuries have been flaunted by overbearing priests before the eyes of starving multitudes, let the People rejoice and dance around that funeral pyre, and above it all let the new Goddess tower smiling and triumphant. The Goddess of Reason! the only deity our new and regenerate France shall acknowledge throughout the centuries which are to come!"

Loud applause greeted the impassioned speech.

"A new goddess, by all means!" shouted the grave gentlemen of the National Assembly, "the Goddess of Reason!"

They were all eager that the People should have this toy; something to play with and to tease, round which to dance the mad Carmagnole and sing the ever-recurring "Ça ira."

Something to distract the minds of the populace from the consequences of its own deeds, and the helplessness of its legislators.

Procureur Chaumette enlarged upon his original idea; like a true artist who sees the broad effect of a picture at a glance and then fills in the minute details, he was already busy elaborating his scheme.

"The goddess must be beautiful—not too young—Reason can only go hand in hand with the riper age of second youth—she must be decked out in classical draperies, severe yet suggestive—she must be rouged and painted—for she is a mere idol—easily to be appeased with incense, music and laughter."

He was getting deeply interested in his subject, seeking minutiae of detail, with which to render his theme more and more attractive.

But patience was never the characteristic of the Revolutionary Government of France. The National Assembly soon tired of Chaumette's dithyrambic utterances. Up aloft on the Mountain, Danton was yawning like a gigantic leopard.

Soon Henriot was on his feet. He had a far finer scheme than that of the *Procureur* to place before his colleagues. A grand National *fête*, semi-religious in character, but of the new religion which destroyed

13

and desecrated and never knelt in worship.

Citizen Chaumette's Goddess of Reason by all means—Henriot conceded that the idea was a good one—but the goddess merely as a figure-head; around her a procession of unfrocked and apostate priests, typifying the destruction of ancient hierarchy, mules carrying loads of sacred vessels, the spoils of ten thousand churches of France, and ballet girls in bacchanalian robes, dancing the Carmagnole around the new deity.

Public Prosecutor Foucquier Tinville thought all these schemes very tame. Why should the People of France be led to think that the era of a new religion would mean an era of milk and water, of pageants and of fireworks? Let every man, woman, and child know that this was an era of blood and again of blood.

"Oh!" he exclaimed in passionate accents, "would that all the traitors in France had but one head, that it might be cut off with one blow of the guillotine!"

He approved of the National *fête*, but he desired an apotheosis of the guillotine; he undertook to find ten thousand traitors to be beheaded on one grand and glorious day; ten thousand heads to adorn the Place de la Revolution on a great, never-to-be-forgotten evening, after the guillotine had accomplished this record work.

But Collot d'Herbois would also have his say. Collot lately hailed from the South, with a reputation for ferocity unparalleled throughout the whole of this horrible decade. He would not be outdone by Tinville's bloodthirsty schemes.

He was the inventor of the *noyades*, which had been so successful at Lyons and Marseilles. "Why not give the inhabitants of Paris one of these exhilarating spectacles?" he asked with a coarse, brutal laugh.

Then he explained his invention, of which he was inordinately proud. Some two or three hundred traitors, men, women, and children, tied securely together with ropes in great, human bundles and thrown upon a barge in the middle of the river; the barge with a hole in her bottom! not too large! only sufficient to cause her to sink slowly, very slowly, in sight of the crowd of delighted spectators.

The cries of the women and children, and even of the men, as they felt the waters rising and gradually enveloping them, as they felt themselves powerless even for a fruitless struggle, had proved most exhilarating, so Citizen Collot declared, to the hearts of the true patriots of Lyons.

Thus, the discussion continued.

This was the era when every man had but one desire, that of out-doing others in ferocity and brutality, and but one care, that of saving his own head by threatening that of his neighbour.

The great duel between the Titanic leaders of these turbulent par-ties, the conflict between hot-headed Danton on the one side and cold-blooded Robespierre on the other, had only just begun; the great, all-devouring monsters had dug their claws into one another, but the issue of the combat was still at stake.

Neither of these two giants had taken part in these deliberations anent the new religion and the new goddess. Danton gave signs now and then of the greatest impatience, and muttered something about a new form of tyranny, a new kind of oppression.

On the left, Robespierre in immaculate sea-green coat and care-fully gauffered linen was quietly polishing the nails of his right hand against the palm of his left.

But nothing escaped him of what was going on. His ferocious ego-ism, his unbounded ambition was even now calculating what advan-tages to himself might accrue from this idea of the new religion and of the National *fête*, what personal aggrandisement he could derive therefrom.

The matter outwardly seemed trivial enough, but already his keen and calculating mind had seen various side issues which might tend to place him—Robespierre—on a yet higher and more unassailable pinnacle.

Surrounded by those who hated him, those who envied and those who feared him, he ruled over them all by the strength of his own cold-blooded savagery, by the resistless power of his merciless cruelty.

He cared about nobody but himself, about nothing but his own exaltation; every action of his career, since he gave up his small prac-tice in a quiet provincial town in order to throw himself into the wild vortex of revolutionary politics, every word he ever uttered had but one aim—Himself.

He saw his colleagues and comrades of the old Jacobin Clubs ruth-lessly destroyed around him; friends he had none, and all left him in-different; and now he had hundreds of enemies in every assembly and club in Paris, and these too one by one were being swept up in that wild whirlpool which they themselves had created.

Impassive, serene, always ready with a calm answer, when passion raged most hotly around him, Robespierre, the most ambitious, most self-seeking demagogue of his time, had acquired the reputation of being incorruptible and self-less, an enthusiastic servant of the Republic.

The sea-green Incorruptible!

And thus, whilst others talked and argued, waxed hot over schemes for processions and pageantry, or loudly denounced the whole matter as the work of a traitor, he, of the sea-green coat, sat quietly polishing his nails.

But he had already weighed all these discussions in the balance of his mind, placed them in the crucible of his ambition, and turned them into something that would benefit him and strengthen his position.

Aye! the feast should be brilliant enough! gay or horrible, mad or fearful, but through it all the people of France must be made to feel that there was a guiding hand which ruled the destinies of all, a head which framed the new laws, which consolidated the new religion and established its new goddess; the Goddess of Reason.

Robespierre, her prophet!

Chapter 2

A Retrospect

The room was close and dark, filled with the smoke from a defective chimney.

A tiny *boudoir*, once the dainty sanctum of imperious Marie Antoinette; a faint and ghostly odour, like unto the perfume of spectres, seemed still to cling to the stained walls, and to the torn Gobelin tapestries.

Everywhere lay the impress of a heavy and destroying hand; that of the great and glorious Revolution.

In the mud-soiled corners of the room a few chairs, with brocaded cushions rudely torn, leant broken and desolate against the walls. A small footstool, once gilt-legged and satin-covered, had been overturned and roughly kicked to one side, and there it lay on its back, like some little animal that had been hurt, stretching its broken limbs upwards, pathetic to behold.

From the delicately wrought Buhl table the silver inlay had been harshly stripped out of its bed of shell.

Across the Lunette, painted by Boucher and representing a chaste Diana surrounded by a bevy of nymphs, an uncouth hand had scribbled in charcoal the device of the Revolution; *Liberté, Egalité, Fraternité ou la Mort*; whilst, as if to give a crowning point to the work of

16

destruction and to emphasise its motto, someone had decorated the portrait of Marie Antoinette with a scarlet cap, and drawn a red and ominous line across her neck.

And at the table two men were sitting in close and eager conclave.

Between them a solitary tallow candle, unsnuffed and weirdly flickering, threw fantastic shadows upon the walls, and illumined with fitful and uncertain light the faces of the two men.

How different were these in character!

One, high cheek-boned, with coarse, sensuous lips, and hair elaborately and carefully powdered; the other pale and thin-lipped, with the keen eyes of a ferret and a high intellectual forehead, from which the sleek brown hair was smoothly brushed away.

The first of these men was Robespierre, the ruthless and incorruptible demagogue; the other was Citizen Chauvelin, ex-ambassador of the Revolutionary Government at the English Court.

The hour was late, and the noises from the great, seething city preparing for sleep came to this remote little apartment in the now deserted Palace of the Tuileries, merely as a faint and distant echo.

It was two days after the *Fructidor* Riots. Paul Déroulède and the woman Juliette Marny, both condemned to death, had been literally spirited away out of the cart which was conveying them from the Hall of Justice to the Luxembourg Prison, and news had just been received by the Committee of Public Safety that at Lyons, the Abbé du Mesnil, with the *ci-devant* Chevalier d'Egremont and the latter's wife and family, had effected a miraculous and wholly incomprehensible escape from the Northern Prison.

But this was not all. When Arras fell into the hands of the Revolutionary Army, and a regular cordon was formed round the town, so that not a single royalist traitor might escape, some three score women and children, twelve priests, the old aristocrats Chermeuil, Delleville and Galipaux and many others, managed to pass the barriers and were never recaptured.

Raids were made on the suspected houses; in Paris chiefly where the escaped prisoners might have found refuge, or better still where their helpers and rescuers might still be lurking. Foucquier Tinville, Public Prosecutor, led and conducted these raids, assisted by that bloodthirsty vampire, Merlin. They heard of a house in the Rue de l'Ancienne Comédie where an Englishmen was said to have lodged for two days.

They demanded admittance and were taken to the rooms where

the Englishman had stayed. These were bare and squalid, like hundreds of other rooms in the poorer quarters of Paris. The landlady, toothless and grimy, had not yet tidied up the one where the Englishman had slept; in fact, she did not know he had left for good.

He had paid for his room, a week in advance, and came and went as he liked, she explained to Citizen Tinville. She never bothered about him, as he never took a meal in the house, and he was only there two days. She did not know her lodger was English until the day he left. She thought he was a Frenchman from the South, as he certainly had a peculiar accent when he spoke.

"It was the day of the riots," she continued; "he would go out, and I told him I did not think that the streets would be safe for a foreigner like him; for he always wore such very fine clothes, and I made sure that the starving men and women of Paris would strip them off his back when their tempers were roused. But he only laughed. He gave me a bit of paper and told me that if he did not return I might conclude that he had been killed, and if the Committee of Public Safety asked me questions about me, I was just to show the bit of paper and there would be no further trouble."

She had talked volubly, more than a little terrified at Merlin's scowls, and the attitude of Citizen Tinville, who was known to be very severe if anyone committed any blunders.

But the Citizeness—her name was Brogard and her husband's brother kept an inn in the neighbourhood of Calais—the Citizeness Brogard had a clear conscience. She held a license from the Committee of Public Safety for letting apartments, and she had always given due notice to the Committee of the arrival and departure of her lodgers. The only thing was that if any lodger paid her more than ordinarily well for the accommodation and he so desired it, she would send in the notice conveniently late, and conveniently vaguely worded as to the description, status and nationality of her more liberal patrons.

This had occurred in the case of her recent English visitor.

But she did not explain it quite like that to Citizen Foucquier Tinville or to Citizen Merlin.

However, she was rather frightened, and produced the scrap of paper which the Englishman had left with her, together with the assurance that when she showed it there would be no further trouble.

Tinville took it roughly out of her hand but would not glance at it. He crushed it into a ball and then Merlin snatched it from him with a coarse laugh, smoothed out the creases on his knee and studied it for a moment.

There were two lines of what looked like poetry, written in a language which Merlin did not understand. English, no doubt.

But what was perfectly clear, and easily comprehended by any one, was the little drawing in the corner, done in red ink and representing a small star-shaped flower.

Then Tinville and Merlin both cursed loudly and volubly, and bidding their men follow them, turned away from the house in the Rue de l'Ancienne Comédie and left its toothless landlady on her own doorstep still volubly protesting her patriotism and her desire to serve the government of the Republic.

Tinville and Merlin, however, took the scrap of paper to Citizen Robespierre, who smiled grimly as he in his turn crushed the offensive little document in the palm of his well-washed hands.

Robespierre did not swear. He never wasted either words or oaths, but he slipped the bit of paper inside the double lid of his silver snuff box and then he sent a special messenger to Citizen Chauvelin in the Rue Corneille, bidding him come that same evening after ten o'clock to room No. 16 in the *ci-devant* Palace of the Tuileries.

It was now half-past ten, and Chauvelin and Robespierre sat opposite one another in the ex-*boudoir* of Queen Marie Antoinette, and between them on the table, just below the tallow-candle, was a much creased, exceedingly grimy bit of paper.

It had passed through several unclean hands before Citizen Robespierre's immaculately white fingers had smoothed it out and placed it before the eyes of ex-Ambassador Chauvelin.

The latter, however, was not looking at the paper, he was not even looking at the pale, cruel face before him. He had closed his eyes and for a moment had lost sight of the small dark room, of Robespierre's ruthless gaze, of the mud-stained walls and greasy floor. He was seeing, as in a bright and sudden vision, the brilliantly-lighted salons of the Foreign Office in London, with beautiful Marguerite Blakeney gliding queenlike on the arm of the Prince of Wales.

He heard the flutter of many fans, the *frou-frou* of silk dresses, and above all the din and sound of dance music; he heard an inane laugh and an affected voice repeating the doggerel rhyme that was even now written on that dirty piece of paper which Robespierre had placed before him;

We seek him here, and we seek him there,

Those Frenchies seek him everywhere!
Is he in heaven, is he in hell,
That demmed elusive Pimpernel?

It was a mere flash! One of memory's swiftly effaced pictures, when she shows us for the fraction of a second, indelible pictures from out our past. Chauvelin, in that same second, while his own eyes were closed and Robespierre's fixed upon him, also saw the lonely cliffs of Calais, heard the same voice singing; "God save the King!" the volley of musketry, the despairing cries of Marguerite Blakeney; and once again he felt the keen and bitter pang of complete humiliation and defeat.

CHAPTER 3

Ex-Ambassador Chauvelin

Robespierre had quietly waited the while. He was in no hurry; being a night-bird of very pronounced tastes, he was quite ready to sit here until the small hours of the morning watching Citizen Chauvelin mentally writhing in the throes of recollections of the past few months.

There was nothing that delighted the sea-green Incorruptible quite so much as the aspect of a man struggling with a hopeless situation and feeling a net of intrigue drawing gradually tighter and tighter around him.

Even now, when he saw Chauvelin's smooth forehead wrinkled into an anxious frown, and his thin hand nervously clutched upon the table, Robespierre heaved a pleasurable sigh, leaned back in his chair, and said with an amiable smile;

"You do agree with me, then, Citizen, that the situation has become intolerable?"

Then as Chauvelin did not reply, he continued, speaking more sharply;

"And how terribly galling it all is, when we could have had that man under the guillotine by now, if you had not blundered so terribly last year."

His voice had become hard and trenchant like that knife to which he was so ready to make constant allusion. But Chauvelin still remained silent. There was really nothing that he could say.

"Citizen Chauvelin, how you must hate that man!" exclaimed Robespierre at last.

Then only did Chauvelin break the silence which up to now he had appeared to have forced himself to keep.

"I do!" he said with unmistakable fervour.

"Then why do you not make an effort to retrieve the blunders of last year?" queried Robespierre blandly. "The Republic has been unusually patient and long-suffering with you, Citizen Chauvelin. She has taken your many services and well-known patriotism into consideration. But you know," he added significantly, "that she has no use for worthless tools."

Then as Chauvelin seemed to have relapsed into sullen silence, he continued with his original ill-omened blandness;

"*Ma foi!* Citizen Chauvelin, were I standing in your buckled shoes, I would not lose another hour in trying to avenge mine own humiliation!"

"Have I ever had a chance?" burst out Chauvelin with ill-suppressed vehemence. "What can I do single-handed? Since war has been declared I cannot go to England unless the government will find some official reason for my doing so. There is much grumbling and wrath over here, and when that damned Scarlet Pimpernel League has been at work, when a score or so of valuable prizes have been snatched from under the very knife of the guillotine, then, there is much gnashing of teeth and useless cursings, but nothing serious or definite is done to smother those accursed English flies which come buzzing about our ears."

"Nay! you forget, Citizen Chauvelin," retorted Robespierre, "that we of the Committee of Public Safety are far more helpless than you. You know the language of these people, we don't. You know their manners and customs, their ways of thought, the methods they are likely to employ; we know none of these things. You have seen and spoken to men in England who are members of that damned League. You have seen the man who is its leader. We have not."

He leant forward on the table and looked more searchingly at the thin, pallid face before him.

"If you named that leader to me now, if you described him, we could go to work more easily. You could name him, and you would, Citizen Chauvelin."

"I cannot," retorted Chauvelin doggedly.

"Ah! but I think you could. But there! I do not blame your silence. You would wish to reap the reward of your own victory, to be the instrument of your own revenge. Passions! I think it natural! But in the name of your own safety, Citizen, do not be too greedy with your

21

secret. If the man is known to you, find him again, find him, lure him to France! We want him—the people want him! And if the people do not get what they want, they will turn on those who have withheld their prey."

"I understand, Citizen, that your own safety and that of your government is involved in this renewed attempt to capture the Scarlet Pimpernel," retorted Chauvelin drily.

"And your head, Citizen Chauvelin," concluded Robespierre.

"Nay! I know that well enough, and you may believe me, and you will, Citizen, when I say that I care but little about that. The question is, if I am to lure that man to France what will you and your government do to help me?"

"Everything," replied Robespierre, "provided you have a definite plan and a definite purpose."

"I have both. But I must go to England in, at least, a semi-official capacity. I can do nothing if I am to hide in disguise in out-of-the-way corners."

"That is easily done. There has been some talk with the British authorities anent the security and welfare of peaceful French subjects settled in England. After a good deal of correspondence, they have suggested our sending a semi-official representative over there to look after the interests of our own people commercially and financially. We can easily send you over in that capacity if it would suit your purpose."

"Admirably. I have only need of a cloak. That one will do as well as another."

"Is that all?"

"Not quite. I have several plans in my head, and I must know that I am fully trusted. Above all, I must have power—decisive, absolute, illimitable power."

There was nothing of the weakling about this small, sable-clad man, who looked the redoubtable Jacobin leader straight in the face and brought a firm fist resolutely down upon the table before him. Robespierre paused awhile ere he replied; he was eying the other man keenly, trying to read if behind that earnest, frowning brow there did not lurk some selfish, ulterior motive along with that demand for absolute power.

But Chauvelin did not flinch beneath that gaze which could make every cheek in France blanch with unnamed terror, and after that slight moment of hesitation Robespierre said quietly;

"You shall have the complete power of a military dictator in every town or borough of France which you may visit. The Revolutionary Government shall create you, before you start for England, Supreme Head of all the Sub-Committees of Public Safety. This will mean that in the name of the safety of the Republic every order given by you, of whatsoever nature it might be, must be obeyed implicitly under pain of an arraignment for treason."

Chauvelin sighed a quick, sharp sigh of intense satisfaction, which he did not even attempt to disguise before Robespierre.

"I shall want agents," he said, "or shall we say spies? and, of course, money."

"You shall have both. We keep a very efficient secret service in England and they do a great deal of good over there. There is much dissatisfaction in their Midland counties—you remember the Birmingham riots? They were chiefly the work of our own spies. Then you know Candeille, the actress? She had found her way among some of those circles in London who have what they call liberal tendencies. I believe they are called Whigs. Funny name, isn't it? It means *perruque*, I think. Candeille has given charity performances in aid of our Paris poor, in one or two of these Whig clubs, and incidentally she has been very useful to us."

"A woman is always useful in such cases. I shall seek out the Citizeness Candeille."

"And if she renders you useful assistance, I think I can offer her what should prove a tempting prize. Women are so vain!" he added, contemplating with rapt attention the enamel-like polish on his finger-nails. "There is a vacancy in the Maison Molière. Or—what might prove more attractive still—in connection with the proposed National *fête*, and the new religion for the people, we have not yet chosen a Goddess of Reason. That should appeal to any feminine mind. The impersonation of a goddess, with processions, pageants, and the rest— Great importance and prominence given to one personality—What say you, Citizen? If you really have need of a woman for the furtherance of your plans, you have that at your disposal which may enhance her zeal."

"I thank you, Citizen," rejoined Chauvelin calmly. "I always entertained a hope that someday the Revolutionary Government would call again on my services. I admit that I failed last year. The Englishman is resourceful. He has wits and he is very rich. He would not have succeeded, I think, but for his money—and corruption and bribery are rife in Paris and on our coasts. He slipped through my fingers at the very moment when I thought that I held him most securely. I do admit all that, but I am prepared to redeem my failure of last year, and—there is nothing more to discuss.—I am ready to start."

He looked round for his cloak and hat, and quietly readjusted the set of his neck-tie. But Robespierre detained him awhile longer; that born mountebank, born torturer of the souls of men, had not gloated sufficiently yet on the agony of mind of this fellow-man.

Chauvelin had always been trusted and respected. His services in connection with the foreign affairs of the Revolutionary Government had been invaluable, both before and since the beginning of the European War. At one time he formed part of that merciless decemvirate which—with Robespierre at its head—meant to govern France by laws of bloodshed and of unparalleled ferocity.

But the sea-green Incorruptible had since tired of him, then had endeavoured to push him on one side, for Chauvelin was keen and clever, and, moreover, he possessed all those qualities of selfless patriotism which were so conspicuously lacking in Robespierre.

His failure in bringing that interfering Scarlet Pimpernel to justice and the guillotine had completed Chauvelin's downfall. Though not otherwise molested, he had been left to moulder in obscurity during this past year. He would soon enough have been completely forgotten.

Now he was not only to be given one more chance to regain public favour, but he had demanded powers which in consideration of the aim in view, Robespierre himself could not refuse to grant him. But the Incorruptible, ever envious and jealous, would not allow him to exult too soon.

With characteristic blandness he seemed to be entering into all Chauvelin's schemes, to be helping in every way he could, for there was something at the back of his mind which he meant to say to the ex-ambassador, before the latter took his leave; something which would show him that he was but on trial once again, and which would demonstrate to him with perfect clearness that over him there hovered the all-powerful hand of a master.

"You have but to name the sum you want, Citizen Chauvelin," said the Incorruptible, with an encouraging smile, "the government will not stint you, and you shall not fail for lack of authority or for lack of funds."

"It is pleasant to hear that the government has such uncounted wealth," remarked Chauvelin with dry sarcasm.

"Oh! the last few weeks have been very profitable," retorted Robespierre; "we have confiscated money and jewels from emigrant royalists to the tune of several million *francs*. You remember the traitor Juliette Marny, who escaped to England lately? Well! her mother's jewels and quite a good deal of gold were discovered by one of our most able spies to be under the care of a certain Abbé Foucquet, a *calotin* from Boulogne—devoted to the family, so it seems."

"Yes?" queried Chauvelin indifferently.

"Our men seized the jewels and gold, that is all. We don't know yet what we mean to do with the priest. The fisherfolk of Boulogne like him, and we can lay our hands on him at any time, if we want his old head for the guillotine. But the jewels were worth having. There's a historic necklace worth half a million at least."

"Could I have it?" asked Chauvelin.

Robespierre laughed and shrugged his shoulders.

"You said it belonged to the Marny family," continued the ex-ambassador. "Juliette Marny is in England. I might meet her. I cannot tell what may happen, but I feel that the historic necklace might prove useful. Just as you please," he added with renewed indifference. "It was a thought that flashed through my mind when you spoke—nothing more."

"And to show you how thoroughly the government trusts you, Citizen Chauvelin," replied Robespierre with perfect urbanity, "I will myself direct that the Marny necklace be placed unreservedly in your hands; and a sum of fifty thousand *francs* for your expenses in England. You see," he added blandly, "we give you no excuse for a second failure."

"I need none," retorted Chauvelin drily, as he finally rose from his seat, with a sigh of satisfaction that this interview was ended at last.

But Robespierre too had risen and pushing his chair aside he took a step or two towards Chauvelin. He was a much taller man than the ex-ambassador. Spare and gaunt, he had a very upright bearing, and in the uncertain light of the candle he seemed to tower strangely and weirdly above the other man; the pale hue of his coat, his light-coloured hair, the whiteness of his linen, all helped to give to his appearance at that moment a curious spectral effect.

Chauvelin somehow felt an unpleasant shiver running down his spine as Robespierre, perfectly urbane and gentle in his manner, placed a long, bony hand upon his shoulder.

"Citizen Chauvelin," said the Incorruptible, with some degree of dignified solemnity, "meseems that we very quickly understood one

another this evening. Your own conscience, no doubt, gave you a premonition of what the purport of my summons to you would be. You
say that you always hoped the Revolutionary Government would give
you one great chance to redeem your failure of last year. I, for one,
always intended that you should have that chance, for I saw, perhaps,
just a little deeper into your heart than my colleagues. I saw not only
enthusiasm for the cause of the People of France, not only abhorrence
for the enemy of your country, I saw a purely personal and deadly hate
of an individual man—the unknown and mysterious Englishman who
proved too clever for you last year. And because I believe that hatred
will prove sharper and more far-seeing than selfless patriotism, therefore I urged the Committee of Public Safety to allow you to work out
your own revenge, and thereby to serve your country more effectually
than any other—perhaps more pure-minded patriot would do. You go
to England well-provided with all that is necessary for the success of
your plans, for the accomplishment of your own personal vengeance.
The Revolutionary Government will help you with money, passports,
safe conducts; it places its spies and agents at your disposal. It gives you
practically unlimited power, wherever you may go. It will not enquire
into your motives, nor yet your means, so long as these lead to success. But private vengeance or patriotism, whatever may actuate you,
we here in France demand you deliver into our hands the man who
is known in two countries as the Scarlet Pimpernel! We want him
alive if possible, or dead if it must be so, and we want as many of his
henchmen as will follow him to the guillotine. Get them to France,
and we'll know how to deal with them, and let the whole of Europe
be damned."

He paused for a while, his hand still resting on Chauvelin's shoulder, his pale green eyes holding those of the other man as if in a trance.
But Chauvelin neither stirred nor spoke. His triumph left him quite
calm; his fertile brain was already busy with his plans. There was no
room for fear in his heart, and it was without the slightest tremor that
he waited for the conclusion of Robespierre's oration.

"Perhaps, Citizen Chauvelin," said the latter at last, "you have already guessed what there is left for me to say. But lest there should
remain in your mind one faint glimmer of doubt or of hope, let me
tell you this. The Revolutionary Government gives you this chance
of redeeming your failure, but this one only; if you fail again, your
outraged country will know neither pardon nor mercy. Whether you
return to France or remain in England, whether you travel North,

South, East or West, cross the Oceans, or traverse the Alps, the hand of an avenging People will be upon you. Your second failure will be punished by death, wherever you may be, either by the guillotine, if you are in France, or if you seek refuge elsewhere, then by the hand of an assassin.

"Look to it, Citizen Chauvelin! for there will be no escape this time, not even if the mightiest tyrant on earth tried to protect you, not even if you succeeded in building up an empire and placing yourself upon a throne."

His thin, strident voice echoed weirdly in the small, close *boudoir*. Chauvelin made no reply. There was nothing that he could say. All that Robespierre had put so emphatically before him, he had fully realised, even whilst he was forming his most daring plans.

It was an "either—or" this time, uttered to *him* now. He thought again of Marguerite Blakeney, and the terrible alternative he had put before *her* less than a year ago.

Well! he was prepared to take the risk. He would not fail again. He was going to England under more favourable conditions this time. He knew who the man was, whom he was bidden to lure to France and to death.

And he returned Robespierre's threatening gaze boldly and un-flinchingly; then he prepared to go. He took up his hat and cloak, opened the door and peered for a moment into the dark corridor, wherein, in the far distance, the steps of a solitary sentinel could be faintly heard; he put on his hat, turned to look once more into the room where Robespierre stood quietly watching him, and went his way.

CHAPTER 4

The Richmond Gala

It was perhaps the most brilliant September ever known in England, where the last days of dying summer are nearly always golden and beautiful.

Strange that in this country, where that same season is so peculiarly radiant with a glory all its own, there should be no special expression in the language with which to accurately name it.

So we needs must call it "*fin d'été*"; the ending of the summer; not the absolute end, nor yet the ultimate departure, but the tender lingering of a friend obliged to leave us *anon*, yet who fain would steal a day here and there, a week or so in which to stay with us; who would make that last pathetic farewell of his endure a little while longer still, and brings forth in gorgeous array for our final gaze all that he has which is most luxuriant, most desirable, most worthy of regret.

And in this year of grace 1793, departing summer had lavished the treasures of her palette upon woodland and river banks; had tinged the once crude green of larch and elm with a tender hue of gold, had brushed the oaks with tones of warm russet, and put patches of sienna and crimson on the beech.

In the gardens the roses were still in bloom, not the delicate blush or lemon ones of June, nor yet the pale Banksias and climbers, but the full-blooded red roses of late summer, and deep-coloured apricot ones, with crinkled outside leaves faintly kissed by the frosty dew. In sheltered spots the purple clematis still lingered, whilst the dahlias, brilliant of hue, seemed overbearing in their gorgeous insolence, flaunting their crudely coloured petals against sober backgrounds of mellow leaves, or the dull, mossy tones of ancient, encircling walls.

The Gala had always been held about the end of September. The weather, on the riverside, was most dependable then, and there was always sufficient sunshine as an excuse for bringing out Madam's last new muslin gown, or her pale-coloured quilted petticoat. Then the ground was dry and hard, good alike for walking and for setting up tents and booths. And of these there was of a truth a most goodly array this year; mountebanks and jugglers from every corner of the world, so it seemed, for there was a man with a face as black as my lord's tricorne, and another with such flat yellow cheeks as made one think of batter pudding, and spring aconite, of eggs and other very yellow things.

There was a tent wherein dogs—all sorts of dogs, big, little, black, white or tan—did things which no Christian with respect for his own backbone would have dared to perform, and another where a weird-faced old man made bean-stalks and walking sticks, coins of the realm and lace kerchiefs vanish into thin air.

And as it was nice and hot one could sit out upon the green and listen to the strains of the band, which discoursed sweet music, and watch the young people tread a measure on the sward.

The quality had not yet arrived; for humbler folk had partaken of very early dinner so as to get plenty of fun, and long hours of delight for the sixpenny toll demanded at the gates.

There was so much to see and so much to do; games of bowls on the green, and a beautiful Aunt Sally, there was a skittle alley, and two merry-go-rounds, there were performing monkeys and dancing bears, a woman so fat that three men with arms outstretched could not get round her, and a man so thin that he could put a lady's bracelet round his neck and her garter around his waist.

There were some funny little dwarfs with pinched faces and a knowing manner, and a giant come all the way from Russia—so 'twas said.

The mechanical toys too were a great attraction. You dropped a penny into a little slit in a box and a doll would begin to dance and play the fiddle; and there was the Magic Mill, where for another modest copper a row of tiny figures, wrinkled and old and dressed in the shabbiest of rags, marched in weary procession up a flight of steps into the Mill, only to emerge again the next moment at a further door of this wonderful building looking young and gay, dressed in gorgeous finery and tripping a dance measure as they descended some steps and were finally lost to view.

But what was most wonderful of all and collected the goodliest crowd of gazers and the largest amount of coins, was a miniature representation of what was going on in France even at this very moment.

And you could not help but be convinced of the truth of it all, so cleverly was it done. There was a background of houses and a very red-looking sky. "Too red!" some people said but were immediately quashed by the *dictum* of the wise, that the sky represented a sunset, as anyone who looked could see. Then there were a number of little figures, no taller than your hand, but with little wooden faces and arms and legs, just beautifully made little dolls, and these were dressed in kirtles and breeches—all rags mostly—and little coats and wooden shoes. They were massed together in groups with their arms all turned upwards.

And in the centre of this little stage on an elevated platform there were miniature wooden posts close together, and with a long flat board at right angles at the foot of the posts, and all painted a bright red. At the further end of the boards was a miniature basket, and between the two posts, at the top, was a miniature knife which ran up and down in a groove and was drawn by a miniature pulley. Folk who knew said that this was a model of a guillotine.

And lo and behold! when you dropped a penny into a slot just below the wooden stage, the crowd of little figures started waving their arms up and down, and another little doll would ascend the elevated platform and lie down on the red board at the foot of the wooden posts. Then a figure dressed in brilliant scarlet put out an arm presumably to touch the pulley, and the tiny knife would rattle down on to the poor little reclining doll's neck, and its head would roll off into the basket beyond.

Then there was a loud whirr of wheels, a buzz of internal mechanism, and all the little figures would stop dead with arms outstretched, whilst the beheaded doll rolled off the board and was lost to view, no doubt preparatory to going through the same gruesome pantomime again.

It was very thrilling, and very terrible; a certain air of hushed awe reigned in the booth where this mechanical wonder was displayed.

The booth itself stood in a secluded portion of the grounds, far from the toll gates, and the band stand and the noise of the merry-go-round, and there were great texts, written in red letters on a black ground, pinned all along the walls.

"Please spare a copper for the starving poor of Paris."

A lady, dressed in grey quilted petticoat and pretty grey and black striped paniers, could be seen walking in the booth from time to time, then disappearing through a partition beyond. She would emerge again presently carrying an embroidered reticule, and would wander round among the crowd, holding out the bag by its chain, and repeating in tones of somewhat monotonous appeal; "For the starving poor of Paris, if you please!"

She had fine, dark eyes, rather narrow and tending upwards at the outer corners, which gave her face a not altogether pleasant expression. Still, they *were* fine eyes, and when she went round soliciting alms, most of the men put a hand into their breeches' pocket and dropped a coin into her embroidered reticule.

She said the word "poor" in rather a funny way, rolling the "r" at the end, and she also said "please" as if it were spelt with a long line of "e's," and so it was concluded that she was French and was begging for her poorer sisters. At stated intervals during the day, the mechanical toy was rolled into a corner, and the lady in grey stood up on a platform and sang queer little songs, the words of which nobody could understand.

Il était une bergère et ron et petit pataplon—

But it all left an impression of sadness and of suppressed awe upon the minds and susceptibilities of the worthy Richmond yokels come with their wives or sweethearts to enjoy the fun of the fair, and gladly did everyone emerge out of that melancholy booth into the sunshine, the brightness and the noise.

"Lud! but she do give me the creeps," said Mistress Polly, the pretty barmaid from the Bell Inn, down by the river. "And I must say that I don't see why we English folk should send our hard-earned pennies to those murdering ruffians over the water. Bein' starving so to speak, don't make a murderer a better man if he goes on murdering," she added with undisputable if ungrammatical logic. "Come, let's look at something more cheerful now."

And without waiting for anyone else's assent, she turned towards the more lively portion of the grounds, closely followed by a ruddy-faced, somewhat sheepish-looking youth, who very obviously was her attendant swain.

It was getting on for three o'clock now, and the quality were beginning to arrive. Lord Anthony Dewhurst was already there, chucking every pretty girl under the chin, to the annoyance of her *beau*. Ladies were arriving all the time, and the humbler feminine hearts were constantly set a-flutter at sight of rich brocaded gowns, and the new Charlottes, all crinkled velvet and soft *marabout*, which were so becoming to the pretty faces beneath.

There was incessant and loud talking and chattering, with here and there the shriller tones of a French voice being distinctly noticeable in the din. There were a good many French ladies and gentlemen present, easily recognisable, even in the distance, for their clothes were of more sober hue and of lesser richness than those of their English compeers.

But they were great lords and ladies, nevertheless, dukes and duchesses and countesses, come to England for fear of being murdered by those devils in their own country. Richmond was full of them just now, as they were made right welcome both at the palace and at the magnificent home of Sir Percy and Lady Blakeney.

Ah! here comes Sir Andrew Ffoulkes with his lady! so pretty and dainty does she look, like a little china doll, in her new-fashioned short-waisted gown, her brown hair in soft waves above her smooth forehead, her great, hazel eyes fixed in unaffected admiration on the gallant husband by her side.

"No wonder she dotes on him!" signed pretty Mistress Polly after she had bobbed her curtsy to my lady. "The brave deeds he did for love of her! Rescued her from those murderers over in France and brought her to England safe and sound, having fought no end of them

31

single-handed, so I've heard it said. Have you not, Master Thomas Jezzard?"

And she looked defiantly at her meek-looking cavalier.

"Bah!" replied Master Thomas with quite unusual vehemence in response to the disparaging look in her brown eyes, "'Tis not he who did it all, as you well know, Mistress Polly. Sir Andrew Ffoulkes is a gallant gentleman, you may take your Bible oath on that, but he that fights the murdering frog-eaters single-handed is he whom they call The Scarlet Pimpernel; the bravest gentleman in all the world."

Then, as at mention of the national hero, he thought that he detected in Mistress Polly's eyes an enthusiasm which he could not very well ascribe to his own individuality, he added with some pique;

"But they do say that this same Scarlet Pimpernel is mightily ill-favoured, and that's why no one ever sees him. They say he is fit to scare the crows away and that no Frenchy can look twice at his face, for it's so ugly, and so they let him get out of the country, rather than look at him again."

"Then they do say a mighty lot of nonsense," retorted Mistress Polly, with a shrug of her pretty shoulders, "and if that be so, then why don't you go over to France and join hands with the Scarlet Pimpernel? I'll warrant no Frenchman'll want to look twice at your face."

A chorus of laughter greeted this sally, for the two young people had in the meanwhile been joined by several of their friends, and now formed part of a merry group near the band, some sitting, others standing, but all bent on seeing as much as there was to see in Richmond Gala this day. There was Johnny Cullen, the grocer's apprentice from Twickenham, and Ursula Quekett, the baker's daughter, and several "young 'uns" from the neighbourhood, as well as some older folk.

And all of them enjoyed a joke when they heard one and thought Mistress Polly's retort mightily smart. But then Mistress Polly was possessed of two hundred pounds, all her own, left to her by her grandmother, and on the strength of this extensive fortune had acquired a reputation for beauty and wit not easily accorded to a wench that had been penniless.

But Mistress Polly was also very kind-hearted. She loved to tease Master Jezzard, who was an indefatigable hanger-on at her pretty skirts, and whose easy conquest had rendered her somewhat contemptuous, but at the look of perplexed annoyance and bewildered distress in the lad's face, her better nature soon got the upper hand. She realised that her remark had been unwarrantably spiteful, and wishing to make atonement, she said with a touch of *coquetry* which quickly spread balm over the honest yokel's injured vanity;

"*La!* Master Jezzard, you do seem to make a body say some queer things. But there! you must own 'tis mighty funny about that Scarlet Pimpernel!" she added, appealing to the company in general, just as if Master Jezzard had been disputing the fact. "Why won't he let anyone see who he is? And those who know him won't tell. Now I have it for a fact from my lady's own maid Lucy, that the young lady as is stopping at Lady Blakeney's house has actually spoken to the man. She came over from France, come a fortnight tomorrow; she and the gentleman they call Mossoo Déroulède. They both saw the Scarlet Pimpernel and spoke to him. *He* brought them over from France. Then why won't they say?"

"Say what?" commented Johnny Cullen, the apprentice.

"Who this mysterious Scarlet Pimpernel is."

"Perhaps he isn't," said old Clutterbuck, who was clerk of the vestry at the church of St. John's the Evangelist.

"Yes!" he added sententiously, for he was fond of his own sayings and usually liked to repeat them before he had quite done with them, "that's it, you may be sure. Perhaps he isn't."

"What do you mean, Master Clutterbuck?" asked Ursula Quekett, for she knew the old man liked to explain his wise saws, and as she wanted to marry his son, she indulged him whenever she could. "What do you mean? He isn't what?"

"He isn't. That's all," explained Clutterbuck with vague solemnity.

Then seeing that he had gained the attention of the little party round him, he condescended to come to more logical phraseology.

"I mean, that perhaps we must not ask, 'who *is* this mysterious Scarlet Pimpernel?' but 'who *was* that poor and unfortunate gentleman?'"

"Then you think—" suggested Mistress Polly, who felt unaccountably low-spirited at this oratorical pronouncement.

"I have it for a fact," said Mr. Clutterbuck solemnly, "that he whom they call the Scarlet Pimpernel no longer exists now; that he was collared by the Frenchies, as far back as last fall, and in the language of the poets, has never been heard of no more."

Mr. Clutterbuck was very fond of quoting from the works of certain writers whose names he never mentioned, but who went by the poetical generality of "the poets." Whenever he made use of phrases which he was supposed to derive from these great and unnamed authors, he solemnly and mechanically raised his hat, as a tribute of respect to these giant minds.

"You think that The Scarlet Pimpernel is dead, Mr. Clutterbuck? That those horrible Frenchies murdered him? Surely you don't mean that?" sighed Mistress Polly ruefully.

Mr. Clutterbuck put his hand up to his hat, preparatory no doubt to making another appeal to the mysterious poets but was interrupted in the very act of uttering great thoughts by a loud and prolonged laugh which came echoing from a distant corner of the grounds.

"Lud! but I'd know that laugh anywhere," said Mistress Quekett, whilst all eyes were turned in the direction whence the merry noise had come.

Half a head taller than any of his friends around him, his lazy blue eyes scanning from beneath their drooping lids the motley throng around him, stood Sir Percy Blakeney, the centre of a gaily-dressed little group which seemingly had just crossed the toll-gate.

"A fine specimen of a man, for sure," remarked Johnnie Cullen, the apprentice.

"Aye! you may take your Bible oath on that!" sighed Mistress Polly, who was inclined to be sentimental.

"Speakin' as the poets," pronounced Mr. Clutterbuck sententiously, "inches don't make a man."

"Nor fine clothes neither," added Master Jezzard, who did not approve of Mistress Polly's sentimental sigh.

"There's my lady!" gasped Miss Barbara suddenly, clutching Master Clutterbuck's arm vigorously. "Lud! but she is beautiful today!"

Beautiful indeed, and radiant with youth and happiness, Marguerite Blakeney had just gone through the gates and was walking along the sward towards the band stand. She was dressed in clinging robes of shimmery green texture, the new-fashioned high-waisted effect suiting her graceful figure to perfection. The large Charlotte, made of velvet to match the gown, cast a deep shadow over the upper part of her face, and gave a peculiar softness to the outline of her forehead and cheeks.

Long lace mittens covered her arms and hands and a scarf of diaphanous material edged with dull gold hung loosely around her shoulders.

Yes! she was beautiful! No captious chronicler has ever denied that! and no one who knew her before, and who saw her again on this late summer's afternoon, could fail to mark the additional charm of her magnetic personality. There was a tenderness in her face as she turned her head to and fro, a joy of living in her eyes that was quite irresistibly fascinating.

Just now she was talking animatedly with the young girl who was walking beside her, and laughing merrily the while;

"Nay! we'll find your Paul, never fear! Lud! child, have you forgotten he is in England now, and that there's no fear of his being kidnapped here on the green in broad daylight."

The young girl gave a slight shudder and her child-like face became a shade paler than before. Marguerite took her hand and gave it a kindly pressure. Juliette Marny, but lately come to England, saved from under the very knife of the guillotine, by a timely and daring rescue, could scarcely believe as yet that she and the man she loved were really out of danger.

"There is Monsieur Déroulède," said Marguerite after a slight pause, giving the young girl time to recover herself and pointing to a group of men close by. "He is among friends, as you see."

They made such a pretty picture, these two women, as they stood together for a moment on the green with the brilliant September sun throwing golden reflections and luminous shadows on their slender forms. Marguerite, tall and queen-like in her rich gown, and costly jewels, wearing with glorious pride the invisible crown of happy wifehood; Juliette, slim and girlish, dressed all in white, with a soft, straw hat on her fair curls, and bearing on an otherwise young and child-like face, the hard imprint of the terrible sufferings she had undergone, of the deathly moral battle her tender soul had had to fight.

Soon a group of friends joined them; Paul Déroulède among these, also Sir Andrew and Lady Ffoulkes, and strolling slowly towards them, his hands buried in the pockets of his fine cloth breeches, his broad shoulders set to advantage in a coat of immaculate cut, priceless lace ruffles at neck and wrist, came the inimitable Sir Percy.

CHAPTER 5

Sir Percy and His Lady

To all appearances he had not changed since those early days of matrimony, when his young wife dazzled London society by her wit and by her beauty, and he was one of the many satellites that helped to bring into bold relief the brilliance of her presence, of her sallies and of her smiles.

His friends alone, mayhap—and of these only an intimate few—

had understood that beneath that self-same lazy manner, those shy and awkward ways, that half-inane, half-cynical laugh, there now lurked an undercurrent of tender and passionate happiness.

That Lady Blakeney was in love with her own husband, nobody could fail to see, and in the more frivolous cliques of fashionable London this extraordinary phenomenon had oft been eagerly discussed.

"A monstrous thing, of a truth, for a woman of fashion to adore her own husband!" was the universal pronouncement of the gaily-decked little world that centred around Carlton House and Ranelagh.

Not that Sir Percy Blakeney was unpopular with the fair sex. Far be it from the veracious chronicler's mind even to suggest such a thing. The ladies would have voted any gathering dull if Sir Percy's witty sallies did not ring from end to end of the dancing hall, if his new satin coat and 'broidered waistcoat did not call for comment or admiration.

But that was the frivolous set, to which Lady Blakeney had never belonged.

It was well known that she had always viewed her good-natured husband as the most willing and most natural butt for her caustic wit; she still was fond of aiming a shaft or two at him, and he was still equally ready to let the shaft glance harmlessly against the flawless shield of his own imperturbable good humour, but now, contrary to all precedent, to all usages and customs of London society, Marguerite seldom was seen at routs or at the opera without her husband; she accompanied him to all the races, and even one night—oh horror!—had danced the gavotte with him.

Society shuddered and wondered! tried to put Lady Blakeney's sudden infatuation down to foreign eccentricity, and finally consoled itself with the thought that after all this nonsense could not last, and that she was too clever a woman and he too perfect a gentleman to keep up this abnormal state of things for any length of time.

In the meanwhile, the ladies averred that this matrimonial love was a very one-sided affair. No one could assert that Sir Percy was anything but politely indifferent to his wife's obvious attentions. His lazy eyes never once lighted up when she entered a ball-room, and there were those who knew for a fact that her ladyship spent many lonely days in her beautiful home at Richmond whilst her lord and master absented himself with persistent if unchivalrous regularity.

His presence at the Gala had been a surprise to everyone, for all thought him still away, fishing in Scotland or shooting in Yorkshire, anywhere save close to the apron strings of his doting wife. He himself seemed conscious of the fact that he had not been expected at this end-of-summer *fête*, for as he strolled forward to meet his wife and Juliette Marny and acknowledge with a bow here and a nod there the many greetings from subordinates and friends, there was quite an apologetic air about his good-looking face, and an obvious shyness in his smile.

But Marguerite gave a happy little laugh when she saw him coming towards her.

"Oh, Sir Percy!" she said gaily, "and pray have you seen the show? I vow 'tis the maddest, merriest throng I've seen for many a day. Nay! but for the sighs and shudders of my poor little Juliette, I should be enjoying one of the liveliest days of my life."

She patted Juliette's arm affectionately.

"Do not shame me before Sir Percy," murmured the young girl, casting shy glances at the elegant cavalier before her, vainly trying to find in the indolent, foppish personality of this society butterfly, some trace of the daring man of action, the bold adventurer who had snatched her and her lover from out the very tumbril that bore them both to death.

"I know I ought to be gay," she continued with an attempt at a smile, "I ought to forget everything, save what I owe to—"

Sir Percy's laugh broke in on her half-finished sentence.

"Lud! and to think of all that I ought not to forget!" he said loudly. "Tony here has been clamouring for iced punch this last half-hour, and I promised to find a booth wherein the noble liquid is properly dispensed. Within half an hour from now His Royal Highness will be here. I assure you, Mlle. Juliette, that from that time onwards I have to endure the qualms of the damned, for the heir to Great Britain's throne always contrives to be thirsty when I am satiated, which is Tantalus' torture magnified a thousandfold, or to be satiated when my parched palate most requires solace; in either case I am a most pitiable man."

"In either case you contrive to talk a deal of nonsense, Sir Percy," said Marguerite gaily.

"What else would your ladyship have me do this lazy, hot afternoon?"

"Come and view the booths with me," she said. "I am dying for a sight of the fat woman and the lean man, the pig-faced child, the dwarfs and the giants. There! Monsieur Déroulède," she added, turning to the young Frenchman who was standing close beside her, "take Mlle. Juliette to hear the clavacin players. I vow she is tired of my company."

The gaily-dressed group was breaking up. Juliette and Paul Déroulède were only too ready to stroll off arm-in-arm together, and Sir Andrew Ffoulkes was ever in attendance on his young wife.

For one moment Marguerite caught her husband's eye. No one was within earshot.

"Percy," she said.

"Yes, m'dear."

"When did you return?"

"Early this morning."

"You crossed over from Calais?"

"From Boulogne."

"Why did you not let me know sooner?"

"I could not, dear. I arrived at my lodgings in town, looking a disgusting object—I could not appear before you until I had washed some of the French mud from off my person. Then His Royal Highness demanded my presence. He wanted news of the Duchesse de Verneuil, whom I had the honour of escorting over from France. By the time I had told him all that he wished to hear, there was no chance of finding you at home, and I thought I should see you here."

Marguerite said nothing for a moment, but her foot impatiently tapped the ground, and her fingers were fidgeting with the gold fringe of her scarf. The look of joy, of exquisite happiness, seemed to have suddenly vanished from her face; there was a deep furrow between her brows.

She sighed a short, sharp sigh, and cast a rapid upward glance at her husband.

He was looking down at her, smiling good-naturedly, a trifle sarcastically perhaps, and the frown on her face deepened.

"Percy," she said abruptly.

"Yes, m'dear."

"These anxieties are terrible to bear. You have been twice over to France within the last month, dealing with your life as lightly as if it did not now belong to me. When will you give up these mad adventures, and leave others to fight their own battles and to save their own lives as best they may?"

She had spoken with increased vehemence, although her voice was scarce raised above a whisper. Even in her sudden, passionate anger she was on her guard not to betray his secret. He did not reply immediately but seemed to be studying the beautiful face on which heartbroken anxiety was now distinctly imprinted.

Then he turned and looked at the solitary booth in the distance, across the frontal of which a large placard had been recently affixed, bearing the words;"Come and see the true representation of the guillotine!"

In front of the booth a man dressed in ragged breeches, with Phrygian cap on his head, adorned with a tri-colour cockade, was vigorously beating a drum, shouting volubly the while;

"Come in and see, come in and see! the only realistic presentation of the original guillotine. Hundreds perish in Paris every day! Come and see! Come and see! the perfectly vivid performance of what goes on hourly in Paris at the present moment."

Marguerite had followed the direction of Sir Percy's eyes. She too was looking at the booth, she heard the man's monotonous, raucous cries. She gave a slight shudder and once more looked imploringly at her husband. His face—though outwardly as lazy and calm as before—had a strange set look about the mouth and firm jaw, and his slender hand, the hand of a dandy accustomed to handle cards and dice and to play lightly with the foils, was clutched tightly beneath the folds of the priceless Mechlin frills.

It was but a momentary stiffening of the whole powerful frame, an instant's flash of the ruling passion hidden within that very secretive soul. Then he once more turned towards her, the rigid lines of his face relaxed, he broke into a pleasant laugh, and with the most elaborate and most courtly bow he took her hand in his and raising her fingers to his lips, he gave the answer to her questions:

"When your ladyship has ceased to be the most admired woman in Europe, namely, when I am in my grave."

Chapter 6

For the Poor of Paris

There was no time to say more then. For the laughing, chatting groups of friends had once more closed up round Marguerite and her husband, and she, ever on the alert, gave neither look nor sign that any serious conversation had taken place between Sir Percy and herself.

Whatever she might feel or dread with regard to the foolhardy adventures in which he still persistently embarked, no member of the League ever guarded the secret of his chief more loyally than did

Marguerite Blakeney.

Though her heart overflowed with a passionate pride in her husband, she was clever enough to conceal every emotion save that which Nature had insisted on imprinting in her face, her present radiant happiness and her irresistible love. And thus, before the world she kept up that bantering way with him, which had characterized her earlier matrimonial life, that good-natured, easy contempt which he had so readily accepted in those days, and which their entourage would have missed and would have enquired after, if she had changed her manner towards him too suddenly.

In her heart she knew full well that within Percy Blakeney's soul she had a great and powerful rival; his wild, mad, passionate love of adventure. For it he would sacrifice everything, even his life; she dared not ask herself if he would sacrifice his love.

Twice in a few weeks he had been over to France; every time he went she could not know if she would ever see him again. She could not imagine how the French Committee of Public Safety could so clumsily allow the hated Scarlet Pimpernel to slip through its fingers. But she never attempted either to warn him or to beg him not to go. When he brought Paul Déroulède and Juliette Marny over from France, her heart went out to the two young people in sheer gladness and pride because of *his* precious life, which *he* had risked for them.

She loved Juliette for the dangers Percy had passed, for the anxieties she herself had endured; only today, in the midst of this beautiful sunshine, this joy of the earth, of summer and of the sky, she had suddenly felt a mad, overpowering anxiety, a deadly hatred of the wild adventurous life, which took him so often away from her side. His pleasant, bantering reply precluded her following up the subject, whilst the merry chatter of people round her warned her to keep her words and looks under control.

But she seemed now to feel the want of being alone, and, somehow, that distant booth with its flaring placard, and the crier in the Phrygian cap, exercised a weird fascination over her.

Instinctively she bent her steps thither, and equally instinctively the idle throng of her friends followed her. Sir Percy alone had halted in order to converse with Lord Hastings, who had just arrived.

"Surely, Lady Blakeney, you have no though of patronising that gruesome spectacle?" said Lord Anthony Dewhurst, as Marguerite almost mechanically had paused within a few yards of the solitary booth.

"I don't know," she said, with enforced gaiety, "the place seems to attract me. And I need not look at the spectacle," she added significantly, as she pointed to a roughly-scribbled notice at the entrance of the tent; "In aid of the starving poor of Paris."

"There's a good-looking woman who sings, and a hideous mechanical toy that moves," said one of the young men in the crowd. "It is very dark and close inside the tent. I was lured in there for my sins and was in a mighty hurry to come out again."

"Then it must be my sins that are helping to lure me too at the present moment," said Marguerite lightly. "I pray you all to let me go in there. I want to hear the good-looking woman sing, even if I do not see the hideous toy on the move."

"May I escort you then, Lady Blakeney?" said Lord Tony.

"Nay! I would rather go in alone," she replied a trifle impatiently. "I beg of you not to heed my whim, and to await my return, there, where the music is at its merriest."

It had been bad manners to insist. Marguerite, with a little comprehensive nod to all her friends, left the young cavaliers still protesting and quickly passed beneath the roughly constructed doorway that gave access into the booth.

A man, dressed in theatrical rags and wearing the characteristic scarlet cap, stood immediately within the entrance, and ostentatiously rattled a money box at regular intervals.

"For the starving poor of Paris," he drawled out in nasal monotonous tones the moment he caught sight of Marguerite and of her rich gown. She dropped some gold into the box and then passed on.

The interior of the booth was dark and lonely-looking after the glare of the hot September sun and the noisy crowd that thronged the sward outside. Evidently a performance had just taken place on the elevated platform beyond, for a few yokels seemed to be lingering in a desultory manner as if preparatory to going out.

A few disjointed comments reached Marguerite's ears as she approached, and the small groups parted to allow her to pass. One or two women gaped in astonishment at her beautiful dress, whilst others bobbed a respectful curtsey.

The mechanical toy arrested her attention immediately. She did not find it as gruesome as she expected, only singularly grotesque, with all those wooden little figures in their quaint, arrested action.

She drew nearer to have a better look, and the yokels who had lingered behind, paused, wondering if she would make any remark.

41

"Her ladyship was born in France," murmured one of the men, close to her, "she would know if the thing really looks like that."

"She do seem interested," quoth another in a whisper.

"Lud love us all!" said a buxom wench, who was clinging to the arm of a nervous-looking youth, "I believe they're coming for more money."

On the elevated platform at the further end of the tent, a slim figure had just made its appearance, that of a young woman dressed in peculiarly sombre colours, and with a black lace hood thrown lightly over her head.

Marguerite thought that the face seemed familiar to her, and she also noticed that the woman carried a large embroidered reticule in her bemittened hand.

There was a general exodus the moment she appeared. The Richmond yokels did not like the look of that reticule. They felt that sufficient demand had already been made upon their scant purses, considering the meagreness of the entertainment, and they dreaded being lured to further extravagance.

When Marguerite turned away from the mechanical toy, the last of the little crowd had disappeared, and she was alone in the booth with the woman in the dark kirtle and black lace hood.

"For the poor of Paris, *Madame*," said the latter mechanically, holding out her reticule.

Marguerite was looking at her intently. The face certainly seemed familiar, recalling to her mind the far-off days in Paris, before she married. Some young actress no doubt driven out of France by that terrible turmoil which had caused so much sorrow and so much suffering. The face was pretty, the figure slim and elegant, and the look of obvious sadness in the dark, almond-shaped eyes was calculated to inspire sympathy and pity.

Yet, strangely enough, Lady Blakeney felt repelled and chilled by this sombrely-dressed young person; an instinct, which she could not have explained and which she felt had no justification, warned her that somehow or other, the sadness was not quite genuine, the appeal for the poor not quite heartfelt.

Nevertheless, she took out her purse, and dropping some few sovereigns into the capacious reticule, she said very kindly;

"I hope that you are satisfied with your day's work, *Madame*; I fear me our British country folk hold the strings of their purses somewhat tightly these times."

The woman sighed and shrugged her shoulders.

"Oh, *Madame!*" she said with a tone of great dejection, "one does what one can for one's starving countrymen, but it is very hard to elicit sympathy over here for them, poor dears!"

"You are a Frenchwoman, of course," rejoined Marguerite, who had noted that though the woman spoke English with a very pronounced foreign accent, she had nevertheless expressed herself with wonderful fluency and correctness.

"Just like Lady Blakeney herself," replied the other.

"You know who I am?"

"Who could come to Richmond and not know Lady Blakeney by sight."

"But what made you come to Richmond on this philanthropic errand of yours?"

"I go where I think there is a chance of earning a little money for the cause which I have at heart," replied the Frenchwoman with the same gentle simplicity, the same tone of mournful dejection.

What she said was undoubtedly noble and selfless. Lady Blakeney felt in her heart that her keenest sympathy should have gone out to this young woman—pretty, dainty, hardly more than a girl—who seemed to be devoting her young life in a purely philanthropic and unselfish cause. And yet in spite of herself, Marguerite seemed unable to shake off that curious sense of mistrust which had assailed her from the first, nor that feeling of unreality and staginess with which the Frenchwoman's attitude had originally struck her.

Yet she tried to be kind and to be cordial, tried to hide that coldness in her manner which she felt was unjustified.

"It is all very praiseworthy on your part, *Madame,*" she said somewhat lamely. "*Madame*—?" she added interrogatively.

"My name is Candeille—Désirée Candeille," replied the Frenchwoman.

"Candeille?" exclaimed Marguerite with sudden alacrity, "Candeille—surely—"

"Yes—of the Variétés."

"Ah! then I know why your face from the first seemed familiar to me," said Marguerite, this time with unaffected cordiality. "I must have applauded you many a time in the olden days. I am an ex-colleague, you know. My name was St. Just before I married, and I was of the Maison Molière."

"I knew that," said Désirée Candeille, "and half hoped that you

43

would remember me."

"Nay! who could forget Demoiselle Candeille, the most popular star in the theatrical firmament?"

"Oh! that was so long ago."

"Only four years."

"A fallen star is soon lost out of sight."

"Why fallen?"

"It was a choice for me between exile from France and the guillotine," rejoined Candeille simply.

"Surely not?" queried Marguerite with a touch of genuine sympathy. With characteristic impulsiveness, she had now cast aside her former misgivings; she had conquered her mistrust, at any rate had relegated it to the background of her mind. This woman was a colleague; she had suffered and was in distress; she had every claim, therefore, on a compatriot's help and friendship. She stretched out her hand and took Désirée Candeille's in her own; she forced herself to feel nothing but admiration for this young woman, whose whole attitude spoke of sorrows nobly borne, of misfortunes proudly endured.

"I don't know why I should sadden you with my story," rejoined Désirée Candeille after a slight pause, during which she seemed to be waging war against her own emotion. "It is not a very interesting one. Hundreds have suffered as I did. I had enemies in Paris. God knows how that happened. I had never harmed anyone, but someone must have hated me and must have wished me ill. Evil is so easily wrought in France these days. A denunciation—a perquisition—an accusation—then the flight from Paris—the forged passports—the disguise—the bribe—the hardships—the squalid hiding places—Oh! I have gone through it all—tasted every kind of humiliation—endured every kind of insult—Remember! that I was not a noble aristocrat—a duchess or an impoverished countess—" she added with marked bitterness, "or perhaps the English cavaliers whom the popular voice has called the League of the Scarlet Pimpernel would have taken some interest in me. I was only a poor actress and had to find my way out of France alone, or else perish on the guillotine."

"I am so sorry!" said Marguerite simply.

"Tell me how you got on, once you were in England," she continued after a while, seeing that Désirée Candeille seemed absorbed in thought.

"I had a few engagements at first," replied the Frenchwoman. "I played at Sadler's Wells and with Mrs. Jordan at Covent Garden, but the Aliens' Bill put an end to my chances of livelihood. No manager cared to give me a part, and so—"

"And so?"

"Oh! I had a few jewels and I sold them—A little money and I live on that—But when I played at Covent Garden I contrived to send part of my salary over to some of the poorer clubs of Paris. My heart aches for those that are starving—Poor wretches, they are misguided and misled by self-seeking demagogues—It hurts me to feel that I can do nothing more to help them—and eases my self-respect if, by singing at public fairs, I can still send a few *francs* to those who are poorer than myself."

She had spoken with ever-increasing passion and vehemence. Marguerite, with eyes fixed into vacancy, seeing neither the speaker nor her surroundings, seeing only visions of those same poor wreckages of humanity, who had been goaded into thirst for blood, when their shrunken bodies should have been clamouring for healthy food,— Marguerite thus absorbed, had totally forgotten her earlier prejudices and now completely failed to note all that was unreal, stagy, theatrical, in the oratorical declamations of the ex-actress from the Variétés.

Pre-eminently true and loyal herself in spite of the many deceptions and treacheries which she had witnessed in her life, she never looked for falsehood or for cant in others. Even now she only saw before her a woman who had been wrongfully persecuted, who had suffered and had forgiven those who had caused her to suffer. She bitterly accused herself for her original mistrust of this noble-hearted, unselfish woman, who was content to tramp around in an alien country, bartering her talents for a few coins, in order that some of those, who were the originators of her sorrows, might have bread to eat and a bed in which to sleep.

"*Mademoiselle*," she said warmly, "truly you shame me, who am also French-born, with the many sacrifices you so nobly make for those who should have first claim on my own sympathy. Believe me, if I have not done as much as duty demanded of me in the cause of my starving compatriots, it has not been for lack of good-will. Is there any way now," she added eagerly, "in which I can help you? Putting aside the question of money, wherein I pray you to command my assistance, what can I do to be of useful service to you?"

"You are very kind, Lady Blakeney—" said the other hesitatingly.

"Well? What is it? I see there is something in your mind—"

"It is perhaps difficult to express—but people say I have a good

45

voice—I sing some French ditties—they are a novelty in England, I think—If I could sing them in fashionable salons—I might perhaps—"

"Nay! you shall sing in fashionable salons," exclaimed Marguerite eagerly, "you shall become the fashion, and I'll swear the Prince of Wales himself shall bid you sing at Carlton House—and you shall name your own fee, *Mademoiselle*—and London society shall vie with the *élite* of Bath, as to which shall lure you to its most frequented routs—There! there! you shall make a fortune for the Paris poor—and to prove to you that I mean every word I say, you shall begin your triumphant career in my own *salon* tomorrow night. His Royal Highness will be present. You shall sing your most engaging songs—and for your fee you must accept a hundred guineas, which you shall send to the poorest workman's club in Paris in the name of Sir Percy and Lady Blakeney."

"I thank your ladyship, but—"

"You'll not refuse?"

"I'll accept gladly—but—you will understand—I am not very old," said Candeille quaintly, "I—I am only an actress—but if a young actress is unprotected—then—"

"I understand," replied Marguerite gently, "that you are far too pretty to frequent the world all alone, and that you have a mother, a sister or a friend—which?—whom you would wish to escort you tomorrow. Is that it?"

"Nay," rejoined the actress, with marked bitterness, "I have neither mother, nor sister, but our Revolutionary Government, with tardy compassion for those it has so relentlessly driven out of France, has deputed a representative of theirs in England to look after the interests of French subjects over here!"

"Yes?"

"They have realised over in Paris that my life here has been devoted to the welfare of the poor people of France. The representative whom the government has sent to England is specially interested in me and in my work. He is a stand-by for me in case of trouble—in case of insults—A woman alone is oft subject to those, even at the hands of so-called gentlemen—and the official representative of my own country becomes in such cases my most natural protector."

"I understand."

"You will receive him?"

"Certainly."

"Then may I present him to your ladyship?"

"Whenever you like."

"Now, and it please you."

"Now?"

"Yes. Here he comes, at your ladyship's service."

Désirée Candeille's almond-shaped eyes were fixed upon a distant part of the tent, behind Lady Blakeney in the direction of the main entrance to the booth. There was a slight pause after she had spoken and then Marguerite slowly turned in order to see who this official representative of France was, whom at the young actress' request she had just agreed to receive in her house. In the doorway of the tent, framed by its gaudy draperies, and with the streaming sunshine as a brilliant background behind him, stood the sable-clad figure of Chauvelin.

Chapter 7

Premonition

Marguerite neither moved nor spoke. She felt two pairs of eyes fixed upon her, and with all the strength of will at her command she forced the very blood in her veins not to quit her cheeks, forced her eyelids not to betray by a single quiver the icy pang of a deadly premonition which at sight of Chauvelin seemed to have chilled her entire soul.

There he stood before her, dressed in his usual sombre garments, a look almost of humility in those keen grey eyes of his, which a year ago on the cliffs of Calais had peered down at her with such relentless hate.

Strange that at this moment she should have felt an instinct of fear. What cause had she to throw more than a pitiful glance at the man who had tried so cruelly to wrong her, and who had so signally failed?

Having bowed very low and very respectfully, Chauvelin advanced towards her, with all the airs of a disgraced courtier craving audience from his queen.

As he approached she instinctively drew back.

"Would you prefer not to speak to me, Lady Blakeney?" he said humbly.

She could scarcely believe her ears or trust her eyes. It seemed impossible that a man could have so changed in a few months. He even looked shorter than last year, more shrunken within himself. His hair, which he wore free from powder, was perceptibly tinged with grey.

"Shall I withdraw?" he added after a pause, seeing that Marguerite made no movement to return his salutation.

"It would be best, perhaps," she replied coldly. "You and I, Monsieur Chauvelin, have so little to say to one another."

"Very little indeed," he rejoined quietly; "the triumphant and happy have ever very little to say to the humiliated and the defeated. But I had hoped that Lady Blakeney in the midst of her victory would have spared one thought of pity and one of pardon."

"I did not know that you had need of either from me, *Monsieur.*"

"Pity perhaps not, but forgiveness certainly."

"You have that, if you so desire it."

"Since I failed, you might try to forget."

"That is beyond my power. But believe me, I have ceased to think of the infinite wrong which you tried to do to me."

"But I failed," he insisted, "and I meant no harm to *you.*"

"To those I care for, Monsieur Chauvelin."

"I had to serve my country as best I could. I meant no harm to your brother. He is safe in England now. And the Scarlet Pimpernel was nothing to you."

She tried to read his face, tried to discover in those inscrutable eyes of his, some hidden meaning to his words. Instinct had warned her of course that this man could be nothing but an enemy, always and at all times. But he seemed so broken, so abject now, that contempt for his dejected attitude, and for the defeat which had been inflicted on him, chased the last remnant of fear from her heart.

"I did not even succeed in harming that enigmatical personage," continued Chauvelin with the same self-abasement. "Sir Percy Blakeney, you remember, threw himself across my plans, quite innocently of course. I failed where you succeeded. Luck has deserted me. Our government offered me a humble post, away from France. I look after the interests of French subjects settled in England. My days of power are over. My failure is complete. I do not complain, for I failed in a combat of wits—but I failed—I failed—I failed—I am almost a fugitive and I am quite disgraced. That is my present history, Lady Blakeney," he concluded, taking once more a step towards her, "and you will understand that it would be a solace if you extended your hand to me just once more, and let me feel that although you would never willingly look upon my face again, you have enough womanly tenderness in you to force your heart to forgiveness and mayhap to pity."

Marguerite hesitated. He held out his hand and her warm, impulsive nature prompted her to be kind. But instinct would not be gainsaid; a curious instinct to which she refused to respond. What had she to fear from this miserable and cringing little worm who had not even in him the pride of defeat? What harm could he do to her, or to those whom she loved? Her brother was in England! Her husband! Bah! not the enmity of the entire world could make her fear for *him!*

Nay! That instinct, which caused her to draw away from Chauvelin, as she would from a venomous asp, was certainly not fear. It was hate! She hated this man! Hated him for all that she had suffered because of him; for that terrible night on the cliffs of Calais! The peril to her husband who had become so infinitely dear! The humiliations and self-reproaches which he had endured.

Yes! it was hate! and hate was of all emotions the one she most despised.

Hate? Does one hate a slimy but harmless toad or a stinging fly? It seemed ridiculous, contemptible and pitiable to think of hate in connection with the melancholy figure of this discomfited intriguer, this fallen leader of revolutionary France.

He was holding out his hand to her. If she placed even the tips of her fingers upon it, she would be making the compact of mercy and forgiveness which he was asking of her. The woman Désirée Candeille roused within her the last lingering vestige of her slumbering wrath. False, theatrical and stagy—as Marguerite had originally suspected—she appeared to have been in league with Chauvelin to bring about this undesirable meeting.

Lady Blakeney turned from one to another, trying to conceal her contempt beneath a mask of passionless indifference. Candeille was standing close by, looking obviously distressed and not a little puzzled. An instant's reflection was sufficient to convince Marguerite that the whilom actress of the Variétés Theatre was obviously ignorant of the events to which Chauvelin had been alluding; she was, therefore, of no serious consequence, a mere tool, mayhap, in the ex-ambassador's hands. At the present moment she looked like a silly child who does not understand the conversation of the "grown-ups."

Marguerite had promised her help and protection, had invited her to her house, and offered her a munificent gift in aid of a deserving cause. She was too proud to go back now on that promise, to rescind the contract because of an unexplainable fear. With regard to Chauvelin, the matter stood differently; she had made him no direct offer of hospitality; she had agreed to receive in her house the official chaperone of an unprotected girl, but she was not called upon to show cordiality to her own and her husband's most deadly enemy.

She was ready to dismiss him out of her life with a cursory word of pardon and a half-expressed promise of oblivion; on that understanding and that only she was ready to let her hand rest for the space of one second in his.

She had looked upon her fallen enemy, seen his discomfiture and his humiliation! Very well! Now let him pass out of her life, all the more easily, since the last vision of him would be one of such utter abjection as would even be unworthy of hate.

All these thoughts, feelings and struggles passed through her mind with great rapidity. Her hesitation had lasted less than five seconds; Chauvelin still wore the look of doubting entreaty with which he had first begged permission to take her hand in his. With an impulsive toss of the head, she had turned straight towards him, ready with the phrase with which she meant to dismiss him from her sight now and forever, when suddenly a well-known laugh broke in upon her ear, and a lazy, drawly voice said pleasantly;

"*La!* I vow the air is fit to poison you! Your Royal Highness, I entreat, let us turn our backs upon these gates of Inferno, where lost souls would feel more at home than doth your humble servant."

The next moment His Royal Highness the Prince of Wales had entered the tent, closely followed by Sir Percy Blakeney.

CHAPTER 8

The Invitation

It was in truth a strange situation, this chance meeting between Percy Blakeney and ex-Ambassador Chauvelin.

Marguerite looked up at her husband. She saw him shrug his broad shoulders as he first caught sight of Chauvelin, and glance down in his usual lazy, good-humoured manner at the shrunken figure of the silent Frenchman. The words she meant to say never crossed her lips; she was waiting to hear what the two men would say to one another.

The instinct of the *grande dame* in her, the fashionable lady accustomed to the exigencies of society, just gave her sufficient presence of mind to make the requisite low curtsey before His Royal Highness. But the prince, forgetting his accustomed gallantry, was also absorbed in the little scene before him. He, too, was looking from the sable-clad figure of Chauvelin to that of gorgeously arrayed Sir Percy. He, too, like Marguerite, was wondering what was passing behind the low, smooth forehead of that inimitable dandy, what behind the inscrutably good-humoured expression of those sleepy eyes.

Of the five persons thus present in the dark and stuffy booth, certainly Sir Percy Blakeney seemed the least perturbed. He had paused just long enough to allow Chauvelin to become fully conscious of a feeling of supreme irritation and annoyance, then he strolled up to the ex-ambassador, with hand outstretched and the most engaging of smiles.

"Ha!" he said, with his usual half-shy, half-pleasant-tempered smile, "my engaging friend from France! I hope, sir, that our demmed climate doth find you well and hearty today."

The cheerful voice seemed to ease the tension. Marguerite sighed a sigh of relief. After all, what was more natural than that Percy with his amazing fund of pleasant irresponsibility should thus greet the man who had once vowed to bring him to the guillotine? Chauvelin, himself, accustomed by now to the audacious coolness of his enemy, was scarcely taken by surprise. He bowed low to His Highness, who, vastly amused at Blakeney's sally, was inclined to be gracious to everyone, even though the personality of Chauvelin as a well-known leader of the regicide government was inherently distasteful to him. But the prince saw in the wizened little figure before him an obvious butt for his friend Blakeney's impertinent shafts, and although historians have been unable to assert positively whether or no George Prince of Wales knew aught of Sir Percy's dual life, yet there is no doubt that he was always ready to enjoy a situation which brought about the discomfiture of any of the Scarlet Pimpernel's avowed enemies.

"I, too, have not met M. Chauvelin for many a long month," said His Royal Highness with an obvious show of irony. "And I mistake not, sir, you left my father's court somewhat abruptly last year."

"Nay, your Royal Highness," said Percy gaily, "my friend Monsieur—er—Chaubertin and I had serious business to discuss, which could only be dealt with in France—Am I not right, *Monsieur?*"

"Quite right, Sir Percy," replied Chauvelin curtly.

"We had to discuss abominable soup in Calais, had we not?" continued Blakeney in the same tone of easy banter, "and wine that I vowed was vinegar. Monsieur—er—Chaubertin—no, no, I beg pardon—Chauvelin—Monsieur Chauvelin and I quite agreed upon that point. The only matter on which we were not quite at one was the question of snuff."

"Snuff?" laughed His Royal Highness, who seemed vastly amused.

"Yes, your Royal Highness—snuff—Monsieur Chauvelin here

had—if I may be allowed to say so—so vitiated a taste in snuff that he prefers it with an admixture of pepper—Is that not so, Monsieur—er—Chaubertin?"

"Chauvelin, Sir Percy," remarked the ex-ambassador drily.

He was determined not to lose his temper and looked urbane and pleasant, whilst his impudent enemy was enjoying a joke at his expense. Marguerite the while had not taken her eyes off the keen, shrewd face. Whilst the three men talked, she seemed suddenly to have lost her sense of the reality of things. The present situation appeared to her strangely familiar, like a dream which she had dreamt ofttimes before.

Suddenly it became absolutely clear to her that the whole scene had been arranged and planned; the booth with its flaring placard, Demoiselle Candeille soliciting her patronage, her invitation to the young actress, Chauvelin's sudden appearance, all, all had been concocted and arranged, not here, not in England at all, but out there in Paris, in some dark gathering of blood-thirsty ruffians, who had invented a final trap for the destruction of the bold adventurer, who went by the name of the Scarlet Pimpernel.

And she also was only a puppet, enacting a part which had been written for her; she had acted just as *they* had anticipated, had spoken the very words they had meant her to say; and when she looked at Percy, he seemed supremely ignorant of it all, unconscious of this trap of the existence of which everyone here present was aware, save indeed himself. She would have fought against this weird feeling of obsession, of being a mechanical toy wound up to do certain things, but this she could not do; her will appeared paralysed; her tongue even refused her service.

As in a dream she heard His Royal Highness ask for the name of the young actress who was soliciting alms for the poor of Paris.

That also had been prearranged. His Royal Highness for the moment was also a puppet, made to dance, to speak and to act as Chauvelin and his colleagues over in France had decided that he should. Quite mechanically Marguerite introduced Demoiselle Candeille to the prince's gracious notice.

"If your Highness will permit," she said, "Mademoiselle Candeille will give us some of her charming old French songs at my rout to-morrow."

"By all means! By all means!" said the prince. "I used to know some in my childhood days. Charming and poetic—I know—I know—We

52

shall be delighted to hear *Mademoiselle* sing, eh, Blakeney?" he added good-humouredly, "and for your rout tomorrow will you not also invite M. Chauvelin?"

"Nay! but that goes without saying, your Royal Highness," responded Sir Percy, with hospitable alacrity and a most approved bow directed at his arch-enemy. "We shall expect M. Chauvelin. He and I have not met for so long, and he shall be made right welcome at Blakeney Manor."

CHAPTER 9

Demoiselle Candeille

Her origin was of the humblest, for her mother—so it was said—had been kitchen-maid in the household of the Duc de Marny, but Désirée had received some kind of education, and though she began life as a dresser in one of the minor theatres of Paris, she became ultimately one of its most popular stars.

She was small and dark, dainty in her manner and ways, and with a graceful little figure, peculiarly supple and sinuous. Her humble origin certainly did not betray itself in her hands and feet, which were exquisite in shape and Lilliputian in size.

Her hair was soft and glossy, always free from powder, and cunningly arranged so as to slightly overshadow the upper part of her face.

The chin was small and round, the mouth extraordinarily red, the neck slender and long. But she was not pretty; so, said all the women. Her skin was rather coarse in texture and darkish in colour, her eyes were narrow and slightly turned upwards at the corners; no! she was distinctly not pretty.

Yet she pleased the men! Perhaps because she was so artlessly determined to please them. The women said that Demoiselle Candeille never left a man alone until she had succeeded in captivating his fancy if only for five minutes; an internal in a dance—the time to cross a muddy road.

But for five minutes she was determined to hold any man's complete attention, and to exact his admiration. And she nearly always succeeded.

Therefore, the women hated her. The men were amused. It is extremely pleasant to have one's admiration compelled, one's attention so determinedly sought after.

And Candeille could be extremely amusing, and as Madelon in Molière's *Les Précieuses* was quite inimitable.

This, however, was in the olden days, just before Paris went quite mad, before the Reign of Terror had set in, and *ci-devant* Louis the King had been executed.

Candeille had taken it into her frolicsome little head that she would like to go to London. The idea was of course in the nature of an experiment. Those dull English people over the water knew so little of what good acting really meant. Tragedy? Well! *passons!* Their heavy, large-boned actresses might manage one or two big scenes where a commanding presence and a powerful voice would not come amiss, and where prominent teeth would pass unnoticed in the agony of a dramatic climax.

But Comedy!

Ah! ça non, par example! Demoiselle Candeille had seen several English gentlemen and ladies in those same olden days at the Tuileries, but she really could not imagine any of them enacting the piquant scenes of Molière or Beaumarchais.

Demoiselle Candeille thought of every English-born individual as having very large teeth. Now large teeth do not lend themselves to well-spoken comedy scenes, to smiles, or to double *entendre*.

Her own teeth were exceptionally small and white, and very sharp, like those of a kitten.

Yes! Demoiselle Candeille thought it would be extremely interesting to go to London and to show to a nation of shopkeepers how daintily one can be amused in a theatre.

Permission to depart from Paris was easy to obtain. In fact, the fair lady had never really found it difficult to obtain anything she very much wanted.

In this case she had plenty of friends in high places. Marat was still alive and a great lover of the theatre. Tallien was a personal admirer of hers; Deputy Dupont would do anything she asked.

She wanted to act in London, at a theatre called Drury Lane. She wanted to play Molière in England in French, and had already spoken with several of her colleagues, who were ready to join her. They would give public representations in aid of the starving population of France; there were plenty of Socialistic clubs in London quite Jacobin and Revolutionary in tendency; their members would give her full support.

She would be serving her country and her countrymen and incidentally see something of the world and amuse herself. She was bored in Paris.

Then she thought of Marguerite St. Just, once of the Maison Molière, who had captivated an English milord of enormous wealth. Demoiselle Candeille had never been of the Maison Molière; she had been the leading star of one of the minor—yet much-frequented—theatres of Paris, but she felt herself quite able and ready to captivate some other unattached *milor*, who would load her with English money and incidentally bestow an English name upon her.

So, she went to London.

The experiment, however, had not proved an unmitigated success. At first, she and her company did obtain a few engagements at one or two of the minor theatres, to give representations of some of the French classical comedies in the original language.

But these never quite became the fashion. The feeling against France and all her doings was far too keen in that very set, which Demoiselle Candeille had desired to captivate with her talents, to allow of the English *jeunesse dorée* to flock and see Molière played in French, by a French troupe, whilst Candeille's own compatriots resident in England had given her but scant support.

One section of these—the aristocrats and *émigrés*—looked upon the actress who was a friend of all the Jacobins in Paris as nothing better than *canaille*. They sedulously ignored her presence in this country and snubbed her whenever they had an opportunity.

The other section—chiefly consisting of agents and spies of the Revolutionary Government—she would gladly have ignored. They had at first made a constant demand on her purse, her talents and her time; then she grew tired of them and felt more and more chary of being identified with a set which was in such ill-odour with that very same *jeunesse dorée* whom Candeille had desired to please.

In her own country she was and always had been a good republican; Marat had given her her first start in life by his violent praises of her talent in his widely-circulated paper; she had been associated in Paris with the whole coterie of artists and actors, every one of them republican to a man. But in London, although one might be snubbed by the *émigrés* and aristocrats, it did not do to be mixed up with the *sans-culotte* journalists and pamphleteers who haunted the Socialistic clubs of the English capital, and who were the prime organisers of all those seditious gatherings and treasonable unions that caused Mr. Pitt and his colleagues so much trouble and anxiety.

One by one, Désirée Candeille's comrades, male and female, who had accompanied her to England, returned to their own country.

When war was declared, some of them were actually sent back under the provisions of the Aliens Bill.

But Désirée had stayed on.

Her old friends in Paris had managed to advise her that she would not be very welcome there just now. The *sans-culotte* journalists of England, the agents and spies of the Revolutionary Government, had taken their revenge of the frequent snubs inflicted upon them by the young actress, and in those days the fact of being unwelcome in France was apt to have a more lurid and more dangerous significant.

Candeille did not dare return; at any rate not for the present.

She trusted to her own powers of intrigue, and her well-known fascinations, to re-conquer the friendship of the Jacobin clique, and she once more turned her attention to the affiliated Socialistic clubs of England. But between the proverbial two stools, Demoiselle Candeille soon came to the ground. Her machinations became known in official quarters, her connection with all the seditious clubs of London was soon bruited abroad, and one evening Désirée found herself confronted with a document addressed to her; "From the Office of His Majesty's Privy Seal," wherein it was set forth that, pursuant to the statute 33 George III. cap. 5, she, Désirée Candeille, a French subject now resident in England, was required to leave this kingdom by order of His Majesty within seven days, and that in the event of the said Désirée Candeille refusing to comply with this order, she would be liable to commitment, brought to trial and sentenced to imprisonment for a month, and afterwards to removal within a limited time under pain of transportation for life.

This meant that Demoiselle Candeille had exactly seven days in which to make complete her reconciliation with her former friends who now ruled Paris and France with a relentless and perpetually bloodstained hand. No wonder that during the night which followed the receipt of this momentous document, Demoiselle Candeille suffered gravely from insomnia.

She dared not go back to France; she was ordered out of England! What was to become of her?

This was just three days before the eventful afternoon of the Richmond Gala, and twenty-four hours after ex-Ambassador Chauvelin had landed in England. Candeille and Chauvelin had since then met at the "*Cercle des Jacobins Français*" in Soho Street, and now fair Désirée found herself in lodgings in Richmond, the evening of the day following the Gala, feeling that her luck had not altogether deserted her.

One conversation with Citizen Chauvelin had brought the fickle jade back to Demoiselle Candeilles' service. Nay, more, the young actress saw before her visions of intrigue, of dramatic situations, of pleasant little bits of revenge;—all of which was meat and drink and air to breathe for Mademoiselle Désirée.

She was to sing in one of the most fashionable *salons* in England; that was very pleasant. The Prince of Wales would hear and see her! that opened out a *vista* of delightful possibilities! And all she had to do was to act a part dictated to her by Citizen Chauvelin, to behave as he directed, to move in the way he wished! Well! that was easy enough, since the part which she would have to play was one peculiarly suited to her talents.

She looked at herself critically in the glass. Her maid Fanchon—a little French waif picked up in the slums of Soho—helped to readjust a stray curl which had rebelled against the comb.

"Now for the necklace, *Mademoiselle*," said Fanchon with suppressed excitement.

It had just arrived by messenger; a large morocco case, which now lay open on the dressing table, displaying its dazzling contents.

Candeille scarcely dared to touch it, and yet it was for her. Citizen Chauvelin had sent a note with it.

"Citizeness Candeille will please accept this gift from the government of France in acknowledgment of useful services past and to come."

The note was signed with Robespierre's own name, followed by that of Citizen Chauvelin. The morocco case contained a necklace of diamonds worth the ransom of a king.

"For useful services past and to come!" and there were promises of still further rewards, a complete pardon for all defalcations, a place within the charmed circle of the *Comédie Française*, a grand pageant and apotheosis with Citizeness Candeille impersonating the Goddess of Reason, in the midst of a grand national fête, and the acclamations of excited Paris; and all in exchange for the enactment of a part—simple and easy—outlined for her by Chauvelin!—

How strange! how inexplicable! Candeille took the necklace up in her trembling fingers and gazed musingly at the priceless gems. She had seen the jewels before, long, long ago! round the neck of the Duchesse de Marny, in whose service her own mother had been. She—as a child—had often gazed at and admired the great lady, who seemed like a wonderful fairy from an altogether world, to the poor little kitchen slut.

How wonderful are the vagaries of fortune! Désirée Candeille, the kitchen-maid's daughter, now wearing her ex-mistress' jewels. She supposed that these had been confiscated when the last of the Marnys—the girl, Juliette—had escaped from France! confiscated and now sent to her—Candeille—as a reward or as a bribe!

In either case they were welcome. The actress' vanity was soothed. She knew Juliette Marny was in England, and that she would meet her tonight at Lady Blakeney's. After the many snubs which she had endured from French aristocrats settled in England, the actress felt that she was about to enjoy an evening of triumph.

The intrigue excited her. She did not quite know what schemes Chauvelin was aiming at, what ultimate end he had had in view when he commanded her services and taught her the part which he wished her to play.

That the schemes were vast and the end mighty, she could not doubt. The reward she had received was proof enough of that.

Little Fanchon stood there in speechless admiration, whilst her mistress still fondly fingered the magnificent necklace.

"*Mademoiselle* will wear the diamond tonight?" she asked with evident anxiety; she would have been bitterly disappointed to have seen the beautiful thing once more relegated to its dark morocco case.

"Oh, yes, Fanchon!" said Candeille with a sigh of great satisfaction; "see that they are fastened quite securely, my girl."

She put the necklace round her shapely neck and Fanchon looked to see that the clasp was quite secure.

There came the sound of loud knocking at the street door.

"That is M. Chauvelin come to fetch me with the chaise. Am I quite ready, Fanchon?" asked Désirée Candeille.

"Oh yes, *Mademoiselle*!" sighed the little maid; "and *Mademoiselle* looks very beautiful tonight."

"Lady Blakeney is very beautiful too, Fanchon," rejoined the actress naively, "but I wonder if she will wear anything as fine as the Marny necklace?"

The knocking at the street door was repeated. Candeille took a final, satisfied survey of herself in the glass. She knew her part and felt that she had dressed well for it. She gave a final, affectionate little tap to the diamonds round her neck, took her cloak and hood from Fanchon, and was ready to go.

CHAPTER 10
Lady Blakeney's Rout

There are several accounts extant, in the fashionable chronicles of the time, of the gorgeous reception given that autumn by Lady Blakeney in her magnificent riverside home.

Never had the spacious apartments of Blakeney Manor looked more resplendent than on this memorable occasion—memorable because of the events which brought the brilliant evening to a close.

The Prince of Wales had come over by water from Carlton House; the royal princesses came early, and all fashionable London was there, chattering and laughing, displaying elaborate gowns and priceless jewels; dancing, flirting, listening to the strains of the string band, or strolling listlessly in the gardens, where the late roses and clumps of heliotrope threw soft fragrance on the balmy air.

But Marguerite was nervous and agitated. Strive how she might, she could not throw off that foreboding of something evil to come, which had assailed her from the first moment when she met Chauvelin face to face.

That unaccountable feeling of unreality was still upon her, that sense that she, and the woman Candeille, Percy and even His Royal Highness were, for the time being, the actors in a play written and stage-managed by Chauvelin. The ex-ambassador's humility, his offers of friendship, his quietude under Sir Percy's good-humoured banter, everything was a sham. Marguerite knew it; her womanly instinct, her passionate love, all cried out to her in warning; but there was that in her husband's nature which rendered her powerless in the face of such dangers, as, she felt sure, were now threatening him.

Just before her guests had begun to assemble, she had been alone with him for a few minutes. She had entered the room in which he sat, looking radiantly beautiful in a shimmering gown of white and silver, with diamonds in her golden hair and round her exquisite neck.

Moments like this, when she was alone with him, were the joy of her life. Then and then only did she see him as he really was, with that wistful tenderness in his deep-set eyes, that occasional flash of passion from beneath the lazily-drooping lids. For a few minutes—seconds, mayhap—the spirit of the reckless adventurer was laid to rest, relegated into the furthermost background of his senses by the powerful emotions of the lover.

Then he would seize her in his arms, and hold her to him, with a

59

strange longing to tear from out his heart all other thoughts, feelings and passions save those which made him a slave to her beauty and her smiles.

"Percy!" she whispered to him tonight when freeing herself from his embrace she looked up at him, and for this one heavenly second felt him all her own. "Percy, you will do nothing rash, nothing foolhardy tonight. That man had planned all that took place yesterday. He hates you, and—"

In a moment his face and attitude had changed, the heavy lids drooped over the eyes, the rigidity of the mouth relaxed, and that quaint, half-shy, half-inane smile played around the firm lips.

"Of course, he does, m'dear," he said in his usual affected, drawly tones, "of course he does, but that is so demmed amusing. He does not really know what or how much he knows, or what I know—In fact—er—we none of us know anything—just at present—"

He laughed lightly and carelessly, then deliberately readjusted the set of his lace tie.

"Percy!" she said reproachfully.

"Yes, m'dear."

"Lately when you brought Déroulède and Juliette Marny to England—I endured agonies of anxiety—and—"

He sighed, a quick, short, wistful sigh, and said very gently;

"I know you did, m'dear, and that is where the trouble lies. I know that you are fretting, so I have to be so demmed quick about the business, so as not to keep you in suspense too long—And now I can't take Ffoulkes away from his young wife, and Tony and the others are so mighty slow."

"Percy!" she said once more with tender earnestness.

"I know, I know," he said with a slight frown of self-reproach. "La! but I don't deserve your solicitude. Heavens know what a brute I was for years, whilst I neglected you, and ignored the noble devotion which I, alas! do even now so little to deserve."

She would have said something more but was interrupted by the entrance of Juliette Marny into the room.

"Some of your guests have arrived, Lady Blakeney," said the young girl, apologising for her seeming intrusion. "I thought you would wish to know."

Juliette looked very young and girlish in a simple white gown, without a single jewel on her arms or neck. Marguerite regarded her with unaffected approval.

"You look charming tonight, *Mademoiselle*, does she not, Sir Percy?"

"Thanks to your bounty," smiled Juliette, a trifle sadly. "Whilst I dressed tonight, I felt how I should have loved to wear my dear mother's jewels, of which she used to be so proud."

"We must hope that you will recover them, dear, some day," said Marguerite vaguely, as she led the young girl out of the small study towards the larger reception rooms.

"Indeed, I hope so," sighed Juliette. "When times became so troublous in France after my dear father's death, his confessor and friend, the Abbé Foucquet, took charge of all my mother's jewels for me. He said they would be safe with the ornaments of his own little church at Boulogne. He feared no sacrilege, and thought they would be most effectually hidden there, for no one would dream of looking for the Marny diamonds in the crypt of a country church."

Marguerite said nothing in reply. Whatever her own doubts might be upon such a subject, it could serve no purpose to disturb the young girl's serenity.

"Dear Abbé Foucquet," said Juliette after a while, "his is the kind of devotion which I feel sure will never be found under the new regimes of anarchy and of so-called equality. He would have laid down his life for my father or for me. And I know that he would never part with the jewels which I entrusted to his care, whilst he had breath and strength to defend them."

Marguerite would have wished to pursue the subject a little further. It was very pathetic to witness poor Juliette's hopes and confidences, which she felt sure would never be realised.

Lady Blakeney knew so much of what was going on in France just now; spoliations, confiscations, official thefts, open robberies, all in the name of equality, of fraternity and of patriotism. She knew nothing, of course, of the Abbé Foucquet, but the tender little picture of the devoted old man, painted by Juliette's words, had appealed strongly to her sympathetic heart.

Instinct and knowledge of the political aspect of France told her that by entrusting valuable family jewels to the old *Abbé*, Juliette had most unwittingly placed the man she so much trusted in danger of persecution at the hands of a government which did not even admit the legality of family possessions. However, there was neither time nor opportunity now to enlarge upon the subject. Marguerite resolved to recur to it a little later, when she would be alone with Mlle. de Marny, and above all when she could take counsel with her husband as to the best means of recovering the young girl's property for her, whilst relieving a devoted old man from the dangerous responsibility which he had so selflessly undertaken.

In the meanwhile, the two women had reached the first of the long line of state apartments wherein the brilliant *fête* was to take place. The staircase and the hall below were already filled with the early arrivals. Bidding Juliette to remain in the ballroom, Lady Blakeney now took up her stand on the exquisitely decorated landing, ready to greet her guests. She had a smile and a pleasant word for all, as, in a constant stream, the elite of London fashionable society began to file past her, exchanging the elaborate greetings which the stilted mode of the day prescribed to this butterfly-world.

The lacqueys in the hall shouted the names of the guests as they passed up the stairs; names celebrated in politics, in worlds of sport, of science or of art, great historic names, humble, newly-made ones, noble illustrious titles. The spacious rooms were filling fast. His Royal Highness, so 'twas said, had just stepped out of his barge. The noise of laughter and chatter was incessant, like unto a crowd of gaily-plumaged birds. Huge bunches of apricot-coloured roses in silver vases made the air heavy with their subtle perfume. Fans began to flutter. The string band struck the preliminary cords of the gavotte. At that moment the lacqueys at the foot of the stairs called out in stentorian tones;

"Mademoiselle Désirée Candeille! and Monsieur Chauvelin!"

Marguerite's heart gave a slight flutter; she felt a sudden tightening of the throat. She did not see Candeille at first, only the slight figure of Chauvelin dressed all in black, as usual, with head bent and hands clasped behind his back; he was slowly mounting the wide staircase, between a double row of brilliantly attired men and women, who looked with no small measure of curiosity at the ex-ambassador from revolutionary France.

Demoiselle Candeille was leading the way up the stairs. She paused on the landing in order to make before her hostess a most perfect and most elaborate curtsey. She looked smiling and radiant, beautifully dressed, a small wreath of wrought gold leaves in her hair, her only jewel an absolutely regal one, a magnificent necklace of diamonds round her shapely throat.

CHAPTER 11

The Challenge

It all occurred just before midnight, in one of the smaller rooms, which lead in enfilade from the principal ballroom.

Dancing had been going on for some time, but the evening was close, and there seemed to be a growing desire on the part of Lady Blakeney's guests to wander desultorily through the gardens and glasshouses or sit about where some measure of coolness could be obtained.

There was a rumour that a new and charming French artiste was to sing a few peculiarly ravishing songs, unheard in England before. Close to the main ballroom was the octagon music-room which was brilliantly illuminated, and in which a large number of chairs had been obviously disposed for the comfort of an audience. Into this room many of the guests had already assembled. It was quite clear that a chamber-concert—select and attractive as were all Lady Blakeney's entertainments—was in contemplation.

Marguerite herself, released for a moment from her constant duties near her royal guests, had strolled through the smaller rooms, accompanied by Juliette, in order to search for Mademoiselle Candeille and to suggest the commencement of the improvised concert.

Désirée Candeille had kept herself very much aloof throughout the evening, only talking to the one or two gentlemen whom her hostess had presented to her on her arrival, and with M. Chauvelin always in close attendance upon her every movement.

Presently, when dancing began, she retired to a small *boudoir*, and there sat down, demurely waiting, until Lady Blakeney should require her services.

When Marguerite and Juliette Marny entered the little room, she rose and came forward a few steps.

"I am ready, *Madame*," she said pleasantly, "whenever you wish me to begin. I have thought out a short programme,—shall I start with the gay or the sentimental songs?"

But before Marguerite had time to utter a reply, she felt her arm nervously clutched by a hot and trembling hand.

"Who—who is this woman?" murmured Juliette Marny close to her ear.

The young girl looked pale and very agitated, and her large eyes were fixed in unmistakable wrath upon the French actress before her. A little startled, not understanding Juliette's attitude, Marguerite tried to reply lightly;

"This is Mademoiselle Candeille, Juliette dear," she said, affecting the usual formal introduction, "of the Variétés Theatre of Paris—Mademoiselle Désirée Candeille, who will sing some charming French ditties for us tonight."

While she spoke, she kept a restraining hand on Juliette's quivering arm. Already, with the keen intuition which had been on the *qui-vive* the whole evening, she scented some mystery in this sudden outburst on the part of her young *protégée*.

But Juliette did not heed her; she felt surging up in her young, overburdened heart all the wrath and the contempt of the persecuted, fugitive aristocrat against the triumphant usurper. She had suffered so much from that particular class of the risen kitchen-wench of which the woman before her was so typical an example; years of sorrow, of poverty were behind her, loss of fortune, of kindred, of friends—she, even now a pauper, living on the bounty of strangers.

And all this through no fault of her own; the fault of her class mayhap! but not hers!

She had suffered much and was still overwrought and nerve-strung; for some reason she could not afterwards have explained, she felt spiteful and uncontrolled, goaded into stupid fury by the look of insolence and of triumph with which Candeille calmly regarded her.

Afterwards she would willingly have bitten out her tongue for her vehemence, but for the moment she was absolutely incapable of checking the torrent of her own emotions.

"Mademoiselle Candeille, indeed?" she said in wrathful scorn, "Désirée Candeille, you mean, Lady Blakeney! my mother's kitchen-maid, flaunting shamelessly my dear mother's jewels which she has stolen mayhap—"

The young girl was trembling from head to foot; tears of anger obscured her eyes; her voice, which fortunately remained low—not much above a whisper—was thick and husky.

"Juliette! Juliette! I entreat you," admonished Marguerite, "you must control yourself, you must, indeed you must. Mademoiselle Candeille, I beg of you to retire—"

But Candeille—well-schooled in the part she had to play—had no intention of quitting the field of battle. The more wrathful and excited Mademoiselle de Marny became, the more insolent and triumphant waxed the young actress' whole attitude. An ironical smile played round the corners of her mouth; her almond-shaped eyes were half-closed, regarding through drooping lashes the trembling figure of the young impoverished aristocrat. Her head was thrown well back, in obvious defiance of the social conventions, which should have forbidden a fracas in Lady Blakeney's hospitable house, and her fingers provocatively toyed with the diamond necklace which glittered and sparkled round her throat.

She had no need to repeat the words of a well-learnt part; her own wit, her own emotions and feelings helped her to act just as her employer would have wished her to do. Her native vulgarity helped her to assume the very bearing which he would have desired. In fact, at this moment Désirée Candeille had forgotten everything save the immediate present; a more than contemptuous snub from one of those penniless aristocrats, who had rendered her own sojourn in London so unpleasant and unsuccessful.

She had suffered from these snubs before but had never had the chance of forcing an *esclandre*, as a result of her own humiliation. That spirit of hatred for the rich and idle classes, which was so characteristic of revolutionary France, was alive and hot within her; she had never had an opportunity—she, the humble fugitive actress from a minor Paris theatre—to retort with forcible taunts to the ironical remarks made at and before her by the various poverty-stricken but haughty emigres who swarmed in those very same circles of London society into which she herself had vainly striven to penetrate.

Now at last, one of this same hated class, provoked beyond self-control, was allowing childish and unreasoning fury to outstrip the usual calm irony of aristocratic rebuffs.

Juliette had paused awhile, in order to check the wrathful tears which, much against her will, were choking the words in her throat and blinding her eyes.

"Hoity! toity!" laughed Candeille, "hark at the young baggage!"

But Juliette had turned to Marguerite and began explaining volubly;

"My mother's jewels!" she said in the midst of her tears, "ask her how she came by them. When I was obliged to leave the home of my fathers,—stolen from me by the Revolutionary Government—I contrived to retain my mother's jewels—you remember, I told you just now—The Abbé Foucquet—dear old man! Saved them for me—that and a little money which I had—he took charge of them—he said he would place them in safety with the ornaments of his church, and now I see them round that woman's neck—I know that he would not have parted with them save with his life."

All the while that the young girl spoke in a voice half-choked with sobs, Marguerite tried with all the physical and mental will at her command to drag her out of the room and thus to put a summary ending to this unpleasant scene. She ought to have felt angry with Juliette for this childish and senseless outburst, were it not for the fact that somehow, she knew within her innermost heart that all this had been arranged and preordained—not by Fate, not by a Higher Hand, but by the most skilful intriguer present-day France had ever known.

And even now, as she was half succeeding in turning Juliette away from the sight of Candeille, she was not the least surprised or startled at seeing Chauvelin standing in the very doorway through which she had hoped to pass. One glance at his face had made her fears tangible and real; there was a look of satisfaction and triumph in his pale, narrow eyes, a flash in them of approbation directed at the insolent attitude of the French actress; he looked like the stage-manager of a play, content with the effect his own well-arranged scenes were producing.

What he hoped to gain by this—somewhat vulgar—quarrel between the two women, Marguerite of course could not guess; that something was lurking in his mind, inimical to herself and to her husband, she did not for a moment doubt, and at this moment she felt that she would have given her very life to induce Candeille and Juliette to cease this passage of arms, without further provocation on either side.

But though Juliette might have been ready to yield to Lady Blakeney's persuasion, Désirée Candeille, under Chauvelin's eye, and fired by her own desire to further humiliate this overbearing aristocrat, did not wish the little scene to end so tamely just yet.

"Your old *calotin* was made to part with his booty, m'dear," she said, with a contemptuous shrug of her bare shoulders. "Paris and France have been starving these many years past; a paternal government seized all it could with which to reward those that served it well, whilst all that would have brought bread and meat for the poor was being greedily stowed away by shameless traitors!"

Juliette winced at the insult.

"Oh!" she moaned, as she buried her flaming face in her hands.

Too late now did she realise that she had deliberately stirred up a mud-heap and sent noisome insects buzzing about her ears.

"*Mademoiselle*," said Marguerite authoritatively, "I must ask you to remember that Mlle. de Marny is my friend and that you are a guest in my house."

"Aye! I try not to forget it," rejoined Candeille lightly, "but of a truth you must admit, Citizeness, that it would require the patience of a saint to put up with the insolence of a penniless baggage, who but lately has had to stand her trial in her own country for impurity of conduct."

There was a moment's silence, whilst Marguerite distinctly heard a short sigh of satisfaction escaping from the lips of Chauvelin. Then a pleasant laugh broke upon the ears of the four actors who were enacting the dramatic little scene, and Sir Percy Blakeney, immaculate in his rich white satin coat and filmy lace ruffles, exquisite in manners and courtesy, entered the little *boudoir*, and with his long back slightly bent, his arm outstretched in a graceful and well-studied curve, he approached Mademoiselle Désirée Candeille.

"May I have the honour," he said with his most elaborate air of courtly deference, "of conducting *Mademoiselle* to her chaise?"

In the doorway just behind him stood His Royal Highness the Prince of Wales chatting with apparent carelessness to Sir Andrew Ffoulkes and Lord Anthony Dewhurst. A curtain beyond the open door was partially drawn aside, disclosing one or two brilliantly dressed groups, strolling desultorily through the further rooms.

The four persons assembled in the little *boudoir* had been so absorbed by their own passionate emotions and the violence of their quarrel that they had not noticed the approach of Sir Percy Blakeney and of his friends. Juliette and Marguerite certainly were startled and Candeille was evidently taken unawares. Chauvelin alone seemed quite indifferent and stood back a little when Sir Percy advanced, in order to allow him to pass.

But Candeille recovered quickly enough from her surprise; without heeding Blakeney's proffered arm, she turned with all the airs of an insulted tragedy queen towards Marguerite.

"So 'tis I," she said with affected calm, "who am to bear every insult in a house in which I was bidden as a guest. I am turned out like some intrusive and importunate beggar, and I, the stranger in this land, am destined to find that amidst all these brilliant English gentlemen there is not one man of honour.

"M. Chauvelin," she added loudly, "our beautiful country has, meseems, deputed you to guard the honour as well as the worldly goods of your unprotected compatriots. I call upon you, in the name of France, to avenge the insults offered to me tonight."

She looked round defiantly from one to the other of the several faces which were now turned towards her, but no one, for the moment, spoke or stirred. Juliette, silent and ashamed, had taken Marguerite's hand in hers, and was clinging to it as if wishing to draw strength of character and firmness of purpose through the pores of the other woman's delicate skin.

Sir Percy with backbone still bent in a sweeping curve had not relaxed his attitude of uttermost deference. The Prince of Wales and his friends were viewing the scene with slightly amused aloofness.

For a moment—seconds at most—there was dead silence in the room, during which time it almost seemed as if the beating of several hearts could be distinctly heard.

Then Chauvelin, courtly and urbane, stepped calmly forward.

"Believe me, Citizeness," he said, addressing Candeille directly and with marked emphasis, "I am entirely at your command, but am I not helpless, seeing that those who have so grossly insulted you are of your own irresponsible, if charming, sex?"

Like a great dog after a nap, Sir Percy Blakeney straightened his long back and stretched it out to its full length.

"*La!*" he said pleasantly, "my ever engaging friend from Calais. Sir, your servant. Meseems we are ever destined to discuss amiable matters, in an amiable spirit—A glass of punch, Monsieur—er—Chauvelin?"

"I must ask you, Sir Percy," rejoined Chauvelin sternly, "to view this matter with becoming seriousness."

"Seriousness is never becoming, sir," said Blakeney, politely smothering a slight yawn, "and it is vastly unbecoming in the presence of ladies."

"Am I to understand then, Sir Percy," said Chauvelin, "that you are prepared to apologize to Mademoiselle Candeille for this insult offered to her by Lady Blakeney?"

Sir Percy again tried to smother that tiresome little yawn, which seemed most distressing, when he desired to be most polite. Then he flicked off a grain of dust from his immaculate lace ruffle and buried his long, slender hands in the capacious pockets of his white satin breeches; finally, he said with the most good-natured of smiles;

"Sir, have you seen the latest fashion in cravats? I would wish to draw your attention to the novel way in which we in England tie a Mechlin-edged bow."

"Sir Percy," retorted Chauvelin firmly, "since you will not offer Mademoiselle Candeille the apology which she has the right to expect from you, are you prepared that you and I should cross swords like honourable gentlemen?"

Blakeney laughed his usual pleasant, somewhat shy laugh, shook his powerful frame and looked from his altitude of six feet three inches down on the small, sable-clad figure of ex-Ambassador Chauvelin.

"The question is, sir," he said slowly, "should we then be two honourable gentlemen crossing swords?"

"Sir Percy—"

"Sir?"

Chauvelin, who for one moment had seemed ready to lose his temper, now made a sudden effort to resume a calm and easy attitude and said quietly;

"Of course, if one of us is coward enough to shirk the contest—"

He did not complete the sentence but shrugged his shoulders expressive of contempt. The other side of the curtained doorway, a little crowd had gradually assembled, attracted hither by the loud and angry voices which came from that small *boudoir*. Host and hostess had been missed from the reception rooms for some time. His Royal Highness, too, had not been seen for the quarter of an hour; like flies attracted by the light, one by one, or in small isolated groups, some of Lady Blakeney's guests had found their way to the room adjoining the royal presence.

As His Highness was standing in the doorway itself, no one could of course cross the threshold, but everyone could see into the room, and could take stock of the various actors in the little comedy. They were witnessing a quarrel between the French envoy and Sir Percy Blakeney wherein the former was evidently in deadly earnest and the latter merely politely bored. Amused comments flew to and fro; laughter and a babel of irresponsible chatter made an incessant chirruping accompaniment to the duologue between the two men.

But at this stage, the Prince of Wales, who hitherto had seemingly kept aloof from the quarrel, suddenly stepped forward and abruptly interposed the weight of his authority and of his social position between the bickering adversaries.

"Tush, man!" he said impatiently, turning more especially towards Chauvelin, "you talk at random. Sir Percy Blakeney is an English gentleman, and the laws of this country do not admit of duelling, as you understand it in France; and I for one certainly could not allow—"

"Pardon, your Royal Highness," interrupted Sir Percy with irresistible *bonhomie*, "your Highness does not understand the situation. My engaging friend here does not propose that I should transgress the laws of this country, but that I should go over to France with him, and fight him there, where duelling and—er—other little matters of that sort are allowed."

"Yes! quite so!" rejoined the prince, "I understand M. Chauvelin's desire—But what about you, Blakeney?"

"Oh!" replied Sir Percy lightly, "I have accepted his challenge, of course!"

CHAPTER 12

Time—Place—Conditions

It would be very difficult indeed to say why—at Blakeney's lightly spoken words—an immediate silence should have fallen upon all those present. All the actors in the little drawing-room drama, who had played their respective parts so unerringly up to now, had paused awhile, just as if an invisible curtain had come down, marking the end of a scene, and the interval during which the players might recover strength and energy to resume their roles. The Prince of Wales as foremost spectator said nothing for the moment, and beyond the doorway, the audience there assembled seemed suddenly to be holding its breath, waiting—eager, expectant, palpitation—for what would follow now.

Only here and there the gentle *frou-frou* of a silk skirt, the rhythmic flutter of a fan, broke those few seconds' deadly, stony silence.

Yet it was all simple enough. A fracas between two ladies, the gentlemen interposing, a few words of angry expostulation, then the inevitable suggestion of Belgium or of some other country where the childish and barbarous custom of settling such matters with a couple of swords had not been as yet systematically stamped out.

The whole scene—with but slight variations—had occurred scores of times in London drawing-rooms. English gentlemen had scores of times crossed the Channel for the purpose of settling similar quarrels in continental fashion.

Why should the present situation appear so abnormal? Sir Percy Blakeney—an accomplished gentleman—was past master in the art of fence and looked more than a match in strength and dexterity for the meagre, sable-clad little opponent who had so summarily challenged him to cross over to France, in order to fight a duel.

But somehow everyone had a feeling at this moment that this proposed duel would be unlike any other combat every fought between two antagonists. Perhaps it was the white, absolutely stony and unexpressive face of Marguerite which suggested a latent tragedy; perhaps it was the look of unmistakable horror in Juliette's eyes, or that of triumph in those of Chauvelin, or even that certain something in His

Royal Highness' face, which seemed to imply that the prince, careless man of the world as he was, would have given much to prevent this particular meeting from taking place.

Be that as it may, there is no doubt that a certain wave of electrical excitement swept over the little crowd assembled there, the while the chief actor in the little drama, the inimitable dandy, Sir Percy Blakeney himself, appeared deeply engrossed in removing a speck of powder from the wide black satin ribbon which held his gold-rimmed eye-glass.

"Gentlemen!" said His Royal Highness suddenly, "we are forgetting the ladies. My lord Hastings," he added, turning to one of the gentlemen who stood close to him, "I pray you to remedy this unpardonable neglect. Men's quarrels are not fit for ladies' dainty ears."

Sir Percy looked up from his absorbing occupation. His eyes met those of his wife; she was like a marble statue, hardly conscious of what was going on round her. But he, who knew every emotion which swayed that ardent and passionate nature, guessed that beneath that stony calm there lay a mad, almost unconquerable impulse, and that was to shout to all these puppets here, the truth, the awful, the unanswerable truth, to tell them what this challenge really meant; a trap wherein one man consumed with hatred and desire for revenge hoped to entice a brave and fearless foe into a death-dealing snare.

Full well did Percy Blakeney guess that for the space of one second his most cherished secret hovered upon his wife's lips; one turn of the balance of Fate, one breath from the mouth of an unseen sprite, and Marguerite was ready to shout;

"Do not allow this monstrous thing to be! The Scarlet Pimpernel, whom you all admire for his bravery, and love for his daring, stands before you now, face to face with his deadliest enemy, who is here to lure him to his doom!"

For that momentous second therefore Percy Blakeney held his wife's gaze with the magnetism of his own; all there was in him of love, of entreaty, of trust, and of command went out to her through that look with which he kept her eyes riveted upon his face.

Then he saw the rigidity of her attitude relax. She closed her eyes in order to shut out the whole world from her suffering soul. She seemed to be gathering all the mental force of which her brain was capable, for one great effort of self-control. Then she took Juliette's hand in hers and turned to go out of the room; the gentlemen bowed as she swept past them, her rich silken gown making a soft hush-sh-sh as she went. She nodded to some, curtseyed to the prince, and had at the last moment the supreme courage and pride to turn her head once more towards her husband, in order to reassure him finally that his secret was as safe with her now, in this hour of danger, as it had been in the time of triumph.

She smiled and passed out of his sight, preceded by Désirée Candeille, who, escorted by one of the gentlemen, had become singularly silent and subdued.

In the little room now there only remained a few men. Sir Andrew Ffoulkes had taken the precaution of closing the door after the ladies had gone.

Then His Royal Highness turned once more to Monsieur Chauvelin and said with an obvious show of indifference;

"Faith, *Monsieur!* meseems we are all enacting a farce, which can have no final act. I vow that I cannot allow my friend Blakeney to go over to France at your bidding. Your government now will not allow my father's subjects to land on your shores without a special passport, and then only for a specific purpose."

"*La*, your Royal Highness," interposed Sir Percy, "I pray you have no fear for me on that score. My engaging friend here has—an I mistake not—a passport ready for me in the pocket of his sable-hued coat, and as we are hoping effectually to spit one another over there—gadzooks! but there's the specific purpose—Is it not true, sir," he added, turning once more to Chauvelin, "that in the pocket of that exquisitely cut coat of yours, you have a passport—name in blank perhaps—which you had specially designed for me?"

It was so carelessly, so pleasantly said, that no one save Chauvelin guessed the real import of Sir Percy's words. Chauvelin, of course, knew their inner meaning; he understood that Blakeney wished to convey to him the fact that he was well aware that the whole scene tonight had been prearranged, and that it was willingly and with eyes wide open that he walked into the trap which the revolutionary patriot had so carefully laid for him.

"The passport will be forthcoming in due course, sir," retorted Chauvelin evasively, "when our seconds have arranged all formalities."

"Seconds be demmed, sir," rejoined Sir Percy placidly, "you do not propose, I trust, that we travel a whole caravan to France."

"Time, place and conditions must be settled, Sir Percy," replied Chauvelin; "you are too accomplished a cavalier, I feel sure, to wish to arrange such formalities yourself."

"Nay! neither you nor I, Monsieur—er—Chauvelin," quoth Sir Percy blandly, "could, I own, settle such things with persistent good-humour; and good-humour in such cases is the most important of all formalities. Is it not so?"

"Certainly, Sir Percy."

"As for seconds? Perish the thought. One second only, I entreat, and that one a lady—the most adorable—the most detestable—the most true—the most fickle amidst all her charming sex—Do you agree, sir?"

"You have not told me her name, Sir Percy?"

"Chance, *Monsieur*, Chance—With His Royal Highness' permission let the wilful jade decide."

"I do not understand."

"Three throws of the dice, *Monsieur*—Time—Place—Conditions, you said—three throws and the winner names them—Do you agree?"

Chauvelin hesitated. Sir Percy's bantering mood did not quite fit in with his own elaborate plans, moreover the ex-ambassador feared a pitfall of some sort and did not quite like to trust to this arbitration of the dice-box.

He turned, quite involuntarily, in appeal to the Prince of Wales and the other gentlemen present.

But the Englishman of those days was a born gambler. He lived with the dice-box in one pocket and a pack of cards in the other. The prince himself was no exception to this rule, and the first gentleman in England was the most avowed worshipper of Hazard in the land.

"Chance, by all means," quoth His Highness gaily.

"Chance! Chance!" repeated the others eagerly.

In the midst of so hostile a crowd, Chauvelin felt it unwise to resist. Moreover, one second's reflection had already assured him that this throwing of the dice could not seriously interfere with the success of his plans. If the meeting took place at all—and Sir Percy now had gone too far to draw back—then of necessity it would have to take place in France.

The question of time and conditions of the fight, which at best would be only a farce—only a means to an end—could not be of paramount importance.

Therefore, he shrugged his shoulders with well-marked indifference, and said lightly;

"As you please."

There was a small table in the centre of the room with a settee and two or three chairs arranged close to it. Around this table now an eager little group had congregated; the Prince of Wales in the fore-front, unwilling to interfere, scarce knowing what madcap plans were floating through Blakeney's adventurous brain, but excited in spite of himself at this momentous game of hazard the issues of which seemed so nebulous, so vaguely fraught with dangers. Close to him were Sir Andrew Ffoulkes, Lord Anthony Dewhurst, Lord Grenville and per-haps a half score gentlemen, young men about town mostly, gay and giddy butterflies of fashion, who did not even attempt to seek in this strange game of chance any hidden meaning save that it was one of Blakeney's irresponsible pranks.

And in the centre of the compact group, Sir Percy Blakeney in his gorgeous suit of shimmering white satin, one knee bent upon a chair, and leaning with easy grace—dice-box in hand—across the small gilt-legged table; beside him ex-Ambassador Chauvelin, stand-ing with arms folded behind his back, watching every movement of his brilliant adversary like some dark-plumaged hawk hovering near a bird of paradise.

"Place first, *Monsieur?*" suggested Sir Percy.

"As you will, sir," assented Chauvelin.

He took up a dice-box which one of the gentlemen handed to him and the two men threw.

"'Tis mine, *Monsieur,*" said Blakeney carelessly, "mine to name the place where shall occur this historic encounter, 'twixt the busiest man in France and the most idle fop that e'er disgraced these three king-doms—Just for the sake of argument, sir, what place would you sug-gest?"

"Oh! the exact spot is immaterial, Sir Percy," replied Chauvelin coldly, "the whole of France stands at your disposal."

"Aye! I thought as much but could not be quite sure of such boundless hospitality," retorted Blakeney imperturbably.

"Do you care for the woods around Paris, sir?"

"Too far from the coast, sir. I might be sea-sick crossing over the Channel, and glad to get the business over as soon as possible—No, not Paris, sir—rather let us say Boulogne—Pretty little place, Bou-logne—do you not think so—?"

"Undoubtedly, Sir Percy."

"Then Boulogne it is, the ramparts, an' you will, on the south side of the town."

"As you please," rejoined Chauvelin drily. "Shall we throw again?"

A murmur of merriment had accompanied this brief colloquy between the adversaries, and Blakeney's bland sallies were received with shouts of laughter. Now the dice rattled again and once more the two men threw.

"'Tis yours this time, Monsieur Chauvelin," said Blakeney, after a rapid glance at the dice. "See how evenly Chance favours us both. Mine, the choice of place—admirably done you'll confess—Now yours the choice of time. I wait upon your pleasure, sir—The southern ramparts at Boulogne—when?"

"The fourth day from this, sir, at the hour when the Cathedral bell chimes the evening Angelus," came Chauvelin's ready reply.

"Nay! but methought that your demmed government had abolished Cathedrals, and bells and chimes—The people of France have now to go to hell their own way—for the way to heaven has been barred by the National Convention—Is that not so?—Methought the Angelus was forbidden to be rung."

"Not at Boulogne, I think, Sir Percy," retorted Chauvelin drily, "and I'll pledge you my word that the evening Angelus shall be rung that night."

"At what hour is that, sir?"

"One hour after sundown."

"But why four days after this? Why not two or three?"

"I might have asked, why the southern ramparts, Sir Percy; why not the western? I chose the fourth day—does it not suit you?" asked Chauvelin ironically.

"Suit me! Why, sir, nothing could suit me better," rejoined Blakeney with his pleasant laugh. "Zounds! but I call it marvellous—demmed marvellous—I wonder now," he added blandly, "what made you think of the Angelus?"

Everyone laughed at this, a little irrelevantly perhaps.

"Ah!" continued Blakeney gaily, "I remember now—Faith! to think that I was nigh forgetting that when last you and I met, sir, you had just taken or were about to take Holy Orders—Ah! how well the thought of the Angelus fits in with your clerical garb—I recollect that the latter was mightily becoming to you, sir—"

"Shall we proceed to settle the conditions of the fight, Sir Percy?" said Chauvelin, interrupting the flow of his antagonist's gibes, and trying to disguise his irritation beneath a mask of impassive reserve.

"The choice of weapons you mean," here interposed His Royal Highness, "but I thought that swords had already been decided on."

"Quite so, your Highness," assented Blakeney, "but there are various little matters in connection with this momentous encounter which are of vast importance—Am I not right, *Monsieur?*—Gentlemen, I appeal to you—Faith! one never knows—my engaging opponent here might desire that I should fight him in green socks, and I that he should wear a scarlet flower in his coat."

"The Scarlet Pimpernel, Sir Percy?"

"Why not, *Monsieur?* It would look so well in your buttonhole, against the black of the clerical coat, which I understand you sometime affect in France—and when it is withered and quite dead you would find that it would leave an overpowering odour in your nostrils, far stronger than that of incense."

There was general laughter after this. The hatred which every member of the French revolutionary government—including, of course, ex-Ambassador Chauvelin—bore to the national hero was well known.

"The conditions then, Sir Percy," said Chauvelin, without seeming to notice the taunt conveyed in Blakeney's last words. "Shall we throw again?"

"After you, sir," acquiesced Sir Percy.

For the third and last time the two opponents rattled the dicebox and threw. Chauvelin was now absolutely unmoved. These minor details quite failed to interest him. What mattered the conditions of the fight which was only intended as a bait with which to lure his enemy in the open? The hour and place were decided on and Sir Percy would not fail to come. Chauvelin knew enough of his opponent's boldly adventurous spirit not to feel in the least doubtful on that point. Even now, as he gazed with grudging admiration at the massive, well-knit figure of his arch-enemy, noted the thin nervy hands and square jaw, the low, broad forehead and deep-set, half-veiled eyes, he knew that in this matter wherein Percy Blakeney was obviously playing with his very life, the only emotion that really swayed him at this moment was his passionate love of adventure.

The ruling passion strong in death!

Yes! Sir Percy would be on the southern ramparts of Boulogne one hour after sunset on the day named, trusting, no doubt, in his usual marvellous good-fortune, his own presence of mind and his great physical and mental strength, to escape from the trap into which he was so ready to walk.

That remained beyond a doubt! Therefore, what mattered details?

But even at this moment, Chauvelin had already resolved on one great thing; namely, that on that eventful day, nothing whatever should be left to chance; he would meet his cunning enemy not only with cunning, but also with power, and if the entire force of the republican army then available in the north of France had to be requisitioned for the purpose, the ramparts of Boulogne would be surrounded and no chance of escape left for the daring Scarlet Pimpernel.

His wave of meditation, however, was here abruptly stemmed by Blakeney's pleasant voice.

"Lud! Monsieur Chauvelin," he said, "I fear me your luck has deserted you. Chance, as you see, has turned to me once more."

"Then it is for you, Sir Percy," rejoined the Frenchman, "to name the conditions under which we are to fight."

"Ah! that is so, is it not, *Monsieur?*" quoth Sir Percy lightly. "By my faith! I'll not plague you with formalities—We'll fight with our coats on if it be cold, in our shirtsleeves if it be sultry—I'll not demand either green socks or scarlet ornaments. I'll even try and be serious for the space of two minutes, sir, and confine my whole attention— the product of my infinitesimal brain—to thinking out some pleasant detail for this duel, which might be acceptable to you. Thus, sir, the thought of weapons springs to my mind—Swords you said, I think. Sir! I will e'en restrict my choice of conditions to that of the actual weapons with which we are to fight—Ffoulkes, I pray you," he added, turning to his friend, "the pair of swords which lie across the top of my desk at this moment—

"We'll not ask a menial to fetch them, eh, *Monsieur?*" he continued gaily, as Sir Andrew Ffoulkes at a sign from him had quickly left the room. "What need to bruit our pleasant quarrel abroad? You will like the weapons, sir, and you shall have your own choice from the pair— You are a fine fencer, I feel sure—and you shall decide if a scratch or two or a more serious wound shall be sufficient to avenge Mademoiselle Candeille's wounded vanity."

Whilst he prattled so gaily on, there was dead silence among all those present. The prince had his shrewd eyes steadily fixed upon him, obviously wondering what this seemingly irresponsible adventurer held at the back of his mind. There is no doubt that everyone felt oppressed, and that a strange murmur of anticipatory excitement went round the little room, when, a few seconds later, Sir Andrew Ffoulkes returned, with two sheathed swords in his hand.

Blakeney took them from his friend and placed them on the little table in front of ex-Ambassador Chauvelin. The spectators strained their necks to look at the two weapons. They were exactly similar one to the other; both encased in plain black leather sheaths, with steel ferrules polished to shine like silver; the handles too were of plain steel, with just the grip fashioned in a twisted basket pattern of the same highly-tempered metal.

"What think you of these weapons, *Monsieur?*" asked Blakeney, who was carelessly leaning against the back of a chair.

Chauvelin took up one of the two swords and slowly drew it from out its scabbard, carefully examining the brilliant, narrow steel blade as he did so.

"A little old-fashioned in style and make, Sir Percy," he said, closely imitating his opponent's easy demeanour, "a trifle heavier, perhaps, than we in France have been accustomed to lately, but, nevertheless, a beautifully tempered piece of steel."

"Of a truth there's not much the matter with the tempering, *Monsieur*," quoth Blakeney, "the blades were fashioned at Toledo just two hundred years ago."

"Ah! here I see an inscription," said Chauvelin, holding the sword close to his eyes, the better to see the minute letters engraved in the steel.

"The name of the original owner. I myself bought them—when I travelled in Italy—from one of his descendants."

"Lorenzo Giovanni Cenci," said Chauvelin, spelling the Italian names quite slowly.

"The greatest blackguard that ever trod this earth. You, no doubt, *Monsieur*, know his history better than we do. Rapine, theft, murder, nothing came amiss to Signor Lorenzo—neither the deadly drug in the cup nor the poisoned dagger."

He had spoken lightly, carelessly, with that same tone of easy banter which he had not forsaken throughout the evening, and the same drawly manner which was habitual to him. But at these last words of his, Chauvelin gave a visible start, and then abruptly replaced the sword—which he had been examining—upon the table.

He threw a quick, suspicious glance at Blakeney, who, leaning back against the chair and one knee resting on the cushioned seat, was idly toying with the other blade, the exact pair to the one which the ex-ambassador had so suddenly put down.

"Well, *Monsieur*," quoth Sir Percy after a slight pause, and meeting with a swift glance of lazy irony his opponent's fixed gaze. "Are you satisfied with the weapons? Which of the two shall be yours, and which mine?"

"Of a truth, Sir Percy—" murmured Chauvelin, still hesitating.

"Nay, *Monsieur*," interrupted Blakeney with pleasant bonhomie, "I know what you would say—of a truth, there is no choice between this pair of perfect twins; one is as exquisite as the other—And yet you must take one and I the other—this or that, whichever you prefer—You shall take it home with you tonight and practise thrusting at a haystack or at a bobbin, as you please—The sword is yours to command until you have used it against my unworthy person—yours until you bring it out four days hence—on the southern ramparts of Boulogne, when the cathedral bells chime the evening Angelus; then you shall cross it against its faithless twin—There, *Monsieur*—they are of equal length—of equal strength and temper—a perfect pair—Yet I pray you choose."

He took up both the swords in his hands and carefully balancing them by the extreme tip of their steel-bound scabbards, he held them out towards the Frenchman. Chauvelin's eyes were fixed upon him, and he from his towering height was looking down at the little sable-clad figure before him.

The Terrorist seemed uncertain what to do. Though he was one of those men whom by the force of their intellect, the strength of their enthusiasm, the power of their cruelty, had built a new anarchical France, had overturned a throne and murdered a king, yet now, face to face with this affected fop, this lazy and *debonnair* adventurer, he hesitated—trying in vain to read what was going on behind that low, smooth forehead or within the depth of those lazy, blue eyes.

He would have given several years of his life at this moment for one short glimpse into the innermost brain cells of this daring mind, to see the man start, quiver but for the fraction of a second, betray himself by a tremor of the eyelid. What counterplan was lurking in Percy Blakeney's head, as he offered to his opponent the two swords which had once belonged to Lorenzo Cenci?

Did any thought of foul play, of dark and deadly poisonings linger in the fastidious mind of this accomplished gentleman?

Surely not!

Chauvelin tried to chide himself for such fears. It seemed madness even to think of Italian poisons, of the Cencis or the Borgias in the midst of this brilliantly lighted English drawing-room.

But because he was above all a diplomatist, a fencer with words and with looks, the envoy of France determined to know, to probe and to read. He forced himself once more to careless laughter and nonchalance of manner and schooled his lips to smile up with gentle irony at the good-humoured face of his arch-enemy.

He tapped one of the swords with his long pointed finger.

"Is this the one you choose, sir?" asked Blakeney.

"Nay! which do you advise, Sir Percy," replied Chauvelin lightly. "Which of those two blades think you is most like to hold after two hundred years the poison of the Cenci?"

But Blakeney neither started nor winced. He broke into a laugh, his own usual pleasant laugh, half shy and somewhat inane, then said in tones of lively astonishment;

"Zounds! sir, but you are full of surprises—Faith! I never would have thought of that—Marvellous, I call it—demmed marvellous— What say you, gentlemen?—Your Royal Highness, what think you?— Is not my engaging friend here of a most original turn of mind—Will you have this sword or that, *Monsieur?*—Nay, I must insist—else we shall weary our friends if we hesitate too long—This one then, sir, since you have chosen it," he continued, as Chauvelin finally took one of the swords in his hand. "And now for a bowl of punch—Nay, *Monsieur*, 'twas demmed smart what you said just now—I must insist on your joining us in a bowl—Such wit as yours, *Monsieur*, must need whetting at times—I pray you repeat that same sally again—"

Then finally turning to the prince and to his friends, he added;

"And after that bowl, gentlemen, shall we rejoin the ladies?"

CHAPTER 13

Reflections

It seemed indeed as if the incident were finally closed, the chief actors in the drama having deliberately vacated the centre of the stage.

The little crowd which had stood in a compact mass round the table, began to break up into sundry small groups; laughter and desultory talk, checked for a moment by that oppressive sense of unknown danger, which had weighed on the spirits of those present, once more became general. Blakeney's light-heartedness had put everyone into good-humour; since he evidently did not look upon the challenge as a matter of serious moment, why then, no one else had any cause for anxiety, and the younger men were right glad to join in that bowl of punch which their genial host had offered with so merry a grace.

Lacqueys appeared, throwing open the doors. From a distance the sound of dance music once more broke upon the ear.

A few of the men only remained silent, deliberately holding aloof from the renewed mirthfulness. Foremost amongst these was His Royal Highness, who was looking distinctly troubled, and who had taken Sir Percy by the arm, and was talking to him with obvious earnestness. Lord Anthony Dewhurst and Lord Hastings were holding converse in a secluded corner of the room, whilst Sir Andrew Ffoulkes, as being the host's most intimate friend, felt it incumbent on him to say a few words to ex-Ambassador Chauvelin.

The latter was desirous of effecting a retreat. Blakeney's invitation to join in the friendly bowl of punch could not be taken seriously, and the Terrorist wanted to be alone, in order to think out the events of the past hour.

A lacquey waited on him, took the momentous sword from his hand, found his hat and cloak and called his coach for him. Chauvelin, having taken formal leave of his host and acquaintances, quickly worked his way to the staircase and hall, through the less frequented apartments.

He sincerely wished to avoid meeting Lady Blakeney face to face. Not that the slightest twinge of remorse disturbed his mind, but he feared some impulsive action on her part, which indirectly might interfere with his future plans. Fortunately, no one took much heed of the darkly-clad, insignificant little figure that glided so swiftly by, obviously determined to escape attention.

In the hall he found Demoiselle Candeille waiting for him. She, too, had evidently been desirous of leaving Blakeney Manor as soon as possible. He saw her to her chaise, then escorted her as far as her lodgings, which were close by; there were still one or two things which he wished to discuss with her, one or two final instructions which he desired to give.

On the whole, he was satisfied with his evening's work; the young actress had well supported him and had played her part so far with marvellous *sang-froid* and skill. Sir Percy, whether willingly or blindly, had seemed only too ready to walk into the trap which was being set for him.

This fact alone disturbed Chauvelin not a little, and as half an hour or so later, having taken final leave of his ally, he sat alone in the coach, which was conveying him back to town, the sword of Lorenzo Cenci close to his hand, he pondered very seriously over it.

That the adventurous Scarlet Pimpernel should have guessed all along, that sooner or later the French Revolutionary Government—whom he had defrauded of some of its most important victims—would desire to be even with him, and to bring him to the scaffold, was not to be wondered at. But that he should be so blind as to imagine that Chauvelin's challenge was anything else but a lure to induce him to go to France, could not possibly be supposed. So, bold an adventurer, so keen an intriguer was sure to have scented the trap immediately, and if he appeared ready to fall into it, it was because there had already sprung up in his resourceful mind some bold coup or subtle counterplan, with which he hoped to gratify his own passionate love of sport, whilst once more bringing his enemies to discomfiture and humiliation.

Undoubtedly Sir Percy Blakeney, as an accomplished gentleman of the period, could not very well under the circumstances which had been so carefully stage-managed and arranged by Chauvelin, refuse the latter's challenge to fight him on the other side of the Channel. Any hesitation on the part of the leader of that daring Scarlet Pimpernel League would have covered him with a faint suspicion of pusillanimity, and a subtle breath of ridicule, and in a moment the prestige of the unknown and elusive hero would have vanished forever.

But apart from the necessity of the fight, Blakeney seemed to enter into the spirit of the plot directed against his own life, with such light-hearted merriment, such zest and joy, that Chauvelin could not help but be convinced that the capture of the Scarlet Pimpernel at Boulogne or elsewhere would not prove quite so easy a matter as he had at first anticipated.

That same night he wrote a long and circumstantial letter to his colleague, Citizen Robespierre, shifting thereby, as it were, some of the responsibility of coming events from his own shoulders on to the executive of the Committee of Public Safety, he wrote:

"I guarantee to you, Citizen Robespierre, and to the members of the Revolutionary Government who have entrusted me with the delicate mission, that four days from this date at one hour after sunset, the man who goes by the mysterious name of the Scarlet Pimpernel, will be on the ramparts of Boulogne on the south side of the town. I have done what has been asked of me. On that day and at that hour, I shall have brought the enemy of the Revolution, the intriguer against the policy of the republic, within the power of the government which he has flouted and outraged. Now look to it, citizens all, that the fruits of my diplomacy and of my skill be not lost to France again. The man will be there at my bidding, 'tis for you to see that he does not escape this time."

This letter he sent by special courier which the National Convention had placed at his disposal in case of emergency. Having sealed it and entrusted it to the man, Chauvelin felt at peace with the world and with himself. Although he was not so sure of success as he would have wished, he yet could not see *how* failure could possibly come about; and the only regret which he felt tonight, when he finally in the early dawn sought a few hours' troubled rest, was that that momentous fourth day was still so very far distant.

CHAPTER 14

The Ruling Passion

In the meanwhile, silence had fallen over the beautiful old manorial house. One by one the guests had departed, leaving that peaceful sense of complete calm and isolation which follows the noisy chatter of any great throng bent chiefly on enjoyment.

The evening had been universally acknowledged to have been brilliantly successful. True, the much talked of French artiste had not sung the promised ditties, but in the midst of the whirl and excitement of dances, of the inspiring tunes of the string band, the elaborate supper and recherche wines, no one had paid much heed to this change in the programme of entertainments.

And everyone had agreed that never had Lady Blakeney looked more radiantly beautiful than on this night. She seemed absolutely indefatigable, a perfect hostess, full of charming little attentions towards every one, although more than ordinarily absorbed by her duties towards her many royal guests.

The dramatic incidents which had taken place in the small *boudoir* had not been much bruited abroad. It was always considered bad form in those courtly days to discuss men's quarrels before ladies, and in this instance, those who were present when it all occurred instinctively felt that their discretion would be appreciated in high circles and held their tongues accordingly.

Thus, the brilliant evening was brought to a happy conclusion without a single cloud to mar the enjoyment of the guests. Marguerite performed a veritable miracle of fortitude, forcing her very smiles to seem natural and gay, chatting pleasantly, even wittily, upon every known fashionable topic of the day, laughing merrily the while her poor, aching heart was filled with unspeakable misery.

Now, when everybody had gone, when the last of her guests had bobbed before her the prescribed curtsey, to which she had invariably responded with the same air of easy self-possession, now at last she felt free to give rein to her thoughts, to indulge in the luxury of looking her own anxiety straight in the face and to let the tension of her nerves relax.

Sir Andrew Ffoulkes had been the last to leave and Percy had strolled out with him as far as the garden gate, for Lady Ffoulkes had left in her chaise some time ago, and Sir Andrew meant to walk to his home, not many yards distant from Blakeney Manor.

In spite of herself Marguerite felt her heartstrings tighten as she thought of this young couple so lately wedded. People smiled a little when Sir Andrew Ffoulkes' name was mentioned; some called him effeminate, others uxorious; his fond attachment for his pretty little wife was thought to pass the bounds of decorum. There was no doubt that since his marriage the young man had greatly changed. His love of sport and adventure seemed to have died out completely, yielding evidently to the great, more overpowering love, that for his young wife.

Suzanne was nervous for her husband's safety. She had sufficient influence over him to keep him at home, when other members of the brave little League of The Scarlet Pimpernel followed their leader with mad zest, on some bold adventure.

Marguerite too at first had smiled in kindly derision when Suzanne Ffoulkes, her large eyes filled with tears, had used her wiles to keep Sir Andrew tied to her own dainty apron-strings. But somehow, lately, with that gentle contempt which she felt for the weaker man, there had mingled a half-acknowledged sense of envy.

How different 'twixt her and her husband.

Percy loved her truly and with a depth of passion proportionate to his own curious dual personality; it were sacrilege, almost, to doubt the intensity of his love. But nevertheless she had at all times a feeling as if he were holding himself and his emotions in check, as if his love, as if she, Marguerite, his wife, were but secondary matters in his life; as if her anxieties, her sorrow when he left her, her fears for his safety were but small episodes in the great book of life which he had planned out and conceived for himself.

Then she would hate herself for such thoughts; they seemed like doubts of him. Did any man ever love a woman, she asked herself, as Percy loved her? He was difficult to understand, and perhaps—oh! that was an awful "perhaps"—perhaps there lurked somewhere in his mind a slight mistrust of her. She had betrayed him once! unwittingly 'tis true! did he fear she might do so again?

And tonight, after her guests had gone she threw open the great windows that gave on the beautiful terrace, with its marble steps leading down to the cool river beyond. Everything now seemed so peaceful and still; the scent of the heliotrope made the midnight air swoon with its intoxicating fragrance, the rhythmic murmur of the waters came gently echoing from below, and from far away there came the melancholy cry of a night-bird on the prowl.

That cry made Marguerite shudder; her thoughts flew back to the episodes of this night and to Chauvelin, the dark bird of prey with his mysterious death-dealing plans, his subtle intrigues which all tended towards the destruction of one man; his enemy, the husband whom Marguerite loved.

Oh! how she hated these wild adventures which took Percy away from her side. Is not a woman who loves—be it husband or child—the most truly selfish, the most cruelly callous creature in the world, there, where the safety and the well-being of the loved one is in direct conflict with the safety and well-being of others.

She would right gladly have closed her eyes to every horror perpetrated in France, she would not have known what went on in Paris, she wanted her husband! And yet month after month, with but short intervals, she saw him risk that precious life of his, which was the very essence of her own soul, for others! for others! always for others!

And she! she! Marguerite, his wife, was powerless to hold him back! powerless to keep him beside her, when that mad fit of passion seized him to go on one of those wild quests, wherefrom she always feared he could not return alive; and this, although she might use every noble artifice, every tender wile of which a loving and beautiful wife is capable.

At times like those her own proud heart was filled with hatred and with envy towards everything that took him away from her; and tonight, all these passionate feelings which she felt were quite unworthy of her and of him, seemed to surge within her soul more tumultuously than ever. She was longing to throw herself in his arms, to pour out into his loving ear all that she suffered, in fear and anxiety, and to make one more appeal to his tenderness and to that passion which had so often made him forget the world at her feet.

And so instinctively she walked along the terrace towards that more secluded part of the garden just above the river bank, where she had so oft wandered hand in hand with him, in the honeymoon of their love. There great clumps of old-fashioned cabbage roses grew in untidy splendour, and belated lilies sent intoxicating odours into the air, whilst the heavy masses of Egyptian and Michaelmas daisies looked like ghostly constellations in the gloom.

She thought Percy must soon be coming this way. Though it was so late, she knew that he would not go to bed. After the events of the night, his ruling passion, strong in death, would be holding him in its thrall.

She too felt wide awake and unconscious of fatigue; when she reached the secluded path beside the river, she peered eagerly up and down, and listened for a sound.

Presently it seemed to her that above the gentle clapper of the waters she could hear a rustle and the scrunching of the fine gravel under carefully measured footsteps. She waited awhile. The footsteps seemed to draw nearer, and soon, although the starlit night was very dark, she perceived a cloaked and hooded figure approaching cautiously toward her.

"Who goes there?" she called suddenly.

The figure paused, then came rapidly forward, and a voice said timidly;

"Ah! Lady Blakeney!"

"Who are you?" asked Marguerite peremptorily.

"It is I—Désirée Candeille," replied the midnight prowler.

"Demoiselle Candeille!" ejaculated Marguerite, wholly taken by surprise. "What are you doing here? alone? and at this hour?"

"Sh-sh-sh—" whispered Candeille eagerly, as she approached quite close to Marguerite and drew her hood still lower over her eyes. "I am all alone—I wanted to see someone—you if possible, Lady Blakeney—for I could not rest—I wanted to know what had happened."

"What had happened? When? I don't understand."

"What happened between Citizen Chauvelin and your husband?" asked Candeille.

"What is that to you?" replied Marguerite haughtily.

"I pray you do not misunderstand me—" pleaded Candeille eagerly. "I know my presence in your house—the quarrel which I provoked must have filled your heart with hatred and suspicion towards me—but oh! how can I persuade you?—I acted unwillingly—will you not believe me?—I was that man's tool—and—Oh God!" she added with sudden, wild vehemence, "if only you could know what

86

tyranny that accursed government of France exercises over poor help-less women or men who happen to have fallen within reach of its relentless clutches—"

Her voice broke down in a sob. Marguerite hardly knew what to say or think. She had always mistrusted this woman with her theatri-cal ways and stagy airs, from the very first moment she saw her in the tent on the green; and she did not wish to run counter against her instinct, in anything pertaining to the present crisis. And yet in spite of her mistrust the actress' vehement words found an echo in the depths of her own heart. How well she knew that tyranny of which Candeille spoke with such bitterness! Had she not suffered from it, endured terrible sorrow and humiliation, when under the ban of that same appalling tyranny she had betrayed the identity—then unknown to her—of the Scarlet Pimpernel?

Therefore, when Candeille paused after those last excited words, she said with more gentleness than she had shown hitherto, though still quite coldly;

"But you have not yet told me why you came back here tonight? If Citizen Chauvelin was your taskmaster, then you must know all that has occurred."

"I had a vague hope that I might see you."

"For what purpose?"

"To warn you if I could."

"I need no warning."

"Or are too proud to take one—Do you know, Lady Blakeney, that Citizen Chauvelin has a personal hatred against your husband?"

"How do you know that?" asked Marguerite, with her suspicions once more on the *qui-vive*. She could not understand Candeille's at-titude. This midnight visit, the vehemence of her language, the strange mixture of knowledge and ignorance which she displayed. What did this woman know of Chauvelin's secret plans? Was she his open ally, or his helpless tool? And was she even now playing a part taught her or commanded her by that prince of intriguers?

Candeille, however, seemed quite unaware of the spirit of antago-nism and mistrust which Marguerite took but little pains now to dis-guise. She clasped her hands together, and her voice shook with the earnestness of her entreaty.

"Oh!" she said eagerly, "have I not seen that look of hatred in Chauvelin's cruel eyes?—He hates your husband, I tell you—Why I know not—but he hates him—and means that great harm shall come to Sir Percy through this absurd duel—Oh! Lady Blakeney, do not let him go—I entreat you, do not let him go!"

But Marguerite proudly drew back a step or two, away from the reach of those hands, stretched out towards her in such vehement appeal.

"You are overwrought, *Mademoiselle*," she said coldly. "Believe me, I have no need either of your entreaties or of your warning—I should like you to think that I have no wish to be ungrateful—that I appreciate any kind thought you may have harboured for me in your mind—But beyond that—please forgive me if I say it somewhat crudely—I do not feel that the matter concerns you in the least—The hour is late," she added more gently, as if desiring to attenuate the harshness of her last words. "Shall I send my maid to escort you home? She is devoted and discreet—"

"Nay!" retorted the other in tones of quiet sadness, "there is no need of discretion—I am not ashamed of my visit to you tonight—You are very proud, and for your sake I will pray to God that sorrow and humiliation may not come to you, as I feared—We are never likely to meet again, Lady Blakeney—you will not wish it, and I shall have passed out of your life as swiftly as I had entered into it—But there was another thought lurking in my mind when I came tonight—In case Sir Percy goes to France—the duel is to take place in or near Boulogne—this much I do know—would you not wish to go with him?"

"Truly, *Mademoiselle*, I must repeat to you—"

"That 'tis no concern of mine—I know—I own that—But, you see when I came back here tonight in the silence and the darkness—I had not guessed that you would be so proud—I thought that I, a woman, would know how to touch your womanly heart—I was clumsy, I suppose—I made so sure that you would wish to go with your husband, in case—in case he insisted on running his head into the noose, which I feel sure Chauvelin has prepared for him—I myself start for France shortly. Citizen Chauvelin has provided me with the necessary passport for myself and my maid, who was to have accompanied me—Then, just now, when I was all alone—and thought over all the mischief which that fiend had forced me to do for him, it seemed to me that perhaps—"

She broke off abruptly and tried to read the other woman's face in the gloom. But Marguerite, who was taller than the Frenchwoman, was standing, very stiff and erect, giving the young actress neither discouragement nor confidence. She did not interrupt Candeille's long and voluble explanation; vaguely she wondered what it was all about, and even now when the Frenchwoman paused, Marguerite said nothing, but watched her quietly as she took a folded paper from the capacious pocket of her cloak and then held it out with a look of timidity towards Lady Blakeney.

"My maid need not come with me," said Désirée Candeille humbly. "I would far rather travel alone—this is her passport and—Oh! you need not take it out of my hand," she added in tones of bitter self-deprecation, as Marguerite made no sign of taking the paper from her. "See! I will leave it here among the roses!—You mistrust me now—it is only natural—presently, perhaps, calmer reflection will come—you will see that my purpose now is selfless—that I only wish to serve you and him."

She stooped and placed the folded paper in the midst of a great clump of centifolium roses, and then without another word she turned and went her way. For a few moments, whilst Marguerite still stood there, puzzled and vaguely moved, she could hear the gentle *frou-frou* of the other woman's skirts against the soft sand of the path, and then a long-drawn sigh that sounded like a sob.

Then all was still again. The gentle midnight breeze caressed the tops of the ancient oaks and elms behind her, drawing murmurs from their dying leaves like unto the whisperings of ghosts.

Marguerite shuddered with a slight sense of cold. Before her, amongst the dark clump of leaves and the roses, invisible in the gloom, there fluttered with a curious, melancholy flapping, the folded paper placed there by Candeille. She watched it for a while, as, disturbed by the wind, it seemed ready to take its flight towards the river. *Anon* it fell to the ground, and Marguerite with sudden overpowering impulse, stooped and picked it up. Then clutching it nervously in her hand, she walked rapidly back towards the house.

CHAPTER 15

Farewell

As she neared the terrace, she became conscious of several forms moving about at the foot of the steps, some few feet below where she was standing. Soon she saw the glimmer of lanthorns, heard whispering voices, and the lapping of the water against the side of a boat.

Anon a figure, laden with cloaks and sundry packages, passed down the steps close beside her. Even in the darkness Marguerite recognised Benyon, her husband's confidential valet. Without a moment's hesitation, she flew along the terrace towards the wing of the house occupied by Sir Percy. She had not gone far before she discerned his tall figure walking leisurely along the path which here skirted part of the house.

He had on his large caped coat, which was thrown open in front, displaying a grey travelling suit of fine cloth; his hands were as usual buried in the pockets of his breeches, and on his head, he wore the folding *chapeau-bras* which he habitually affected.

Before she had time to think, or to realise that he was going, before she could utter one single word, she was in his arms, clinging to him with passionate intensity, trying in the gloom to catch every expression of his eyes, every quiver of the face now bent down so close to her.

"Percy, you cannot go—you cannot go!—" she pleaded.

She had felt his strong arms closing round her, his lips seeking hers, her eyes, her hair, her clinging hands, which dragged at his shoulders in a wild agony of despair.

"If you really loved me, Percy," she murmured, "you would not go, you would not go—"

He would not trust himself to speak; it well-nigh seemed as if his sinews cracked with the violent effort at self-control. Oh! how she loved him, when she felt in him the passionate lover, the wild, un-tamed creature that he was at heart, on whom the frigid courtliness of manner sat but as a thin veneer. This was his own real personality, and there was little now of the elegant and accomplished gentleman of fashion, schooled to hold every emotion in check, to hide every thought, every desire save that for amusement or for display.

She—feeling her power and his weakness now—gave herself wholly to his embrace, not grudging one single, passionate caress, yielding her lips to him, the while she murmured;

"You cannot go—you cannot—why should you go?—It is mad-ness to leave me—I cannot let you go—"

Her arms clung tenderly round him, her voice was warm and faint-ly shaken with suppressed tears, and as he wildly murmured; "Don't! for pity's sake!" she almost felt that her love would be triumphant.

"For pity's sake, I'll go on pleading, Percy!" she whispered. "Oh! my love, my dear! do not leave me!—we have scarce had time to sa-vour our happiness.. we have such arrears of joy to make up—Do not go, Percy—there's so much I want to say to you—Nay! you shall not!

you shall not!" she added with sudden vehemence. "Look me straight in the eyes, my dear, and tell me if you can leave now?"

He did not reply, but, almost roughly, he placed his hand over her tear-dimmed eyes, which were turned up to his, in an agony of tender appeal. Thus, he blindfolded her with that wild caress. She should not see—no, not even she!—that for the space of a few seconds stern manhood was well-nigh vanquished by the magic of her love.

All that was most human in him, all that was weak in this strong and untamed nature, cried aloud for peace and luxury and idleness; for long summer afternoons spent in lazy content, for the companionship of horses and dogs and of flowers, with no thought or cares save those for the next evening's gavotte, no graver occupation save that of sitting at *her* feet.

And during these few seconds, whilst his hand lay across her eyes, the lazy, idle fop of fashionable London was fighting a hand-to-hand fight with the bold leader of a band of adventurers; and his own passionate love for his wife ranged itself with fervent intensity on the side of his weaker self. Forgotten were the horrors of the guillotine, the calls of the innocent, the appeal of the helpless; forgotten the daring adventures, the excitements, the hair's-breadth escapes; for those few seconds, heavenly in themselves, he only remembered her—his wife—her beauty and her tender appeal to him.

She would have pleaded again, for she felt that she was winning in this fight; her instinct—that unerring instinct of the woman who loves and feels herself beloved—told her that for the space of an infinitesimal fraction of time, his iron will was inclined to bend; but he checked her pleading with a kiss.

Then there came a change.

Like a gigantic wave carried inwards by the tide, his turbulent emotion seemed suddenly to shatter itself against a rock of self-control. Was it a call from the boatmen below? a distant scrunching of feet upon the gravel?—who knows, perhaps only a sigh in the midnight air, a ghostly summons from the land of dreams that recalled him to himself.

Even as Marguerite was still clinging to him, with the ardent fervour of her own passion, she felt the rigid tension of his arms relax, the power of his embrace weaken, the wild love-light become dim in his eyes.

He kissed her fondly, tenderly, and with infinite gentleness smoothed away the little damp curls from her brow. There was a wistfulness now in his caress, and in his kiss, there was the finality of a long farewell.

"'Tis time I went," he said, "or we shall miss the tide."

These were the first coherent words he had spoken since first she had met him here in this lonely part of the garden, and his voice was perfectly steady, conventional and cold. An icy pang shot through Marguerite's heart. It was as if she had been abruptly wakened from a beautiful dream.

"You are not going, Percy!" she murmured, and her own voice now sounded hollow and forced. "Oh! if you loved me you would not go!"

"If I love you!"

Nay! in this at least there was no dream! no coldness in his voice when he repeated those words with such a sigh of tenderness, such a world of longing, that the bitterness of her great pain vanished, giving place to tears. He took her hand in his. The passion was momentarily conquered, forced within his innermost soul, by his own alter ego, that second personality in him, the cold-blooded and coolly-calculating adventurer who juggled with his life and tossed it recklessly upon the sea of chance 'twixt a doggerel and a smile. But the tender love lingered on, fighting the enemy awhile longer, the wistful desire was there for her kiss, the tired longing for the exquisite repose of her embrace.

He took her hand in his, and bent his lips to it, and with the warmth of his kiss upon it, she felt a moisture like a tear.

"I must go, dear," he said, after a little while.

"Why? Why?" she repeated obstinately. "Am I nothing then? Is my life of no account? My sorrows? My fears? My misery? Oh!" she added with vehement bitterness, "why should it always be others? What are others to you and to me, Percy?—Are we not happy here?—Have you not fulfilled to its uttermost that self-imposed duty to people who can be nothing to us?—Is not your life ten thousand times more precious to me than the lives of ten thousand others?"

Even through the darkness, and because his face was so close to hers, she could see a quaint little smile playing round the corners of his mouth.

"Nay, m'dear," he said gently, "'tis not ten thousand lives that call to me today—only one at best—Don't you hate to think of that poor little old _curé_ sitting in the midst of his ruined pride and hopes; the jewels so confidently entrusted to his care, stolen from him, he waiting, perhaps, in his little presbytery for the day when those brutes will march him to prison and to death—Nay! I think a little sea voyage and English country air would suit the Abbé Foucquet, m'dear, and I only mean to ask him to cross the Channel with me!—"

"Percy!" she pleaded.

"Oh! I know! I know!" he rejoined with that short deprecatory sigh of his, which seemed always to close any discussion between them on that point, "you are thinking of that absurd duel—" He laughed lightly, good-humouredly, and his eyes gleamed with merriment.

"La, m'dear!" he said gaily, "will you not reflect a moment? Could I refuse the challenge before His Royal Highness and the ladies? I couldn't—Faith! that was it—Just a case of couldn't—Fate did it all—the quarrel—my interference—the challenge—*he* had planned it all of course—Let us own that he is a brave man, seeing that he and I are not even yet, for that beating he gave me on the Calais cliffs."

"Yes! he has planned it all," she retorted vehemently. "The quarrel tonight, your journey to France, your meeting with him face to face at a given hour and place where he can most readily, most easily close the death-trap upon you."

This time he broke into a laugh. A good, hearty laugh, full of the joy of living, of the madness and intoxication of a bold adventure, a laugh that had not one particle of anxiety or of tremor in it.

"Nay! m'dear!" he said, "but your ladyship is astonishing—Close a death-trap upon your humble servant?—Nay! the governing citizens of France will have to be very active and mighty wide-awake ere they succeed in stealing a march on me—Zounds! but we'll give them an exciting chase this time—Nay! little woman, do not fear!" he said with sudden infinite gentleness, "those demmed murderers have not got me yet."

Oh! how often she had fought with him thus; with him, the adventurer, the part of his dual nature that was her bitter enemy, and which took him, the lover, away from her side. She knew so well the finality of it all, the amazing hold which that unconquerable desire for these mad adventures had upon him. Impulsive, ardent as she was, Marguerite felt in her very soul an overwhelming fury against herself for her own weakness, her own powerlessness in the face of that which forever threatened to ruin her life and her happiness.

Yes! and his also! for he loved her! he loved her! he loved her! the thought went on hammering in her mind, for she knew of its great truth! He loved her and went away! And she, poor, puny weakling, was unable to hold him back; the tendrils which fastened his soul to hers were not so tenacious as those which made him cling to suffering humanity, over there in France, where men and women were in fear of death and torture and looked upon the elusive and mysterious Scarlet Pimpernel as a heaven-born hero sent to save them from their doom. To them at these times his very heartstrings seemed to turn with unconquerable force, and when, with all the ardour of her own passion, she tried to play upon the cords of his love for her, he could not respond, for they—the strangers—had the stronger claim.

And yet through it all she knew that this love of humanity, this mad desire to serve and to help, in no way detracted from his love for her. Nay, it intensified it, made it purer and better, adding to the joy of perfect intercourse the poetic and subtle fragrance of ever-recurring pain.

But now at last she felt weary of the fight; her heart was aching, bruised and sore. An infinite fatigue seemed to weigh like lead upon her very soul. This seemed so different to any other parting, that had perforce been during the past year. The presence of Chauvelin in her house, the obvious planning of this departure for France, had filled her with a foreboding, nay, almost a certitude of a gigantic and deadly cataclysm.

Her senses began to reel; she seemed not to see anything very distinctly; even the loved form took on a strange and ghostlike shape. He now looked preternaturally tall, and there was a mist between her and him.

She thought that he spoke to her again, but she was not quite sure, for his voice sounded like some weird and mysterious echo. A bosquet of climbing heliotrope close by threw a fragrance into the evening air, which turned her giddy with its overpowering sweetness.

She closed her eyes, for she felt as if she must die, if she held them open any longer; and as she closed them it seemed to her as if he folded her in one last, long, heavenly embrace.

He felt her graceful figure swaying in his arms like a tall and slender lily bending to the wind. He saw that she was but half-conscious, and thanked heaven for this kindly solace to his heart-breaking farewell.

There was a sloping, mossy bank close by, there where the marble terrace yielded to the encroaching shrubbery; a tangle of pale pink monthly roses made a bower overhead. She was just sufficiently conscious to enable him to lead her to this soft green couch. There he laid her amongst the roses, kissed the dear, tired eyes, her hands, her lips, her tiny feet, and went.

CHAPTER 16

The Passport

The rhythmic clapper of oars roused Marguerite from this trance-like swoon.

In a moment she was on her feet, all her fatigue gone, her numbness of soul and body vanished as in a flash. She was fully conscious now! conscious that he had gone! that according to every probability under heaven and every machination concocted in hell, he would never return from France alive, and that she had failed to hear the last words which he spoke to her, had failed to glean his last look or to savour his final kiss.

Though the night was starlit and balmy it was singularly dark, and vainly did Marguerite strain her eyes to catch sight of that boat which was bearing him away so swiftly now; she strained her ears, vaguely hoping to catch one last, lingering echo of his voice. But all was silence, save that monotonous clapper, which seemed to beat against her heart like a rhythmic knell of death.

She could hear the oars distinctly; there were six or eight, she thought, certainly no fewer. Eight oarsmen probably, which meant the larger boat, and undoubtedly the longer journey—not to London only with a view to posting to Dover, but to Tilbury Fort, where the *Daydream* would be in readiness to start with a favourable tide.

Thought was returning to her, slowly and coherently; the pain of the last farewell was still there, bruising her very senses with its dull and heavy weight, but it had become numb and dead, leaving her, herself, her heart and soul, stunned and apathetic, whilst her brain was gradually resuming its activity.

And the more she thought it over, the more certain she grew that her husband was going as far as Tilbury by river and would embark on the *Daydream* there. Of course, he would go to Boulogne at once. The duel was to take place there, Candeille had told her that—adding that she thought she, Marguerite, would wish to go with him.

To go with him!

Heavens above! was not that the only real, tangible thought in that whirling chaos which was raging in her mind?

To go with him! Surely there must be some means of reaching him yet! Fate, Nature, God Himself would never permit so monstrous a thing as this; that she should be parted from her husband, now when his life was not only in danger, but forfeited already—lost—a precious thing all but gone from this world.

Percy was going to Boulogne—she must go too. By posting at
once to Dover, she could get the tidal boat on the morrow and reach
the French coast quite as soon as the *Daydream*. Once at Boulogne,
she would have no difficulty in finding her husband, of that she felt
sure. She would have but to dog Chauvelin's footsteps, find out something of his plans, of the orders he gave to troops or to spies,—oh! she
would find him! of that she was never for a moment in doubt!

How well she remembered her journey to Calais just a year ago, in
company with Sir Andrew Ffoulkes! Chance had favoured her then,
had enabled her to be of service to her husband if only by distracting
Chauvelin's attention for a while to herself. Heaven knows! she had
but little hope of being of use to him now; an aching sense was in her
that fate had at last been too strong! that the daring adventurer had
staked once too often, had cast the die and had lost.

In the bosom of her dress she felt the sharp edge of the paper
left for her by Désirée Candeille among the roses in the park. She
had picked it up almost mechanically then, and tucked it away, hardly heeding what she was doing. Whatever the motive of the French
actress had been in placing the passport at her disposal, Marguerite
blessed her in her heart for it. To the woman she had mistrusted, she
would owe the last supreme happiness of her life.

Her resolution never once wavered. Percy would not take her with
him; that was understandable. She could neither expect it nor think
it. But she, on the other hand, could not stay in England, at Blakeney
Manor, whilst any day, any hour, the death-trap set by Chauvelin for
the Scarlet Pimpernel might be closing upon the man whom she
worshipped. She would go mad if she stayed. As there could be no
chance of escape for Percy now, as he had agreed to meet his deadly
enemy face to face at a given place, and a given hour, she could not
be a hindrance to him; and she knew enough subterfuge, enough
machinations and disguises by now, to escape Chauvelin's observation,
unless—unless Percy wanted her, and then she would be there.

No! she could not be a hindrance. She had a passport in her pocket, everything *en règle*; nobody could harm her, and she could come
and go as she pleased. There were plenty of swift horses in the stables,
plenty of devoted servants to do her bidding quickly and discreetly;
moreover, at moments like these, conventionalities and the possible
conjectures and surmises of others became of infinitesimally small
importance. The household of Blakeney Manor were accustomed to

the master's sudden journeys and absences of several days, presumably on some shooting or other sporting expeditions, with no one in attendance on him, save Benyon, his favourite valet. These passed without any comments now! Bah! let everyone marvel for once at her ladyship's sudden desire to go to Dover and let it all be a nine days' wonder; she certainly did not care. Skirting the house, she reached the stables beyond. One or two men were astir. To these she gave the necessary orders for her coach and four, then she found her way back to the house.

Walking along the corridor, she went past the room occupied by Juliette de Marny. For a moment she hesitated, then she turned and knocked at the door.

Juliette was not yet in bed, for she went to the door herself and opened it. Obviously, she had been quite unable to rest, her hair was falling loosely over her shoulders, and there was a look of grave anxiety on her young face.

"Juliette," said Marguerite in a hurried whisper, the moment she had closed the door behind her and she and the young girl were alone, "I am going to France to be near my husband. He has gone to meet that fiend in a duel which is nothing but a trap, set to capture him, and lead him to his death. I want you to be of help to me, here in my house, in my absence."

"I would give my life for you, Lady Blakeney," said Juliette simply, "is it not *his* since he saved it?"

"It is only a little presence of mind, a little coolness and patience, which I will ask of you, dear," said Marguerite. "You of course know who your rescuer was, therefore you will understand my fears. Until tonight, I had vague doubts as to how much Chauvelin really knew, but now these doubts have naturally vanished. He and the French Revolutionary Government know that the Scarlet Pimpernel and Percy Blakeney are one and the same. The whole scene tonight was prearranged; you and I and all the spectators, and that woman Candeille—we were all puppets piping to that devil's tune. The duel, too, was prearranged!—that woman wearing your mother's jewels!—Had you not provoked her, a quarrel between her and me, or one of my guests would have been forced somehow—I wanted to tell you this, lest you should fret, and think that you were in any way responsible for what has happened—You were not—He had arranged it all—You were only the tool—just as I was—You must understand and believe that— Percy would hate to think that you felt yourself to blame—you are not that, in any way—The challenge was bound to come—Chauvelin had arranged that it should come, and if you had failed him as a tool, he soon would have found another! Do you believe that?"

"I believe that you are an angel of goodness, Lady Blakeney," replied Juliette, struggling with her tears, "and that you are the only woman in the world worthy to be his wife."

"But," insisted Marguerite firmly, as the young girl took her cold hand in her own, and gently fondling it, covered it with grateful kisses, "but if—if anything happens—*anon*—you will believe firmly that you were in no way responsible?—that you were innocent.. and merely a blind tool?—"

"God bless you for that!"

"You will believe it?"

"I will."

"And now for my request," rejoined Lady Blakeney in a more quiet, more matter-of-fact tone of voice. "You must represent me, here, when I am gone; explain as casually and as naturally as you can, that I have gone to join my husband on his yacht for a few days. Lucie, my maid, is devoted and a tower of secrecy; she will stand between you and the rest of the household, in concocting some plausible story. To every friend who calls, to anyone of our world whom you may meet, you must tell the same tale, and if you note an air of incredulity in anyone, if you hear whispers of there being some mystery, well! let the world wag its busy tongue—I care less than naught; it will soon tire of me and my doings, and having torn my reputation to shreds will quickly leave me in peace. But to Sir Andrew Ffoulkes," she added earnestly, "tell the whole truth from me. He will understand and do as he thinks right."

"I will do all you ask, Lady Blakeney, and am proud to think that I shall be serving you, even in so humble and easy a capacity. When do you start?"

"At once. Goodbye, Juliette."

She bent down to the young girl and kissed her tenderly on the forehead, then she glided out of the room as rapidly as she had come. Juliette, of course, did not try to detain her, or to force her help of companionship on her when obviously she would wish to be alone.

Marguerite quickly reached her room. Her maid Lucie was already waiting for her. Devoted and silent as she was, one glance at her mistress' face told her that trouble—grave and imminent—had reached Blakeney Manor.

Marguerite, whilst Lucie undressed her, took up the passport and carefully perused the personal description of one, Céline Dumont, maid to Citizeness Désirée Candeille, which was given therein; tall, blue eyes, light hair, age about twenty-five. It all might have been vaguely meant for her. She had a dark cloth gown, and long black cloak with hood to come well over the head. These she now donned, with some thick shoes, and a dark-coloured handkerchief tied over her head under the hood, so as to hide the golden glory of her hair.

She was quite calm and in no haste. She made Lucie pack a small hand valise with some necessaries for the journey and provided herself plentifully with money—French and English notes—which she tucked well away inside her dress.

Then she bade her maid, who was struggling with her tears, a kindly farewell, and quickly went down to her coach.

CHAPTER 17

Boulogne

During the journey Marguerite had not much leisure to think. The discomforts and petty miseries incidental on cheap travelling had the very welcome effect of making her forget, for the time being, the soul-rendering crisis through which she was now passing.

For, of necessity, she had to travel at the cheap rate, among the crowd of poorer passengers who were herded aft the packet boat, leaning up against one another, sitting on bundles and packages of all kinds; that part of the deck, reeking with the smell of tar and sea-water, damp, squally and stuffy, was an abomination of hideous discomfort to the dainty, fastidious lady of fashion, yet she almost welcomed the intolerable propinquity, the cold douches of salt water, which every now and then wetted her through and through, for it was the consequent sense of physical wretchedness that helped her to forget the intolerable anguish of her mind.

And among these poorer travellers she felt secure from observation. No one took much notice of her. She looked just like one of the herd, and in the huddled-up little figure, in the dark bedraggled clothes, no one would for a moment have recognised the dazzling personality of Lady Blakeney.

Drawing her hood well over her head, she sat in a secluded corner of the deck, upon the little black valise which contained the few belongings she had brought with her. Her cloak and dress, now mud-stained and dank with splashings of salt-water, attracted no one's attention. There was a keen north-easterly breeze, cold and penetrating, but favourable to a rapid crossing. Marguerite, who had gone through several hours of weary travelling by coach, before she had embarked at Dover in the late afternoon, was unspeakably tired. She had watched the golden sunset out at sea until her eyes were burning with pain, and as the dazzling crimson and orange and purple gave place to the soft grey tones of evening, she descried the round cupola of the church of Our Lady of Boulogne against the dull background of the sky.

After that her mind became a blank. A sort of torpor fell over her sense; she was wakeful and yet half-asleep, unconscious of everything around her, seeing nothing but the distant massive towers of old Boulogne churches gradually detaching themselves one by one from out the fast gathering gloom.

The town seemed like a dream city, a creation of some morbid imagination, presented to her mind's eye as the city of sorrow and death.

When the boat finally scraped her sides along the rough wooden jetty, Marguerite felt as if she were forcibly awakened. She was numb and stiff and thought she must have fallen asleep during the last half hour of the journey. Everything round her was dark. The sky was overcast, and the night seemed unusually sombre. Figures were moving all around her, there was noise and confusion of voices, and a general pushing and shouting which seemed strangely weird in this gloom. Here among the poorer passengers, there had not been thought any necessity for a light; one solitary lantern fixed to a mast only enhanced the intense blackness of everything around. Now and then a face would come within range of this meagre streak of yellow light, looking strangely distorted, with great, elongated shadows across the brow and chin, a grotesque, ghostly apparition which quickly vanished again, scurrying off like some frightened gnome, giving place to other forms, other figures all equally grotesque and equally weird.

Marguerite watched them all half stupidly and motionlessly for a while. She did not quite know what she ought to do and did not like to ask any questions; she was dazed and the darkness blinded her. Then gradually things began to detach themselves more clearly. On looking straight before her, she began to discern the landing place, the little wooden bridge across which the passengers walked one by one from the boat unto the jetty. The first-class passengers were evidently all alighting now; the crowd, of which Marguerite formed a unit, had been pushed back in a more compact herd, out of the way for the moment, so that their betters might get along more comfortably.

Beyond the landing stage a little booth had been erected, a kind of tent, open in front and lighted up within by a couple of lanthorns. Under this tent there was a table, behind which sat a man dressed in some sort of official looking clothes and wearing the tricolour scarf across his chest.

All the passengers from the boat had apparently to file past this tent. Marguerite could see them now quite distinctly, the profiles of the various faces, as they paused for a moment in front of the table, being brilliantly illuminated by one of the lanterns. Two sentinels wearing the uniform of the National Guard stood each side of the table. The passengers one by one took out their passport as they went by, handed it to the man in the official dress, who examined it carefully, very lengthily, then signed it and returned the paper to its owner; but at times, he appeared doubtful, folded the passport and put it down in front of him; the passenger would protest; Marguerite could not hear what was said, but she could see that some argument was attempted, quickly dismissed by a peremptory order from the official. The doubtful passport was obviously put on one side for further examination, and the unfortunate owner thereof detained, until he or she had been able to give more satisfactory references to the representatives of the Committee of Public Safety, stationed at Boulogne.

This process of examination necessarily took a long time. Marguerite was getting horribly tired; her feet ached and she scarcely could hold herself upright, yet she watched all these people mechanically, making absurd little guesses in her weary mind as to whose passport would find favour in the eyes of the official, and whose would be found suspect and inadequate.

Suspect! a terrible word these times! since Merlin's terrible law decreed now that every man, woman, or child who was suspected by the Republic of being a traitor was a traitor in fact.

How sorry she felt for those whose passports were detained, who tried to argue—so needlessly!—and who were finally led off by a soldier, who had stepped out from somewhere in the dark, and had to await further examination, probably imprisonment and often death.

As to herself, she felt quite safe; the passport given to her by Chauvelin's own accomplice was sure to be quite *en règle*.

Then suddenly her heart seemed to give a sudden leap and then to stop in its beating for a second or two. In one of the passengers, a man who was just passing in front of the tent, she had recognised the form and profile of Chauvelin.

He had no passport to show, but evidently the official knew who he was, for he stood up and saluted, and listened deferentially whilst the ex-ambassador apparently gave him a few instructions. It seemed to Marguerite that these instructions related to two women who were close behind Chauvelin at the time, and who presently seemed to file past without going through the usual formalities of showing their passports. But of this she could not be quite sure. The women were closely hooded and veiled and her own attention had been completely absorbed by this sudden appearance of her deadly enemy.

Yet what more natural than that Chauvelin should be here now? His object accomplished, he had no doubt posted to Dover, just as she had done. There was no difficulty in that, and a man of his type and importance would always have unlimited means and money at his command to accomplish any journey he might desire to undertake.

There was nothing strange or even unexpected in the man's presence here; and yet somehow it had made the whole, awful reality more tangible, more wholly unforgettable. Marguerite remembered his abject words to her, when first she had seen him at the Richmond fête; he said that he had fallen into disgrace, that, having failed in his service to the Republic, he had been relegated to a subordinate position, pushed aside with contumely to make room for better, abler men.

Well! all that was a lie, of course, a cunning method of gaining access into her house; of that she had already been convinced, when Candeille provoked the *esclandre* which led to the challenge.

That on French soil he seemed in anything but a subsidiary position, that he appeared to rule rather than to obey, could in no way appear to Marguerite in the nature of surprise.

As the actress had been a willing tool in the cunning hands of Chauvelin, so were probably all these people around her. Where others cringed in the face of officialism, the ex-ambassador had stepped forth as a master; he had shown a badge, spoken a word mayhap, and the man in the tent who had made other people tremble, stood up deferentially and obeyed all commands.

It was all very simple and very obvious, but Marguerite's mind had been asleep, and it was the sight of the sable-clad little figure which had roused it from its happy torpor.

In a moment now, her brain was active and alert, and presently it seemed to her as if another figure—taller than those around—had crossed the barrier immediately in the wake of Chauvelin. Then she chided herself for her fancies!

It could not be her husband. Not yet! He had gone by water and would scarce be in Boulogne before the morning!

Ah! now at last came the turn of the second-class passengers! There was a general *bousculade* and the human bundle began to move. Marguerite lost sight of the tent and its awe-inspiring appurtenances; she was a mere unit again in this herd on the move. She too progressed along slowly, one step at a time; it was wearisome and she was deadly tired. She was beginning to form plans now that she had arrived in France. All along she had made up her mind that she would begin by seeking out the Abbé Foucquet, for he would prove a link 'twixt her husband and herself. She knew that Percy would communicate with the abbe; had he not told her that the rescue of the devoted old man from the clutches of the Terrorists would be one of the chief objects of his journey? It had never occurred to her what she would do if she found the Abbé Foucquet gone from Boulogne.

"*Hé! la mère!* your passport!"

The rough words roused her from her meditations. She had moved forward, quite mechanically, her mind elsewhere, her thoughts not following the aim of her feet. Thus, she must have crossed the bridge along with some of the crowd, must have landed on the jetty, and reached the front of the tent, without really knowing what she was doing.

Ah yes! her passport! She had quite forgotten that! But she had it by her, quite in order, given to her in a fit of tardy remorse by Demoiselle Candeille, the intimate friend of one of the most influential members of the Revolutionary Government of France.

She took the passport from the bosom of her dress and handed it to the man in the official dress.

"Your name?" he asked peremptorily.

"Céline Dumont," she replied unhesitatingly, for had she not rehearsed all this in her mind dozens of times, until her tongue could rattle off the borrowed name as easily as it could her own; "servitor to Citizeness Désirée Candeille!"

The man who had very carefully been examining the paper the while, placed it down on the table deliberately in front of him, and said;

"*Céline Dumont! Eh! la mère!* what tricks are you up to now?"

"Tricks? I don't understand!" she said quietly, for she was not afraid. The passport was *en règle*; she knew she had nothing to fear.

"Oh! but I think you do!" retorted the official with a sneer, "and 'tis a mighty clever one, I'll allow. Céline Dumont, *ma foi!* Not badly imagined, *ma petite mère*; and all would have passed off splendidly; unfortunately, Céline Dumont, servitor to Citizeness Désirée Candeille, passed through these barriers along with her mistress not half an hour ago."

And with long, grimy finger he pointed to an entry in the large book which lay open before him, and wherein he had apparently been busy making notes of the various passengers who had filed past him.

Then he looked up with a triumphant leer at the calm face of Marguerite. She still did not feel really frightened, only puzzled and perturbed; but all the blood had rushed away from her face, leaving her cheeks ashen white, and pressing against her heart, until it almost choked her.

"You are making a mistake, Citizen," she said very quietly. "I am Citizeness Candeille's maid. She gave me the passport herself, just before I left for England; if you will ask her the question, she will confirm what I say, and she assured me that it was quite *en règle*."

But the man only shrugged his shoulders and laughed derisively. The incident evidently amused him, yet he must have seen many of the same sort; in the far corner of the tent Marguerite seemed to discern a few moving forms, soldiers, she thought, for she caught sight of a glint like that of steel. One or two men stood close behind the official at the desk, and the sentinels were to the right and left of the tent.

With an instinctive sense of appeal, Marguerite looked round from one face to the other; but each looked absolutely impassive and stolid, quite uninterested in this little scene, the exact counterpart of a dozen others, enacted on this very spot within the last hour.

"*Hé! là! là! petite mère!*" said the official in the same tone of easy persiflage which he had adopted all along, "but we do know how to concoct a pretty lie, aye! and so circumstantially too! Unfortunately, it was Citizeness Désirée Candeille herself who happened to be standing just where you are at the present moment, along with her maid, Céline Dumont, both of whom were specially signed for and recommended as perfectly trustworthy, by no less a person than Citoyen Chauvelin of the Committee of Public Safety."

"But I assure you that there is a mistake," pleaded Marguerite earnestly, "'Tis the other woman who lied, I have my passport and—"

"A truce on this," retorted the man peremptorily. "If everything is as you say, and if you have nothing to hide, you'll be at liberty to continue your journey tomorrow, after you have explained yourself before the citizen governor. Next one now, quick!"

Marguerite tried another protest, just as those others had done, whom she had watched so mechanically before. But already she knew that that would be useless, for she had felt that a heavy hand was being placed on her shoulder, and that she was being roughly led away.

In a flash she had understood and seen the whole sequel of the awful trap which had all along been destined to engulf her as well as her husband.

What a clumsy, blind fool she had been!

What a miserable antagonist the subtle schemes of a past master of intrigue as was Chauvelin. To have enticed the Scarlet Pimpernel to France was a great thing! The challenge was clever, the acceptance of it by the bold adventurer a forgone conclusion, but the master stroke of the whole plan was done, when she, the wife, was enticed over too with the story of Candeille's remorse and the offer of the passport.

Fool! fool that she was!

And how well did Chauvelin know feminine nature! How cleverly he had divined her thoughts, her feelings, the impulsive way in which she would act; how easily he had guessed that, knowing her husband's danger, she, Marguerite, would immediately follow him.

Now the trap had closed on her—and she saw it all, when it was too late.

Percy Blakeney in France! His wife a prisoner! Her freedom and safety in exchange for his life!

The hopelessness of it all struck her with appalling force, and her senses reeled with the awful finality of the disaster.

Yet instinct in her still struggled for freedom. Ahead of her, and all around, beyond the tent and in the far distance there was a provocative alluring darkness; if she only could get away, only could reach the shelter of that remote and sombre distance, she would hide, and wait, not blunder again, oh no! she would be prudent and wary, if only she could get away!

One woman's struggles, against five men! It was pitiable, sublime, absolutely useless.

The man in the tent seemed to be watching her with much amusement for a moment or two, as her whole graceful body stiffened for that absurd and unequal physical contest. He seemed vastly entertained at the sight of this good-looking young woman striving to pit her strength against five sturdy soldiers of the Republic.

"*Allons!* that will do now!" he said at last roughly. "We have no time to waste! Get the jade away, and let her cool her temper in No. 6, until the citizen governor gives further orders.

"Take her away!" he shouted more loudly, banging a grimy fist down on the table before him, as Marguerite still struggled on with the blind madness of despair. "*Pardi!* can none of you rid us of that turbulent baggage?"

The crowd behind were pushing forward; the guard within the tent were jeering at those who were striving to drag Marguerite away; these latter were cursing loudly and volubly, until one of them, tired out, furious and brutal, raised his heavy fist and with an obscene oath brought it crashing down upon the unfortunate woman's head.

Perhaps, though it was the work of a savage and cruel creature, the blow proved more merciful than it had been intended; it had caught Marguerite full between the eyes; her aching senses, wearied and reeling already, gave way beneath this terrible violence; her useless struggles ceased, her arms fell inert by her side; and losing consciousness completely, her proud, unbendable spirit was spared the humiliating knowledge of her final removal by the rough soldiers, and of the complete wreckage of her last, lingering hopes.

CHAPTER 18

No. 6

Consciousness returned very slowly, very painfully.

It was night when last Marguerite had clearly known what was going on around her; it was daylight before she realised that she still lived, that she still knew and suffered.

Her head ached intolerably—that was the first conscious sensation which came to her; then she vaguely perceived a pale ray of sunshine, very hazy and narrow, which came from somewhere in front of her and struck her in the face. She kept her eyes tightly shut, for that filmy light caused her an increase of pain.

She seemed to be lying on her back, and her fingers wandering restlessly around felt a hard paillasse, beneath their touch, then a rough pillow, and her own cloak laid over her; thought had not yet returned, only the sensation of great suffering and of infinite fatigue.

Anon she ventured to open her eyes, and gradually one or two objects detached themselves from out the haze which still obscured her vision.

Firstly, the narrow aperture—scarcely a window—filled in with tiny squares of coarse, unwashed glass, through which the rays of the morning sun were making kindly efforts to penetrate, then the cloud of dust illumined by those same rays, and made up—so it seemed to the poor tired brain that strove to perceive—of myriads of abnormally large molecules, over-abundant, and over-active, for they appeared to be dancing a kind of wild saraband before Marguerite's aching eyes, advancing and retreating, forming themselves into groups and taking on funny shapes of weird masques and grotesque faces which grinned at the unconscious figure lying helpless on the rough paillasse.

Through and beyond them Marguerite gradually became aware of three walls of a narrow room, dank and grey, half covered with white-wash and half with greenish mildew! Yes! and there, opposite to her and immediately beneath that semblance of a window, was another paillasse, and on it something dark, that moved.

The words; "*Liberté, Egalité, Fraternité ou la Mort!*" stared out at her from somewhere beyond those active molecules of dust, but she also saw just above the other paillasse the vague outline of a dark crucifix.

It seemed a terrible effort to co-ordinate all these things, and to try and realise what the room was, and what was the meaning of the pail-lasse, the narrow window and the stained walls, too much altogether for the aching head to take in save very slowly, very gradually.

Marguerite was content to wait and to let memory creep back as reluctantly as it would.

"Do you think, my child, you could drink a little of this now?"

It was a gentle, rather tremulous voice which struck upon her ear. She opened her eyes and noticed that the dark something which had previously been on the opposite paillasse was no longer there, and that there appeared to be a presence close to her only vaguely defined, someone kindly and tender who had spoken to her in French, with that soft sing-song accent peculiar to the Normandy peasants, and who now seemed to be pressing something cool and soothing to her lips.

"They gave me this for you!" continued the tremulous voice close to her ear. "I think it would do you good, if you tried to take it."

A hand and arm was thrust underneath the rough pillow, causing her to raise her head a little. A glass was held to her lips and she drank.

The hand that held the glass was all wrinkled, brown and dry, and trembled slightly, but the arm which supported her head was firm and very kind.

"There! I am sure you feel better now. Close your eyes and try to go to sleep."

She did as she was bid and was ready enough to close her eyes. It seemed to her presently as if something had been interposed between her aching head and that trying ray of white September sun.

Perhaps she slept peacefully for a little while after that, for though her head was still very painful, her mouth and throat felt less parched and dry. Through this sleep or semblance of sleep, she was conscious of the same pleasant voice softly droning *Paters* and *Aves* close to her ear.

Thus, she lay, during the greater part of the day. Not quite fully conscious, not quite awake to the awful memories which *anon* would crowd upon her thick and fast.

From time to time the same kind and trembling hands would with gentle pressure force a little liquid food through her unwilling lips; some warm soup, or *anon* a glass of milk. Beyond the pain in her head, she was conscious of no physical ill; she felt at perfect peace, and an extraordinary sense of quiet and repose seemed to pervade this small room, with its narrow window through which the rays of the sun came gradually in more golden splendour as the day drew towards noon, and then they vanished altogether.

The drony voice close beside her acted as a soporific upon her nerves. In the afternoon she fell into a real and beneficent sleep—

But after that, she woke to full consciousness!

Oh! the horror, the folly of it all!

It came back to her with all the inexorable force of an appalling certainty.

She was a prisoner in the hands of those who long ago had sworn to bring The Scarlet Pimpernel to death!

She! his wife, a hostage in their hands! her freedom and safety offered to him as the price of his own! Here there was no question of dreams or of nightmares, no illusions as to the ultimate intentions of her husband's enemies. It was all a reality, and even now, before she had the strength fully to grasp the whole nature of this horrible situation, she knew that by her own act of mad and passionate impulse, she had hopelessly jeopardised the life of the man she loved.

For with that sublime confidence in him begotten of her love, she never for a moment doubted which of the two alternatives he would choose, when once they were placed before him. He would sacrifice himself for her; he would prefer to die a thousand deaths so long as they set her free.

For herself, her own sufferings, her danger or humiliation she cared nothing! Nay! at this very moment she was conscious of a wild passionate desire for death—In this sudden onrush of memory and of thought she wished with all her soul and heart and mind to die here suddenly, on this hard paillasse, in this lonely and dark prison—so that she should be out of the way once and for all—so that she should *not* be the hostage to be bartered against his precious life and freedom.

He would suffer acutely, terribly at her loss, because he loved her above everything else on earth; he would suffer in every fibre of his passionate and ardent nature, but he would not then have to endure the humiliations, the awful alternatives, the galling impotence and miserable death, the relentless "either—or" which his enemies were even now preparing for him.

And then came a revulsion of feeling. Marguerite's was essentially a buoyant and active nature, a keen brain which worked and schemed and planned, rather than one ready to accept the inevitable.

Hardly had these thoughts of despair and of death formulated themselves in her mind, than with brilliant swiftness, a new train of ideas began to take root.

What if matters were not so hopeless after all?

Already her mind had flown instinctively to thoughts of escape. Had she the right to despair? She, the wife and intimate companion of the man who had astonished the world with his daring, his prowess, his amazing good luck, she to imagine for a moment that in this all-supreme moment of adventurous life the Scarlet Pimpernel would fail!

Was not English society peopled with men, women and children whom his ingenuity had rescued from plights quite as seemingly hopeless as her own, and would not all the resources of that inventive brain be brought to bear upon this rescue which touched him nearer and more deeply than any which he had attempted hitherto?

Now Marguerite was chiding herself for her doubts and for her fears. Already she remembered that amongst the crowd on the landing stage she had perceived a figure—unusually tall—following in the wake of Chauvelin and his companions. Awakened hope had already assured her that she had not been mistaken, that Percy, contrary to her own surmises, had reached Boulogne last night; he always acted so differently to what anyone might expect, that it was quite possible that he had crossed over in the packet-boat after all unbeknown to Marguerite as well as to his enemies.

Oh yes! the more she thought about it all, the more sure was she that Percy was already in Boulogne, and that he knew of her capture and her danger.

What right had she to doubt even for a moment that he would know how to reach her, how—when the time came—to save himself and her?

A warm glow began to fill her veins, she felt excited and alert, absolutely unconscious now of pain or fatigue, in this radiant joy of reawakened hope.

She raised herself slightly, leaning on her elbow; she was still very weak and the slight movement had made her giddy, but soon she would be strong and well—she must be strong and well and ready to do his bidding when the time for escape would have come.

"Ah! you are better, my child, I see—" said that quaint, tremulous voice again, with its soft sing-song accent, "but you must not be so venturesome, you know. The physician said that you had received a cruel blow. The brain has been rudely shaken—and you must lie quite still all today, or your poor little head will begin to ache again."

Marguerite turned to look at the speaker, and in spite of her excitement, of her sorrow and of her anxieties, she could not help smiling at the whimsical little figure which sat opposite to her, on a very rickety chair, solemnly striving with slow and measured movement of hand and arm, and a large supply of breath, to get up a polish on the worn-out surface of an ancient pair of buckled shoes.

The figure was slender and almost wizened, the thin shoulders round with an habitual stoop, the lean shanks were encased in a pair of much-darned, coarse black stockings. It was the figure of an old man, with a gentle, clear-cut face furrowed by a forest of wrinkles, and surmounted by scanty white locks above a smooth forehead which looked yellow and polished like an ancient piece of ivory.

He had looked across at Marguerite as he spoke, and a pair of innately kind and mild blue eyes were fixed with tender reproach upon her. Marguerite thought that she had never seen quite so much goodness and simple-heartedness portrayed on any face before. It literally beamed out of those pale blue eyes, which seemed quite full of unshed tears.

The old man wore a tattered garment, a miracle of shining cleanliness, which had once been a soutane of smooth black cloth but was now a mass of patches and threadbare at shoulders and knees. He seemed deeply intent in the task of polishing his shoes, and having delivered himself of his little admonition, he very solemnly and earnestly resumed his work.

Marguerite's first and most natural instinct had, of course, been one of dislike and mistrust of anyone who appeared to be in some way on guard over her. But when she took in every detail of the quaint figure of the old man, his scrupulous tidiness of apparel, the resigned stoop of his shoulders, and met in full the gaze of those moist eyes, she felt that the whole aspect of the man, as he sat there polishing his shoes, was infinitely pathetic and, in its simplicity, commanding of respect.

"Who are you?" asked Lady Blakeney at last, for the old man after looking at her with a kind of appealing wonder, seemed to be waiting for her to speak.

"A priest of the good God, my dear child," replied the old man with a deep sigh and a shake of his scanty locks, "who is not allowed to serve his divine Master any longer. A poor old fellow, very harmless and very helpless, who had been set here to watch over you.

"You must not look upon me as a jailer because of what I say, my child," he added with a quaint air of deference and apology. "I am very old and very small, and only take up a very little room. I can make myself very scarce; you shall hardly know that I am here. They forced me to it much against my will—But they are strong and I am weak, how could I deny them since they put me here. After all," he concluded naively, "perhaps it is the will of *le bon Dieu,* and He knows best, my child, He knows best."

The shoes evidently refused to respond any further to the old man's efforts at polishing them. He contemplated them now, with a whimsical look of regret on his furrowed face, then set them down on the floor and slipped his stockinged feet into them.

Marguerite was silently watching him, still leaning on her elbow. Evidently her brain was still numb and fatigued, for she did not seem able to grasp all that the old man said. She smiled to herself too as she watched him. How could she look upon him as a jailer? He did not seem at all like a Jacobin or a Terrorist, there was nothing of the dissatisfied democrat, of the snarling anarchist ready to lend his hand to any act of ferocity directed against a so-called aristocrat, about this pathetic little figure in the ragged soutane and worn shoes.

He seemed singularly bashful too and ill at ease, and loath to meet Marguerite's great, ardent eyes, which were fixed questioningly upon him.

"You must forgive me, my daughter," he said shyly, "for concluding my toilet before you. I had hoped to be quite ready before you woke, but I had some trouble with my shoes; except for a little water and soap the prison authorities will not provide us poor captives with any means of cleanliness and tidiness, and *le bon Dieu* does love a tidy body as well as a clean soul.

"But there, there," he added fussily, "I must not continue to gossip like this. You would like to get up, I know, and refresh your face and hands with a little water. Oh! you will see how well I have thought it out. I need not interfere with you at all, and when you make your little bit of *toilette*, you will feel quite alone—just as if the old man was not there."

He began busying himself about the room, dragging the rickety, rush-bottomed chairs forward. There were four of these in the room, and he began forming a kind of bulwark with them, placing two side by side, then piling the two others up above.

"You will see, my child, you will see!" he kept repeating at intervals as the work of construction progressed. It was no easy matter, for he was of low stature, and his hands were unsteady from apparently uncontrollable nervousness.

Marguerite, leaning slightly forward, her chin resting in her hand, was too puzzled and anxious to grasp the humour of this comical situation. She certainly did not understand. This old man had in some sort of way, and for a hitherto unexplained reason, been set as a guard over her; it was not an unusual device on the part of the inhuman wretches who now ruled France, to add to the miseries and terrors of captivity, where a woman of refinement was concerned, the galling outrage of never leaving her alone for a moment.

That peculiar form of mental torture, surely the invention of brains rendered mad by their own ferocious cruelty, was even now being inflicted on the hapless, dethroned Queen of France. Marguerite, in far-off England, had shuddered when she heard of it, and in her heart had prayed, as indeed every pure-minded woman did then, that proud, unfortunate Marie Antoinette might soon find release from such torments in death.

There was evidently some similar intention with regard to Marguerite herself in the minds of those who now held her prisoner. But this old man seemed so feeble and so helpless, his very delicacy of thought as he built up a screen to divide the squalid room in two, proved him to be singularly inefficient for the task of a watchful jailer.

When the four chairs appeared fairly steady, and in comparatively little danger of toppling, he dragged the paillasse forward and propped it up against the chairs. Finally, he drew the table along, which held the cracked ewer and basin, and placed it against this improvised partition; then he surveyed the whole construction with evident gratification and delight.

"There now!" he said, turning a face beaming with satisfaction to Marguerite, "I can continue my prayers on the other side of the fortress. Oh! it is quite safe——" he added, as with a fearsome hand he touched his engineering feat with gingerly pride, "and you will be quite private—Try and forget that the old *abbé* is in the room—He does not count—really he does not count—he has ceased to be of any moment these many months now that Saint Joseph is closed and he may no longer say Mass."

He was obviously prattling on in order to hide his nervous bashfulness. He ensconced himself behind his own finely constructed bulwark, drew a breviary from his pocket and having found a narrow ledge on one of the chairs, on which he could sit, without much danger of bringing the elaborate screen onto the top of his head, he soon became absorbed in his orisons.

Marguerite watched him for a little while longer; he was evidently endeavouring to make her think that he had become oblivious of her presence, and his transparent little manoeuvres amused and puzzled her not a little.

He looked so comical with his fussy and shy ways, yet withal so gentle and so kindly that she felt completely reassured and quite calm.

She tried to raise herself still further and found the process astonishingly easy. Her limbs still ached and the violent, intermittent pain in her head certainly made her feel sick and giddy at times, but otherwise she was not ill. She sat up on the paillasse, then put her feet to the ground and presently walked up to the improvised dressing-room and bathed her face and hands. The rest had done her good, and she felt quite capable of co-ordinating her thoughts, of moving about without too much pain, and of preparing herself both mentally and physically for the grave events which she knew must be imminent.

While she busied herself with her toilet her thoughts dwelt on the one all-absorbing theme; Percy was in Boulogne, he knew that she was here, in prison, he would reach her without fail, in fact he might communicate with her at any moment now, and had without a doubt already evolved a plan of escape for her, more daring and ingenious than any which he had conceived hitherto; therefore, she must be ready, and prepared for any eventuality, she must be strong and eager, in no way despondent, for if he were here, would he not chide her for her want of faith?

By the time she had smoothed her hair and tidied her dress, Marguerite caught herself singing quite cheerfully to herself.

So full of buoyant hope was she.

CHAPTER 19

The Strength of the Weak

"*M. L'Abbé!*—" said Marguerite gravely.

"Yes, *mon enfant.*"

The old man looked up from his breviary and saw Marguerite's great earnest eyes fixed with obvious calm and trust upon him. She had finished her toilet as well as she could, had shaken up and tidied the paillasse, and was now sitting on the edge of it, her hands clasped between her knees. There was something which still puzzled her, and impatient and impulsive as she was, she had watched the *abbé* as he calmly went on reading the Latin prayers for the last five minutes, and now she could contain her questionings no longer.

"You said just now that they set you to watch over me—"

"So, they did, my child, so they did—" he replied with a sigh, as he quietly closed his book and slipped it back into his pocket. "Ah! they are very cunning—and we must remember that they have the power. No doubt," added the old man, with his own, quaint philosophy, "no doubt *le bon Dieu* meant them to have the power, or they would not have it, would they?"

"By 'they' you mean the Terrorists and Anarchists of France, *M. L'Abbé*—The Committee of Public Safety who pillage and murder, outrage women, and desecrate religion—Is that not so?"

"Alas! my child!" he sighed.

"And it is 'they' who have set you to watch over me?—I confess I don't understand—"

She laughed, quite involuntarily indeed, for in spite of the reassurance in her heart her brain was still in a whirl of passionate anxiety.

"You don't look at all like one of 'them,' *M. l'Abbé*," she said.

"The good God forbid!" ejaculated the old man, raising protesting hands up toward the very distant, quite invisible sky. "How could I, a humble priest of the Lord, range myself with those who would flout and defy Him."

"Yet I am a prisoner of the Republic and you are my jailer, *M. l'Abbé*."

114

"Ah, yes!" he sighed. "But I am very helpless. This was my cell. I had been here with François and Félicité, my sister's children, you know. Innocent lambs, whom those fiends would lead to slaughter. Last night," he continued, speaking volubly, "the soldiers came in and dragged François and Félicité out of this room, where, in spite of the danger before us, in spite of what we suffered, we had contrived to be quite happy together. I could read the Mass, and the dear children would say their prayers night and morning at my knee."

He paused awhile. The unshed tears in his mild blue eyes struggled for freedom now, and one or two flowed slowly down his wrinkled cheek. Marguerite, though heartsore and full of agonising sorrow herself, felt her whole noble soul go out to this kind old man, so pathetic, so high and simple-minded in his grief.

She said nothing, however, and the *abbé* continued after a few seconds' silence.

"When the children had gone, they brought you in here, *mon enfant*, and laid you on the paillasse where Félicité used to sleep. You looked very white, and stricken down, like one of God's lambs attacked by the ravening wolf. Your eyes were closed and you were blissfully unconscious. I was taken before the governor of the prison, and he told me that you would share the cell with me for a time, and that I was to watch you night and day, because—"

The old man paused again. Evidently what he had to say was very difficult to put into words. He groped in his pockets and brought out a large bandana handkerchief, red and yellow and green, with which he began to mop his moist forehead. The quaver in his voice and the trembling of his hands became more apparent and pronounced.

"Yes, *M. l'Abbé*? Because?—" queried Marguerite gently.

"They said that if I guarded you well, Félicité and François would be set free," replied the old man after a while, during which he made vigorous efforts to overcome his nervousness, "and that if you escaped the children and I would be guillotined the very next day."

There was silence in the little room now. The *abbé* was sitting quite still, clasping his trembling fingers, and Marguerite neither moved nor spoke. What the old man had just said was very slowly finding its way to the innermost cells of her brain. Until her mind had thoroughly grasped the meaning of it all, she could not trust herself to make a single comment.

It was some seconds before she fully understood it all, before she realised what it meant not only to her, but indirectly to her husband.

Until now she had not been fully conscious of the enormous wave of hope which almost in spite of herself had risen triumphant above the dull, grey sea of her former despair; only now when it had been shattered against this deadly rock of almost superhuman devilry and cunning did she understand what she had hoped, and what she must now completely forswear.

No bolts and bars, no fortified towers or inaccessible fortresses could prove so effectual a prison for Marguerite Blakeney as the dictum which morally bound her to her cell.

"If you escape the children and I would be guillotined the very next day."

This meant that even if Percy knew, even if he could reach her, he could never set her free, since her safety meant death to two innocent children and to this simple-hearted man.

It would require more than the ingenuity of the Scarlet Pimpernel himself to untie this Gordian knot.

"I don't mind for myself, of course," the old man went on with gentle philosophy. "I have lived my life. What matters if I die tomorrow, or if I linger on until my earthly span is legitimately run out? I am ready to go home whenever my Father calls me. But it is the children, you see. I have to think of them. François is his mother's only son, the bread-winner of the household, a good lad and studious too, and Félicité has always been very delicate. She is blind from birth and—"

"Oh! don't—for pity's sake, don't—" moaned Marguerite in an agony of helplessness. "I understand—you need not fear for your children, M. l'Abbé; no harm shall come to them through me."

"It is as the good God wills!" replied the old man quietly.

Then, as Marguerite had once more relapsed into silence, he fumbled for his beads, and his gentle voice began droning the *Paters* and *Aves* wherein no doubt his childlike heart found peace and solace.

He understood that the poor woman would not wish to speak; he knew as well as she did the overpowering strength of his helpless appeal. Thus the minutes sped on; the jailer and the captive, tied to one another by the strongest bonds that hand of man could forge, had nothing to say to one another, he, the old priest, imbued with the traditions of his calling, could pray and resign himself to the will of the Almighty, but she was young and ardent and passionate, she loved and was beloved, and an impassable barrier was built up between her and the man she worshipped!

A barrier fashioned by the weak hands of children, one of whom was delicate and blind. Outside was air and freedom, reunion with her husband, an agony of happy remorse, a kiss from his dear lips, and trembling held her back from it all, because of François who was the bread-winner and of Félicité who was blind.

Mechanically now Marguerite rose again, and like an automaton—lifeless and thoughtless—she began putting the dingy, squalid room to rights. The *abbé* helped her demolish the improvised screen; with the same gentle delicacy of thought which had caused him to build it up, he refrained from speaking to her now; he would not intrude himself on her grief and her despair.

Later on, she forced herself to speak again, and asked the old man his name.

"My name is Foucquet," he replied, "Jean Baptiste Marie Foucquet, late parish priest of the Church of Saint Joseph, the patron saint of Boulogne."

Foucquet! This was l'Abbé Foucquet! the faithful friend and servant of the de Marny family.

Marguerite gazed at him with great, questioning eyes.

What a wealth of memories crowded in on her mind at sound of that name! Her beautiful home at Richmond, her brilliant array of servants and guests, His Royal Highness at her side! life in free, joyous happy England—how infinitely remote it now seemed. Her ears were filled with the sound of a voice, drawly and quaint and gentle, a voice and a laugh half shy, wholly mirthful, and oh! so infinitely dear;

"I think a little sea voyage and English country air would suit the Abbé Foucquet, m'dear, and I only mean to ask him to cross the Channel with me—"

Oh! the joy and confidence expressed in those words! the daring, the ambition! the pride! and the soft, languorous air of the old-world garden round her then, the passion of his embrace! the heavy scent of late roses and of heliotrope, which caused her to swoon in his arms!

And now a narrow prison cell, and that pathetic, tender little creature there, with trembling hands and tear-dimmed eyes, the most powerful and most relentless jailer which the ferocious cunning of her deadly enemies could possible have devised.

Then she talked to him of Juliette Marny.

The *abbé* did not know that Mlle. de Marny had succeeded in reaching England safely and was overjoyed to hear it.

He recounted to Marguerite the story of the Marny jewels; how he had put them safely away in the crypt of his little church, until the

Assembly of the Convention had ordered the closing of the churches and placed before every minister of *le bon Dieu* the alternative of apostasy or death.

"With me it has only been prison so far," continued the old man simply, "but prison has rendered me just as helpless as the guillotine would have done, for the enemies of *le bon Dieu* have ransacked the Church of Saint Joseph and stolen the jewels which I should have guarded with my life."

But it was obvious joy for the *abbé* to talk of Juliette Marny's happiness. Vaguely, in his remote little provincial cure, he had heard of the prowess and daring of the Scarlet Pimpernel and liked to think that Juliette owed her safety to him.

"The good God will reward him and those whom he cares for," added Abbé Foucquet with that earnest belief in divine interference which seemed so strangely pathetic under these present circumstances.

Marguerite sighed, and for the first time in this terrible soul-stirring crisis through which she was passing so bravely, she felt a beneficent moisture in her eyes; the awful tension of her nerves relaxed. She went up to the old man, took his wrinkled hand in hers, and falling on her knees beside him, she eased her overburdened heart in a flood of tears.

CHAPTER 20

Triumph

The day that Citizen Chauvelin's letter was received by the members of the Committee of Public Safety was indeed one of great rejoicing.

The *Moniteur* tells us that in the *Séance* of September 22nd, 1793, or *Vendemiaire* 1st of the Year 1 it was decreed that sixty prisoners, not absolutely proved guilty of treason against the Republic—only suspected—were to be set free.

Sixty!—at the mere news of the possible capture of the Scarlet Pimpernel.

The Committee was inclined to be magnanimous. Ferocity yielded for the moment to the elusive joy of anticipatory triumph.

A glorious prize was about to fall into the hands of those who had the welfare of the people at heart.

Robespierre and his decemvirs rejoiced, and sixty persons had cause to rejoice with them. So be it! There were plans evolved already as to national *fêtes* and wholesale pardons when that impudent and meddlesome Englishman at last got his deserts.

Wholesale pardons which could easily be rescinded afterwards. Even with those sixty it was a mere respite. Those of le Salut Public only loosened their hold for a while, were nobly magnanimous for a day, quite prepared to be doubly ferocious the next.

In the meanwhile, let us heartily rejoice!

The Scarlet Pimpernel is in France or will be very soon, and on an appointed day he will present himself conveniently to the soldiers of the Republic for capture and for subsequent guillotine. England is at war with us; there is nothing therefore further to fear from her. We might hang every Englishman we can lay hands on, and England could do no more than she is doing at the present moment; bombard our ports, bluster and threaten, join hands with Flanders, and Austria and Sardinia, and the devil if she choose.

Allons! vogue la galère! The Scarlet Pimpernel is perhaps on our shores at this very moment! Our most stinging, most irritating foe is about to be delivered into our hands.

Citizen Chauvelin's letter is very categorical;

"I guarantee to you, Citizen Robespierre, and to the Members of the Revolutionary Government who have entrusted me with the delicate mission—"

Robespierre's sensuous lips curl into a sarcastic smile. Citizen Chauvelin's pen was very florid in its style; "entrusted me with the delicate mission," is hardly the way to describe an order given under penalty of death.

But let it pass.

"—that four days from this date, at one hour after sunset, the man who goes by the mysterious name of the Scarlet Pimpernel will be on the southern ramparts of Boulogne, at the extreme southern corner of the town."

"Four days from this date—" and Citizen Chauvelin's letter is dated the nineteenth of September, 1793.

"Too much of an aristocrat—Monsieur le Marquis Chauvelin—" sneers Merlin, the Jacobin. "He does not know that all good citizens had called that date the 28th *Fructidor*, Year I of the Republic."

"No matter," retorts Robespierre with impatient frigidity, "whatever we may call the day it was forty-eight hours ago, and in forty-eight hours more than that damned Englishman will have run his head into a noose, from which, an I mistake not, he'll not find it easy to extricate himself."

"And you believe in Citizen Chauvelin's assertion," commented Danton with a lazy shrug of the shoulders.

"Only because he asks for help from us," quoth Robespierre drily; "he is sure that the man will be there, but not sure if he can tackle him."

But many were inclined to think that Chauvelin's letter was an idle boast. They knew nothing of the circumstances which had caused that letter to be written; they could not conjecture how it was that the ex-ambassador could be so precise in naming the day and hour when the enemy of France would be at the mercy of those whom he had outraged and flouted.

Nevertheless, Citizen Chauvelin asks for help, and help must not be denied him. There must be no shadow of blame upon the actions of the Committee of Public Safety.

Chauvelin had been weak once, had allowed the prize to slip through his fingers; it must not occur again. He has a wonderful head for devising plans, but he needs a powerful hand to aid him, so that he may not fail again.

Collot d'Herbois, just home from Lyons and Tours, is the right man in an emergency like this. Citizen Collot is full of ideas; the inventor of the *noyades* is sure to find a means of converting Boulogne into one gigantic prison out of which the mysterious English adventurer will find it impossible to escape.

And whilst the deliberations go on, whilst this committee of butchers are busy slaughtering in imagination the game they have not yet succeeded in bringing down, there comes another messenger from Citizen Chauvelin.

He must have ridden hard on the other one's heels, and something very unexpected and very sudden must have occurred to cause the Citizen to send this second note.

This time it is curt and to the point. Robespierre unfolds it and reads it to his colleagues.

"We have caught the woman—his wife—there may be murder attempted against my person, send me someone at once who will carry out my instructions in case of my sudden death."

Robespierre's lips curl in satisfaction, showing a row of yellowish teeth, long and sharp like the fangs of a wolf. A murmur like unto the snarl of a pack of hyenas rises round the table, as Chauvelin's letter is handed round.

Everyone has guessed the importance of this preliminary capture;

"*the woman—his wife.*" Chauvelin evidently thinks much of it, for he anticipates an attempt against his life, nay! he is quite prepared for it, ready to sacrifice it for the sake of his revenge.

Who had accused him of weakness?

He only thinks of his duty, not of his life; he does not fear for himself, only that the fruits of his skill might be jeopardized through assassination.

Well! this English adventurer is capable of any act of desperation to save his wife and himself, and Citizen Chauvelin must not be left in the lurch.

Thus, Citizen Collot d'Herbois is despatched forthwith to Boulogne to be a helpmeet and counsellor to Citizen Chauvelin.

Everything that can humanly be devised must be done to keep the woman secure and to set the trap for that elusive Pimpernel.

Once he is caught the whole of France shall rejoice, and Boulogne, who had been instrumental in running the quarry to earth, must be specially privileged on that day.

A general amnesty for all prisoners the day the Scarlet Pimpernel is captured. A public holiday and a pardon for all natives of Boulogne who are under sentence of death; they shall be allowed to find their way to the various English boats—trading and smuggling craft—that always lie at anchor in the roads there.

The Committee of Public Safety feels amazingly magnanimous towards Boulogne; a proclamation embodying the amnesty and the pardon is at once drawn up and signed by Robespierre and his blood-thirsty Council of Ten; it is entrusted to Citizen Collot d'Herbois, to be read out at every corner of the ramparts as an inducement to the little town to do its level best. The Englishman and his wife—captured in Boulogne—will both be subsequently brought to Paris, formally tried on a charge of conspiring against the Republic, and guillotined as English spies, but Boulogne shall have the greater glory and shall reap the first and richest reward.

And armed with the magnanimous proclamation, the orders for general rejoicings and a grand local *fête*, armed also with any and every power over the entire city, its municipality, its garrisons, its forts, for himself and his colleague Chauvelin, Citizen Collot d'Herbois starts for Boulogne forthwith.

Needless to tell him not to let the grass grow under his horse's hoofs. The capture of the Scarlet Pimpernel, though not absolutely an accomplished fact, is nevertheless a practical certainty, and no one rejoices over this great event more than the man who is to be present and see all the fun.

Riding and driving, getting what relays of horses or waggons from roadside farms that he can, Collot is not likely to waste much time on the way.

It is 157 miles to Boulogne by road, and Collot, burning with ambition to be in at the death, rides or drives as no messenger of good tidings has ever ridden or driven before.

He does not stop to eat, but munches chunks of bread and cheese in the recess of the lumbering chaise or waggon that bears him along whenever his limbs refuse him service and he cannot mount a horse.

The chronicles tell us that twenty-four hours after he left Paris, half-dazed with fatigue, but ferocious and eager still, he is borne to the gates of Boulogne by an old cart horse requisitioned from some distant farm, and which falls down, dead, at the Porte Gayole, whilst its rider, with a last effort, loudly clamours for admittance into the town "in the name of the Republic."

CHAPTER 21

Suspense

In his memorable interview with Robespierre, the day before he left for England, Chauvelin had asked that absolute power be given him, in order that he might carry out the plans for the capture of the Scarlet Pimpernel, which he had in his mind. Now that he was back in France he had no cause to complain that the revolutionary government had grudged him this power for which he had asked.

Implicit obedience had followed whenever he had commanded.

As soon as he heard that a woman had been arrested in the act of uttering a passport in the name of Céline Dumont, he guessed at once that Marguerite Blakeney had, with characteristic impulse, fallen into the trap which, with the aid of the woman Candeille, he had succeeded in laying for her.

He was not the least surprised at that. He knew human nature, feminine nature, far too well, ever to have been in doubt for a moment that Marguerite would follow her husband without calculating either costs or risks.

Ye gods! the irony of it all! Had she not been called the cleverest woman in Europe at one time? Chauvelin himself had thus acclaimed her, in those olden days, before she and he became such mortal enemies, and when he was one of the many satellites that revolved round brilliant Marguerite St. Just. And tonight, when a sergeant of the town guards brought him news of her capture, he smiled grimly to himself; the cleverest woman in Europe had failed to perceive the trap laid temptingly open for her.

Once more she had betrayed her husband into the hands of those who would not let him escape a second time. And now she had done it with her eyes open, with loving, passionate heart which ached for self-sacrifice, and only succeeded in imperilling the loved one more hopelessly than before.

The sergeant was waiting for orders. Citizen Chauvelin had come to Boulogne, armed with more full and more autocratic powers than any servant of the new republic had ever been endowed with before. The governor of the town, the captain of the guard, the fort and municipality were all as abject slaves before him.

As soon as he had taken possession of the quarters organised for him in the town hall, he had asked for a list of prisoners who for one cause or another were being detained pending further investigations.

The list was long and contained many names which were of not the slightest interest to Chauvelin; he passed them over impatiently.

"To be released at one," he said curtly.

He did not want the guard to be burdened with unnecessary duties, nor the prisons of the little sea-port town to be inconveniently encumbered. He wanted room, space, air, the force and intelligence of the entire town at his command for the one capture which meant life and revenge to him.

"A woman—name unknown—found in possession of a forged passport in the name of Céline Dumont, maid to the Citizeness Désirée Candeille—attempted to land—was interrogated and failed to give satisfactory explanation of herself—detained in room No. 6 of the Gayole prison."

This was one of the last names on the list, the only one of any importance to Citizen Chauvelin. When he read it he nearly drove his nails into the palms of his hands, so desperate an effort did he make not to betray before the sergeant by look or sigh the exultation which he felt.

For a moment he shaded his eyes against the glare of the lamp, but it was not long before he had formulated a plan and was ready to give his orders.

He asked for a list of prisoners already detained in the various forts. The name of l'Abbé Foucquet with those of his niece and nephew attracted his immediate attention. He asked for further information respecting these people, heard that the boy was a widow's only son, the sole supporter of his mother's declining years; the girl was ailing, suffering from incipient phthisis, and was blind.

Pardi! the very thing! *L'Abbé* himself, the friend of Juliette Marny, the pathetic personality around which this final adventure of the Scarlet Pimpernel was intended to revolve! and these two young people! his sister's children! one of them blind and ill, the other full of vigour and manhood.

Citizen Chauvelin had soon made up his mind.

A few quick orders to the sergeant of the guard, and l'Abbé Foucquet, weak, helpless and gentle, became the relentless jailer who would guard Marguerite more securely than a whole regiment of loyal soldiers could have done.

Then, having despatched a messenger to the Committee of Public Safety, Chauvelin laid himself down to rest. Fate had not deceived him. He had thought and schemed and planned, and events had shaped themselves exactly as foreseen, and the fact that Marguerite Blakeney was at the present moment a prisoner in his hands was merely the result of his own calculations.

As for the Scarlet Pimpernel, Chauvelin could not very well conceive what he would do under these present circumstances. The duel on the southern ramparts had of course become a farce, not likely to be enacted now that Marguerite's life was at stake. The daring adventurer was caught in a network at last, from which all his ingenuity, all his wit, his impudence and his amazing luck could never extricate him.

And in Chauvelin's mind there was still something more. Revenge was the sweetest emotion his bruised and humbled pride could know; he had not yet tasted its complete intoxicating joy, but every hour now his cup of delight became more and more full; in a few days it would overflow.

In the meanwhile, he was content to wait. The hours sped by and there was no news yet of that elusive Pimpernel. Of Marguerite he knew nothing save that she was well guarded; the sentry who passed up and down outside room No. 6 had heard her voice and that of the Abbé Foucquet, in the course of the afternoon.

Chauvelin had asked the Committee of Public Safety for aid in his difficult task, but forty-eight hours at least must elapse before such aid could reach him. Forty-eight hours, during which the hand of an assassin might be lurking for him and might even reach him ere his vengeance was fully accomplished.

That was the only thought which really troubled him. He did not want to die before he had seen the Scarlet Pimpernel a withered abject creature, crushed in fame and honour, too debased to find glorification even in death.

At this moment he only cared for his life because it was needed for the complete success of his schemes. No one else he knew would have that note of personal hatred towards the enemy of France which was necessary now in order to carry out successfully the plans which he had formed.

Robespierre and all the others only desired the destruction of a man who had intrigued against the reign of terror which they had established; his death on the guillotine, even if it were surrounded with the halo of martyrdom, would have satisfied them completely. Chauvelin looked further than that. He hated the man! He had suffered humiliation through him individually. He wished to see him as an object of contempt rather than of pity. And because of the anticipation of this joy, he was careful of his life, and throughout those two days which elapsed between the capture of Marguerite and the arrival of Collot d'Herbois at Boulogne, Chauvelin never left his quarters at the Hotel de Ville, and requisitioned a special escort consisting of proved soldiers of the town guard to attend his every footstep.

On the evening of the 22nd, after the arrival of Citizen Collot in Boulogne, he gave orders that the woman from No. 6 cell be brought before him in the ground floor room of the Fort Gayole.

CHAPTER 22

Not Death

Two days of agonising suspense, of alternate hope and despair, had told heavily on Marguerite Blakeney.

Her courage was still indomitable, her purpose firm and her faith secure, but she was without the slightest vestige of news, entirely shut off from the outside world, left to conjecture, to scheme, to expect and to despond alone.

The Abbé Foucquet had tried in his gentle way to be of comfort to her, and she in her turn did her very best not to render his position more cruel than it already was.

A message came to him twice during those forty-eight hours from François and Félicité, a little note scribbled by the boy, or a token sent by the blind girl, to tell the *abbé* that the children were safe and well, that they would be safe and well so long as the Citizeness with the name unknown remained closely guarded by him in room No. 6.

When these messages came, the old man would sigh and murmur something about the good God; and hope, which perhaps had faintly risen in Marguerite's heart within the last hour or so, would once more sink back into the abyss of uttermost despair.

Outside the monotonous walk of the sentry sounded like the perpetual thud of a hammer beating upon her bruised temples.

"What's to be done? My God? what's to be done?"

Where was Percy now?

"How to reach him!—Oh, God! grant me light!"

The one real terror which she felt was that she would go mad. Nay! that she was in a measure mad already. For hours now,—or was it days?—or years?—she had heard nothing save that rhythmic walk of the sentinel, and the kindly, tremulous voice of the *abbé* whispering consolations, or murmuring prayers in her ears; she had seen nothing save that prison door, of rough deal, painted a dull grey, with great old-fashioned lock, and hinges rusty with the damp of ages.

She had kept her eyes fixed on that door until they burned and ached with well-nigh intolerable pain; yet she felt that she could not look elsewhere, lest she missed the golden moment when the bolts would be drawn, and that dull, grey door would swing slowly on its rusty hinges.

Surely, surely, that was the commencement of madness!

Yet for Percy's sake, because he might want her, because he might have need of her courage and of her presence of mind, she tried to keep her wits about her. But it was difficult! oh! terribly difficult! especially when the shade of evening began to gather in, and peopled the squalid, whitewashed room with innumerable threatening ghouls.

Then when the moon came up, a silver ray crept in through the tiny window and struck full upon that grey door, making it look weird and spectral like the entrance to a house of ghosts.

Even now as there was a distinct sound of the pushing of bolts and bars, Marguerite thought that she was the prey of hallucinations. The Abbé Foucquet was sitting in the remote and darkest corner of the room, quietly telling his beads. His serene philosophy and gentle placidity could in no way be disturbed by the opening or shutting of a door, or by the bearer of good or evil tidings.

The room now seemed strangely gloomy and cavernous, with

those deep, black shadows all around and that white ray of the moon which struck so weirdly on the door.

Marguerite shuddered with one of those unaccountable premonitions of something evil about to come, which ofttimes assail those who have a nervous and passionate temperament.

The door swung slowly open upon its hinges; there was a quick word of command, and the light of a small oil lamp struck full into the gloom. Vaguely Marguerite discerned a group of men, soldiers no doubt, for there was a glint of arms and the suggestion of tricolour cockades and scarves. One of the men was holding the lamp aloft; another took a few steps forward into the room. He turned to Marguerite, entirely ignoring the presence of the old priest, and addressed her peremptorily.

"Your presence is desired by the citizen governor," he said curtly; "stand up and follow me."

"Whither am I to go?" she asked.

"To where my men will take you. Now then, quick's the word. The citizen governor does not like to wait."

At a word of command from him, two more soldiers now entered the room and placed themselves one on each side of Marguerite, who, knowing that resistance was useless, had already risen and was prepared to go.

The *abbé* tried to utter a word of protest and came quickly forward towards Marguerite, but he was summarily and very roughly pushed aside.

"Now then, *calotin*," said the first soldier with an oath, "this is none of your business. Forward! march!" he added, addressing his men, "and you, Citizeness, will find it wiser to come quietly along and not to attempt any tricks with me, or the gag and manacles will have to be used."

But Marguerite had no intention of resisting. She was too tired even to wonder as to what they meant to do with her or whither they were going; she moved as in a dream and felt a hope within her that she was being led to death; summary executions were the order of the day, she knew that, and sighed for this simple solution of the awful problem which had been harassing her these past two days.

She was being led along a passage, stumbling ever and *anon* as she walked, for it was but dimly lighted by the same little oil lamp, which one of the soldiers was carrying in front, holding it high up above his head; then they went down a narrow flight of stone steps, until she and her escort reached a heavy oak door.

A halt was ordered at this point, and the man in command of the little party pushed the door open and walked in. Marguerite caught sight of a room beyond, dark and gloomy-looking, as was her own prison cell. Somewhere on the left there was obviously a window; she could not see it but guessed that it was there because the moon struck full upon the floor, ghost-like and spectral, well fitting in with the dream-like state in which Marguerite felt herself to be.

In the centre of the room she could discern a table with a chair close beside it, also a couple of tallow candles, which flickered in the draught caused no doubt by that open window which she could not see.

All these little details impressed themselves on Marguerite's mind, as she stood there, placidly waiting until she should once more be told to move along. The table, the chair, that unseen window, trivial objects though they were, assumed before her overwrought fancy an utterly disproportionate importance. She caught herself presently counting up the number of boards visible on the floor and watching the smoke of the tallow-candles rising up towards the grimy ceiling.

After a few minutes' weary waiting which seemed endless to Marguerite, there came a short word of command from within and she was roughly pushed forward into the room by one of the men. The cool air of a late September's evening gently fanned her burning temples. She looked round her and now perceived that someone was sitting at the table, the other side of the tallow-candles—a man, with head bent over a bundle of papers and shading his face against the light with his hand.

He rose as she approached, and the flickering flame of the candles played weirdly upon the slight, sable-clad figure, illumining the keen, ferret-like face, and throwing fitful gleams across the deep-set eyes and the narrow, cruel mouth.

It was Chauvelin.

Mechanically Marguerite took the chair which the soldier drew towards her, ordering her curtly to sit down. She seemed to have but little power to move. Though all her faculties had suddenly become preternaturally alert at sight of this man, whose very life now was spent in doing her the most grievous wrong that one human being can do to another, yet all these faculties were forcefully centred in the one mighty effort not to flinch before him, not to let him see for a moment that she was afraid.

She compelled her eyes to look at him fully and squarely, her lips not to tremble, her very heart to stop its wild, excited beating. She felt his keen eyes fixed intently upon her, but more in curiosity than in hatred or satisfied vengeance.

When she had sat down he came round the table and moved towards her. When he drew quite near, she instinctively recoiled. It had been an almost imperceptible action on her part and certainly an involuntary one, for she did not wish to betray a single thought or emotion, until she knew what he wished to say.

But he had noted her movement—a sort of drawing up and stiffening of her whole person as he approached. He seemed pleased to see it, for he smiled sarcastically but with evident satisfaction, and—as if his purpose was now accomplished—he immediately withdrew and went back to his former seat on the other side of the table. After that he ordered the soldiers to go.

"But remain at attention outside, you and your men," he added, "ready to enter if I call."

It was Marguerite's turn to smile at this obvious sign of a lurking fear on Chauvelin's part, and a line of sarcasm and contempt curled her full lips.

The soldiers having obeyed and the oak door having closed upon them, Marguerite was now alone with the man whom she hated and loathed beyond every living thing on earth.

She wondered when he would begin to speak and why he had sent for her. But he seemed in no hurry to begin. Still shading his face with his hand, he was watching her with utmost attention; she, on the other hand, was looking through and beyond him, with contemptuous indifference, as if his presence here did not interest her in the least.

She would give him no opening for this conversation which he had sought and which she felt would prove either purposeless or else deeply wounding to her heart and to her pride. She sat, therefore, quite still with the flickering and yellow light fully illuminating her delicate face, with its child-like curves, and delicate features, the noble, straight brow, the great blue eyes and halo of golden hair.

"My desire to see you here tonight, must seem strange to you, Lady Blakeney," said Chauvelin at last.

Then, as she did not reply, he continued, speaking quite gently, almost deferentially;

"There are various matters of grave importance, which the events of the next twenty-four hours will reveal to your ladyship; and believe me that I am actuated by motives of pure friendship towards you in this my effort to mitigate the unpleasantness of such news as you might hear tomorrow perhaps, by giving you due warning of what its nature might be."

She turned great questioning eyes upon him, and in their expression, she tried to put all the contempt which she felt, all the bitterness, all the defiance and the pride.

He quietly shrugged his shoulders.

"Ah! I fear me," he said, "that your ladyship, as usual doth me grievous wrong. It is but natural that you should misjudge me, yet believe me—"

"A truce on this foolery, M. Chauvelin," she broke in, with sudden impatient vehemence, "pray leave your protestations of friendship and courtesy alone; there is no one here to hear them. I pray you proceed with what you have to say."

"Ah!" It was a sigh of satisfaction on the part of Chauvelin. Her anger and impatience even at this early stage of the interview proved sufficiently that her icy restraint was only on the surface.

And Chauvelin always knew how to deal with vehemence. He loved to play with the emotions of a passionate fellow-creature; it was only the imperturbable calm of a certain enemy of his that was wont to shake his own impenetrable armour of reserve.

"As your ladyship desires," he said, with a slight and ironical bow of the head. "But before proceeding according to your wish, I am compelled to ask your ladyship just one question."

"And that is?"

"Have you reflected what your present position means to that inimitable prince of dandies, Sir Percy Blakeney?"

"Is it necessary for your present purpose, *Monsieur*, that you should mention my husband's name at all?" she asked.

"It is indispensable, fair lady," he replied suavely, "for is not the fate of your husband so closely intertwined with yours, that his actions will inevitably be largely influenced by your own."

Marguerite gave a start of surprise, and as Chauvelin had paused, she tried to read what hidden meaning lay behind these last words of his. Was it his intention then to propose some bargain, one of those terrible "either-or's" of which he seemed to possess the malignant secret? Oh! if that was so, if indeed he had sent for her in order to suggest one of those terrible alternatives of his, then—be it what it may, be it the wildest conception which the insane brain of a fiend could invent—she would accept it, so long as the man she loved were given one single chance of escape.

Therefore, she turned to her arch-enemy in a more conciliatory spirit now, and even endeavoured to match her own diplomatic cunning against his.

"I do not understand," she said tentatively. "How can my actions influence those of my husband? I am a prisoner in Boulogne; he probably is not aware of that fact yet, and—"

"Sir Percy Blakeney may be in Boulogne at any moment now," he interrupted quietly. "And I mistake not, few places can offer such great attractions to that peerless gentleman of fashion than doth this humble provincial town of France just at this present—Hath it not the honour of harbouring Lady Blakeney within its gates?—And your ladyship may indeed believe me when I say that the day that Sir Percy lands in our hospitable port, two hundred pairs of eyes will be fixed upon him, lest he should wish to quit it again."

"And if there were two thousand, sir," she said impulsively, "they would not stop his coming or going as he pleased."

"Nay, fair lady," he said, with a smile, "are you then endowing Sir Percy Blakeney with the attributes which, as popular fancy has it, belong exclusively to that mysterious English hero, the Scarlet Pimpernel?"

"A truce to your diplomacy, Monsieur Chauvelin," she retorted, goaded by his sarcasm, "why should we try to fence with one another? What was the object of your journey to England? of the farce which you enacted in my house, with the help of the woman Candeille? of that duel and that challenge, save that you desired to entice Sir Percy Blakeney to France?"

"And also, his charming wife," he added with an ironical bow.

She bit her lip and made no comment.

"Shall we say that I succeeded admirably?" he continued, speaking with persistent urbanity and calm, "and that I have strong cause to hope that the elusive Pimpernel will soon be a guest on our friendly shores?—There! you see I too have laid down the foils—As you say, why should we fence? Your ladyship is now in Boulogne, soon Sir Percy will come to try and take you away from us, but believe me, fair lady, that it would take more than the ingenuity and the daring of the Scarlet Pimpernel magnified a thousandfold to get him back to England again—unless—"

"Unless?—"

Marguerite held her breath. She felt now as if the whole universe must stand still during the next supreme moment, until she had heard what Chauvelin's next words would be.

There was to be an "unless" then? An "either-or" more terrible no doubt than the one he had formulated before her just a year ago.

Chauvelin, she knew, was past master in the art of putting a knife at his victim's throat and of giving it just the necessary twist with his cruel and relentless "unless"!

But she felt quite calm, because her purpose was resolute. There is no doubt that during this agonising moment of suspense she was absolutely firm in her determination to accept any and every condition which Chauvelin would put before her as the price of her husband's safety. After all, these conditions, since he placed them before *her*, could resolve themselves into questions of her own life against her husband's.

With that unreasoning impulse which was one of her most salient characteristics, she never paused to think that, to Chauvelin, her own life or death were only the means to the great end which he had in view; the complete annihilation of the Scarlet Pimpernel.

That end could only be reached by Percy Blakeney's death—not by her own.

Even now as she was watching him with eyes glowing and lips tightly closed, lest a cry of impatient agony should escape her throat, he,—like a snail that has shown its slimy horns too soon, and is not ready to face the enemy as yet,—seemed suddenly to withdraw within his former shell of careless suavity. The earnestness of his tone vanished, giving place to light and easy conversation, just as if he were discussing social topics with a woman of fashion in a Paris drawing-room.

"Nay!" he said pleasantly, "is not your ladyship taking this matter in too serious a spirit? Of a truth you repeated my innocent word 'unless' even as if I were putting knife at your dainty throat. Yet I meant naught that need disturb you yet. Have I not said that I am your friend? Let me try and prove it to you."

"You will find that a difficult task, *Monsieur*," she said drily.

"Difficult tasks always have had a great fascination for your humble servant. May I try?"

"Certainly."

"Shall we then touch at the root of this delicate matter? Your ladyship, so I understand, is at this moment under the impression that I desire to encompass—shall I say?—the death of an English gentleman for whom, believe me, I have the greatest respect. That is so, is it not?"

"What is so, M. Chauvelin?" she asked almost stupidly, for truly she had not even begun to grasp his meaning. "I do not understand."

"You think that I am at this moment taking measures for sending the Scarlet Pimpernel to the guillotine? Eh?"

"I do."

"Never was so great an error committed by a clever woman. Your ladyship must believe me when I say that the guillotine is the very last place in the world where I would wish to see that enigmatic and elusive personage."

"Are you trying to fool me, M. Chauvelin? If so, for what purpose? And why do you lie to me like that?"

"On my honour, 'tis the truth. The death of Sir Percy Blakeney—I may call him that, may I not?—would ill suit the purpose which I have in view."

"What purpose? You must pardon me, Monsieur Chauvelin," she added with a quick, impatient sigh, "but of a truth I am getting confused, and my wits must have become dull in the past few days. I pray to you to add to your many protestations of friendship a little more clearness in your speech and, if possible, a little more brevity. What then is the purpose which you had in view when you enticed my husband to come over to France?"

"My purpose was the destruction of the Scarlet Pimpernel, not the death of Sir Percy Blakeney. Believe me, I have a great regard for Sir Percy. He is a most accomplished gentleman, witty, brilliant, an inimitable dandy. Why should he not grace with his presence the drawing-rooms of London or of Brighton for many years to come?"

She looked at him with puzzled inquiry. For one moment the thought flashed through her mind that, after all, Chauvelin might be still in doubt as to the identity of the Scarlet Pimpernel—But no! that hope was madness—It was preposterous and impossible—But then, why? why? why?—Oh God! for a little more patience!

"What I have just said may seem a little enigmatic to your ladyship," he continued blandly, "but surely so clever a woman as yourself, so great a lady as is the wife of Sir Percy Blakeney, Baronet, will be aware that there are other means of destroying an enemy than the taking of his life."

"For instance, Monsieur Chauvelin?"

"There is the destruction of his honour," he replied slowly.

A long, bitter laugh, almost hysterical in its loud outburst, broke from the very depths of Marguerite's convulsed heart.

"The destruction of his honour!—ha! ha! ha! ha!—of a truth, Monsieur Chauvelin, your inventive powers have led you beyond the bounds of dreamland!—Ha! ha! ha! ha!—It is in the land of madness that you are wandering, sir, when you talk in one breath of Sir Percy Blakeney and the possible destruction of his honour!"

But he remained apparently quite unruffled, and when her laughter had somewhat subsided, he said placidly;

"Perhaps!—"

Then he rose from his chair, and once more approached her. This time she did not shrink from him. The suggestion which he had made just now, this talk of attacking her husband's honour rather than his life, seemed so wild and preposterous—the conception truly of a mind unhinged—that she looked upon it as a sign of extreme weakness on his part, almost as an acknowledgement of impotence.

But she watched him as he moved round the table more in curiosity now than in fright. He puzzled her, and she still had a feeling at the back of her mind that there must be something more definite and more evil lurking at the back of that tortuous brain.

"Will your ladyship allow me to conduct you to yonder window?" he said, "the air is cool, and what I have to say can best be done in sight of yonder sleeping city."

His tone was one of perfect courtesy, even of respectful deference through which not the slightest trace of sarcasm could be discerned, and she, still actuated by curiosity and interest, not in any way by fear, quietly rose to obey him. Though she ignored the hand which he was holding out towards her, she followed him readily enough as he walked up to the window.

All through this agonising and soul-stirring interview she had felt heavily oppressed by the close atmosphere of the room, rendered nauseous by the evil smell of the smoky tallow-candles which were left to spread their grease and smoke abroad unchecked. Once or twice she had gazed longingly towards the suggestion of pure air outside.

Chauvelin evidently had still much to say to her; the torturing, mental rack to which she was being subjected had not yet fully done its work. It still was capable of one or two turns, a twist or so which might succeed in crushing her pride and her defiance. Well! so be it! she was in the man's power—had placed herself therein through her own unreasoning impulse. This interview was but one of the many soul-agonies which she had been called upon to endure, and if by submitting to it all she could in a measure mitigate her own faults and be of help to the man she loved, she would find the sacrifice small and the mental torture easy to bear.

Therefore, when Chauvelin beckoned to her to draw near, she went up to the window, and leaning her head against the deep stone embrasure, she looked out into the night.

CHAPTER 23

The Hostage

Chauvelin, without speaking, extended his hand out towards the city as if to invite Marguerite to gaze upon it.

She was quite unconscious what hour of the night it might be, but it must have been late, for the little town, encircled by the stony arms of its forts, seemed asleep. The moon, now slowly sinking in the west, edged the towers and spires with filmy lines of silver. To the right Marguerite caught sight of the frowning *beffroi*, which even as she gazed out began tolling its heavy bell. It sounded like the tocsin, dull and muffled. After ten strokes it was still.

Ten o'clock! At this hour in far-off England, in fashionable London, the play was just over; crowds of gaily dressed men and women poured out of the open gates of the theatres calling loudly for attendant or chaise. Thence to balls or routs, gaily fluttering like so many butterflies, brilliant and irresponsible—

And in England also, in the beautiful gardens of her Richmond home, ofttimes at ten o'clock she had wandered alone with Percy, when he was at home, and the spirit of adventure in him momentarily laid to rest. Then, when the night was very dark and the air heavy with the scent of roses and lilies, she lay quiescent in his arms in that little arbour beside the river. The rhythmic lapping of the waves was the only sound that stirred the balmy air. He seldom spoke then, for his voice would shake whenever he uttered a word; but his impenetrable armour of flippancy was pierced through and he did not speak because his lips were pressed to hers, and his love had soared beyond the domain of speech.

A shudder of intense mental pain went through her now as she gazed on the sleeping city, and sweet memories of the past turned to bitterness in this agonising present. One by one as the moon gradually disappeared behind a bank of clouds, the towers of Boulogne were merged in the gloom. In front of her far, far away, beyond the

135

flat sand dunes, the sea seemed to be calling to her with a ghostly and melancholy moan.

The window was on the ground floor of the Fort, and gave direct onto the wide and shady walk which runs along the crest of the city walls; from where she stood Marguerite was looking straight along the ramparts, some thirty metres wide at this point, flanked on either side by the granite balustrade, and adorned with a double row of ancient elms stunted and twisted into grotesque shapes by the persistent action of the wind.

"These wide ramparts are a peculiarity of this city—" said a voice close to her ear, "at times of peace they form an agreeable promenade under the shade of the trees, and a delightful meeting-place for lovers—or enemies—"

The sound brought her back to the ugly realities of the present; the rose-scented garden at Richmond, the lazily flowing river, the tender memories which for that brief moment had confronted her from out a happy past, suddenly vanished from her ken. Instead of these the brine-laden sea-air struck her quivering nostrils, the echo of the old *beffroi* died away in her ear, and now from out one of the streets or open places of the sleeping city there came the sound of a raucous voice, shouting in monotonous tones a string of words, the meaning of which failed to reach her brain.

Not many feet below the window, the southern ramparts of the town stretched away into the darkness. She felt unaccountably cold suddenly as she looked down upon them and, with aching eyes, tried to pierce the gloom. She was shivering in spite of the mildness of this early autumnal night; her overwrought fancy was peopling the lonely walls with unearthly shapes strolling along, discussing in spectral language a strange duel which was to take place here between a noted butcher of men and a mad Englishman overfond of adventure.

The ghouls seemed to pass and repass along in front of her and to be laughing audibly because that mad Englishman had been offered his life in exchange for his honour. They laughed and laughed, no doubt because he refused the bargain—Englishmen were always eccentric, and in these days of equality and other devices of a free and glorious revolution, honour was such a very marketable commodity that it seemed ridiculous to prize it quite so highly. Then they strolled away again and disappeared, whilst Marguerite distinctly heard the scrunching of the path beneath their feet. She leant forward to peer still further into the darkness, for this sound had seemed so absolutely real, but immediately a detaining hand was placed upon her arm and a sarcastic voice murmured at her elbow;

"The result, fair lady, would only be a broken leg or arm; the height is not great enough for picturesque suicides, and believe me these ramparts are only haunted by ghosts."

She drew back as if a viper had stung her; for the moment she had become oblivious of Chauvelin's presence. However, she would not take notice of his taunt, and, after a slight pause, he asked her if she could hear the town crier over in the public streets.

"Yes," she replied.

"What he says at this present moment is of vast importance to your ladyship," he remarked drily.

"How so?"

"Your ladyship is a precious hostage. We are taking measures to guard our valuable property securely."

Marguerite thought of the Abbé Foucquet, who no doubt was still quietly telling his beads, even if in his heart he had begun to wonder what had become of her. She thought of François, who was the bread-winner, and of Félicité, who was blind.

"Methinks you and your colleagues have done that already," she said.

"Not as completely as we would wish. We know the daring of the Scarlet Pimpernel. We are not even ashamed to admit that we fear his luck, his impudence and his marvellous ingenuity—Have I not told you that I have the greatest possible respect for that mysterious English hero—An old priest and two young children might be spir- ited away by that enigmatical adventurer, even whilst Lady Blakeney herself is made to vanish from our sight."

"Ah! I see your ladyship is taking my simple words as a confession of weakness," he continued, noting the swift sigh of hope which had involuntarily escaped her lips. "Nay! and it please you, you shall de- spise me for it. But a confession of weakness is the first sign of strength. The Scarlet Pimpernel is still at large, and whilst we guard our hostage securely, he is bound to fall into our hands."

"Aye! still at large!" she retorted with impulsive defiance. "Think you that all your bolts and bars, the ingenuity of yourself and your colleagues, the collaboration of the devil himself, would succeed in outwitting the Scarlet Pimpernel, now that his purpose will be to try and drag *me* from out your clutches."

She felt hopeful and proud. Now that she had the pure air of heaven in her lungs, that from afar she could smell the sea, and could feel that perhaps in a straight line of vision from where she stood, the *Daydream* with Sir Percy on board, might be lying out there in the roads, it seemed impossible that he should fail in freeing her and those poor people—an old man and two children—whose lives depended on her own.

But Chauvelin only laughed a dry, sarcastic laugh and said;

"Hm! perhaps not!—It of course will depend on you and your personality—your feelings in such matters—and whether an English gentleman likes to save his own skin at the expense of others."

Marguerite shivered as if from cold.

"Ah! I see," resumed Chauvelin quietly, "that your ladyship has not quite grasped the position. That public crier is a long way off; the words have lingered on the evening breeze and have failed to reach your brain. Do you suppose that I and my colleagues do not know that all the ingenuity of which the Scarlet Pimpernel is capable will now be directed in piloting Lady Blakeney, and incidentally the Abbé Foucquet with his nephew and niece, safely across the Channel! Four people!—Bah! a bagatelle, for this mighty conspirator, who but lately snatched twenty aristocrats from the prisons of Lyons—Nay! nay! two children and an old man were not enough to guard our precious hostage, and I was not thinking of either the Abbé Foucquet or of the two children, when I said that an English gentleman would not save himself at the expense of others."

"Of whom then were you thinking, Monsieur Chauvelin? Whom else have you set to guard the prize which you value so highly?"

"The whole city of Boulogne," he replied simply.

"I do not understand."

"Let me make my point clear. My colleague, Citizen Collot d'Herbois, rode over from Paris yesterday; like myself he is a member of the Committee of Public Safety whose duty it is to look after the welfare of France by punishing all those who conspire against her laws and the liberties of the people. Chief among these conspirators, whom it is our duty to punish is, of course, that impudent adventurer who calls himself the Scarlet Pimpernel. He has given the government of France a great deal of trouble through his attempts—mostly successful, as I have already admitted,—at frustrating the just vengeance which an oppressed country has the right to wreak on those who have proved themselves to be tyrants and traitors."

"Is it necessary to recapitulate all this, Monsieur Chauvelin?" she asked impatiently.

"I think so," he replied blandly. "You see, my point is this. We feel that in a measure now the Scarlet Pimpernel is in our power. Within the next few hours he will land at Boulogne—Boulogne, where he has agreed to fight a duel with me—Boulogne, where Lady Blakeney happens to be at this present moment—as you see, Boulogne has a great responsibility to bear; just now she is to a certain extent the proudest city in France, since she holds within her gates a hostage for the appearance on our shores of her country's most bitter enemy. But she must not fall from that high estate. Her double duty is clear before her; she must guard Lady Blakeney and capture the Scarlet Pimpernel; if she fail in the former she must be punished, if she succeed in the latter she shall be rewarded."

He paused and leaned out of the window again, whilst she watched him, breathless and terrified. She was beginning to understand.

"Hark!" he said, looking straight at her. "Do you hear the crier now? He is proclaiming the punishment and the reward. He is making it clear to the citizens of Boulogne that on the day when the Scarlet Pimpernel falls into the hands of the Committee of Public Safety a general amnesty will be granted to all natives of Boulogne who are under arrest at the present time, and a free pardon to all those who, born within these city walls, are today under sentence of death—A noble reward, eh? well-deserved you'll admit—Should you wonder then if the whole town of Boulogne were engaged just now in finding that mysterious hero, and delivering him into our hands?—How many mothers, sisters, wives, think you, at the present moment, would fail to lay hands on the English adventurer, if a husband's or a son's life or freedom happened to be at stake?—I have some records there," he continued, pointing in the direction of the table, "which tell me that there are five and thirty natives of Boulogne in the local prisons, a dozen more in the prisons of Paris; of these at least twenty have been tried already and are condemned to death. Every hour that the Scarlet Pimpernel succeeds in evading his captors so many deaths lie at his door. If he succeeds in once more reaching England safely three score lives mayhap will be the price of his escape—Nay! but I see your ladyship is shivering with cold—" he added with a dry little laugh, "shall I close the window? or do you wish to hear what punishment will be meted out to Boulogne, if on the day that the Scarlet Pimpernel is captured, Lady Blakeney happens to have left the shelter of these city walls?"

"I pray you proceed, *Monsieur*," she rejoined with perfect calm.

"The Committee of Public Safety," he resumed, "would look upon this city as a nest of traitors if on the day that the Scarlet Pimpernel becomes our prisoner Lady Blakeney herself, the wife of that notorious English spy, had already quitted Boulogne. The whole town knows by now that you are in our hands—you, the most precious hostage we can hold for the ultimate capture of the man whom we all fear and detest. Virtually the town-crier is at the present moment proclaiming to the inhabitants of this city; 'We want that man, but we already have his wife, see to it, citizens, that she does not escape! for if she do, we shall summarily shoot the breadwinner in every family in the town!'"

A cry of horror escaped Marguerite's parched lips.

"Are you devils then, all of you," she gasped, "that you should think of such things?"

"Aye! some of us are devils, no doubt," said Chauvelin drily; "but why should you honour us in this case with so flattering an epithet? We are mere men striving to guard our property and mean no harm to the citizens of Boulogne. We have threatened them, true! but is it not for you and that elusive Pimpernel to see that the threat is never put into execution?"

"You would not do it!" she repeated, horror-stricken.

"Nay! I pray you, fair lady, do not deceive yourself. At present the proclamation sounds like a mere threat, I'll allow, but let me assure you that if we fail to capture the Scarlet Pimpernel and if you on the other hand are spirited out of this fortress by that mysterious adventurer we shall undoubtedly shoot or guillotine every able-bodied man and woman in this town."

He had spoken quietly and emphatically, neither with bombast, nor with rage, and Marguerite saw in his face nothing but a calm and ferocious determination, the determination of an entire nation embodied in this one man, to be revenged at any cost. She would not let him see the depth of her despair, nor would she let him read in her face the unutterable hopelessness which filled her soul. It were useless to make an appeal to him; she knew full well that from him she could obtain neither gentleness nor mercy.

"I hope at last I have made the situation quite clear to your ladyship?" he was asking quite pleasantly now. "See how easy is your position; you have but to remain quiescent in room No. 6, and if any chance of escape be offered you ere the Scarlet Pimpernel is captured, you need but to think of all the families of Boulogne, who would be deprived of their breadwinner—fathers and sons mostly, but there are girls too, who support their mothers or sisters; the fish curers of Boulogne are mostly women, and there are the net-makers and the seamstresses, all would suffer if your ladyship were no longer to be found in No. 6 room of this ancient fort, whilst all would be included in the amnesty if the Scarlet Pimpernel fell into our hands—"

He gave a low, satisfied chuckle which made Marguerite think of the evil spirits in hell exulting over the torments of unhappy lost souls.

"I think, Lady Blakeney," he added drily and making her an ironical bow, "that your humble servant hath outwitted the elusive hero at last."

Quietly he turned on his heel and went back into the room, Marguerite remaining motionless beside the open window, where the soft, brine-laden air, the distant murmur of the sea, the occasional cry of a sea-mew, all seemed to mock her agonising despair.

The voice of the town-crier came nearer and nearer now; she could hear the words he spoke quite distinctly; something about "amnesty" and pardon, the reward for the capture of the Scarlet Pimpernel, the lives of men, women and children in exchange for his.

Oh! she knew what all that meant! that Percy would not hesitate one single instant to throw his life into the hands of his enemies, in exchange for that of others. Others! others! always others! this sigh that had made her heart ache so often in England, what terrible significance it bore now!

And how he would suffer in his heart and in his pride, because of her whom he could not even attempt to save since it would mean the death of others! of others, always of others!

She wondered if he had already landed in Boulogne! Again, she remembered the vision on the landing stage; his massive figure, the glimpse she had of the loved form, in the midst of the crowd!

The moment he entered the town he would hear the proclamation read, see it posted up no doubt on every public building, and realise that she had been foolish enough to follow him, that she was a prisoner and that he could do nothing to save her.

What would he do? Marguerite at the thought instinctively pressed her hands to her heart; the agony of it all had become physically painful. She hoped that perhaps this pain meant approaching death! oh! how easy would this simple solution be!

The moon peered out from beneath the bank of clouds which had obscured her for so long; smiling, she drew her pencilled silver lines along the edge of towers and pinnacles, the frowning *beffroi* and those stony walls which seemed to Marguerite as if they encircled a gigantic graveyard.

The town-crier had evidently ceased to read the proclamation. One by one the windows in the public square were lighted up from within. The citizens of Boulogne wanted to think over the strange events which had occurred without their knowledge, yet which were apparently to have such direful or such joyous consequences for them.

A man to be captured! the mysterious English adventurer of whom they had all heard, but whom nobody had seen. And a woman—his wife—to be guarded until the man was safely under lock and key.

Marguerite felt as if she could almost hear them talking it over and vowing that she should not escape, and that the Scarlet Pimpernel should soon be captured.

A gentle wind stirred the old gnarled trees on the southern ramparts, a wind that sounded like the sigh of swiftly dying hope.

What could Percy do now? His hands were tied, and he was inevitably destined to endure the awful agony of seeing the woman he loved die a terrible death beside him.

Having captured him, they would not keep him long; no necessity for a trial, for detention, for formalities of any kind. A summary execution at dawn on the public place, a roll of drums, a public holiday to mark the joyful event, and a brave man will have ceased to live, a noble heart have stilled its beatings forever, whilst a whole nation gloried over the deed.

"Sleep, citizens of Boulogne! all is still!"

The night watchman had replaced the town-crier. All was quiet within the city walls; the inhabitants could sleep in peace; a beneficent government was wakeful and guarding their rest.

But many of the windows of the town remained lighted up, and at a little distance below her, round the corner so that she could not see it, a small crowd must have collected in front of the gateway which led into the courtyard of the Gayole Fort. Marguerite could hear a persistent murmur of voices, mostly angry and threatening, and once there were loud cries of; "English spies," and "à *la lanterne!*"

"The citizens of Boulogne are guarding the treasures of France!" commented Chauvelin drily, as he laughed again, that cruel, mirthless laugh of his.

Then she roused herself from her torpor; she did not know how long she had stood beside the open window, but the fear seized her that that man must have seen and gloated over the agony of her mind. She straightened her graceful figure, threw back her proud head defiantly, and quietly walked up to the table, where Chauvelin seemed once more absorbed in the perusal of his papers.

"Is this interview over?" she asked quietly, and without the slightest tremor in her voice. "May I go now?"

"As soon as you wish," he replied with gentle irony.

He regarded her with obvious delight, for truly she was beautiful; grand in this attitude of defiant despair. The man, who had spent the last half-hour in martyrizing her, gloried over the misery which he had wrought, and which all her strength of will could not entirely banish from her face.

"Will you believe me, Lady Blakeney?" he added, "that there is no personal animosity in my heart towards you or your husband? Have I not told you that I do not wish to compass his death?"

"Yet you propose to send him to the guillotine as soon as you have laid hands on him."

"I have explained to you the measures which I have taken in order to make sure that we *do* lay hands on the Scarlet Pimpernel. Once he is in our power, it will rest with him to walk to the guillotine or to embark with you on board his yacht."

"You propose to place an alternative before Sir Percy Blakeney?"

"Certainly."

"To offer him his life?"

"And that of his charming wife."

"In exchange for what?"

"His honour."

"He will refuse, *Monsieur.*"

"We shall see."

Then he touched a hand-bell which stood on the table, and within a few seconds the door was opened and the soldier who had led Marguerite hither, re-entered the room.

The interview was at an end. It had served its purpose. Marguerite knew now that she must not even think of escape for herself or hope for safety for the man she loved. Of Chauvelin's talk of a bargain which would touch Percy's honour, she would not even think; and she was too proud to ask anything further from him.

Chauvelin stood up and made her a deep bow, as she crossed the room and finally went out of the door. The little company of soldiers closed in around her and she was once more led along the dark passages, back to her own prison cell.

Colleagues

As soon as the door had closed behind Marguerite, there came from somewhere in the room the sound of a yawn, a grunt and a volley of oaths.

The flickering light of the tallow candles had failed to penetrate into all the corners, and now from out one of these dark depths, a certain something began to detach itself, and to move forward towards the table at which Chauvelin had once more resumed his seat.

"Has the damned aristocrat gone at last?" queried a hoarse voice, as a burly body clad in loose-fitting coat and mud-stained boots and breeches appeared within the narrow circle of light.

"Yes," replied Chauvelin curtly.

"And a cursed long time you have been with the baggage," grunted the other surlily. "Another five minutes and I'd have taken the matter in my own hands.

"An assumption of authority," commented Chauvelin quietly, "to which your position here does not entitle you, Citizen Collot."

Collot d'Herbois lounged lazily forward, and presently he threw his ill-knit figure into the chair lately vacated by Marguerite. His heavy, square face bore distinct traces of the fatigue endured in the past twenty-four hours on horseback or in jolting market waggons. His temper too appeared to have suffered on the way, and, at Chauvelin's curt and dictatorial replies, he looked as surly as a chained dog.

"You were wasting your breath over that woman," he muttered, bringing a large and grimy fist heavily down on the table, "and your measures are not quite so sound as your fondly imagine, Citizen Chauvelin."

"They were mostly of your imagining, Citizen Collot," rejoined the other quietly, "and of your suggestion."

"I added a touch of strength and determination to your mild milk-and-water notions, Citizen," snarled Collot spitefully. "I'd have knocked that intriguing woman's brains out at the very first possible opportunity, had I been consulted earlier than this."

"Quite regardless of the fact that such violent measures would completely damn all our chances of success as far as the capture of the Scarlet Pimpernel is concerned," remarked Chauvelin drily, with a contemptuous shrug of the shoulders. "Once his wife is dead, the

144

Englishman will never run his head into the noose which I have so carefully prepared for him."

"So, you say, Chauvelin; and therefore, I suggested to you certain measures to prevent the woman escaping which you will find adequate, I hope."

"You need have no fear, Citizen Collot," said Chauvelin curtly, "this woman will make no attempt at escape now."

"If she does—" and Collot d'Herbois swore an obscene oath.

"I think she understands that we mean to put our threat in execution."

"Threat?—It was no empty threat, Citizen—*Sacré tonnerre!* if that woman escapes now, by all the devils in hell I swear that I'll wield the guillotine myself and cut off the head of every able-bodied man or woman in Boulogne, with my own hands."

As he said this his face assumed such an expression of inhuman cruelty, such a desire to kill, such a savage lust for blood, that instinctively Chauvelin shuddered and shrank away from his colleague. All through his career there is no doubt that this man, who was of gentle birth, of gentle breeding, and who had once been called M. le Marquis de Chauvelin, must have suffered in his susceptibilities and in his pride when in contact with the revolutionaries with whom he had chosen to cast his lot. He could not have thrown off all his old ideas of refinement quite so easily, as to feel happy in the presence of such men as Collot d'Herbois, or Marat in his day—men who had become brute beasts, more ferocious far than any wild animal, more scientifically cruel than any feline prowler in jungle or desert.

One look in Collot's distorted face was sufficient at this moment to convince Chauvelin that it were useless for him to view the proclamation against the citizens of Boulogne merely as an idle threat, even if he had wished to do so. That Marguerite would not, under the circumstances, attempt to escape, that Sir Percy Blakeney himself would be forced to give up all thoughts of rescuing her, was a foregone conclusion in Chauvelin's mind, but if this high-born English gentleman had not happened to be the selfless hero that he was, if Marguerite Blakeney were cast in a different, a rougher mould—if, in short, the Scarlet Pimpernel in the face of the proclamation did succeed in dragging his wife out of the clutches of the Terrorists, then it was equally certain that Collot d'Herbois would carry out his rabid and cruel reprisals to the full. And if in the course of the wholesale butchery of the able-bodied and wage-earning inhabitants of Boulogne, the headsman should sink worn out, then would this ferocious sucker of blood put his own hand to the guillotine, with the same joy and lust which he had felt when he ordered one hundred and thirty-eight women of Nantes to be stripped naked by the soldiery before they were flung helter-skelter into the river.

A touch of strength and determination! Aye! Citizen Collot d'Herbois had plenty of that. Was it he, or Carriere who at Arras commanded mothers to stand by while their children were being guillotined? And surely it was Maignet, Collot's friend and colleague, who at Bedouin, because the Red Flag of the Republic had been mysteriously torn down over night, burnt the entire little village down to the last hovel and guillotined every one of the three hundred and fifty inhabitants.

And Chauvelin knew all that. Nay, more! he was himself a member of that so-called government which had countenanced these butcheries, by giving unlimited powers to men like Collot, like Maignet and Carrière. He was at one with them in their republican ideas and he believed in the regeneration and the purification of France, through the medium of the guillotine, but he propounded his theories and carried out his most bloodthirsty schemes with physically clean hands and in an immaculately cut coat.

Even now when Collot d'Herbois lounged before him, with mud-bespattered legs stretched out before him, with dubious linen at neck and wrists, and an odour of rank tobacco and stale, cheap wine pervading his whole personality, the more fastidious man of the world, who had consorted with the dandies of London and Brighton, winced at the enforced proximity.

But it was the joint characteristic of all these men who had turned France into a vast butchery and charnel-house, that they all feared and hated one another, even more whole-heartedly than they hated the aristocrats and so-called traitors whom they sent to the guillotine. Citizen Lebon is said to have dipped his sword into the blood which flowed from the guillotine, whilst exclaiming; "*Comme je l'aime ce sang coulé de traître!*" but he and Collot and Danton and Robespierre, all of them in fact would have regarded with more delight still the blood of any one of their colleagues.

At this very moment Collot d'Herbois and Chauvelin would with utmost satisfaction have denounced, one the other, to the tender mercies of the Public Prosecutor. Collot made no secret of his hatred for Chauvelin, and the latter disguised it but thinly under the veneer of contemptuous indifference.

"As for that dammed Englishman," added Collot now, after a slight pause, and with another savage oath, "if 'tis my good fortune to lay hands on him, I'd shoot him then and there like a mad dog, and rid France once and forever of this accursed spy."

"And think you, Citizen Collot," rejoined Chauvelin with a shrug of the shoulders, "that France would be rid of all English adventurers by the summary death of this one man?"

"He is the ringleader, at any rate—"

"And has at least nineteen disciples to continue his traditions of conspiracy and intrigue. None perhaps so ingenious as himself, none with the same daring and good luck perhaps, but still a number of ardent fools only too ready to follow in the footsteps of their chief. Then there's the halo of martyrdom around the murdered hero, the enthusiasm created by his noble death—Nay! nay, Citizen, you have not lived among these English people, you do not understand them, or you would not talk of sending their popular hero to an honoured grave."

But Collot d'Herbois only shook his powerful frame like some big, sulky dog, and spat upon the floor to express his contempt of this wild talk which seemed to have no real tangible purpose.

"You have not caught your Scarlet Pimpernel yet, Citizen," he said with a snort.

"No, but I will, after sundown tomorrow."

"How do you know?"

"I have ordered the Angelus to be rung at one of the closed churches, and he agreed to fight a duel with me on the southern ramparts at that hour and on that day," said Chauvelin simply.

"You take him for a fool?" sneered Collot.

"No, only for a foolhardy adventurer."

"You imagine that with his wife as hostage in our hands, and the whole city of Boulogne on the lookout for him for the sake of the amnesty, that the man would be fool enough to walk on those ramparts at a given hour, for the express purpose of getting himself caught by you and your men?"

"I am quite sure that if we do not lay hands on him before that given hour, that he will be on the ramparts at the Angelus tomorrow," said Chauvelin emphatically.

Collot shrugged his broad shoulders.

"Is the man mad?" he asked with an incredulous laugh.

"Yes, I think so," rejoined the other with a smile.

"And having caught your hare," queried Collot, "how do you propose to cook him?"

"Twelve picked men will be on the ramparts ready to seize him the moment he appears."

"And to shoot him at sight, I hope."

"Only as a last resource, for the Englishman is powerful and may cause our half-famished men a good deal of trouble. But I want him alive, if possible—"

"Why? a dead lion is safer than a live one any day."

"Oh! we'll kill him right enough, Citizen. I pray you have no fear. I hold a weapon ready for that meddlesome Scarlet Pimpernel, which will be a thousand times more deadly and more effectual than a chance shot, or even a guillotine."

"What weapon is that, Citizen Chauvelin?"

Chauvelin leaned forward across the table and rested his chin in his hands; instinctively Collot too leaned towards him, and both men peered furtively round them as if wondering if prying eyes happened to be lurking round. It was Chauvelin's pale eyes which now gleamed with hatred and with an insatiable lust for revenge at least as powerful as Collot's lust for blood; the unsteady light of the tallow candles threw grotesque shadows across his brows, and his mouth was set in such rigid lines of implacable cruelty that the brutish sot beside him gazed on him amazed, vaguely scenting here a depth of feeling which was beyond his power to comprehend. He repeated his question under his breath;

"What weapon do you mean to use against that accursed spy, Citizen Chauvelin?"

"Dishonour and ridicule!" replied the other quietly.

"Bah!"

"In exchange for his life and that of his wife."

"As the woman told you just now—he will refuse."

"We shall see, Citizen."

"You are mad to think such things, Citizen, and ill serve the Republic by sparing her bitterest foe."

A long, sarcastic laugh broke from Chauvelin's parted lips.

"Spare him?—spare the Scarlet Pimpernel!—" he ejaculated. "Nay, Citizen, you need have no fear of that. But believe me, I have schemes in my head by which the man whom we all hate will be more truly destroyed than your guillotine could ever accomplish; schemes, whereby the hero who is now worshipped in England as a demi-god will suddenly become an object of loathing and of contempt—Ah! I see you understand me now—I wish to so cover him with ridicule that the very name of the small wayside flower will become a term of derision and of scorn. Only then shall we be rid of these pestilential English spies, only then will the entire League of the Scarlet Pimpernel become a thing of the past when its whilom leader, now thought akin to a god, will have found refuge in a suicide's grave, from the withering contempt of the entire world."

Chauvelin had spoken low, hardly above a whisper, and the echo of his last words died away in the great, squalid room like a long-drawn-out sigh. There was dead silence for a while save for the murmur in the wind outside and from the floor above the measured tread of the sentinel guarding the precious hostage in No. 6.

Both men were staring straight in front of them. Collot d'Herbois incredulous, half-contemptuous, did not altogether approve of these schemes which seemed to him wild and uncanny; he liked the direct simplicity of a summary trial, of the guillotine, or of his own well stage-managed *noyades*. He did not feel that any ridicule or dishonour would necessarily paralyze a man in his efforts at intrigue, and would have liked to set Chauvelin's authority aside, to behead the woman upstairs and then to take his chances of capturing the man later on.

But the orders of the Committee of Public Safety had been peremptory; he was to be Chauvelin's help, not his master, and to obey in all things. He did not dare to take any initiative in the matter, for in that case, if he failed, the reprisals against him would indeed be terrible.

He was fairly satisfied now that Chauvelin had accepted his suggestion of summarily sending to the guillotine one member of every family resident in Boulogne, if Marguerite succeeded in effecting an escape, and, of a truth, Chauvelin had hailed the fiendish suggestion with delight. The old *abbé* with his nephew and niece were undoubtedly not sufficient deterrents against the daring schemes of the Scarlet Pimpernel, who, as a matter of fact, could spirit them out of Boulogne just as easily as he would his own wife.

Collot's plan tied Marguerite to her own prison cell more completely than any other measure could have done, more so indeed than the originator thereof knew or believed. A man like this d'Herbois—born in the gutter, imbued with every brutish tradition, which generations of jail-birds had bequeathed to him—would not perhaps fully realise the fact that neither Sir Percy nor Marguerite Blakeney would ever save themselves at the expense of others. He had merely made the suggestion, because he felt that Chauvelin's plans were complicated and obscure, and above all insufficient, and that perhaps after all the English adventurer and his wife would succeed in once more outwitting him, when there would remain the grand and bloody compensation of a wholesale butchery in Boulogne.

But Chauvelin was quite satisfied. He knew that under present circumstances neither Sir Percy nor Marguerite would make any attempt to escape. The ex-ambassador had lived in England; he understood the class to which these two belonged and was quite convinced that no attempt would be made on either side to get Lady Blakeney away whilst the present ferocious order against the bread-winner of every family in the town held good.

Aye! the measures were sound enough. Chauvelin was easy in his mind about that. In another twenty-four hours he would hold the man completely in his power who had so boldly outwitted him last year; tonight, he would sleep in peace, an entire city was guarding the precious hostage.

"We'll go to bed now, Citizen," he said to Collot, who, tired and sulky, was moodily fingering the papers on the table. The scraping sound which he made thereby grated on Chauvelin's overstrung nerves. He wanted to be alone, and the sleepy brute's presence here jarred on his own solemn mood.

To his satisfaction, Collot grunted a surly assent. Very leisurely he rose from his chair, stretched out his loose limbs, shook himself like a shaggy cur, and without uttering another word he gave his colleague a curt nod, and slowly lounged out of the room.

CHAPTER 25

The Unexpected

Chauvelin heaved a deep sigh of satisfaction when Collot d'Herbois finally left him to himself. He listened for a while until the heavy footsteps died away in the distance, then leaning back in his chair, he gave himself over to the delights of the present situation.

Marguerite in his power. Sir Percy Blakeney compelled to treat for her rescue if he did not wish to see her die a miserable death.

"Aye! my elusive hero," he muttered to himself, "methinks that we shall be able to cry quits at last."

Outside everything had become still. Even the wind in the trees out there on the ramparts had ceased their melancholy moaning. The man was alone with his thoughts. He felt secure and at peace, sure of victory, content to await the events of the next twenty-four hours. The other side of the door the guard which he had picked out from amongst the more feeble and ill-fed garrison of the little city for attendance on his own person were ranged ready to respond to his call.

"Dishonour and ridicule! Derision and scorn!" he murmured, gloating over the very sound of these words, which expressed all that he hoped to accomplish, "utter abjections, then perhaps a suicide's grave—"

He loved the silence around him, for he could murmur these words and hear them echoing against the bare stone walls like the whisperings of all the spirits of hate which were waiting to lend him their aid.

How long he had remained thus absorbed in his meditations, he could not afterwards have said; a minute or two perhaps at most, whilst he leaned back in his chair with eyes closed, savouring the sweets of his own thoughts, when suddenly the silence was interrupted by a loud and pleasant laugh and a drawly voice speaking in merry accents;

"The lud love you, Monsieur Chaubertin, and pray how do you propose to accomplish all these pleasant things?"

In a moment Chauvelin was on his feet and with eyes dilated, lips parted in awed bewilderment, he was gazing towards the open window, where astride upon the sill, one leg inside the room, the other out, and with the moon shining full on his suit of delicate-coloured cloth, his wide caped coat and elegant *chapeau-bras*, sat the imperturbable Sir Percy.

"I heard you muttering such pleasant words, *Monsieur*," continued Blakeney calmly, "that the temptation seized me to join in the conversation. A man talking to himself is ever in a sorry plight—he is either a mad man or a fool—"

He laughed his own quaint and inane laugh and added apologetically;

"Far be it from me, sir, to apply either epithet to you—demmed bad form calling another fellow names—just when he does not quite feel himself, eh?—You don't feel quite yourself, I fancy just now—eh, Monsieur Chauberin—er—beg pardon, Chauvelin—"

He sat there quite comfortably, one slender hand resting on the gracefully-fashioned hilt of his sword—the sword of Lorenzo Cenci—the other holding up the gold-rimmed eyeglass through which he was regarding his avowed enemy; he was dressed as for a ball, and his perpetually amiable smile lurked round the corners of his firm lips.

Chauvelin had undoubtedly for the moment lost his presence of mind. He did not even think of calling to his picked guard, so completely taken aback was he by this unforeseen move on the part of Sir Percy. Yet, obviously, he should have been ready for this eventuality. Had he not caused the town-crier to loudly proclaim throughout the city that if *one* female prisoner escaped from Fort Gayole the entire able-bodied population of Boulogne would suffer?

The moment Sir Percy entered the gates of the town, he could not help but hear the proclamation, and hear at the same time that this one female prisoner who was so precious a charge, was the wife of the English spy; the Scarlet Pimpernel.

Moreover, was it not a fact that whenever or wherever the Scarlet Pimpernel was least expected there and then would he surely appear? Having once realised that it was his wife who was incarcerated in Fort Gayole, was it not natural that he would go and prowl around the prison, and along the avenue on the summit of the southern ramparts, which was accessible to every passer-by? No doubt he had lain in hiding among the trees, had perhaps caught snatches of Chauvelin's recent talk with Collot.

Aye! it was all so natural, so simple! Strange that it should have been so unexpected!

Furious at himself for his momentary stupor, he now made a vigorous effort to face his impudent enemy with the same *sang-froid* of which the latter had so inexhaustible a fund.

He walked quietly towards the window, compelling his nerves to perfect calm and his mood to indifference. The situation had ceased to astonish him; already his keen mind had seen its possibilities, its grimness and its humour, and he was quite prepared to enjoy these to the full.

Sir Percy now was dusting the sleeve of his coat with a lace-edged handkerchief, but just as Chauvelin was about to come near him, he stretched out one leg, turning the point of a dainty boot towards the ex-ambassador.

"Would you like to take hold of me by the leg, Monsieur Chaubertin?" he said gaily. "'Tis more effectual than a shoulder, and your picked guard of six stalwart fellows can have the other leg—Nay! I pray you, sir, do not look at me like that—I vow that it is myself and not my ghost—But if you still doubt me, I pray you call the guard—ere I fly out again towards that fitful moon—"

"Nay, Sir Percy," said Chauvelin, with a steady voice, "I have no thought that you will take flight just yet—Methinks you desire conversation with me, or you had not paid me so unexpected a visit."

"Nay, sir, the air is too oppressive for lengthy conversation—I was strolling along these ramparts, thinking of our pleasant encounter at the hour of the Angelus tomorrow—when this light attracted me—feared I had lost my way and climbed the window to obtain information."

"As to your way to the nearest prison cell, Sir Percy?" queried Chauvelin drily.

"As to anywhere, where I could sit more comfortably than on this demmed sill—It must be very dusty, and I vow 'tis terribly hard—"

"I presume, Sir Percy, that you did my colleague and myself the honour of listening to our conversation?"

"An' you desired to talk secrets, Monsieur—er—Chaubertin—you should have shut this window—and closed this avenue of trees against the chance passer-by."

"What we said was no secret, Sir Percy. It is all over the town to-night."

"Quite so—you were only telling the devil your mind—eh?"

"I had also been having conversation with Lady Blakeney—Pray did you hear any of that, sir?"

But Sir Percy had evidently not heard the question, for he seemed quite absorbed in the task of removing a speck of dust from his immaculate *chapeau-bras*.

"These hats are all the rage in England just now," he said airily, "but they have had their day, do you not think so, *Monsieur?* When I return to town, I shall have to devote my whole mind to the invention of a new headgear—"

"When will you return to England, Sir Percy?" queried Chauvelin with good-natured sarcasm.

"At the turn of the tide tomorrow eve, *Monsieur*," replied Blakeney.

"In company with Lady Blakeney?"

"Certainly, sir—and yours if you will honour us with your company."

"If you return to England tomorrow, Sir Percy, Lady Blakeney, I fear me, cannot accompany you."

"You astonish me, sir," rejoined Blakeney with an exclamation of genuine and unaffected surprise. "I wonder now what would prevent her?"

"All those whose death would be the result of her flight, if she succeeded in escaping from Boulogne—"

But Sir Percy was staring at him, with wide open eyes expressive of utmost amazement.

"Dear, dear, dear—Lud! but that sounds most unfortunate—"

"You have not heard of the measures which I have taken to prevent Lady Blakeney quitting this city without our leave?"

"No, Monsieur Chaubertin—no—I have heard nothing—" rejoined Sir Percy blandly. "I lead a very retired life when I come abroad and—"

"Would you wish to hear them now?"

"Quite unnecessary, sir, I assure you—and the hour is getting late—"

"Sir Percy, are you aware of the fact that unless you listen to what I have to say, your wife will be dragged before the Committee of Public Safety in Paris within the next twenty-four hours?" said Chauvelin firmly.

"What swift horses you must have, sir," quoth Blakeney pleasantly. "Lud! to think of it!—I always heard that these demmed French horses would never beat ours across country."

But Chauvelin now would not allow himself to be ruffled by Sir Percy's apparent indifference. Keen reader of emotions as he was, he had not failed to note a distinct change in the drawly voice, a sound of something hard and trenchant in the flippant laugh, ever since Marguerite's name was first mentioned. Blakeney's attitude was apparently as careless, as audacious as before, but Chauvelin's keen eyes had not missed the almost imperceptible tightening of the jaw and the rapid clenching of one hand on the sword hilt even whilst the other toyed in graceful idleness with the filmy Mechlin lace cravat.

Sir Percy's head was well thrown back, and the pale rays of the moon caught the edge of the clear-cut profile, the low massive brow, the drooping lids through which the audacious plotter was lazily regarding the man who held not only his own life, but that of the woman who was infinitely dear to him, in the hollow of his hand.

"I am afraid, Sir Percy," continued Chauvelin drily, "that you are under the impression that bolts and bars will yield to your usual good luck, now that so precious a life is at stake as that of Lady Blakeney."

"I am a greater believer in impressions, Monsieur Chauvelin."

"I told her just now that if she quitted Boulogne ere the Scarlet Pimpernel is in our hands, we should summarily shoot one member of every family in the town—the bread-winner."

"A pleasant conceit, *Monsieur*—and one that does infinite credit to your inventive faculties."

"Lady Blakeney, therefore, we hold safely enough," continued Chauvelin, who no longer heeded the mocking observations of his enemy; "as for the Scarlet Pimpernel—"

"You have but to ring a bell, to raise a voice, and he too will be under lock and key within the next two minutes, eh?—*Passons, Monsieur*—you are dying to say something further—I pray you proceed—your engaging countenance is becoming quite interesting in its seriousness."

"What I wish to say to you, Sir Percy, is in the nature of a proposed bargain."

"Indeed?—*Monsieur*, you are full of surprises—like a pretty woman—And pray what are the terms of this proposed bargain?"

"Your side of the bargain, Sir Percy, or mine? Which will you hear first?"

"Oh yours, *Monsieur*—yours, I pray you—Have I not said that you are like a pretty woman?—*Place aux dames*, sir! always!"

"My share of the bargain, sir, is simple enough; Lady Blakeney, escorted by yourself and any of your friends who might be in this city at the time, shall leave Boulogne harbour at sunset tomorrow, free and unmolested, if you on the other hand will do your share—"

"I don't yet know what my share in this interesting bargain is to be, sir—but for the sake of argument let us suppose that I do not carry it out—What then?—"

"Then, Sir Percy—putting aside for the moment the question of the Scarlet Pimpernel altogether—then, Lady Blakeney will be taken to Paris, and will be incarcerated in the prison of the Temple lately vacated by Marie Antoinette—there she will be treated in exactly the same way as the ex-queen is now being treated in the *Conciergerie*—Do you know what that means, Sir Percy?—It does not mean a summary trial and a speedy death, with the halo and glory of martyrdom thrown in—it means days, weeks, nay, months, perhaps, of misery and humiliation—it means, that like Marie Antoinette, she will never be allowed solitude for one single instant of the day or night—it means the constant proximity of soldiers, drunk with cruelty and with hate—the insults, the shame—"

"You hound!—you dog!—you cur!—do you not see that I must strangle you for this!—"

The attack had been so sudden and so violent that Chauvelin had not the time to utter the slightest call for help. But a second ago, Sir Percy Blakeney had been sitting on the window-sill, outwardly listening with perfect calm to what his enemy had to say; now he was at the latter's throat, pressing with long and slender hands the breath out of the Frenchman's body, his usually placid face distorted into a mask of hate.

"You cur!—you cur!—" he repeated, "am I to kill you or will you unsay those words?"

Then suddenly he relaxed his grip. The habits of a lifetime would not be gainsaid even now. A second ago his face had been livid with rage and hate, now a quick flush overspread it, as if he were ashamed of this loss of self-control. He threw the little Frenchman away from him like he would a beast which had snarled and passed his hand across his brow.

"Lud forgive me!" he said quaintly, "I had almost lost my temper."

Chauvelin was not slow in recovering himself. He was plucky and alert, and his hatred for this man was so great that he had actually ceased to fear him. Now he quietly readjusted his cravat, made a vigorous effort to re-conquer his breath, and said firmly as soon as he could contrive to speak at all;

"And if you did strangle me, Sir Percy, you would do yourself no good. The fate which I have mapped out for Lady Blakeney, would then irrevocably be hers, for she is in our power and none of my colleagues are disposed to offer you a means of saving her from it, as I am ready to do."

Blakeney was now standing in the middle of the room, with his hands buried in the pockets of his breeches, his manner and attitude once more calm, *debonnair*, expressive of lofty self-possession and of absolute indifference. He came quite close to the meagre little figure of his exultant enemy, thereby forcing the latter to look up at him.

"Oh!—ah!—yes!" he said airily, "I had nigh forgotten—you were talking of a bargain—my share of it—eh?—Is it me you want?—Do you wish to see me in your Paris prisons?—I assure you, sir, that the propinquity of drunken soldiers may disgust me, but it would in no way disturb the equanimity of my temper."

"I am quite sure of that, Sir Percy—and I can but repeat what I had the honour of saying to Lady Blakeney just now—I do not desire the death of so accomplished a gentleman as yourself."

"Strange, *Monsieur*," retorted Blakeney, with a return of his accustomed flippancy. "Now I do desire your death very strongly indeed—there would be so much less vermin on the face of the earth—But pardon me—I was interrupting you—Will you be so kind as to proceed?"

Chauvelin had not winced at the insult. His enemy's attitude now left him completely indifferent. He had seen that self-possessed man of the world, that dainty and fastidious dandy, in the throes of an overmastering passion. He had very nearly paid with his life for the joy of having roused that supercilious and dormant lion. In fact, he was ready to welcome any insults from Sir Percy Blakeney now, since these would be only additional evidences that the Englishman's temper was not yet under control.

"I will try to be brief, Sir Percy," he said, setting himself the task of imitating his antagonist's affected manner. "Will you not sit down?—We must try and discuss these matters like two men of the world—As for me, I am always happiest beside a board littered with papers—I am not an athlete, Sir Percy—and serve my country with my pen rather than with my fists."

Whilst he spoke he had reached the table and once more took the chair whereon he had been sitting lately, when he dreamed the dreams which were so near realisation now. He pointed with a graceful gesture to the other vacant chair, which Blakeney took without a word.

"Ah!" said Chauvelin with a sigh of satisfaction, "I see that we are about to understand one another—I have always felt it was a pity, Sir Percy, that you and I could not discuss certain matters pleasantly with one another—Now, about this unfortunate incident of Lady Blakeney's incarceration, I would like you to believe that I had no part in the arrangements which have been made for her detention in Paris. My colleagues have arranged it all—and I have vainly tried to protest against the rigorous measures which are to be enforced against her in the Temple prison—But these are answering so completely in the case of the ex-queen, they have so completely broken her spirit and her pride, that my colleagues felt that they would prove equally useful in order to bring the Scarlet Pimpernel—through his wife—to an humbler frame of mind."

He paused a moment, distinctly pleased with his peroration, satisfied that his voice had been without a tremor and his face impassive, and wondering what effect this somewhat lengthy preamble had upon Sir Percy, who through it all had remained singularly quiet. Chauvelin was preparing himself for the next effect which he hoped to produce and was vaguely seeking for the best words with which to fully express his meaning, when he was suddenly startled by a sound as unexpected as it was disconcerting.

It was the sound of a loud and prolonged snore. He pushed the candle aside, which somewhat obstructed his line of vision, and casting a rapid glance at the enemy, with whose life he was toying even as a cat doth with that of a mouse, he saw that the aforesaid mouse was calmly and unmistakably asleep.

An impatient oath escaped Chauvelin's lips, and he brought his fist heavily down on the table, making the metal candlesticks rattle and causing Sir Percy to open one sleepy eye.

"A thousand pardons, sir," said Blakeney with a slight yawn. "I am so demmed fatigued, and your preface was unduly long—Beastly bad form, I know, going to sleep during a sermon—but I haven't had a wink of sleep all day—I pray you to excuse me—"

"Will you condescend to listen, Sir Percy?" queried Chauvelin peremptorily, "or shall I call the guard and give up all thoughts of treating with you?"

"Just whichever you demmed well prefer, sir," rejoined Blakeney impatiently.

And once more stretching out his long limbs, he buried his hands in the pockets of his breeches and apparently prepared himself for another quiet sleep. Chauvelin looked at him for a moment, vaguely wondering what to do next. He felt strangely irritated at what he firmly believed was mere affectation on Blakeney's part, and although he was burning with impatience to place the terms of the proposed bargain before this man, yet he would have preferred to be interrogated, to deliver his "either-or" with becoming sternness and decision, rather than to take the initiative in this discussion, where he should have been calm and indifferent, whilst his enemy should have been nervous and disturbed.

Sir Percy's attitude had disconcerted him, a touch of the grotesque had been given to what should have been a tense moment, and it was terribly galling to the pride of the ex-diplomatist that with this elusive enemy and in spite of his own preparedness for any eventuality, it was invariably the unforeseen that happened.

After a moment's reflection, however, he decided upon a fresh course of action. He rose and crossed the room, keeping as much as possible an eye upon Sir Percy, but the latter sat placid and dormant and evidently in no hurry to move. Chauvelin having reached the door, opened it noiselessly, and to the sergeant in command of his bodyguard who stood at attention outside, he whispered hurriedly;

"The prisoner from No. 6—Let two of the men bring her hither back to me at once."

CHAPTER 26

The Terms of the Bargain

Less than three minutes later, there came to Chauvelin's expectant ears the soft sound made by a woman's skirts against the stone floor. During those three minutes, which had seemed an eternity to his impatience, he had sat silently watching the slumber—affected or real—of his enemy.

Directly he heard the word; "Halt!" outside the door, he jumped to his feet. The next moment Marguerite had entered the room.

Hardly had her foot crossed the threshold than Sir Percy rose, quietly and without haste but evidently fully awake, and turning towards her, made her a low obeisance.

She, poor woman, had of course caught sight of him at once. His presence here, Chauvelin's demand for her reappearance, the soldiers in a small compact group outside the door, all these were unmistakable proofs that the awful cataclysm had at last occurred.

The Scarlet Pimpernel, Percy Blakeney, her husband, was in the hands of the Terrorists of France, and though face to face with her now, with an open window close to him, and an apparently helpless enemy under his hand, he could not—owing to the fiendish measures taken by Chauvelin—raise a finger to save himself and her.

Mercifully for her, nature—in the face of this appalling tragedy—deprived her of the full measure of her senses. She could move and speak and see, she could hear and, in a measure, understand what was said, but she was really an automaton or a sleep-walker, moving and speaking mechanically and without due comprehension.

Possibly, if she had then and there fully realised all that the future meant, she would have gone mad with the horror of it all.

"Lady Blakeney," began Chauvelin after he had quickly dismissed the soldiers from the room, "when you and I parted from one another just now, I had no idea that I should so soon have the pleasure of a personal conversation with Sir Percy—There is no occasion yet, believe me, for sorrow or fear—Another twenty-four hours at most, and you will be on board the *Daydream*' outward bound for England. Sir Percy himself might perhaps accompany you; he does not desire that you should journey to Paris, and I may safely say, that in his mind, he has already accepted certain little conditions which I have been forced to impose upon him ere I sign the order for your absolute release."

"Conditions?" she repeated vaguely and stupidly, looking in bewilderment from one to the other.

"You are tired, m'dear," said Sir Percy quietly, "will you not sit down?"

He held the chair gallantly for her. She tried to read his face but could not catch even a flash from beneath the heavy lids which obstinately veiled his eyes.

"Oh! it is a mere matter of exchanging signatures," continued Chauvelin in response to her inquiring glance and toying with the papers which were scattered on the table. "Here you see is the order to allow Sir Percy Blakeney and his wife, nee Marguerite St. Just, to quit the town of Boulogne unmolested."

He held a paper out towards Marguerite, inviting her to look at it. She caught sight of an official-looking document, bearing the motto and seal of the Republic of France, and of her own name and Percy's written thereon in full.

"It is perfectly *en règle*, I assure you," continued Chauvelin, "and only awaits my signature."

He now took up another paper which looked like a long closely-written letter. Marguerite watched his every movement, for instinct told her that the supreme moment had come. There was a look of almost superhuman cruelty and malice in the little Frenchman's eyes as he fixed them on the impassive figure of Sir Percy, the while with slightly trembling hands he fingered that piece of paper and smoothed out its creases with loving care.

"I am quite prepared to sign the order for your release, Lady Blakeney," he said, keeping his gaze still keenly fixed upon Sir Percy. "When it is signed you will understand that our measures against the citizens of Boulogne will no longer hold good, and that on the contrary, the general amnesty and free pardon will come into force."

"Yes, I understand that," she replied.

"And all that will come to pass, Lady Blakeney, the moment Sir Percy will write me in his own hand a letter, in accordance with the draft which I have prepared, and sign it with his name.

"Shall I read it to you?" he asked.

"If you please."

"You will see how simple it all is—A mere matter of form—I

pray you do not look upon it with terror, but only as the prelude to that general amnesty and free pardon, which I feel sure will satisfy the philanthropic heart of the noble Scarlet Pimpernel, since three score at least of the inhabitants of Boulogne will owe their life and freedom to him."

"I am listening, *Monsieur*," she said calmly.

"As I have already had the honour of explaining, this little document is in the form of a letter addressed personally to me and of course in French," he said finally, and then he looked down on the paper and began to read;

"Citizen Chauvelin—

"In consideration of a further sum of one million *francs* and on the understanding that this ridiculous charge brought against me of conspiring against the Republic of France is immediately withdrawn, and I am allowed to return to England unmolested, I am quite prepared to acquaint you with the names and whereabouts of certain persons who under the guise of the League of the Scarlet Pimpernel are even now conspiring to free the woman Marie Antoinette and her son from prison and to place the latter upon the throne of France. You are quite well aware that under the pretence of being the leader of a gang of English adventurers, who never did the Republic of France and her people any real harm, I have actually been the means of unmasking many a royalist plot before you, and of bringing many persistent conspirators to the guillotine. I am surprised that you should cavil at the price I am asking this time for the very important information with which I am able to furnish you, whilst you have often paid me similar sums for work which was a great deal less difficult to do. In order to serve your government effectually, both in England and in France, I must have a sufficiency of money, to enable me to live in a costly style befitting a gentleman of my rank. Were I to alter my mode of life I could not continue to mix in that same social milieu to which all my friends belong and wherein, as you are well aware, most of the royalist plots are hatched.

"Trusting therefore to receive a favourable reply to my just demands within the next twenty-four hours, whereupon the names in question shall be furnished you forthwith,

"I have the honour to remain, Citizen,

"Your humble and obedient servant,

When he had finished reading, Chauvelin quietly folded the paper up again, and then only did he look at the man and the woman before him.

Marguerite sat very erect, her head thrown back, her face very pale and her hands tightly clutched in her lap. She had not stirred whilst Chauvelin read out the infamous document, with which he desired to brand a brave man with the ineradicable stigma of dishonour and of shame. After she heard the first words, she looked up swiftly and questioningly at her husband, but he stood at some little distance from her, right out of the flickering circle of yellowish light made by the burning tallow-candle. He was as rigid as a statue, standing in his usual attitude with legs apart and hands buried in his breeches pockets.

She could not see his face.

Whatever she may have felt with regard to the letter, as the meaning of it gradually penetrated into her brain, she was, of course, convinced of one thing, and that was that never for a moment would Percy dream of purchasing his life or even hers at such a price. But she would have liked some sign from him, some look by which she could be guided as to her immediate conduct; as, however, he gave neither look nor sign, she preferred to assume an attitude of silent contempt.

But even before Chauvelin had had time to look from one face to the other, a prolonged and merry laugh echoed across the squalid room.

Sir Percy, with head thrown back, was laughing whole-heartedly.

"A magnificent epistle, sir," he said gaily, "Lud love you, where did you wield the pen so gracefully?—I vow that if I signed this interesting document no one will believe I could have expressed myself with perfect ease.. and in French too—"

"Nay, Sir Percy," rejoined Chauvelin drily, "I have thought of all that, and lest in the future there should be any doubt as to whether your own hand had or had not penned the whole of this letter, I also make it a condition that you write out every word of it yourself, and sign it here in this very room, in the presence of Lady Blakeney, of myself, of my colleagues and of at least half a dozen other persons whom I will select."

"It is indeed admirably thought out, *Monsieur*," rejoined Sir Percy, "and what is to become of the charming epistle, may I ask, after I have written and signed it?—Pardon my curiosity—I take a natural interest in the matter—and truly your ingenuity passes belief—"

"Oh! the fate of this letter will be as simple as was the writing thereof—A copy of it will be published in our *Gazette de Paris* as a bait for enterprising English journalists—They will not be backward in getting hold of so much interesting matter—Can you not see the attractive headlines in *The London Gazette*, Sir Percy? 'The League of the Scarlet Pimpernel unmasked! A gigantic hoax! The origin of the Blakeney millions!'—I believe that journalism in England has reached a high standard of excellence—and even the 'Gazette de Paris' is greatly read in certain towns of your charming country—His Royal Highness the Prince of Wales, and various other influential gentlemen in London, will, on the other hand, be granted a private view of the original through the kind offices of certain devoted friends whom we possess in England—I don't think that you need have any fear, Sir Percy, that your calligraphy will sink into oblivion. It will be our business to see that it obtains the full measure of publicity which it deserves—"

He paused a moment, then his manner suddenly changed; the sarcastic tone died out of his voice, and there came back into his face that look of hatred and cruelty which Blakeney's persiflage had always the power to evoke.

"You may rest assured of one thing, Sir Percy," he said with a harsh laugh, "that enough mud will be thrown at that erstwhile glorious Scarlet Pimpernel—some of it will be bound to stick—"

"Nay, Monsieur—er—Chaubertin," quoth Blakeney lightly, "I have no doubt that you and your colleagues are past masters in the graceful art of mud-throwing—But pardon me—er—I was interrupting you—Continue, *Monsieur*—continue, I pray. 'Pon my honour, the matter is vastly diverting."

"Nay, sir, after the publication of this diverting epistle, meseems your honour will cease to be a marketable commodity."

"Undoubtedly, sir," rejoined Sir Percy, apparently quite unruffled, "pardon a slip of the tongue—we are so much the creatures of habit— As you were saying—?"

"I have but little more to say, sir—But lest there should even now be lurking in your mind a vague hope that, having written this letter, you could easily in the future deny its authorship, let me tell you this; my measures are well taken, there will be witnesses to your writing of it—You will sit here in this room, unfettered, uncoerced in any way, and the money spoken of in the letter will be handed over to you by my colleague, after a few suitable words spoken by him, and you will take the money from him, Sir Percy—and the witnesses will see you take it after having seen you write the letter—they will understand that you are being *paid* by the French Government for giving information anent royalist plots in this country and in England—they will understand that your identity as the leader of that so-called band is not only known to me and to my colleague, but that it also covers your real character and profession as the paid spy of France."

"Marvellous, I call it—demmed marvellous," quoth Sir Percy blandly.

Chauvelin had paused, half-choked by his own emotion, his hatred and prospective revenge. He passed his handkerchief over his forehead, which was streaming with perspiration.

"Warm work, this sort of thing—eh—Monsieur—er—Chaubertin?—" queried his imperturbable enemy.

Marguerite said nothing; the whole thing was too horrible for words, but she kept her large eyes fixed upon her husband's face—waiting for that look, that sign from him which would have eased the agonising anxiety in her heart, and which never came.

With a great effort now, Chauvelin pulled himself together and, though his voice still trembled, he managed to speak with a certain amount of calm;

"Probably, Sir Percy, you know," he said, "that throughout the whole of France we are inaugurating a series of national *fêtes*, in honour of the new religion which the people are about to adopt—Demoiselle Désirée Candeille, whom you know, will at these festivals impersonate the Goddess of Reason, the only deity whom we admit now in France—She has been specially chosen for this honour, owing to the services which she has rendered us recently—and as Boulogne happens to be the lucky city in which we have succeeded in bringing the Scarlet Pimpernel to justice, the National *fête* will begin within these city walls, with Demoiselle Candeille as the thrice-honoured goddess."

"And you will be very merry here in Boulogne, I dare swear—"

"Aye, merry, sir," said Chauvelin with an involuntary and savage snarl, as he placed a long claw-like finger upon the momentous paper before him, "merry, for we here in Boulogne will see that which will fill the heart of every patriot in France with gladness—Nay! 'twas not the death of the Scarlet Pimpernel we wanted—not the noble martyrdom of England's chosen hero—but his humiliation and defeat—derision and scorn—contumely and contempt. You asked me airily just now, Sir Percy, how I proposed to accomplish this object—Well! you know it now—by forcing you—aye, *forcing*—to write and sign a letter and to take money from my hands which will brand you forever as a liar and informer, and cover you with the thick and slimy mud of irreclaimable infamy—"

"Lud! sir," said Sir Percy pleasantly, "what a wonderful command you have of our language—I wish I could speak French half as well—"

Marguerite had risen like an automaton from her chair. She felt that she could no longer sit still, she wanted to scream out at the top of her voice, all the horror she felt for this dastardly plot, which surely must have had its origin in the brain of devils. She could not understand Percy. This was one of those awful moments, which she had been destined to experience once or twice before, when the whole personality of her husband seemed to become shadowy before her, to slip, as it were, past her comprehension, leaving her indescribably lonely and wretched, trusting yet terrified.

She thought that long ere this he would have flung back every insult in his opponent's teeth; she did not know what inducements Chauvelin had held out in exchange for the infamous letter, what threats he had used. That her own life and freedom were at stake, was, of course, evident, but she cared nothing for life, and he should know that certainly she would care still less if such a price had to be paid for it.

She longed to tell him all that was in her heart, longed to tell him how little she valued her life, how highly she prized his honour! but how could she, before this fiend who snarled and sneered in his anticipated triumph, and surely, surely Percy knew!

And knowing all that, why did he not speak? Why did he not tear that infamous paper from out that devil's hands and fling it in his face? Yet, though her loving ear caught every intonation of her husband's voice, she could not detect the slightest harshness in his airy laugh; his tone was perfectly natural and he seemed to be, indeed, just as he appeared—vastly amused.

Then she thought that perhaps he would wish her to go now, that he felt desire to be alone with this man, who had outraged him in everything that he held most holy and most dear, his honour and his wife—that perhaps, knowing that his own temper was no longer under control, he did not wish her to witness the rough and ready chastisement which he was intending to mete out to this dastardly intriguer.

Yes! that was it no doubt! Herein she could not be mistaken; she knew his fastidious notions of what was due and proper in the presence of a woman, and that even at a moment like this, he would wish the manners of London drawing-rooms to govern his every action.

Therefore, she rose to go, and as she did so, once more tried to read the expression in his face—to guess what was passing in his mind.

"Nay, Madam," he said, whilst he bowed gracefully before her, "I fear me this lengthy conversation hath somewhat fatigued you—This merry jest 'twixt my engaging friend and myself should not have been prolonged so far into the night—*Monsieur*, I pray you, will you not give orders that her ladyship be escorted back to her room?"

He was still standing outside the circle of light, and Marguerite instinctively went up to him. For this one second, she was oblivious of Chauvelin's presence; she forgot her well-schooled pride, her firm determination to be silent and to be brave; she could no longer restrain the wild beatings of her heart, the agony of her soul, and with sudden impulse she murmured in a voice broken with intense love and subdued, passionate appeal;

"Percy!"

He drew back a step further into the gloom; this made her realise the mistake she had made in allowing her husband's most bitter enemy to get this brief glimpse into her soul. Chauvelin's thin lips curled with satisfaction; the brief glimpse had been sufficient for him; the rapidly whispered name, the broken accent had told him what he had not known hitherto; namely, that between this man and woman there was a bond far more powerful than that which usually existed between husband and wife, and merely made up of chivalry on the one side and trustful reliance on the other.

Marguerite having realised her mistake, ashamed of having betrayed her feelings even for a moment, threw back her proud head and gave her exultant foe a look of defiance and of scorn. He responded with one of pity, not altogether unmixed with deference. There was something almost unearthly and sublime in this beautiful woman's agonising despair.

He lowered his head and made her a deep obeisance, lest she should see the satisfaction and triumph which shone through his pity.

As usual Sir Percy remained quite imperturbable, and now it was he, who, with characteristic impudence, touched the hand-bell on the table;

"Excuse this intrusion, *Monsieur*," he said lightly, "her ladyship is overfatigued and would be best in her room."

Marguerite threw him a grateful look. After all she was only a woman and was afraid of breaking down. In her mind there was no issue to the present deadlock save in death. For this she was prepared and had but one great hope that she could lie in her husband's arms just once again before she died. Now, since she could not speak to him, scarcely dared to look into the loved face, she was quite ready to go.

In answer to the bell, the soldier had entered.

"If Lady Blakeney desires to go—" said Chauvelin.

She nodded and Chauvelin gave the necessary orders; two soldiers stood at attention ready to escort Marguerite back to her prison cell. As she went towards the door she came to within a couple of steps from where her husband was standing, bowing to her as she passed. She stretched out an icy cold hand towards him, and he, in the most approved London fashion, with the courtly grace of a perfect English gentleman, took the little hand in his and stooping very low kissed the delicate finger-tips.

Then only did she notice that the strong, nervy hand which held hers trembled perceptibly, and that his lips—which for an instant rested on her fingers—were burning hot.

CHAPTER 27

The Decision

Once more the two men were alone.

As far as Chauvelin was concerned he felt that everything was not yet settled, and until a moment ago he had been in doubt as to whether Sir Percy would accept the infamous conditions which had been put before him or allow his pride and temper to get the better of him and throw the deadly insults back into his adversary's teeth.

But now a new secret had been revealed to the astute diplomatist. A name, softly murmured by a broken-hearted woman, had told him a tale of love and passion, which he had not even suspected before.

Since he had made this discovery he knew that the ultimate issue was no longer in doubt. Sir Percy Blakeney, the bold adventurer, ever ready for a gamble where lives were at stake, might have demurred before he subscribed to his own dishonour, in order to save his wife from humiliation and the shame of the terrible fate that had been mapped out for her. But the same man passionately in love with such a woman as Marguerite Blakeney would count the world well lost for her sake.

One sudden fear alone had shot through Chauvelin's heart when he stood face to face with the two people whom he had so deeply and cruelly wronged, and that was that Blakeney, throwing aside all thought of the scores of innocent lives that were at stake, might forget everything, risk everything, dare everything, in order to get his wife away there and then.

For the space of a few seconds Chauvelin had felt that his own life was in jeopardy, and that the Scarlet Pimpernel would indeed make a desperate effort to save himself and his wife. But the fear was short-lived; Marguerite—as he had well foreseen—would never save herself at the expense of others, and she was tied! tied! tied! That was his triumph and his joy!

When Marguerite finally left the room, Sir Percy made no motion to follow her, but turned once more quietly to his antagonist.

"As you were saying, *Monsieur?*—" he queried lightly.

"Oh! there is nothing more to say, Sir Percy," rejoined Chauvelin; "my conditions are clear to you, are they not? Lady Blakeney's and your own immediate release in exchange for a letter written to me by your own hand and signed here by you—in this room—in my presence and that of sundry other persons whom I need not name just now. Also, certain money passing from my hand to yours. Failing the letter, a long, hideously humiliating sojourn in the Temple prison for your wife, a prolonged trial and the guillotine as a happy release!—I would add, the same thing for yourself, only that I will do you the justice to admit that you probably do not care."

"Nay! a grave mistake, *Monsieur*—I do care—vastly care, I assure you—and would seriously object to ending my life on your demmed guillotine—a nasty, uncomfortable thing, I should say—and I am told that an inexperienced barber is deputed to cut one's hair—Brrr!—Now, on the other hand, I like the idea of a national *fête*—that pretty wench Candeille, dressed as a goddess—the boom of the cannon when your amnesty comes into force—You *will* boom the cannon, will you not, *Monsieur?*—Cannon are demmed noisy, but they are effective sometimes, do you not think so, *Monsieur?*"

"Very effective certainly, Sir Percy," sneered Chauvelin, "and we will certainly boom the cannon from this very fort, an' it so please you—"

"At what hour, *Monsieur*, is my letter to be ready?"

"Why! at any hour you please, Sir Percy."

"The *Daydream* could weigh anchor at eight o'clock—would an hour before that be convenient to yourself?"

"Certainly, Sir Percy—if you will honour me by accepting my hospitality in these uncomfortable quarters until seven o'clock tomorrow eve?—"

"I thank you, *Monsieur*—"

"Then am I to understand, Sir Percy, that—"

A loud and ringing laugh broke from Blakeney's lips.

"That I accept your bargain, man!—Zounds! I tell you I accept—I'll write the letter, I'll sign it—an' you have our free passes ready for us in exchange—At seven o'clock tomorrow eve, did you say?—Man! do not look so astonished—The letter, the signature, the money—all your witnesses—have everything ready—I accept, I say—And now, in the name of all the evil spirits in hell, let me have some supper and a bed, for I vow that I am demmed fatigued."

And without more ado Sir Percy once more rang the hand-bell, laughing boisterously the while; then suddenly, with quick transition of mood, his laugh was lost in a gigantic yawn, and throwing his long body onto a chair, he stretched out his legs, buried his hands in his pockets, and the next moment was peacefully asleep.

CHAPTER 28

The Midnight Watch

Boulogne had gone through many phases, in its own languid and sleepy way, whilst the great upheaval of a gigantic revolution shook other cities of France to their very foundations.

At first the little town had held somnolently aloof, and whilst Lyons and Tours conspired and rebelled, whilst Marseilles and Toulon opened their ports to the English and Dunkirk was ready to surrender to the allied forces, she had gazed through half-closed eyes at all the turmoil, and then quietly turned over and gone to sleep again.

Boulogne fished and mended nets, built boats and manufactured boots with placid content, whilst France murdered her king and butchered her citizens.

The initial noise of the great revolution was only wafted on the southerly breezes from Paris to the little seaport towns of Northern France and lost much of its volume and power in this aerial transit; the fisher folk were too poor to worry about the dethronement of kings; the struggle for daily existence, the perils and hardships of deep-sea fishing engrossed all the faculties they possessed.

As for the *burghers* and merchants of the town, they were at first content with reading an occasional article in the *Gazette de Paris* or the *Gazette des Tribunaux*, brought hither by one or other of the many travellers who crossed the city on their way to the harbour. They were interested in these articles, at times even comfortably horrified at the doings in Paris, the executions and the tumbrils, but on the whole they liked the idea that the country was in future to be governed by duly chosen representatives of the people, rather than be a prey to the despotism of kings, and they were really quite pleased to see the tricolour flag hoisted on the old *beffroi*, there where the snow-white standard of the Bourbons had erstwhile flaunted its golden *fleur-de-lis* in the glare of the midday sun.

The worthy *burgesses* of Boulogne were ready to shout; "*Vive la République!*" with the same cheerful and raucous Normandy accent as they had lately shouted "*Dieu protège le Roi!*"

The first awakening from this happy torpor came when that tent was put up on the landing stage in the harbour. Officials, dressed in shabby uniforms and wearing tricolour cockades and scarves, were now quartered in Town Hall, and repaired daily to that roughly erected tent, accompanied by so many soldiers from the garrison.

There installed, they busied themselves with examining carefully the passports of all those who desired to leave or enter Boulogne. Fisher-folk who had dwelt in the city—father and son and grandfather and many generations before that—and had come and gone in and out of their own boats as they pleased, were now stopped as they beached their craft and made to give an account of themselves to these officials from Paris.

It was, of a truth, more than ridiculous, that these strangers should ask of Jean-Marie who he was, or of Pierre what was his business, or of Désiré François whither he was going, when Jean-Marie and Pierre and Désiré François had plied their nets in the roads outside Boulogne harbour for more years than they would care to count.

It also caused no small measure of annoyance that fishermen were ordered to wear tricolour cockades on their caps. They had no special ill-feeling against tricolour cockades, but they did not care about them. Jean-Marie flatly refused to have one pinned on and being admonished somewhat severely by one of the Paris officials, he became obstinate about the whole thing and threw the cockade violently on the ground and spat upon it, not from any sentiment of anti-republicanism, but just from a feeling of Norman doggedness.

He was arrested, shut up in Fort Gayole, tried as a traitor and publicly guillotined.

The consternation in Boulogne was appalling.

The one little spark had found its way to a barrel of blasting powder and caused a terrible explosion. Within twenty-four hours of Jean-

Marie's execution the whole town was in the throes of the Revolution. What the death of King Louis, the arrest of Marie Antoinette, the massacres of September had failed to do, that the arrest and execution of an elderly fisherman accomplished in a trice.

People began to take sides in politics. Some families realised that they came from ancient lineage, and that their ancestors had helped to build up the throne of the Bourbons. Others looked up ancient archives and remembered past oppressions at the hands of the aristocrats.

Thus, some *burghers* of Boulogne became ardent reactionaries, whilst others secretly nursed enthusiastic royalist convictions; some were ready to throw in their lot with the anarchists, to deny the religion of their fathers, to scorn the priests and close the places of worship; others adhered strictly still to the usages and practices of the Church.

Arrests became frequent; the guillotine, erected in the Place de la Sénéchaussée, had plenty of work to do. Soon the cathedral was closed, the priests thrown into prison, whilst scores of families hoped to escape a similar fate by summary flight.

Vague rumours of a band of English adventurers soon reached the little sea-port town. The Scarlet Pimpernel—English spy or hero, as he was alternately called—had helped many a family with pronounced royalist tendencies to escape the fury of the blood-thirsty Terrorists.

Thus, gradually the anti-revolutionaries had been weeded out of the city; some by death and imprisonment, others by flight. Boulogne became the hotbed of anarchism; the idlers and loafers, inseparable from any town where there is a garrison and a harbour, practically ruled the city now. Denunciations were the order of the day. Everyone who owned any money, or lived with any comfort, was accused of being a traitor and suspected of conspiracy. The fisher folk wandered about the city, surly and discontented; their trade was at a standstill, but there was a trifle to be earned by giving information; information which meant the arrest, ofttimes the death of men, women and even children who had tried to seek safety in flight, and to denounce whom—as they were trying to hire a boat anywhere along the coast— meant a good square meal for a starving family.

Then came the awful cataclysm.

A woman—a stranger—had been arrested and imprisoned in the Fort Gayole and the town-crier publicly proclaimed that if she escaped from jail, one member of every family in the town—rich or poor, republican or royalist, Catholic or free-thinker—would be sum-

171

marily guillotined.

That member, the bread-winner!

"Why, then, with the Duvals it would be young François-Auguste. He keeps his old mother with his boot-making—"

"And it would be Marie Lebon, she has her blind father dependent on her net-mending."

"And old Mother Laferrière, whose grandchildren were left penniless—she keeps them from starvation by her wash-tub."

"But Francois-Auguste is a real Republican; he belongs to the Jacobin Club."

"And look at Pierre, who never meets a *calotin* but he must needs spit on him."

"Is there no safety anywhere?—are we to be butchered like so many cattle?—"

Somebody makes the suggestion;

"It is a threat—they would not dare!—"

"Would not dare?—"

'Tis old Andre Lemoine who has spoken, and he spits vigorously on the ground. André Lemoine has been a soldier; he was in La Vendee. He was wounded at Tours—and he knows!

"Would not dare?—" he says in a whisper. "I tell you, friends, that there's nothing the present government would not dare. There was the Plaine Saint Mauve—Did you ever hear about that?—little children fusilladed by the score—little ones, I say, and women with babies at their breasts—weren't they innocent?—Five hundred innocent people butchered in La Vendée—until the Headsman sank—worn out—I could tell worse than that—for I know—There's nothing they would not dare!—"

Consternation was so great that the matter could not even be discussed.

"We'll go to Gayole and see this woman at any rate."

Angry, sullen crowds assembled in the streets. The proclamation had been read just as the men were leaving the public houses, preparing to go home for the night.

They brought the news to the women, who, at home, were setting the soup and bread on the table for their husbands' supper. There was no thought of going to bed or of sleeping that night. The breadwinner in every family and all those dependent on him for daily sustenance were trembling for their lives.

Resistance to the barbarous order would have been worse than useless, nor did the thought of it enter the heads of these humble and ignorant fisher folk, wearied out with the miserable struggle for existence. There was not sufficient spirit left in this half-starved population of a small provincial city to suggest open rebellion. A regiment of soldiers come up from the South were quartered in the *château*, and the natives of Boulogne could not have mustered more than a score of disused blunderbusses between them.

Then they remembered tales which André Lemoine had told, the fate of Lyons, razed to the ground, of Toulon burnt to ashes, and they did not dare rebel.

But brothers, fathers, sons trooped out towards Gayole, in order to have a good look at the frowning pile, which held the hostage for their safety. It looked dark and gloomy enough, save for one window which gave on the southern ramparts. This window was wide open and a feeble light flickered from the room beyond, and as the men stood about, gazing at the walls in sulky silence, they suddenly caught the sound of a loud laugh proceeding from within, and of a pleasant voice speaking quite gaily in a language which they did not understand, but which sounded like English.

Against the heavy oaken gateway, leading to the courtyard of the prison, the proclamation written on stout parchment had been pinned up. Beside it hung a tiny lantern, the dim light of which flickered in the evening breeze and brought at times into sudden relief the bold writing and heavy signature, which stood out, stern and grim, against the yellowish background of the paper, like black signs of approaching death.

Facing the gateway and the proclamation, the crowd of men took its stand. The moon, from behind them, cast fitful, silvery glances at the weary heads bent in anxiety and watchful expectancy; on old heads and young heads, dark, curly heads and heads grizzled with age, on backs bent with toil, and hands rough and gnarled like seasoned timber.

All night the men stood and watched.

Sentinels from the town guard were stationed at the gates, but these might prove inattentive or insufficient; they had not the same price at stake, so the entire able-bodied population of Boulogne watched the gloomy prison that night, lest anyone escaped by wall or window.

They were guarding the precious hostage whose safety was the stipulation for their own.

There was dead silence among them, and dead silence all around, save for that monotonous *tok-tok-tok* of the parchment flapping in the breeze. The moon, who all along had been capricious and chary of her light, made a final retreat behind a gathering bank of clouds, and the crowd, the soldiers and the great grim walls were all equally wrapped in gloom.

Only the little lantern on the gateway now made a ruddy patch of light and tinged that fluttering parchment with the colour of blood. Every now and then an isolated figure would detach itself from out the watching throng, and go up to the heavy, oaken door, in order to gaze at the proclamation. Then the light of the lantern illumined a dark head or a grey one, for a moment or two; black or white locks were stirred gently in the wind, and a sigh of puzzlement and disappointment would be distinctly heard.

At times a group of three or four would stand there for a while, not speaking, only sighing and casting eager questioning glances at one another, whilst trying vainly to find some hopeful word, some turn of phrase of meaning that would be less direful, in that grim and ferocious proclamation. Then a rough word from the sentinel, a push from the butt-end of a bayonet would disperse the little group and send the men, sullen and silent, back into the crowd.

Thus, they watched for hours whilst the bell of the *beffroi* tolled all the hours of that tedious night. A thin rain began to fall in the small hours of the morning, a wetting, soaking drizzle which chilled the weary watchers to the bone.

But they did not care.

"We must not sleep, for the woman might escape."

Some of them squatted down in the muddy road; the luckier ones managed to lean their backs against the slimy walls.

Twice before the hour of midnight they heard that same quaint and merry laugh proceeding from the lighted room, through the open window. Once it sounded very low and very prolonged, as if in response to a delightful joke.

Anon the heavy gateway of Gayole was opened from within, and half a dozen soldiers came walking out of the courtyard. They were dressed in the uniform of the town-guard but had evidently been picked out of the rank and file, for all six were exceptionally tall and stalwart, and towered above the sentinel, who saluted and presented arms as they marched out of the gate.

In the midst of them walked a slight, dark figure, clad entirely in black, save for the tricolour scarf round his waist.

The crowd of watchers gazed on the little party with suddenly awakened interest.

"Who is it?" whispered some of the men.

"The citizen-governor," suggested one.

"The new public executioner," ventured another.

"No! no!" quoth Pierre Maxime, the doyen of Boulogne fishermen, and a great authority on every matter public or private with the town; "no, no, he is the man who has come down from Paris, the friend of Robespierre. He makes the laws now, the citizen-governor even must obey him. 'Tis he who made the law that if the woman up yonder should escape—"

"Hush!—sh!—sh!—" came in frightened accents from the crowd.

"Hush, Pierre Maxime!—the Citizen might hear thee," whispered the man who stood closest to the old fisherman; "the Citizen might hear thee, and think that we rebelled—"

"What are these people doing here?' queried Chauvelin as he passed out into the street.

"They are watching the prison, Citizen," replied the sentinel, whom he had thus addressed, "lest the female prisoner should attempt to escape."

With a satisfied smile, Chauvelin turned toward the Town Hall, closely surrounded by his escort. The crowd watched him and the soldiers as they quickly disappeared in the gloom, then they resumed the stolid, wearisome vigil of the night.

The old *beffroi* now tolled the midnight hour, the one solitary light in the old fort was extinguished, and after that the frowning pile remained dark and still.

CHAPTER 29

The National Fête

"Citizens of Boulogne, awake!"

They had not slept; only some of them had fallen into drowsy somnolence, heavy and nerve-racking, worse indeed than any wakefulness.

Within the houses, the women too had kept the tedious vigil, listening for every sound, dreading every bit of news, which the wind might waft in through the small, open windows.

If one prisoner escaped, every family in Boulogne would be deprived of the bread-winner. Therefore, the women wept, and tried to remember those *Paters* and *Aves* which the tyranny of liberty, fraternity and equality had ordered them to forget.

Broken rosaries were fetched out from neglected corners, and knees stiff with endless, thankless toil were bent once more in prayer.

"Oh God! Good God! Do not allow that woman to flee!"

"Holy Virgin! Mother of God! Make that she should not escape!"

Some of the women went out in the early dawn to take hot soup and coffee to their men who were watching outside the prison.

"Has anything been seen?"

"Have ye seen the woman?"

"Which room is she in?"

"Why won't they let us see her?"

"Are you sure she hath not already escaped?"

Questions and surmises went round in muffled whispers as the steaming cans were passed round. No one had a definite answer to give, although Desire Melun declared that he had, once during the night, caught sight of a woman's face at one of the windows above; but as he could not describe the woman's face, nor locate with any degree of precision the particular window at which she was supposed to have appeared, it was unanimously decided that Desire must have been dreaming.

"Citizens of Boulogne, awake!"

The cry came first from the Town Hall, and therefore from behind the crowd of men and women, whose faces had been so resolutely set for all these past hours towards the Gayole prison.

They were all awake! but too tired and cramped to move as yet, and to turn in the direction whence arose that cry.

"Citizens of Boulogne, awake!"

It was just the voice of Auguste Moleux, the town-crier of Boulogne, who, bell in hand, was trudging his way along the Rue Daumont, closely followed by two fellows of the municipal guard.

Auguste was in the very midst of the sullen crowd, before the men even troubled about his presence here, but now with many a vigorous "*Allons donc!*" and "*Voyez-moi ça, fais donc place, voyons!*" he elbowed his way through the throng.

He was neither tired nor cramped; he served the Republic in comfort and ease and had slept soundly on his paillasse in the little garret allotted to him in the Town Hall.

The crowd parted in silence, to allow him to pass. Auguste was lean and powerful; the scanty and meagre food, doled out to him by a paternal government, had increased his muscular strength whilst reducing his fat. He had very hard elbows, and soon he managed, by dint of pushing and cursing to reach the gateway of Gayole.

"*Voyons! enlevez-moi ça,*" he commanded in stentorian tones, pointing to the proclamation.

The fellows of the municipal guard fell to and tore the parchment away from the door whilst the crowd looked on with stupid amazement.

What did it all mean?

Then Auguste Moleux turned and faced the men.

"*Mes enfants,*" he said, "my little cabbages! wake up! the government of the Republic has decreed that today is to be a day of gaiety and public rejoicings!"

"Gaiety?—Public rejoicings forsooth, when the bread-winner of every family—"

"Hush! Hush! Be silent, all of you," quoth Auguste impatiently, "you do not understand!—All that is at an end—There is no fear that the woman shall escape—You are all to dance and rejoice—The Scarlet Pimpernel has been captured in Boulogne, last night—"

"*Qui ça* the Scarlet Pimpernel?"

"*Mais!* 'tis that mysterious English adventurer who rescued people from the guillotine!"

"A hero? *quoi?*"

"No! no! only an English spy, a friend of aristocrats—he would have cared nothing for the breadwinners of Boulogne—"

"He would not have raised a finger to save them."

"Who knows?" sighed a feminine voice, "perhaps he came to Boulogne to help them."

"And he has been caught anyway," concluded Auguste Moleux sententiously, "and, my little cabbages, remember this, that so great is the pleasure of the all-powerful Committee of Public Safety at this capture, that because he has been caught in Boulogne, therefore Boulogne is to be specially rewarded!"

"Holy Virgin, who'd have thought it?"

"Sh—Jeanette, dost not know that there's no Holy Virgin now?"

"And dost know, Auguste, how we are to be rewarded?"

It is a difficult matter for the human mind to turn very quickly from despair to hope, and the fishermen of Boulogne had not yet grasped the fact that they were to make merry and that thoughts of anxiety must be abandoned for those of gaiety.

Auguste Moleux took out a parchment from the capacious pocket of his coat; he put on his most solemn air of officialdom, and pointing with extended forefinger to the parchment, he said;

"A general amnesty to all natives of Boulogne who are under arrest at the present moment; a free pardon to all natives of Boulogne who are under sentence of death; permission to all natives of Boulogne to quit the town with their families, to embark on any vessel they please, in or out of the harbour, and to go whithersoever they choose, without passports, formalities or question of any kind."

Dead silence followed this announcement. Hope was just beginning to crowd anxiety and sullenness out of the way.

"Then poor André Legrand will be pardoned," whispered a voice suddenly; "he was to have been guillotined today."

"And Denise Latour! she was innocent enough, the gentle pigeon."

"And they'll let poor Abbé Foucquet out of prison too."

"And François!"

"And poor Félicité, who is blind!"

"*M. l'Abbé* would be wise to leave Boulogne with the children."

"He will too; thou canst be sure of that!"

"It is not good to be a priest just now!"

"Bah! *calotins* are best dead than alive."

But some in the crowd were silent; others whispered eagerly.

"Thinkest thou it would be safer for us to get out of the country whilst we can?" said one of the men in a muffled tone and clutching nervously at a woman's wrist.

"Aye! aye! it might leak out about that boat we procured for—"

"Sh!—I was thinking of that—"

"We can go to my Aunt Lebrun in Belgium—"

Others talked in whispers of England or the New Land across the seas; they were those who had something to hide, money received from refugee aristocrats, boats sold to would-be emigres, information withheld, denunciations shirked; the amnesty would not last long, 'twas best to be safely out of the way.

"In the meanwhile, my cabbages," quoth Auguste sententiously, "are you not grateful to Citizen Robespierre, who has sent this order specially down from Paris?"

"Aye! aye!" assented the crowd cheerfully.

"Hurrah for Citizen Robespierre!"

"*Viva la République!*"

"And you will enjoy yourselves today?"

"That we will!"

"Processions?"

"Aye! with music and dancing."

Out there, far away, beyond the harbour, the grey light of dawn was yielding to the crimson glow of morning. The rain had ceased and heavy slaty clouds parted here and there, displaying glints of delicate turquoise sky, and tiny ethereal vapours in the dim and remote distance of infinity, flecked with touches of rose and gold.

The towers and pinnacles of old Boulogne detached themselves one by one from the misty gloom of night. The old bell of the *beffroi* tolled the hour of six. Soon the massive cupola of Notre Dame was clothed in purple hues, and the gilt cross on St. Joseph threw back across the square a blinding ray of gold.

The town sparrows began to twitter, and from far out at sea in the direction of Dunkirk there came the muffled boom of cannon.

"And remember, my pigeons," admonished Auguste Moleux solemnly, "that in this order which Robespierre has sent from Paris, it also says that from today onwards *le bon Dieu* has ceased to be!"

Many faces were turned towards the East just then, for the rising sun, tearing with one gigantic sweep the banks of cloud asunder, now displayed his magnificence in a gorgeous immensity of flaming crimson. The sea, in response, turned to liquid fire beneath the glow, whilst the whole sky was irradiated with the first blush of morning.

Le bon Dieu has ceased to be!

"There is only one religion in France now," explained Auguste Moleux, "the religion of Reason! We are all citizens! We are all free and all able to think for ourselves. Citizen Robespierre has decreed that there is no good God. *Le bon Dieu* was a tyrant and an aristocrat, and, like all tyrants and aristocrats, He has been deposed. There is no good God, there is no Holy Virgin and no Saints, only Reason, who is a goddess and whom we all honour."

And the townsfolk of Boulogne, with eyes still fixed on the gorgeous East, shouted with sullen obedience;

"Hurrah! for the Goddess of Reason!"

"Hurrah for Robespierre!"

Only the women, trying to escape the town-crier's prying eyes, or the soldiers' stern gaze, hastily crossed themselves behind their husbands' backs, terrified lest *le bon Dieu* had, after all, not altogether ceased to exist at the bidding of Citizen Robespierre.

Thus, the worthy natives of Boulogne, forgetting their anxieties and fears, were ready enough to enjoy the national fête ordained for them by the Committee of Public Safety, in honour of the capture of the Scarlet Pimpernel. They were even willing to accept this new religion which Robespierre had invented; a religion which was only a mockery, with an actress to represent its supreme deity.

Mais, que voulez-vous? Boulogne had long ago ceased to have faith in God; the terrors of the Revolution, which culminated in that agonising watch of last night, had smothered all thoughts of worship and of prayer.

The Scarlet Pimpernel must indeed be a dangerous spy that his arrest should cause so much joy in Paris!

Even Boulogne had learned by experience that the Committee of Public Safety did not readily give up a prey, once its vulture-like claws had closed upon it. The proportion of condemnations as against acquittals was as a hundred to one.

But because this one man was taken, scores today were to be set free!

In the evening at a given hour—seven o'clock had Auguste Moleux, the town-crier, understood—the boom of the cannon would be heard, the gates of the town would be opened, the harbour would become a free port.

The inhabitants of Boulogne were ready to shout;

"*Vive* the Scarlet Pimpernel!"

Whatever he was—hero or spy—he was undoubtedly the primary cause of all their joy.

By the time Auguste Moleux had cried out the news throughout the town and pinned the new proclamation of mercy up on every public building, all traces of fatigue and anxiety had vanished. In spite of the fact that wearisome vigils had been kept in every home that night, and that hundreds of men and women had stood about for hours in the vicinity of the Gayole Fort, no sooner was the joyful news known, than all lassitude was forgotten and everyone set to with a right merry will to make the great *fête*-day a complete success.

There is in every native of Normandy, be he peasant or gentleman, an infinite capacity for enjoyment, and at the same time a marvellous faculty for co-ordinating and systematizing his pleasures.

In a trice the surly crowds had vanished. Instead of these, there were groups of gaily-visaged men pleasantly chattering outside every eating and drinking place in the town. The national holiday had come upon these people quite unawares, so the early part of it had to be spent in thinking out a satisfactory programme for it. Sipping their

beer or coffee, or munching their cherries à *l'eau-de-vie*, the townsfolk
of Boulogne, so lately threatened with death, were quietly organising
processions.

There was to be a grand muster on the Place de la Sénéchaussée,
then a torchlight and lanthorn-light march, right round the Ramparts, culminating in a gigantic assembly outside the Town Hall, where
the Citizen Chauvelin, representing the Committee of Public Safety,
would receive an address of welcome from the entire population of
Boulogne.

The procession was to be in costume! There were to be Pierrots
and Pierettes, Harlequins and English clowns, aristocrats and goddess-
es! All day the women and girls were busy contriving travesties of all
sorts, and the little tumbledown shops in the Rue de Château and the
Rue Frédéric Sauvage—kept chiefly by Jews and English traders—
were ransacked for old bits of finery, and for remnants of costumes,
worn in the days when Boulogne was still a gay city and carnivals
were held every year.

And then, of course, there would be the Goddess of Reason, in her
triumphal car! the apotheosis of the new religion, which was to make
everybody happy, rich and free.

Forgotten were the anxieties of the night, the fears of death, the
great and glorious Revolution, which for this one day would cease
her perpetual demand for the toll of blood.

Nothing was remembered save the pleasures and joys of the moment, and at times the name of that Englishman—spy, hero or adventurer—the cause of all this bounty; the Scarlet Pimpernel.

CHAPTER 30

The Procession

The grandfathers of the present generation of Boulonnese remembered the great day of the National *fête*, when all Boulogne, for
twenty-four hours, went crazy with joy. So many families had fathers,
brothers, sons, languishing in prison under some charge of treason, real
or imaginary; so many had dear ones for whom already the guillotine
loomed ahead, that the feast on this memorable day of September,
1793, was one of never-to-be-forgotten relief and thanksgiving.

The weather all day had been exceptionally fine. After that glorious sunrise, the sky had remained all day clad in its gorgeous mantle of
blue and the sun had continued to smile benignly on the many varied
doings of this gay, little seaport town. When it began to sink slowly

towards the West a few little fluffy clouds appeared on the horizon, and from a distance, although the sky remained clear and blue, the sea looked quite dark and slaty against the brilliance of the firmament.

Gradually, as the splendour of the sunset gave place to the delicate purple and grey tints of evening, the little fluffy clouds merged themselves into denser masses, and these too soon became absorbed in the great, billowy banks which the south-westerly wind was blowing seawards.

By the time that the last grey streak of dusk vanished in the West, the whole sky looked heavy with clouds, and the evening set in, threatening and dark.

But this by no means mitigated the anticipation of pleasure to come. On the contrary, the fast-gathering gloom was hailed with delight, since it would surely help to show off the coloured lights of the lanthorns and give additional value to the glow of the torches.

Of a truth 'twas a motley throng which began to assemble on the Place de la Sénéchaussée, just as the old bell of the *beffroi* tolled the hour of six. Men, women and children in ragged finery, Pierrots with neck frills and floured faces, hideous masks of impossible beasts roughly besmeared in crude colours. There were gaily-coloured dominoes, blue, green, pink and purple, harlequins combining all the colours of the rainbow in one tight-fitting garment, and Columbines with short, tarlatan skirts, beneath which peeped bare feet and ankles. There were judges' *perruques*, and soldiers' helmets of past generations, tall Normandy caps adorned with hundreds of streaming ribbons, and powdered headgear which recalled the glories of Versailles.

Everything was torn and dirty, the dominoes were in rags, the Pierrot frills, mostly made up of paper, already hung in strips over the wearers' shoulders. But what mattered that?

The crowd pushed and jolted, shouted and laughed, the girls screamed as the men snatched a kiss here and there from willing or unwilling lips, or stole an arm round a gaily accoutred waist. The spirit of Old King Carnival was in the evening air—a spirit just awakened from a long Rip van Winkle-like sleep.

In the centre of the Place stood the guillotine, grim and gaunt with long, thin arms stretched out towards the sky, the last glimmer of waning light striking the triangular knife, there, where it was not rusty with stains of blood.

For weeks now, Madame Guillotine had been much occupied plying her gruesome trade; she now stood there in the gloom, passive and immovable, seeming to wait placidly for the end of this holiday, ready to begin her work again on the morrow. She towered above these merrymakers, hoisted up on the platform whereon many an innocent foot had trodden, the tattered basket beside her, into which many an innocent head had rolled.

What cared they tonight for Madame Guillotine and the horrors of which she told? A crowd of Pierrots with floured faces and tattered neck-frills had just swarmed up the wooden steps, shouting and laughing, chasing each other round and round on the platform, until one of them lost his footing and fell into the basket, covering himself with bran and staining his clothes with blood.

"*Ah! vogue la galère!* We must be merry tonight!"

And all these people who for weeks past had been staring death and the guillotine in the face, had denounced each other with savage callousness in order to save themselves, or hidden for days in dark cellars to escape apprehension, now laughed, and danced and shrieked with gladness in a sudden, hysterical outburst of joy.

Close beside the guillotine stood the triumphal car of the Goddess of Reason, the special feature of this great National *fête*. It was only a rough market cart, painted by an unpractised hand with bright, crimson paint and adorned with huge clusters of autumn-tinted leaves, and the scarlet berries of mountain ash and rowan, culled from the town gardens, or the country side outside the city walls.

In the cart the goddess reclined on a crimson-draped seat, she, herself, swathed in white, and wearing a gorgeous necklace around her neck. Désirée Candeille, a little pale, a little apprehensive of all this noise, had obeyed the final dictates of her taskmaster. She had been the means of bringing the Scarlet Pimpernel to France and vengeance; she was to be honoured therefore above every other woman in France.

She sat in the car, vaguely thinking over the events of the past few days, whilst watching the throng of rowdy merrymakers seething around her. She thought of the noble-hearted, proud woman whom she had helped to bring from her beautiful English home to sorrow and humiliation in a dank French prison; she thought of the gallant English gentleman with his pleasant voice and courtly, *debonnair* manners.

Chauvelin had roughly told her, only this morning, that both were now under arrest as English spies, and that their fate no longer concerned her. Later on, the governor of the city had come to tell her that Citizen Chauvelin desired her to take part in the procession and the national *fête*, as the Goddess of Reason, and that the people of Boulogne were ready to welcome her as such. This had pleased Candeille's vanity, and all day, whilst arranging the finery which she meant to wear for the occasion, she had ceased to think of England and of Lady Blakeney.

But now, when she arrived on the Place de la Sénéchaussée, and mounting her car, found herself on a level with the platform of the guillotine, her memory flew back to England, to the lavish hospitality of Blakeney Manor, Marguerite's gentle voice, the pleasing grace of Sir Percy's manners, and she shuddered a little when that cruel glint of evening light caused the knife of the guillotine to glisten from out the gloom.

But *anon* her reflections were suddenly interrupted by loud and prolonged shouts of joy. A whole throng of Pierrots had swarmed into the Place from every side, carrying lighted torches and tall staves, on which were hung lanthorns with many-coloured lights.

The procession was ready to start. A stentorian voice shouted out in resonant accents;

"*En avant, la grosse caisse!*"

A man now, portly and gorgeous in scarlet and blue, detached himself from out the crowd. His head was hidden beneath the monstrous mask of a cardboard lion, roughly painted in brown and yellow, with crimson for the widely open jaws and the corners of the eyes, to make them seem ferocious and bloodshot. His coat was of bright crimson cloth, with cuts and slashings in it, through which bunches of bright blue paper were made to protrude, in imitation of the costume of mediaeval times.

He had blue stockings on and bright scarlet slippers, and behind him floated a large strip of scarlet flannel, on which moons and suns and stars of gold had been showered in plenty.

Upon his portly figure in front he was supporting the big drum, which was securely strapped round his shoulders with tarred cordages, the spoil of some fishing vessel.

There was a merciful slit in the jaw of the cardboard lion, through which the portly drummer puffed and spluttered as he shouted lustily;

"*En avant!*"

And wielding the heavy drumstick with a powerful arm, he brought it crashing down against the side of the mighty instrument.

"Hurrah! Hurrah! *en avant les trompettes!*"

A fanfare of brass instruments followed, lustily blown by twelve young men in motley coats of green, and tall, peaked hats adorned with feathers.

The drummer had begun to march, closely followed by the trumpeters. Behind them a bevy of Columbines in many-coloured tarlatan skirts and hair flying wildly in the breeze, giggling, pushing, exchanging ribald jokes with the men behind, and getting kissed or slapped for their pains.

Then the triumphal car of the goddess, with Demoiselle Candeille standing straight up in it, a tall gold wand in one hand, the other resting in a mass of scarlet berries. All round the car, helter-skelter, tumbling, pushing, came Pierrots and Pierrettes, carrying lanthorns, and Harlequins bearing the torches.

And after the car the long line of more sober folk, the older fishermen, the women in caps and many-hued skirts, the serious townfolk who had scorned the travesty, yet would not be left out of the procession. They all began to march, to the tune of those noisy brass trumpets which were thundering forth snatches from the newly composed "*Marseillaise.*"

Above the sky became more heavy with clouds. *Anon* a few drops of rain began to fall, making the torches sizzle and splutter, and scattering grease and tar around, and wetting the lightly-covered shoulders of tarlatan-clad Columbines. But no one cared! The glow of so much merrymaking kept the blood warm and the skin dry.

The flour all came off the Pierrots' faces; the blue paper slashings of the drummer-in-chief hung in pulpy lumps against his gorgeous scarlet cloak. The trumpeters' feathers became streaky and bedraggled.

But in the name of that good God who had ceased to exist, who in the world or out of it cared if it rained or thundered and stormed! This was a national holiday, for an English spy was captured, and all natives of Boulogne were free of the guillotine tonight.

The revellers were making the circuit of the town, with lanthorns fluttering in the wind, and flickering torches held up aloft illumining laughing faces, red with the glow of a drunken joy, young faces that only enjoyed the moment's pleasure, serious ones that withheld a frown at thought of the morrow.

The fitful light played on the grotesque masques of beasts and reptiles, on the diamond necklace of a very earthly goddess, on God's glorious spoils from gardens and country-side, on smothered anxiety and repressed cruelty.

The crowd had turned its back on the guillotine, and the trumpets now changed the inspiriting tune of the "*Marseillaise*" to the ribald vulgarity of the "Ça *ira!*"

Everyone yelled and shouted. Girls with flowing hair produced broomsticks, and astride on these, broke from the ranks and danced a mad and obscene *saraband*, a dance of witches in the weird glow of sizzling torches, to the accompaniment of raucous laughter and of coarse jokes.

Thus, the procession passed on, a sight to gladden the eyes of those who had desired to smother all thought of the Infinite, of Eternity and of God in the minds of those to whom they had nothing to offer in return. A threat of death yesterday, misery, starvation and squalor! all the hideousness of a destroying anarchy, that had nothing to give save a national fête, a tinsel goddess, some shallow laughter and momentary intoxication, a travesty of clothes and of religion and a dance on the ashes of the past.

And there along the ramparts where the massive walls of the city encircled the frowning prisons of Gayole and the old *château*, dark groups were crouching, huddled together in compact masses, which in the gloom seemed to vibrate with fear. Like hunted quarry seeking for shelter, sombre figures flattened themselves in the angles of the dank walls, as the noisy carousers drew nigh. Then as the torches and lanthorns detached themselves from out the evening shadows, hand would clutch hand and hearts would beat with agonised suspense, whilst the dark and shapeless forms would try to appear smaller, flatter, less noticeable than before.

And when the crowd had passed noisily along, leaving behind it a trail of torn finery, of glittering tinsel and of scarlet berries, when the boom of the big drum and the grating noise of the brass trumpets had somewhat died away, wan faces, pale with anxiety, would peer from out the darkness, and nervous hands would grasp with trembling fingers the small bundles of poor belongings tied up hastily in view of flight.

At seven o'clock, so 'twas said, the cannon would boom from the old *beffroi*. The guard would throw open the prison gates, and those who had something or somebody to hide, and those who had a great deal to fear, would be free to go whithersoever they chose.

And mothers, sisters, sweethearts stood watching by the gates, for loved ones tonight would be set free, all along of the capture of that English spy, the Scarlet Pimpernel.

CHAPTER 31

Final Dispositions

To Chauvelin the day had been one of restless inquietude and
nervous apprehension.

Collot d'Herbois harassed him with questions and complaints
intermixed with threats but thinly veiled. At his suggestion Gayole
had been transformed into a fully-manned, well-garrisoned fortress.
Troops were to be seen everywhere, on the stairs and in the passages,
the guard-rooms and offices; picked men from the municipal guard,
and the company which had been sent down from Paris some time
ago.

Chauvelin had not resisted these orders given by his colleague. He
knew quite well that Marguerite would make no attempt at escape,
but he had long ago given up all hope of persuading a man of the
type of Collot d'Herbois that a woman of her temperament would
never think of saving her own life at the expense of others, and that Sir
Percy Blakeney, in spite of his adoration for his wife, would sooner see
her die before him, than allow the lives of innocent men and women
to be the price of hers.

Collot was one of those brutish sots—not by any means infrequent
among the Terrorists of that time—who, born in the gutter, still loved
to wallow in his native element, and who measured all his fellow-crea-
tures by the same standard which he had always found good enough
for himself. In this man there was neither the enthusiastic patriotism
of a Chauvelin, nor the ardent selflessness of a Danton. He served the
revolution and fostered the anarchical spirit of the times only because
these brought him a competence and a notoriety, which an orderly
and fastidious government would obviously have never offered him.

History shows no more despicable personality than that of Collot
d'Herbois, one of the most hideous products of that utopian Revolution, whose grandly conceived theories of a universal levelling of
mankind only succeeded in dragging into prominence a number of
half-brutish creatures who, revelling in their own abasement, would
otherwise have remained content in inglorious obscurity.

Chauvelin tolerated and half feared Collot, knowing full well that
if now the Scarlet Pimpernel escaped from his hands, he could expect
no mercy from his colleagues.

The scheme by which he hoped to destroy not only the heroic
leader but the entire League by bringing opprobrium and ridicule

upon them, was wonderfully subtle in its refined cruelty, and Chauvelin, knowing by now something of Sir Percy Blakeney's curiously blended character, was never for a moment in doubt but that he would write the infamous letter, save his wife by sacrificing his honour, and then seek oblivion and peace in suicide.

With so much disgrace, so much mud cast upon their chief, the League of the Scarlet Pimpernel would cease to be. *That* had been Chauvelin's plan all along. For the end he had schemed and thought and planned, from the moment that Robespierre had given him the opportunity of redeeming his failure of last year. He had built up the edifice of his intrigue, bit by bit, from the introduction of his tool, Candeille, to Marguerite at the Richmond gala, to the arrest of Lady Blakeney in Boulogne. All that remained for him to see now, would be the attitude of Sir Percy Blakeney tonight, when, in exchange for the stipulated letter, he would see his wife set free.

All day Chauvelin had wondered how it would all go off. He had stage-managed everything, but he did not know how the chief actor would play his part.

From time to time, when his feeling of restlessness became quite unendurable, the ex-ambassador would wander round Fort Gayole and on some pretext or other demand to see one or the other of his prisoners. Marguerite, however, observed complete silence in his presence; she acknowledged his greeting with a slight inclination of the head, and in reply to certain perfunctory queries of his—which he put to her in order to justify his appearance—she either nodded or gave curt monosyllabic answers through partially closed lips.

"I trust that everything is arranged for your comfort, Lady Blakeney."

"I thank you, sir."

"You will be rejoining the *Daydream* tonight. Can I send a messenger over to the yacht for you?"

"I thank you. No."

"Sir Percy is well. He is fast asleep, and hath not asked for your ladyship. Shall I let him know that you are well?"

A nod of acquiescence from Marguerite and Chauvelin's string of queries was at an end. He marvelled at her quietude and thought that she should have been as restless as himself.

Later on in the day, and egged on by Collot d'Herbois and by his own fears, he had caused Marguerite to be removed from No. 6.

This change he heralded by another brief visit to her, and his attitude this time was one of deferential apology.

"A matter of expediency, Lady Blakeney," he explained, "and I trust that the change will be for your comfort."

Again, the same curt nod of acquiescence on her part, and a brief; "As you command, *Monsieur!*"

But when he had gone, she turned with a sudden passionate outburst towards the Abbé Foucquet, her faithful companion through the past long, weary hours. She fell on her knees beside him and sobbed in an agony of grief.

"Oh! if I could only know—if I could only see him!—for a minute—a second!—if I could only know!—"

She felt as if the awful uncertainty would drive her mad.

If she could only know! If she could only know what he meant to do.

"The good God knows!" said the old man, with his usual simple philosophy, "and perhaps it is all for the best."

The room which Chauvelin had now destined for Marguerite was one which gave from the larger one, wherein last night he had had his momentous interview with her and with Sir Percy.

It was small, square and dark, with no window in it; only a small ventilating hole high up in the wall and heavily grated. Chauvelin, who desired to prove to her that there was no wish on his part to add physical discomfort to her mental tortures, had given orders that the little place should be made as habitable as possible. A thick, soft carpet had been laid on the ground; there was an easy chair and a comfortable-looking couch with a couple of pillows and a rug upon it, and oh, marvel! on the round central table, a vase with a huge bunch of many-coloured dahlias which seemed to throw a note as if of gladness into this strange and gloomy little room.

At the furthest corner, too, a construction of iron uprights and crossway bars had been hastily contrived and fitted with curtains, forming a small recess, behind which was a tidy washstand, fine clean towels and plenty of fresh water. Evidently the shops of Boulogne had been commandeered in order to render Marguerite's sojourn here outwardly agreeable.

But as the place was innocent of window, so was it innocent of doors. The one that gave into the large room had been taken out of its hinges, leaving only the frame, on each side of which stood a man from the municipal guard with fixed bayonet.

Chauvelin himself had conducted Marguerite to her new prison.

She followed him—silent and apathetic—with not a trace of that awful torrent of emotion which had overwhelmed her but half-an-hour ago when she had fallen on her knees beside the old priest and sobbed her heart out in a passionate fit of weeping. Even the sight of the soldiers left her outwardly indifferent. As she stepped across the threshold she noticed that the door itself had been taken away; then she gave another quick glance at the soldiers, whose presence there would control her every movement.

The thought of Queen Marie Antoinette in the *Conciergerie* prison with the daily, hourly humiliation and shame which this constant watch imposed upon her womanly pride and modesty, flashed suddenly across Marguerite's mind, and a deep blush of horror rapidly suffused her pale cheeks, whilst an almost imperceptible shudder shook her delicate frame.

Perhaps, as in a flash, she had at this moment received an inkling of what the nature of that terrible "either—or" might be, with which Chauvelin was trying to force an English gentleman to dishonour. Sir Percy Blakeney's wife had been threatened with Marie Antoinette's fate.

"You see, *Madame*," said her cruel enemy's unctuous voice close to her ear, "that we have tried our humble best to make your brief sojourn here as agreeable as possible. May I express a hope that you will be quite comfortable in this room, until the time when Sir Percy will be ready to accompany you to the *Daydream*."

"I thank you, sir," she replied quietly.

"And if there is anything you require, I pray you to call. I shall be in the next room all day and entirely at your service."

A young orderly now entered bearing a small collation—eggs, bread, milk and wine—which he set on the central table. Chauvelin bowed low before Marguerite and withdrew. *Anon* he ordered the two sentinels to stand the other side of the doorway, against the wall of his own room, and well out of sight of Marguerite, so that, as she moved about her own narrow prison, if she ate or slept, she might have the illusion that she was unwatched.

The sight of the soldiers had had the desired effect on her. Chauvelin had seen her shudder and knew that she understood of that she guessed. He was now satisfied and really had no wish to harass her beyond endurance.

Moreover, there was always the proclamation which threatened the bread-winners of Boulogne with death if Marguerite Blakeney escaped, and which would be in full force until Sir Percy had written, signed and delivered into Chauvelin's hands the letter which was to be the signal for the general amnesty.

Chauvelin had indeed cause to be satisfied with his measures. There was no fear that his prisoners would attempt to escape.

Even Collot d'Herbois had to admit everything was well done. He had read the draft of the proposed letter and was satisfied with its contents. Gradually now into his loutish brain there had filtrated the conviction that Citizen Chauvelin was right, that that accursed Scarlet Pimpernel and his brood of English spies would be more effectually annihilated by all the dishonour and ridicule which such a letter written by the mysterious hero would heap upon them all, than they could ever be through the relentless work of the guillotine. His only anxiety now was whether the Englishman would write that letter.

"Bah! he'll do it," he would say whenever he thought the whole matter over; "*Sacré tonnerre!* but 'tis an easy means to save his own skin."

"You would sign such a letter without hesitation, eh, Citizen Collot," said Chauvelin, with well-concealed sarcasm, on one occasion when his colleague discussed the all-absorbing topic with him; "you would show no hesitation, if your life were at stake, and you were given the choice between writing that letter and—the guillotine?"

"*Parbleu!*" responded Collot with conviction.

"More especially," continued Chauvelin drily, "if a million *francs* were promised you as well?"

"*Sacré Anglis!*" swore Collot angrily, "you don't propose giving him that money, do you?"

"We'll place it ready to his hand, at any rate, so that it should appear as if he had actually taken it."

Collot looked up at his colleague in ungrudging admiration. Chauvelin had indeed left nothing undone, had thought everything out in this strangely conceived scheme for the destruction of the enemy of France.

"But in the name of all the dwellers in hell, Citizen," admonished Collot, "guard that letter well, once it is in your hands."

"I'll do better than that," said Chauvelin, "I will hand it over to you, Citizen Collot, and you shall ride with it to Paris at once."

"Tonight!" assented Collot with a shout of triumph, as he brought his grimy fist crashing down on the table, "I'll have a horse ready saddled at this very gate, and an escort of mounted men—we'll ride like hell's own furies and not pause to breathe until that letter is in Citizen Robespierre's hands."

"Well thought of, Citizen," said Chauvelin approvingly. "I pray you give the necessary orders, that the horses be ready saddled, and the men booted and spurred, and waiting at the Gayole gate, at seven o'clock this evening."

"I wish the letter were written and safely in our hands by now."

"Nay! the Englishman will have it ready by this evening, never fear. The tide is high at half-past seven, and he will be in haste for his wife to be aboard his yacht, ere the turn, even if he—"

He paused, savouring the thoughts which had suddenly flashed across his mind, and a look of intense hatred and cruel satisfaction for a moment chased away the studied impassiveness of his face.

"What do you mean, Citizen?" queried Collot anxiously, "even if he—what?—"

"Oh! nothing, nothing! I was only trying to make vague guesses as to what the Englishman will do *after* he has written the letter," quoth Chauvelin reflectively.

"*Morbleu!* he'll return to his own accursed country—glad enough to have escaped with his skin—I suppose," added Collot with sudden anxiety, "you have no fear that he will refuse at the last moment to write that letter?"

The two men were sitting in the large room, out of which opened the one which was now occupied by Marguerite. They were talking at the further end of it, close to the window, and though Chauvelin had mostly spoken in a whisper, Collot had ofttimes shouted, and the ex-ambassador was wondering how much Marguerite had heard.

Now at Collot's anxious query he gave a quick furtive glance in the direction of the further room wherein she sat, so silent and so still, that it seemed almost as if she must be sleeping.

"You don't think that the Englishman will refuse to write the letter?" insisted Collot with angry impatience.

"No!" replied Chauvelin quietly.

"But if he does?" persisted the other.

"If he does, I send the woman to Paris tonight and have him hanged as a spy in this prison yard without further formality or trial—" replied Chauvelin firmly; "so either way, you see, Citizen," he added in a whisper, "the Scarlet Pimpernel is done for—But I think that he will write the letter."

"*Parbleu!* so do I!—" rejoined Collot with a coarse laugh.

CHAPTER 32

The Letter

Later on, when his colleague left him in order to see to the horses and to his escort for tonight, Chauvelin called Sergeant Hébert, his old and trusted familiar, to him and gave him some final orders.

"The Angelus must be rung at the proper hour, friend Hébert," he began with a grim smile.

"The Angelus, Citizen?" quoth the Sergeant, with complete stupefaction, "'tis months now since it has been rung. It was forbidden by a decree of the Convention, and I doubt me if any of our men would know how to set about it."

Chauvelin's eyes were fixed before him in apparent vacancy, while the same grim smile still hovered round his thin lips. Something of that irresponsible spirit of adventure which was the mainspring of all Sir Percy Blakeney's actions, must for the moment have pervaded the mind of his deadly enemy.

Chauvelin had thought out this idea of having the Angelus rung tonight and was thoroughly pleased with the notion. This was the day when the duel was to have been fought; seven o'clock would have been the very hour, and the sound of the Angelus to have been the signal for combat, and there was something very satisfying in the thought, that that same Angelus should be rung, as a signal that the Scarlet Pimpernel was withered and broken at last.

In answer to Hébert's look of bewilderment Chauvelin said quietly;

"We must have some signal between ourselves and the guard at the different gates, also with the harbour officials; at a given moment the general amnesty must take effect and the harbour become a free port. I have a fancy that the signal shall be the ringing of the Angelus; the cannons at the gates and the harbour can boom in response; then the prisons can be thrown open and prisoners can either participate in the evening fête or leave the city immediately, as they choose. The Committee of Public Safety has promised the amnesty; it will carry out its promise to the full, and when Citizen Collot d'Herbois arrives in Paris with the joyful news, all natives of Boulogne in the prisons there will participate in the free pardon too."

"I understand all that, Citizen," said Hébert, still somewhat bewildered, "but not the Angelus."

"A fancy, friend Hébert, and I mean to have it."

193

"But who is to ring it, Citizen?"

"*Morbleu!* haven't you one *calotin* left in Boulogne whom you can press into doing this service?"

"Aye! *calotins* enough! there's the Abbé Foucquet in this very building—in No. 6 cell—"

"*Sacré tonnerre!*" ejaculated Chauvelin exultingly, "the very man! I know his dossier well! Once he is free, he will make straightway for England—he and his family—and will help to spread the glorious news of the dishonour and disgrace of the much-vaunted Scarlet Pimpernel!—The very man, friend Hébert!—Let him be stationed here—to see the letter written—to see the money handed over—for we will go through with that farce—and make him understand that the moment I give him the order, he can run over to his old church St. Joseph and ring the Angelus—The old fool will be delighted—more especially when he knows that he will thereby be giving the very signal which will set his own sister's children free—You understand?—"

"I understand, Citizen."

"And you can make the old *calotin* understand?"

"I think so, Citizen—You want him in this room—At what time?"

"A quarter before seven."

"Yes. I'll bring him along myself, and stand over him, lest he play any pranks."

"Oh! he'll not trouble you," sneered Chauvelin, "he'll be deeply interested in the proceedings. The woman will be here too, remember," he added with a jerky movement of the hand in the direction of Marguerite's room, "the two might be made to stand together, with four of your fellows round them."

"I understand, Citizen. Are any of us to escort the Citizen Foucquet when he goes to St. Joseph?"

"Aye! two men had best go with him. There will be a crowd in the streets by then—How far is it from here to the church?"

"Less than five minutes."

"Good. See to it that the doors are opened and the bell ropes easy of access."

"It shall be seen to, Citizen. How many men will you have inside this room tonight?"

"Let the walls be lined with men whom you can trust. I anticipate neither trouble nor resistance. The whole thing is a simple formality to which the Englishman has already intimated his readiness to submit. If he changes his mind at the last moment there will be no Angelus rung, no booming of the cannons or opening of the prison doors; there will be no amnesty, and no free pardon. The woman will be at once conveyed to Paris, and—But he'll not change his mind, friend Hébert," he concluded in suddenly altered tones, and speaking quite lightly, "he'll not change his mind."

The conversation between Chauvelin and his familiar had been carried on in whispers; not that the Terrorist cared whether Marguerite overheard or not, but whispering had become a habit with this man, whose tortuous ways and subtle intrigues did not lend themselves to discussion in a loud voice.

Chauvelin was sitting at the central table, just where he had been last night when Sir Percy Blakeney's sudden advent broke in on his meditations. The table had been cleared of the litter of multitudinous papers which had encumbered it before. On it now there were only a couple of heavy pewter candlesticks, with the tallow candles fixed ready in them, a leather-pad, an ink-well, a sand-box and two or three quill pens; everything disposed, in fact, for the writing and signing of the letter.

Already in imagination, Chauvelin saw his impudent enemy, the bold and daring adventurer, standing there beside that table and putting his name to the consummation of his own infamy. The mental picture thus evoked brought a gleam of cruel satisfaction and of satiated lust into the keen, ferret-like face, and a smile of intense joy lit up the narrow, pale-coloured eyes.

He looked round the room where the great scene would be enacted; two soldiers were standing guard outside Marguerite's prison, two more at attention near the door which gave on the passage; his own half-dozen picked men were waiting his commands in the corridor. Presently the whole room would be lined with troops, himself and Collot standing with eyes fixed on the principal actor of the drama! Hébert with specially selected troopers standing on guard over Marguerite!

No, no! he had left nothing to chance this time, and down below the horses would be ready saddled, that were to convey Collot and the precious document to Paris.

No! nothing was left to chance, and in either case he was bound to win. Sir Percy Blakeney would either write the letter in order to save his wife, and heap dishonour on himself, or he would shrink from the terrible ordeal at the last moment and let Chauvelin and the Committee of Public Safety work their will with her and him.

"In that case the pillory as a spy and summary hanging for you, my friend," concluded Chauvelin in his mind, "and for your wife—Bah, once you are out of the way, even she will cease to matter."

He left Hébert on guard in the room. An irresistible desire seized him to go and have a look at his discomfited enemy, and from the latter's attitude make a shrewd guess as to what he meant to do tonight.

Sir Percy had been given a room on one of the upper floors of the old prison. He had in no way been closely guarded, and the room itself had been made as comfortable as may be. He had seemed quite happy and contented when he had been conducted hither by Chauvelin, the evening before.

"I hope you quite understand, Sir Percy, that you are my guest here tonight," Chauvelin had said suavely, "and that you are free to come and go, just as you please."

"Lud love you, sir," Sir Percy had replied gaily, "but I verily believe that I am."

"It is only Lady Blakeney whom we have cause to watch until tomorrow," added Chauvelin with quiet significance. "Is that not so, Sir Percy?"

But Sir Percy seemed, whenever his wife's name was mentioned, to lapse into irresistible somnolence. He yawned now with his usual affectation and asked at what hour gentlemen in France were wont to breakfast.

Since then Chauvelin had not seen him. He had repeatedly asked how the English prisoner was faring, and whether he seemed to be sleeping and eating heartily. The orderly in charge invariably reported that the Englishman seemed well but did not eat much. On the other hand, he had ordered, and lavishly paid for, measure after measure of brandy and bottle after bottle of wine.

"Hm! how strange these Englishmen are!" mused Chauvelin; "this so-called hero is nothing but a wine-sodden brute, who seeks to nerve himself for a trying ordeal by drowning his faculties in brandy—Perhaps after all he doesn't care!—"

But the wish to have a look at that strangely complex creature—hero, adventurer or mere lucky fool—was irresistible, and Chauvelin in the latter part of the afternoon went up to the room which had been allotted to Sir Percy Blakeney.

He never moved now without his escort, and this time also two of his favourite bodyguard accompanied him to the upper floor. He knocked at the door, but received no answer, and after a second or two he bade his men wait in the corridor and, gently turning the latch, walked in.

There was an odour of brandy in the air; on the table two or three empty bottles of wine and a glass half filled with cognac testified to the truth of what the orderly had said, whilst sprawling across the camp bedstead, which obviously was too small for his long limbs, his head thrown back, his mouth open for a vigorous snore, lay the imperturbable Sir Percy fast asleep.

Chauvelin went up to the bedstead and looked down upon the reclining figure of the man who had oft been called the most dangerous enemy of Republican France.

Of a truth, a fine figure of a man, Chauvelin was ready enough to admit that; the long, hard limbs, the wide chest, and slender, white hands, all bespoke the man of birth, breeding and energy; the face too looked strong and clearly-cut in repose, now that the perpetually inane smile did not play round the firm lips, nor the lazy, indolent expression mar the seriousness of the straight brow. For one moment—it was a mere flash—Chauvelin felt almost sorry that so interesting a career should be thus ignominiously brought to a close.

The Terrorist felt that if his own future, his own honour and integrity were about to be so hopelessly crushed, he would have wandered up and down this narrow room like a caged beast, eating out his heart with self-reproach and remorse, and racking his nerves and brain for an issue out of the terrible alternative which meant dishonour or death.

But this man drank and slept.

"Perhaps he doesn't care!"

And as if in answer to Chauvelin's puzzled musing a deep snore escaped the sleeping adventurer's parted lips.

Chauvelin sighed, perplexed and troubled. He looked round the little room, then went up to a small side table which stood against the wall and on which were two or three quill pens and an ink-well, also some loosely scattered sheets of paper. These he turned over with a careless hand and presently came across a closely written page;

"Citizen Chauvelin;—In consideration of a further sum of one million *francs*—"

It was the beginning of the letter!—only a few words so far—with several corrections of misspelt words—and a line left out here and there which confused the meaning—a beginning made by the unsteady hand of that drunken fool—an attempt only at present—

But still—a beginning.

Close by was the draft of it as written out by Chauvelin, and which Sir Percy had evidently begun to copy.

He had made up his mind then—He meant to subscribe with his own hand to his lasting dishonour—and meaning it, he slept!

Chauvelin felt the paper trembling in his hand. He felt strangely agitated and nervous, now that the issue was so near—so sure!—

"There's no demmed hurry for that, is there—er—Monsieur Chaubertin?—" came from the slowly wakening Sir Percy in somewhat thick, heavy accents, accompanied by a prolonged yawn. "I haven't got the demmed thing quite ready—"

Chauvelin had been so startled that the paper dropped from his hand. He stooped to pick it up.

"Nay! why should you be so scared, sir?" continued Sir Percy lazily, "did you think I was drunk?—I assure you, sir, on my honour, I am not so drunk as you think I am."

"I have no doubt, Sir Percy," replied Chauvelin ironically, "that you have all your marvellous faculties entirely at your command—I must apologise for disturbing your papers," he added, replacing the half-written page on the table, "I thought perhaps that if the letter was ready—"

"It will be, sir—it will be—for I am not drunk, I assure you—and can write with a steady hand—and do honour to my signature—"

"When will you have the letter ready, Sir Percy?"

"The *Daydream* must leave the harbour at the turn of the tide," quoth Sir Percy thickly. "It'll be demmed well time by then—won't it, sir?—"

"About sundown, Sir Percy—not later—"

"About sundown—not later—" muttered Blakeney, as he once more stretched his long limbs along the narrow bed.

He gave a loud and hearty yawn.

"I'll not fail you—" he murmured, as he closed his eyes, and gave a final struggle to get his head at a comfortable angle, "the letter will be written in my best cali—calig—Lud! but I'm not so drunk as you think I am—"

But as if to belie his own oft-repeated assertion, hardly was the last word out of his mouth than his stertorous and even breathing proclaimed the fact that he was once more fast asleep.

With a shrug of the shoulders and a look of unutterable contempt at his broken-down enemy, Chauvelin turned on his heel and went out of the room.

But outside in the corridor he called the orderly to him and gave strict commands that no more wine or brandy was to be served to the Englishman under any circumstances whatever.

"He has two hours in which to sleep off the effects of all that brandy which he has consumed," he mused as he finally went back to his own quarters, "and by that time he will be able to write with a steady hand."

CHAPTER 33

The English Spy

And now at last the shades of evening were drawing in thick and fast. Within the walls of Fort Gayole the last rays of the setting sun had long ago ceased to shed their dying radiance, and through the thick stone embrasures and the dusty panes of glass, the grey light of dusk soon failed to penetrate.

In the large ground-floor room with its window opened upon the wide promenade of the southern ramparts, a silence reigned which was oppressive. The air was heavy with the fumes of the two tallow candles on the table, which smoked persistently.

Against the walls a row of figures in dark blue uniforms with scarlet facings, drab breeches and heavy riding boots, silent and immovable, with fixed bayonets like so many automatons lining the room all round; at some little distance from the central table and out of the immediate circle of light, a small group composed of five soldiers in the same blue and scarlet uniforms. One of these was Sergeant Hébert. In the centre of this group two persons were sitting; a woman and an old man.

The Abbé Foucquet had been brought down from his prison cell a few minutes ago and told to watch what would go on around him, after which he would be allowed to go to his old church of St. Joseph and ring the Angelus once more before he and his family left Boulogne forever.

The Angelus would be the signal for the opening of all the prison gates in the town. Everyone tonight could come and go as they pleased, and having rung the Angelus, the *abbé* would be at liberty to join François and Félicité and their old mother, his sister, outside the purlieus of the town.

The Abbé Foucquet did not quite understand all this, which was very rapidly and roughly explained to him. It was such a very little

199

while ago that he had expected to see the innocent children mounting up those awful steps which lead to the guillotine, whilst he himself was looking death quite near in the face, that all this talk of amnesty and of pardon had not quite fully reached his brain.

But he was quite content that it had all been ordained by *le bon Dieu*, and very happy at the thought of ringing the dearly-loved Angelus in his own old church once again. So, when he was peremptorily pushed into the room and found himself close to Marguerite, with four or five soldiers standing round them, he quietly pulled his old rosary from his pocket and began murmuring gentle *"Paters"* and *"Aves"* under his breath.

Beside him sat Marguerite, rigid as a statue, her cloak thrown over her shoulders, so that its hood might hide her face. She could not now have said how that awful day had passed, how she had managed to survive the terrible, nerve-racking suspense, the agonising doubt as to what was going to happen. But above all, what she had found most unendurable was the torturing thought that in this same grim and frowning building her husband was there—somewhere—how far or how near she could not say—but she knew that she was parted from him and perhaps would not see him again, not even at the hour of death.

That Percy would never write that infamous letter and *live*, she knew. That he might write it in order to save her, she feared was possible, whilst the look of triumph on Chauvelin's face had aroused her most agonising terrors.

When she was summarily ordered to go into the next room, she realised at once that all hope now was more than futile. The walls lined with troops, the attitude of her enemies, and above all that table with paper, ink and pens ready as it were for the accomplishment of the hideous and monstrous deed, all made her very heart numb, as if it were held within the chill embrace of death.

"If the woman moves, speaks or screams, gag her at once!" said Collot roughly the moment she sat down, and Sergeant Hébert stood over her, gag and cloth in hand, whilst two soldiers placed heavy hands on her shoulders.

But she neither moved nor spoke, not even presently when a loud and cheerful voice came echoing from a distant corridor, and *anon* the door opened and her husband came in, accompanied by Chauvelin.

The ex-ambassador was very obviously in a state of acute nervous tension; his hands were tightly clasped behind his back, and his movements were curiously irresponsible and jerky. But Sir Percy Blakeney looked a picture of calm unconcern; the lace bow at his throat was tied with scrupulous care, his eyeglass upheld at quite the correct angle, and his delicate-coloured caped coat was thrown back just sufficiently to afford a glimpse of the dainty cloth suit and exquisitely embroidered waistcoat beneath.

He was the perfect presentation of a London dandy, and might have been entering a royal drawing-room in company with an honoured guest. Marguerite's eyes were riveted on him as he came well within the circle of light projected by the candles, but not even with that acute sixth sense of a passionate and loving woman could she detect the slightest tremor in the aristocratic hands which held the gold-rimmed eyeglass, nor the faintest quiver of the firmly moulded lips.

This had occurred just as the bell of the old *beffroi* chimed three-quarters after six. Now it was close on seven, and in the centre of the room and with his face and figure well lighted up by the candles, at the table pen in hand sat Sir Percy writing.

At his elbow just behind him stood Chauvelin on the one side and Collot d'Herbois on the other, both watching with fixed and burning eyes the writing of that letter.

Sir Percy seemed in no hurry. He wrote slowly and deliberately, carefully copying the draft of the letter which was propped up in front of him. The spelling of some of the French words seemed to have troubled him at first, for when he began he made many facetious and self-deprecatory remarks anent his own want of education, and carelessness in youth in acquiring the gentle art of speaking so elegant a language.

Presently, however, he appeared more at his ease, or perhaps less inclined to talk, since he only received curt monosyllabic answers to his pleasant sallies. Five minutes had gone by without any other sound, save the spasmodic creak of Sir Percy's pen upon the paper, the while Chauvelin and Collot watched every word he wrote.

But gradually from afar there had arisen in the stillness of evening a distant, rolling noise like that of surf breaking against the cliffs. Nearer and louder it grew, and as it increased in volume, so it gained now in diversity. The monotonous, roll-like, far-off thunder was just as continuous as before, but now shriller notes broke out from amongst the more remote sounds, a loud laugh seemed ever and *anon* to pierce the distance and to rise above the persistent hubbub, which became the mere accompaniment to these isolated tones.

The merrymakers of Boulogne, having started from the Place de la Sénéchaussée, were making the round of the town by the wide avenue which tops the ramparts. They were coming past the Fort Gayole, shouting, singing, brass trumpets in front, big drum ahead, drenched, hot, and hoarse, but supremely happy.

Sir Percy looked up for a moment as the noise drew near, then turned to Chauvelin and pointing to the letter, he said;

"I have nearly finished!"

The suspense in the smoke-laden atmosphere of this room was becoming unendurable, and four hearts at least were beating wildly with overpowering anxiety. Marguerite's eyes were fixed with tender intensity on the man she so passionately loved. She did not understand his actions or his motives, but she felt a wild longing in her, to drink in every line of that loved face, as if with this last, long look she was bidding an eternal farewell to all hopes of future earthly happiness.

The old priest had ceased to tell his beads. Feeling in his kindly heart the echo of the appalling tragedy which was being enacted before him, he had put out a fatherly, tentative hand towards Marguerite, and given her icy fingers a comforting pressure.

And in the hearts of Chauvelin and his colleague there was satisfied revenge, eager, exultant triumph and that terrible nerve-tension which immediately precedes the long-expected climax.

But who can say what went on within the heart of that bold adventurer, about to be brought to the lowest depths of humiliation which it is in the power of man to endure? What behind that smooth unruffled brow still bent laboriously over the page of writing?

The crowd was now on the Place Daumont; some of the foremost in the ranks were ascending the stone steps which lead to the southern ramparts. The noise had become incessant; Pierrots and Pierrettes, Harlequins and Columbines had worked themselves up into a veritable intoxication of shouts and laughter.

Now as they all swarmed up the steps and caught sight of the open window almost on a level with the ground, and of the large dimly-lighted room, they gave forth one terrific and voluminous "Hurrah!" for the paternal government up in Paris, who had given them cause for all this joy. Then they recollected how the amnesty, the pardon, the National *fête*, this brilliant procession had come about, and somebody in the crowd shouted;

"*Allons!* les us have a look at that English spy!—"

"Let us see the Scarlet Pimpernel!"

"Yes! yes! let us see what he is like!"

They shouted and stamped and swarmed round the open window, swinging their lanthorns and demanding in a loud tone of voice that the English spy be shown to them.

Faces wet with rain and perspiration tried to peep in at the window. Collot gave brief orders to the soldiers to close the shutters at once and to push away the crowd, but the crowd would not be pushed. It would not be gainsaid, and when the soldiers tried to close the window, twenty angry fists broke the panes of glass.

"I can't finish this writing in your lingo, sir, whilst this demmed row is going on," said Sir Percy placidly.

"You have not much more to write, Sir Percy," urged Chauvelin with nervous impatience, "I pray you, finish the matter now, and get you gone from out this city."

"Send that demmed lot away, then," rejoined Sir Percy calmly.

"They won't go—They want to see you—"

Sir Percy paused a moment, pen in hand, as if in deep reflection.

"They want to see me," he said with a laugh. "Why, demn it all—then, why not let 'em?—"

And with a few rapid strokes of the pen, he quickly finished the letter, adding his signature with a bold flourish, whilst the crowd, pushing, jostling, shouting and cursing the soldiers, still loudly demanded to see the Scarlet Pimpernel.

Chauvelin felt as if his heart would veritably burst with the wildness of its beating.

Then Sir Percy, with one hand lightly pressed on the letter, pushed his chair away and with his pleasant ringing voice, said once again;

"Well! demn it—let 'em see me!—"

With that he sprang to his feet and up to his full height, and as he did so he seized the two massive pewter candlesticks, one in each hand, and with powerful arms well outstretched he held them high above his head.

"The letter—" murmured Chauvelin in a hoarse whisper.

But even as he was quickly reaching out a hand, which shook with the intensity of his excitement, towards the letter on the table, Blakeney, with one loud and sudden shout, threw the heavy candlesticks onto the floor. They rattled down with a terrific crash, the lights were extinguished, and the whole room was immediately plunged in utter darkness.

The crowd gave a wild yell of fear; they had only caught sight for one instant of that gigantic figure—which, with arms outstretched had seemed supernaturally tall—weirdly illuminated by the flickering light of the tallow candles and the next moment disappearing into utter darkness before their very gaze. Overcome with sudden superstitious fear, Pierrots and Pierrettes, drummer and trumpeters turned and fled in every direction.

Within the room all was wild confusion. The soldiers had heard a cry;

"*La fenêtre! La fenêtre!*"

Who gave it no one knew, no one could afterwards recollect; certain it is that with one accord the majority of the men made a rush for the open window, driven thither partly by the wild instinct of the chase after an escaping enemy, and partly by the same superstitious terror which had caused the crowd to flee. They clambered over the sill and dropped down on to the ramparts below, then started in wild pursuit.

But when the crash came, Chauvelin had given one frantic shout;

"The letter!!!—Collot!!—À *moi*—In his hand—The letter!—"

There was the sound of a heavy thud, of a terrible scuffle there on the floor in the darkness and then a yell of victory from Collot d'Herbois.

"I have the letter! À *Paris!*"

"Victory!" echoed Chauvelin, exultant and panting, "victory!! The Angelus, friend Hébert! Take the *calotin* to ring the Angelus!!!"

It was instinct which caused Collot d'Herbois to find the door; he tore it open, letting in a feeble ray of light from the corridor. He stood in the doorway one moment, his slouchy, ungainly form distinctly outlined against the lighter background beyond, a look of exultant and malicious triumph, of deadly hate and cruelty distinctly imprinted on his face and with upraised hand wildly flourishing the precious document, the brand of dishonour for the enemy of France.

"À *Paris!*" shouted Chauvelin to him excitedly. "Into Robespierre's hands—The letter!—"

Then he fell back panting, exhausted on the nearest chair.

Collot, without looking again behind him, called wildly for the men who were to escort him to Paris. They were picked troopers, stalwart veterans from the old municipal guard. They had not broken their ranks throughout the turmoil and fell into line in perfect order as they followed Citizen Collot out of the room.

Less than five minutes later there was the noise of stamping and champing of bits in the courtyard below, a shout from Collot, and the sound of a cavalcade galloping at break-neck speed towards the distant Paris gate.

CHAPTER 34

The Angelus

And gradually all noises died away around the old Fort Gayole. The shouts and laugher of the merrymakers, who had quickly recovered from their fright, now came only as the muffled rumble of a distant storm, broken here and there by the shrill note of a girl's loud laughter, or a vigorous fanfare from the brass trumpets.

The room where so much turmoil had taken place, where so many hearts had beaten with torrent-like emotions, where the awesome tragedy of revenge and hate, of love and passion had been consummated, was now silent and at peace.

The soldiers had gone, some in pursuit of the revellers, some with Collot d'Herbois, others with Hébert and the *calotin* who was to ring the Angelus.

Chauvelin, overcome with the intensity of his exultation and the agony of the suspense which he had endured, sat, vaguely dreaming, hardly conscious, but wholly happy and content. Fearless, too, for his triumph was complete, and he cared not now if he lived or died.

He had lived long enough to see the complete annihilation and dishonour of his enemy.

What happened to Sir Percy Blakeney now, what to Marguerite, he neither knew nor cared. No doubt the Englishman had picked himself up and got away through the window or the door; he would be anxious to get his wife out of the town as quickly as possible. The Angelus would ring directly, the gates would be opened, the harbour made free to everyone—

And Collot was a league outside Boulogne by now—a league nearer to Paris.

So what mattered the humbled wayside English flower?—the damaged and withered Scarlet Pimpernel?—

A slight noise suddenly caused him to start. He had been dreaming, no doubt, having fallen into some kind of torpor, akin to sleep, after the deadly and restless fatigue of the past four days. He certainly had been unconscious of everything around him, of time and of place. But now he felt fully awake.

And again, he heard that slight noise, as if something or someone

205

was moving in the room.

He tried to peer into the darkness but could distinguish nothing. He rose and went to the door. It was still open, and close behind it against the wall a small oil lamp was fixed which lit up the corridor.

Chauvelin detached the lamp and came back with it into the room. Just as he did so there came to his ears the first sound of the little church bell ringing the Angelus.

He stepped into the room holding the lamp high above his head; its feeble rays fell full upon the brilliant figure of Sir Percy Blakeney.

He was smiling pleasantly, bowing slightly towards Chauvelin, and in his hand he held the sheathed sword, the blade of which had been fashioned in Toledo for Lorenzo Cenci, and the fellow of which was lying now—Chauvelin himself knew not where.

"The day and hour, *Monsieur*, I think," said Sir Percy with courtly grace, "when you and I are to cross swords together; those are the southern ramparts, meseems. Will you precede, sir? and I will follow."

At sight of this man, of his impudence and of his daring, Chauvelin felt an icy grip on his heart. His cheeks became ashen white, his thin lips closed with a snap, and the hand which held the lamp aloft trembled visibly. Sir Percy stood before him, still smiling and with a graceful gesture pointing towards the ramparts.

From the Church of St. Joseph, the gentle, melancholy tones of the Angelus sounding the second *Ave Maria* came faintly echoing in the evening air.

With a violent effort Chauvelin forced himself to self-control and tried to shake off the strange feeling of obsession which had overwhelmed him in the presence of this extraordinary man. He walked quite quietly up to the table and placed the lamp upon it. As in a flash recollection had come back to him, the past few minutes!—the letter! and Collot well on his way to Paris!

Bah! he had nothing to fear now, save perhaps death at the hand of this adventurer turned assassin in his misery and humiliation!

"A truce on this folly, Sir Percy," he said roughly, "as you well know, I had never any intention of fighting you with these poisoned swords of yours and—"

"I knew that, M. Chauvelin—But do *you* know that I have the intention of killing you now—as you stand—like a dog!—"

And throwing down the sword with one of those uncontrolled outbursts of almost animal passion, which for one instant revealed the real, inner man, he went up to Chauvelin and towering above him like

206

a great avenging giant, he savoured for one second the joy of looking down on that puny, slender figure which he could crush with sheer brute force, with one blow from his powerful hands.

But Chauvelin at this moment was beyond fear.

"And if you killed me now, Sir Percy," he said quietly and looking the man whom he so hated fully in the eyes, "you could not destroy that letter which my colleague is taking to Paris at this very moment."

As he had anticipated, his words seemed to change Sir Percy's mood in an instant. The passion in the handsome, aristocratic face faded in a trice, the hard lines round the jaw and lips relaxed, the fire of revenge died out from the lazy blue eyes, and the next moment a long, loud, merry laugh raised the dormant echoes of the old fort.

"Nay, Monsieur Chaubertin," said Sir Percy gaily, "but this is marvellous—demmed marvellous—do you hear that, m'dear?—Gad-zooks! but 'tis the best joke I have heard this past twelve-months—*Monsieur* here thinks—Lud! but I shall die of laughing—*Monsieur* here thinks—that 'twas that demmed letter which went to Paris—and that an English gentleman lay scuffling on the floor and allowed a letter to be filched from him—"

"Sir Percy!—" gasped Chauvelin, as an awful thought seemed suddenly to flash across his fevered brain.

"Lud, sir, you are astonishing!" said Sir Percy, taking a very much crumpled sheet of paper from the capacious pocket of his elegant caped coat, and holding it close to Chauvelin's horror-stricken gaze. "*This* is the letter which I wrote at that table yonder in order to gain time and in order to fool you—But, by the Lord, you are a bigger demmed fool than ever I took you to be, if you thought it would serve any other purpose save that of my hitting you in the face with it."

And with a quick and violent gesture he struck Chauvelin full in the face with the paper.

"You would like to know, Monsieur Chaubertin, would you not?—" he added pleasantly, "what letter it is that your friend, Citizen Collot, is taking in such hot haste to Paris for you—Well! the letter is not long and 'tis written in verse—I wrote it myself upstairs today whilst you thought me sodden with brandy and three-parts asleep. But brandy is easily flung out of the window—Did you think I drank it all?—Nay! as you remember, I told you that I was not so drunk as you thought?—Aye! the letter is writ in English verse, *Monsieur*, and it reads thus;

"We seek him here! we seek him there!
Those Frenchies seek him everywhere!
Is he in heaven? Is he in hell?
That demmed elusive Pimpernel!

"A neat rhyme, I fancy, *Monsieur*, and one which will, if rightly translated, greatly please your friend and ruler, Citizen Robespierre— Your colleague Citizen Collot is well on his way to Paris with it by now—No, no, *Monsieur*—as you rightly said just now—I really could not kill you—God having blessed me with the saving sense of humour—"

Even as he spoke the third *Ave Maria* of the Angelus died away on the morning air. From the harbour and the old *château* there came the loud boom of cannon.

The hour of the opening of the gates, of the general amnesty and free harbour was announced throughout Boulogne.

Chauvelin was livid with rage, fear and baffled revenge. He made a sudden rush for the door in a blind desire to call for help, but Sir Percy had toyed long enough with his prey. The hour was speeding on; Hébert and some of the soldiers might return, and it was time to think of safety and of flight. Quick as a hunted panther, he had interposed his tall figure between his enemy and the latter's chance of calling for aid, then, seizing the little man by the shoulders, he pushed him back into that portion of the room where Marguerite and the Abbé Foucquet had been lately sitting.

The gag, with cloth and cord, which had been intended for a woman were lying on the ground close by, just where Hébert had dropped them, when he marched the old *abbé* off to the Church.

With quick and dexterous hands, Sir Percy soon reduced Chauvelin to an impotent and silent bundle. The ex-ambassador after four days of harrowing nerve-tension, followed by so awful a climax, was weakened physically and mentally, whilst Blakeney, powerful, athletic and always absolutely unperturbed, was fresh in body and spirit. He had slept calmly all the afternoon, having quietly thought out all his plans, left nothing to chance, and acted methodically and quickly, and invariably with perfect repose.

Having fully assured himself that the cords were well fastened, the gag secure and Chauvelin completely helpless, he took the now inert mass up in his arms and carried it into the adjoining room, where Marguerite for twelve hours had endured a terrible martyrdom.

He laid his enemy's helpless form upon the couch, and for one moment looked down on it with a strange feeling of pity quite unmixed with contempt. The light from the lamp in the further room struck vaguely upon the prostrate figure of Chauvelin. He seemed to have lost consciousness, for the eyes were closed; only the hands, which were tied securely to his body, had a spasmodic, nervous twitch in them.

With a good-natured shrug of the shoulders the imperturbable Sir Percy turned to go, but just before he did so, he took a scrap of paper from his waistcoat pocket and slipped it between Chauvelin's trembling fingers. On the paper were scribbled the four lines of verse which in the next four and twenty hours Robespierre himself and his colleagues would read.

Then Blakeney finally went out of the room.

Chapter 35

Marguerite

As he re-entered the large room, she was standing beside the table, with one dainty hand resting against the back of the chair, her whole graceful figure bent forward as if in an agony of ardent expectation.

Never for an instant, in that supreme moment when his precious life was at stake, did she waver in courage or presence of mind. From the moment that he jumped up and took the candlesticks in his hands, her sixth sense showed her as in a flash what he meant to do and how he would wish her to act.

When the room was plunged in darkness she stood absolutely still; when she heard the scuffle on the floor she never trembled, for her passionate heart had already told her that he never meant to deliver that infamous letter into his enemies' hands. Then, when there was the general scramble, when the soldiers rushed away, when the room became empty and Chauvelin alone remained, she shrank quietly into the darkest corner of the room, hardly breathing, only waiting—Waiting for a sign from him!

She could not see him, but she felt the beloved presence there, somewhere close to her, and she knew that he would wish her to wait—She watched him silently—ready to help if he called—equally ready to remain still and to wait.

Only when the helpless body of her deadly enemy was well out of the way did she come from out the darkness, and now she stood with the full light of the lamp illumining her ruddy golden hair, the delicate blush on her cheek, the flame of love dancing in her glorious eyes.

Thus, he saw her as he re-entered the room, and for one second, he paused at the door, for the joy of seeing her there seemed greater than he could bear.

Forgotten was the agony of mind which he had endured, the humiliations and the dangers which still threatened; he only remembered that she loved him and that he worshipped her.

The next moment she lay clasped in his arms. All was still around them, save for the gentle pitter-patter of the rain on the trees of the ramparts, and from very far away the echo of laughter and music from the distant revellers.

And then the cry of the sea-mew thrice repeated from just beneath the window.

Blakeney and Marguerite awoke from their brief dream; once more the passionate lover gave place to the man of action.

"'Tis Tony, an' I mistake not," he said hurriedly, as with loving fingers still slightly trembling with suppressed passion, he readjusted the hood over her head.

"Lord Tony?" she murmured.

"Aye! with Hastings and one or two others. I told them to be ready for us tonight as soon as the place was quiet."

"You were so sure of success then, Percy?" she asked in wonderment.

"So sure," he replied simply.

Then he led her to the window and lifted her onto the sill. It was not high from the ground and two pairs of willing arms were there ready to help her down.

Then he, too, followed, and quietly the little party turned to walk toward the gate. The ramparts themselves now looked strangely still and silent; the merrymakers were far away; only one or two passers-by hurried swiftly past here and there, carrying bundles, evidently bent on making use of that welcome permission to leave this dangerous soil.

The little party walked on in silence, Marguerite's small hand resting on her husband's arm. *Anon* they came upon a group of soldiers who were standing somewhat perfunctorily and irresolutely close by the open gate of the fort.

"*Tiens c'est l'Anglais!*" said one.

"*Morbleu!* he is on his way back to England," commented another lazily.

The gates of Boulogne had been thrown open to everyone when the Angelus was rung and the cannon boomed. The general amnesty had been proclaimed; everyone had the right to come and go as they pleased; the sentinels had been ordered to challenge no one and to let everyone pass.

No one knew that the great and glorious plans for the complete annihilation of the Scarlet Pimpernel and his League had come to naught, that Collot was taking a mighty hoax to Paris, and that the man who had thought out and nearly carried through the most fiendishly cruel plan ever conceived for the destruction of an enemy, lay helpless, bound and gagged, within his own stronghold.

And so the little party, consisting of Sir Percy and Marguerite, Lord Anthony Dewhurst and my Lord Hastings, passed unchallenged through the gates of Boulogne.

Outside the precincts of the town they met my Lord Everingham and Sir Philip Glynde, who had met the Abbé Foucquet outside his little church and escorted him safely out of the city, whilst François and Félicité with their old mother had been under the charge of other members of the League.

"We were all in the procession, dressed up in all sorts of ragged finery, until the last moment," explained Lord Tony to Marguerite as the entire party now quickly made its way to the harbour. "We did not know what was going to happen—All we knew was that we should be wanted about this time—the hour when the duel was to have been fought—and somewhere near here on the southern ramparts—and we always have strict orders to mix with the crowd if there happens to be one. When we saw Blakeney raise the candlesticks we guessed what was coming, and we each went to our respective posts. It was all quite simple."

The young man spoke gaily and lightly, but through the easy banter of his tone, there pierced the enthusiasm and pride of the soldier in the glory and daring of his chief.

Between the city walls and the harbour there was much bustle and agitation. The English packet-boat would lift anchor at the turn of the tide, and as everyone was free to get aboard without leave or passport, there were a very large number of passengers, bound for the land of freedom.

Two boats from the *Daydream* were waiting in readiness for Sir Percy and my lady and those whom they would bring with them.

Silently the party embarked, and as the boats pushed off and the sailors from Sir Percy's yacht bent to their oars, the old Abbé Foucquet began gently droning a *Pater* and *Ave* to the accompaniment of his beads.

He accepted joy, happiness and safety with the same gentle philosophy as he would have accepted death, but Marguerite's keen and loving ears caught at the end of each "*Pater*" a gently murmured request to *le bon Dieu* to bless and protect our English rescuer.

★★★★★★

Only once did Marguerite make allusion to that terrible time which had become the past.

They were wandering together down the chestnut alley in the beautiful garden at Richmond. It was evening, and the air was heavy with the rich odour of wet earth, of belated roses and dying mignonette. She had paused in the alley, and placed a trembling hand upon his arm, whilst raising her eyes filled with tears of tender passion up to his face.

"Percy!" she murmured, "have you forgiven me?"

"What, m'dear?"

"That awful evening in Boulogne—what that fiend demanded—his awful 'either—or'—I brought it all upon you—it was all my fault."

"Nay, my dear, for that 'tis I should thank you—"

"Thank me?"

"Aye," he said, whilst in the fast-gathering dusk she could only just perceive the sudden hardening of his face, the look of wild passion in his eyes, "but for that evening in Boulogne, but for that alternative which that devil placed before me, I might never have known how much you meant to me."

Even the recollection of all the sorrow, the anxiety, the torturing humiliations of that night seemed completely to change him; the voice became trenchant, the hands were tightly clenched. But Marguerite drew nearer to him; her two hands were on his breast; she murmured gently;

"And now?—"

He folded her in his arms, with an agony of joy, and said earnestly;

"Now I know."

Eldorado

Mon état présent, mon cher ami, est
devenu tel qu'il m'est impossible d[e]
supporter Le citoyen Héron ain[si que]
M. Chauvelin ont transform[é ...]
en un véritable enfer. De[main]
nous quittons ces lieux e[t je]
guiderai le citoyen H[éron au lieu]
connu de nous où se [trouve ...]
Mais l'autorité administ[rative]
exige que l'un de mes am[is ...] restant
[...]
Nous partons à première heure e[t il est]
nécessaire que vous soyez devan[t la]
porte de la maison de Justice à [...]
de relevée. L'autorité administrative
donne assurance que votre vie restera sauv[e]
mais si vous refusez de me suivre, la
guillotine sera dès demain prête à [vous]
recevoir en ses bras.

Percy Bl[akeney]

II. 19 Pluviôse

Contents

Introduction

There has of late years crept so much confusion into the mind of the student as well as of the general reader as to the identity of the Scarlet Pimpernel with that of the Gascon Royalist plotter known to history as the Baron de Batz, that the time seems opportune for setting all doubts on that subject at rest.

The identity of the Scarlet Pimpernel is in no way whatever connected with that of the Baron de Batz, and even superficial reflection will soon bring the mind to the conclusion that great fundamental differences existed in these two men, in their personality, in their character, and, above all, in their aims.

According to one or two enthusiastic historians, the Baron de Batz was the chief agent in a vast network of conspiracy, entirely supported by foreign money—both English and Austrian—and which had for its object the overthrow of the Republican Government and the restoration of the monarchy in France.

In order to attain this political goal, it is averred that he set himself the task of pitting the members of the Revolutionary Government one against the other, and bringing hatred and dissensions amongst them, until the cry of "Traitor!" resounded from one end of the Assembly of the Convention to the other, and the Assembly itself became as one vast den of wild beasts wherein wolves and hyenas devoured one another and, still unsatiated, licked their streaming jaws hungering for more prey.

Those same enthusiastic historians, who have a firm belief in the so-called "Foreign Conspiracy," ascribe every important event of the Great Révolution—be that event the downfall of the Girondins, the escape of the Dauphin from the Temple, or the death of Robespierre—to the intrigues of Baron de Batz. He it was, so they say, who egged the Jacobins on against the Mountain, Robespierre against Danton, Hebert against Robespierre. He it was who instigated the massacres of September, the atrocities of Nantes, the horrors of *Thermidor*, the sacrileges, the *noyades*: all with the view of causing every

217

section of the National Assembly to vie with the other in excesses and in cruelty, until the makers of the *Révolution*, satiated with their own lust, turned on one another, and Sardanapalus-like buried themselves and their orgies in the vast hecatomb of a self-consumed anarchy.

Whether the power thus ascribed to Baron de Batz by his historians is real or imaginary it is not the purpose of this preface to investigate. Its sole object is to point out the difference between the career of this plotter and that of the Scarlet Pimpernel.

The Baron de Batz himself was an adventurer without substance, save that which he derived from abroad. He was one of those men who have nothing to lose and everything to gain by throwing themselves headlong in the seething cauldron of internal politics.

Though he made several attempts at rescuing King Louis first, and then the queen and royal family from prison and from death, he never succeeded, as we know, in any of these undertakings, and he never once so much as attempted the rescue of other equally innocent, if not quite so distinguished, victims of the most bloodthirsty revolution that has ever shaken the foundations of the civilised world.

Nay more; when on the 29th *Prairial* those unfortunate men and women were condemned and executed for alleged complicity in the so-called "Foreign Conspiracy," de Batz, who is universally admitted to have been the head and prime-mover of that conspiracy—if, indeed, conspiracy there was—never made either the slightest attempt to rescue his confederates from the guillotine, or at least the offer to perish by their side if he could not succeed in saving them.

And when we remember that the martyrs of the 29th *Prairial* included women like Grandmaison, the devoted friend of de Batz, the beautiful Emilie de St. Amaranthe, little Cécile Renault—a mere child not sixteen years of age—also men like Michonis and Roussell, faithful servants of de Batz, the Baron de Lézardière, and the Comte de St. Maurice, his friends, we no longer can have the slightest doubt that the Gascon plotter and the English gentleman are indeed two very different persons.

The latter's aims were absolutely non-political. He never intrigued for the restoration of the monarchy, or even for the overthrow of that Republic which he loathed.

His only concern was the rescue of the innocent, the stretching out of a saving hand to those unfortunate creatures who had fallen into the nets spread out for them by their fellow-men; by those who—godless, lawless, penniless themselves—had sworn to exterminate all those who clung to their belongings, to their religion, and to their beliefs.

The Scarlet Pimpernel did not take it upon himself to punish the guilty; his care was solely of the helpless and of the innocent.

For this aim he risked his life every time that he set foot on French soil, for it he sacrificed his fortune, and even his personal happiness, and to it he devoted his entire existence.

Moreover, whereas the French plotter is said to have had confederates even in the Assembly of the Convention, confederates who were sufficiently influential and powerful to secure his own immunity, the Englishman when he was bent on his errands of mercy had the whole of France against him.

The Baron de Batz was a man who never justified either his own ambitions or even his existence; the Scarlet Pimpernel was a personality of whom an entire nation might justly be proud.

PART 1

CHAPTER 1

In the Théâtre National

And yet people found the opportunity to amuse themselves, to dance and to go to the theatre, to enjoy music and open-air *cafés* and promenades in the Palais Royal.

New fashions in dress made their appearance, milliners produced fresh "creations," and jewellers were not idle. A grim sense of humour, born of the very intensity of ever-present danger, had dubbed the cut of certain tunics "*tête tranchée*," or a favourite *ragoût* was called "à *la guillotine.*"

On three evenings only during the past memorable four and a half years did the theatres close their doors, and these evenings were the ones immediately following that terrible 2nd of September the day of the butchery outside the Abbaye prison, when Paris herself was aghast with horror, and the cries of the massacred might have drowned the calls of the audience whose hands upraised for plaudits would still be dripping with blood.

On all other evenings of these same four and a half years the theatres in the Rue de Richelieu, in the Palais Royal, the Luxembourg, and others, had raised their curtains and taken money at their doors. The same audience that earlier in the day had whiled away the time by witnessing the ever-recurrent dramas of the Place de la Révolution assembled here in the evenings and filled stalls, boxes, and tiers, laughing over the satires of Voltaire or weeping over the sentimental tragedies of persecuted Romeos and innocent Juliets.

Death knocked at so many doors these days! He was so constant a guest in the houses of relatives and friends that those who had merely shaken him by the hand, those on whom he had smiled, and whom he, still smiling, had passed indulgently by, looked on him with that subtle contempt born of familiarity, shrugged their shoulders at his passage, and envisaged his probable visit on the morrow with light-hearted indifference.

Paris—despite the horrors that had stained her walls had remained a city of pleasure, and the knife of the guillotine did scarce descend more often than did the drop-scenes on the stage.

On this bitterly cold evening of the 27th *Nivôse*, in the second year of the Republic—or, as we of the old style still persist in calling it, the 16th of January, 1794—the auditorium of the *Théâtre National* was filled with a very brilliant company.

The appearance of a favourite actress in the part of one of Molière's volatile heroines had brought pleasure-loving Paris to witness this revival of "*Le Misanthrope*," with new scenery, dresses, and the aforesaid charming actress to add piquancy to the master's mordant wit.

The *Moniteur*, which so impartially chronicles the events of those times, tells us under that date that the Assembly of the Convention voted on that same day a new law giving fuller power to its spies, enabling them to effect domiciliary searches at their discretion without previous reference to the Committee of General Security, authorising them to proceed against all enemies of public happiness, to send them to prison at their own discretion, and assuring them the sum of thirty-five *livres* "for every piece of game thus beaten up for the guillotine." Under that same date the *Moniteur* also puts it on record that the *Théâtre National* was filled to its utmost capacity for the revival of the late Citoyen Molière's comedy.

The Assembly of the Convention having voted the new law which placed the lives of thousands at the mercy of a few human blood-hounds, adjourned its sitting and proceeded to the Rue de Richelieu.

Already the house was full when the fathers of the people made their way to the seats which had been reserved for them. An awed hush descended on the throng as one by one the men whose very names inspired horror and dread filed in through the narrow gangways of the stalls or took their places in the tiny boxes around.

Citizen Robespierre's neatly bewigged head soon appeared in one of these; his bosom friend St. Just was with him, and also his sister Charlotte. Danton, like a big, shaggy-coated lion, elbowed his way into the stalls, whilst Santerre, the handsome butcher and idol of the people of Paris, was loudly acclaimed as his huge frame, gorgeously clad in the uniform of the National Guard, was sighted on one of the tiers above.

The public in the *parterre* and in the galleries whispered excitedly; the awe-inspiring names flew about hither and thither on the wings of the overheated air. Women craned their necks to catch sight of heads which mayhap on the morrow would roll into the gruesome basket at the foot of the guillotine.

In one of the tiny *avant-scène* boxes two men had taken their seats long before the bulk of the audience had begun to assemble in the house. The inside of the box was in complete darkness, and the narrow opening which allowed but a sorry view of one side of the stage helped to conceal rather than display the occupants.

The younger one of these two men appeared to be something of a stranger in Paris, for as the public men and the well-known members of the government began to arrive he often turned to his companion for information regarding these notorious personalities.

"Tell me, de Batz," he said, calling the other's attention to a group of men who had just entered the house, "that creature there in the green coat—with his hand up to his face now—who is he?"

"Where? Which do you mean?"

"There! He looks this way now, and he has a playbill in his hand. The man with the protruding chin and the convex forehead, a face like a marmoset, and eyes like a jackal. What?"

The other leaned over the edge of the box, and his small, restless eyes wandered over the now closely-packed auditorium.

"Oh!" he said as soon as he recognised the face which his friend had pointed out to him, "that is Citizen Foucquier-Tinville."

"The Public Prosecutor?"

"Himself. And Héron is the man next to him."

"Héron?" said the younger man interrogatively.

"Yes. He is chief agent to the Committee of General Security now."

"What does that mean?"

Both leaned back in their chairs, and their sombrely-clad figures were once more merged in the gloom of the narrow box. Instinctively, since the name of the Public Prosecutor had been mentioned between them, they had allowed their voices to sink to a whisper.

The older man—a stoutish, florid-looking individual, with small, keen eyes, and skin pitted with smallpox—shrugged his shoulders at his friend's question, and then said with an air of contemptuous indifference:

"It means, my good St. Just, that these two men whom you see down there, calmly conning the programme of this evening's entertainment, and preparing to enjoy themselves tonight in the company of the late M. de Molière, are two hell-hounds as powerful as they are cunning."

"Yes, yes," said St. Just, and much against his will a slight shudder ran through his slim figure as he spoke. "Foucquier-Tinville I know; I know his cunning, and I know his power—but the other?"

"The other?" retorted de Batz lightly. "Héron? Let me tell you, my friend, that even the might and lust of that damned Public Prosecutor pale before the power of Héron!"

"But how? I do not understand."

"Ah! you have been in England so long, you lucky dog, and though no doubt the main plot of our hideous tragedy has reached your ken, you have no cognisance of the actors who play the principal parts on this arena flooded with blood and carpeted with hate. They come and go, these actors, my good St. Just—they come and go. Marat is already the man of yesterday, Robespierre is the man of tomorrow. Today we still have Danton and Foucquier-Tinville; we still have Père Duchesne, and your own good cousin Antoine St. Just, but Héron and his like are with us always."

"Spies, of course?"

"Spies," assented the other. "And what spies! Were you present at the sitting of the Assembly today?"

"I was. I heard the new decree which already has passed into law. Ah! I tell you, friend, that we do not let the grass grow under our feet these days. Robespierre wakes up one morning with a whim; by the afternoon that whim has become law, passed by a servile body of men too terrified to run counter to his will, fearful lest they be accused of moderation or of humanity—the greatest crimes that can be committed nowadays."

"But Danton?"

"Ah! Danton? He would wish to stem the tide that his own passions have let loose; to muzzle the raging beasts whose fangs he him-

222

self has sharpened. I told you that Danton is still the man of today; tomorrow he will be accused of moderation. Danton and moderation!—ye gods! Eh? Danton, who thought the guillotine too slow in its work, and armed thirty soldiers with swords, so that thirty heads might fall at one and the same time. Danton, friend, will perish tomorrow accused of treachery against the Révolution, of moderation towards her enemies; and curs like Héron will feast on the blood of lions like Danton and his crowd."

He paused a moment, for he dared not raise his voice, and his whispers were being drowned by the noise in the auditorium. The curtain, timed to be raised at eight o'clock, was still down, though it was close on half-past, and the public was growing impatient. There was loud stamping of feet, and a few shrill whistles of disapproval proceeded from the gallery.

"If Héron gets impatient," said de Batz lightly, when the noise had momentarily subsided, "the manager of this theatre and mayhap his leading actor and actress will spend an unpleasant day tomorrow."

"Always Héron!" said St. Just, with a contemptuous smile.

"Yes, my friend," rejoined the other imperturbably, "always Héron. And he has even obtained a longer lease of existence this afternoon."

"By the new decree?"

"Yes. The new decree. The agents of the Committee of General Security, of whom Héron is the chief, have from today powers of domiciliary search; they have full powers to proceed against all enemies of public welfare. Isn't that beautifully vague? And they have absolute discretion; every one may become an enemy of public welfare, either by spending too much money or by spending too little, by laughing today or crying tomorrow, by mourning for one dead relative or rejoicing over the execution of another. He may be a bad example to the public by the cleanliness of his person or by the filth upon his clothes, he may offend by walking today and by riding in a carriage next week; the agents of the Committee of General Security shall alone decide what constitutes enmity against public welfare. All prisons are to be opened at their bidding to receive those whom they choose to denounce; they have henceforth the right to examine prisoners privately and without witnesses, and to send them to trial without further warrants; their duty is clear—they must 'beat up game for the guillotine.' Thus is the decree worded; they must furnish the Public Prosecutor with work to do, the tribunals with victims to condemn, the Place de la Révolution with death-scenes to amuse the people, and for their work they will be rewarded thirty-five livres for every head that falls under the guillotine Ah! if Héron and his like and his myrmidons work hard and well they can make a comfortable income of four or five thousand *livres* a week. We are getting on, friend St. Just—we are getting on."

He had not raised his voice while he spoke, nor in the recounting of such inhuman monstrosity, such vile and bloodthirsty conspiracy against the liberty, the dignity, the very life of an entire nation, did he appear to feel the slightest indignation; rather did a tone of amusement and even of triumph strike through his speech; and now he laughed good-humouredly like an indulgent parent who is watching the naturally cruel antics of a spoilt boy.

"Then from this hell let loose upon earth," exclaimed St. Just hotly, "must we rescue those who refuse to ride upon this tide of blood."

His cheeks were glowing, his eyes sparkled with enthusiasm. He looked very young and very eager. Armand St. Just, the brother of Lady Blakeney, had something of the refined beauty of his lovely sister, but the features though manly—had not the latent strength expressed in them which characterised every line of Marguerite's exquisite face. The forehead suggested a dreamer rather than a thinker, the blue-grey eyes were those of an idealist rather than of a man of action.

De Batz's keen piercing eyes had no doubt noted this, even whilst he gazed at his young friend with that same look of good-humoured indulgence which seemed habitual to him.

"We have to think of the future, my good St. Just," he said after a slight pause, and speaking slowly and decisively, like a father rebuking a hot-headed child, "not of the present. What are a few lives worth beside the great principles which we have at stake?"

"The restoration of the monarchy—I know," retorted St. Just, still unsobered, "but, in the meanwhile—"

"In the meanwhile," rejoined de Batz earnestly, "every victim to the lust of these men is a step towards the restoration of law and or- der—that is to say, of the monarchy. It is only through these violent excesses perpetrated in its name that the nation will realise how it is being fooled by a set of men who have only their own power and their own advancement in view, and who imagine that the only way to that power is over the dead bodies of those who stand in their way. Once the nation is sickened by these orgies of ambition and of hate, it will turn against these savage brutes, and gladly acclaim the restora- tion of all that they are striving to destroy. This is our only hope for the future, and, believe me, friend, that every head snatched from the guillotine by your romantic hero, the Scarlet Pimpernel, is a stone laid for the consolidation of this infamous Republic."

"I'll not believe it," protested St. Just emphatically.

De Batz, with a gesture of contempt indicative also of complete self-satisfaction and unalterable self-belief, shrugged his broad shoulders. His short fat fingers, covered with rings, beat a tattoo upon the ledge of the box.

Obviously, he was ready with a retort. His young friend's attitude irritated even more than it amused him. But he said nothing for the moment, waiting while the traditional three knocks on the floor of the stage proclaimed the rise of the curtain. The growing impatience of the audience subsided as if by magic at the welcome call; everybody settled down again comfortably in their seats, they gave up the contemplation of the fathers of the people and turned their full attention to the actors on the boards.

Chapter 2
Widely Divergent Aims

This was Armand St. Just's first visit to Paris since that memorable day when first he decided to sever his connection from the Republican party, of which he and his beautiful sister Marguerite had at one time been amongst the most noble, most enthusiastic followers. Already a year and a half ago the excesses of the party had horrified him, and that was long before they had degenerated into the sickening orgies which were culminating today in wholesale massacres and bloody hecatombs of innocent victims.

With the death of Mirabeau, the moderate Republicans, whose sole and entirely pure aim had been to free the people of France from the autocratic tyranny of the Bourbons, saw the power go from their clean hands to the grimy ones of lustful demagogues, who knew no law save their own passions of bitter hatred against all classes that were not as self-seeking, as ferocious as themselves.

It was no longer a question of a fight for political and religious liberty only, but one of class against class, man against man, and let the weaker look to himself. The weaker had proved himself to be, firstly, the man of property and substance, then the law-abiding citizen, lastly the man of action who had obtained for the people that very same liberty of thought and of belief which soon became so terribly misused.

Armand St. Just, one of the apostles of liberty, fraternity, and equality, soon found that the most savage excesses of tyranny were being perpetrated in the name of those same ideals which he had worshipped.

His sister Marguerite, happily married in England, was the final temptation which caused him to quit the country the destinies of which he no longer could help to control. The spark of enthusiasm which he and the followers of Mirabeau had tried to kindle in the hearts of an oppressed people had turned to raging tongues of unquenchable flames. The taking of the Bastille had been the prelude to the massacres of September, and even the horror of these had since paled beside the holocausts of today.

Armand, saved from the swift vengeance of the revolutionaries by the devotion of the Scarlet Pimpernel, crossed over to England and enrolled himself under the banner of the heroic chief. But he had been unable hitherto to be an active member of the League. The chief was loath to allow him to run foolhardy risks. The St. Justs—both Marguerite and Armand—were still very well-known in Paris. Marguerite was not a woman easily forgotten, and her marriage with an English "*aristo*" did not please those republican circles who had looked upon her as their queen. Armand's secession from his party into the ranks of the *émigrés* had singled him out for special reprisals, if and whenever he could be got hold of, and both brother and sister had an unusually bitter enemy in their cousin Antoine St. Just—once an aspirant to Marguerite's hand, and now a servile adherent and imitator of Robespierre, whose ferocious cruelty he tried to emulate with a view to ingratiating himself with the most powerful man of the day.

Nothing would have pleased Antoine St. Just more than the opportunity of showing his zeal and his patriotism by denouncing his own kith and kin to the Tribunal of the Terror, and the Scarlet Pimpernel, whose own slender fingers were held on the pulse of that reckless revolution, had no wish to sacrifice Armand's life deliberately, or even to expose it to unnecessary dangers.

Thus, it was that more than a year had gone by before Armand St. Just—an enthusiastic member of the League of the Scarlet Pimpernel—was able to do aught for its service. He had chafed under the enforced restraint placed upon him by the prudence of his chief, when, indeed, he was longing to risk his life with the comrades whom he loved and beside the leader whom he revered.

At last, in the beginning of '94 he persuaded Blakeney to allow him to join the next expedition to France. What the principal aim of that expedition was the members of the League did not know as yet, but what they did know was that perils—graver even than hitherto—would attend them on their way.

The circumstances had become very different of late. At first the impenetrable mystery which had surrounded the personality of the chief had been a full measure of safety, but now one tiny corner of that veil of mystery had been lifted by two rough pairs of hands at least; Chauvelin, ex-ambassador at the English Court, was no longer in any doubt as to the identity of the Scarlet Pimpernel, whilst Collot d'Herbois had seen him at Boulogne, and had there been effectually foiled by him.

Four months had gone by since that day, and the Scarlet Pimpernel was hardly ever out of France now; the massacres in Paris and in the provinces had multiplied with appalling rapidity, the necessity for the selfless devotion of that small band of heroes had become daily, hourly more pressing. They rallied round their chief with unbounded enthusiasm, and let it be admitted at once that the sporting instinct—inherent in these English gentlemen—made them all the more keen, all the more eager now that the dangers which beset their expeditions were increased tenfold.

At a word from the beloved leader, these young men—the spoilt darlings of society—would leave the gaieties, the pleasures, the luxuries of London or of Bath, and, taking their lives in their hands, they placed them, together with their fortunes, and even their good names, at the service of the innocent and helpless victims of merciless tyranny. The married men—Ffoulkes, my Lord Hastings, Sir Jeremiah Walles-court—left wife and children at a call from the chief, at the cry of the wretched. Armand—unattached and enthusiastic—had the right to demand that he should no longer be left behind.

He had only been away a little over fifteen months, and yet he found Paris a different city from the one he had left immediately after the terrible massacres of September. An air of grim loneliness seemed to hang over her despite the crowds that thronged her streets; the men whom he was wont to meet in public places fifteen months ago—friends and political allies—were no longer to be seen; strange faces surrounded him on every side—sullen, glowering faces, all wearing a certain air of horrified surprise and of vague, terrified wonder, as if life had become one awful puzzle, the answer to which must be found in the brief interval between the swift passages of death.

Armand St. Just, having settled his few simple belongings in the squalid lodgings which had been assigned to him, had started out after dark to wander somewhat aimlessly through the streets. Instinctively he seemed to be searching for a familiar face, someone who would come to him out of that merry past which he had spent with Marguerite in their pretty apartment in the Rue St. Honoré.

For an hour he wandered thus and met no one whom he knew. At times it appeared to him as if he did recognise a face or figure that passed him swiftly by in the gloom, but even before he could fully make up his mind to that, the face or figure had already disappeared, gliding furtively down some narrow unlighted by-street, without turning to look to right or left, as if dreading fuller recognition. Armand felt a total stranger in his own native city.

The terrible hours of the execution on the *Place de la Révolution* were fortunately over, the tumbrils no longer rattled along the uneven pavements, nor did the death-cry of the unfortunate victims resound through the deserted streets. Armand was, on this first day of his arrival, spared the sight of this degradation of the once lovely city; but her desolation, her general appearance of shamefaced indigence and of cruel aloofness struck a chill in the young man's heart.

It was no wonder, therefore, when *anon* he was wending his way slowly back to his lodging he was accosted by a pleasant, cheerful voice, that he responded to it with alacrity. The voice, of a smooth, oily *timbre*, as if the owner kept it well greased for purposes of amiable speech, was like an echo of the past, when jolly, irresponsible Baron de Batz, erstwhile officer of the Guard in the service of the late king, and since then known to be the most inveterate conspirator for the restoration of the monarchy, used to amuse Marguerite by his vapid, senseless plans for the overthrow of the newly-risen power of the people.

Armand was quite glad to meet him, and when de Batz suggested that a good talk over old times would be vastly agreeable, the younger man gladly acceded. The two men, though certainly not mistrustful of one another, did not seem to care to reveal to each other the place where they lodged. De Batz at once proposed the *avant-scène* box of one of the theatres as being the safest place where old friends could talk without fear of spying eyes or ears.

"There is no place so safe or so private nowadays, believe me, my young friend," he said, "I have tried every sort of nook and cranny in this accursed town, now riddled with spies, and I have come to the conclusion that a small *avant-scène* box is the most perfect den of privacy there is in the entire city. The voices of the actors on the stage and the hum among the audience in the house will effectually drown all individual conversation to every ear save the one for whom it is intended."

It is not difficult to persuade a young man who feels lonely and somewhat forlorn in a large city to while away an evening in the companionship of a cheerful talker, and de Batz was essentially good company. His vapourings had always been amusing, but Armand now gave him credit for more seriousness of purpose; and though the chief had warned him against picking up acquaintances in Paris, the young man felt that that restriction would certainly not apply to a man like de Batz, whose hot partisanship of the Royalist cause and hare-brained schemes for its restoration must make him at one with the League of the Scarlet Pimpernel.

Armand accepted the other's cordial invitation. He, too, felt that he would indeed be safer from observation in a crowded theatre than in the streets. Among a closely packed throng bent on amusement the sombrely-clad figure of a young man, with the appearance of a student or of a journalist, would easily pass unperceived.

But somehow, after the first ten minutes spent in de Batz' company within the gloomy shelter of the small *avant-scène* box, Armand already repented of the impulse which had prompted him to come to the theatre tonight, and to renew acquaintanceship with the ex-officer of the late King's Guard. Though he knew de Batz to be an ardent Royalist, and even an active adherent of the monarchy, he was soon conscious of a vague sense of mistrust of this pompous, self-complacent individual, whose every utterance breathed selfish aims rather than devotion to a forlorn cause.

Therefore, when the curtain rose at last on the first act of Molière's witty comedy, St. Just turned deliberately towards the stage and tried to interest himself in the wordy quarrel between Philinte and Alceste.

But this attitude on the part of the younger man did not seem to suit his newly-found friend. It was clear that de Batz did not consider the topic of conversation by any means exhausted, and that it had been more with a view to a discussion like the present interrupted one that he had invited St. Just to come to the theatre with him tonight, rather than for the purpose of witnessing Mlle. Lange's *début* in the part of Célimène.

The presence of St. Just in Paris had as a matter of fact astonished de Batz not a little and had set his intriguing brain busy on conjectures. It was in order to turn these conjectures into certainties that he had desired private talk with the young man.

He waited silently now for a moment or two, his keen, small eyes resting with evident anxiety on Armand's averted head, his fingers still beating the impatient tattoo upon the velvet-covered cushion of the box. Then at the first movement of St. Just towards him he was ready in an instant to re-open the subject under discussion.

With a quick nod of his head he called his young friend's attention back to the men in the auditorium.

"Your good cousin Antoine St. Just is hand and glove with Robespierre now," he said. "When you left Paris more than a year ago you could afford to despise him as an empty-headed windbag; now, if you desire to remain in France, you will have to fear him as a power and a menace."

"Yes, I knew that he had taken to herding with the wolves," rejoined Armand lightly. "At one time he was in love with my sister. I thank God that she never cared for him."

"They say that he herds with the wolves because of this disappointment," said de Batz. "The whole pack is made up of men who have been disappointed, and who have nothing more to lose. When all these wolves will have devoured one another, then and then only can we hope for the restoration of the monarchy in France. And they will not turn on one another whilst prey for their greed lies ready to their jaws. Your friend the Scarlet Pimpernel should feed this bloody revolution of ours rather than starve it, if indeed he hates it as he seems to do."

His restless eyes peered with eager interrogation into those of the younger man. He paused as if waiting for a reply; then, as St. Just remained silent, he reiterated slowly, almost in the tones of a challenge:

"If indeed he hates this bloodthirsty revolution of ours as he seems to do."

The reiteration implied a doubt. In a moment St. Just's loyalty was up in arms.

"The Scarlet Pimpernel," he said, "cares naught for your political aims. The work of mercy that he does, he does for justice and for humanity."

"And for sport," said de Batz with a sneer, "so I've been told."

"He is English," assented St. Just, "and as such will never own to sentiment. Whatever be the motive, look at the result!

"Yes! a few lives stolen from the guillotine."

"Women and children—innocent victims—would have perished

230

but for his devotion."

"The more innocent they were, the more helpless, the more pitiable, the louder would their blood have cried for reprisals against the wild beasts who sent them to their death."

St. Just made no reply. It was obviously useless to attempt to argue with this man, whose political aims were as far apart from those of the Scarlet Pimpernel as was the North Pole from the South.

"If any of you have influence over that hot-headed leader of yours," continued de Batz, unabashed by the silence of his friend, "I wish to God you would exert it now."

"In what way?" queried St. Just, smiling in spite of himself at the thought of his or anyone else's control over Blakeney and his plans.

It was de Batz' turn to be silent. He paused for a moment or two, then he asked abruptly:

"Your Scarlet Pimpernel is in Paris now, is he not?"

"I cannot tell you," replied Armand.

"Bah! there is no necessity to fence with me, my friend. The moment I set eyes on you this afternoon I knew that you had not come to Paris alone."

"You are mistaken, my good de Batz," rejoined the young man earnestly; "I came to Paris alone."

"Clever parrying, on my word—but wholly wasted on my unbelieving ears. Did I not note at once that you did not seem over-pleased today when I accosted you?"

"Again, you are mistaken. I was very pleased to meet you, for I had felt singularly lonely all day, and was glad to shake a friend by the hand. What you took for displeasure was only surprise."

"Surprise? Ah, yes! I don't wonder that you were surprised to see me walking unmolested and openly in the streets of Paris—whereas you had heard of me as a dangerous conspirator, eh?—and as a man who has the entire police of his country at his heels—on whose head there is a price—what?"

"I knew that you had made several noble efforts to rescue the unfortunate king and queen from the hands of these brutes."

"All of which efforts were unsuccessful," assented de Batz imperturbably, "every one of them having been either betrayed by some d——d confederate or ferreted out by some astute spy eager for gain. Yes, my friend, I made several efforts to rescue King Louis and Queen Marie Antoinette from the scaffold, and every time I was foiled, and yet here I am, you see, unscathed and free. I walk about the streets boldly and talk to my friends as I meet them."

"You are lucky," said St. Just, not without a tinge of sarcasm.

"I have been prudent," retorted de Batz. "I have taken the trouble to make friends there where I thought I needed them most—the Mammon of unrighteousness, you know-what?"

And he laughed a broad, thick laugh of perfect self-satisfaction.

"Yes, I know," rejoined St. Just, with the tone of sarcasm still more apparent in his voice now. "You have Austrian money at your disposal."

"Any amount," said the other complacently, "and a great deal of it sticks to the grimy fingers of these patriotic makers of revolutions. Thus, do I ensure my own safety. I buy it with the emperor's money, and thus am I able to work for the restoration of the monarchy in France."

Again St. Just was silent. What could he say? Instinctively now, as the fleshy personality of the Gascon Royalist seemed to spread itself out and to fill the tiny box with his ambitious schemes and his far-reaching plans, Armand's thoughts flew back to that other plotter, the man with the pure and simple aims, the man whose slender fingers had never handled alien gold, but were ever there ready stretched out to the helpless and the weak, whilst his thoughts were only of the help that he might give them, but never of his own safety.

De Batz, however, seemed blandly unconscious of any such disparaging thoughts in the mind of his young friend, for he continued quite amiably, even though a note of anxiety seemed to make itself felt now in his smooth voice:

"We advance slowly, but step by step, my good St. Just," he said. "I have not been able to save the monarchy in the person of the king or the queen, but I may yet do it in the person of the *Dauphin*."

"The *Dauphin*," murmured St. Just involuntarily.

That involuntary murmur, scarcely audible, so soft was it, seemed in some way to satisfy de Batz, for the keenness of his gaze relaxed, and his fat fingers ceased their nervous, intermittent tattoo on the ledge of the box.

"Yes! the *Dauphin*," he said, nodding his head as if in answer to his own thoughts, "or rather, let me say, the reigning King of France— Louis XVII, by the grace of God—the most precious life at present upon the whole of this earth."

"You are right there, friend de Batz," assented Armand fervently, "the most precious life, as you say, and one that must be saved at all costs."

"Yes," said de Batz calmly, "but not by your friend the Scarlet Pimpernel."

"Why not?"

Scarce were those two little words out of St. Just's mouth than he repented of them. He bit his lip, and with a dark frown upon his face he turned almost defiantly towards his friend.

But de Batz smiled with easy *bonhomie*.

"Ah, friend Armand," he said, "you were not cut out for diplomacy, nor yet for intrigue. So then," he added more seriously, "that gallant hero, the Scarlet Pimpernel, has hopes of rescuing our young king from the clutches of Simon the cobbler and of the herd of hyenas on the watch for his attenuated little corpse, eh?"

"I did not say that," retorted St. Just sullenly.

"No. But I say it. Nay! nay! do not blame yourself, my over-loyal young friend. Could I, or anyone else, doubt for a moment that sooner or later your romantic hero would turn his attention to the most pathetic sight in the whole of Europe—the child-martyr in the Temple prison? The wonder were to me if the Scarlet Pimpernel ignored our little king altogether for the sake of his subjects. No, no; do not think for a moment that you have betrayed your friend's secret to me. When I met you so luckily today I guessed at once that you were here under the banner of the enigmatical little red flower, and, thus guessing, I even went a step further in my conjecture. The Scarlet Pimpernel is in Paris now in the hope of rescuing Louis XVII from the Temple prison."

"If that is so, you must not only rejoice but should be able to help."

"And yet, my friend, I do neither the one now nor mean to do the other in the future," said de Batz placidly. "I happen to be a Frenchman, you see."

"What has that to do with such a question?"

"Everything; though you, Armand, despite that you are a Frenchman too, do not look through my spectacles. Louis XVII is King of France, my good St. Just; he must owe his freedom and his life to us Frenchmen, and to no one else."

"That is sheer madness, man," retorted Armand. "Would you have the child perish for the sake of your own selfish ideas?"

"You may call them selfish if you will; all patriotism is in a measure selfish. What does the rest of the world care if we are a republic or a monarchy, an oligarchy or hopeless anarchy? We work for ourselves and to please ourselves, and I for one will not brook foreign interference."

"Yet you work with foreign money!"

"That is another matter. I cannot get money in France, so I get it where I can; but I can arrange for the escape of Louis XVII from the Temple Prison, and to us Royalists of France should belong the honour and glory of having saved our king."

For the third time now, St. Just allowed the conversation to drop; he was gazing wide-eyed, almost appalled at this impudent display of well-nigh ferocious selfishness and vanity. De Batz, smiling and complacent, was leaning back in his chair, looking at his young friend with perfect contentment expressed in every line of his pock-marked face and in the very attitude of his well-fed body. It was easy enough now to understand the remarkable immunity which this man was enjoying, despite the many foolhardy plots which he hatched, and which had up to now invariably come to naught.

A regular braggart and empty windbag, he had taken but one good care, and that was of his own skin. Unlike other less fortunate Royalists of France, he neither fought in the country nor braved dangers in town. He played a safer game—crossed the frontier and constituted himself agent of Austria; he succeeded in gaining the emperor's money for the good of the Royalist cause, and for his own most especial benefit.

Even a less astute man of the world than was Armand St. Just would easily have guessed that de Batz' desire to be the only instrument in the rescue of the poor little *Dauphin* from the Temple was not actuated by patriotism, but solely by greed. Obviously, there was a rich reward waiting for him in Vienna the day that he brought Louis XVII safely into Austrian territory; that reward he would miss if a meddlesome Englishman interfered in this affair. Whether in this wrangle he risked the life of the child-king or not mattered to him not at all. It was de Batz who was to get the reward, and whose welfare and prosperity mattered more than the most precious life in Europe.

Chapter 3

The Demon Chance

St. Just would have given much to be back in his lonely squalid lodgings now. Too late did he realise how wise had been the dictum which had warned him against making or renewing friendships in France.

Men had changed with the times. How terribly they had changed!

Personal safety had become a fetish with most—a goal so difficult to attain that it had to be fought for and striven for, even at the expense of humanity and of self-respect.

Selfishness—the mere, cold-blooded insistence for self-advancement—ruled supreme. De Batz, surfeited with foreign money, used it firstly to ensure his own immunity, scattering it to right and left to still the ambition of the Public Prosecutor or to satisfy the greed of innumerable spies.

What was left over he used for the purpose of pitting the blood-thirsty demagogues one against the other, making of the National Assembly a gigantic bear-den, wherein wild beasts could rend one another limb from limb.

In the meanwhile, what cared he—he said it himself—whether hundreds of innocent martyrs perished miserably and uselessly? They were the necessary food whereby the *Révolution* was to be satiated and de Batz' schemes enabled to mature. The most precious life in Europe even was only to be saved if its price went to swell the pockets of de Batz, or to further his future ambitions.

Times had indeed changed an entire nation. St. Just felt as sickened with this self-seeking Royalist as he did with the savage brutes who struck to right or left for their own delectation. He was meditating immediate flight back to his lodgings, with a hope of finding there a word for him from the chief—a word to remind him that men did live nowadays who had other aims besides their own advancement—other ideals besides the deification of self.

The curtain had descended on the first act, and traditionally, as the works of M. de Molière demanded it, the three knocks were heard again without any interval. St. Just rose ready with a pretext for parting with his friend. The curtain was being slowly drawn up on the second act, and disclosed Alceste in wrathful conversation with Célimène.

Alceste's opening speech is short. Whilst the actor spoke it Armand had his back to the stage; with hand outstretched, he was murmuring what he hoped would prove a polite excuse for thus leaving his amiable host while the entertainment had only just begun.

De Batz—vexed and impatient—had not by any means finished with his friend yet. He thought that his specious arguments—delivered with boundless conviction—had made some impression on the mind of the young man. That impression, however, he desired to deepen, and whilst Armand was worrying his brain to find a plausible excuse for going away, de Batz was racking his to find one for keeping him here.

Then it was that the wayward demon Chance intervened. Had St. Just risen but two minutes earlier, had his active mind suggested the desired excuse more readily, who knows what unspeakable sorrow, what heartrending misery, what terrible shame might have been spared both him and those for whom he cared? Those two minutes—did he but know it—decided the whole course of his future life. The excuse hovered on his lips, de Batz reluctantly was preparing to bid him goodbye, when Célimène, speaking common-place words enough in answer to her quarrelsome lover, caused him to drop the hand which he was holding out to his friend and to turn back towards the stage.

It was an exquisite voice that had spoken—a voice mellow and tender, with deep tones in it that betrayed latent power. The voice had caused Armand to look, the lips that spoke forged the first tiny link of that chain which riveted him forever after to the speaker.

It is difficult to say if such a thing really exists as love at first sight. Poets and romancists will have us believe that it does; idealists swear by it as being the only true love worthy of the name.

I do not know if I am prepared to admit their theory with regard to Armand St. Just. Mlle. Lange's exquisite voice certainly had charmed him to the extent of making him forget his mistrust of de Batz and his desire to get away. Mechanically almost he sat down again and leaning both elbows on the edge of the box, he rested his chin in his hand, and listened. The words which the late M. de Molière puts into the mouth of Célimène are trite and flippant enough, yet every time that Mlle. Lange's lips moved Armand watched her, entranced.

There, no doubt, the matter would have ended: a young man fascinated by a pretty woman on the stage—'tis a small matter, and one from which there doth not often spring a weary trail of tragic circumstances. Armand, who had a passion for music, would have worshipped at the shrine of Mlle. Lange's perfect voice until the curtain came down on the last act, had not his friend de Batz seen the keen enchantment which the actress had produced on the young enthusiast.

Now de Batz was a man who never allowed an opportunity to slip by, if that opportunity led towards the furtherance of his own desires. He did not want to lose sight of Armand just yet, and here the good demon Chance had given him an opportunity for obtaining what he wanted.

He waited quietly until the fall of the curtain at the end of Act 2; then, as Armand, with a sigh of delight, leaned back in his chair, and closing his eyes appeared to be living the last half-hour all over again, de Batz remarked with well-assumed indifference:

"Mlle. Lange is a promising young actress. Do you not think so, my friend?"

"She has a perfect voice—it was exquisite melody to the ear," replied Armand. "I was conscious of little else."

"She is a beautiful woman, nevertheless," continued de Batz with a smile. "During the next act, my good St. Just, I would suggest that you open your eyes as well as your ears."

Armand did as he was bidden. The whole appearance of Mlle. Lange seemed in harmony with her voice. She was not very tall, but eminently graceful, with a small, oval face and slender, almost childlike figure, which appeared still more so above the wide hoops and draped panniers of the fashions of Molière's time.

Whether she was beautiful or not the young man hardly knew. Measured by certain standards, she certainly was not so, for her mouth was not small, and her nose anything but classical in outline. But the eyes were brown, and they had that half-veiled look in them—shaded with long lashes that seemed to make a perpetual tender appeal to the masculine heart: the lips, too, were full and moist, and the teeth dazzling white. Yes!—on the whole we might easily say that she was exquisite, even though we did not admit that she was beautiful.

Painter David has made a sketch of her; we have all seen it at the Musée Carnavalet, and all wondered why that charming, if irregular, little face made such an impression of sadness.

There are five acts in *Le Misanthrope*, during which Célimène is almost constantly on the stage. At the end of the fourth act de Batz said casually to his friend:

"I have the honour of personal acquaintanceship with Mlle. Lange. An' you care for an introduction to her, we can go round to the green-room after the play."

Did prudence then whisper, "Desist"? Did loyalty to the leader murmur, "Obey"? It were indeed difficult to say. Armand St. Just was not five-and-twenty, and Mlle. Lange's melodious voice spoke louder than the whisperings of prudence or even than the call of duty.

He thanked de Batz warmly, and during the last half-hour, while the misanthropical lover spurned repentant Célimène, he was conscious of a curious sensation of impatience, a tingling of his nerves, a wild, mad longing to hear those full moist lips pronounce his name, and have those large brown eyes throw their half-veiled look into his own.

CHAPTER 4

Mademoiselle Lange

The green-room was crowded when de Batz and St. Just arrived there after the performance. The older man cast a hasty glance through the open door. The crowd did not suit his purpose, and he dragged his companion hurriedly away from the contemplation of Mlle. Lange, sitting in a far corner of the room, surrounded by an admiring throng, and by innumerable floral tributes offered to her beauty and to her success.

De Batz without a word led the way back towards the stage. Here, by the dim light of tallow candles fixed in sconces against the surrounding walls, the scene-shifters were busy moving drop-scenes, back cloths and wings, and paid no heed to the two men who strolled slowly up and down silently, each wrapped in his own thoughts.

Armand walked with his hands buried in his breeches pockets, his head bent forward on his chest; but every now and again he threw quick, apprehensive glances round him whenever a firm step echoed along the empty stage or a voice rang clearly through the now de-serted theatre.

"Are we wise to wait here?" he asked, speaking to himself rather than to his companion.

He was not anxious about his own safety; but the words of de Batz had impressed themselves upon his mind: "Héron and his spies we have always with us."

From the green-room a separate *foyer* and exit led directly out into the street. Gradually the sound of many voices, the loud laugh-ter and occasional snatches of song which for the past half-hour had proceeded from that part of the house, became more subdued and more rare. One by one the friends of the artists were leaving the theatre, after having paid the usual banal compliments to those whom they favoured or presented the accustomed offering of flowers to the brightest star of the night.

The actors were the first to retire, then the older actresses, the ones who could no longer command a court of admirers round them. They all filed out of the green-room and crossed the stage to where, at the back, a narrow, rickety, wooden stairs led to their so-called dressing-rooms—tiny, dark cubicles, ill-lighted, unventilated, where some half-dozen of the lesser stars tumbled over one another while removing wigs and grease-paint.

238

Armand and de Batz watched this exodus, both with equal impatience. Mlle. Lange was the last to leave the green-room. For some time, since the crowd had become thinner round her, Armand had contrived to catch glimpses of her slight, elegant figure. A short passage led from the stage to the green-room door, which was wide open, and at the corner of this passage the young man had paused from time to time in his walk, gazing with earnest admiration at the dainty outline of the young girl's head, with its wig of powdered curls that seemed scarcely whiter than the creamy brilliance of her skin.

De Batz did not watch Mlle. Lange beyond casting impatient looks in the direction of the crowd that prevented her leaving the green-room. He did watch Armand, however—noted his eager look, his brisk and alert movements, the obvious glances of admiration which he cast in the direction of the young actress, and this seemed to afford him a considerable amount of contentment.

The best part of an hour had gone by since the fall of the curtain before Mlle. Lange finally dismissed her many admirers, and de Batz had the satisfaction of seeing her running down the passage, turning back occasionally in order to bid gay "goodnights" to the loiterers who were loath to part from her. She was a child in all her movements, quite unconscious of self or of her own charms, but frankly delighted with her success. She was still dressed in the ridiculous hoops and panniers pertaining to her part, and the powdered peruke hid the charm of her own hair; the costume gave a certain stilted air to her unaffected personality, which, by this very sense of contrast, was essentially fascinating.

In her arms she held a huge sheaf of sweet-scented narcissi, the spoils of some favoured spot far away in the South. Armand thought that never in his life had he seen anything so winsome or so charming.

Having at last said the positively final *adieu*, Mlle. Lange with a happy little sigh turned to run down the passage.

She came face to face with Armand and gave a sudden little gasp of terror. It was not good these days to come on any loiterer unawares.

But already de Batz had quickly joined his friend, and his smooth, pleasant voice, and podgy, beringed hand extended towards Mlle. Lange, were sufficient to reassure her.

"You were so surrounded in the green-room, *mademoiselle*," he said courteously, "I did not venture to press in among the crowd of your admirers. Yet I had the great wish to present my respectful congratulations in person."

"*Ah! c'est ce cher de Batz!*" exclaimed *mademoiselle* gaily, in that exquisitely rippling voice of hers. "And where in the world do you spring from, my friend?

"Hush-sh-sh!" he whispered, holding her small bemittened hand in his, and putting one finger to his lips with an urgent entreaty for discretion; "not my name, I beg of you, fair one."

"Bah!" she retorted lightly, even though her full lips trembled now as she spoke and belied her very words. "You need have no fear whilst you are in this part of the house. It is an understood thing that the Committee of General Security does not send its spies behind the curtain of a theatre. Why, if all of us actors and actresses were sent to the guillotine there would be no play on the morrow. Artistes are not replaceable in a few hours; those that are in existence must perforce be spared, or the citizens who govern us now would not know where to spend their evenings."

But though she spoke so airily and with her accustomed gaiety, it was easily perceived that even on this childish mind the dangers which beset everyone these days had already imprinted their mark of suspicion and of caution.

"Come into my dressing-room," she said. "I must not tarry here any longer, for they will be putting out the lights. But I have a room to myself, and we can talk there quite agreeably."

She led the way across the stage towards the wooden stairs. Armand, who during this brief colloquy between his friend and the young girl had kept discreetly in the background, felt undecided what to do. But at a peremptory sign from de Batz he, too, turned in the wake of the gay little lady, who ran swiftly up the rickety steps, humming snatches of popular songs the while, and not turning to see if indeed the two men were following her.

She had the sheaf of narcissi still in her arms, and the door of her tiny dressing-room being open, she ran straight in and threw the flowers down in a confused, sweet-scented mass upon the small table that stood at one end of the room, littered with pots and bottles, letters, mirrors, powder-puffs, silk stockings, and cambric handkerchiefs.

Then she turned and faced the two men, a merry look of unalterable gaiety dancing in her eyes.

"Shut the door, *mon ami*," she said to de Batz, "and after that sit down where you can, so long as it is not on my most precious pot of unguent or a box of costliest powder."

While de Batz did as he was told, she turned to Armand and said with a pretty tone of interrogation in her melodious voice:

"*Monsieur?*"

"St. Just, at your service, *mademoiselle*," said Armand, bowing very low in the most approved style obtaining at the English Court.

"St. Just?" she repeated, a look of puzzlement in her brown eyes. "Surely—"

"A kinsman of citizen St. Just, whom no doubt you know, *mademoiselle*," he exclaimed.

"My friend Armand St. Just," interposed de Batz, "is practically a newcomer in Paris. He lives in England habitually."

"In England?" she exclaimed. "Oh! do tell me all about England. I would love to go there. Perhaps I may have to go someday. Oh! do sit down, de Batz," she continued, talking rather volubly, even as a delicate blush heightened the colour in her cheeks under the look of obvious admiration from Armand St. Just's expressive eyes.

She swept a handful of delicate cambric and silk from off a chair, making room for de Batz' portly figure. Then she sat upon the sofa, and with an inviting gesture and a call from the eyes she bade Armand sit down next to her. She leaned back against the cushions, and the table being close by, she stretched out a hand and once more took up the bunch of narcissi, and while she talked to Armand she held the snow-white blooms quite close to her face—so close, in fact, that he could not see her mouth and chin, only her dark eyes shone across at him over the heads of the blossoms.

"Tell me all about England," she reiterated, settling herself down among the cushions like a spoilt child who is about to listen to an oft-told favourite story.

Armand was vexed that de Batz was sitting there. He felt he could have told this dainty little lady quite a good deal about England if only his pompous, fat friend would have had the good sense to go away.

As it was, he felt unusually timid and *gauche*, not quite knowing what to say, a fact which seemed to amuse Mlle. Lange not a little.

"I am very fond of England," he said lamely; "my sister is married to an Englishman, and I myself have taken up my permanent residence there."

"Among the society of *émigrés?*" she queried.

Then, as Armand made no reply, de Batz interposed quickly:

"Oh! you need not fear to admit it, my good Armand; Mademoiselle Lange, has many friends among the *émigrés*—have you not, *mademoiselle?*"

241

"Yes, of course," she replied lightly; "I have friends everywhere. Their political views have nothing to do with me. Artistes, I think, should have naught to do with politics. You see, Citizen St. Just, I never inquired of you what were your views. Your name and kinship would proclaim you a partisan of Citizen Robespierre, yet I find you in the company of M. de Batz; and you tell me that you live in England."

"He is no partisan of Citizen Robespierre," again interposed de Batz; "in fact, *mademoiselle*, I may safely tell you, I think, that my friend has but one ideal on this earth, whom he has set up in a shrine, and whom he worships with all the ardour of a Christian for his God."

"How romantic!" she said, and she looked straight at Armand. "Tell me, *monsieur*, is your ideal a woman or a man?"

His look answered her, even before he boldly spoke the two words: "A woman."

She took a deep draught of sweet, intoxicating scent from the narcissi, and his gaze once more brought blushes to her cheeks. De Batz' good-humoured laugh helped her to hide this unwonted access of confusion.

"That was well turned, friend Armand," he said lightly; "but I assure you, *mademoiselle*, that before I brought him here tonight his ideal was a man."

"A man!" she exclaimed, with a contemptuous little pout. "Who was it?"

"I know no other name for him but that of a small, insignificant flower—the Scarlet Pimpernel," replied de Batz.

"The Scarlet Pimpernel!" she ejaculated, dropping the flowers suddenly, and gazing on Armand with wide, wondering eyes. "And do you know him, *monsieur*?"

He was frowning despite himself, despite the delight which he felt at sitting so close to this charming little lady and feeling that in a measure his presence and his personality interested her. But he felt irritated with de Batz and angered at what he considered the latter's indiscretion. To him the very name of his leader was almost a sacred one; he was one of those enthusiastic devotees who only care to name the idol of their dreams with bated breath, and only in the ears of those who would understand and sympathise.

Again, he felt that if only he could have been alone with *mademoiselle* he could have told her all about the Scarlet Pimpernel, knowing that in her he would find a ready listener, a helping and a loving heart; but as it was he merely replied tamely enough:

"Yes, *mademoiselle*, I do know him."

"You have seen him?" she queried eagerly; "spoken to him?"

"Yes."

"Oh! do tell me all about him. You know quite a number of us in France have the greatest possible admiration for your national hero. We know, of course, that he is an enemy of our government—but, oh! we feel that he is not an enemy of France because of that. We are a nation of heroes, too, *monsieur*," she added with a pretty, proud toss of the head; "we can appreciate bravery and resource, and we love the mystery that surrounds the personality of your Scarlet Pimpernel. But since you know him, *monsieur*, tell me what is he like?"

Armand was smiling again. He was yielding himself up wholly to the charm which emanated from this young girl's entire being, from her gaiety and her unaffectedness, her enthusiasm, and that obvious artistic temperament which caused her to feel every sensation with superlative keenness and thoroughness.

"What is he like?" she insisted.

"That, *mademoiselle*," he replied, "I am not at liberty to tell you."

"Not at liberty to tell me!" she exclaimed; "but *monsieur*, if I command you—"

"At risk of falling forever under the ban of your displeasure, *mademoiselle*, I would still remain silent on that subject."

She gazed on him with obvious astonishment. It was quite an unusual thing for this spoilt darling of an admiring public to be thus openly thwarted in her whims.

"How tiresome and pedantic!" she said, with a shrug of her pretty shoulders and a *moue* of discontent. "And, oh! how ungallant! You have learnt ugly, English ways, *monsieur*, for there, I am told, men hold their womenkind in very scant esteem. There!" she added, turning with a mock air of hopelessness towards de Batz, "am I not a most unlucky woman? For the past two years I have used my best endeavours to catch sight of that interesting Scarlet Pimpernel; here do I meet *monsieur*, who actually knows him (so he says), and he is so ungallant that he even refuses to satisfy the first cravings of my just curiosity."

"Citizen St. Just will tell you nothing now, *mademoiselle*," rejoined de Batz with his good-humoured laugh; "it is my presence, I assure you, which is setting a seal upon his lips. He is, believe me, aching to confide in you, to share in your enthusiasm, and to see your beautiful eyes glowing in response to his ardour when he describes to you the exploits of that prince of heroes. *En tête-à-tête* one day, you will, I know, worm every secret out of my discreet friend Armand."

Mademoiselle made no comment on this—that is to say, no audible comment—but she buried the whole of her face for a few seconds among the flowers, and Armand from amongst those flowers caught sight of a pair of very bright brown eyes which shone on him with a puzzled look.

She said nothing more about the Scarlet Pimpernel or about England just then, but after a while she began talking of more indifferent subjects: the state of the weather, the price of food, the discomforts of her own house, now that the servants had been put on perfect equality with their masters.

Armand soon gathered that the burning questions of the day, the horrors of massacres, the raging turmoil of politics, had not affected her very deeply as yet. She had not troubled her pretty head very much about the social and humanitarian aspect of the present seething revolution. She did not really wish to think about it at all. An artist to her finger-tips, she was spending her young life in earnest work, striving to attain perfection in her art, absorbed in study during the day, and in the expression of what she had learnt in the evenings.

The terrors of the guillotine affected her a little, but somewhat vaguely still. She had not realised that any dangers could assail her whilst she worked for the artistic delectation of the public.

It was not that she did not understand what went on around her, but that her artistic temperament and her environment had kept her aloof from it all. The horrors of the Place de la Révolution made her shudder, but only in the same way as the tragedies of M. Racine or of Sophocles which she had studied caused her to shudder, and she had exactly the same sympathy for poor Queen Marie Antoinette as she had for Mary Stuart and shed as many tears for King Louis as she did for Polyeucte.

Once de Batz mentioned the *Dauphin*, but *mademoiselle* put up her hand quickly and said in a trembling voice, whilst the tears gathered in her eyes:

"Do not speak of the child to me, de Batz. What can I, a lonely, hard-working woman, do to help him? I try not to think of him, for if I did, knowing my own helplessness, I feel that I could hate my countrymen, and speak my bitter hatred of them across the footlights; which would be more than foolish," she added naively, "for it would not help the child, and I should be sent to the guillotine. But oh, sometimes I feel that I would gladly die if only that poor little child-martyr were restored to those who love him and given back once more to joy and happiness. But they would not take my life for his, I am afraid," she concluded, smiling through her tears. "My life is of no value in comparison with his."

Soon after this she dismissed her two visitors. De Batz, well content with the result of this evening's entertainment, wore an urbane, bland smile on his rubicund face. Armand, somewhat serious and not a little in love, made the hand-kiss with which he took his leave last as long as he could.

"You will come and see me again, citizen St. Just?" she asked after that preliminary leave-taking.

"At your service, *mademoiselle*," he replied with alacrity.

"How long do you stay in Paris?"

"I may be called away at any time."

"Well, then, come tomorrow. I shall be free towards four o'clock. Square du Roule. You cannot miss the house. Anyone there will tell you where lives Citizeness Lange."

"At your service, *mademoiselle*," he replied.

The words sounded empty and meaningless, but his eyes, as they took final leave of her, spoke the gratitude and the joy which he felt.

CHAPTER 5

The Temple Prison

It was close on midnight when the two friends finally parted company outside the doors of the theatre. The night air struck with biting keenness against them when they emerged from the stuffy, overheated building, and both wrapped their caped cloaks tightly round their shoulders. Armand—more than ever now—was anxious to rid himself of de Batz. The Gascon's platitudes irritated him beyond the bounds of forbearance, and he wanted to be alone, so that he might think over the events of this night, the chief event being a little lady with an enchanting voice and the most fascinating brown eyes he had ever seen.

Self-reproach, too, was fighting a fairly even fight with the excitement that had been called up by that same pair of brown eyes. Armand for the past four or five hours had acted in direct opposition to the earnest advice given to him by his chief; he had renewed one friendship which had been far better left in oblivion, and he had made an acquaintance which already was leading him along a path that he felt sure his comrade would disapprove. But the path was so profusely strewn with scented narcissi that Armand's sensitive conscience was quickly lulled to rest by the intoxicating fragrance.

Looking neither to right nor left, he made his way very quickly up the Rue Richelieu towards the Montmartre quarter, where he lodged.

De Batz stood and watched him for as long as the dim lights of the street lamps illumined his slim, soberly-clad figure; then he turned on his heel and walked off in the opposite direction.

His florid, pock-marked face wore an air of contentment not altogether unmixed with a kind of spiteful triumph.

"So, my pretty Scarlet Pimpernel," he muttered between his closed lips, "you wish to meddle in my affairs, to have for yourself and your friends the credit and glory of snatching the golden prize from the clutches of these murderous brutes. Well, we shall see! We shall see which is the wiliest—the French ferret or the English fox."

He walked deliberately away from the busy part of the town, turning his back on the river, stepping out briskly straight before him, and swinging his gold-beaded cane as he walked.

The streets which he had to traverse were silent and deserted, save occasionally where a drinking or an eating house had its swing-doors still invitingly open. From these places, as de Batz strode rapidly by, came sounds of loud voices, rendered raucous by outdoor oratory; volleys of oaths hurled irreverently in the midst of impassioned speeches; interruptions from rowdy audiences that vied with the speaker in invectives and blasphemies; wordy war-fares that ended in noisy vituperations; accusations hurled through the air heavy with tobacco smoke and the fumes of cheap wines and of raw spirits.

De Batz took no heed of these as he passed, anxious only that the crowd of eating-house politicians did not, as often was its wont, turn out *pêle-mêle* into the street, and settle its quarrel by the weight of fists. He did not wish to be embroiled in a street fight, which invariably ended in denunciations and arrests, and was glad when presently he had left the purlieus of the Palais Royal behind him and could strike on his left toward the lonely Faubourg du Temple.

From the dim distance far away came at intervals the mournful sound of a roll of muffled drums, half veiled by the intervening hubbub of the busy night life of the great city. It proceeded from the Place de la Révolution, where a company of the National Guard were on night watch round the guillotine. The dull, intermittent notes of the drum came as a reminder to the free people of France that the watchdog of a vengeful revolution was alert night and day, never sleeping, ever wakeful, "beating up game for the guillotine," as the new decree framed today by the government of the people had ordered that it should do.

From time to time now the silence of this lonely street was broken by a sudden cry of terror, followed by the clash of arms, the inevitable volley of oaths, the call for help, the final moan of anguish. They were the ever-recurring brief tragedies which told of denunciations, of domiciliary search, of sudden arrests, of an agonising desire for life and for freedom—for life under these same horrible conditions of brutality and of servitude, for freedom to breathe, if only a day or two longer, this air, polluted by filth and by blood.

De Batz, hardened to these scenes, paid no heed to them. He had heard it so often, that cry in the night, followed by death-like silence; it came from comfortable *bourgeois* houses, from squalid lodgings, or lonely *cul-de-sac*, wherever some hunted quarry was run to earth by the newly-organised spies of the Committee of General Security.

Five and thirty *livres* for every head that falls trunkless into the basket at the foot of the guillotine! Five and thirty pieces of silver, now as then, the price of innocent blood. Every cry in the night, every call for help, meant game for the guillotine, and five and thirty *livres* in the hands of a Judas.

And de Batz walked on unmoved by what he saw and heard, swinging his cane and looking satisfied. Now he struck into the *Place de la Victoire* and looked on one of the open-air camps that had recently been established where men, women, and children were working to provide arms and accoutrements for the Republican Army that was fighting the whole of Europe.

The people of France were up in arms against tyranny; and on the open places of their mighty city they were encamped day and night forging those arms which were destined to make them free, and in the meantime were bending under a yoke of tyranny more complete, more grinding and absolute than any that the most despotic kings had ever dared to inflict.

Here by the light of resin torches, at this late hour of the night, raw lads were being drilled into soldiers, half-naked under the cutting blast of the north wind, their knees shaking under them, their arms and legs blue with cold, their stomachs empty, and their teeth chattering with fear; women were sewing shirts for the great improvised army, with eyes straining to see the stitches by the flickering light of the torches, their throats parched with the continual inhaling of smoke-laden air; even children, with weak, clumsy little fingers, were picking rags to be woven into cloth again—all, all these slaves were working far into the night, tired, hungry, and cold, but working unceasingly, as the country had demanded it: "the people of France in arms against tyranny!" The people of France had to set to work to make arms, to clothe the soldiers, the defenders of the people's liberty.

And from this crowd of people—men, women, and children—there came scarcely a sound, save raucous whispers, a moan or a sigh quickly suppressed. A grim silence reigned in this thickly-peopled camp; only the crackling of the torches broke that silence now and then, or the flapping of canvas in the wintry gale. They worked on sullen, desperate, and starving, with no hope of payment save the miserable rations wrung from poor tradespeople or miserable farmers, as wretched, as oppressed as themselves; no hope of payment, only fear of punishment, for that was ever present.

The people of France in arms against tyranny were not allowed to forget that grim taskmaster with the two great hands stretched upwards, holding the knife which descended mercilessly, indiscriminately on necks that did not bend willingly to the task.

A grim look of gratified desire had spread over de Batz' face as he skirted the open-air camp. Let them toil, let them groan, let them starve! The more these clouts suffer, the more brutal the heel that grinds them down, the sooner will the emperor's money accomplish its work, the sooner will these wretches be clamouring for the monarchy, which would mean a rich reward in de Batz' pockets.

To him everything now was for the best: the tyranny, the brutality, the massacres. He gloated in the holocausts with as much satisfaction as did the most bloodthirsty Jacobin in the Convention. He would with his own hands have wielded the guillotine that worked too slowly for his ends. Let that end justify the means, was his motto. What matter if the future King of France walked up to his throne over steps made of headless corpses and rendered slippery with the blood of martyrs?

The ground beneath de Batz' feet was hard and white with the frost. Overhead the pale, wintry moon looked down serene and placid on this giant city wallowing in an ocean of misery.

There, had been but little snow as yet this year, and the cold was intense. On his right now the Cimetière des SS. Innocents lay peaceful and still beneath the wan light of the moon. A thin covering of snow lay evenly alike on grass mounds and smooth stones. Here and there a broken cross with chipped arms still held pathetically outstretched, as if in a final appeal for human love, bore mute testimony to senseless excesses and spiteful desire for destruction.

But here within the precincts of the dwelling of the eternal Master a solemn silence reigned; only the cold north wind shook the branches of the yew, causing them to send forth a melancholy sigh into the night, and to shed a shower of tiny crystals of snow like the frozen tears of the dead.

And round the precincts of the lonely graveyard, and down narrow streets or open places, the night watchmen went their rounds, lanthorn in hand, and every five minutes their monotonous call rang clearly out in the night:

"Sleep, citizens! everything is quiet and at peace!"

We may take it that de Batz did not philosophise over-much on what went on around him. He had walked swiftly up the Rue St. Martin, then turning sharply to his right he found himself beneath the tall, frowning walls of the Temple prison, the grim guardian of so many secrets, such terrible despair, such unspeakable tragedies.

Here, too, as in the Place de la Révolution, an intermittent roll of muffled drums proclaimed the ever-watchful presence of the National Guard. But with that exception not a sound stirred round the grim and stately edifice; there were no cries, no calls, no appeals around its walls. All the crying and wailing was shut in by the massive stone that told no tales.

Dim and flickering lights shone behind several of the small windows in the *façade* of the huge labyrinthine building. Without any hesitation de Batz turned down the Rue du Temple, and soon found himself in front of the main gates which gave on the courtyard beyond. The sentinel challenged him, but he had the pass-word, and explained that he desired to have speech with Citizen Héron.

With a surly gesture the guard pointed to the heavy bell-pull up against the gate, and de Batz pulled it with all his might. The long clang of the brazen bell echoed and re-echoed round the solid stone walls. *Anon* a tiny judas in the gate was cautiously pushed open, and a peremptory voice once again challenged the midnight intruder.

De Batz, more peremptorily this time, asked for Citizen Héron, with whom he had immediate and important business, and a glimmer of a piece of silver which he held up close to the judas secured him the necessary admittance.

The massive gates slowly swung open on their creaking hinges, and as de Batz passed beneath the archway they closed again behind him.

The *concierge's* lodge was immediately on his left. Again, he was challenged, and again gave the pass-word. But his face was apparently known here, for no serious hindrance to proceed was put in his way.

A man, whose wide, lean frame was but ill-covered by a threadbare coat and ragged breeches, and with soleless shoes on his feet, was told off to direct the *citoyen* to Citizen Héron's rooms. The man walked slowly along with bent knees and arched spine and shuffled his feet as he walked; the bunch of keys which he carried rattled ominously in his long, grimy hands; the passages were badly lighted, and he also carried a lanthorn to guide himself on the way.

Closely followed by de Batz, he soon turned into the central corridor, which is open to the sky above, and was spectrally alight now with flag-stones and walls gleaming beneath the silvery sheen of the moon and throwing back the fantastic elongated shadows of the two men as they walked.

On the left, heavily barred windows gave on the corridor, as did here and there the massive oaken doors, with their gigantic hinges and bolts, on the steps of which squatted groups of soldiers wrapped in their cloaks, with wild, suspicious eyes beneath their capotes, peering at the midnight visitor as he passed.

There was no thought of silence here. The very walls seemed alive with sounds, groans and tears, loud wails and murmured prayers; they exuded from the stones and trembled on the frost-laden air.

Occasionally at one of the windows a pair of white hands would appear, grasping the heavy iron bar, trying to shake it in its socket, and mayhap, above the hands, the dim vision of a haggard face, a man's or a woman's, trying to get a glimpse of the outside world, a final look at the sky, before the last journey to the place of death tomorrow. Then one of the soldiers, with a loud, angry oath, would struggle to his feet, and with the butt-end of his gun strike at the thin, wan fingers till their hold on the iron bar relaxed, and the pallid face beyond would sink back into the darkness with a desperate cry of pain.

A quick, impatient sigh escaped de Batz' lips. He had skirted the wide courtyard in the wake of his guide, and from where he was he could see the great central tower, with its tiny windows lighted from within, the grim walls behind which the descendant of the world's conquerors, the bearer of the proudest name in Europe, and wearer of its most ancient crown, had spent the last days of his brilliant life in abject shame, sorrow, and degradation.

The memory had swiftly surged up before him of that night when he all but rescued King Louis and his family from this same miserable prison: the guard had been bribed, the keeper corrupted, everything had been prepared, save the reckoning with the one irresponsible factor—chance!

He had failed then and had tried again, and again had failed; a fortune had been his reward if he had succeeded. He had failed, but even now, when his footsteps echoed along the flagged courtyard, over which an unfortunate king and queen had walked on their way to their last ignominious Calvary, he hugged himself with the satisfying thought that where he had failed at least no one else had succeeded.

Whether that meddlesome English adventurer, who called himself the Scarlet Pimpernel, had planned the rescue of King Louis or of Queen Marie Antoinette at any time or not—that he did not know; but on one point at least he was more than ever determined, and that was that no power on earth should snatch from him the golden prize offered by Austria for the rescue of the little *Dauphin*.

"I would sooner see the child perish, if I cannot save him myself," was the burning thought in this man's tortuous brain. "And let that accursed Englishman look to himself and to his d——d confederates," he added, muttering a fierce oath beneath his breath.

A winding, narrow stone stair, another length or two of corridor, and his guide's shuffling footsteps paused beside a low iron-studded door let into the solid stone. De Batz dismissed his ill-clothed guide and pulled the iron bell-handle which hung beside the door.

The bell gave forth a dull and broken clang, which seemed like an echo of the wails of sorrow that peopled the huge building with their weird and monotonous sounds.

De Batz—a thoroughly unimaginative person—waited patiently beside the door until it was opened from within, and he was confronted by a tall stooping figure, wearing a greasy coat of snuff-brown cloth, and holding high above his head a lanthorn that threw its feeble light on de Batz' jovial face and form.

"It is even I, Citizen Héron," he said, breaking in swiftly on the other's ejaculation of astonishment, which threatened to send his name echoing the whole length of corridors and passages, until round every corner of the labyrinthine house of sorrow the murmur would be borne on the wings of the cold night breeze: "Citizen Héron is in parley with *ci-devant* Baron de Batz!"

A fact which would have been equally unpleasant for both these worthies.

"Enter!" said Héron curtly.

He banged the heavy door to behind his visitor; and de Batz, who seemed to know his way about the place, walked straight across the narrow landing to where a smaller door stood invitingly open.

He stepped boldly in, the while Citizen Héron put the lanthorn down on the floor of the *couloir*, and then followed his nocturnal visitor into the room.

CHAPTER 6

The Committee's Agent

It was a narrow, ill-ventilated place, with but one barred window that gave on the courtyard. An evil-smelling lamp hung by a chain from the grimy ceiling, and in a corner of the room a tiny iron stove shed more unpleasant vapour than warm glow around.

There was but little furniture: two or three chairs, a table which was littered with papers, and a corner-cupboard—the open doors of which revealed a miscellaneous collection—bundles of papers, a tin saucepan, a piece of cold sausage, and a couple of pistols. The fumes of stale tobacco-smoke hovered in the air and mingled most unpleasantly with those of the lamp above, and of the mildew that penetrated through the walls just below the roof.

Héron pointed to one of the chairs, and then sat down on the other, close to the table, on which he rested his elbow. He picked up a short-stemmed pipe, which he had evidently laid aside at the sound of the bell, and having taken several deliberate long-drawn puffs from it, he said abruptly:

"Well, what is it now?"

In the meanwhile, de Batz had made himself as much at home in this uncomfortable room as he possibly could. He had deposited his hat and cloak on one rickety rush-bottomed chair and drawn another close to the fire. He sat down with one leg crossed over the other, his podgy be-ringed hand wandering with loving gentleness down the length of his shapely calf.

He was nothing if not complacent, and his complacency seemed highly to irritate his friend Héron.

"Well, what is it?" reiterated the latter, drawing his visitor's attention roughly to himself by banging his fist on the table. "Out with it! What do you want? Why have you come at this hour of the night to compromise me, I suppose—bring your own d—d neck and mine into the same noose—what?"

"Easy, easy, my friend," responded de Batz imperturbably; "waste not so much time in idle talk. Why do I usually come to see you? Surely you have had no cause to complain hitherto of the unprofitableness of my visits to you?"

"They will have to be still more profitable to me in the future," growled the other across the table. "I have more power now."

"I know you have," said de Batz suavely. "The new decree? What? You may denounce whom you please, search whom you please, arrest whom you please, and send whom you please to the Supreme Tribunal without giving them the slightest chance of escape."

"Is it in order to tell me all this that you have come to see me at this hour of the night?" queried Héron with a sneer.

"No; I came at this hour of the night because I surmised that in the future you and your hell-hounds would be so busy all day 'beating up game for the guillotine' that the only time you would have at the disposal of your friends would be the late hours of the night. I saw you at the theatre a couple of hours ago, friend Héron; I didn't think to find you yet abed."

"Well, what do you want?"

"Rather," retorted de Batz blandly, "shall we say, what do *you* want, Citizen Héron?"

"For what?

"For my continued immunity at the hands of yourself and your pack?"

Héron pushed his chair brusquely aside and strode across the narrow room deliberately facing the portly figure of de Batz, who with head slightly inclined on one side, his small eyes narrowed till they appeared mere slits in his pockmarked face, was steadily and quite placidly contemplating this inhuman monster who had this very day been given uncontrolled power over hundreds of thousands of human lives.

Héron was one of those tall men who look mean in spite of their height. His head was small and narrow, and his hair, which was sparse and lank, fell in untidy strands across his forehead. He stooped slightly from the neck, and his chest, though wide, was hollow between the shoulders. But his legs were big and bony, slightly bent at the knees, like those of an ill-conditioned horse.

The face was thin and the cheeks sunken; the eyes, very large and prominent, had a look in them of cold and ferocious cruelty, a look which contrasted strangely with the weakness and petty greed apparent in the mouth, which was flabby, with full, very red lips, and chin that sloped away to the long thin neck.

Even at this moment as he gazed on de Batz the greed and the cruelty in him were fighting one of those battles the issue of which is always uncertain in men of his stamp.

"I don't know," he said slowly, "that I am prepared to treat with you any longer. You are an intolerable bit of vermin that has annoyed the Committee of General Security for over two years now. It would be excessively pleasant to crush you once and for all, as one would a buzzing fly."

"Pleasant, perhaps, but immeasurably foolish," rejoined de Batz coolly; "you would only get thirty-five *livres* for my head, and I offer you ten times that amount for the self-same commodity."

"I know, I know; but the whole thing has become too dangerous."

"Why? I am very modest. I don't ask a great deal. Let your hounds keep off my scent."

"You have too many d—d confederates."

"Oh! Never mind about the others. I am not bargaining about them. Let them look after themselves."

"Every time we get a batch of them, one or the other denounces you."

"Under torture, I know," rejoined de Batz placidly, holding his podgy hands to the warm glow of the fire. "For you have started torture in your house of Justice now, eh, friend Héron? You and your friend the Public Prosecutor have gone the whole gamut of devilry—eh?"

"What's that to you?" retorted the other gruffly.

"Oh, nothing, nothing! I was even proposing to pay you three thousand five hundred *livres* for the privilege of taking no further interest in what goes on inside this prison!"

"Three thousand five hundred!" ejaculated Héron involuntarily, and this time even his eyes lost their cruelty; they joined issue with the mouth in an expression of hungering avarice.

"Two little zeros added to the thirty-five, which is all you would get for handing me over to your accursed Tribunal," said de Batz, and, as if thoughtlessly, his hand wandered to the inner pocket of his coat, and a slight rustle as of thin crisp paper brought drops of moisture to the lips of Héron.

"Leave me alone for three weeks and the money is yours," concluded de Batz pleasantly.

There was silence in the room now. Through the narrow, barred window, the steely rays of the moon fought with the dim yellow light of the oil lamp, and lit up the pale face of the Committee's agent with its lines of cruelty in sharp conflict with those of greed.

"Well! is it a bargain?" asked de Batz at last in his usual smooth, oily voice, as he half drew from out his pocket that tempting little bundle of crisp printed paper. "You have only to give me the usual receipt for the money and it is yours."

Héron gave a vicious snarl.

"It is dangerous, I tell you. That receipt, if it falls into some cursed meddler's hands, would send me straight to the guillotine."

"The receipt could only fall into alien hands," rejoined de Batz blandly, "if I happened to be arrested, and even in that case they could but fall into those of the chief agent of the Committee of General Security, and he hath name Héron. You must take some risks, my friend. I take them too. We are each in the other's hands. The bargain is quite fair."

For a moment or two longer Héron appeared to be hesitating whilst de Batz watched him with keen intentness. He had no doubt himself as to the issue. He had tried most of these patriots in his own golden crucible, and had weighed their patriotism against Austrian money, and had never found the latter wanting.

He had not been here tonight if he were not quite sure. This inveterate conspirator in the Royalist cause never took personal risks. He looked on Héron now, smiling to himself the while with perfect satisfaction.

"Very well," said the Committee's agent with sudden decision, "I'll take the money. But on one condition."

"What is it?"

"That you leave little *Capet* alone."

"The *Dauphin!*"

"Call him what you like," said Héron, taking a step nearer to de Batz, and from his great height glowering down in fierce hatred and rage upon his accomplice; "call the young devil what you like, but leave us to deal with him."

"To kill him, you mean? Well, how can I prevent it, my friend?"

"You and your like are always plotting to get him out of here. I won't have it. I tell you I won't have it. If the brat disappears I am a dead man. Robespierre and his gang have told me as much. So, you leave him alone, or I'll not raise a finger to help you, but will lay my own hands on your accursed neck."

He looked so ferocious and so merciless then, that despite himself, the selfish adventurer, the careless self-seeking intriguer, shuddered with a quick wave of unreasoning terror. He turned away from Héron's piercing gaze, the gaze of a hyena whose prey is being snatched from beneath its nails. For a moment he stared thoughtfully into the fire.

He heard the other man's heavy footsteps cross and re-cross the narrow room and was conscious of the long, curved shadow creeping up the mildewed wall or retreating down upon the carpetless floor.

Suddenly, without any warning he felt a grip upon his shoulder. He gave a start and almost uttered a cry of alarm which caused Héron to laugh. The Committee's agent was vastly amused at his friend's obvious access of fear. There was nothing that he liked better than that he should inspire dread in the hearts of all those with whom he came in contact.

"I am just going on my usual nocturnal round," he said abruptly. "Come with me, Citizen de Batz."

A certain grim humour was apparent in his face as he proffered this invitation, which sounded like a rough command. As de Batz seemed to hesitate he nodded peremptorily to him to follow. Already he had gone into the hall and picked up his lanthorn. From beneath his waistcoat he drew forth a bunch of keys, which he rattled impatiently, calling to his friend to come.

"Come, citizen," he said roughly. "I wish to show you the one treasure in this house which your d—d fingers must not touch."

Mechanically de Batz rose at last. He tried to be master of the terror which was invading his very bones. He would not own to himself even that he was afraid, and almost audibly he kept murmuring to himself that he had no cause for fear.

Héron would never touch him. The spy's avarice, his greed of money were a perfect safeguard for any man who had the control of millions, and Héron knew, of course, that he could make of this inveterate plotter a comfortable source of revenue for himself. Three weeks would soon be over, and fresh bargains could be made time and again, while de Batz was alive and free.

Héron was still waiting at the door, even whilst de Batz wondered what this nocturnal visitation would reveal to him of atrocity and of outrage. He made a final effort to master his nervousness, wrapped his cloak tightly around him, and followed his host out of the room.

CHAPTER 7
The Most Precious Life in Europe

Once more he was being led through the interminable corridors of the gigantic building. Once more from the narrow, barred windows close by him he heard the heart-breaking sighs, the moans, the curses which spoke of tragedies that he could only guess.

Héron was walking on ahead of him, preceding him by some fifty metres or so, his long legs covering the distances more rapidly than de Batz could follow them. The latter knew his way well about the old prison. Few men in Paris possessed that accurate knowledge of its intricate passages and its network of cells and halls which de Batz had acquired after close and persevering study.

He himself could have led Héron to the doors of the tower where the little *Dauphin* was being kept imprisoned, but unfortunately, he did not possess the keys that would open all the doors which led to it. There were sentinels at every gate, groups of soldiers at each end of every corridor, the great—now empty—courtyards, thronged with prisoners in the daytime, were alive with soldiery even now. Some walked up and down with fixed bayonet on shoulder, others sat in groups on the stone copings or squatted on the ground, smoking or playing cards, but all of them were alert and watchful.

Héron was recognised everywhere the moment he appeared, and though in these days of equality no one presented arms, nevertheless every guard stood aside to let him pass, or when necessary opened a gate for the powerful chief agent of the Committee of General Security.

Indeed, de Batz had no keys such as these to open the way for him to the presence of the martyred little king.

Thus, the two men wended their way on in silence, one preceding the other. De Batz walked leisurely, thought-fully, taking stock of everything he saw—the gates, the barriers, the positions of sentinels and warders, of everything in fact that might prove a help or a hindrance presently, when the great enterprise would be hazarded. At last—still in the wake of Héron—he found himself once more behind the main entrance gate, underneath the archway on which gave the *guichet* of the *concierge*.

Here, too, there seemed to be an unnecessary number of soldiers: two were doing sentinel outside the *guichet*, but there were others in a file against the wall.

Héron rapped with his keys against the door of the *concierge's* lodge, then, as it was not immediately opened from within, he pushed it open with his foot.

"The *concierge?*" he queried peremptorily.

From a corner of the small panelled room there came a grunt and a reply:

"Gone to bed, *quoi!*"

The man who previously had guided de Batz to Héron's door slowly struggled to his feet. He had been squatting somewhere in the gloom and had been roused by Héron's rough command. He slouched forward now still carrying a boot in one hand and a blacking brush in the other.

"Take this lanthorn, then," said the chief agent with a snarl directed at the sleeping *concierge*, "and come along. Why are you still here?" he added, as if in after-thought.

"The citizen *concierge* was not satisfied with the way I had done his boots," muttered the man, with an evil leer as he spat contemptuously on the floor; "an *aristo, quoi?* A hell of a place this—twenty cells to sweep out every day—and boots to clean for every *aristo* of a *concierge* or warder who demands it—Is that work for a free born patriot, I ask?"

"Well, if you are not satisfied, Citoyen Dupont," retorted Héron dryly, "you may go when you like, you know there are plenty of others ready to do your work—"

"Nineteen hours a day, and nineteen *sous* by way of payment—I have had fourteen days of this convict work—"

He continued to mutter under his breath, whilst Héron, paying no further heed to him, turned abruptly towards a group of soldiers stationed outside.

"*En avant*, corporal!" he said; "bring four men with you—we go up to the tower."

The small procession was formed. On ahead the lanthorn-bearer, with arched spine and shaking knees, dragging shuffling footsteps along the corridor, then the corporal with two of his soldiers, then Héron closely followed by de Batz, and finally two more soldiers bringing up the rear.

Héron had given the bunch of keys to the man Dupont. The latter, on ahead, holding the lanthorn aloft, opened one gate after another. At each gate he waited for the little procession to file through, then he re-locked the gate and passed on.

Up two or three flights of winding stairs set in the solid stone, and the final heavy door was reached.

De Batz was meditating. Héron's precautions for the safe-guarding of the most precious life in Europe were more complete than he had anticipated. What lavish liberality would be required! what superhuman ingenuity and boundless courage in order to break down all the barriers that had been set up round that young life that flickered inside this grim tower!

Of these three requisites the corpulent, complacent intriguer possessed only the first in a considerable degree. He could be exceedingly liberal with the foreign money which he had at his disposal. As for courage and ingenuity, he believed that he possessed both, but these qualities had not served him in very good stead in the attempts which he had made at different times to rescue the unfortunate members of the Royal Family from prison. His overwhelming egotism would not admit for a moment that in ingenuity and pluck the Scarlet Pimpernel and his English followers could outdo him, but he did wish to make quite sure that they would not interfere with him in the highly remunerative work of saving the *Dauphin*.

Héron's impatient call roused him from these meditations. The little party had come to a halt outside a massive iron-studded door.

At a sign from the chief agent the soldiers stood at attention. He then called de Batz and the lanthorn-bearer to him.

He took a key from his breeches pocket, and with his own hand unlocked the massive door. He curtly ordered the lanthorn-bearer and de Batz to go through, then he himself went in, and finally once more re-locked the door behind him, the soldiers remaining on guard on the landing outside.

Now the three men were standing in a square antechamber, dank and dark, devoid of furniture save for a large cupboard that filled the whole of one wall; the others, mildewed and stained, were covered with a greyish paper, which here and there hung away in strips.

Héron crossed this ante-chamber, and with his knuckles rapped against a small door opposite.

"*Hola!*" he shouted, "Simon, *mon vieux, tu es là?*"

From the inner room came the sound of voices, a man's and a woman's, and now, as if in response to Héron's call, the shrill tones of a child. There was some shuffling, too, of footsteps, and some pushing about of furniture, then the door was opened, and a gruff voice invited the belated visitors to enter.

The atmosphere in this further room was so thick that at first de Batz was only conscious of the evil smells that pervaded it; smells which were made up of the fumes of tobacco, of burning coke, of a smoky lamp, and of stale food, and mingling through it all the pungent odour of raw spirits.

Héron had stepped briskly in, closely followed by de Batz. The man Dupont with a mutter of satisfaction put down his lanthorn and curled himself up in a corner of the antechamber. His interest in the spectacle so favoured by Citizen Héron had apparently been exhausted by constant repetition.

De Batz looked round him with keen curiosity with which disgust was ready enough to mingle.

The room itself might have been a large one; it was almost impossible to judge of its size, so crammed was it with heavy and light furniture of every conceivable shape and type. There was a monumental wooden bedstead in one corner, a huge sofa covered in black horsehair in another. A large table stood in the centre of the room, and there were at least four capacious armchairs round it. There were wardrobes and cabinets, a diminutive washstand and a huge pier-glass, there were innumerable boxes and packing-cases, cane-bottomed chairs and what-nots everywhere. The place looked like a depot for second-hand furniture.

In the midst of all the litter de Batz at last became conscious of two people who stood staring at him and at Héron. He saw a man before him, somewhat fleshy of build, with smooth, mouse-coloured hair brushed away from a central parting and ending in a heavy curl above each ear; the eyes were wide open and pale in colour, the lips unusually thick and with a marked downward droop. Close beside him stood a youngish-looking woman, whose unwieldy bulk, however, and pallid skin revealed the sedentary life and the ravages of ill-health.

Both appeared to regard Héron with a certain amount of awe, and de Batz with a vast measure of curiosity.

Suddenly the woman stood aside, and in the far corner of the room there was displayed to the Gascon Royalist's cold, calculating gaze the pathetic figure of the uncrowned King of France.

"How is it Capet is not yet in bed?" queried Héron as soon as he caught sight of the child.

"He wouldn't say his prayers this evening," replied Simon with a coarse laugh, "and wouldn't drink his medicine. Bah!" he added with a snarl, "this is a place for dogs and not for human folk."

"If you are not satisfied, *mon vieux*," retorted Héron curtly, "you can send in your resignation when you like. There are plenty who will be glad of the place."

The ex-cobbler gave another surly growl and expectorated on the floor in the direction where stood the child.

"Little vermin," he said, "he is more trouble than man or woman can bear."

The boy in the meanwhile seemed to take but little notice of the vulgar insults put upon him by his guardian. He stood, a quaint, impassive little figure, more interested apparently in de Batz, who was a stranger to him, than in the three others whom he knew. De Batz noted that the child looked well nourished, and that he was warmly clad in a rough woollen shirt and cloth breeches, with coarse grey stockings and thick shoes; but he also saw that the clothes were indescribably filthy, as were the child's hands and face. The golden curls, among which a young and queenly mother had once loved to pass her slender perfumed fingers, now hung bedraggled, greasy, and lank round the little face, from the lines of which every trace of dignity and of simplicity had long since been erased.

There was no look of the martyr about this child now, even though, mayhap, his small back had often smarted under his vulgar tutor's rough blows; rather did the pale young face wear the air of sullen indifference, and an abject desire to please, which would have appeared heart-breaking to any spectator less self-seeking and egotistic than was this Gascon conspirator.

Madame Simon had called him to her while her man and the Citizen Héron were talking, and the child went readily enough, without any sign of fear. She took the corner of her coarse dirty apron in her hand, and wiped the boy's mouth and face with it.

"I can't keep him clean," she said with an apologetic shrug of the shoulders and a look at de Batz. "There now," she added, speaking once more to the child, "drink like a good boy, and say your lesson to please *maman*, and then you shall go to bed."

She took a glass from the table, which was filled with a clear liquid that de Batz at first took to be water and held it to the boy's lips. He turned his head away and began to whimper.

"Is the medicine very nasty?" queried de Batz.

"*Mon Dieu!* but no, citizen," exclaimed the woman, "it is good strong *eau de vie,* the best that can be procured. Capet likes it really— don't you, Capet? It makes you happy and cheerful, and sleep well of nights. Why, you had a glassful yesterday and enjoyed it. Take it now," she added in a quick whisper, seeing that Simon and Héron were in close conversation together; "you know it makes papa angry if you don't have at least half a glass now and then."

The child wavered for a moment longer, making a quaint little grimace of distaste. But at last he seemed to make up his mind that it was wisest to yield over so small a matter, and he took the glass from Madame Simon.

And thus, did de Batz see the descendant of St. Louis quaffing a glass of raw spirit at the bidding of a rough cobbler's wife, whom he called by the fond and foolish name sacred to childhood, *maman!*

Selfish egoist though he was, de Batz turned away in loathing.

Simon had watched the little scene with obvious satisfaction. He chuckled audibly when the child drank the spirit, and called Héron's attention to him, whilst a look of triumph lit up his wide, pale eyes.

"And now, *mon petit*," he said jovially, "let the citizen hear you say your prayers!"

He winked toward de Batz, evidently anticipating a good deal of enjoyment for the visitor from what was coming. From a heap of litter in a corner of the room he fetched out a greasy red bonnet adorned with a tricolour cockade, and a soiled and tattered flag, which had once been white, and had golden *fleur-de-lys* embroidered upon it.

The cap he set on the child's head, and the flag he threw upon the floor.

"Now, Capet—your prayers!" he said with another chuckle of amusement.

All his movements were rough, and his speech almost ostenta-tiously coarse. He banged against the furniture as he moved about the room, kicking a footstool out of the way or knocking over a chair. De Batz instinctively thought of the perfumed stillness of the rooms at Versailles, of the army of elegant high-born ladies who had ministered to the wants of this child, who stood there now before him, a cap on his yellow hair, and his shoulder held up to his ear with that gesture of careless indifference peculiar to children when they are sullen or uncared for.

Obediently, quite mechanically it seemed, the boy trod on the flag which Henri IV had borne before him at Ivry, and *le Roi Soleil* had flaunted in the face of the armies of Europe. The son of the Bourbons was spitting on their flag and wiping his shoes upon its tattered folds. With shrill cracked voice he sang the Carmagnole, "*Ça ira! Ça ira! les aristos à la lanterne!*" until de Batz himself felt inclined to stop his ears and to rush from the place in horror.

Louis XVII, whom the hearts of many had proclaimed King of France by the grace of God, the child of the Bourbons, the eldest son of the Church, was stepping a vulgar dance over the flag of St. Louis, which he had been taught to defile. His pale cheeks glowed as he danced, his eyes shone with the unnatural light kindled in them by the intoxicating liquor; with one slender hand he waved the red cap with the tricolour cockade and shouted "*Vive la République!*"

Madame Simon was clapping her hands, looking on the child with obvious pride, and a kind of rough maternal affection. Simon was gazing on Héron for approval, and the latter nodded his head, murmuring words of encouragement and of praise.

"Thy catechism now, Capet—thy catechism," shouted Simon in a hoarse voice.

The boy stood at attention, cap on head, hands on his hips, legs wide apart, and feet firmly planted on the *fleur-de-lys*, the glory of his forefathers.

"Thy name?" queried Simon.

"Louis Capet," replied the child in a clear, high-pitched voice.

"What art thou?"

"A citizen of the Republic of France."

"What was thy father?"

"Louis Capet, *ci-devant* king, a tyrant who perished by the will of the people!"

"What was thy mother?"

"A ——"

De Batz involuntarily uttered a cry of horror. Whatever the man's private character was, he had been born a gentleman, and his every instinct revolted against what he saw and heard. The scene had positively sickened him. He turned precipitately towards the door.

"How now, citizen?" queried the Committee's agent with a sneer. "Are you not satisfied with what you see?"

"Mayhap the citizen would like to see Capet sitting in a golden chair," interposed Simon the cobbler with a sneer, "and me and my wife kneeling and kissing his hand—what?"

"'Tis the heat of the room," stammered de Batz, who was fumbling with the lock of the door; "my head began to swim."

"Spit on their accursed flag, then, like a good patriot, like Capet," retorted Simon gruffly. "Here, Capet, my son," he added, pulling the

263

boy by the arm with a rough gesture, "get thee to bed; thou art quite drunk enough to satisfy any good Republican."

By way of a caress he tweaked the boy's ear and gave him a prod in the back with his bent knee. He was not wilfully unkind, for just now he was not angry with the lad; rather was he vastly amused with the effect Capet's prayer and Capet's recital of his catechism had had on the visitor.

As to the lad, the intensity of excitement in him was immediately followed by an overwhelming desire for sleep. Without any preliminary of undressing or of washing, he tumbled, just as he was, on to the sofa. Madame Simon, with quite pleasing solicitude, arranged a pillow under his head, and the very next moment the child was fast asleep.

"'Tis well, Citoyen Simon," said Héron in his turn, going towards the door. "I'll report favourably on you to the Committee of Public Security. As for the *citoyenne*, she had best be more careful," he added, turning to the woman Simon with a snarl on his evil face. "There was no cause to arrange a pillow under the head of that vermin's spawn. Many good patriots have no pillows to put under their heads. Take that pillow away; and I don't like the shoes on the brat's feet; sabots are quite good enough."

Citoyenne Simon made no reply. Some sort of retort had apparently hovered on her lips, but had been checked, even before it was uttered, by a peremptory look from her husband. Simon the cobbler, snarling in speech but obsequious in manner, prepared to accompany the citizen agent to the door.

De Batz was taking a last look at the sleeping child; the uncrowned King of France was wrapped in a drunken sleep, with the last spoken insult upon his dead mother still hovering on his childish lips.

Chapter 8

Arcades Ambo

"That is the way we conduct our affairs, citizen," said Héron gruffly, as he once more led his guest back into his office.

It was his turn to be complacent now. De Batz, for once in his life cowed by what he had seen, still wore a look of horror and disgust upon his florid face.

"What devils you all are!" he said at last.

"We are good patriots," retorted Héron, "and the tyrant's spawn leads but the life that hundreds of thousands of children led whilst his father oppressed the people. Nay! what am I saying? He leads a far better, far happier life. He gets plenty to eat and plenty of warm clothes. Thousands of innocent children, who have not the crimes of a despot father upon their conscience, have to starve whilst he grows fat."

The leer in his face was so evil that once more de Batz felt that eerie feeling of terror creeping into his bones. Here were cruelty and bloodthirsty ferocity personified to their utmost extent. At thought of the Bourbons, or of all those whom he considered had been in the past the oppressors of the people, Héron was nothing but a wild and ravenous beast, hungering for revenge, longing to bury his talons and his fangs into the body of those whose heels had once pressed on his own neck.

And de Batz knew that even with millions or countless money at his command he could not purchase from this carnivorous brute the life and liberty of the son of King Louis. No amount of bribery would accomplish that; it would have to be ingenuity pitted against animal force, the wiliness of the fox against the power of the wolf.

Even now Héron was darting savagely suspicious looks upon him.

"I shall get rid of the Simons," he said; "there's something in that woman's face which I don't trust. They shall go within the next few hours, or as soon as I can lay my hands upon a better patriot than that mealy-mouthed cobbler. And it will be better not to have a woman about the place. Let me see—today is Thursday, or else Friday morning. By Sunday I'll get those Simons out of the place. Methought I saw you ogling that woman," he added, bringing his bony fist crashing down on the table so that papers, pen, and inkhorn rattled loudly; "and if I thought that you—"

De Batz thought it well at this point to finger once more nonchalantly the bundle of crisp paper in the pocket of his coat.

"Only on that one condition," reiterated Héron in a hoarse voice; "if you try to get at Capet, I'll drag you to the Tribunal with my own hands."

"Always presuming that you can get me, my friend," murmured de Batz, who was gradually regaining his accustomed composure.

Already his active mind was busily at work. One or two things which he had noted in connection with his visit to the *Dauphin's* prison had struck him as possibly useful in his schemes. But he was disappointed that Héron was getting rid of the Simons. The woman might have been very useful and more easily got at than a man. The avarice of the French *bourgeoise* would have proved a promising factor.

But this, of course, would now be out of the question. At the same time, it was not because Héron raved and stormed and uttered cries like a hyena that he, de Batz, meant to give up an enterprise which, if successful, would place millions into his own pocket.

As for that meddling Englishman, the Scarlet Pimpernel, and his crack-brained followers, they must be effectually swept out of the way first of all. De Batz felt that they were the real, the most likely hindrance to his schemes. He himself would have to go very cautiously to work, since apparently Héron would not allow him to purchase immunity for himself in that one matter, and whilst he was laying his plans with necessary deliberation so as to ensure his own safety, that accursed Scarlet Pimpernel would mayhap snatch the golden prize from the Temple prison right under his very nose.

When he thought of that the Gascon Royalist felt just as vindictive as did the chief agent of the Committee of General Security.

While these thoughts were coursing through de Batz' head, Héron had been indulging in a volley of vituperation.

"If that little vermin escapes," he said, "my life will not be worth an hour's purchase. In twenty-four hours I am a dead man, thrown to the guillotine like those dogs of aristocrats! You say I am a night-bird, citizen. I tell you that I do not sleep night or day thinking of that brat and the means to keep him safely under my hand. I have never trusted those Simons—"

"Not trusted them!" exclaimed de Batz; "surely you could not find anywhere more inhuman monsters!"

"Inhuman monsters?" snarled Héron. "Bah! they don't do their business thoroughly; we want the tyrant's spawn to become a true Republican and a patriot—aye! to make of him such a one that even if you and your cursed confederates got him by some hellish chance, he would be no use to you as a king, a tyrant to set above the people, to set up in your Versailles, your Louvre, to eat off golden plates and wear satin clothes. You have seen the brat! By the time he is a man he should forget how to eat save with his fingers and get roaring drunk every night. That's what we want!—to make him so that he shall be no use to you, even if you did get him away; but you shall not! You shall not, not if I have to strangle him with my own hands."

He picked up his short-stemmed pipe and pulled savagely at it for a while. De Batz was meditating.

"My friend," he said after a little while, "you are agitating yourself quite unnecessarily, and gravely jeopardising your prospects of getting a comfortable little income through keeping your fingers off my person. Who said I wanted to meddle with the child?"

"You had best not," growled Héron.

"Exactly. You have said that before. But do you not think that you would be far wiser, instead of directing your undivided attention to my unworthy self, to turn your thoughts a little to one whom, believe me, you have far greater cause to fear?"

"Who is that?"

"The Englishman."

"You mean the man they call the Scarlet Pimpernel?"

"Himself. Have you not suffered from his activity, friend Héron? I fancy that Citizen Chauvelin and citizen Collot would have quite a tale to tell about him."

"They ought both to have been guillotined for that blunder last autumn at Boulogne."

"Take care that the same accusation be not laid at your door this year, my friend," commented de Batz placidly.

"Bah!"

"The Scarlet Pimpernel is in Paris even now."

"The devil he is!"

"And on what errand, think you?"

There was a moment's silence, and then de Batz continued with slow and dramatic emphasis:

"That of rescuing your most precious prisoner from the Temple."

"How do you know?" Héron queried savagely.

"I guessed."

"How?"

"I saw a man in the *Théâtre National* today—"

"Well?"

"Who is a member of the League of the Scarlet Pimpernel."

"D—— him! Where can I find him?"

"Will you sign a receipt for the three thousand five hundred *livres*, which I am pining to hand over to you, my friend, and I will tell you?"

"Where's the money?"

"In my pocket."

Without further words Héron dragged the inkhorn and a sheet of paper towards him, took up a pen, and wrote a few words rapidly in a loose, scrawly hand. He strewed sand over the writing, then handed it across the table to de Batz.

"Will that do?" he asked briefly.

The other was reading the note through carefully.

"I see you only grant me a fortnight," he remarked casually.

"For that amount of money, it is sufficient. If you want an extension you must pay more."

"So be it," assented de Batz coolly, as he folded the paper across. "On the whole a fortnight's immunity in France these days is quite a pleasant respite. And I prefer to keep in touch with you, friend Héron. I'll call on you again this day fortnight."

He took out a letter-case from his pocket. Out of this he drew a packet of bank-notes, which he laid on the table in front of Héron, then he placed the receipt carefully into the letter-case, and this back into his pocket.

Héron in the meanwhile was counting over the banknotes. The light of ferocity had entirely gone from his eyes; momentarily the whole expression of the face was one of satisfied greed.

"Well!" he said at last when he had assured himself that the number of notes was quite correct, and he had transferred the bundle of crisp papers into an inner pocket of his coat—"well, what about your friend?"

"I knew him years ago," rejoined de Batz coolly; "he is a kinsman of citizen St. Just. I know that he is one of the confederates of the Scarlet Pimpernel."

"Where does he lodge?"

"That is for you to find out. I saw him at the theatre, and afterwards in the green-room; he was making himself agreeable to the Citizeness Lange. I heard him ask for leave to call on her tomorrow at four o'clock. You know where she lodges, of course!"

He watched Héron while the latter scribbled a few words on a scrap of paper, then he quietly rose to go. He took up his cloak and once again wrapped it round his shoulders. There was nothing more to be said, and he was anxious to go.

The leave-taking between the two men was neither cordial nor more than barely courteous. De Batz nodded to Héron, who escorted him to the outside door of his lodging, and there called loudly to a soldier who was doing sentinel at the further end of the corridor.

"Show this citizen the way to the *guichet*," he said curtly. "Good-night, citizen," he added finally, nodding to de Batz.

Ten minutes later the Gascon once more found himself in the Rue du Temple between the great outer walls of the prison and the silent little church and convent of St. Elizabeth. He looked up to where in the central tower a small grated window lighted from within showed the place where the last of the Bourbons was being taught to desecrate the traditions of his race, at the bidding of a mender of shoes—a naval officer cashiered for misconduct and fraud.

Such is human nature in its self-satisfied complacency that de Batz, calmly ignoring the vile part which he himself had played in the last quarter of an hour of his interview with the Committee's agent, found it in him to think of Héron with loathing, and even of the cobbler Simon with disgust.

Then with a self-righteous sense of duty performed, and an indifferent shrug of the shoulders, he dismissed Héron from his mind.

"That meddlesome Scarlet Pimpernel will find his hands over-full tomorrow, and mayhap will not interfere in my affairs for some time to come," he mused; "meseems that that will be the first time that a member of his precious League has come within the clutches of such unpleasant people as the sleuth-hounds of my friend Héron!"

CHAPTER 9

What Love Can Do

"Yesterday you were unkind and ungallant. How could I smile when you seemed so stern?"

"Yesterday I was not alone with you. How could I say what lay next my heart, when indifferent ears could catch the words that were meant only for you?"

"Ah, *monsieur*, do they teach you in England how to make pretty speeches?"

"No, *mademoiselle*, that is an instinct that comes into birth by the fire of a woman's eyes."

Mademoiselle Lange was sitting upon a small sofa of antique design, with cushions covered in faded silks heaped round her pretty head. Armand thought that she looked like that carved cameo which his sister Marguerite possessed.

He himself sat on a low chair at some distance from her. He had brought her a large bunch of early violets, for he knew that she was fond of flowers, and these lay upon her lap, against the opalescent grey of her gown.

She seemed a little nervous and agitated, his obvious admiration bringing a ready blush to her cheeks.

The room itself appeared to Armand to be a perfect frame for the charming picture which she presented. The furniture in it was small and old; tiny tables of antique Vernis-Martin, softly faded tapestries, a pale-toned Aubusson carpet. Everything mellow and in a measure pathetic. Mademoiselle Lange, who was an orphan, lived alone under the *duennaship* of a middle-aged relative, a penniless hanger-on of the successful young actress, who acted as her chaperone, housekeeper, and maid, and kept unseemly or over-bold gallants at bay.

She told Armand all about her early life, her childhood in the back-shop of Maître Mézière, the jeweller, who was a relative of her mother's; of her desire for an artistic career, her struggles with the middle-class prejudices of her relations, her bold defiance of them, and final independence.

She made no secret of her humble origin, her want of education in those days; on the contrary, she was proud of what she had accomplished for herself. She was only twenty years of age, and already held a leading place in the artistic world of Paris.

Armand listened to her chatter, interested in everything she said, questioning her with sympathy and discretion. She asked him a good deal about himself, and about his beautiful sister Marguerite, who, of course, had been the most brilliant star in that most brilliant constellation, the *Comédie Française*. She had never seen Marguerite St. Just act, but, of course, Paris still rang with her praises, and all art-lovers regretted that she should have married and left them to mourn for her.

Thus, the conversation drifted naturally back to England. *Mademoiselle* professed a vast interest in the citizen's country of adoption.

"I had always," she said, "thought it an ugly country, with the noise and bustle of industrial life going on everywhere, and smoke and fog to cover the landscape and to stunt the trees."

"Then, in future, *mademoiselle*," he replied, "must you think of it as one carpeted with verdure, where in the spring the orchard trees covered with delicate blossom would speak to you of fairyland, where the dewy grass stretches its velvety surface in the shadow of ancient monumental oaks, and ivy-covered towers rear their stately crowns to the sky."

"And the Scarlet Pimpernel? Tell me about him, *monsieur*."

"Ah, *mademoiselle*, what can I tell you that you do not already know? The Scarlet Pimpernel is a man who has devoted his entire existence to the benefit of suffering mankind. He has but one thought, and that is for those who need him; he hears but one sound the cry of the oppressed."

"But they do say, *monsieur*, that philanthropy plays but a sorry part in your hero's schemes. They aver that he looks on his own efforts and the adventures through which he goes only in the light of sport."

"Like all Englishmen, *mademoiselle*, the Scarlet Pimpernel is a little ashamed of sentiment. He would deny its very existence with his lips, even whilst his noble heart brimmed over with it. Sport? Well! mayhap the sporting instinct is as keen as that of charity—the race for lives, the tussle for the rescue of human creatures, the throwing of a life on the hazard of a die."

"They fear him in France, *monsieur*. He has saved so many whose death had been decreed by the Committee of Public Safety."

"Please God, he will save many yet."

"Ah, *monsieur*, the poor little boy in the Temple prison!"

"He has your sympathy, *mademoiselle?*"

"Of every right-minded woman in France, *monsieur*. Oh!" she added with a pretty gesture of enthusiasm, clasping her hands together, and looking at Armand with large eyes filled with tears, "if your noble Scarlet Pimpernel will do aught to save that poor innocent lamb, I would indeed bless him in my heart, and help him with all my humble might if I could."

"May God's saints bless you for those words, *mademoiselle*," he said, whilst, carried away by her beauty, her charm, her perfect femininity, he stooped towards her until his knee touched the carpet at her feet. "I had begun to lose my belief in my poor misguided country, to think all men in France vile, and all women base. I could thank you on my knees for your sweet words of sympathy, for the expression of tender motherliness that came into your eyes when you spoke of the poor forsaken *Dauphin* in the Temple."

She did not restrain her tears; with her they came very easily, just as with a child, and as they gathered in her eyes and rolled down her fresh cheeks they in no way marred the charm of her face. One hand lay in her lap fingering a diminutive bit of cambric, which from time to time she pressed to her eyes. The other she had almost unconsciously yielded to Armand.

The scent of the violets filled the room. It seemed to emanate from her, a fitting attribute of her young, wholly unsophisticated girlhood. The citizen was goodly to look at; he was kneeling at her feet, and his lips were pressed against her hand.

Armand was young and he was an idealist. I do not for a moment imagine that just at this moment he was deeply in love. The stronger feeling had not yet risen up in him; it came later when tragedy encompassed him and brought passion to sudden maturity. Just now he was merely yielding himself up to the intoxicating moment, with all the abandonment, all the enthusiasm of the Latin race. There was no reason why he should not bend the knee before this exquisite little cameo, that by its very presence was giving him an hour of perfect pleasure and of aesthetic joy.

Outside the world continued its hideous, relentless way; men butchered one another, fought and hated. Here in this small old-world salon, with its faded satins and bits of ivory-tinted lace, the outer universe had never really penetrated. It was a tiny world—quite apart from the rest of mankind, perfectly peaceful and absolutely beautiful.

If Armand had been allowed to depart from here now, without having been the cause as well as the chief actor in the events that followed, no doubt that Mademoiselle Lange would always have remained a charming memory with him, an exquisite bouquet of violets pressed reverently between the leaves of a favourite book of poems, and the scent of spring flowers would in after years have ever brought her dainty picture to his mind.

He was murmuring pretty words of endearment; carried away by emotion, his arm stole round her waist; he felt that if another tear came like a dewdrop rolling down her cheek he must kiss it away at its very source. Passion was not sweeping them off their feet—not yet, for they were very young, and life had not as yet presented to them its most unsolvable problem.

But they yielded to one another, to the springtime of their life, calling for Love, which would come presently hand in hand with his grim attendant, Sorrow.

Even as Armand's glowing face was at last lifted up to hers asking with mute lips for that first kiss which she already was prepared to give, there came the loud noise of men's heavy footsteps tramping up the old oak stairs, then some shouting, a woman's cry, and the next moment Madame Belhomme, trembling, wide-eyed, and in obvious terror, came rushing into the room.

"Jeanne! Jeanne! My child! It is awful! It is awful! *Mon Dieu—mon Dieu!* What is to become of us?"

She was moaning and lamenting even as she ran in, and now she threw her apron over her face and sank into a chair, continuing her moaning and her lamentations.

Neither *Mademoiselle* nor Armand had stirred. They remained like graven images, he on one knee, she with large eyes fixed upon his face.

They had neither of them looked on the old woman; they seemed even now unconscious of her presence. But their ears had caught the sound of that measured tramp of feet up the stairs of the old house, and the halt upon the landing; they had heard the brief words of command:

"Open, in the name of the people!"

They knew quite well what it all meant; they had not wandered so far in the realms of romance that reality—the grim, horrible reality of the moment—had not the power to bring them back to earth.

That peremptory call to open in the name of the people was the prologue these days to a drama which had but two concluding acts: arrest, which was a certainty; the guillotine, which was more than probable. Jeanne and Armand, these two young people who but a moment ago had tentatively lifted the veil of life, looked straight into each other's eyes and saw the hand of death interposed between them: they looked straight into each other's eyes and knew that nothing but the hand of death would part them now. Love had come with its attendant, Sorrow; but he had come with no uncertain footsteps. Jeanne looked on the man before her, and he bent his head to imprint a glowing kiss upon her hand.

"Aunt Marie!"

It was Jeanne Lange who spoke, but her voice was no longer that of an irresponsible child; it was firm, steady and hard. Though she spoke to the old woman, she did not look at her; her luminous brown eyes rested on the bowed head of Armand St. Just.

"Aunt Marie!" she repeated more peremptorily, for the old woman, with her apron over her head, was still moaning, and unconscious of all save an overmastering fear.

"Open, in the name of the people!" came in a loud harsh voice once more from the other side of the front door.

"Aunt Marie, as you value your life and mine, pull yourself together," said Jeanne firmly.

"What shall we do? Oh! what shall we do?" moaned Madame Belhomme. But she had dragged the apron away from her face, and was looking with some puzzlement at meek, gentle little Jeanne, who had suddenly become so strange, so dictatorial, all unlike her habitual somewhat diffident self.

"You need not have the slightest fear, Aunt Marie, if you will only do as I tell you," resumed Jeanne quietly; "if you give way to fear, we are all of us undone. As you value your life and mine," she now repeated authoritatively, "pull yourself together, and do as I tell you."

The girl's firmness, her perfect quietude had the desired effect. Madame Belhomme, though still shaken up with sobs of terror, made a great effort to master herself; she stood up, smoothed down her apron, passed her hand over her ruffled hair, and said in a quaking voice:

"What do you think we had better do?"

"Go quietly to the door and open it."

"But—the soldiers—"

"If you do not open quietly they will force the door open within the next two minutes," interposed Jeanne calmly. "Go quietly and open the door. Try and hide your fears, grumble in an audible voice at being interrupted in your cooking and tell the soldiers at once that they will find *mademoiselle* in the *boudoir*. Go, for God's sake!" she added, whilst suppressed emotion suddenly made her young voice vibrate; "go, before they break open that door!"

Madame Belhomme, impressed and cowed, obeyed like an automaton. She turned and marched fairly straight out of the room. It was not a minute too soon. From outside had already come the third and final summons:

"Open, in the name of the people!"

After that a crowbar would break open the door.

Madame Belhomme's heavy footsteps were heard crossing the ante-chamber. Armand still knelt at Jeanne's feet, holding her trembling little hand in his.

"A love-scene," she whispered rapidly, "a love-scene—quick—do you know one?"

And even as he had tried to rise she held him back, down on his knees.

He thought that fear was making her distracted.

"*Mademoiselle*—" he murmured, trying to soothe her.

"Try and understand," she said with wonderful calm, "and do as I tell you. Aunt Marie has obeyed. Will you do likewise?"

"To the death!" he whispered eagerly.

"Then a love-scene," she entreated. "Surely you know one. Rodrigue and Chimène! Surely—surely," she urged, even as tears of anguish rose into her eyes, "you must—you must, or, if not that, something else. Quick! The very seconds are precious!"

They were indeed! Madame Belhomme, obedient as a frightened dog, had gone to the door and opened it; even her well-feigned grumblings could now be heard and the rough interrogations from the soldiery.

"Citizeness Lange!" said a gruff voice.

"In her *boudoir, quoi!*"

Madame Belhomme, braced up apparently by fear, was playing her part remarkably well.

"Bothering good citizens! On baking day, too!" she went on grumbling and muttering.

"Oh, think—think!" murmured Jeanne now in an agonised whisper, her hot little hand grasping his so tightly that her nails were driven into his flesh. "You must know something that will do—anything—for dear life's sake—Armand!"

His name—in the tense excitement of this terrible moment—had escaped her lips.

All in a flash of sudden intuition he understood what she wanted, and even as the door of the *boudoir* was thrown violently open Armand—still on his knees, but with one hand pressed to his heart, the other stretched upwards to the ceiling in the most approved dramatic style, was loudly declaiming:

> *"Pour venger son honneur il perdit son amour,*
> *Pour venger sa maitresse il a quitté le jour!"*

Whereupon Mademoiselle Lange feigned the most perfect impatience.

"No, no, my good cousin," she said with a pretty *moue* of disdain, "that will never do! You must not thus emphasise the end of every line; the verses should flow more evenly, as thus—"

Héron had paused at the door. It was he who had thrown it open—he who, followed by a couple of his sleuth-hounds, had thought to find here the man denounced by de Batz as being one of the followers of that irrepressible Scarlet Pimpernel. The obviously Parisian intonation of the man kneeling in front of Citizeness Lange in an attitude no ways suggestive of personal admiration, and coolly reciting verses out of a play, had somewhat taken him aback.

"What does this mean?" he asked gruffly, striding forward into the room and glaring first at *mademoiselle*, then at Armand.

Mademoiselle gave a little cry of surprise.

"Why, if it isn't Citizen Héron!" she cried, jumping up with a dainty movement of coquetry and embarrassment. "Why did not Aunt Marie announce you?—It is indeed remiss of her, but she is so ill-tempered on baking days I dare not even rebuke her. Won't you sit down, Citizen Héron? And you, cousin," she added, looking down airily on Armand, "I pray you maintain no longer that foolish attitude."

The *febrileness* of her manner, the glow in her cheeks were easily attributable to natural shyness in face of this unexpected visit. Héron, completely bewildered by this little scene, which was so unlike what he expected, and so unlike those to which he was accustomed in the exercise of his horrible duties, was practically speechless before the little lady who continued to prattle along in a simple, unaffected manner.

"Cousin," she said to Armand, who in the meanwhile had risen to his knees, "this is Citizen Héron, of whom you have heard me speak. My cousin Belhomme," she continued, once more turning to Héron, "is fresh from the country, citizen. He hails from Orléans, where he has played leading parts in the tragedies of the late citizen Corneille. But, ah me! I fear that he will find Paris audiences vastly more critical than the good Orléanese. Did you hear him, citizen, declaiming those beautiful verses just now? He was murdering them, say I—yes, murdering them—the *gaby!*"

Then only did it seem as if she realised that there was something amiss, that Citizen Héron had come to visit her, not as an admirer of her talent who would wish to pay his respects to a successful actress, but as a person to be looked on with dread.

She gave a quaint, nervous little laugh, and murmured in the tones of a frightened child:

"*La*, citizen, how glum you look! I thought you had come to compliment me on my latest success. I saw you at the theatre last night, though you did not afterwards come to see me in the green-room. Why! I had a regular ovation! Look at my flowers!" she added more gaily, pointing to several bouquets in vases about the room. "Citizen Danton brought me the violets himself, and Citizen Santerre the narcissi, and that laurel wreath—is it not charming?—that was a tribute from Citizen Robespierre himself."

She was so artless, so simple, and so natural that Héron was completely taken off his usual mental balance. He had expected to find the usual setting to the dramatic episodes which he was wont to conduct—screaming women, a man either at bay, sword in hand, or hiding in a linen cupboard or up a chimney.

Now everything puzzled him. De Batz—he was quite sure—had spoken of an Englishman, a follower of the Scarlet Pimpernel; every thinking French patriot knew that all the followers of the Scarlet Pimpernel were Englishmen with red hair and prominent teeth, whereas this man—

Armand—who deadly danger had primed in his improvised *rôle*—was striding up and down the room declaiming with ever-varying intonations:

"Joignez tous vos efforts contre un espoir si doux
Pour en venir à bout, c'est trop peu que de vous."

"No! no!" said *mademoiselle* impatiently; "you must not make that ugly pause midway in the last line: *'pour en venir à bout, c'est trop peu que de vous!'"*

She mimicked Armand's diction so quaintly, imitating his stride, his awkward gesture, and his faulty phraseology with such funny exaggeration that Héron laughed in spite of himself.

"So that is a cousin from Orléans, is it?" he asked, throwing his lanky body into an armchair, which creaked dismally under his weight.

"Yes! a regular *gaby*—what?" she said archly. "Now, Citizen Héron, you must stay and take coffee with me. Aunt Marie will be bringing it in directly. Hector," she added, turning to Armand, "come down from the clouds and ask Aunt Marie to be quick."

This certainly was the first time in the whole of his experience that Héron had been asked to stay and drink coffee with the quarry he was hunting down. *Mademoiselle's* innocent little ways, her desire for the prolongation of his visit, further addled his brain. De Batz had undoubtedly spoken of an Englishman, and the cousin from Orleans was certainly a Frenchman every inch of him.

Perhaps had the denunciation come from anyone else but de Batz, Héron might have acted and thought more circumspectly; but, of course, the chief agent of the Committee of General Security was more suspicious of the man from whom he took a heavy bribe than of anyone else in France. The thought had suddenly crossed his mind that mayhap de Batz had sent him on a fool's errand in order to get him safely out of the way of the Temple prison at a given hour of the day.

The thought took shape, crystallised, caused him to see a rapid vision of de Batz sneaking into his lodgings and stealing his keys, the guard being slack, careless, inattentive, allowing the adventurer to pass barriers that should have been closed against all comers.

Now Héron was sure of it; it was all a conspiracy invented by de

Batz. He had forgotten all about his theories that a man under arrest is always safer than a man that is free. Had his brain been quite normal, and not obsessed, as it always was now by thoughts of the *Dauphin's* escape from prison, no doubt he would have been more suspicious of Armand, but all his worst suspicions were directed against de Batz. Armand seemed to him just a fool, an actor *quoi?* and so obviously not an Englishman.

He jumped to his feet, curtly declining *mademoiselle's* offers of hospitality. He wanted to get away at once. Actors and actresses were always, by tacit consent of the authorities, more immune than the rest of the community. They provided the only amusement in the intervals of the horrible scenes around the scaffolds; they were irresponsible, harmless creatures who did not meddle in politics.

Jeanne the while was gaily prattling on, her luminous eyes fixed upon the all-powerful enemy, striving to read his thoughts, to understand what went on behind those cruel, prominent eyes, the chances that Armand had of safety and of life.

She knew, of course, that the visit was directed against Armand—someone had betrayed him, that odious de Batz mayhap—and she was fighting for Armand's safety, for his life. Her armoury consisted of her presence of mind, her cool courage, her self-control; she used all these weapons for his sake, though at times she felt as if the strain on her nerves would snap the thread of life in her. The effort seemed more than she could bear.

But she kept up her part, rallying Héron for the shortness of his visit, begging him to tarry for another five minutes at least, throwing out—with subtle feminine intuition—just those very hints anent little Capet's safety that were most calculated to send him flying back towards the Temple.

"I felt so honoured last night, citizen," she said coquettishly, "that you even forgot little Capet in order to come and watch my *début* as Célimène."

"Forget him!" retorted Héron, smothering a curse, "I never forget the vermin. I must go back to him; there are too many cats nosing round my mouse. Good day to you, citizeness. I ought to have brought flowers, I know; but I am a busy man—a harassed man."

"*Je te crois*," she said with a grave nod of the head; "but do come to the theatre tonight. I am playing Camille—such a fine part! one of my greatest successes."

"Yes, yes, I'll come—mayhap, mayhap—but I'll go now—glad to

have seen you, citizeness. Where does your cousin lodge?" he asked abruptly.

"Here," she replied boldly, on the spur of the moment.

"Good. Let him report himself tomorrow morning at the *Conciergerie* and get his certificate of safety. It is a new decree, and you should have one, too."

"Very well, then. Hector and I will come together, and perhaps Aunt Marie will come too. Don't send us to *maman* guillotine yet awhile, citizen," she said lightly; "you will never get such another Camille, nor yet so good a Célimène."

She was gay, artless to the last. She accompanied Héron to the door herself, chaffing him about his escort.

"You are an *aristo*, citizen," she said, gazing with well-feigned admiration on the two sleuth-hounds who stood in wait in the anteroom; "it makes me proud to see so many citizens at my door. Come and see me play Camille—come tonight, and don't forget the greenroom door—it will always be kept invitingly open for you."

She bobbed him a curtsey, and he walked out, closely followed by his two men; then at last she closed the door behind them. She stood there for a while, her ear glued against the massive panels, listening for their measured tread down the oak staircase. At last it rang more sharply against the flagstones of the courtyard below; then she was satisfied that they had gone and went slowly back to the *boudoir*.

Chapter 10

Shadows

The tension on her nerves relaxed; there was the inevitable reaction. Her knees were shaking under her, and she literally staggered into the room.

But Armand was already near her, down on both his knees this time, his arms clasping the delicate form that swayed like the slender stems of narcissi in the breeze.

"Oh! you must go out of Paris at once—at once," she said through sobs which no longer would be kept back.

"He'll return—I know that he will return—and you will not be safe until you are back in England."

But he could not think of himself or of anything in the future. He had forgotten Héron, Paris, the world; he could only think of her.

"I owe my life to you!" he murmured. "Oh, how beautiful you are—how brave! How I love you!"

It seemed that he had always loved her, from the moment that first in his boyish heart he had set up an ideal to worship, and then, last night, in the box of the theatre—he had his back turned toward the stage, and was ready to go—her voice had called him back; it had held him spellbound; her voice, and also her eyes—He did not know then that it was Love which then and there had enchained him. Oh, how foolish he had been! for now he knew that he had loved her with all his might, with all his soul, from the very instant that his eyes had rested upon her.

He babbled along—incoherently—in the intervals of covering her hands and the hem of her gown with kisses. He stooped right down to the ground and kissed the arch of her instep; he had become a devotee worshipping at the shrine of his saint, who had performed a great and a wonderful miracle.

Armand the idealist had found his ideal in a woman. That was the great miracle which the woman herself had performed for him. He found in her all that he had admired most, all that he had admired in the leader who hitherto had been the only personification of his ideal. But Jeanne possessed all those qualities which had roused his enthusiasm in the noble hero whom he revered. Her pluck, her ingenuity, her calm devotion which had averted the threatened danger from him!

What had he done that she should have risked her own sweet life for his sake?

But Jeanne did not know. She could not tell. Her nerves now were somewhat unstrung, and the tears that always came so readily to her eyes flowed quite unchecked. She could not very well move, for he held her knees imprisoned in his arms, but she was quite content to remain like this, and to yield her hands to him so that he might cover them with kisses.

Indeed, she did not know at what precise moment love for him had been born in her heart. Last night, perhaps—she could not say—but when they parted she felt that she must see him again—and then today—perhaps it was the scent of the violets—they were so exquisitely sweet—perhaps it was his enthusiasm and his talk about England—but when Héron came she knew that she must save Armand's life at all cost—that she would die if they dragged him away to prison.

Thus, these two children philosophised, trying to understand the mystery of the birth of Love. But they were only children; they did not really understand. Passion was sweeping them off their feet, because a common danger had bound them irrevocably to one another.

The womanly instinct to save and to protect had given the young girl strength to bear a difficult part, and now she loved him for the dangers from which she had rescued him, and he loved her because she had risked her life for him.

The hours sped on; there was so much to say, so much that was exquisite to listen to. The shades of evening were gathering fast; the room, with its pale-toned hangings and faded tapestries, was sinking into the arms of gloom. Aunt Marie was no doubt too terrified to stir out of her kitchen; she did not bring the lamps, but the darkness suited Armand's mood, and Jeanne was glad that the gloaming effectually hid the perpetual blush in her cheeks.

In the evening air the dying flowers sent their heady fragrance around. Armand was intoxicated with the perfume of violets that clung to Jeanne's fingers, with the touch of her satin gown that brushed his cheek, with the murmur of her voice that quivered through her tears.

No noise from the ugly outer world reached this secluded spot. In the tiny square outside a street lamp had been lighted, and its feeble rays came peeping in through the lace curtains at the window. They caught the dainty silhouette of the young girl, playing with the loose tendrils of her hair around her forehead, and outlining with a thin band of light the contour of neck and shoulder, making the satin of her gown shimmer with an opalescent glow.

Armand rose from his knees. Her eyes were calling to him, her lips were ready to yield.

"*Tu m'aimes?*" he whispered.

And like a tired child she sank upon his breast.

He kissed her hair, her eyes, her lips; her skin was fragrant as the flowers of spring, the tears on her cheeks glistened like morning dew.

Aunt Marie came in at last, carrying the lamp. She found them sitting side by side, like two children, hand in hand, mute with the eloquence which comes from boundless love. They were under a spell, forgetting even that they lived, knowing nothing except that they loved.

The lamp broke the spell, and Aunt Marie's still trembling voice:

"Oh, my dear! how did you manage to rid yourself of those brutes?"

But she asked no other question, even when the lamp showed up quite clearly the glowing cheeks of Jeanne and the ardent eyes of Armand. In her heart, long since atrophied, there were a few memories, carefully put away in a secret cell, and those memories caused the old woman to understand.

Neither Jeanne nor Armand noticed what she did; the spell had been broken, but the dream lingered on; they did not see Aunt Marie putting the room tidy, and then quietly tiptoeing out by the door.

But through the dream, reality was struggling for recognition. After Armand had asked for the hundredth time: "*Tu m'aimes?*" and Jeanne for the hundredth time had replied mutely with her eyes, her fears for him suddenly returned.

Something had awakened her from her trance—a heavy footstep, mayhap, in the street below, the distant roll of a drum, or only the clash of steel saucepans in Aunt Marie's kitchen. But suddenly Jeanne was alert, and with her alertness came terror for the beloved.

"Your life," she said—for he had called her his life just then, "your life—and I was forgetting that it is still in danger—your dear, your precious life!"

"Doubly dear now," he replied, "since I owe it to you."

"Then I pray you, I entreat you, guard it well for my sake—make all haste to leave Paris—oh, this I beg of you!" she continued more earnestly, seeing the look of demur in his eyes; "every hour you spend in it brings danger nearer to your door."

"I could not leave Paris while you are here."

"But I am safe here," she urged; "quite, quite safe, I assure you. I am only a poor actress, and the government takes no heed of us mimes. Men must be amused, even between the intervals of killing one another. Indeed, indeed, I should be far safer here now, waiting quietly for a while, while you make preparations to go—My hasty departure at this moment would bring disaster on us both."

There was logic in what she said. And yet how could he leave her? now that he had found this perfect woman—this realisation of his highest ideals, how could he go and leave her in this awful Paris, with brutes like Héron forcing their hideous personality into her sacred presence, threatening that very life he would gladly give his own to keep inviolate?

"Listen, sweetheart," he said after a while, when presently reason struggled back for first place in his mind. "Will you allow me to consult with my chief, with the Scarlet Pimpernel, who is in Paris at the present moment? I am under his orders; I could not leave France just now. My life, my entire person are at his disposal. I and my comrades are here under his orders, for a great undertaking which he has not yet unfolded to us, but which I firmly believe is framed for the rescue of the Dauphin from the Temple."

She gave an involuntary exclamation of horror.

"No, no!" she said quickly and earnestly; "as far as you are concerned, Armand, that has now become an impossibility. Someone has betrayed you, and you are henceforth a marked man. I think that odious de Batz had a hand in Héron's visit of this afternoon. We succeeded in putting these spies off the scent, but only for a moment—within a few hours—less perhaps—Héron will repent him of his carelessness; he'll come back—I know that he will come back. He may leave me, personally, alone; but he will be on your track; he'll drag you to the *Conciergerie* to report yourself, and there your true name and history are bound to come to light. If you succeed in evading him, he will still be on your track. If the Scarlet Pimpernel keeps you in Paris now, your death will be at his door."

Her voice had become quite hard and trenchant as she said these last words; womanlike, she was already prepared to hate the man whose mysterious personality she had hitherto admired, now that the life and safety of Armand appeared to depend on the will of that elusive hero.

"You must not be afraid for me, Jeanne," he urged. "The Scarlet Pimpernel cares for all his followers; he would never allow me to run unnecessary risks."

She was unconvinced, almost jealous now of his enthusiasm for that unknown man. Already she had taken full possession of Armand; she had purchased his life, and he had given her his love. She would share neither treasure with that nameless leader who held Armand's allegiance.

"It is only for a little while, sweetheart," he reiterated again and again. "I could not, anyhow, leave Paris whilst I feel that you are here, maybe in danger. The thought would be horrible. I should go mad if I had to leave you."

Then he talked again of England, of his life there, of the happiness and peace that were in store for them both.

"We will go to England together," he whispered, "and there we will be happy together, you and I. We will have a tiny house among the Kentish hills, and its walls will be covered with honeysuckle and roses. At the back of the house there will be an orchard, and in May, when the fruit-blossom is fading and soft spring breezes blow among the trees, showers of sweet-scented petals will envelop us as we walk along, falling on us like fragrant snow. You will come, sweetheart, will you not?"

"If you still wish it, Armand," she murmured.

Still wish it! He would gladly go tomorrow if she would come with him. But, of course, that could not be arranged. She had her contract to fulfil at the theatre, then there would be her house and furniture to dispose of, and there was Aunt Marie—But, of course, Aunt Marie would come too—She thought that she could get away some time before the spring; and he swore that he could not leave Paris until she came with him.

It seemed a terrible deadlock, for she could not bear to think of him alone in those awful Paris streets, where she knew that spies would always be tracking him. She had no illusions as to the impression which she had made on Héron; she knew that it could only be a momentary one, and that Armand would henceforth be in daily, hourly danger.

At last she promised him that she would take the advice of his chief; they would both be guided by what he said. Armand would confide in him tonight, and if it could be arranged she would hurry on her preparations and, mayhap, be ready to join him in a week.

"In the meanwhile, that cruel man must not risk your dear life," she said. "Remember, Armand, your life belongs to me. Oh, I could hate him for the love you bear him!"

"Sh—sh—sh!" he said earnestly. "Dear heart, you must not speak like that of the man whom, next to your perfect self, I love most upon earth."

"You think of him more than of me. I shall scarce live until I know that you are safely out of Paris."

Though it was horrible to part, yet it was best, perhaps, that he should go back to his lodgings now, in case Héron sent his spies back to her door, and since he meant to consult with his chief. She had a vague hope that if the mysterious hero was indeed the noble-hearted man whom Armand represented him to be, surely, he would take compassion on the anxiety of a sorrowing woman and release the man she loved from bondage.

This thought pleased her and gave her hope. She even urged Armand now to go.

"When may I see you tomorrow?" he asked.

"But it will be so dangerous to meet," she argued.

"I must see you. I could not live through the day without seeing you."

"The theatre is the safest place."

"I could not wait till the evening. May I not come here?"

"No, no. Héron's spies may be about."

"Where then?"

She thought it over for a moment.

"At the stage-door of the theatre at one o'clock," she said at last. "We shall have finished rehearsal. Slip into the *guichet* of the *concierge*. I will tell him to admit you and send my dresser to meet you there; she will bring you along to my room, where we shall be undisturbed for at least half an hour."

He had perforce to be content with that, though he would so much rather have seen her here again, where the faded tapestries and soft-toned hangings made such a perfect background for her delicate charm. He had every intention of confiding in Blakeney, and of asking his help for getting Jeanne out of Paris as quickly as may be.

Thus, this perfect hour was past; the most pure, the fullest of joy that these two young people were ever destined to know. Perhaps they felt within themselves the consciousness that their great love would rise anon to yet greater, fuller perfection when Fate had crowned it with his halo of sorrow. Perhaps, too, it was that consciousness that gave to their kisses now the solemnity of a last farewell.

Chapter 11

The League of the Scarlet Pimpernel

Armand never could say definitely afterwards whither he went when he left the Square du Roule that evening. No doubt he wandered about the streets for some time in an absent, mechanical way, paying no heed to the passers-by, none to the direction in which he was going.

His mind was full of Jeanne, her beauty, her courage, her attitude in face of the hideous bloodhound who had come to pollute that charming old-world *boudoir* by his loathsome presence. He recalled every word she uttered, every gesture she made.

He was a man in love for the first time—wholly, irremediably in love.

I suppose that it was the pangs of hunger that first recalled him to himself. It was close on eight o'clock now, and he had fed on his imaginings—first on anticipation, then on realisation, and lastly on memory—during the best part of the day. Now he awoke from his day-dream to find himself tired and hungry, but fortunately not very far from that quarter of Paris where food is easily obtainable.

He was somewhere near the Madeleine—a quarter he knew well.

Soon he saw in front of him a small eating-house which looked fairly clean and orderly. He pushed open its swing-door and seeing an empty table in a secluded part of the room, he sat down and ordered some supper.

The place made no impression upon his memory. He could not have told you an hour later where it was situated, who had served him, what he had eaten, or what other persons were present in the dining-room at the time that he himself entered it.

Having eaten, however, he felt more like his normal self—more conscious of his actions. When he finally left the eating-house, he realised, for instance, that it was very cold—a fact of which he had for the past few hours been totally unaware. The snow was falling in thin close flakes, and a biting north-easterly wind was blowing those flakes into his face and down his collar. He wrapped his cloak tightly around him. It was a good step yet to Blakeney's lodgings, where he knew that he was expected.

He struck quickly into the Rue St. Honoré, avoiding the great open places where the grim horrors of this magnificent city in revolt against civilisation were displayed in all their grim nakedness—on the Place de la Révolution the guillotine, on the Carrousel the open-air camps of workers under the lash of slave-drivers more cruel than the uncivilised brutes of the Far West.

And Armand had to think of Jeanne in the midst of all these horrors. She was still a petted actress today, but who could tell if on the morrow the terrible law of the "suspect" would not reach her in order to drag her before a tribunal that knew no mercy, and whose sole justice was a condemnation?

The young man hurried on; he was anxious to be among his own comrades, to hear his chief's pleasant voice, to feel assured that by all the sacred laws of friendship Jeanne henceforth would become the special care of the Scarlet Pimpernel and his league.

Blakeney lodged in a small house situated on the Quai de l'Ecole, at the back of St. Germain l'Auxerrois, from whence he had a clear and uninterrupted view across the river, as far as the irregular block of buildings of the Châtelet prison and the house of Justice.

The same tower-clock that two centuries ago had tolled the signal for the massacre of the Huguenots was even now striking nine. Armand slipped through the half-open *porte cochère*, crossed the narrow dark courtyard, and ran up two flights of winding stone stairs. At the top of these, a door on his right allowed a thin streak of light to filtrate between its two folds. An iron bell handle hung beside it; Armand gave it a pull.

Two minutes later he was amongst his friends. He heaved a great sigh of content and relief. The very atmosphere here seemed to be different. As far as the lodging itself was concerned, it was as bare, as devoid of comfort as those sort of places—so-called *chambres garnies*—usually were in these days. The chairs looked rickety and uninviting, the sofa was of black horsehair, the carpet was threadbare, and in places in actual holes; but there was a certain something in the air which revealed, in the midst of all this squalor, the presence of a man of fastidious taste.

To begin with, the place was spotlessly clean; the stove, highly polished, gave forth a pleasing warm glow, even whilst the window, slightly open, allowed a modicum of fresh air to enter the room. In a rough earthenware jug on the table stood a large bunch of Christmas roses, and to the educated nostril the slight scent of perfumes that hovered in the air was doubly pleasing after the fetid air of the narrow streets.

Sir Andrew Ffoulkes was there, also my Lord Tony, and Lord Hastings. They greeted Armand with whole-hearted cheeriness.

"Where is Blakeney?" asked the young man as soon as he had shaken his friends by the hand.

"Present!" came in loud, pleasant accents from the door of an inner room on the right.

And there he stood under the lintel of the door, the man against whom was raised the giant hand of an entire nation—the man for whose head the revolutionary government of France would gladly pay out all the savings of its Treasury—the man whom human bloodhounds were tracking, hot on the scent—for whom the nets of a bitter revenge and relentless reprisals were constantly being spread.

Was he unconscious of it, or merely careless? His closest friend, Sir Andrew Ffoulkes, could not say. Certain it is that, as he now appeared before Armand, picturesque as ever in perfectly tailored clothes, with priceless lace at throat and wrists, his slender fingers holding an enamelled snuff-box and a handkerchief of delicate cambric, his whole personality that of a dandy rather than a man of action, it seemed impossible to connect him with the foolhardy escapades which had set one nation glowing with enthusiasm and another clamouring for revenge.

But it was the magnetism that emanated from him that could not be denied; the light that now and then, swift as summer lightning, flashed out from the depths of the blue eyes usually veiled by heavy, lazy lids, the sudden tightening of firm lips, the setting of the square jaw, which in a moment—but only for the space of a second—transformed the entire face, and revealed the born leader of men.

Just now there was none of that in the *débonnair*, easy-going man of the world who advanced to meet his friend. Armand went quickly up to him, glad to grasp his hand, slightly troubled with remorse, no doubt, at the recollection of his adventure of today. It almost seemed to him that from beneath his half-closed lids Blakeney had shot a quick inquiring glance upon him. The quick flash seemed to light up the young man's soul from within, and to reveal it, naked, to his friend.

It was all over in a moment, and Armand thought that mayhap his conscience had played him a trick: there was nothing apparent in him—of this he was sure—that could possibly divulge his secret just yet.

"I am rather late, I fear," he said. "I wandered about the streets in the late afternoon and lost my way in the dark. I hope I have not kept you all waiting."

They all pulled chairs closely round the fire, except Blakeney, who preferred to stand. He waited awhile until they were all comfortably settled, and all ready to listen, then:

"It is about the *Dauphin*," he said abruptly without further preamble.

They understood. All of them had guessed it, almost before the summons came that had brought them to Paris two days ago. Sir Andrew Ffoulkes had left his young wife because of that, and Armand had demanded it as a right to join hands in this noble work. Blakeney had not left France for over three months now. Backwards and forwards between Paris, or Nantes, or Orleans to the coast, where his friends would meet him to receive those unfortunates whom one man's whole-hearted devotion had rescued from death; backwards and forwards into the very hearts of those cities wherein an army of sleuth-hounds were on his track, and the guillotine was stretching out her arms to catch the foolhardy adventurer.

Now it was about the *Dauphin*. They all waited, breathless and eager, the fire of a noble enthusiasm burning in their hearts. They waited in silence, their eyes fixed on the leader, lest one single word from him should fail to reach their ears.

The full magnetism of the man was apparent now. As he held these four men at this moment, he could have held a crowd. The man of the world—the fastidious dandy—had shed his mask; there stood the leader, calm, serene in the very face of the most deadly danger that had ever encompassed any man, looking that danger fully in the face, not striving to belittle it or to exaggerate it, but weighing it in the balance with what there was to accomplish: the rescue of a martyred, innocent child from the hands of fiends who were destroying his very soul even more completely than his body.

"Everything, I think, is prepared," resumed Sir Percy after a slight pause. "The Simons have been summarily dismissed; I learned that today. They remove from the Temple on Sunday next, the nineteenth. Obviously, that is the one day most likely to help us in our operations. As far as I am concerned, I cannot make any hard-and-fast plans. Chance at the last moment will have to dictate. But from every one of you I must have co-operation, and it can only be by your following my directions implicitly that we can even remotely hope to succeed."

He crossed and recrossed the room once or twice before he spoke again, pausing now and again in his walk in front of a large map of Paris and its environs that hung upon the wall, his tall figure erect, his hands behind his back, his eyes fixed before him as if he saw right through the walls of this squalid room, and across the darkness that overhung the city, through the grim bastions of the mighty building far away, where the descendant of an hundred kings lived at the mercy of human fiends who worked for his abasement.

The man's face now was that of a seer and a visionary; the firm lines were set and rigid as those of an image carved in stone—the statue of heart-whole devotion, with the self-imposed task beckoning sternly to follow, there where lurked danger and death.

"The way, I think, in which we could best succeed would be this," he resumed after a while, sitting now on the edge of the table and directly facing his four friends. The light from the lamp which stood upon the table behind him fell full upon those four glowing faces fixed eagerly upon him, but he himself was in shadow, a massive silhouette broadly cut out against the light-coloured map on the wall beyond.

"I remain here, of course, until Sunday," he said, "and will closely watch my opportunity, when I can with the greatest amount of safety enter the Temple building and take possession of the child. I shall, of course choose the moment when the Simons are actually on the move, with their successors probably coming in at about the same time. God alone knows," he added earnestly, "how I shall contrive to get possession of the child; at the moment I am just as much in the dark about that as you are."

He paused a moment, and suddenly his grave face seemed flooded with sunshine, a kind of lazy merriment danced in his eyes, effacing all trace of solemnity within them.

"*La!*" he said lightly, "on one point I am not at all in the dark, and that is that His Majesty King Louis XVII will come out of that ugly house in my company next Sunday, the nineteenth day of January in this year of grace seventeen hundred and ninety-four; and this, too, do I know—that those murderous blackguards shall not lay hands on me whilst that precious burden is in my keeping. So, I pray you, my good Armand, do not look so glum," he added with his pleasant, merry laugh; "you'll need all your wits about you to help us in our undertaking."

"What do you wish me to do, Percy?" said the young man simply.

"In one moment I will tell you. I want you all to understand the situation first. The child will be out of the Temple on Sunday, but at what hour I know not. The later it will be the better would it suit my purpose, for I cannot get him out of Paris before evening with any chance of safety. Here we must risk nothing; the child is far better off as he is now than he would be if he were dragged back after an abortive attempt at rescue. But at this hour of the night, between nine and ten o'clock, I can arrange to get him out of Paris by the Villette gate, and that is where I want you, Ffoulkes, and you, Tony, to be, with some kind of covered cart, yourselves in any disguise your ingenuity will suggest. Here are a few certificates of safety; I have been making a collection of them for some time, as they are always useful."

He dived into the wide pocket of his coat and drew forth a number of cards, greasy, much-fingered documents of the usual pattern which the Committee of General Security delivered to the free citizens of the new republic, and without which no one could enter or leave any town or country commune without being detained as "suspect." He glanced at them and handed them over to Ffoulkes.

"Choose your own identity for the occasion, my good friend," he said lightly; "and you too, Tony. You may be stonemasons or coal-carriers, chimney-sweeps or farm-labourers, I care not which so long as you look sufficiently grimy and wretched to be unrecognisable, and so long as you can procure a cart without arousing suspicions and can wait for me punctually at the appointed spot."

Ffoulkes turned over the cards, and with a laugh handed them over to Lord Tony. The two fastidious gentlemen discussed for a while the respective merits of a chimney-sweep's uniform as against that of a coal-carrier.

"You can carry more grime if you are a sweep," suggested Blakeney; "and if the soot gets into your eyes it does not make them smart like coal does."

"But soot adheres more closely," argued Tony solemnly, "and I know that we shan't get a bath for at least a week afterwards."

"Certainly, you won't, you sybarite!" asserted Sir Percy with a laugh.

"After a week soot might become permanent," mused Sir Andrew, wondering what, under the circumstance, my lady would say to him.

"If you are both so fastidious," retorted Blakeney, shrugging his broad shoulders, "I'll turn one of you into a reddleman, and the other into a dyer. Then one of you will be bright scarlet to the end of his days, as the reddle never comes off the skin at all, and the other will have to soak in turpentine before the dye will consent to move—In either case—oh, my dear Tony!—the smell—"

He laughed like a schoolboy in anticipation of a prank and held his scented handkerchief to his nose. My Lord Hastings chuckled audibly, and Tony punched him for this unseemly display of mirth.

Armand watched the little scene in utter amazement. He had been in England over a year, and yet he could not understand these Englishmen. Surely, they were the queerest, most inconsequent people in the world. Here were these men, who were engaged at this very moment in an enterprise which for cool-headed courage and foolhardy daring had probably no parallel in history. They were literally taking their lives in their hands, in all probability facing certain death; and yet they now sat chaffing and fighting like a crowd of third-form schoolboys, talking utter, silly nonsense, and making foolish jokes that would have shamed a Frenchman in his teens. Vaguely he wondered what fat, pompous de Batz would think of this discussion if he could overhear it. His contempt, no doubt, for the Scarlet Pimpernel and his followers would be increased tenfold.

Then at last the question of the disguise was effectually dismissed. Sir Andrew Ffoulkes and Lord Anthony Dewhurst had settled their differences of opinion by solemnly agreeing to represent two over-grimy and overheated coal-heavers. They chose two certificates of safety that were made out in the names of Jean Lepetit and Achille Grospierre, labourers.

"Though you don't look at all like an Achille, Tony," was Blakeney's parting shot to his friend.

Then without any transition from this schoolboy nonsense to the serious business of the moment, Sir Andrew Ffoulkes said abruptly:

"Tell us exactly, Blakeney, where you will want the cart to stand on Sunday."

Blakeney rose and turned to the map against the wall, Ffoulkes and Tony following him. They stood close to his elbow whilst his slender, nervy hand wandered along the shiny surface of the varnished paper. At last he placed his finger on one spot.

"Here you see," he said, "is the Villette gate. Just outside it a narrow street on the right leads down in the direction of the canal. It is just at the bottom of that narrow street at its junction with the tow-path there that I want you two and the cart to be. It had better be a coal-car by the way; they will be unloading coal close by there tomorrow," he added with one of his sudden irrepressible outbursts of merriment. "You and Tony can exercise your muscles coal-heaving, and incidentally make yourselves known in the neighbourhood as good if somewhat grimy patriots."

"We had better take up our parts at once then," said Tony. "I'll take a fond farewell of my clean shirt tonight."

"Yes, you will not see one again for some time, my good Tony. After your hard day's work tomorrow, you will have to sleep either inside your cart, if you have already secured one, or under the arches of the canal bridge, if you have not."

"I hope you have an equally pleasant prospect for Hastings," was my Lord Tony's grim comment.

It was easy to see that he was as happy as a schoolboy about to start for a holiday. Lord Tony was a true sportsman. Perhaps there was in him less sentiment for the heroic work which he did under the guidance of his chief than an inherent passion for dangerous adventures. Sir Andrew Ffoulkes, on the other hand, thought perhaps a little less of the adventure, but a great deal of the martyred child in the Temple. He was just as buoyant, just as keen as his friend, but the leaven of sentiment raised his sporting instincts to perhaps a higher plane of self-devotion.

"Well, now, to recapitulate," he said, in turn following with his finger the indicated route on the map. "Tony and I and the coal-cart will await you on this spot, at the corner of the towpath on Sunday evening at nine o'clock."

"And your signal, Blakeney?" asked Tony.

"The usual one," replied Sir Percy, "the seamew's cry thrice repeated at brief intervals. But now," he continued, turning to Armand and Hastings, who had taken no part in the discussion hitherto, "I want your help a little further afield."

"I thought so," nodded Hastings.

"The coal-cart, with its usual miserable nag, will carry us a distance of fifteen or sixteen kilometres, but no more. My purpose is to cut along the north of the city, and to reach St. Germain, the nearest point where we can secure good mounts. There is a farmer just outside the commune; his name is Achard. He has excellent horses, which I have borrowed before now; we shall want five, of course, and he has one powerful beast that will do for me, as I shall have, in addition to my own weight, which is considerable, to take the child with me on the pillion. Now you, Hastings and Armand, will have to start early tomorrow morning, leave Paris by the Neuilly gate, and from there make your way to St. Germain by any conveyance you can contrive to obtain. At St. Germain you must at once find Achard's farm; disguised as labourers you will not arouse suspicion by so doing. You will find the farmer quite amenable to money, and you must secure the best horses you can get for our own use, and, if possible, the powerful mount I spoke of just now. You are both excellent horse-men, therefore I selected you amongst the others for this special errand, for you two, with the five horses, will have to come and meet our coal-cart some seventeen kilometres out of St. Germain, to where the first sign-post indicates the road to Courbevoie. Some two hundred metres down this road on the right there is a small spinney, which will afford splendid shelter for yourselves and your horses. We hope to be there at about one o'clock after midnight of Monday morning. Now, is all that quite clear, and are you both satisfied?"

"It is quite clear," exclaimed Hastings placidly; "but I, for one, am not at all satisfied."

"And why not?"

"Because it is all too easy. We get none of the danger."

"Oho! I thought that you would bring that argument forward, you incorrigible grumbler," laughed Sir Percy good-humouredly. "Let me tell you that if you start tomorrow from Paris in that spirit you will run your head and Armand's into a noose long before you reach the gate of Neuilly. I cannot allow either of you to cover your faces with too much grime; an honest farm labourer should not look over-dirty, and your chances of being discovered and detained are, at the outset, far greater than those which Ffoulkes and Tony will run—"

Armand had said nothing during this time. While Blakeney was unfolding his plan for him and for Lord Hastings—a plan which practically was a command—he had sat with his arms folded across his chest, his head sunk upon his breast. When Blakeney had asked if they were satisfied, he had taken no part in Hastings' protest nor responded to his leader's good-humoured banter.

Though he did not look up even now, yet he felt that Percy's eyes were fixed upon him, and they seemed to scorch into his soul. He made a great effort to appear eager like the others, and yet from the first a chill had struck at his heart. He could not leave Paris before he had seen Jeanne.

He looked up suddenly, trying to seem unconcerned; he even looked his chief fully in the face.

"When ought we to leave Paris?" he asked calmly.

"You *must* leave at daybreak," replied Blakeney with a slight, almost imperceptible emphasis on the word of command. "When the gates are first opened, and the work-people go to and fro at their work, that is the safest hour. And you must be at St. Germain as soon as may be, or the farmer may not have a sufficiency of horses available at a moment's notice. I want you to be spokesman with Achard, so that Hastings' British accent should not betray you both. Also, you might not get a conveyance for St. Germain immediately. We must think of every eventuality, Armand. There is so much at stake."

Armand made no further comment just then. But the others looked astonished. Armand had but asked a simple question, and Blakeney's reply seemed almost like a rebuke—so circumstantial too, and so explanatory. He was so used to being obeyed at a word, so accustomed that the merest wish, the slightest hint from him was understood by his band of devoted followers, that the long explanation of his orders which he gave to Armand struck them all with a strange sense of unpleasant surprise.

Hastings was the first to break the spell that seemed to have fallen over the party.

"We leave at daybreak, of course," he said, "as soon as the gates are open. We can, I know, get one of the carriers to give us a lift as far as St. Germain. There, how do we find Achard?"

"He is a well-known farmer," replied Blakeney. "You have but to ask."

"Good. Then we bespeak five horses for the next day, find lodgings in the village that night, and make a fresh start back towards Paris in the evening of Sunday. Is that right?"

"Yes. One of you will have two horses on the lead, the other one. Pack some fodder on the empty saddles and start at about ten o'clock. Ride straight along the main road, as if you were making back for Paris, until you come to four cross-roads with a sign-post pointing to Courbevoie. Turn down there and go along the road until you meet a close spinney of fir-trees on your right. Make for the interior of that. It gives splendid shelter, and you can dismount there and give the horses a feed. We'll join you one hour after midnight. The night will be dark, I hope, and the moon anyhow will be on the wane."

"I think I understand. Anyhow, it's not difficult, and we'll be as careful as may be."

"You will have to keep your heads clear, both of you," concluded Blakeney.

He was looking at Armand as he said this; but the young man had not made a movement during this brief colloquy between Hastings and the chief. He still sat with arms folded, his head falling on his breast.

Silence had fallen on them all. They all sat round the fire buried in thought. Through the open window there came from the quay beyond the hum of life in the open-air camp; the tramp of the sentinels around it, the words of command from the drill-sergeant, and through it all the moaning of the wind and the beating of the sleet against the window-panes.

A whole world of wretchedness was expressed by those sounds! Blakeney gave a quick, impatient sigh, and going to the window he pushed it further open, and just then there came from afar the muffled roll of drums, and from below the watchman's cry that seemed such dire mockery:

"Sleep, citizens! Everything is safe and peaceful."

"Sound advice," said Blakeney lightly. "Shall we also go to sleep? What say you all—eh?"

He had with that sudden rapidity characteristic of his every action, already thrown off the serious air which he had worn a moment ago when giving instructions to Hastings. His usual *débonnair* manner was on him once again, his laziness, his careless *insouciance*. He was even at this moment deeply engaged in flicking off a grain of dust from the immaculate Mechlin ruff at his wrist. The heavy lids had fallen over the tell-tale eyes as if weighted with fatigue, the mouth appeared ready for the laugh which never was absent from it very long.

It was only Ffoulkes's devoted eyes that were sharp enough to pierce the mask of light-hearted gaiety which enveloped the soul of his leader at the present moment. He saw—for the first time in all the years that he had known Blakeney—a frown across the habitually smooth brow, and though the lips were parted for a laugh, the lines round mouth and chin were hard and set.

With that intuition born of whole-hearted friendship Sir Andrew guessed what troubled Percy. He had caught the look which the latter had thrown on Armand and knew that some explanation would have to pass between the two men before they parted tonight. Therefore, he gave the signal for the breaking up of the meeting.

"There is nothing more to say, is there, Blakeney?" he asked.

"No, my good fellow, nothing," replied Sir Percy. "I do not know how you all feel, but I am demmed fatigued."

"What about the rags for tomorrow?" queried Hastings.

"You know where to find them. In the room below. Ffoulkes has the key. Wigs and all are there. But don't use false hair if you can help it—it is apt to shift in a scrimmage."

He spoke jerkily, more curtly than was his wont. Hastings and Tony thought that he was tired. They rose to say goodnight. Then the three men went away together, Armand remaining behind.

CHAPTER 12

What Love Is

"Well, now, Armand, what is it?" asked Blakeney, the moment the footsteps of his friends had died away down the stone stairs, and their voices had ceased to echo in the distance.

"You guessed, then, that there was—something?" said the younger man, after a slight hesitation.

"Of course."

Armand rose, pushing the chair away from him with an impatient nervy gesture. Burying his hands in the pockets of his breeches, he began striding up and down the room, a dark, troubled expression in his face, a deep frown between his eyes.

Blakeney had once more taken up his favourite position, sitting on the corner of the table, his broad shoulders interposed between the lamp and the rest of the room. He was apparently taking no notice of Armand, but only intent on the delicate operation of polishing his nails.

296

Suddenly the young man paused in his restless walk and stood in front of his friend—an earnest, solemn, determined figure.

"Blakeney," he said, "I cannot leave Paris tomorrow."

Sir Percy made no reply. He was contemplating the polish which he had just succeeded in producing on his thumbnail.

"I must stay here for a while longer," continued Armand firmly. "I may not be able to return to England for some weeks. You have the three others here to help you in your enterprise outside Paris. I am entirely at your service within the compass of its walls."

Still no comment from Blakeney, not a look from beneath the fallen lids. Armand continued, with a slight tone of impatience apparent in his voice:

"You must want someone to help you here on Sunday. I am entirely at your service—here or anywhere in Paris—but I cannot leave this city—at any rate, not just yet—"

Blakeney was apparently satisfied at last with the result of his polishing operations. He rose, gave a slight yawn, and turned toward the door.

"Goodnight, my dear fellow," he said pleasantly; "it is time we were all abed. I am so demmed fatigued."

"Percy!" exclaimed the young man hotly.

"Eh? What is it?" queried the other lazily.

"You are not going to leave me like this—without a word?"

"I have said a great many words, my good fellow. I have said 'goodnight,' and remarked that I was demmed fatigued."

He was standing beside the door which led to his bedroom, and now he pushed it open with his hand.

"Percy, you cannot go and leave me like this!" reiterated Armand with rapidly growing irritation.

"Like what, my dear fellow?" queried Sir Percy with good-humoured impatience.

"Without a word—without a sign. What have I done that you should treat me like a child, unworthy even of attention?"

Blakeney had turned back and was now facing him, towering above the slight figure of the younger man. His face had lost none of its gracious air, and beneath their heavy lids his eyes looked down not unkindly on his friend.

"Would you have preferred it, Armand," he said quietly, "if I had said the word that your ears have heard even though my lips have not uttered it?"

"I don't understand," murmured Armand defiantly.

"What sign would you have had me make?" continued Sir Percy, his pleasant voice falling calm and mellow on the younger man's supersensitive consciousness: "That of branding you, Marguerite's brother, as a liar and a cheat?"

"Blakeney!" retorted the other, as with flaming cheeks and wrathful eyes he took a menacing step toward his friend; "had any man but you dared to speak such words to me—"

"I pray to God, Armand, that no man but I has the right to speak them."

"You have no right."

"Every right, my friend. Do I not hold your oath?—Are you not prepared to break it?"

"I'll not break my oath to you. I'll serve and help you in every way you can command—my life I'll give to the cause—give me the most dangerous—the most difficult task to perform—I'll do it—I'll do it gladly."

"I have given you an over-difficult and dangerous task."

"Bah! To leave Paris in order to engage horses, while you and the others do all the work. That is neither difficult nor dangerous."

"It will be difficult for you, Armand, because your head is not sufficiently cool to foresee serious eventualities and to prepare against them. It is dangerous, because you are a man in love, and a man in love is apt to run his head—and that of his friends—blindly into a noose."

"Who told you that I was in love?"

"You yourself, my good fellow. Had you not told me so at the outset," he continued, still speaking very quietly and deliberately and never raising his voice, "I would even now be standing over you, dog-whip in hand, to thrash you as a defaulting coward and a perjurer—Bah!" he added with a return to his habitual *bonhomie*, "I would no doubt even have lost my temper with you. Which would have been purposeless and excessively bad form. Eh?"

A violent retort had sprung to Armand's lips. But fortunately, at that very moment his eyes, glowing with anger, caught those of Blakeney fixed with lazy good-nature upon his. Something of that irresistible dignity which pervaded the whole personality of the man checked Armand's hot-headed words on his lips.

"I cannot leave Paris tomorrow," he reiterated more calmly.

"Because you have arranged to see her again?"

"Because she saved my life today and is herself in danger."

"She is in no danger," said Blakeney simply, "since she saved the life of my friend."

"Percy!"

The cry was wrung from Armand St. Just's very soul. Despite the tumult of passion which was raging in his heart, he was conscious again of the magnetic power which bound so many to this man's service. The words he had said—simple though they were—had sent a thrill through Armand's veins. He felt himself disarmed. His resistance fell before the subtle strength of an unbendable will; nothing remained in his heart but an overwhelming sense of shame and of impotence.

He sank into a chair and rested his elbows on the table, burying his face in his hands. Blakeney went up to him and placed a kindly hand upon his shoulder.

"The difficult task, Armand," he said gently.

"Percy, cannot you release me? She saved my life. I have not thanked her yet."

"There will be time for thanks later, Armand. Just now over yonder the son of kings is being done to death by savage brutes."

"I would not hinder you if I stayed."

"God knows you have hindered us enough already."

"How?"

"You say she saved your life—then you were in danger—Héron and his spies have been on your track; your track leads to mine, and I have sworn to save the *Dauphin* from the hands of thieves—A man in love, Armand, is a deadly danger among us—Therefore at daybreak you must leave Paris with Hastings on your difficult and dangerous task."

"And if I refuse?" retorted Armand.

"My good fellow," said Blakeney earnestly, "in that admirable lexicon which the League of the Scarlet Pimpernel has compiled for itself there is no such word as refuse."

"But if I do refuse?" persisted the other.

"You would be offering a tainted name and tarnished honour to the woman you pretend to love."

"And you insist upon my obedience?"

"By the oath which I hold from you."

"But this is cruel—inhuman!"

"Honour, my good Armand, is often cruel and seldom human. He is a godlike taskmaster, and we who call ourselves men are all of us his slaves."

"The tyranny comes from you alone. You could release me an' you would."

"And to gratify the selfish desire of immature passion, you would wish to see me jeopardise the life of those who place infinite trust in me."

"God knows how you have gained their allegiance, Blakeney. To me now you are selfish and callous."

"There is the difficult task you craved for, Armand," was all the answer that Blakeney made to the taunt—"to obey a leader whom you no longer trust."

But this Armand could not brook. He had spoken hotly, impetuously, smarting under the discipline which thwarted his desire, but his heart was loyal to the chief whom he had reverenced for so long.

"Forgive me, Percy," he said humbly; "I am distracted. I don't think I quite realised what I was saying. I trust you, of course—implicitly—and you need not even fear—I shall not break my oath, though your orders now seem to me needlessly callous and selfish—I will obey—you need not be afraid."

"I was not afraid of that, my good fellow."

"Of course, you do not understand—you cannot. To you, your honour, the task which you have set yourself, has been your only fetish—Love in its true sense does not exist for you—I see it now—you do not know what it is to love."

Blakeney made no reply for the moment. He stood in the centre of the room, with the yellow light of the lamp falling full now upon his tall powerful frame, immaculately dressed in perfectly-tailored clothes, upon his long, slender hands half hidden by filmy lace, and upon his face, across which at this moment a heavy strand of curly hair threw a curious shadow. At Armand's words his lips had imperceptibly tightened, his eyes had narrowed as if they tried to see something that was beyond the range of their focus.

Across the smooth brow the strange shadow made by the hair seemed to find a reflex from within. Perhaps the reckless adventurer, the careless gambler with life and liberty, saw through the walls of this squalid room, across the wide, ice-bound river, and beyond even the gloomy pile of buildings opposite, a cool, shady garden at Richmond, a velvety lawn sweeping down to the river's edge, a bower of clematis and roses, with a carved stone seat half covered with moss. There sat an exquisitely beautiful woman with great sad eyes fixed on the far-distant horizon. The setting sun was throwing a halo of gold all round her hair, her white hands were clasped idly on her lap.

She gazed out beyond the river, beyond the sunset, toward an unseen bourne of peace and happiness, and her lovely face had in it a look of utter hopelessness and of sublime self-abnegation. The air was still. It was late autumn, and all around her the russet leaves of beech and chestnut fell with a melancholy hush-sh-sh about her feet.

She was alone, and from time to time heavy tears gathered in her eyes and rolled slowly down her cheeks.

Suddenly a sigh escaped the man's tightly-pressed lips. With a strange gesture, wholly unusual to him, he passed his hand right across his eyes.

"Mayhap you are right, Armand," he said quietly; "mayhap I do not know what it is to love."

Armand turned to go. There was nothing more to be said. He knew Percy well enough by now to realise the finality of his pronouncements. His heart felt sore, but he was too proud to show his hurt again to a man who did not understand. All thoughts of disobedience he had put resolutely aside; he had never meant to break his oath. All that he had hoped to do was to persuade Percy to release him from it for a while.

That by leaving Paris he risked to lose Jeanne he was quite convinced, but it is nevertheless a true fact that in spite of this he did not withdraw his love and trust from his chief. He was under the influence of that same magnetism which enchained all his comrades to the will of this man; and though his enthusiasm for the great cause had somewhat waned, his allegiance to its leader was no longer tottering.

But he would not trust himself to speak again on the subject.

"I will find the others downstairs," was all he said, "and will arrange with Hastings for tomorrow. Goodnight, Percy."

"Goodnight, my dear fellow. By the way, you have not told me yet who she is."

"Her name is Jeanne Lange," said St. Just half reluctantly. He had not meant to divulge his secret quite so fully as yet.

"The young actress at the *Théâtre National?*"

"Yes. Do you know her?"

"Only by name."

"She is beautiful, Percy, and she is an angel—Think of my sister Marguerite—she, too, was an actress—Goodnight, Percy."

"Goodnight."

The two men grasped one another by the hand. Armand's eyes proffered a last desperate appeal. But Blakeney's eyes were impassive and unrelenting, and Armand with a quick sigh finally took his leave.

For a long while after he had gone Blakeney stood silent and motionless in the middle of the room. Armand's last words lingered in his ear:

"Think of Marguerite!"

The walls had fallen away from around him—the window, the river below, the Temple prison had all faded away, merged in the chaos of his thoughts.

Now he was no longer in Paris; he heard nothing of the horrors that even at this hour of the night were raging around him; he did not hear the call of murdered victims, of innocent women and children crying for help; he did not see the descendant of St. Louis, with a red cap on his baby head, stamping on the *fleur-de-lys*, and heaping insults on the memory of his mother. All that had faded into nothingness.

He was in the garden at Richmond, and Marguerite was sitting on the stone seat, with branches of the rambler roses twining themselves in her hair.

He was sitting on the ground at her feet, his head pillowed in her lap, lazily dreaming whilst at his feet the river wound its graceful curves beneath overhanging willows and tall stately elms.

A swan came sailing majestically down the stream, and Marguerite, with idle, delicate hands, threw some crumbs of bread into the water. Then she laughed, for she was quite happy, and anon she stooped, and he felt the fragrance of her lips as she bent over him and savoured the perfect sweetness of her caress. She was happy because her husband was by her side. He had done with adventures, with risking his life for others' sake. He was living only for her.

The man, the dreamer, the idealist that lurked behind the adventurous soul, lived an exquisite dream as he gazed upon that vision. He closed his eyes so that it might last all the longer, so that through the open window opposite he should not see the great gloomy walls of the labyrinthine building packed to overflowing with innocent men, women, and children waiting patiently and with a smile on their lips for a cruel and unmerited death; so that he should not see even through the vista of houses and of streets that grim Temple prison far away, and the light in one of the tower windows, which illumined the final martyrdom of a boy-king.

Thus, he stood for fully five minutes, with eyes deliberately closed and lips tightly set. Then the neighbouring tower-clock of St. Germain l'Auxerrois slowly tolled the hour of midnight. Blakeney woke from his dream. The walls of his lodging were once more around him, and through the window the ruddy light of some torch in the street below fought with that of the lamp.

He went deliberately up to the window and looked out into the night. On the quay, a little to the left, the outdoor camp was just breaking up for the night. The people of France in arms against tyranny were allowed to put away their work for the day and to go to their miserable homes to gather rest in sleep for the morrow. A band of soldiers, rough and brutal in their movements, were hustling the women and children. The little ones, weary, sleepy, and cold, seemed too dazed to move. One woman had two little children clinging to her skirts; a soldier suddenly seized one of them by the shoulders and pushed it along roughly in front of him to get it out of the way. The woman struck at the soldier in a stupid, senseless, useless way, and then gathered her trembling chicks under her wing, trying to look defiant.

In a moment she was surrounded. Two soldiers seized her, and two more dragged the children away from her. She screamed and the children cried, the soldiers swore and struck out right and left with their bayonets. There was a general *mêlée*, calls of agony rent the air, rough oaths drowned the shouts of the helpless. Some women, panic-stricken, started to run.

And Blakeney from his window looked down upon the scene. He no longer saw the garden at Richmond, the lazily-flowing river, the bowers of roses; even the sweet face of Marguerite, sad and lonely, appeared dim and far away.

He looked across the ice-bound river, past the quay where rough soldiers were brutalising a number of wretched defenceless women, to that grim Châtelet prison, where tiny lights shining here and there behind barred windows told the sad tale of weary vigils, of watches through the night, when dawn would bring martyrdom and death.

And it was not Marguerite's blue eyes that beckoned to him now, it was not her lips that called, but the wan face of a child with matted curls hanging above a greasy forehead, and small hands covered in grime that had once been fondled by a queen.

The adventurer in him had chased away the dream.

"While there is life in me I'll cheat those brutes of prey," he murmured.

CHAPTER 13

Then Everything Was Dark

The night that Armand St. Just spent tossing about on a hard, narrow bed was the most miserable, agonising one he had ever passed in his life. A kind of fever ran through him, causing his teeth to chatter and the veins in his temples to throb until he thought that they must burst.

Physically he certainly was ill; the mental strain caused by two great conflicting passions had attacked his bodily strength, and whilst his brain and heart fought their battles together, his aching limbs found no repose.

His love for Jeanne! His loyalty to the man to whom he owed his life, and to whom he had sworn allegiance and implicit obedience!

These super-acute feelings seemed to be tearing at his very heart-strings, until he felt that he could no longer lie on the miserable pal-liasse which in these squalid lodgings did duty for a bed.

He rose long before daybreak, with tired back and burning eyes, but unconscious of any pain save that which tore at his heart.

The weather, fortunately, was not quite so cold—a sudden and very rapid thaw had set in; and when after a hurried toilet Armand, carrying a bundle under his arm, emerged into the street, the mild south wind struck pleasantly on his face.

It was then pitch dark. The street lamps had been extinguished long ago, and the feeble January sun had not yet tinged with pale col-our the heavy clouds that hung over the sky.

The streets of the great city were absolutely deserted at this hour. It lay, peaceful and still, wrapped in its mantle of gloom. A thin rain was falling, and Armand's feet, as he began to descend the heights of Montmartre, sank ankle deep in the mud of the road. There was but scanty attempt at pavements in this outlying quarter of the town, and Armand had much ado to keep his footing on the uneven and inter-mittent stones that did duty for roads in these parts. But this discom-fort did not trouble him just now. One thought—and one alone—was clear in his mind: he must see Jeanne before he left Paris.

He did not pause to think how he could accomplish that at this hour of the day. All he knew was that he must obey his chief, and that he must see Jeanne. He would see her, explain to her that he must leave Paris immediately, and beg her to make her preparations quickly, so that she might meet him as soon as maybe, and accompany him to England straight away.

He did not feel that he was being disloyal by trying to see Jeanne. He had thrown prudence to the winds, not realising that his impru-dence would and did jeopardise, not only the success of his chief's plans, but also his life and that of his friends. He had before parting from Hastings last night arranged to meet him in the neighbourhood of the Neuilly Gate at seven o'clock; it was only six now. There was plenty of time for him to rouse the *concierge* at the house of the Square du Roule, to see Jeanne for a few moments, to slip into Madame Belhomme's kitchen, and there into the labourer's clothes which he was carrying in the bundle under his arm, and to be at the gate at the appointed hour.

The Square du Roule is shut off from the Rue St. Honoré, on which it abuts, by tall iron gates, which a few years ago, when the secluded little square was a fashionable quarter of the city, used to be kept closed at night, with a watchman in uniform to intercept midnight prowlers. Now these gates had been rudely torn away from their sockets, the iron had been sold for the benefit of the ever-empty Treasury, and no one cared if the homeless, the starving, or the evil-doer found shelter under the porticoes of the houses, from whence wealthy or aristocratic owners had long since thought it wise to flee.

No one challenged Armand when he turned into the square, and though the darkness was intense, he made his way fairly straight for the house where lodged Mademoiselle Lange.

So far, he had been wonderfully lucky. The foolhardiness with which he had exposed his life and that of his friends by wandering about the streets of Paris at this hour without any attempt at disguise, though carrying one under his arm, had not met with the untoward fate which it undoubtedly deserved. The darkness of the night and the thin sheet of rain as it fell had effectually wrapped his progress through the lonely streets in their beneficent mantle of gloom; the soft mud below had drowned the echo of his footsteps. If spies were on his track, as Jeanne had feared and Blakeney prophesied, he had certainly succeeded in evading them.

He pulled the *concierge's* bell, and the latch of the outer door, ma-nipulated from within, duly sprang open in response. He entered, and from the lodge the *concierge's* voice emerging, muffled from the depths of pillows and blankets, challenged him with an oath directed at the unseemliness of the hour.

"Mademoiselle Lange," said Armand boldly, as without hesitation he walked quickly past the lodge making straight for the stairs.

It seemed to him that from the *concierge's* room loud vituperations followed him, but he took no notice of these; only a short flight of stairs and one more door separated him from Jeanne.

He did not pause to think that she would in all probability be still in bed, that he might have some difficulty in rousing Madame Belhomme, that the latter might not even care to admit him; nor did he reflect on the glaring imprudence of his actions. He wanted to see Jeanne, and she was the other side of that wall.

"*Hé*, citizen! *Holà!* Here! Curse you! Where are you?" came in a gruff voice to him from below.

He had mounted the stairs and was now on the landing just outside Jeanne's door. He pulled the bell-handle and heard the pleasing echo of the bell that would presently wake Madame Belhomme and bring her to the door.

"Citizen! *Holà!* Curse you for an *aristo!* What are you doing there?"

The *concierge*, a stout, elderly man, wrapped in a blanket, his feet thrust in slippers, and carrying a guttering tallow candle, had appeared upon the landing.

He held the candle up so that its feeble flickering rays fell on Armand's pale face, and on the damp cloak which fell away from his shoulders.

"What are you doing there?" reiterated the *concierge* with another oath from his prolific vocabulary.

"As you see, citizen," replied Armand politely, "I am ringing Mademoiselle Lange's front door bell."

"At this hour of the morning?" queried the man with a sneer.

"I desire to see her."

"Then you have come to the wrong house, citizen," said the *concierge* with a rude laugh.

"The wrong house? What do you mean?" stammered Armand, a little bewildered.

"She is not here—*quoi!*" retorted the *concierge*, who now turned deliberately on his heel. "Go and look for her, citizen; it'll take you some time to find her."

He shuffled off in the direction of the stairs. Armand was vainly trying to shake himself free from a sudden, an awful sense of horror.

He gave another vigorous pull at the bell, then with one bound he overtook the *concierge*, who was preparing to descend the stairs, and gripped him peremptorily by the arm.

"Where is Mademoiselle Lange?" he asked.

His voice sounded quite strange in his own ear; his throat felt parched, and he had to moisten his lips with his tongue before he was able to speak.

"Arrested," replied the man.

"Arrested? When? Where? How?"

"When—late yesterday evening. Where?—here in her room. How?—by the agents of the Committee of General Security. She and the old woman! *Basta!* that's all I know. Now I am going back to bed, and you clear out of the house. You are making a disturbance, and I shall be reprimanded. I ask you, is this a decent time for rousing honest patriots out of their morning sleep?"

He shook his arm free from Armand's grasp and once more began to descend.

Armand stood on the landing like a man who has been stunned by a blow on the head. His limbs were paralysed. He could not for the moment have moved or spoken if his life had depended on a sign or on a word. His brain was reeling, and he had to steady himself with his hand against the wall or he would have fallen headlong on the floor. He had lived in a whirl of excitement for the past twenty-four hours; his nerves during that time had been kept at straining point. Passion, joy, happiness, deadly danger, and moral fights had worn his mental endurance threadbare; want of proper food and a sleepless night had almost thrown his physical balance out of gear. This blow came at a moment when he was least able to bear it.

Jeanne had been arrested! Jeanne was in the hands of those brutes, whom he, Armand, had regarded yesterday with insurmountable loathing! Jeanne was in prison—she was arrested—she would be tried, condemned, and all because of him!

The thought was so awful that it brought him to the verge of mania. He watched as in a dream the form of the *concierge* shuffling his way down the oak staircase; his portly figure assumed Gargantuan proportions, the candle which he carried looked like the dancing flames of hell, through which grinning faces, hideous and contortioned, mocked at him and leered.

Then suddenly everything was dark. The light had disappeared round the bend of the stairs; grinning faces and ghoulish visions vanished; he only saw Jeanne, his dainty, exquisite Jeanne, in the hands of those brutes. He saw her as he had seen a year and a half ago the victims of those bloodthirsty wretches being dragged before a tribunal that was but a mockery of justice; he heard the quick interrogatory, and the responses from her perfect lips, that exquisite voice of hers veiled by tones of anguish. He heard the condemnation, the rattle of the tumbril on the ill-paved streets—saw her there with hands clasped together, her eyes—

Great God! he was really going mad!

Like a wild creature driven forth he started to run down the stairs, past the *concierge*, who was just entering his lodge, and who now turned in surly anger to watch this man running away like a lunatic or a fool, out by the front door and into the street. In a moment he was out of the little square; then like a hunted hare he still ran down the Rue St. Honoré, along its narrow, interminable length. His hat had fallen from his head, his hair was wild all round his face, the rain weighted the cloak upon his shoulders; but still he ran.

His feet made no noise on the muddy pavement. He ran on and on, his elbows pressed to his sides, panting, quivering, intent but upon one thing—the goal which he had set himself to reach.

Jeanne was arrested. He did not know where to look for her, but he did know whither he wanted to go now as swiftly as his legs would carry him.

It was still dark, but Armand St. Just was a born Parisian, and he knew every inch of this quarter, where he and Marguerite had years ago lived. Down the Rue St. Honoré, he had reached the bottom of the interminably long street at last. He had kept just a sufficiency of reason—or was it merely blind instinct?—to avoid the places where the night patrols of the National Guard might be on the watch. He avoided the Place du Carrousel, also the quay, and struck sharply to his right until he reached the facade of St. Germain l'Auxerrois.

Another effort; round the corner, and there was the house at last. He was like the hunted creature now that has run to earth. Up the two flights of stone stairs, and then the pull at the bell; a moment of tense anxiety, whilst panting, gasping, almost choked with the sustained effort and the strain of the past half-hour, he leaned against the wall, striving not to fall.

Then the well-known firm step across the rooms beyond, the open door, the hand upon his shoulder.

After that he remembered nothing more.

CHAPTER 14

The Chief

He had not actually fainted, but the exertion of that long run had rendered him partially unconscious. He knew now that he was safe, that he was sitting in Blakeney's room, and that something hot and vivifying was being poured down his throat.

"Percy, they have arrested her!" he said, panting, as soon as speech returned to his paralysed tongue.

"All right. Don't talk now. Wait till you are better."

With infinite care and gentleness Blakeney arranged some cushions under Armand's head, turned the sofa towards the fire, and *anon* brought his friend a cup of hot coffee, which the latter drank with avidity.

He was really too exhausted to speak. He had contrived to tell Blakeney, and now Blakeney knew, so everything would be all right. The inevitable reaction was asserting itself; the muscles had relaxed, the nerves were numbed, and Armand lay back on the sofa with eyes half closed, unable to move, yet feeling his strength gradually returning to him, his vitality asserting itself, all the feverish excitement of the past twenty-four hours yielding at last to a calmer mood.

Through his half-closed eyes he could see his brother-in-law moving about the room. Blakeney was fully dressed. In a sleepy kind of way Armand wondered if he had been to bed at all; certainly, his clothes set on him with their usual well-tailored perfection, and there was no suggestion in his brisk step and alert movements that he had passed a sleepless night.

Now he was standing by the open window. Armand, from where he lay, could see his broad shoulders sharply outlined against the grey background of the hazy winter dawn. A wan light was just creeping up from the east over the city; the noises of the streets below came distinctly to Armand's ear.

He roused himself with one vigorous effort from his lethargy, feeling quite ashamed of himself and of this breakdown of his nervous system. He looked with frank admiration on Sir Percy, who stood immovable and silent by the window—a perfect tower of strength, serene and impassive, yet kindly in distress.

"Percy," said the young man, "I ran all the way from the top of the Rue St. Honoré. I was only breathless. I am quite all right. May I tell you all about it?"

Without a word Blakeney closed the window and came across to the sofa; he sat down beside Armand, and to all outward appearances he was nothing now but a kind and sympathetic listener to a friend's tale of woe. Not a line in his face or a look in his eyes betrayed the thoughts of the leader who had been thwarted at the outset of a dangerous enterprise, or of the man, accustomed to command, who had been so flagrantly disobeyed.

Armand, unconscious of all save of Jeanne and of her immediate need, put an eager hand on Percy's arm.

"Héron and his hell-hounds went back to her lodgings last night," he said, speaking as if he were still a little out of breath. "They hoped to get me, no doubt; not finding me there, they took her. Oh, my God!"

It was the first time that he had put the whole terrible circumstance into words, and it seemed to gain in reality by the recounting. The agony of mind which he endured was almost unbearable; he hid his face in his hands lest Percy should see how terribly he suffered.

"I knew that," said Blakeney quietly. Armand looked up in surprise.

"How? When did you know it?" he stammered.

"Last night when you left me. I went down to the Square du Roule. I arrived there just too late."

"Percy!" exclaimed Armand, whose pale face had suddenly flushed scarlet, "you did that?—last night you—"

"Of course," interposed the other calmly; "had I not promised you to keep watch over her? When I heard the news, it was already too late to make further inquiries, but when you arrived just now I was on the point of starting out, in order to find out in what prison Mademoiselle Lange is being detained. I shall have to go soon, Armand, before the guard is changed at the Temple and the Tuileries. This is the safest time, and God knows we are all of us sufficiently compromised already."

The flush of shame deepened in St. Just's cheek. There had not been a hint of reproach in the voice of his chief, and the eyes which regarded him now from beneath the half-closed lids showed nothing but lazy *bonhomie*.

In a moment now, Armand realised all the harm which his recklessness had done, was still doing to the work of the League. Every one of his actions since his arrival in Paris two days ago had jeopardised a plan or endangered a life: his friendship with de Batz, his connection with Mademoiselle Lange, his visit to her yesterday afternoon, the repetition of it this morning, culminating in that wild run through the streets of Paris, when at any moment a spy lurking round a corner might either have barred his way, or, worse still, have followed him to Blakeney's door. Armand, without a thought of anyone save of his beloved, might easily this morning have brought an agent of the Committee of General Security face to face with his chief.

"Percy," he murmured, "can you ever forgive me?"

"Pshaw, man!" retorted Blakeney lightly; "there is naught to forgive, only a great deal that should no longer be forgotten; your duty to the others, for instance, your obedience, and your honour."

"I was mad, Percy. Oh! if you only could understand what she means to me!"

Blakeney laughed, his own light-hearted careless laugh, which so often before now had helped to hide what he really felt from the eyes of the indifferent, and even from those of his friends.

"No! no!" he said lightly, "we agreed last night, did we not? that in matters of sentiment I am a cold-blooded fish. But will you at any rate concede that I am a man of my word? Did I not pledge it last night that Mademoiselle Lange would be safe? I foresaw her arrest the moment I heard your story. I hoped that I might reach her before that brute Héron's return; unfortunately, he forestalled me by less than half an hour. Mademoiselle Lange has been arrested, Armand; but why should you not trust me on that account? Have we not succeeded, I and the others, in worse cases than this one? They mean no harm to Jeanne Lange," he added emphatically; "I give you my word on that. They only want her as a decoy. It is you they want. You through her, and me through you. I pledge you my honour that she will be safe. You must try and trust me, Armand. It is much to ask, I know, for you will have to trust me with what is most precious in the world to you; and you will have to obey me blindly, or I shall not be able to keep my word."

"What do you wish me to do?"

"Firstly, you must be outside Paris within the hour. Every minute that you spend inside the city now is full of danger—oh, no! not for you," added Blakeney, checking with a good-humoured gesture Armand's words of protestation, "danger for the others—and for our scheme tomorrow."

"How can I go to St. Germain, Percy, knowing that she—"

"Is under my charge?" interposed the other calmly. "That should not be so very difficult. Come," he added, placing a kindly hand on the other's shoulder, "you shall not find me such an inhuman monster after all. But I must think of the others, you see, and of the child whom I have sworn to save. But I won't send you as far as St. Germain. Go down to the room below and find a good bundle of rough clothes that will serve you as a disguise, for I imagine that you have lost those which you had on the landing or the stairs of the house in the Square du Roule. In a tin box with the clothes downstairs you will find the packet of miscellaneous certificates of safety. Take an appropriate one, and then start out immediately for Villette. You understand?"

"Yes, yes!" said Armand eagerly. "You want me to join Ffoulkes and Tony."

"Yes! You'll find them probably unloading coal by the canal. Try and get private speech with them as early as may be and tell Tony to set out at once for St. Germain, and to join Hastings there, instead of you, whilst you take his place with Ffoulkes."

"Yes, I understand; but how will Tony reach St. Germain?"

"La, my good fellow," said Blakeney gaily, "you may safely trust Tony to go where I send him. Do you but do as I tell you and leave him to look after himself. And now," he added, speaking more earnestly, "the sooner you get out of Paris the better it will be for us all. As you see, I am only sending you to La Villette, because it is not so far, but that I can keep in personal touch with you. Remain close to the gates for an hour after nightfall. I will contrive before they close to bring you news of Mademoiselle Lange."

Armand said no more. The sense of shame in him deepened with every word spoken by his chief. He felt how untrustworthy he had been, how undeserving of the selfless devotion which Percy was showing him even now. The words of gratitude died on his lips; he knew that they would be unwelcome. These Englishmen were so devoid of sentiment, he thought, and his brother-in-law, with all his unselfish and heroic deeds, was, he felt, absolutely callous in matters of the heart.

But Armand was a noble-minded man, and with the true sporting instinct in him, despite the fact that he was a creature of nerves, highly strung and imaginative. He could give ungrudging admiration to his chief, even whilst giving himself up entirely to the sentiment for Jeanne.

He tried to imbue himself with the same spirit that actuated my Lord Tony and the other members of the League. How gladly would he have chaffed and made senseless schoolboy jokes like those which—in face of their hazardous enterprise and the dangers which they all ran—had horrified him so much last night.

But somehow, he knew that jokes from him would not ring true. How could he smile when his heart was brimming over with his love for Jeanne, and with solicitude on her account? He felt that Percy was regarding him with a kind of indulgent amusement; there was a look of suppressed merriment in the depths of those lazy blue eyes.

So he braced up his nerves, trying his best to look cool and unconcerned, but he could not altogether hide from his friend the burning anxiety which was threatening to break his heart.

"I have given you my word, Armand," said Blakeney in answer to the unspoken prayer; "cannot you try and trust me—as the others do? Then with sudden transition he pointed to the map behind him.

"Remember the gate of Villette, and the corner by the towpath. Join Ffoulkes as soon as may be and send Tony on his way and wait for news of Mademoiselle Lange some time tonight."

"God bless you, Percy!" said Armand involuntarily. "Goodbye!"

"Goodbye, my dear fellow. Slip on your disguise as quickly as you can and be out of the house in a quarter of an hour."

He accompanied Armand through the ante-room, and finally closed the door on him. Then he went back to his room and walked up to the window, which he threw open to the humid morning air. Now that he was alone the look of trouble on his face deepened to a dark, anxious frown, and as he looked out across the river a sigh of bitter impatience and disappointment escaped his lips.

CHAPTER 15

The Gate of La Villette

And now the shades of evening had long since yielded to those of night. The gate of La Villette, at the northeast corner of the city, was about to close. Armand, dressed in the rough clothes of a labouring man, was leaning against a low wall at the angle of the narrow street which abuts on the canal at its further end; from this point of vantage he could command a view of the gate and of the life and bustle around it.

He was dog-tired. After the emotions of the past twenty-four hours, a day's hard manual toil to which he was unaccustomed had caused him to ache in every limb. As soon as he had arrived at the canal wharf in the early morning he had obtained the kind of casual work that ruled about here, and soon was told off to unload a cargo of coal which had arrived by barge overnight. He had set to with a will, half hoping to kill his anxiety by dint of heavy bodily exertion. During the course of the morning he had suddenly become aware of Sir Andrew Ffoulkes and of Lord Anthony Dewhurst working not far away from him, and as fine a pair of coalheavers as any shipper could desire.

It was not very difficult in the midst of the noise and activity that reigned all about the wharf for the three men to exchange a few words together, and Armand soon communicated the chief's new instructions to my Lord Tony, who effectually slipped away from his work sometime during the day. Armand did not even see him go, it had all been so neatly done.

Just before five o'clock in the afternoon the labourers were paid off. It was then too dark to continue work. Armand would have liked to talk to Sir Andrew, if only for a moment. He felt lonely and desperately anxious. He had hoped to tire out his nerves as well as his body, but in this he had not succeeded. As soon as he had given up his tools, his brain began to work again more busily than ever. It followed Percy in his peregrinations through the city, trying to discover where those brutes were keeping Jeanne.

That task had suddenly loomed up before Armand's mind with all its terrible difficulties. How could Percy—a marked man if ever there was one—go from prison to prison to inquire about Jeanne? The very idea seemed preposterous. Armand ought never to have consented to such an insensate plan. The more he thought of it, the more impossible did it seem that Blakeney could find anything out.

Sir Andrew Ffoulkes was nowhere to be seen. St. Just wandered about in the dark, lonely streets of this outlying quarter vainly trying to find the friend in whom he could confide, who, no doubt, would reassure him as to Blakeney's probable movements in Paris. Then as the hour approached for the closing of the city gates Armand took up his stand at an angle of the street from whence he could see both the gate on one side of him and the thin line of the canal intersecting the street at its further end.

Unless Percy came within the next five minutes the gates would be closed and the difficulties of crossing the barrier would be increased a hundredfold. The market gardeners with their covered carts filed out of the gate one by one; the labourers on foot were returning to their homes; there was a group of stonemasons, a few road-makers, also a number of beggars, ragged and filthy, who herded somewhere in the neighbourhood of the canal.

In every form, under every disguise, Armand hoped to discover Percy. He could not stand still for very long but strode up and down the road that skirts the fortifications at this point.

There were a good many idlers about at this hour; some men who had finished their work, and meant to spend an hour or so in one of the drinking shops that abounded in the neighbourhood of the wharf; others who liked to gather a small knot of listeners around them, whilst they discoursed on the politics of the day, or rather raged against the Convention, which was all made up of traitors to the people's welfare.

Armand, trying manfully to play his part, joined one of the groups that stood gaping round a street orator. He shouted with the best of them, waved his cap in the air, and applauded or hissed in unison with the majority. But his eyes never wandered for long away from the gate whence Percy must come now at any moment—now or not at all.

At what precise moment the awful doubt took birth in his mind the young man could not afterwards have said. Perhaps it was when he heard the roll of drums proclaiming the closing of the gates and witnessed the changing of the guard.

Percy had not come. He could not come now, and he (Armand) would have the night to face without news of Jeanne. Something, of course, had detained Percy; perhaps he had been unable to get definite information about Jeanne; perhaps the information which he had obtained was too terrible to communicate.

If only Sir Andrew Ffoulkes had been there, and Armand had had someone to talk to, perhaps then he would have found sufficient strength of mind to wait with outward patience, even though his nerves were on the rack.

Darkness closed in around him, and with the darkness came the full return of the phantoms that had assailed him in the house of the Square du Roule when first he had heard of Jeanne's arrest. The open place facing the gate had transformed itself into the Place de la Révolution, the tall rough post that held a flickering oil lamp had become the gaunt arm of the guillotine, the feeble light of the lamp was the knife that gleamed with the reflection of a crimson light.

And Armand saw himself, as in a vision, one of a vast and noisy throng—they were all pressing round him so that he could not move; they were brandishing caps and tricolour flags, also pitchforks and scythes. He had seen such a crowd four years ago rushing towards the Bastille. Now they were all assembled here around him and around the guillotine.

Suddenly a distant rattle caught his subconscious ear: the rattle of wheels on rough cobble-stones. Immediately the crowd began to cheer and to shout; some sang the "Ça ira!" and others screamed:

"*Les aristos! à la lanterne! à mort! à mort! les aristos!*"

He saw it all quite plainly, for the darkness had vanished, and the vision was more vivid than even reality could have been. The rattle of wheels grew louder, and presently the cart debouched on the open place.

Men and women sat huddled up in the cart; but in the midst of them a woman stood, and her eyes were fixed upon Armand. She wore her pale-grey satin gown, and a white kerchief was folded across her bosom. Her brown hair fell in loose soft curls all round her head. She looked exactly like the exquisite cameo which Marguerite used to wear. Her hands were tied with cords behind her back, but between her fingers she held a small bunch of violets.

Armand saw it all. It was, of course, a vision, and he knew that it was one, but he believed that the vision was prophetic. No thought of the chief whom he had sworn to trust and to obey came to chase away these imaginings of his fevered fancy. He saw Jeanne, and only Jeanne, standing on the tumbril and being led to the guillotine. Sir Andrew was not there, and Percy had not come. Armand believed that a direct message had come to him from heaven to save his beloved.

Therefore, he forgot his promise—his oath; he forgot those very things which the leader had entreated him to remember—his duty to the others, his loyalty, his obedience. Jeanne had first claim on him. It were the act of a coward to remain in safety whilst she was in such deadly danger.

Now he blamed himself severely for having quitted Paris. Even Percy must have thought him a coward for obeying quite so readily. Maybe the command had been but a test of his courage, of the strength of his love for Jeanne.

A hundred conjectures flashed through his brain; a hundred plans presented themselves to his mind. It was not for Percy, who did not know her, to save Jeanne or to guard her. That task was Armand's, who worshipped her, and who would gladly die beside her if he failed to rescue her from threatened death.

Resolution was not slow in coming. A tower clock inside the city struck the hour of six, and still no sign of Percy.

Armand, his certificate of safety in his hand, walked boldly up to the gate.

The guard challenged him, but he presented the certificate. There was an agonising moment when the card was taken from him, and he was detained in the guard-room while it was being examined by the sergeant in command.

But the certificate was in good order, and Armand, covered in coal-dust, with the perspiration streaming down his face, did certainly not look like an aristocrat in disguise. It was never very difficult to enter the great city; if one wished to put one's head in the lion's mouth, one was welcome to do so; the difficulty came when the lion thought fit to close his jaws.

Armand, after five minutes of tense anxiety, was allowed to cross the barrier, but his certificate of safety was detained. He would have to get another from the Committee of General Security before he would be allowed to leave Paris again.

The lion had thought fit to close his jaws.

CHAPTER 16

The Weary Search

Blakeney was not at his lodgings when Armand arrived there that evening, nor did he return, whilst the young man haunted the precincts of St. Germain l'Auxerrois and wandered along the quays hours and hours at a stretch, until he nearly dropped under the portico of a house and realised that if he loitered longer he might lose consciousness completely and be unable on the morrow to be of service to Jeanne.

He dragged his weary footsteps back to his own lodgings on the heights of Montmartre. He had not found Percy, he had no news of Jeanne; it seemed as if hell itself could hold no worse tortures than this intolerable suspense.

He threw himself down on the narrow palliasse and, tired nature asserting herself, at last fell into a heavy, dreamless torpor, like the sleep of a drunkard, deep but without the beneficent aid of rest.

It was broad daylight when he awoke. The pale light of a damp, wintry morning filtered through the grimy panes of the window. Armand jumped out of bed, aching of limb but resolute of mind. There was no doubt that Percy had failed in discovering Jeanne's whereabouts; but where a mere friend had failed a lover was more likely to succeed.

The rough clothes which he had worn yesterday were the only ones he had. They would, of course, serve his purpose better than his own, which he had left at Blakeney's lodgings yesterday. In half an hour he was dressed, looking a fairly good imitation of a labourer out of work.

He went to a humble eating house of which he knew, and there, having ordered some hot coffee with a hunk of bread, he set himself to think.

It was quite a usual thing these days for relatives and friends of prisoners to go wandering about from prison to prison to find out where the loved ones happened to be detained. The prisons were over full just now; convents, monasteries, and public institutions had all been requisitioned by the government for the housing of the hundreds of so-called traitors who had been arrested on the barest suspicion, or at the mere denunciation of an evil-wisher.

There were the Abbaye and the Luxembourg, the erstwhile convents of the Visitation and the Sacré-Coeur, the cloister of the Oratorians, the Salpêtrière, and the St. Lazare hospitals, and there was, of course, the Temple, and, lastly, the *Conciergerie*, to which those prisoners were brought whose trial would take place within the next few days, and whose condemnation was practically assured.

Persons under arrest at some of the other prisons did sometimes come out of them alive, but the *Conciergerie* was only the ante-chamber of the guillotine.

Therefore Armand's idea was to visit the *Conciergerie* first. The sooner he could reassure himself that Jeanne was not in immediate danger the better would he be able to endure the agony of that heartbreaking search, that knocking at every door in the hope of finding his beloved.

If Jeanne was not in the *Conciergerie*, then there might be some hope that she was only being temporarily detained, and through Armand's excited brain there had already flashed the thought that mayhap the Committee of General Security would release her if he gave himself up.

These thoughts, and the making of plans, fortified him mentally and physically; he even made a great effort to eat and drink, knowing that his bodily strength must endure if it was going to be of service to Jeanne.

He reached the Quai de l'Horloge soon after nine. The grim, irregular walls of the Châtelet and the house of Justice loomed from out the mantle of mist that lay on the river banks. Armand skirted the square clock-tower and passed through the monumental gateways of the house of Justice.

He knew that his best way to the prison would be through the halls and corridors of the Tribunal, to which the public had access whenever the court was sitting. The sittings began at ten, and already the usual crowd of idlers were assembling—men and women who apparently had no other occupation save to come day after day to this theatre of horrors and watch the different acts of the heartrending dramas that were enacted here with a kind of awful monotony.

Armand mingled with the crowd that stood about the courtyard, and anon moved slowly up the gigantic flight of stone steps, talking lightly on indifferent subjects. There was quite a goodly sprinkling of workingmen amongst this crowd, and Armand in his toil-stained clothes attracted no attention.

Suddenly a word reached his ear—just a name flippantly spoken by spiteful lips—and it changed the whole trend of his thoughts. Since he had risen that morning he had thought of nothing but of Jeanne, and—in connection with her—of Percy and his vain quest of her. Now that name spoken by someone unknown brought his mind back to more definite thoughts of his chief.

"Capet!" the name—intended as an insult, but actually merely irrelevant—whereby the uncrowned little King of France was designated by the revolutionary party.

Armand suddenly recollected that today was Sunday, the 19th of January. He had lost count of days and of dates lately, but the name, "Capet," had brought everything back: the child in the Temple; the conference in Blakeney's lodgings; the plans for the rescue of the boy. That was to take place today—Sunday, the 19th. The Simons would be moving from the Temple, at what hour Blakeney did not know, but it would be today, and he would be watching his opportunity.

Now Armand understood everything; a great wave of bitterness swept over his soul. Percy had forgotten Jeanne! He was busy thinking of the child in the Temple, and whilst Armand had been eating out his heart with anxiety, the Scarlet Pimpernel, true only to his mission, and impatient of all sentiment that interfered with his schemes, had left Jeanne to pay with her life for the safety of the uncrowned king.

But the bitterness did not last long; on the contrary, a kind of wild exultation took its place. If Percy had forgotten, then Armand could stand by Jeanne alone. It was better so! He would save the loved one; it was his duty and his right to work for her sake. Never for a moment did he doubt that he could save her, that his life would be readily accepted in exchange for hers.

The crowd around him was moving up the monumental steps, and Armand went with the crowd. It lacked but a few minutes to ten now; soon the court would begin to sit. In the olden days, when he was studying for the law, Armand had often wandered about at will along the corridors of the house of Justice. He knew exactly where the different prisons were situated about the buildings, and how to reach the courtyards where the prisoners took their daily exercise.

To watch those *aristos* who were awaiting trial and death taking their recreation in these courtyards had become one of the sights of Paris. Country cousins on a visit to the city were brought hither for entertainment. Tall iron gates stood between the public and the prisoners, and a row of sentinels guarded these gates; but if one was enterprising and eager to see, one could glue one's nose against the ironwork and watch the *ci-devant* aristocrats in threadbare clothes trying to cheat their horror of death by acting a farce of light-heartedness which their wan faces and tear-dimmed eyes effectually belied.

All this Armand knew, and on this he counted. For a little while he joined the crowd in the Salle des Pas Perdus and wandered idly up and down the majestic colonnaded hall. He even, at one time, formed part of the throng that watched one of those quick tragedies that were enacted within the great chamber of the court. A number of prisoners brought in, in a batch; hurried interrogations, interrupted answers, a quick indictment, monstrous in its flaring injustice, spoken by Fouc-quier-Tinville, the public prosecutor, and listened to in all seriousness by men who dared to call themselves judges of their fellows.

The accused had walked down the Champs Elysées without wearing a tricolour cockade; the other had invested some savings in an English industrial enterprise; yet another had sold public funds, causing them to depreciate rather suddenly in the market!

Sometimes from one of these unfortunates led thus wantonly to butchery there would come an excited protest, or from a woman screams of agonised entreaty. But these were quickly silenced by rough blows from the butt-ends of muskets, and condemnations—wholesale sentences of death—were quickly passed amidst the cheers of the spectators and the howls of derision from infamous jury and judge.

Oh! the mockery of it all—the awful, the hideous ignominy, the blot of shame that would forever sully the historic name of France. Armand, sickened with horror, could not bear more than a few minutes of this monstrous spectacle. The same fate might even now be awaiting Jeanne. Among the next batch of victims to this sacrilegious butchery he might suddenly spy his beloved with her pale face and cheeks stained with her tears.

He fled from the great chamber, keeping just a sufficiency of presence of mind to join a knot of idlers who were drifting leisurely towards the corridors. He followed in their wake and soon found himself in the long *Galerie des Prisonniers*, along the flagstones of which two days ago de Batz had followed his guide towards the lodgings of Héron.

On his left now were the arcades shut off from the courtyard beyond by heavy iron gates. Through the ironwork Armand caught sight of a number of women walking or sitting in the courtyard. He heard a man next to him explaining to his friend that these were the female prisoners who would be brought to trial that day, and he felt that his heart must burst at the thought that mayhap Jeanne would be among them.

He elbowed his way cautiously to the front rank. Soon he found himself beside a sentinel who, with a good-humoured jest, made way for him that he might watch the *aristos*. Armand leaned against the grating, and his every sense was concentrated in that of sight.

At first, he could scarcely distinguish one woman from another amongst the crowd that thronged the courtyard, and the close ironwork hindered his view considerably. The women looked almost like phantoms in the grey misty air, gliding slowly along with noiseless tread on the flag-stones.

Presently, however, his eyes, which mayhap were somewhat dim with tears, became more accustomed to the hazy grey light and the moving figures that looked so like shadows. He could distinguish isolated groups now, women and girls sitting together under the colonnaded arcades, some reading, others busy, with trembling fingers, patching and darning a poor, torn gown. Then there were others who were actually chatting and laughing together, and—oh, the pity of it! the pity and the shame!—a few children, shrieking with delight, were playing hide and seek in and out amongst the columns.

And, between them all, in and out like the children at play, unseen, yet familiar to all, the spectre of Death, scythe and hour-glass in hand, wandered, majestic and sure.

Armand's very soul was in his eyes. So far, he had not yet caught sight of his beloved, and slowly—very slowly—a ray of hope was filtering through the darkness of his despair.

The sentinel, who had stood aside for him, chaffed him for his intentness.

"Have you a sweetheart among these *aristos*, citizen?" he asked. "You seem to be devouring them with your eyes."

Armand, with his rough clothes soiled with coal-dust, his face grimy and streaked with sweat, certainly looked to have but little in common with the *ci-devant aristos* who formed the hulk of the groups in the courtyard. He looked up; the soldier was regarding him with obvious amusement, and at sight of Armand's wild, anxious eyes he gave vent to a coarse jest.

"Have I made a shrewd guess, citizen?" he said. "Is she among that lot?"

"I do not know where she is," said Armand almost involuntarily.

"Then why don't you find out?" queried the soldier.

The man was not speaking altogether unkindly. Armand, devoured with the maddening desire to know, threw the last fragment of prudence to the wind. He assumed a more careless air, trying to look as like a country bumpkin in love as he could.

"I would like to find out," he said, "but I don't know where to inquire. My sweetheart has certainly left her home," he added lightly; "some say that she has been false to me, but I think that, mayhap, she has been arrested."

"Well, then, you *gaby*," said the soldier good-humouredly, "go straight to *La Tournelle*; you know where it is?"

Armand knew well enough but thought it more prudent to keep up the air of the ignorant lout.

"Straight down that first corridor on your right," explained the other, pointing in the direction which he had indicated, "you will find the *guichet* of *La Tournelle* exactly opposite to you. Ask the *concierge* for the register of female prisoners—every freeborn citizen of the Republic has the right to inspect prison registers. It is a new decree framed for safeguarding the liberty of the people. But if you do not press half a *livre* in the hand of the *concierge*," he added, speaking confidentially, "you will find that the register will not be quite ready for your inspection."

"Half a *livre!*" exclaimed Armand, striving to play his part to the end. "How can a poor devil of a labourer have half a *livre* to give away?"

"Well! a few *sous* will do in that case; a few *sous* are always welcome these hard times."

Armand took the hint, and as the crowd had drifted away momentarily to a further portion of the corridor, he contrived to press a few copper coins into the hand of the obliging soldier.

Of course, he knew his way *to La Tournelle*, and he would have covered the distance that separated him from the *guichet* there with steps flying like the wind, but, commending himself for his own prudence, he walked as slowly as he could along the interminable corridor, past the several minor courts of justice, and skirting the courtyard where the male prisoners took their exercise.

At last, having struck sharply to his left and ascended a short flight of stairs, he found himself in front of the *guichet*—a narrow wooden box, wherein the clerk in charge of the prison registers sat nominally at the disposal of the citizens of this free republic.

But to Armand's almost overwhelming chagrin he found the place entirely deserted. The *guichet* was closed down; there was not a soul in sight. The disappointment was doubly keen, coming as it did in the wake of hope that had refused to be gainsaid. Armand himself did not realise how sanguine he had been until he discovered that he must wait and wait again—wait for hours, all day mayhap, before he could get definite news of Jeanne.

He wandered aimlessly in the vicinity of that silent, deserted, cruel spot, where a closed trapdoor seemed to shut off all his hopes of a speedy sight of Jeanne. He inquired of the first sentinels whom he came across at what hour the clerk of the registers would be back at his post; the soldiers shrugged their shoulders and could give no information. Then began Armand's aimless wanderings round *La Tournelle*, his fruitless inquiries, his wild, excited search for the hide-bound official who was keeping from him the knowledge of Jeanne.

He went back to his sentinel well-wisher by the women's courtyard but found neither consolation nor encouragement there.

"It is not the hour—*quoi?*" the soldier remarked with laconic philosophy.

It apparently was not the hour when the prison registers were placed at the disposal of the public. After much fruitless inquiry, Armand at last was informed by a *bon bourgeois*, who was wandering about the house of Justice and who seemed to know its multifarious rules, that the prison registers all over Paris could only be consulted by the public between the hours of six and seven in the evening.

There was nothing for it but to wait. Armand, whose temples were throbbing, who was footsore, hungry, and wretched, could gain nothing by continuing his aimless wanderings through the labyrinthine building. For close upon another hour he stood with his face glued against the ironwork which separated him from the female prisoners' courtyard. Once it seemed to him as if from its further end he caught the sound of that exquisitely melodious voice which had rung forever in his ear since that memorable evening when Jeanne's dainty footsteps had first crossed the path of his destiny. He strained his eyes to look in the direction whence the voice had come, but the centre of the courtyard was planted with a small garden of shrubs, and Armand could not see across it. At last, driven forth like a wandering and lost soul, he turned back and out into the streets. The air was mild and damp. The sharp thaw had persisted through the day, and a thin, misty rain was falling and converting the ill-paved roads into seas of mud.

But of this Armand was wholly unconscious. He walked along the quay holding his cap in his hand, so that the mild south wind should cool his burning forehead.

How he contrived to kill those long, weary hours he could not afterwards have said. Once he felt very hungry, and turned almost mechanically into an eating-house, and tried to eat and drink. But most of the day he wandered through the streets, restlessly, unceasingly, feeling neither chill nor fatigue. The hour before six o'clock found him on the *Quai de l'Horloge* in the shadow of the great towers of the Hall of Justice, listening for the clang of the clock that would sound the hour of his deliverance from this agonising torture of suspense.

He found his way to *La Tournelle* without any hesitation. There before him was the wooden box, with its *guichet* open at last, and two stands upon its ledge, on which were placed two huge leather-bound books.

Though Armand was nearly an hour before the appointed time, he saw when he arrived a number of people standing round the *guichet*. Two soldiers were there keeping guard and forcing the patient, long-suffering inquirers to stand in a queue, each waiting his or her turn at the books.

It was a curious crowd that stood there, in single file, as if waiting at the door of the cheaper part of a theatre; men in substantial cloth clothes, and others in ragged blouse and breeches; there were a few women, too, with black shawls on their shoulders and kerchiefs round their wan, tear-stained faces.

They were all silent and absorbed, submissive under the rough handling of the soldiery, humble and deferential when *anon* the clerk of the registers entered his box and prepared to place those fateful books at the disposal of those who had lost a loved one—father, brother, mother, or wife—and had come to search through those cruel pages.

From inside his box the clerk disputed every inquirer's right to consult the books; he made as many difficulties as he could, demanding the production of certificates of safety, or permits from the section. He was as insolent as he dared, and Armand from where he stood could see that a continuous if somewhat thin stream of coppers flowed from the hands of the inquirers into those of the official.

It was quite dark in the passage where the long queue continued to swell with amazing rapidity. Only on the ledge in front of the *guichet* there was a guttering tallow candle at the disposal of the inquirers.

Now it was Armand's turn at last. By this time his heart was beating so strongly and so rapidly that he could not have trusted himself to speak. He fumbled in his pocket, and without unnecessary preliminaries he produced a small piece of silver, and pushed it towards the clerk, then he seized on the register marked "*Femmes*" with voracious avidity.

The clerk had with stolid indifference pocketed the half-*livre*; he looked on Armand over a pair of large bone-rimmed spectacles, with the air of an old hawk that sees a helpless bird and yet is too satiated to eat. He was apparently vastly amused at Armand's trembling hands, and the clumsy, aimless way with which he fingered the book and held up the tallow candle.

"What date?" he asked curtly in a piping voice.

"What date?" reiterated Armand vaguely.

"What day and hour was she arrested?" said the man, thrusting his beak-like nose closer to Armand's face. Evidently the piece of silver had done its work well; he meant to be helpful to this country lout.

"On Friday evening," murmured the young man.

The clerk's hands did not in character gainsay the rest of his appearance; they were long and thin, with nails that resembled the talons of a hawk. Armand watched them fascinated as from above they turned over rapidly the pages of the book; then one long, grimy finger pointed to a row of names down a column.

"If she is here," said the man curtly, "her name should be amongst these."

Armand's vision was blurred. He could scarcely see. The row of names was dancing a wild dance in front of his eyes; perspiration stood out on his forehead, and his breath came in quick, stertorous gasps.

He never knew afterwards whether he actually saw Jeanne's name there in the book, or whether his fevered brain was playing his aching senses a cruel and mocking trick. Certain it is that suddenly amongst a row of indifferent names hers suddenly stood clearly on the page, and to him it seemed as if the letters were writ out in blood.

582. Belhomme, Louise, aged sixty. Discharged.

And just below, the other entry:

583. Lange, Jeanne, aged twenty, actress. Square du Roule
No. 5. Suspected of harbouring traitors and ci-devants.
Transferred 29th Nivose to the Temple, cell 29.

He saw nothing more, for suddenly it seemed to him as if someone held a vivid scarlet veil in front of his eyes, whilst a hundred claw-like hands were tearing at his heart and at his throat.

"Clear out now! it is my turn—what? Are you going to stand there all night?"

A rough voice seemed to be speaking these words; rough hands apparently were pushing him out of the way, and someone snatched the candle out of his hand; but nothing was real. He stumbled over a corner of a loose flagstone, and would have fallen, but something seemed to catch hold of him and to lead him away for a little distance, until a breath of cold air blew upon his face.

This brought him back to his senses.

Jeanne was a prisoner in the Temple; then his place was in the prison of the Temple, too. It could not be very difficult to run one's head into the noose that caught so many necks these days. A few cries of "*Vive le roi!*" or "*À bas la république!*" and more than one prison door would gape invitingly to receive another guest.

The hot blood had rushed into Armand's head. He did not see clearly before him, nor did he hear distinctly. There was a buzzing in his ears as of myriads of mocking birds' wings, and there was a veil in front of his eyes—a veil through which he saw faces and forms flitting ghost-like in the gloom, men and women jostling or being jostled, soldiers, sentinels; then long, interminable corridors, more crowd and more soldiers, winding stairs, courtyards and gates; finally the open street, the quay, and the river beyond.

An incessant hammering went on in his temples, and that veil never lifted from before his eyes. Now it was lurid and red, as if stained with blood; *anon* it was white like a shroud but it was always there.

Through it he saw the Pont-au-Change, which he crossed, then far down on the Quai de l'Ecole to the left the corner house behind St. Germain l'Auxerrois, where Blakeney lodged—Blakeney, who for the sake of a stranger had forgotten all about his comrade and Jeanne.

Through it he saw the network of streets which separated him from the neighbourhood of the Temple, the gardens of ruined habitations, the closely-shuttered and barred windows of ducal houses, then the mean streets, the crowded drinking bars, the tumble-down shops with their dilapidated awnings.

He saw with eyes that did not see, heard the tumult of daily life round him with ears that did not hear. Jeanne was in the Temple prison, and when its grim gates closed finally for the night, he—Armand, her chevalier, her lover, her defender—would be within its walls as near to cell No. 29 as bribery, entreaty, promises would help him to attain.

Ah! there at last loomed the great building, the pointed bastions cut through the surrounding gloom as with a sable knife.

Armand reached the gate; the sentinels challenged him; he replied: "*Vive le roi!*" shouting wildly like one who is drunk.

He was hatless, and his clothes were saturated with moisture. He tried to pass, but crossed bayonets barred the way. Still he shouted: "*Vive le roi!*" and "*À bas la république!*"

"*Allons!* the fellow is drunk!" said one of the soldiers.

Armand fought like a madman; he wanted to reach that gate. He shouted, he laughed, and he cried, until one of the soldiers in a fit of rage struck him heavily on the head.

Armand fell backwards, stunned by the blow; his foot slipped on the wet pavement. Was he indeed drunk, or was he dreaming? He put his hand up to his forehead; it was wet, but whether with the rain or with blood he did not know; but for the space of one second, he tried to collect his scattered wits.

"Citizen St. Just!" said a quiet voice at his elbow.

Then, as he looked round dazed, feeling a firm, pleasant grip on his arm, the same quiet voice continued calmly:

"Perhaps you do not remember me, citizen St. Just. I had not the honour of the same close friendship with you as I had with your charming sister. My name is Chauvelin. Can I be of any service to you?"

Chapter 17

Chauvelin

Chauvelin! The presence of this man here at this moment made the events of the past few days seem more absolutely like a dream. Chauvelin!—the most deadly enemy he, Armand, and his sister Marguerite had in the world. Chauvelin!—the evil genius that presided over the Secret Service of the Republic. Chauvelin—the aristocrat turned revolutionary, the diplomat turned spy, the baffled enemy of the Scarlet Pimpernel.

He stood there vaguely outlined in the gloom by the feeble rays of an oil lamp fixed into the wall just above. The moisture on his sable clothes glistened in the flickering light like a thin veil of crystal; it clung to the rim of his hat, to the folds of his cloak; the ruffles at his throat and wrist hung limp and soiled.

He had released Armand's arm, and held his hands now underneath his cloak; his pale, deep-set eyes rested gravely on the younger man's face.

"I had an idea, somehow," continued Chauvelin calmly, "that you and I would meet during your sojourn in Paris. I heard from my friend Héron that you had been in the city; he, unfortunately, lost your track almost as soon as he had found it, and I, too, had begun to fear that our mutual and ever enigmatical friend, the Scarlet Pimpernel, had spirited you away, which would have been a great disappointment to me."

Now he once more took hold of Armand by the elbow, but quite gently, more like a comrade who is glad to have met another and is preparing to enjoy a pleasant conversation for a while. He led the way back to the gate, the sentinel saluting at sight of the tricolour scarf which was visible underneath his cloak. Under the stone rampart Chauvelin paused.

It was quiet and private here. The group of soldiers stood at the further end of the archway, but they were out of hearing, and their forms were only vaguely discernible in the surrounding darkness.

Armand had followed his enemy mechanically like one bewitched and irresponsible for his actions. When Chauvelin paused he too stood still, not because of the grip on his arm, but because of that curious numbing of his will.

Vague, confused thoughts were floating through his brain, the most dominant one among them being that Fate had effectually ordained everything for the best. Here was Chauvelin, a man who hated him, who, of course, would wish to see him dead. Well, surely it must be an easier matter now to barter his own life for that of Jeanne; she had only been arrested on suspicion of harbouring him, who was a known traitor to the Republic; then, with his capture and speedy death, her supposed guilt would, he hoped, be forgiven. These people could have no ill-will against her, and actors and actresses were always leniently dealt with when possible. Then surely, surely, he could serve Jeanne best by his own arrest and condemnation, than by working to rescue her from prison.

In the meanwhile, Chauvelin shook the damp from off his cloak, talking all the time in his own peculiar, gently ironical manner.

"Lady Blakeney?" he was saying—"I hope that she is well!"

"I thank you, sir," murmured Armand mechanically.

"And my dear friend, Sir Percy Blakeney? I had hoped to meet him in Paris. Ah! but no doubt he has been busy very busy; but I live in hopes—I live in hopes. See how kindly Chance has treated me," he continued in the same bland and mocking tones. "I was taking a stroll in these parts, scarce hoping to meet a friend, when, passing the postern-gate of this charming hostelry, whom should I see but my amiable friend St. Just striving to gain admission. But, *la!* here am I talking of myself, and I am not reassured as to your state of health. You felt faint just now, did you not? The air about this building is very dank and close. I hope you feel better now. Command me, pray, if I can be of service to you in any way."

Whilst Chauvelin talked he had drawn Armand after him into the lodge of the *concierge*. The young man now made a great effort to pull himself vigorously together and to steady his nerves.

He had his wish. He was inside the Temple prison now, not far from Jeanne, and though his enemy was older and less vigorous than himself, and the door of the *concierge's* lodge stood wide open, he knew that he was indeed as effectually a prisoner already as if the door of one of the numerous cells in this gigantic building had been bolted and barred upon him.

This knowledge helped him to recover his complete presence of mind. No thought of fighting or trying to escape his fate entered his head for a moment. It had been useless probably, and undoubtedly it was better so. If he only could see Jeanne and assure himself that she would be safe in consequence of his own arrest, then, indeed, life could hold no greater happiness for him.

Above all now he wanted to be cool and calculating, to curb the excitement which the Latin blood in him called forth at every mention of the loved one's name. He tried to think of Percy, of his calmness, his easy banter with an enemy; he resolved to act as Percy would act under these circumstances.

Firstly, he steadied his voice, and drew his well-knit, slim figure upright. He called to mind all his friends in England, with their rigid manners, their impassiveness in the face of trying situations. There was Lord Tony, for instance, always ready with some boyish joke, with boyish impertinence always hovering on his tongue. Armand tried to emulate Lord Tony's manner, and to borrow something of Percy's calm impudence.

"Citizen Chauvelin," he said, as soon as he felt quite sure of the steadiness of his voice and the calmness of his manner, "I wonder if you are quite certain that that light grip which you have on my arm is sufficient to keep me here walking quietly by your side instead of knocking you down, as I certainly feel inclined to do, for I am a younger, more vigorous man than you."

"H'm!" said Chauvelin, who made pretence to ponder over this difficult problem; "like you, citizen St. Just, I wonder—"

"It could easily be done, you know."

"Fairly easily," rejoined the other; "but there is the guard; it is numerous and strong in this building, and—"

"The gloom would help me; it is dark in the corridors, and a desperate man takes risks, remember—"

"Quite so! And you, citizen St. Just, are a desperate man just now."

"My sister Marguerite is not here, Citizen Chauvelin. You cannot barter my life for that of your enemy."

"No! no! no!" rejoined Chauvelin blandly; "not for that of my enemy, I know, but—"

Armand caught at his words like a drowning man at a reed.

"For hers!" he exclaimed.

"For hers?" queried the other with obvious puzzlement.

"Mademoiselle Lange," continued Armand with all the egoistic ardour of the lover who believes that the attention of the entire world is concentrated upon his beloved.

"Mademoiselle Lange! You will set her free now that I am in your power."

Chauvelin smiled, his usual suave, enigmatical smile.

"Ah, yes!" he said. "Mademoiselle Lange. I had forgotten."

"Forgotten, man?—forgotten that those murderous dogs have arrested her?—the best, the purest, this vile, degraded country has ever produced. She sheltered me one day just for an hour. I am a traitor to the Republic—I own it. I'll make full confession; but she knew nothing of this. I deceived her; she is quite innocent, you understand? I'll make full confession, but you must set her free."

He had gradually worked himself up again to a state of feverish excitement. Through the darkness which hung about in this small room he tried to peer in Chauvelin's impassive face.

"Easy, easy, my young friend," said the other placidly; "you seem to imagine that I have something to do with the arrest of the lady

330

in whom you take so deep an interest. You forget that now I am but a discredited servant of the Republic whom I failed to serve in her need. My life is only granted me out of pity for my efforts, which were genuine if not successful. I have no power to set anyone free."

"Nor to arrest me now, in that case!" retorted Armand.

Chauvelin paused a moment before he replied with a deprecating smile:

"Only to denounce you, perhaps. I am still an agent of the Committee of General Security."

"Then all is for the best!" exclaimed St. Just eagerly. "You shall denounce me to the Committee. They will be glad of my arrest, I assure you. I have been a marked man for some time. I had intended to evade arrest and to work for the rescue of Mademoiselle Lange; but I will give up all thought of that—I will deliver myself into your hands absolutely; nay, more, I will give you my most solemn word of honour that not only will I make no attempt at escape, but that I will not allow anyone to help me to do so. I will be a passive and willing prisoner if you, on the other hand, will effect Mademoiselle Lange's release."

"H'm!" mused Chauvelin again, "it sounds feasible."

"It does! it does!" rejoined Armand, whose excitement was at fever-pitch. "My arrest, my condemnation, my death, will be of vast deal more importance to you than that of a young and innocent girl against whom unlikely charges would have to be tricked up, and whose acquittal mayhap public feeling might demand. As for me, I shall be an easy prey; my known counter-revolutionary principles, my sister's marriage with a foreigner—"

"Your connection with the Scarlet Pimpernel," suggested Chauvelin blandly.

"Quite so. I should not defend myself—"

"And your enigmatical friend would not attempt your rescue. C'est entendu," said Chauvelin with his wonted blandness. "Then, my dear, enthusiastic young friend, shall we adjourn to the office of my colleague, Citizen Héron, who is chief agent of the Committee of General Security, and will receive your—did you say confession?—and note the conditions under which you place yourself absolutely in the hands of the Public Prosecutor and subsequently of the executioner. Is that it?"

Armand was too full of schemes, too full of thoughts of Jeanne to note the tone of quiet irony with which Chauvelin had been speaking all along. With the unreasoning egoism of youth, he was quite convinced that his own arrest, his own affairs were as important to this entire nation in revolution as they were to himself. At moments like these it is difficult to envisage a desperate situation clearly, and to a young man in love the fate of the beloved never seems desperate whilst he himself is alive and ready for every sacrifice for her sake. "My life for hers" is the sublime if often foolish battle-cry that has so often resulted in whole-sale destruction. Armand at this moment, when he fondly believed that he was making a bargain with the most astute, most unscrupulous spy this Revolutionary Government had in its pay—Armand just then had absolutely forgotten his chief, his friends, the league of mercy and help to which he belonged.

Enthusiasm and the spirit of self-sacrifice were carrying him away. He watched his enemy with glowing eyes as one who looks on the arbiter of his fate.

Chauvelin, without another word, beckoned to him to follow. He led the way out of the lodge, then, turning sharply to his left, he reached the wide quadrangle with the covered passage running right round it, the same which de Batz had traversed two evenings ago when he went to visit Héron.

Armand, with a light heart and springy step, followed him as if he were going to a feast where he would meet Jeanne, where he would kneel at her feet, kiss her hands, and lead her triumphantly to freedom and to happiness.

CHAPTER 18

The Removal

Chauvelin no longer made any pretence to hold Armand by the arm. By temperament as well as by profession a spy, there was one subject at least which he had mastered thoroughly: that was the study of human nature. Though occasionally an exceptionally complex mental organisation baffled him—as in the case of Sir Percy Blakeney—he prided himself, and justly, too, on reading natures like that of Armand St. Just as he would an open book.

The excitable disposition of the Latin races he knew out and out; he knew exactly how far a sentimental situation would lead a young Frenchman like Armand, who was by disposition chivalrous, and by temperament essentially passionate. Above all things, he knew when and how far he could trust a man to do either a sublime action or an essentially foolish one.

Therefore, he walked along contentedly now, not even looking back to see whether St. Just was following him. He knew that he did.

His thoughts only dwelt on the young enthusiast—in his mind he called him the young fool—in order to weigh in the balance, the mighty possibilities that would accrue from the present sequence of events. The fixed idea ever working in the man's scheming brain had already transformed a vague belief into a certainty. That the Scarlet Pimpernel was in Paris at the present moment Chauvelin had now become convinced. How far he could turn the capture of Armand St. Just to the triumph of his own ends remained to be seen.

But this he did know: The Scarlet Pimpernel—the man whom he had learned to know, to dread, and even in a grudging manner to admire—was not like to leave one of his followers in the lurch. Marguerite's brother in the Temple would be the surest decoy for the elusive meddler who still, and in spite of all care and precaution, continued to baffle the army of spies set upon his track.

Chauvelin could hear Armand's light, elastic footsteps resounding behind him on the flagstones. A world of intoxicating possibilities surged up before him. Ambition, which two successive dire failures had atrophied in his breast, once more rose up buoyant and hopeful. Once he had sworn to lay the Scarlet Pimpernel by the heels, and that oath was not yet wholly forgotten; it had lain dormant after the catastrophe of Boulogne, but with the sight of Armand St. Just it had re-awakened and confronted him again with the strength of a likely fulfilment.

The courtyard looked gloomy and deserted. The thin drizzle which still fell from a persistently leaden sky effectually held every outline of masonry, of column, or of gate hidden as beneath a shroud. The corridor which skirted it all round was ill-lighted save by an occasional oil-lamp fixed in the wall.

But Chauvelin knew his way well. Héron's lodgings gave on the second courtyard, the Square du Nazaret, and the way thither led past the main square tower, in the top floor of which the uncrowned King of France eked out his miserable existence as the plaything of a rough cobbler and his wife.

Just beneath its frowning bastions Chauvelin turned back towards Armand. He pointed with a careless hand upwards to the central tower.

"We have got little Capet in there," he said dryly. "Your chivalrous Scarlet Pimpernel has not ventured in these precincts yet, you see."

Armand was silent. He had no difficulty in looking unconcerned;

his thoughts were so full of Jeanne that he cared but little at this moment for any Bourbon king or for the destinies of France.

Now the two men reached the postern gate. A couple of sentinels were standing by, but the gate itself was open, and from within there came the sound of bustle and of noise, of a good deal of swearing, and also of loud laughter.

The guard-room gave on the left of the gate, and the laughter came from there. It was brilliantly lighted, and Armand, peering in, in the wake of Chauvelin, could see groups of soldiers sitting and standing about. There was a table in the centre of the room, and on it a number of jugs and pewter mugs, packets of cards, and overturned boxes of dice.

But the bustle did not come from the guard-room; it came from the landing and the stone stairs beyond.

Chauvelin, apparently curious, had passed through the gate, and Armand followed him. The light from the open door of the guard-room cut sharply across the landing, making the gloom beyond appear more dense and almost solid. From out the darkness, fitfully intersected by a lanthorn apparently carried to and fro, moving figures loomed out ghost-like and weirdly gigantic. Soon Armand distinguished a number of large objects that encumbered the landing, and as he and Chauvelin left the sharp light of the guard-room behind them, he could see that the large objects were pieces of furniture of every shape and size; a wooden bedstead—dismantled—leaned against the wall, a black horsehair sofa blocked the way to the tower stairs, and there were numberless chairs and several tables piled one on the top of the other.

In the midst of this litter a stout, flabby-cheeked man stood, apparently giving directions as to its removal to persons at present unseen.

"*Holà*, Papa Simon!" exclaimed Chauvelin jovially; "moving out today? What?"

"Yes, thank the Lord!—if there be a Lord!" retorted the other curtly. "Is that you, Citizen Chauvelin?"

"In person, citizen. I did not know you were leaving quite so soon. Is Citizen Héron anywhere about?"

"Just left," replied Simon. "He had a last look at Capet just before my wife locked the brat up in the inner room. Now he's gone back to his lodgings."

A man carrying a chest, empty of its drawers, on his back now came stumbling down the tower staircase. Madame Simon followed close on his heels, steadying the chest with one hand.

"We had better begin to load up the cart," she called to her husband in a high-pitched querulous voice; "the corridor is getting too much encumbered."

She looked suspiciously at Chauvelin and at Armand, and when she encountered the former's bland, unconcerned gaze she suddenly shivered and drew her black shawl closer round her shoulders.

"Bah!" she said, "I shall be glad to get out of this God-forsaken hole. I hate the very sight of these walls."

"Indeed, the citizeness does not look over robust in health," said Chauvelin with studied politeness. "The stay in the tower did not, mayhap, bring forth all the fruits of prosperity which she had anticipated."

The woman eyed him with dark suspicion lurking in her hollow eyes.

"I don't know what you mean, citizen," she said with a shrug of her wide shoulders.

"Oh! I meant nothing," rejoined Chauvelin, smiling. "I am so interested in your removal; busy man as I am, it has amused me to watch you. Whom have you got to help you with the furniture?"

"Dupont, the man-of-all-work, from the *concierge*," said Simon curtly. "Citizen Héron would not allow anyone to come in from the outside."

"Rightly too. Have the new commissaries come yet?"

"Only Citizen Cochefer. He is waiting upstairs for the others."

"And Capet?"

"He is all safe. Citizen Héron came to see him, and then he told me to lock the little vermin up in the inner room. Citizen Cochefer had just arrived by that time, and he has remained in charge."

During all this while the man with the chest on his back was waiting for orders. Bent nearly double, he was grumbling audibly at his uncomfortable position.

"Does the citizen want to break my back?" he muttered.

"We had best get along—*quoi?*"

He asked if he should begin to carry the furniture out into the street.

"Two *sous* have I got to pay every ten minutes to the lad who holds my nag," he said, muttering under his breath; "we shall be all night at this rate."

"Begin to load then," commanded Simon gruffly. "Here!—begin

with this sofa."

"You'll have to give me a hand with that," said the man. "Wait a bit; I'll just see that everything is all right in the cart. I'll be back directly."

"Take something with you then as you are going down," said Madame Simon in her querulous voice.

The man picked up a basket of linen that stood in the angle by the door. He hoisted it on his back and shuffled away with it across the landing and out through the gate.

"How did Capet like parting from his papa and *maman?*" asked Chauvelin with a laugh.

"H'm!" growled Simon laconically. "He will find out soon enough how well off he was under our care."

"Have the other commissaries come yet?"

"No. But they will be here directly. Citizen Cochefer is upstairs mounting guard over Capet."

"Well, good-bye, Papa Simon," concluded Chauvelin jovially. "Citizeness, your servant!"

He bowed with unconcealed irony to the cobbler's wife, and nodded to Simon, who expressed by a volley of motley oaths his exact feelings with regard to all the agents of the Committee of General Security.

"Six months of this penal servitude have we had," he said roughly, "and no thanks or pension. I would as soon serve a *ci-devant aristo* as your accursed Committee."

The man Dupont had returned. Stolidly, after the fashion of his kind, he commenced the removal of citizen Simon's goods. He seemed a clumsy enough creature, and Simon and his wife had to do most of the work themselves.

Chauvelin watched the moving forms for a while, then he shrugged his shoulders with a laugh of indifference and turned on his heel.

CHAPTER 19

It Is About the Dauphin

Héron was not at his lodgings when, at last, after vigorous pulls at the bell, a great deal of waiting and much cursing, Chauvelin, closely followed by Armand, was introduced in the chief agent's office.

The soldier who acted as servant said that Citizen Héron had gone out to sup but would surely be home again by eight o'clock. Armand by this time was so dazed with fatigue that he sank on a chair like a log, and remained there staring into the fire, unconscious of the flight of time.

Anon Héron came home. He nodded to Chauvelin and threw but a cursory glance on Armand.

"Five minutes, citizen," he said, with a rough attempt at an apology. "I am sorry to keep you waiting, but the new commissaries have arrived who are to take charge of Capet. The Simons have just gone, and I want to assure myself that everything is all right in the Tower. Cochefer has been in charge, but I like to cast an eye over the brat every day myself."

He went out again, slamming the door behind him. His heavy footsteps were heard treading the flagstones of the corridor, and gradually dying away in the distance. Armand had paid no heed either to his entrance or to his exit. He was only conscious of an intense weariness and would at this moment gladly have laid his head on the scaffold if on it he could find rest.

A white-faced clock on the wall ticked off the seconds one by one. From the street below came the muffled sounds of wheeled traffic on the soft mud of the road; it was raining more heavily now, and from time to time a gust of wind rattled the small windows in their dilapidated frames or hurled a shower of heavy drops against the panes.

The heat from the stove had made Armand drowsy; his head fell forward on his chest. Chauvelin, with his hands held behind his back, paced ceaselessly up and down the narrow room.

Suddenly Armand started—wide awake now. Hurried footsteps on the flagstones outside, a hoarse shout, a banging of heavy doors, and the next moment Héron stood once more on the threshold of the room. Armand, with wide-opened eyes, gazed on him in wonder. The whole appearance of the man had changed. He looked ten years older, with lank, dishevelled hair hanging matted over a moist forehead, the cheeks ashen-white, the full lips bloodless and hanging, flabby and parted, displaying both rows of yellow teeth that shook against each other. The whole figure looked bowed, as if shrunk within itself.

Chauvelin had paused in his restless walk. He gazed on his colleague, a frown of puzzlement on his pale, set face.

"Capet!" he exclaimed, as soon as he had taken in every detail of Héron's altered appearance and seen the look of wild terror that literally distorted his face.

Héron could not speak; his teeth were chattering in his mouth, and his tongue seemed paralysed. Chauvelin went up to him. He was several inches shorter than his colleague, but at this moment he seemed to be towering over him like an avenging spirit. He placed a firm hand on the other's bowed shoulders.

"Capet has gone—is that it?" he queried peremptorily.

The look of terror increased in Héron's eyes, giving its mute reply. "How? When?"

But for the moment the man was speechless. An almost maniacal fear seemed to hold him in its grip. With an impatient oath Chauvelin turned away from him.

"Brandy!" he said curtly, speaking to Armand.

A bottle and glass were found in the cupboard. It was St. Just who poured out the brandy and held it to Héron's lips. Chauvelin was once more pacing up and down the room in angry impatience.

"Pull yourself together, man," he said roughly after a while, "and try and tell me what has occurred."

Héron had sunk into a chair. He passed a trembling hand once or twice over his forehead.

"Capet has disappeared," he murmured; "he must have been spirited away while the Simons were moving their furniture. That accursed Cochefer was completely taken in."

Héron spoke in a toneless voice, hardly above a whisper, and like one whose throat is dry and mouth parched. But the brandy had revived him somewhat, and his eyes lost their former glassy look.

"How?" asked Chauvelin curtly.

"I was just leaving the Tower when he arrived. I spoke to him at the door. I had seen Capet safely installed in the room and gave orders to the woman Simon to let Citizen Cochefer have a look at him, too, and then to lock up the brat in the inner room and install Cochefer in the antechamber on guard. I stood talking to Cochefer for a few moments in the antechamber. The woman Simon and the man-of-all-work, Dupont—whom I know well—were busy with the furniture. There could not have been anyone else concealed about the place—that I'll swear. Cochefer, after he took leave of me, went straight into the room; he found the woman Simon in the act of turning the key in the door of the inner chamber. I have locked Capet in there,' she said, giving the key to Cochefer; 'he will be quite safe until tonight; when the other commissaries come.'"

"Didn't Cochefer go into the room and ascertain whether the woman was lying?"

"Yes, he did! He made the woman re-open the door and peeped in over her shoulder. She said the child was asleep. He vows that he saw the child lying fully dressed on a rug in the further corner of the room. The room, of course, was quite empty of furniture and only lighted by one candle, but there was the rug and the child asleep on it. Cochefer swears he saw him, and now—when I went up—"

"Well?"

"The commissaries were all there—Cochefer and Lasnière, Lorinet and Legrand. We went into the inner room, and I had a candle in my hand. We saw the child lying on the rug, just as Cochefer had seen him, and for a while we took no notice of it. Then someone—I think it was Lorinet—went to have a closer look at the brat. He took up the candle and went up to the rug. Then he gave a cry, and we all gathered round him. The sleeping child was only a bundle of hair and of clothes, a dummy—what?"

There was silence now in the narrow room, while the white-faced clock continued to tick off each succeeding second of time. Héron had once more buried his head in his hands; a trembling—like an attack of ague—shook his wide, bony shoulders. Armand had listened to the narrative with glowing eyes and a beating heart. The details which the two Terrorists here could not probably understand he had already added to the picture which his mind had conjured up.

He was back in thought now in the small lodging in the rear of St. Germain l'Auxerrois; Sir Andrew Ffoulkes was there, and my Lord Tony and Hastings, and a man was striding up and down the room, looking out into the great space beyond the river with the eyes of a seer, and a firm voice said abruptly:

"It is about the *Dauphin!*"

"Have you any suspicions?" asked Chauvelin now, pausing in his walk beside Héron, and once more placing a firm, peremptory hand on his colleague's shoulder.

"Suspicions!" exclaimed the chief agent with a loud oath. "Suspicions! Certainties, you mean. The man sat here but two days ago, in that very chair, and bragged of what he would do. I told him then that if he interfered with Capet I would wring his neck with my own hands."

And his long, talon-like fingers, with their sharp, grimy nails, closed and unclosed like those of feline creatures when they hold the coveted prey.

"Of whom do you speak?" queried Chauvelin curtly.

"Of whom? Of whom but that accursed de Batz? His pockets are bulging with Austrian money, with which, no doubt, he has bribed the Simons and Cochefer and the sentinels—"

"And Lorinet and Lasnière and you," interposed Chauvelin dryly.

"It is false!" roared Héron, who already at the suggestion was foaming at the mouth, and had jumped up from his chair, standing at bay as if prepared to fight for his life.

"False, is it?" retorted Chauvelin calmly; "then be not so quick, friend Héron, in slashing out with senseless denunciations right and left. You'll gain nothing by denouncing anyone just now. This is too intricate a matter to be dealt with a sledge-hammer. Is anyone up in the Tower at this moment?" he asked in quiet, business-like tones.

"Yes. Cochefer and the others are still there. They are making wild schemes to cover their treachery. Cochefer is aware of his own danger, and Lasnière and the others know that they arrived at the Tower several hours too late. They are all at fault, and they know it. As for that de Batz," he continued with a voice rendered raucous with bitter passion, "I swore to him two days ago that he should not escape me if he meddled with Capet. I'm on his track already. I'll have him before the hour of midnight, and I'll torture him—yes! I'll torture him—the Tribunal shall give me leave. We have a dark cell down below here where my men know how to apply tortures worse than the rack—where they know just how to prolong life long enough to make it unendurable. I'll torture him! I'll torture him!"

But Chauvelin abruptly silenced the wretch with a curt command; then, without another word, he walked straight out of the room.

In thought Armand followed him. The wild desire was suddenly born in him to run away at this moment, while Héron, wrapped in his own meditations, was paying no heed to him. Chauvelin's footsteps had long ago died away in the distance; it was a long way to the upper floor of the Tower, and some time would be spent, too, in interrogating the commissaries. This was Armand's opportunity. After all, if he were free himself he might more effectually help to rescue Jeanne. He knew, too, now where to join his leader. The corner of the street by the canal, where Sir Andrew Ffoulkes would be waiting with the coal-cart; then there was the spinney on the road to St. Germain. Armand hoped that, with good luck, he might yet overtake his comrades, tell them of Jeanne's plight, and entreat them to work for her rescue.

He had forgotten that now he had no certificate of safety, that undoubtedly, he would be stopped at the gates at this hour of the night; that his conduct proving suspect he would in all probability he detained, and, mayhap, be brought back to this self-same place within an hour. He had forgotten all that, for the primeval instinct for freedom had suddenly been aroused. He rose softly from his chair and crossed the room. Héron paid no attention to him. Now he had traversed the antechamber and unlatched the outer door.

Immediately a couple of bayonets were crossed in front of him, two more further on ahead scintillated feebly in the flickering light. Chauvelin had taken his precautions. There was no doubt that Armand St. Just was effectually a prisoner now.

With a sigh of disappointment, he went back to his place beside the fire. Héron had not even moved whilst he had made this futile attempt at escape. Five minutes later Chauvelin re-entered the room.

CHAPTER 20

The Certificate of Safety

"You can leave de Batz and his gang alone, Citizen Héron," said Chauvelin, as soon as he had closed the door behind him; "he had nothing to do with the escape of the *Dauphin*."

Héron growled out a few words of incredulity. But Chauvelin shrugged his shoulders and looked with unutterable contempt on his colleague. Armand, who was watching him closely, saw that in his hand he held a small piece of paper, which he had crushed into a shapeless mass.

"Do not waste your time, citizen," he said, "in raging against an empty wind-bag. Arrest de Batz if you like, or leave him alone an' you please—we have nothing to fear from that braggart."

With nervous, slightly shaking fingers he set to work to smooth out the scrap of paper which he held. His hot hands had soiled it and pounded it until it was a mere rag and the writing on it illegible. But, such as it was, he threw it down with a blasphemous oath on the desk in front of Héron's eyes.

"It is that accursed Englishman who has been at work again," he said more calmly; "I guessed it the moment I heard your story. Set your whole army of sleuth-hounds on his track, citizen; you'll need them all."

Héron picked up the scrap of torn paper and tried to decipher the writing on it by the light from the lamp. He seemed almost dazed now with the awful catastrophe that had befallen him, and the fear that his own wretched life would have to pay the penalty for the disappearance of the child.

As for Armand—even in the midst of his own troubles, and of his own anxiety for Jeanne, he felt a proud exultation in his heart. The Scarlet Pimpernel had succeeded; Percy had not failed in his self-imposed undertaking. Chauvelin, whose piercing eyes were fixed on him at that moment, smiled with contemptuous irony.

"As you will find your hands overfull for the next few hours, Citizen Héron," he said, speaking to his colleague and nodding in the direction of Armand, "I'll not trouble you with the voluntary confession this young citizen desired to make to you. All I need tell you is that he is an adherent of the Scarlet Pimpernel—I believe one of his most faithful, most trusted officers."

Héron roused himself from the maze of gloomy thoughts that were again paralysing his tongue. He turned bleary, wild eyes on Armand.

"We have got one of them, then?" he murmured incoherently, babbling like a drunken man.

"M'yes!" replied Chauvelin lightly; "but it is too late now for a formal denunciation and arrest. He cannot leave Paris anyhow, and all that your men need to do is to keep a close look-out on him. But I should send him home tonight if I were you."

Héron muttered something more, which, however, Armand did not understand. Chauvelin's words were still ringing in his ear. Was he, then, to be set free tonight? Free in a measure, of course, since spies were to be set to watch him—but free, nevertheless? He could not understand Chauvelin's attitude, and his own self-love was not a little wounded at the thought that he was of such little account that these men could afford to give him even this provisional freedom. And, of course, there was still Jeanne.

"I must, therefore, bid you goodnight, citizen," Chauvelin was saying in his bland, gently ironical manner. "You will be glad to return to your lodgings. As you see, the chief agent of the Committee of General Security is too much occupied just now to accept the sacrifice of your life which you were prepared so generously to offer him."

"I do not understand you, citizen," retorted Armand coldly, "nor do I desire indulgence at your hands. You have arrested an innocent woman on the trumped-up charge that she was harbouring me. I came here tonight to give myself up to justice so that she might be set free."

"But the hour is somewhat late, citizen," rejoined Chauvelin urbanely. "The lady in whom you take so fervent an interest is no doubt asleep in her cell at this hour. It would not be fitting to disturb her now. She might not find shelter before morning, and the weather is quite exceptionally unpropitious."

"Then, sir," said Armand, a little bewildered, "am I to understand that if I hold myself at your disposition Mademoiselle Lange will be set free as early tomorrow morning as may be?"

"No doubt, sir—no doubt," replied Chauvelin with more than his accustomed blandness; "if you will hold yourself entirely at our disposition, Mademoiselle Lange will be set free tomorrow. I think that we can safely promise that, Citizen Héron, can we not?" he added, turning to his colleague.

But Héron, overcome with the stress of emotions, could only murmur vague, unintelligible words.

"Your word on that, Citizen Chauvelin?" asked Armand.

"My word on it an' you will accept it."

"No, I will not do that. Give me an unconditional certificate of safety and I will believe you."

"Of what use were that to you?" asked Chauvelin.

"I believe my capture to be of more importance to you than that of Mademoiselle Lange," said Armand quietly.

"I will use the certificate of safety for myself or one of my friends if you break your word to me anent Mademoiselle Lange."

"H'm! the reasoning is not illogical, citizen," said Chauvelin, whilst a curious smile played round the corners of his thin lips. "You are quite right. You are a more valuable asset to us than the charming lady who, I hope, will for many a day and year to come delight pleasure-loving Paris with her talent and her grace."

"Amen to that, citizen," said Armand fervently.

"Well, it will all depend on you, sir! Here," he added, coolly running over some papers on Héron's desk until he found what he wanted, "is an absolutely unconditional certificate of safety. The Committee of General Security issue very few of these. It is worth the cost of a human life. At no barrier or gate of any city can such a certificate be disregarded, nor even can it be detained. Allow me to hand it to you, citizen, as a pledge of my own good faith."

Smiling, urbane, with a curious look that almost expressed amusement lurking in his shrewd, pale eyes, Chauvelin handed the momentous document to Armand.

The young man studied it very carefully before he slipped it into the inner pocket of his coat.

"How soon shall I have news of Mademoiselle Lange?" he asked finally.

"In the course of tomorrow. I myself will call on you and redeem that precious document in person. You, on the other hand, will hold yourself at my disposition. That's understood, is it not?"

"I shall not fail you. My lodgings are——"

"Oh! do not trouble," interposed Chauvelin, with a polite bow; "we can find that out for ourselves."

Héron had taken no part in this colloquy. Now that Armand prepared to go he made no attempt to detain him, or to question his colleague's actions. He sat by the table like a log; his mind was obviously a blank to all else save to his own terrors engendered by the events of this night.

With bleary, half-veiled eyes he followed Armand's progress through the room and seemed unaware of the loud slamming of the outside door. Chauvelin had escorted the young man past the first line of sentry, then he took cordial leave of him.

"Your certificate will, you will find, open every gate to you. Goodnight, citizen. *À demain.*"

"Goodnight."

Armand's slim figure disappeared in the gloom. Chauvelin watched him for a few moments until even his footsteps had died away in the distance; then he turned back towards Héron's lodgings.

"*À nous deux,*" he muttered between tightly clenched teeth; "à *nous deux* once more, my enigmatical Scarlet Pimpernel."

Chapter 21

Back to Paris

It was an exceptionally dark night, and the rain was falling in torrents. Sir Andrew Ffoulkes, wrapped in a piece of sacking, had taken shelter right underneath the coal-cart; even then he was getting wet through to the skin.

He had worked hard for two days coal-heaving, and the night before he had found a cheap, squalid lodging where at any rate he was protected from the inclemencies of the weather; but tonight, he was expecting Blakeney at the appointed hour and place. He had secured a cart of the ordinary ramshackle pattern used for carrying coal. Unfortunately, there were no covered ones to be obtained in the neighbourhood, and equally unfortunately the thaw had set in with a blustering wind and driving rain, which made waiting in the open air for hours at a stretch and in complete darkness excessively unpleasant.

But for all these discomforts Sir Andrew Ffoulkes cared not one jot. In England, in his magnificent Suffolk home, he was a confirmed sybarite, in whose service every description of comfort and luxury had to be enrolled. Here tonight in the rough and tattered clothes of a coal-heaver, drenched to the skin, and crouching under the body of a cart that hardly sheltered him from the rain, he was as happy as a schoolboy out for a holiday.

Happy, but vaguely anxious.

He had no means of ascertaining the time. So many of the church-bells and clock towers had been silenced recently that not one of those welcome sounds penetrated to the dreary desolation of this canal wharf, with its abandoned carts standing ghostlike in a row. Darkness had set in very early in the afternoon, and the heavers had given up work soon after four o'clock.

For about an hour after that a certain animation had still reigned round the wharf, men crossing and going, one or two of the barges moving in or out alongside the quay. But for some time now darkness and silence had been the masters in this desolate spot, and that time had seemed to Sir Andrew an eternity. He had hobbled and tethered his horse and stretched himself out at full length under the cart. Now and again he had crawled out from under this uncomfortable shelter and walked up and down in ankle-deep mud, trying to restore circulation in his stiffened limbs; now and again a kind of torpor had come over him, and he had fallen into a brief and restless sleep. He would at this moment have given half his fortune for knowledge of the exact time.

But through all this weary waiting he was never for a moment in doubt. Unlike Armand St. Just, he had the simplest, most perfect faith in his chief. He had been Blakeney's constant companion in all these adventures for close upon four years now; the thought of failure, however vague, never once entered his mind.

He was only anxious for his chief's welfare. He knew that he would succeed, but he would have liked to have spared him much of the physical fatigue and the nerve-racking strain of these hours that lay between the daring deed and the hope of safety. Therefore, he was conscious of an acute tingling of his nerves, which went on even during the brief patches of fitful sleep, and through the numbness that invaded his whole body while the hours dragged wearily and slowly along.

Then, quite suddenly, he felt wakeful and alert; quite a while—even before he heard the welcome signal—he knew, with a curious, subtle sense of magnetism, that the hour had come, and that his chief was somewhere nearby, not very far.

Then he heard the cry—a seamew's call—repeated thrice at intervals, and five minutes later something loomed out of the darkness quite close to the hind wheels of the cart.

"Hist! Ffoulkes!" came in a soft whisper, scarce louder than the wind.

"Present!" came in quick response.

"Here, help me to lift the child into the cart. He is asleep and has been a dead weight on my arm for close on an hour now. Have you a dry bit of sacking or something to lay him on?"

"Not very dry, I am afraid."

With tender care the two men lifted the sleeping little King of France into the rickety cart. Blakeney laid his cloak over him and listened for a while to the slow regular breathing of the child.

"St. Just is not here—you know that?" said Sir Andrew after a while.

"Yes, I knew it," replied Blakeney curtly.

It was characteristic of these two men that not a word about the adventure itself, about the terrible risks and dangers of the past few hours, was exchanged between them. The child was here and was safe, and Blakeney knew the whereabouts of St. Just—that was enough for Sir Andrew Ffoulkes, the most devoted follower, the most perfect friend the Scarlet Pimpernel would ever know.

Ffoulkes now went to the horse, detached the nose-bag, and undid the nooses of the hobble and of the tether.

"Will you get in now, Blakeney?" he said; "we are ready."

And in unbroken silence they both got into the cart; Blakeney sitting on its floor beside the child, and Ffoulkes gathering the reins in his hands.

The wheels of the cart and the slow jog-trot of the horse made scarcely any noise in the mud of the roads, what noise they did make was effectually drowned by the soughing of the wind in the bare branches of the stunted acacia trees that edged the towpath along the line of the canal.

Sir Andrew had studied the topography of this desolate neighbourhood well during the past twenty-four hours; he knew of a detour that would enable him to avoid the La Villette gate and the neighbourhood of the fortifications, and yet bring him out soon on the road leading to St. Germain.

Once he turned to ask Blakeney the time.

"It must be close on ten now," replied Sir Percy. "Push your nag along, old man. Tony and Hastings will be waiting for us."

It was very difficult to see clearly even a metre or two ahead, but the road was a straight one, and the old nag seemed to know it almost as well and better than her driver. She shambled along at her own pace, covering the ground very slowly for Ffoulkes's burning impatience. Once or twice he had to get down and lead her over a rough piece of ground. They passed several groups of dismal, squalid, houses, in some of which a dim light still burned, and as they skirted St. Ouen the church clock slowly tolled the hour of midnight.

But for the greater part of the way derelict, uncultivated spaces of *terres vagues*, and a few isolated houses lay between the road and the fortifications of the city. The darkness of the night, the late hour, the soughing of the wind, were all in favour of the adventurers; and a coal-cart slowly trudging along in this neighbourhood, with two labourers sitting in it, was the least likely of any vehicle to attract attention.

Past Clichy, they had to cross the river by the rickety wooden bridge that was unsafe even in broad daylight. They were not far from their destination now. Half a dozen kilometres further on they would be leaving Courbevoie on their left, and then the sign-post would come in sight. After that the spinney just off the road, and the welcome presence of Tony, Hastings, and the horses. Ffoulkes got down in order to make sure of the way. He walked at the horse's head now, fearful lest he missed the cross-roads and the sign-post.

The horse was getting over-tired; it had covered fifteen kilometres, and it was close on three o'clock of Monday morning.

Another hour went by in absolute silence. Ffoulkes and Blakeney took turns at the horse's head. Then at last they reached the cross-roads; even through the darkness the sign-post showed white against the surrounding gloom.

"This looks like it," murmured Sir Andrew. He turned the horse's head sharply towards the left, down a narrower road, and leaving the sign-post behind him. He walked slowly along for another quarter of an hour, then Blakeney called a halt.

"The spinney must be sharp on our right now," he said.

He got down from the cart, and while Ffoulkes remained beside the horse, he plunged into the gloom. A moment later the cry of the seamew rang out three times into the air. It was answered almost immediately.

The spinney lay on the right of the road. Soon the soft sounds that to a trained ear invariably betray the presence of a number of horses reached Ffoulkes' straining senses. He took his old nag out of the shafts, and the shabby harness from off her, then he turned her out on the piece of waste land that faced the spinney. Someone would find her in the morning, her and the cart with the shabby harness laid in it, and, having wondered if all these things had perchance dropped down from heaven, would quietly appropriate them, and mayhap thank much-maligned heaven for its gift.

Blakeney in the meanwhile had lifted the sleeping child out of the cart. Then he called to Sir Andrew and led the way across the road and into the spinney.

Five minutes later Hastings received the uncrowned King of France in his arms.

Unlike Ffoulkes, my Lord Tony wanted to hear all about the adventure of this afternoon. A thorough sportsman, he loved a good story of hairbreadth escapes, of dangers cleverly avoided, risks taken and conquered.

"Just in ten words, Blakeney," he urged entreatingly; "how did you actually get the boy away?"

Sir Percy laughed—despite himself—at the young man's eagerness.

"Next time we meet, Tony," he begged; "I am so demmed fatigued, and there's this beastly rain—"

"No, no—now! while Hastings sees to the horses. I could not exist long without knowing, and we are well sheltered from the rain under this tree."

"Well, then, since you will have it," he began with a laugh, which despite the weariness and anxiety of the past twenty-four hours had forced itself to his lips, "I have been sweeper and man-of-all-work at the Temple for the past few weeks, you must know—"

"No!" ejaculated my Lord Tony lustily. "By gum!"

"Indeed, you old sybarite, whilst you were enjoying yourself heaving coal on the canal wharf, I was scrubbing floors, lighting fires, and doing a number of odd jobs for a lot of demmed murdering villains, and"—he added under his breath—"incidentally, too, for our league. Whenever I had an hour or two off duty I spent them in my lodgings and asked you all to come and meet me there."

"By Gad, Blakeney! Then the day before yesterday?—when we all met—"

"I had just had a bath—sorely needed, I can tell you. I had been

348

cleaning boots half the day, but I had heard that the Simons were removing from the Temple on the Sunday and had obtained an order from them to help them shift their furniture."

"Cleaning boots!" murmured my Lord Tony with a chuckle. "Well! and then?"

"Well, then everything worked out splendidly. You see by that time I was a well-known figure in the Temple. Héron knew me well. I used to be his lanthorn-bearer when at nights he visited that poor mite in his prison. It was 'Dupont, here! Dupont there!' all day long. 'Light the fire in the office, Dupont! Dupont, brush my coat! Dupont, fetch me a light!' When the Simons wanted to move their household goods they called loudly for Dupont. I got a covered laundry cart, and I brought a dummy with me to substitute for the child. Simon himself knew nothing of this, but *Madame* was in my pay. The dummy was just splendid, with real hair on its head; *Madame* helped me to substitute it for the child; we laid it on the sofa and covered it over with a rug, even while those brutes Héron and Cochefer were on the landing outside, and we stuffed His Majesty the King of France into a linen basket. The room was badly lighted, and an one would have been deceived. No one was suspicious of that type of trickery, so it went off splendidly. I moved the furniture of the Simons out of the Tower. His Majesty King Louis XVII was still concealed in the linen basket. I drove the Simons to their new lodgings—the man still suspects nothing—and there I helped them to unload the furniture—with the exception of the linen basket, of course. After that I drove my laundry cart to a house I knew of and collected a number of linen baskets, which I had arranged should be in readiness for me. Thus, loaded up I left Paris by the Vincennes gate, and drove as far as Bagnolet, where there is no road except past the *octroi*, where the officials might have proved unpleasant. So, I lifted His Majesty out of the basket and we walked on hand in hand in the darkness and the rain until the poor little feet gave out. Then the little fellow—who has been wonderfully plucky throughout, indeed, more a Capet than a Bourbon—snuggled up in my arms and went fast asleep, and—and—well, I think that's all, for here we are, you see."

"But if Madame Simon had not been amenable to bribery?" suggested Lord Tony after a moment's silence.

"Then I should have had to think of something else."

"If during the removal of the furniture Héron had remained resolutely in the room?"

"Then, again, I should have had to think of something else; but remember that in life there is always one supreme moment when Chance—who is credited to have but one hair on her head—stands by you for a brief space of time; sometimes that space is infinitesimal—one minute, a few seconds—just the time to seize Chance by that one hair. So, I pray you all give me no credit in this or any other matter in which we all work together, but the quickness of seizing Chance by the hair during the brief moment when she stands by my side. If Madame Simon had been un-amenable, if Héron had remained in the room all the time, if Cochefer had had two looks at the dummy instead of one—well, then, something else would have helped me, something would have occurred; something—I know not what—but surely something which Chance meant to be on our side, if only we were quick enough to seize it—and so you see how simple it all is."

So simple, in fact, that it was sublime. The daring, the pluck, the ingenuity and, above all, the super-human heroism and endurance which rendered the hearers of this simple narrative, simply told, dumb with admiration.

Their thoughts now were beyond verbal expression.

"How soon was the hue and cry for the child about the streets?" asked Tony, after a moment's silence.

"It was not out when I left the gates of Paris," said Blakeney meditatively; "so quietly has the news of the escape been kept, that I am wondering what devilry that brute Héron can be after. And now no more chattering," he continued lightly; "all to horse, and you, Hastings, have a care. The destinies of France, mayhap, will be lying asleep in your arms."

"But you, Blakeney?" exclaimed the three men almost simultaneously.

"I am not going with you. I entrust the child to you. For God's sake guard him well! Ride with him to Mantes. You should arrive there at about ten o'clock. One of you then go straight to No. 9 Rue la Tour. Ring the bell; an old man will answer it. Say the one word to him, '*Enfant*'; he will reply, '*De roi!*' Give him the child, and may Heaven bless you all for the help you have given me this night!"

"But you, Blakeney?" reiterated Tony with a note of deep anxiety in his fresh young voice.

"I am straight for Paris," he said quietly.

"Impossible!"

"Therefore feasible."

"But why? Percy, in the name of Heaven, do you realise what you are doing?"

"Perfectly."

"They'll not leave a stone unturned to find you—they know by now, believe me, that your hand did this trick."

"I know that."

"And yet you mean to go back?"

"And yet I am going back."

"Blakeney!"

"It's no use, Tony. Armand is in Paris. I saw him in the corridor of the Temple prison in the company of Chauvelin."

"Great God!" exclaimed Lord Hastings.

The others were silent. What was the use of arguing? One of themselves was in danger. Armand St. Just, the brother of Marguerite Blakeney! Was it likely that Percy would leave him in the lurch.

"One of us will stay with you, of course?" asked Sir Andrew after a while.

"Yes! I want Hastings and Tony to take the child to Mantes, then to make all possible haste for Calais, and there to keep in close touch with the *Daydream*; the skipper will contrive to open communication. Tell him to remain in Calais waters. I hope I may have need of him soon.

"And now to horse, both of you," he added gaily. "Hastings, when you are ready, I will hand up the child to you. He will be quite safe on the pillion with a strap round him and you."

Nothing more was said after that. The orders were given, there was nothing to do but to obey; and the uncrowned King of France was not yet out of danger. Hastings and Tony led two of the horses out of the spinney; at the roadside they mounted, and then the little lad for whose sake so much heroism, such selfless devotion had been expended, was hoisted up, still half asleep, on the pillion in front of my Lord Hastings.

"Keep your arm round him," admonished Blakeney; "your horse looks quiet enough. But put on speed as far as Mantes and may Heaven guard you both!"

The two men pressed their heels to their horses' flanks, the beasts snorted and pawed the ground anxious to start. There were a few whispered farewells, two loyal hands were stretched out at the last, eager to grasp the leader's hand.

Then horses and riders disappeared in the utter darkness which

351

comes before the dawn.

Blakeney and Ffoulkes stood side by side in silence for as long as the pawing of hoofs in the mud could reach their ears, then Ffoulkes asked abruptly:

"What do you want me to do, Blakeney?"

"Well, for the present, my dear fellow, I want you to take one of the three horses we have left in the spinney and put him into the shafts of our old friend the coal-cart; then I am afraid that you must go back the way we came."

"Yes?"

"Continue to heave coal on the canal wharf by La Villette; it is the best way to avoid attention. After your day's work keep your cart and horse in readiness against my arrival, at the same spot where you were last night. If after having waited for me like this for three consecutive nights you neither see nor hear anything from me, go back to England and tell Marguerite that in giving my life for her brother I gave it for her!"

"Blakeney—!"

"I spoke differently to what I usually do, is that it?" he interposed, placing his firm hand on his friend's shoulder. "I am degenerating, Ffoulkes—that's what it is. Pay no heed to it. I suppose that carrying that sleeping child in my arms last night softened some nerves in my body. I was so infinitely sorry for the poor mite, and vaguely wondered if I had not saved it from one misery only to plunge it in another. There was such a fateful look on that wan little face, as if destiny had already writ its veto there against happiness. It came on me then how futile were our actions, if God chooses to interpose His will between us and our desires."

Almost as he left off speaking the rain ceased to patter down against the puddles in the road. Overhead the clouds flew by at terrific speed, driven along by the blustering wind. It was less dark now, and Sir Andrew, peering through the gloom, could see his leader's face. It was singularly pale and hard, and the deep-set lazy eyes had in them just that fateful look which he himself had spoken of just now.

"You are anxious about Armand, Percy?" asked Ffoulkes softly.

"Yes. He should have trusted me, as I had trusted him. He missed me at the Villette gate on Friday, and without a thought left me—left us all in the lurch; he threw himself into the lion's jaws, thinking that he could help the girl he loved. I knew that I could save her. She is in comparative safety even now. The old woman, Madame Belhomme, was released the day after her arrest, and Jeanne Lange is still in the house in the Rue St. Germain l'Auxerrois, close to my own lodgings. I got her there early this morning. It was easy for me, of course: 'Holà, Dupont! my boots, Dupont!' 'One moment, citizen, my daughter—' 'Curse thy daughter, bring me my boots!' and Jeanne Lange walked out of the Temple prison her hand in that of that lout Dupont."

"But Armand does not know that she is in safety?"

"No. I have not seen him since that early morning on Saturday when he came to tell me that she had been arrested. Having sworn that he would obey me, he went to meet you and Tony at La Villette, but returned to Paris a few hours later, and drew the undivided attention of all the committees on Jeanne Lange by his senseless, foolish inquiries. But for his action throughout the whole of yesterday I could have smuggled Jeanne out of Paris, got her to join you at Villette, or Hastings in St. Germain. But the barriers were being closely watched for her, and I had the Dauphin to think of. She is in comparative safety; the people in the Rue St. Germain l'Auxerrois are friendly for the moment; but for how long? Who knows? I must look after her of course. And Armand! Poor old Armand! The lion's jaws have snapped over him, and they hold him tight. Chauvelin and his gang are using him as a decoy to trap me, of course. All that had not happened if Armand had trusted me."

He sighed a quick sigh of impatience, almost of regret. Ffoulkes was the one man who could guess the bitter disappointment that this had meant. Percy had longed to be back in England soon, back to Marguerite, to a few days of unalloyed happiness and a few days of peace.

Now Armand's actions had retarded all that; they were a deliberate bar to the future as it had been mapped out by a man who foresaw everything, who was prepared for every eventuality.

In this case, too, he had been prepared, but not for the want of trust which had brought on disobedience akin to disloyalty. That absolutely unforeseen eventuality had changed Blakeney's usual irresponsible gaiety into a consciousness of the inevitable, of the inexorable decrees of Fate.

With an anxious sigh, Sir Andrew turned away from his chief and went back to the spinney to select for his own purpose one of the three horses which Hastings and Tony had unavoidably left behind.

"And you, Blakeney—how will you go back to that awful Paris?" he said, when he had made his choice and was once more back beside

Percy.

"I don't know yet," replied Blakeney, "but it would not be safe to ride. I'll reach one of the gates on this side of the city and contrive to slip in somehow. I have a certificate of safety in my pocket in case I need it.

"We'll leave the horses here," he said presently, whilst he was helping Sir Andrew to put the horse in the shafts of the coal-cart; "they cannot come to much harm. Some poor devil might steal them, in order to escape from those vile brutes in the city. If so, God speed him, say I. I'll compensate my friend the farmer of St. Germain for their loss at an early opportunity. And now, goodbye, my dear fellow! Some time tonight, if possible, you shall hear direct news of me—if not, then tomorrow or the day after that. Goodbye, and Heaven guard you!"

"God guard you, Blakeney!" said Sir Andrew fervently.

He jumped into the cart and gathered up the reins. His heart was heavy as lead, and a strange mist had gathered in his eyes, blurring the last dim vision which he had of his chief standing all alone in the gloom, his broad, magnificent figure looking almost weirdly erect and defiant, his head thrown back, and his kind, lazy eyes watching the final departure of his most faithful comrade and friend.

CHAPTER 22

Of That There Could Be No Question

Blakeney had more than one *pied-à-terre* in Paris, and never stayed longer than two or three days in any of these. It was not difficult for a single man, be he labourer or *bourgeois*, to obtain a night's lodging, even in these most troublous times, and in any quarter of Paris, provided the rent—out of all proportion to the comfort and accommodation given—was paid ungrudgingly and in advance.

Emigration and, above all, the enormous death-roll of the past eighteen months, had emptied the apartment houses of the great city, and those who had rooms to let were only too glad of a lodger, always providing they were not in danger of being worried by the committees of their section.

The laws framed by these same committees now demanded that all keepers of lodging or apartment houses should within twenty-four hours give notice at the bureau of their individual sections of the advent of new lodgers, together with a description of the personal appearance of such lodgers, and an indication of their presumed civil status and occupation. But there was a margin of twenty-four hours, which could on pressure be extended to forty-eight, and, therefore, anyone could obtain shelter for forty-eight hours, and have no questions asked, provided he or she was willing to pay the exorbitant sum usually asked under the circumstances.

Thus, Blakeney had no difficulty in securing what lodgings he wanted when he once more found himself inside Paris at somewhere about noon of that same Monday.

The thought of Hastings and Tony speeding on towards Mantes with the royal child safely held in Hastings' arms had kept his spirits buoyant and caused him for a while to forget the terrible peril in which Armand St. Just's thoughtless egoism had placed them both.

Blakeney was a man of abnormal physique and iron nerve, else he could never have endured the fatigues of the past twenty-four hours, from the moment when on the Sunday afternoon he began to play his part of furniture-remover at the Temple, to that when at last on Monday at noon he succeeded in persuading the sergeant at the Maillot gate that he was an honest stonemason residing at Neuilly, who was come to Paris in search of work.

After that matters became more simple. Terribly foot-sore, though he would never have admitted it, hungry and weary, he turned into an unpretentious eating-house and ordered some dinner. The place when he entered was occupied mostly by labourers and workmen, dressed very much as he was himself, and quite as grimy as he had become after having driven about for hours in a laundry-cart and in a coal-cart, and having walked twelve kilometres, some of which he had covered whilst carrying a sleeping child in his arms.

Thus, Sir Percy Blakeney, Bart., the friend and companion of the Prince of Wales, the most fastidious fop the salons of London and Bath had ever seen, was in no way distinguishable outwardly from the tattered, half-starved, dirty, and out-at-elbows products of this fraternising and equalising Republic.

He was so hungry that the ill-cooked, badly-served meal tempted him to eat; and he ate on in silence, seemingly more interested in boiled beef than in the conversation that went on around him. But he would not have been the keen and daring adventurer that he was if he did not all the while keep his ears open for any fragment of news that the desultory talk of his fellow-diners was likely to yield to him.

Politics were, of course, discussed; the tyranny of the sections, the slavery that this free Republic had brought on its citizens. The names of the chief personages of the day were all mentioned in turns Focquier-Tinville, Santerre, Danton, Robespierre. Héron and his sleuth-hounds were spoken of with execrations quickly suppressed, but of little Capet not one word.

Blakeney could not help but infer that Chauvelin, Héron and the commissaries in charge were keeping the escape of the child a secret for as long as they could.

He could hear nothing of Armand's fate, of course. The arrest—if arrest there had been—was not like to be bruited abroad just now. Blakeney having last seen Armand in Chauvelin's company, whilst he himself was moving the Simons' furniture, could not for a moment doubt that the young man was imprisoned,—unless, indeed, he was being allowed a certain measure of freedom, whilst his every step was being spied on, so that he might act as a decoy for his chief.

At thought of that all weariness seemed to vanish from Blakeney's powerful frame. He set his lips firmly together, and once again the light of irresponsible gaiety danced in his eyes.

He had been in as tight a corner as this before now; at Boulogne his beautiful Marguerite had been used as a decoy, and twenty-four hours later he had held her in his arms on board his yacht the *Daydream*. As he would have put it in his own forcible language:

"Those d—d murderers have not got me yet."

The battle mayhap would this time be against greater odds than before, but Blakeney had no fear that they would prove overwhelming.

There was in life but one odd that was overwhelming, and that was treachery.

But of that there could be no question.

In the afternoon Blakeney started off in search of lodgings for the night. He found what would suit him in the Rue de l'Arcade, which was equally far from the House of Justice as it was from his former lodgings. Here he would be safe for at least twenty-four hours, after which he might have to shift again. But for the moment the landlord of the miserable apartment was over-willing to make no fuss and ask no questions, for the sake of the money which this *aristo* in disguise dispensed with a lavish hand.

Having taken possession of his new quarters and snatched a few hours of sound, well-deserved rest, until the time when the shades of evening and the darkness of the streets would make progress through the city somewhat more safe, Blakeney sallied forth at about six o'clock having a threefold object in view.

Primarily, of course, the threefold object was concentrated on Armand. There was the possibility of finding out at the young man's lodgings in Montmartre what had become of him; then there were the usual inquiries that could be made from the registers of the various prisons; and, thirdly, there was the chance that Armand had succeeded in sending some kind of message to Blakeney's former lodgings in the Rue St. Germain l'Auxerrois.

On the whole, Sir Percy decided to leave the prison registers alone for the present. If Armand had been actually arrested, he would almost certainly be confined in the Châtelet prison, where he would be closer to hand for all the interrogatories to which, no doubt, he would be subjected.

Blakeney set his teeth and murmured a good, sound, British oath when he thought of those interrogatories. Armand St. Just, highly strung, a dreamer and a bundle of nerves—how he would suffer under the mental rack of questions and cross-questions, cleverly-laid traps to catch information from him unawares!

His next objective, then, was Armand's former lodging, and from six o'clock until close upon eight Sir Percy haunted the slopes of Montmartre, and more especially the neighbourhood of the Rue de la Croix Blanche, where Armand had lodged these former days. At the house itself he could not inquire as yet; obviously it would not have been safe; tomorrow, perhaps, when he knew more, but not tonight. His keen eyes had already spied at least two figures clothed in the rags of out-of-work labourers like himself, who had hung with suspicious persistence in this same neighbourhood, and who during the two hours that he had been in observation had never strayed out of sight of the house in the Rue de la Croix Blanche.

That these were two spies on the watch was, of course, obvious; but whether they were on the watch for St. Just or for some other unfortunate wretch it was at this stage impossible to conjecture.

Then, as from the Tour des Dames close by the clock solemnly struck the hour of eight, and Blakeney prepared to wend his way back to another part of the city, he suddenly saw Armand walking slowly up the street.

The young man did not look either to right or left; he held his head forward on his chest, and his hands were hidden underneath his cloak. When he passed immediately under one of the street lamps Blakeney caught sight of his face; it was pale and drawn. Then he turned his head, and for the space of two seconds his eyes across the narrow street encountered those of his chief. He had the presence of mind not to make a sign or to utter a sound; he was obviously being followed, but in that brief moment Sir Percy had seen in the young man's eyes a look that reminded him of a hunted creature.

"What have those brutes been up to with him, I wonder?" he muttered between clenched teeth.

Armand soon disappeared under the doorway of the same house where he had been lodging all along. Even as he did so Blakeney saw the two spies gather together like a pair of slimy lizards, and whisper excitedly one to another. A third man, who obviously had been dogging Armand's footsteps, came up and joined them after a while.

Blakeney could have sworn loudly and lustily, had it been possible to do so without attracting attention. The whole of Armand's history in the past twenty-four hours was perfectly clear to him. The young man had been made free that he might prove a decoy for more important game.

His every step was being watched, and he still thought Jeanne Lange in immediate danger of death. The look of despair in his face proclaimed these two facts, and Blakeney's heart ached for the mental torture which his friend was enduring. He longed to let Armand know that the woman he loved was in comparative safety.

Jeanne Lange first, and then Armand himself; and the odds would be very heavy against the Scarlet Pimpernel! But that Marguerite should not have to mourn an only brother, of that Sir Percy made oath.

He now turned his steps towards his own former lodgings by St. Germain l'Auxerrois. It was just possible that Armand had succeeded in leaving a message there for him. It was, of course, equally possible that when he did so Héron's men had watched his movements, and that spies would be stationed there, too, on the watch.

But that risk must, of course, be run. Blakeney's former lodging was the one place that Armand would know of to which he could send a message to his chief, if he wanted to do so. Of course, the unfortunate young man could not have known until just now that Percy would come back to Paris, but he might guess it, or wish it, or only vaguely hope for it; he might want to send a message, he might long to communicate with his brother-in-law, and, perhaps, feel sure that the latter would not leave him in the lurch.

With that thought in his mind, Sir Percy was not likely to give up the attempt to ascertain for himself whether Armand had tried to communicate with him or not. As for spies—well, he had dodged some of them often enough in his time—the risks that he ran tonight were no worse than the ones to which he had so successfully run counter in the Temple yesterday.

Still keeping up the slouchy gait peculiar to the out-at-elbows working man of the day, hugging the houses as he walked along the streets, Blakeney made slow progress across the city. But at last he reached the *façade* of St. Germain l'Auxerrois, and turning sharply to his right he soon came in sight of the house which he had only quitted twenty-four hours ago.

We all know that house—all of us who are familiar with the Paris of those terrible days. It stands quite detached—a vast quadrangle, facing the Quai de l'Ecole and the river, backing on the Rue St. Germain l'Auxerrois, and shouldering the Carrefour des Trois Manes. The *porte-cochère*, so-called, is but a narrow doorway, and is actually situated in the Rue St. Germain l'Auxerrois.

Blakeney made his way cautiously right round the house; he peered up and down the quay, and his keen eyes tried to pierce the dense gloom that hung at the corners of the Pont Neuf immediately opposite. Soon he assured himself that for the present, at any rate, the house was not being watched.

Armand presumably had not yet left a message for him here; but he might do so at any time now that he knew that his chief was in Paris and on the look-out for him.

Blakeney made up his mind to keep this house in sight. This art of watching he had acquired to a masterly extent and could have taught Héron's watch-dogs a remarkable lesson in it. At night, of course, it was a comparatively easy task. There were a good many unlighted doorways along the quay, whilst a street lamp was fixed on a bracket in the wall of the very house which he kept in observation.

Finding temporary shelter under various doorways, or against the dank walls of the houses, Blakeney set himself resolutely to a few hours' weary waiting. A thin, drizzly rain fell with unpleasant persistence, like a damp mist, and the thin blouse which he wore soon became wet through and clung hard and chilly to his shoulders.

It was close on midnight when at last he thought it best to give up his watch and to go back to his lodgings for a few hours' sleep; but at seven o'clock the next morning he was back again at his post.

The *porte-cochère* of his former lodging-house was not yet open; he took up his stand close beside it. His woollen cap pulled well over his forehead, the grime cleverly plastered on his hair and face, his lower jaw thrust forward, his eyes looking lifeless and bleary, all gave him an expression of sly villainy, whilst the short clay pipe struck at a sharp angle in his mouth, his hands thrust into the pockets of his ragged breeches, and his bare feet in the mud of the road, gave the final touch to his representation of an out-of-work, ill-conditioned, and supremely discontented loafer.

He had not very long to wait. Soon the *porte-cochère* of the house was opened, and the *concierge* came out with his broom, making a show of cleaning the pavement in front of the door. Five minutes later a lad, whose clothes consisted entirely of rags, and whose feet and head were bare, came rapidly up the street from the quay, and walked along looking at the houses as he went, as if trying to decipher their number. The cold grey dawn was just breaking, dreary and damp, as all the past days had been. Blakeney watched the lad as he approached, the small, naked feet falling noiselessly on the cobblestones of the road. When the boy was quite close to him and to the house, Blakeney shifted his position and took the pipe out of his mouth.

"Up early, my son!" he said gruffly.

"Yes," said the pale-faced little creature; "I have a message to deliver at No. 9 Rue St. Germain l'Auxerrois. It must be somewhere near here."

"It is. You can give me the message."

"Oh, no, citizen!" said the lad, into whose pale, circled eyes a look of terror had quickly appeared. "It is for one of the lodgers in No. 9. I must give it to him."

With an instinct which he somehow felt could not err at this moment, Blakeney knew that the message was one from Armand to himself; a written message, too, since—instinctively when he spoke—the boy clutched at his thin shirt, as if trying to guard something precious that had been entrusted to him.

"I will deliver the message myself, sonny," said Blakeney gruffly. "I know the citizen for whom it is intended. He would not like the *concierge* to see it."

"Oh! I would not give it to the *concierge*," said the boy. "I would take it upstairs myself."

"My son," retorted Blakeney, "let me tell you this. You are going to give that message up to me and I will put five whole *livres* into your hand."

Blakeney, with all his sympathy aroused for this poor pale-faced lad, put on the airs of a ruffianly bully. He did not wish that message to be taken indoors by the lad, for the *concierge* might get hold of it, despite the boy's protests and tears, and after that Blakeney would perforce have to disclose himself before it would be given up to him. During the past week the *concierge* had been very amenable to bribery. Whatever suspicions he had had about his lodger he had kept to himself for the sake of the money which he received; but it was impossible to gauge any man's trend of thought these days from one hour to the next. Something—for aught Blakeney knew—might have occurred in the past twenty-four hours to change an amiable and accommodating lodging-house keeper into a surly or dangerous spy.

Fortunately, the *concierge* had once more gone within; there was no one abroad, and if there were, no one probably would take any notice of a burly ruffian brow-beating a child.

"*Allons!*" he said gruffly, "give me the letter, or that five *livres* goes back into my pocket."

"Five *livres!*" exclaimed the child with pathetic eagerness. "Oh, citizen!"

The thin little hand fumbled under the rags, but it reappeared again empty, whilst a faint blush spread over the hollow cheeks.

"The other citizen also gave me five *livres*," he said humbly. "He lodges in the house where my mother is *concierge*. It is in the Rue de la Croix Blanche. He has been very kind to my mother. I would rather do as he bade me."

"Bless the lad," murmured Blakeney under his breath; "his loyalty redeems many a crime of this God-forsaken city. Now I suppose I shall have to bully him, after all."

He took his hand out of his breeches pocket; between two very dirty fingers he held a piece of gold. The other hand he placed quite roughly on the lad's chest.

"Give me the letter," he said harshly, "or—"

He pulled at the ragged blouse, and a scrap of soiled paper soon fell into his hand. The lad began to cry.

"Here," said Blakeney, thrusting the piece of gold into the thin small palm, "take this home to your mother, and tell your lodger that a big, rough man took the letter away from you by force. Now run, before I kick you out of the way."

The lad, terrified out of his poor wits, did not wait for further commands; he took to his heels and ran, his small hand clutching the piece of gold. Soon he had disappeared round the corner of the street.

Blakeney did not at once read the paper; he thrust it quickly into his breeches pocket and slouched away slowly down the street, and thence across the Place du Carrousel, in the direction of his new lodgings in the Rue de l'Arcade.

It was only when he found himself alone in the narrow, squalid room which he was occupying that he took the scrap of paper from his pocket and read it slowly through. It said:

Percy, you cannot forgive me, nor can I ever forgive myself, but if you only knew what I have suffered for the past two days you would, I think, try and forgive. I am free and yet a prisoner; my every footstep is dogged. What they ultimately mean to do with me I do not know. And when I think of Jeanne I long for the power to end mine own miserable existence. Percy! she is still in the hands of those fiends—I saw the prison register; her name written there has been like a burning brand on my heart ever since. She was still in prison the day that you left Paris; tomorrow, tonight mayhap, they will try her, condemn her, torture her, and I dare not go to see you, for I would only be bringing spies to your door. But will you come to me, Percy? It should be safe in the hours of the night, and the *concierge* is devoted to me. Tonight at ten o'clock she will leave the *porte-cochère* unlatched. If you find it so, and if on the ledge of the window immediately on your left as you enter you find a candle alight, and beside it a scrap of paper with your initials S. P. traced on it, then it will be quite safe for you to come up to my room. It is on the second landing—a door on your right—that too I will leave on the latch. But in the name of the woman you love best in all the world come at once to me then, and bear in mind, Percy, that the woman I love is threatened with immediate death, and that I am powerless to save her. Indeed, believe me, I would gladly die even now but for the thought of Jeanne, whom I should be leaving in the hands of those fiends. For God's sake, Percy, remember that Jeanne is all the world to me.

"Poor old Armand," murmured Blakeney with a kindly smile directed at the absent friend, "he won't trust me even now. He won't trust his Jeanne in my hands. Well," he added after a while, "after all, I would not entrust Marguerite to anybody else either."

CHAPTER 23

The Overwhelming Odds

At half-past ten that same evening, Blakeney, still clad in a workman's tattered clothes, his feet bare so that he could tread the streets unheard, turned into the Rue de la Croix Blanche.

The *porte-cochère* of the house where Armand lodged had been left on the latch; not a soul was in sight. Peering cautiously round, he slipped into the house. On the ledge of the window, immediately on his left when he entered, a candle was left burning, and beside it there was a scrap of paper with the initials S. P. roughly traced in pencil. No one challenged him as he noiselessly glided past it, and up the narrow stairs that led to the upper floor. Here, too, on the second landing the door on the right had been left on the latch. He pushed it open and entered.

As is usual even in the meanest lodgings in Paris houses, a small antechamber gave between the front door and the main room. When Percy entered the antechamber was unlighted, but the door into the inner room beyond was ajar. Blakeney approached it with noiseless tread, and gently pushed it open.

That very instant he knew that the game was up; he heard the footsteps closing up behind him, saw Armand, deathly pale, leaning against the wall in the room in front of him, and Chauvelin and Héron standing guard over him.

The next moment the room and the antechamber were literally alive with soldiers—twenty of them to arrest one man.

It was characteristic of that man that when hands were laid on him from every side he threw back his head and laughed—laughed mirthfully, light-heartedly, and the first words that escaped his lips were:

"Well, I am d—d!"

"The odds are against you, Sir Percy," said Chauvelin to him in English, whilst Héron at the further end of the room was growling like a contented beast.

"By the Lord, sir," said Percy with perfect *sang-froid*, "I do believe that for the moment they are."

"Have done, my men—have done!" he added, turning good-humouredly to the soldiers round him. "I never fight against over-whelming odds. Twenty to one, eh? I could lay four of you out easily enough, perhaps even six, but what then?"

But a kind of savage lust seemed to have rendered these men temporarily mad, and they were being egged on by Héron. The mysterious Englishman, about whom so many eerie tales were told! Well, he had supernatural powers, and twenty to one might be nothing to him if the devil was on his side. Therefore, a blow on his forearm with the butt-end of a bayonet was useful for disabling his right hand, and soon the left arm with a dislocated shoulder hung limp by his side. Then he was bound with cords.

The vein of luck had given out. The gambler had staked more than usual and had lost; but he knew how to lose, just as he had always known how to win.

"Those d—d brutes are trussing me like a fowl," he murmured with irrepressible gaiety at the last.

Then the wrench on his bruised arms as they were pulled roughly back by the cords caused the veil of unconsciousness to gather over his eyes.

"And Jeanne was safe, Armand," he shouted with a last desperate effort; "those devils have lied to you and tricked you into this—Since yesterday she is out of prison—in the house—you know—"

After that he lost consciousness.

And this occurred on Tuesday, January 21st, in the year 1794, or, in accordance with the new calendar, on the 2nd *Pluviose*, year 2 of the Republic.

It is chronicled in the *Moniteur* of the 3rd *Pluviose* that:

> On the previous evening, at half-past ten of the clock, the Eng-
> lishman known as the Scarlet Pimpernel, who for three years
> has conspired against the safety of the Republic, was arrested
> through the patriotic exertions of Citizen Chauvelin, and con-
> veyed to the *Conciergerie*, where he now lies—sick, but closely
> guarded. Long live the Republic!

PART 2

Chapter 24

The News

The grey January day was falling, drowsy, and dull into the arms of night.

Marguerite, sitting in the dusk beside the fire in her small *boudoir*, shivered a little as she drew her scarf closer round her shoulders.

Edwards, the butler, entered with the lamp. The room looked pe-culiarly cheery now, with the delicate white panelling of the wall glowing under the soft kiss of the flickering firelight and the steadier glow of the rose-shaded lamp.

"Has the courier not arrived yet, Edwards?" asked Marguerite, fixing the impassive face of the well-drilled servant with her large

Plan of a portion of Old Paris, showing the house at the corner of the Quai de l'Ecole and the Carrefour des Trois Maries where Sir Percy Blakeney lodged, and the Conciergerie Prison where he was incarcerated. Reconstructed from old prints and documents

purple-rimmed eyes.

"Not yet, m'lady," he replied placidly.

"It is his day, is it not?"

"Yes, m'lady. And the forenoon is his time. But there have been heavy rains, and the roads must be rare muddy. He must have been delayed, m'lady."

"Yes, I suppose so," she said listlessly. "That will do, Edwards. No, don't close the shutters. I'll ring presently."

The man went out of the room as automatically as he had come. He closed the door behind him, and Marguerite was once more alone.

She picked up the book which she had fingered idly before the light gave out. She tried once more to fix her attention on this tale of love and adventure written by Mr. Fielding; but she had lost the thread of the story, and there was a mist between her eyes and the printed pages.

With an impatient gesture she threw down the book and passed her hand across her eyes, then seemed astonished to find that her hand was wet.

She rose and went to the window. The air outside had been singularly mild all day; the thaw was persisting, and a south wind came across the Channel—from France.

Marguerite threw open the casement and sat down on the wide sill, leaning her head against the window-frame, and gazing out into the fast gathering gloom. From far away, at the foot of the gently sloping lawns, the river murmured softly in the night; in the borders to the right and left a few snowdrops still showed like tiny white specks through the surrounding darkness. Winter had begun the process of slowly shedding its mantle, coquetting with Spring, who still lingered in the land of Infinity. Gradually the shadows drew closer and closer; the reeds and rushes on the river bank were the first to sink into their embrace, then the big cedars on the lawn, majestic and defiant, but yielding still unconquered to the power of night.

The tiny stars of snowdrop blossoms vanished one by one, and at last the cool, grey ribbon of the river surface was wrapped under the mantle of evening.

Only the south wind lingered on, soughing gently in the drowsy reeds, whispering among the branches of the cedars, and gently stirring the tender corollas of the sleeping snowdrops.

Marguerite seemed to open out her lungs to its breath. It had come all the way from France, and on its wings had brought something of Percy—a murmur as if he had spoken—a memory that was as intangible as a dream.

She shivered again, though of a truth it was not cold. The courier's delay had completely unsettled her nerves. Twice a week he came especially from Dover, and always he brought some message, some token which Percy had contrived to send from Paris. They were like tiny scraps of dry bread thrown to a starving woman, but they did just help to keep her heart alive—that poor, aching, disappointed heart that so longed for enduring happiness which it could never get.

The man whom she loved with all her soul, her mind and her body, did not belong to her; he belonged to suffering humanity over there in terror-stricken France, where the cries of the innocent, the persecuted, the wretched called louder to him than she in her love could do.

He had been away three months now, during which time her starving heart had fed on its memories, and the happiness of a brief visit from him six weeks ago, when—quite unexpectedly—he had appeared before her—home between two desperate adventures that had given life and freedom to a number of innocent people, and nearly cost him his—and she had lain in his arms in a swoon of perfect happiness.

But he had gone away again as suddenly as he had come, and for six weeks now she had lived partly in anticipation of the courier with messages from him, and partly on the fitful joy engendered by these messages. Today she had not even that, and the disappointment seemed just now more than she could bear.

She felt unaccountably restless and could she but have analysed her feelings—had she dared so to do—she would have realised that the weight which oppressed her heart so that she could hardly breathe, was one of vague yet dark foreboding.

She closed the window and returned to her seat by the fire, taking up her book with the strong resolution not to allow her nerves to get the better of her. But it was difficult to pin one's attention down to the adventures of Master Tom Jones when one's mind was fully engrossed with those of Sir Percy Blakeney.

The sound of carriage wheels on the gravelled forecourt in the front of the house suddenly awakened her drowsy senses. She threw down the book, and with trembling hands clutched the arms of her chair, straining her ears to listen. A carriage at this hour—and on this damp winter's evening! She racked her mind wondering who it could be.

Lady Ffoulkes was in London, she knew. Sir Andrew, of course, was in Paris. His Royal Highness, ever a faithful visitor, would surely not venture out to Richmond in this inclement weather—and the courier always came on horseback.

There was a murmur of voices; that of Edwards, mechanical and placid, could be heard quite distinctly saying:

"I'm sure that her ladyship will be at home for you, m'lady. But I'll go and ascertain."

Marguerite ran to the door and with joyful eagerness tore it open.

"Suzanne!" she called "my little Suzanne! I thought you were in London. Come up quickly! In the *boudoir*—yes. Oh! what good fortune hath brought you?"

Suzanne flew into her arms, holding the friend whom she loved so well close and closer to her heart, trying to hide her face, which was wet with tears, in the folds of Marguerite's kerchief.

"Come inside, my darling," said Marguerite. "Why, how cold your little hands are!"

She was on the point of turning back to her *boudoir*, drawing Lady Ffoulkes by the hand, when suddenly she caught sight of Sir Andrew, who stood at a little distance from her, at the top of the stairs.

"Sir Andrew!" she exclaimed with unstinted gladness.

Then she paused. The cry of welcome died on her lips, leaving them dry and parted. She suddenly felt as if some fearful talons had gripped her heart and were tearing at it with sharp, long nails; the blood flew from her cheeks and from her limbs, leaving her with a sense of icy numbness.

She backed into the room, still holding Suzanne's hand, and drawing her in with her. Sir Andrew followed them, then closed the door behind him. At last the word escaped Marguerite's parched lips:

"Percy! Something has happened to him! He is dead?"

"No, no!" exclaimed Sir Andrew quickly.

Suzanne put her loving arms round her friend and drew her down into the chair by the fire. She knelt at her feet on the hearthrug and pressed her own burning lips on Marguerite's icy-cold hands. Sir Andrew stood silently by, a world of loving friendship, of heartbroken sorrow, in his eyes.

There was silence in the pretty white-panelled room for a while. Marguerite sat with her eyes closed, bringing the whole armoury of her will power to bear her up outwardly now.

"Tell me!" she said at last, and her voice was toneless and dull, like one that came from the depths of a grave—"tell me—exactly—eve-rything. Don't be afraid. I can bear it. Don't be afraid."

Sir Andrew remained standing, with bowed head and one hand resting on the table. In a firm, clear voice he told her the events of the past few days as they were known to him. All that he tried to hide was Armand's disobedience, which, in his heart, he felt was the primary cause of the catastrophe. He told of the rescue of the *Dauphin* from the Temple, the midnight drive in the coal-cart, the meeting with Hastings and Tony in the spinney. He only gave vague explanations of Armand's stay in Paris which caused Percy to go back to the city, even at the moment when his most daring plan had been so successfully carried through.

"Armand, I understand, has fallen in love with a beautiful woman in Paris, Lady Blakeney," he said, seeing that a strange, puzzled look had appeared in Marguerite's pale face. "She was arrested the day be-fore the rescue of the *Dauphin* from the Temple. Armand could not join us. He felt that he could not leave her. I am sure that you will understand."

Then as she made no comment, he resumed his narrative:

"I had been ordered to go back to La Villette, and there to resume my duties as a labourer in the daytime, and to wait for Percy during the night. The fact that I had received no message from him for two days had made me somewhat worried, but I have such faith in him, such belief in his good luck and his ingenuity, that I would not allow myself to be really anxious. Then on the third day I heard the news."

"What news?" asked Marguerite mechanically.

"That the Englishman who was known as the Scarlet Pimpernel had been captured in a house in the Rue de la Croix Blanche and had been imprisoned in the *Conciergerie*."

"The Rue de la Croix Blanche? Where is that?"

"In the Montmartre quarter. Armand lodged there. Percy, I imag-ine, was working to get him away; and those brutes captured him."

"Having heard the news, Sir Andrew, what did you do?"

"I went into Paris and ascertained its truth."

"And there is no doubt of it?"

"Alas, none! I went to the house in the Rue de la Croix Blanche. Armand had disappeared. I succeeded in inducing the *concierge* to talk. She seems to have been devoted to her lodger. Amidst tears she told me some of the details of the capture. Can you bear to hear them, Lady Blakeney?"

"Yes—tell me everything—don't be afraid," she reiterated with the same dull monotony.

"It appears that early on the Tuesday morning the son of the *concierge*—a lad about fifteen—was sent off by her lodger with a message to No. 9 Rue St. Germain l'Auxerrois. That was the house where Percy was staying all last week, where he kept disguises and so on for us all, and where some of our meetings were held. Percy evidently expected that Armand would try and communicate with him at that address, for when the lad arrived in front of the house he was accosted—so he says—by a big, rough workman, who browbeat him into giving up the lodger's letter, and finally pressed a piece of gold into his hand. The workman was Blakeney, of course. I imagine that Armand, at the time that he wrote the letter, must have been under the belief that Mademoiselle Lange was still in prison; he could not know then that Blakeney had already got her into comparative safety.

"In the letter he must have spoken of the terrible plight in which he stood, and also of his fears for the woman whom he loved. Percy was not the man to leave a comrade in the lurch! He would not be the man whom we all love and admire, whose word we all obey, for whose sake we would gladly all of us give our life—he would not be that man if he did not brave even certain dangers in order to be of help to those who call on him. Armand called and Percy went to him. He must have known that Armand was being spied upon, for Armand, alas! was already a marked man, and the watch-dogs of those infernal committees were already on his heels.

"Whether these sleuth-hounds had followed the son of the *concierge* and seen him give the letter to the workman in the Rue St. Germain l'Auxerrois, or whether the *concierge* in the Rue de la Croix Blanche was nothing but a spy of Héron's, or, again whether the Committee of General Security kept a company of soldiers in constant alert in that house, we shall, of course, never know. All that I do know is that Percy entered that fatal house at half-past ten, and that a quarter of an hour later the *concierge* saw some of the soldiers descending the stairs, carrying a heavy burden. She peeped out of her lodge, and by the light in the corridor she saw that the heavy burden was the body of a man bound closely with ropes: his eyes were closed, his clothes were stained with blood. He was seemingly unconscious. The next day the official organ of the hovernment proclaimed the capture of the Scarlet Pimpernel, and there was a public holiday in honour of the event."

Marguerite had listened to this terrible narrative dry-eyed and silent. Now she still sat there, hardly conscious of what went on around her—of Suzanne's tears, that fell unceasingly upon her fingers—of Sir Andrew, who had sunk into a chair, and buried his head in his hands. She was hardly conscious that she lived; the universe seemed to have stood still before this awful, monstrous cataclysm.

But, nevertheless, she was the first to return to the active realities of the present.

"Sir Andrew," she said after a while, "tell me, where are my Lords Tony and Hastings?"

"At Calais, madam," he replied. "I saw them there on my way hither. They had delivered the *Dauphin* safely into the hands of his adherents at Mantes, and were awaiting Blakeney's further orders, as he had commanded them to do."

"Will they wait for us there, think you?"

"For us, Lady Blakeney?" he exclaimed in puzzlement.

"Yes, for us, Sir Andrew," she replied, whilst the ghost of a smile flitted across her drawn face; "you had thought of accompanying me to Paris, had you not?"

"But Lady Blakeney—"

"Ah! I know what you would say, Sir Andrew. You will speak of dangers, of risks, of death, mayhap; you will tell me that I as a woman can do nothing to help my husband—that I could be but a hindrance to him, just as I was in Boulogne. But everything is so different now. Whilst those brutes planned his capture he was clever enough to outwit them, but now they have actually got him, think you they'll let him escape? They'll watch him night and day, my friend, just as they watched the unfortunate queen; but they'll not keep him months, weeks, or even days in prison—even Chauvelin now will no longer attempt to play with the Scarlet Pimpernel. They have him, and they will hold him until such time as they take him to the guillotine."

Her voice broke in a sob; her self-control was threatening to leave her. She was but a woman, young and passionately in love with the man who was about to die an ignominious death, far away from his country, his kindred, his friends.

"I cannot let him die alone, Sir Andrew; he will be longing for me, and—and, after all, there is you, and my Lord Tony, and Lord Hastings and the others; surely—surely we are not going to let him die, not like that, and not alone."

"You are right, Lady Blakeney," said Sir Andrew earnestly; "we are not going to let him die, if human agency can do aught to save him.

Already Tony, Hastings and I have agreed to return to Paris. There are one or two hidden places in and around the city known only to Percy and to the members of the League where he must find one or more of us if he succeeds in getting away. All the way between Paris and Calais we have places of refuge, places where any of us can hide at a given moment; where we can find disguises when we want them, or horses in an emergency. No! no! we are not going to despair, Lady Blakeney; there are nineteen of us prepared to lay down our lives for the Scarlet Pimpernel. Already I, as his lieutenant, have been selected as the leader of as determined a gang as has ever entered on a work of rescue before. We leave for Paris tomorrow, and if human pluck and devotion can destroy mountains then we'll destroy them. Our watchword is: 'God save the Scarlet Pimpernel.'"

He knelt beside her chair and kissed the cold fingers which, with a sad little smile, she held out to him.

"And God bless you all!" she murmured.

Suzanne had risen to her feet when her husband knelt; now he stood up beside her. The dainty young woman hardly more than a child—was doing her best to restrain her tears.

"See how selfish I am," said Marguerite. "I talk calmly of taking your husband from you, when I myself know the bitterness of such partings."

"My husband will go where his duty calls him," said Suzanne with charming and simple dignity. "I love him with all my heart, because he is brave and good. He could not leave his comrade, who is also his chief, in the lurch. God will protect him, I know. I would not ask him to play the part of a coward."

Her brown eyes glowed with pride. She was the true wife of a soldier, and with all her dainty ways and childlike manners she was a splendid woman and a staunch friend. Sir Percy Blakeney had saved her entire family from death, the Comte and Comtesse de Tournai, the *Vicomte*, her brother, and she herself all owed their lives to the Scarlet Pimpernel.

This she was not like to forget.

"There is but little danger for us, I fear me," said Sir Andrew lightly; "the Revolutionary Government only wants to strike at a head, it cares nothing for the limbs. Perhaps it feels that without our leader we are enemies not worthy of persecution. If there are any dangers, so much the better," he added; "but I don't anticipate any, unless we succeed in freeing our chief; and having freed him, we fear nothing more."

"The same applies to me, Sir Andrew," rejoined Marguerite earnestly. "Now that they have captured Percy, those human fiends will care naught for me. If you succeed in freeing Percy I, like you, will have nothing more to fear, and if you fail——"

She paused and put her small, white hand on Sir Andrew's arm.

"Take me with you, Sir Andrew," she entreated; "do not condemn me to the awful torture of weary waiting, day after day, wondering, guessing, never daring to hope, lest hope deferred be more hard to bear than dreary hopelessness."

Then as Sir Andrew, very undecided, yet half inclined to yield, stood silent and irresolute, she pressed her point, gently but firmly insistent.

"I would not be in the way, Sir Andrew; I would know how to efface myself so as not to interfere with your plans. But, oh!" she added, while a quivering note of passion trembled in her voice, "can't you see that I must breathe the air that he breathes else I shall stifle or mayhap go mad?"

Sir Andrew turned to his wife, a mute query in his eyes.

"You would do an inhuman and a cruel act," said Suzanne with seriousness that sat quaintly on her baby face, "if you did not afford your protection to Marguerite, for I do believe that if you did not take her with you tomorrow she would go to Paris alone."

Marguerite thanked her friend with her eyes. Suzanne was a child in nature, but she had a woman's heart. She loved her husband, and, therefore, knew and understood what Marguerite must be suffering now.

Sir Andrew no longer could resist the unfortunate woman's earnest pleading. Frankly, he thought that if she remained in England while Percy was in such deadly peril she ran the grave risk of losing her reason before the terrible strain of suspense. He knew her to be a woman of courage, and one capable of great physical endurance; and really, he was quite honest when he said that he did not believe there would be much danger for the headless League of the Scarlet Pimpernel unless they succeeded in freeing their chief. And if they did succeed, then indeed there would be nothing to fear, for the brave and loving wife who, like every true woman does, and has done in like circumstances since the beginning of time, was only demanding with passionate insistence the right to share the fate, good or ill, of the man whom she loved.

CHAPTER 25

Paris Once More

Sir Andrew had just come in. He was trying to get a little warmth into his half-frozen limbs, for the cold had set in again, and this time with renewed vigour, and Marguerite was pouring out a cup of hot coffee which she had been brewing for him. She had not asked for news. She knew that he had none to give her, else he had not worn that wearied, despondent look in his kind face.

"I'll just try one more place this evening," he said as soon as he had swallowed some of the hot coffee—"a restaurant in the Rue de la Harpe; the members of the Cordeliers' Club often go there for supper, and they are usually well informed. I might glean something definite there."

"It seems very strange that they are so slow in bringing him to trial," said Marguerite in that dull, toneless voice which had become habitual to her. "When you first brought me the awful news that—I made sure that they would bring him to trial at once and was in terror lest we arrived here too late to—to see him."

She checked herself quickly, bravely trying to still the quiver of her voice.

"And of Armand?" she asked.

He shook his head sadly.

"With regard to him I am at a still greater loss," he said: "I cannot find his name on any of the prison registers, and I know that he is not in the *Conciergerie.* They have cleared out all the prisoners from there; there is only Percy—"

"Poor Armand!" she sighed; "it must be almost worse for him than for any of us; it was his first act of thoughtless disobedience that brought all this misery upon our heads."

She spoke sadly but quietly. Sir Andrew noted that there was no bitterness in her tone. But her very quietude was heart-breaking; there was such an infinity of despair in the calm of her eyes.

"Well! though we cannot understand it all, Lady Blakeney," he said with forced cheerfulness, "we must remember one thing—that whilst there is life there is hope."

"Hope!" she exclaimed with a world of pathos in her sigh, her large eyes dry and circled, fixed with indescribable sorrow on her friend's face.

Ffoulkes turned his head away, pretending to busy himself with the coffee-making utensils. He could not bear to see that look of hope-lessness in her face, for in his heart he could not find the wherewithal to cheer her. Despair was beginning to seize on him too, and this he would not let her see.

They had been in Paris three days now, and it was six days since Blakeney had been arrested. Sir Andrew and Marguerite had found temporary lodgings inside Paris, Tony and Hastings were just out-side the gates, and all along the route between Paris and Calais, at St. Germain, at Mantes, in the villages between Beauvais and Amiens, wherever money could obtain friendly help, members of the devoted League of the Scarlet Pimpernel lay in hiding, waiting to aid their chief.

Ffoulkes had ascertained that Percy was kept a close prisoner in the *Conciergerie*, in the very rooms occupied by Marie Antoinette dur-ing the last months of her life. He left poor Marguerite to guess how closely that elusive Scarlet Pimpernel was being guarded, the precau-tions surrounding him being even more minute than those which had made the unfortunate queen's closing days a martyrdom for her.

But of Armand he could glean no satisfactory news, only the nega-tive probability that he was not detained in any of the larger prisons of Paris, as no register which he, Ffoulkes, so laboriously consulted bore record of the name of St. Just.

Haunting the restaurants and drinking booths where the most ad-vanced Jacobins and Terrorists were wont to meet, he had learned one or two details of Blakeney's incarceration which he could not possi-bly impart to Marguerite. The capture of the mysterious Englishman known as the Scarlet Pimpernel had created a great deal of popular satisfaction; but it was obvious that not only was the public mind not allowed to associate that capture with the escape of little Capet from the Temple, but it soon became clear to Ffoulkes that the news of that escape was still being kept a profound secret.

On one occasion he had succeeded in spying on the Chief Agent of the Committee of General Security, whom he knew by sight, while the latter was sitting at dinner in the company of a stout, florid man with pock-marked face and podgy hands covered with rings.

Sir Andrew marvelled who this man might be. Héron spoke to him in ambiguous phrases that would have been unintelligible to anyone who did not know the circumstances of the *Dauphin's* escape and the part that the League of the Scarlet Pimpernel had played in it. But to Sir Andrew Ffoulkes, who—cleverly disguised as a farrier, grimy after his day's work—was straining his ears to listen whilst apparently consuming huge slabs of boiled beef, it soon became clear that the chief agent and his fat friend were talking of the *Dauphin* and of Blakeney.

"He won't hold out much longer, citizen," the chief agent was saying in a confident voice; "our men are absolutely unremitting in their task. Two of them watch him night and day; they look after him well, and practically never lose sight of him, but the moment he tries to get any sleep one of them rushes into the cell with a loud banging of bayonet and sabre, and noisy tread on the flagstones, and shouts at the top of his voice: 'Now then, *aristo*, where's the brat? Tell us now, and you shall be down and go to sleep.' I have done it myself all through one day just for the pleasure of it. It's a little tiring for you to have to shout a good deal now, and sometimes give the cursed Englishman a good shake-up. He has had five days of it, and not one wink of sleep during that time—not one single minute of rest—and he only gets enough food to keep him alive. I tell you he can't last. Citizen Chauvelin had a splendid idea there. It will all come right in a day or two."

"H'm!" grunted the other sulkily; "those Englishmen are tough."

"Yes!" retorted Héron with a grim laugh and a leer of savagery that made his gaunt face look positively hideous—"you would have given out after three days, friend de Batz, would you not? And I warned you, didn't I? I told you if you tampered with the brat I would make you cry in mercy to me for death."

"And I warned you," said the other imperturbably, "not to worry so much about me, but to keep your eyes open for those cursed Englishmen."

"I am keeping my eyes open for you, nevertheless, my friend. If I thought you knew where the vermin's spawn was at this moment I would—"

"You would put me on the same rack that you or your precious friend, Chauvelin, have devised for the Englishman. But I don't know where the lad is. If I did I would not be in Paris."

"I know that," assented Héron with a sneer; "you would soon be after the reward—over in Austria, what?—but I have your movements tracked day and night, my friend. I dare say you are as anxious as we are as to the whereabouts of the child. Had he been taken over the frontier you would have been the first to hear of it, eh? No," he added confidently, and as if anxious to reassure himself, "my firm belief is that the original idea of these confounded Englishmen was to try and get the child over to England, and that they alone know where he is. I tell you it won't be many days before that very withered Scarlet Pimpernel will order his followers to give little Capet up to us. Oh! they are hanging about Paris some of them, I know that; Citizen Chauvelin is convinced that the wife isn't very far away. Give her a sight of her husband now, say I, and she'll make the others give the child up soon enough."

The man laughed like some hyena gloating over its prey. Sir Andrew nearly betrayed himself then. He had to dig his nails into his own flesh to prevent himself from springing then and there at the throat of that wretch whose monstrous ingenuity had invented torture for the fallen enemy far worse than any that the cruelties of medieval Inquisitions had devised.

So, they would not let him sleep! A simple idea born in the brain of a fiend. Héron had spoken of Chauvelin as the originator of the devilry; a man weakened deliberately day by day by insufficient food, and the horrible process of denying him rest. It seemed inconceivable that human, sentient beings should have thought of such a thing. Perspiration stood up in beads on Sir Andrew's brow when he thought of his friend, brought down by want of sleep to—what? His physique was splendidly powerful, but could it stand against such racking torment for long? And the clear, the alert mind, the scheming brain, the reckless daring—how soon would these become enfeebled by the slow, steady torture of an utter want of rest?

Ffoulkes had to smother a cry of horror, which surely must have drawn the attention of that fiend on himself had he not been so engrossed in the enjoyment of his own devilry. As it is, he ran out of the stuffy eating-house, for he felt as if its fetid air must choke him.

For an hour after that he wandered about the streets, not daring to face Marguerite, lest his eyes betrayed some of the horror which was shaking his very soul.

That was twenty-four hours ago. Today he had learnt little else. It was generally known that the Englishman was in the *Conciergerie* prison, that he was being closely watched, and that his trial would come on within the next few days; but no one seemed to know exactly when. The public was getting restive, demanding that trial and execution to which everyone seemed to look forward as to a holiday. In the meanwhile, the escape of the *Dauphin* had been kept from the knowledge of the public; Héron and his gang, fearing for their lives, had still hopes of extracting from the Englishman the secret of the lad's hiding-place, and the means they employed for arriving at this end was worthy of Lucifer and his host of devils in hell.

From other fragments of conversation which Sir Andrew Ffoulkes had gleaned that same evening, it seemed to him that in order to hide their defalcations Héron and the four commissaries in charge of little Capet had substituted a deaf and dumb child for the escaped little prisoner. This miserable small wreck of humanity was reputed to be sick and kept in a darkened room, in bed, and was in that condition exhibited to any member of the Convention who had the right to see him. A partition had been very hastily erected in the inner room once occupied by the Simons, and the child was kept behind that partition, and no one was allowed to come too near to him. Thus, the fraud was succeeding fairly well. Héron and his accomplices only cared to save their skins, and the wretched little substitute being really ill, they firmly hoped that he would soon die, when no doubt they would bruit abroad the news of the death of Capet, which would relieve them of further responsibility.

That such ideas, such thoughts, such schemes should have engendered in human minds it is almost impossible to conceive, and yet we know from no less important a witness than Madame Simon herself that the child who died in the Temple a few weeks later was a poor little imbecile, a deaf and dumb child brought hither from one of the asylums and left to die in peace. There was nobody but kindly Death to take him out of his misery, for the giant intellect that had planned and carried out the rescue of the uncrowned King of France, and which alone might have had the power to save him too, was being broken on the rack of enforced sleeplessness.

CHAPTER 26

The Bitterest Foe

That same evening Sir Andrew Ffoulkes, having announced his intention of gleaning further news of Armand, if possible, went out shortly after seven o'clock, promising to be home again about nine.

Marguerite, on the other hand, had to make her friend a solemn promise that she would try and eat some supper which the landlady of these miserable apartments had agreed to prepare for her. So far, they had been left in peaceful occupation of these squalid lodgings in a tumble-down house on the Quai de la Ferraille, facing the house of Justice, the grim walls of which Marguerite would watch with wide-open dry eyes for as long as the grey wintry light lingered over them.

Even now, though the darkness had set in, and snow, falling in close, small flakes, threw a thick white veil over the landscape, she sat at the open window long after Sir Andrew had gone out, watching the few small flicks of light that blinked across from the other side of the river, and which came from the windows of the Châtelet towers. The windows of the *Conciergerie* she could not see, for these gave on one of the inner courtyards; but there was a melancholy consolation even in the gazing on those walls that held in their cruel, grim embrace all that she loved in the world.

It seemed so impossible to think of Percy—the laughter-loving, irresponsible, light-hearted adventurer—as the prey of those fiends who would revel in their triumph, who would crush him, humiliate him, insult him—ye gods alive! even torture him, perhaps—that they might break the indomitable spirit that would mock them even on the threshold of death.

Surely, surely God would never allow such monstrous infamy as the deliverance of the noble soaring eagle into the hands of those preying jackals! Marguerite—though her heart ached beyond what human nature could endure, though her anguish on her husband's account was doubled by that which she felt for her brother—could not bring herself to give up all hope. Sir Andrew said it rightly; while there was life there was hope. While there was life in those vigorous limbs, spirit in that daring mind, how could puny, rampant beasts gain the better of the immortal soul? As for Armand—why, if Percy were free she would have no cause to fear for Armand.

She sighed a sigh of deep, of passionate regret and longing. If she could only see her husband; if she could only look for one second into those laughing, lazy eyes, wherein she alone knew how to fathom the infinity of passion that lay within their depths; if she could but once feel his—ardent kiss on her lips, she could more easily endure this agonising suspense, and wait confidently and courageously for the issue.

She turned away from the window, for the night was getting bitterly cold. From the tower of St. Germain l'Auxerrois the clock slowly struck eight. Even as the last sound of the historic bell died away in the distance she heard a timid knocking at the door.

"Enter!" she called unthinkingly.

She thought it was her landlady, come up with more wood, mayhap, for the fire, so she did not turn to the door when she heard it being slowly opened, then closed again, and presently a soft tread on the threadbare carpet.

"May I crave your kind attention, Lady Blakeney?" said a harsh voice, subdued to tones of ordinary courtesy.

She quickly repressed a cry of terror. How well she knew that voice! When last she heard it it was at Boulogne, dictating that infamous letter—the weapon wherewith Percy had so effectually foiled his enemy. She turned and faced the man who was her bitterest foe— hers in the person of the man she loved.

"Chauvelin!" she gasped.

"Himself at your service, dear lady," he said simply.

He stood in the full light of the lamp, his trim, small figure boldly cut out against the dark wall beyond. He wore the usual sable-coloured clothes which he affected, with the primly-folded jabot and cuffs edged with narrow lace.

Without waiting for permission from her he quietly and deliberately placed his hat and cloak on a chair. Then he turned once more toward her and made a movement as if to advance into the room; but instinctively she put up a hand as if to ward off the calamity of his approach.

He shrugged his shoulders, and the shadow of a smile, that had neither mirth nor kindliness in it, hovered round the corners of his thin lips.

"Have I your permission to sit?" he asked.

"As you will," she replied slowly, keeping her wide-open eyes fixed upon him as does a frightened bird upon the serpent whom it loathes and fears.

"And may I crave a few moments of your undivided attention, Lady Blakeney?" he continued, taking a chair, and so placing it beside the table that the light of the lamp when he sat remained behind him and his face was left in shadow.

"Is it necessary?" asked Marguerite.

"It is," he replied curtly, "if you desire to see and speak with your husband—to be of use to him before it is too late."

"Then, I pray you, speak, citizen, and I will listen."

She sank into a chair, not heeding whether the light of the lamp fell on her face or not, whether the lines in her haggard cheeks, or her tear-dimmed eyes showed plainly the sorrow and despair that had traced them. She had nothing to hide from this man, the cause of all the tortures which she endured. She knew that neither courage nor sorrow would move him, and that hatred for Percy—personal deadly hatred for the man who had twice foiled him—had long crushed the last spark of humanity in his heart.

"Perhaps, Lady Blakeney," he began after a slight pause and in his smooth, even voice, "it would interest you to hear how I succeeded in procuring for myself this pleasure of an interview with you?"

"Your spies did their usual work, I suppose," she said coldly.

"Exactly. We have been on your track for three days, and yesterday evening an unguarded movement on the part of Sir Andrew Ffoulkes gave us the final clue to your whereabouts."

"Of Sir Andrew Ffoulkes?" she asked, greatly puzzled.

"He was in an eating-house, cleverly disguised, I own, trying to glean information, no doubt as to the probable fate of Sir Percy Blakeney. As chance would have it, my friend Héron, of the Committee of General Security, chanced to be discussing with reprehensible openness—er—certain—what shall I say?—certain measures which, at my advice, the Committee of Public Safety have been forced to adopt with a view to—"

"A truce on your smooth-tongued speeches, Citizen Chauvelin," she interposed firmly. "Sir Andrew Ffoulkes has told me naught of this—so I pray you speak plainly and to the point, if you can."

He bowed with marked irony.

"As you please," he said. "Sir Andrew Ffoulkes, hearing certain matters of which I will tell you *anon*, made a movement which betrayed him to one of our spies. At a word from Citizen Héron this man followed on the heels of the young farrier who had shown such interest in the conversation of the Chief Agent. Sir Andrew, I imagine, burning with indignation at what he had heard, was perhaps not quite so cautious as he usually is. Anyway, the man on his track followed him to this door. It was quite simple, as you see. As for me, I had guessed a week ago that we would see the beautiful Lady Blakeney in Paris before long. When I knew where Sir Andrew Ffoulkes lodged, I had no difficulty in guessing that Lady Blakeney would not be far off."

"And what was there in Citizen Héron's conversation last night," she asked quietly, "that so aroused Sir Andrew's indignation?"

"He has not told you?" "Oh! it is very simple. Let me tell you, Lady Blakeney, exactly how matters stand. Sir Percy Blakeney—before lucky chance at last delivered him into our hands—thought fit, as no doubt you know, to meddle with our most important prisoner of State."

"A child. I know it, sir—the son of a murdered father whom you and your friends were slowly doing to death."

"That is as it may be, Lady Blakeney," rejoined Chauvelin calmly;

"but it was none of Sir Percy Blakeney's business. This, however, he chose to disregard. He succeeded in carrying little Capet from the Temple, and two days later we had him under lock, and key."

"Through some infamous and treacherous trick, sir," she retorted.

Chauvelin made no immediate reply; his pale, inscrutable eyes were fixed upon her face, and the smile of irony round his mouth appeared more strongly marked than before.

"That, again, is as it may be," he said suavely; "but anyhow for the moment we have the upper hand. Sir Percy is in the *Conciergerie*, guarded day and night, more closely than Marie Antoinette even was guarded."

"And he laughs at your bolts and bars, sir," she rejoined proudly. "Remember Calais, remember Boulogne. His laugh at your discomfiture, then, must resound in your ear even today."

"Yes; but for the moment laughter is on our side. Still we are willing to forego even that pleasure, if Sir Percy will but move a finger towards his own freedom."

"Again, some infamous letter?" she asked with bitter contempt; "some attempt against his honour?"

"No, no, Lady Blakeney," he interposed with perfect blandness. "Matters are so much simpler now, you see. We hold Sir Percy at our mercy. We could send him to the guillotine tomorrow, but we might be willing—remember, I only say we might—to exercise our prerogative of mercy if Sir Percy Blakeney will on his side accede to a request from us."

"And that request?"

"Is a very natural one. He took Capet away from us, and it is but credible that he knows at the present moment exactly where the child is. Let him instruct his followers—and I mistake not, Lady Blakeney, there are several of them not very far from Paris just now—let him, I say, instruct these followers of his to return the person of young Capet to us, and not only will we undertake to give these same gentlemen a safe conduct back to England, but we even might be inclined to deal somewhat less harshly with the gallant Scarlet Pimpernel himself."

She laughed a harsh, mirthless, contemptuous laugh.

"I don't think that I quite understand," she said after a moment or two, whilst he waited calmly until her out-break of hysterical mirth had subsided. "You want my husband—the Scarlet Pimpernel, citizen—to deliver the little King of France to you after he has risked his life to save the child out of your clutches? Is that what you are trying to say?"

"It is," rejoined Chauvelin complacently, "just what we have been saying to Sir Percy Blakeney for the past six days, *Madame*."

"Well! then you have had your answer, have you not?"

"Yes," he replied slowly; "but the answer has become weaker day by day."

"Weaker? I don't understand."

"Let me explain, Lady Blakeney," said Chauvelin, now with measured emphasis. He put both elbows on the table and leaned well forward, peering into her face, lest one of its varied expressions escaped him. "Just now you taunted me with my failure in Calais, and again at Boulogne, with a proud toss of the head, which I own is excessive becoming; you threw the name of the Scarlet Pimpernel in my face like a challenge which I no longer dare to accept. 'The Scarlet Pimpernel,' you would say to me, 'stands for loyalty, for honour, and for indomitable courage. Think you he would sacrifice his honour to obtain your mercy? Remember Boulogne and your discomfiture!' All of which, dear lady, is perfectly charming and womanly and enthusiastic, and I, bowing my humble head, must own that I was fooled in Calais and baffled in Boulogne. But in Boulogne I made a grave mistake, and one from which I learned a lesson, which I am putting into practice now."

He paused a while as if waiting for her reply. His pale, keen eyes had already noted that with every phrase he uttered the lines in her beautiful face became more hard and set. A look of horror was gradually spreading over it, as if the icy-cold hand of death had passed over her eyes and cheeks, leaving them rigid like stone.

"In Boulogne," resumed Chauvelin quietly, satisfied that his words were hitting steadily at her heart—"in Boulogne Sir Percy and I did not fight an equal fight. Fresh from a pleasant sojourn in his own magnificent home, full of the spirit of adventure which puts the essence of life into a man's veins, Sir Percy Blakeney's splendid physique was pitted against my feeble powers. Of course, I lost the battle. I made the mistake of trying to subdue a man who was in the zenith of his strength, whereas now—"

"Yes, Citizen Chauvelin," she said, "whereas now—"

"Sir Percy Blakeney has been in the prison of the *Conciergerie* for exactly one week, Lady Blakeney," he replied, speaking very slowly, and letting every one of his words sink individually into her mind. "Even before he had time to take the bearings of his cell or to plan on his own behalf one of those remarkable escapes for which he is so justly famous, our men began to work on a scheme which I am proud to say originated with myself. A week has gone by since then, Lady Blakeney, and during that time a special company of prison guard, acting under the orders of the Committee of General Security and of Public Safety, have questioned the prisoner unremittingly—unremittingly, remember—day and night. Two by two these men take it in turns to enter the prisoner's cell every quarter of an hour—lately it has had to be more often—and ask him the one question, 'Where is little Capet?' Up to now we have received no satisfactory reply, although we have explained to Sir Percy that many of his followers are honouring the neighbourhood of Paris with their visit, and that all we ask for from him are instructions to those gallant gentlemen to bring young Capet back to us. It is all very simple, unfortunately the prisoner is somewhat obstinate. At first, even, the idea seemed to amuse him; he used to laugh and say that he always had the faculty of sleeping with his eyes open. But our soldiers are untiring in their efforts, and the want of sleep as well as of a sufficiency of food and of fresh air is certainly beginning to tell on Sir Percy Blakeney's magnificent physique. I don't think that it will be very long before he gives way to our gentle persuasions; and in any case now, I assure you, dear lady, that we need not fear any attempt on his part to escape. I doubt if he could walk very steadily across this room—"

Marguerite had sat quite silent and apparently impassive all the while that Chauvelin had been speaking; even now she scarcely stirred. Her face expressed absolutely nothing but deep puzzlement. There was a frown between her brows, and her eyes, which were always of such liquid blue, now looked almost black. She was trying to visualise that which Chauvelin had put before her: a man harassed day and night, unceasingly, unremittingly, with one question allowed neither respite nor sleep—his brain, soul, and body fagged out at every hour, every moment of the day and night, until mind and body and soul must inevitably give way under anguish ten thousand times more unendurable than any physical torment invented by monsters in barbaric times.

That man thus harassed, thus fagged out, thus martyrised at all hours of the day and night, was her husband, whom she loved with every fibre of her being, with every throb of her heart.

Torture? Oh, no! these were advanced and civilised times that could afford to look with horror on the excesses of medieval days. This was a revolution that made for progress and challenged the opinion of the world. The cells of the Temple of La Force or the *Conciergerie* held no secret inquisition with iron maidens and racks and thumbscrews; but a few men had put their tortuous brains together and had said one to another: "We want to find out from that man where we can lay our hands on little Capet, so we won't let him sleep until he has told us. It is not torture—oh, no! Who would dare to say that we torture our prisoners? It is only a little horseplay, worrying to the prisoner, no doubt; but, after all, he can end the unpleasantness at any moment. He need but to answer our question, and he can go to sleep as comfortably as a little child. The want of sleep is very trying, the want of proper food and of fresh air is very weakening; the prisoner must give way sooner or later—"

So these fiends had decided it between them, and they had put their idea into execution for one whole week. Marguerite looked at Chauvelin as she would on some monstrous, inscrutable Sphinx, marvelling if God—even in His anger—could really have created such a fiendish brain, or, having created it, could allow it to wreak such devilry unpunished.

Even now she felt that he was enjoying the mental anguish which he had put upon her, and she saw his thin, evil lips curled into a smile.

"So, you came tonight to tell me all this?" she asked as soon as she could trust herself to speak. Her impulse was to shriek out her indignation, her horror of him, into his face. She longed to call down God's eternal curse upon this fiend; but instinctively she held herself in check. Her indignation, her words of loathing would only have added to his delight.

"You have had your wish," she added coldly; "now, I pray you, go."

"Your pardon, Lady Blakeney," he said with all his habitual blandness; "my object in coming to see you tonight was twofold. Methought that I was acting as your friend in giving you authentic news of Sir Percy, and in suggesting the possibility of your adding your persuasion to ours."

"My persuasion? You mean that I—"

"You would wish to see your husband, would you not, Lady Blakeney?"

"Yes."

"Then I pray you command me. I will grant you the permission whenever you wish to go."

"You are in the hope, citizen," she said, "that I will do my best to break my husband's spirit by my tears or my prayers—is that it?"

"Not necessarily," he replied pleasantly. "I assure you that we can manage to do that ourselves, in time."

"You devil!" The cry of pain and of horror was involuntarily wrung from the depths of her soul. "Are you not afraid that God's hand will strike you where you stand?"

"No," he said lightly; "I am not afraid, Lady Blakeney. You see, I do not happen to believe in God. Come!" he added more seriously, "have I not proved to you that my offer is disinterested? Yet I repeat it even now. If you desire to see Sir Percy in prison, command me, and the doors shall be open to you."

She waited a moment, looking him straight and quite dispassionately in the face; then she said coldly:

"Very well! I will go."

"When?" he asked.

"This evening."

"Just as you wish. I would have to go and see my friend Héron first and arrange with him for your visit."

"Then go. I will follow in half an hour."

"*C'est entendu.* Will you be at the main entrance of the *Conciergerie* at half-past nine? You know it, perhaps—no? It is in the Rue de la Barillerie, immediately on the right at the foot of the great staircase of the house of Justice."

"Of the house of Justice!" she exclaimed involuntarily, a world of bitter contempt in her cry. Then she added in her former matter-of-fact tones:

"Very good, citizen. At half-past nine I will be at the entrance you name."

"And I will be at the door prepared to escort you."

He took up his hat and coat and bowed ceremoniously to her. Then he turned to go. At the door a cry from her—involuntarily enough, God knows!—made him pause.

"My interview with the prisoner," she said, vainly trying, poor soul! to repress that quiver of anxiety in her voice, "it will be private?"

"Oh, yes! Of course," he replied with a reassuring smile. "*Au revoir,* Lady Blakeney! Half-past nine, remember—"

She could no longer trust herself to look on him as he finally took his departure. She was afraid—yes, absolutely afraid that her fortitude would give way—meanly, despicably, uselessly give way; that she would suddenly fling herself at the feet of that sneering, inhuman wretch, that she would pray, implore—Heaven above! what might she not do in the face of this awful reality, if the last lingering shred of vanishing reason, of pride, and of courage did not hold her in check?

Therefore, she forced herself not to look on that departing, sable-clad figure, on that evil face, and those hands that held Percy's fate in their cruel grip; but her ears caught the welcome sound of his departure—the opening and shutting of the door, his light footstep echoing down the stone stairs.

When at last she felt that she was really alone she uttered a loud cry like a wounded doe and falling on her knees she buried her face in her hands in a passionate fit of weeping. Violent sobs shook her entire frame; it seemed as if an overwhelming anguish was tearing at her heart—the physical pain of it was almost unendurable. And yet even through this paroxysm of tears her mind clung to one root idea: when she saw Percy, she must be brave and calm, be able to help him if he wanted her, to do his bidding if there was anything that she could do, or any message that she could take to the others. Of hope she had none. The last lingering ray of it had been extinguished by that fiend when he said, "We need not fear that he will escape. I doubt if he could walk very steadily across this room now."

CHAPTER 27

In the Conciergerie

Marguerite, accompanied by Sir Andrew Ffoulkes, walked rapidly along the quay. It lacked ten minutes to the half hour; the night was dark and bitterly cold. Snow was still falling in sparse, thin flakes, and lay like a crisp and glittering mantle over the parapets of the bridges and the grim towers of the Châtelet prison.

They walked on silently now. All that they had wanted to say to one another had been said inside the squalid room of their lodgings when Sir Andrew Ffoulkes had come home and learned that Chauvelin had been.

"They are killing him by inches, Sir Andrew," had been the heart-rending cry which burst from Marguerite's oppressed heart as soon as her hands rested in the kindly ones of her best friend. "Is there aught that we can do?"

There was, of course, very little that could be done. One or two fine steel files which Sir Andrew gave her to conceal beneath the folds of her kerchief; also, a tiny dagger with sharp, poisoned blade, which for a moment she held in her hand hesitating, her eyes filling with tears, her heart throbbing with unspeakable sorrow.

Then slowly—very slowly—she raised the small, death-dealing instrument to her lips, and reverently kissed the narrow blade.

"If it must be!" she murmured, "God in His mercy will forgive!"

She sheathed the dagger, and this, too, she hid in the folds of her gown.

"Can you think of anything else, Sir Andrew, that he might want?" she asked. "I have money in plenty, in case those soldiers—"

Sir Andrew sighed, and turned away from her so as to hide the hopelessness which he felt. Since three days now he had been exhausting every conceivable means of getting at the prison guard with bribery and corruption. But Chauvelin and his friends had taken excellent precautions. The prison of the *Conciergerie*, situated as it was in the very heart of the labyrinthine and complicated structure of the Châtelet and the house of Justice, and isolated from every other group of cells in the building, was inaccessible save from one narrow doorway which gave on the guard-room first, and thence on the inner cell beyond. Just as all attempts to rescue the late unfortunate queen from that prison had failed, so now every attempt to reach the imprisoned Scarlet Pimpernel was equally doomed to bitter disappointment.

The guard-room was filled with soldiers, day and night; the windows of the inner cell, heavily barred, were too small to admit of the passage of a human body, and they were raised twenty feet from the corridor below. Sir Andrew had stood in the corridor two days ago, he had looked on the window behind which he knew that his friend must be eating out his noble heart in a longing for liberty, and he had realised then that every effort at help from the outside was foredoomed to failure.

"Courage, Lady Blakeney," he said to Marguerite, when *anon* they had crossed the Pont au Change, and were wending their way slowly along the Rue de la Barillerie; "remember our proud *dictum*: the Scarlet Pimpernel never fails! and also this, that whatever messages Blakeney gives you for us, whatever he wishes us to do, we are to a man ready to do it, and to give our lives for our chief. Courage! Something tells me that a man like Percy is not going to die at the hands of such vermin as Chauvelin and his friends."

They had reached the great iron gates of the house of Justice. Marguerite, trying to smile, extended her trembling band to this faithful, loyal comrade.

"I'll not be far," he said. "When you come out do not look to the right or left but make straight for home; I'll not lose sight of you for a moment, and as soon as possible will overtake you. God bless you both."

He pressed his lips on her cold little hand, and watched her tall, elegant figure as she passed through the great gates until the veil of falling snow hid her from his gaze. Then with a deep sigh of bitter anguish and sorrow he turned away and was soon lost in the gloom.

Marguerite found the gate at the bottom of the monumental stairs open when she arrived. Chauvelin was standing immediately inside the building waiting for her.

"We are prepared for your visit, Lady Blakeney," he said, "and the prisoner knows that you are coming."

He led the way down one of the numerous and interminable corridors of the building, and she followed briskly, pressing her hand against her bosom there where the folds of her kerchief hid the steel files and the precious dagger.

Even in the gloom of these ill-lighted passages she realised that she was surrounded by guards. There were soldiers everywhere; two had stood behind the door when first she entered and had immediately closed it with a loud clang behind her; and all the way down the corridors, through the half-light engendered by feebly flickering lamps, she caught glimpses of the white facings on the uniforms of the town guard, or occasionally the glint of steel of a bayonet. Presently Chauvelin paused beside a door, which he had just reached. His hand was on the latch, for it did not appear to be locked, and he turned toward Marguerite.

"I am very sorry, Lady Blakeney," he said in simple, deferential tones, "that the prison authorities, who at my request are granting you this interview at such an unusual hour, have made a slight condition to your visit."

"A condition?" she asked. "What is it?"

"You must forgive me," he said, as if purposely evading her question, "for I give you my word that I had nothing to do with a regulation that you might justly feel was derogatory to your dignity. If you will kindly step in here a wardress in charge will explain to you what is required."

He pushed open the door, and stood aside ceremoniously in order to allow her to pass in. She looked on him with deep puzzlement and a look of dark suspicion in her eyes. But her mind was too much engrossed with the thought of her meeting with Percy to worry over any trifle that might—as her enemy had inferred—offend her womanly dignity.

She walked into the room, past Chauvelin, who whispered as she went by:

"I will wait for you here. And, I pray you, if you have aught to complain of summon me at once."

Then he closed the door behind her. The room in which Marguerite now found herself was a small unventilated quadrangle, dimly lighted by a hanging lamp. A woman in a soiled cotton gown and lank grey hair brushed away from a parchment-like forehead rose from the chair in which she had been sitting when Marguerite entered and put away some knitting on which she had apparently been engaged.

"I was to tell you, citizeness," she said the moment the door had been closed and she was alone with Marguerite, "that the prison authorities have given orders that I should search you before you visit the prisoner."

She repeated this phrase mechanically like a child who has been taught to say a lesson by heart. She was a stoutish middle-aged woman, with that pasty, flabby skin peculiar to those who live in want of fresh air; but her small, dark eyes were not unkindly, although they shifted restlessly from one object to another as if she were trying to avoid looking the other woman straight in the face.

"That you should search me!" reiterated Marguerite slowly, trying to understand.

"Yes," replied the woman. "I was to tell you to take off your clothes, so that I might look them through and through. I have often had to do this before when visitors have been allowed inside the prison, so it is no use your trying to deceive me in any way. I am very sharp at finding out if anyone has papers, or files or ropes concealed in an underpetticoat. Come," she added more roughly, seeing that Marguerite had remained motionless in the middle of the room; "the quicker you are about it the sooner you will be taken to see the prisoner."

These words had their desired effect. The proud Lady Blakeney, inwardly revolting at the outrage, knew that resistance would be worse than useless. Chauvelin was the other side of the door. A call from the woman would bring him to her assistance, and Marguerite was only longing to hasten the moment when she could be with her husband.

She took off her kerchief and her gown and calmly submitted to the woman's rough hands as they wandered with sureness and accuracy to the various pockets and folds that might conceal prohibited articles. The woman did her work with peculiar stolidity; she did not utter a word when she found the tiny steel files and placed them on a table beside her. In equal silence she laid the little dagger beside them, and the purse which contained twenty gold pieces. These she counted in front of Marguerite and then replaced them in the purse. Her face expressed neither surprise, nor greed nor pity. She was obviously beyond the reach of bribery—just a machine paid by the prison authorities to do this unpleasant work, and no doubt terrorised into doing it conscientiously.

When she had satisfied herself that Marguerite had nothing further concealed about her person, she allowed her to put her dress on once more. She even offered to help her on with it. When Marguerite was fully dressed she opened the door for her. Chauvelin was standing in the passage waiting patiently. At sight of Marguerite, whose pale, set face betrayed nothing of the indignation which she felt, he turned quick, inquiring eyes on the woman.

"Two files, a dagger and a purse with twenty *louis*," said the latter curtly.

Chauvelin made no comment. He received the information quite placidly, as if it had no special interest for him. Then he said quietly:

"This way, citizeness!"

Marguerite followed him, and two minutes later he stood beside a heavy nail-studded door that had a small square grating let into one of the panels, and said simply:

"This is it."

Two soldiers of the National Guard were on sentry at the door, two more were pacing up and down outside it, and had halted when Citizen Chauvelin gave his name and showed his tricolour scarf of office. From behind the small grating in the door a pair of eyes peered at the newcomers.

"*Qui va là?*" came the quick challenge from the guard-room within.

"Citizen Chauvelin of the Committee of Public Safety," was the prompt reply.

There was the sound of grounding of arms, of the drawing of bolts and the turning of a key in a complicated lock. The prison was kept locked from within, and very heavy bars had to be moved ere the ponderous door slowly swung open on its hinges.

Two steps led up into the guard-room. Marguerite mounted them with the same feeling of awe and almost of reverence as she would have mounted the steps of a sacrificial altar.

The guard-room itself was more brilliantly lighted than the corridor outside. The sudden glare of two or three lamps placed about the room caused her momentarily to close her eyes that were aching with many shed and unshed tears. The air was rank and heavy with the fumes of tobacco, of wine and stale food. A large barred window gave on the corridor immediately above the door.

When Marguerite felt strong enough to look around her, she saw that the room was filled with soldiers. Some were sitting, others standing, others lay on rugs against the wall, apparently asleep. There was one who appeared to be in command, for with a word he checked the noise that was going on in the room when she entered, and then he said curtly:

"This way, citizeness!"

He turned to an opening in the wall on the left, the stone-lintel of a door, from which the door itself had been removed; an iron bar ran across the opening, and this the sergeant now lifted, nodding to Marguerite to go within.

Instinctively she looked round for Chauvelin.

But he was nowhere to be seen.

CHAPTER 28

The Caged Lion

Was there some instinct of humanity left in the soldier who allowed Marguerite through the barrier into the prisoner's cell? Had the wan face of this beautiful woman stirred within his heart the last chord of gentleness that was not wholly atrophied by the constant cruelties, the excesses, the mercilessness which his service under this fraternising republic constantly demanded of him?

Perhaps some recollection of former years, when first he served his king and country, recollection of wife or sister or mother pleaded within him in favour of this sorely-stricken woman with the look of unspeakable sorrow in her large blue eyes.

Certain it is that as soon as Marguerite passed the barrier he put himself on guard against it with his back to the interior of the cell and to her.

Marguerite had paused on the threshold.

After the glaring light of the guard-room the cell seemed dark, and at first, she could hardly see. The whole length of the long, narrow cubicle lay to her left, with a slight recess at its further end, so that from the threshold of the doorway she could not see into the distant corner.

Swift as a lightning flash the remembrance came back to her of proud Marie Antoinette narrowing her life to that dark corner where the insolent eyes of the rabble soldiery could not spy her every movement.

Marguerite stepped further into the room. Gradually by the dim light of an oil lamp placed upon a table in the recess she began to distinguish various objects: one or two chairs, another table, and a small but very comfortable-looking camp bedstead.

Just for a few seconds she only saw these inanimate things, then she became conscious of Percy's presence.

He sat on a chair, with his left arm half-stretched out upon the table, his head hidden in the bend of the elbow.

Marguerite did not utter a cry; she did not even tremble. Just for one brief instant she closed her eyes, so as to gather up all her courage before she dared to look again. Then with a steady and noiseless step she came quite close to him. She knelt on the flagstones at his feet and raised reverently to her lips the hand that hung nerveless and limp by his side.

He gave a start; a shiver seemed to go right through him; he half raised his head and murmured in a hoarse whisper:

"I tell you that I do not know, and if I did—"

She put her arms round him and pillowed her head upon his breast. He turned his head slowly toward her, and now his eyes—hollowed and rimmed with purple—looked straight into hers.

"My beloved," he said, "I knew that you would come." His arms closed round her. There was nothing of lifelessness or of weariness in the passion of that embrace; and when she looked up again it seemed to her as if that first vision which she had had of him with weary head bent, and wan, haggard face was not reality, only a dream born of her own anxiety for him, for now the hot, ardent blood coursed just as swiftly as ever through his veins, as if life—strong, tenacious, pulsating life—throbbed with unabated vigour in those massive limbs, and behind that square, clear brow as though the body, but half subdued, had transferred its vanishing strength to the kind and noble heart that was beating with the fervour of self-sacrifice.

"Percy," she said gently, "they will only give us a few moments together. They thought that my tears would break your spirit where their devilry had failed."

He held her glance with his own, with that close, intent look which binds soul to soul, and in his deep blue eyes there danced the restless flames of his own undying mirth:

"*La!* little woman," he said with enforced lightness, even whilst his voice quivered with the intensity of passion engendered by her presence, her nearness, the perfume of her hair, "how little they know you, eh? Your brave, beautiful, exquisite soul, shining now through your glorious eyes, would defy the machinations of Satan himself and his horde. Close your dear eyes, my love. I shall go mad with joy if I drink their beauty in any longer."

He held her face between his two hands, and indeed it seemed as if he could not satiate his soul with looking into her eyes. In the midst of so much sorrow, such misery and such deadly fear, never had Marguerite felt quite so happy, never had she felt him so completely her own. The inevitable bodily weakness, which of necessity had invaded even his splendid physique after a whole week's privations, had made a severe breach in the invincible barrier of self-control with which the soul of the inner man was kept perpetually hidden behind a mask of indifference and of irresponsibility.

And yet the agony of seeing the lines of sorrow so plainly writ on the beautiful face of the woman he worshipped must have been the keenest that the bold adventurer had ever experienced in the whole course of his reckless life. It was he—and he alone—who was making her suffer; her for whose sake he would gladly have shed every drop of his blood, endured every torment, every misery and every humiliation; her whom he worshipped only one degree less than he worshipped his honour and the cause which he had made his own.

Yet, in spite of that agony, in spite of the heartrending pathos of her pale wan face, and through the anguish of seeing her tears, the ruling passion—strong in death—the spirit of adventure, the mad, wild, devil-may-care irresponsibility was never wholly absent.

"Dear heart," he said with a quaint sigh, whilst he buried his face in the soft masses of her hair, "until you came I was so d——d fatigued."

He was laughing, and the old look of boyish love of mischief illumined his haggard face.

"Is it not lucky, dear heart," he said a moment or two later, "that those brutes do not leave me unshaved? I could not have faced you with a week's growth of beard round my chin. By dint of promises and bribery I have persuaded one of that rabble to come and shave me every morning. They will not allow me to handle a razor myself. They are afraid I should cut my throat—or one of theirs. But mostly I am too d——d sleepy to think of such a thing."

"Percy!" she exclaimed with tender and passionate reproach.

"I know—I know, dear," he murmured, "what a brute I am! Ah, God did a cruel thing the day that He threw me in your path. To think that once—not so very long ago—we were drifting apart, you and I. You would have suffered less, dear heart, if we had continued to drift."

Then as he saw that his bantering tone pained her, he covered her hands with kisses, entreating her forgiveness.

"Dear heart," he said merrily, "I deserve that you should leave me to rot in this abominable cage. They haven't got me yet, little woman, you know; I am not yet dead—only d—d sleepy at times. But I'll cheat them even now, never fear."

"How, Percy—how?" she moaned, for her heart was aching with intolerable pain; she knew better than he did the precautions which were being taken against his escape, and she saw more clearly than he realised it himself the terrible barrier set up against that escape by ever encroaching physical weakness.

"Well, dear," he said simply, "to tell you the truth I have not yet thought of that all-important 'how.' I had to wait, you see, until you came. I was so sure that you would come! I have succeeded in putting on paper all my instructions for Ffoulkes and the others. I will give them to you *anon*. I knew that you would come, and that I could give them to you; until then I had but to think of one thing, and that was of keeping body and soul together. My chance of seeing you was to let them have their will with me. Those brutes were sure, sooner or later, to bring you to me, that you might see the caged fox worn down to imbecility, eh? That you might add your tears to their persuasion and succeed where they have failed."

He laughed lightly with an unstrained note of gaiety, only Marguerite's sensitive ears caught the faint tone of bitterness which rang through the laugh.

"Once I know that the little King of France is safe," he said, "I can think of how best to rob those d—d murderers of my skin."

Then suddenly his manner changed. He still held her with one arm closely to, him, but the other now lay across the table, and the slender, emaciated hand was tightly clutched. He did not look at her, but straight ahead; the eyes, unnaturally large now, with their deep purple rims, looked far ahead beyond the stone walls of this grim, cruel prison.

The passionate lover, hungering for his beloved, had vanished; there sat the man with a purpose, the man whose firm hand had snatched men and women and children from death, the reckless enthusiast who tossed his life against an ideal.

For a while he sat thus, while in his drawn and haggard face she could trace every line formed by his thoughts—the frown of anxiety, the resolute setting of the lips, the obstinate look of will around the firm jaw. Then he turned again to her.

"My beautiful one," he said softly, "the moments are very precious. God knows I could spend eternity thus with your dear form nestling against my heart. But those d——d murderers will only give us half an hour, and I want your help, my beloved, now that I am a helpless cur caught in their trap. Will you listen attentively, dear heart, to what I am going to say?

"Yes, Percy, I will listen," she replied.

"And have you the courage to do just what I tell you, dear?"

"I would not have courage to do aught else," she said simply.

"It means going from hence today, dear heart, and perhaps not meeting again. Hush-sh-sh, my beloved," he said, tenderly placing his thin hand over her mouth, from which a sharp cry of pain had well-nigh escaped; "your exquisite soul will be with me always. Try—try not to give way to despair. Why! your love alone, which I see shining from your dear eyes, is enough to make a man cling to life with all his might. Tell me! will you do as I ask you?"

And she replied firmly and courageously:

"I will do just what you ask, Percy."

"God bless you for your courage, dear. You will have need of it."

CHAPTER 29

For the Sake of That Helpless Innocent

The next instant he was kneeling on the floor and his hands were wandering over the small, irregular flagstones immediately underneath the table. Marguerite had risen to her feet; she watched her husband with intent and puzzled eyes; she saw him suddenly pass his slender fingers along a crevice between two flagstones, then raise one of these slightly and from beneath it extract a small bundle of papers, each carefully folded and sealed. Then he replaced the stone and once more rose to his knees.

He gave a quick glance toward the doorway. That corner of his cell, the recess wherein stood the table, was invisible to anyone who had not actually crossed the threshold. Reassured that his movements could not have been and were not watched, he drew Marguerite closer to him.

"Dear heart," he whispered, "I want to place these papers in your care. Look upon them as my last will and testament. I succeeded in fooling those brutes one day by pretending to be willing to accede to their will. They gave me pen and ink and paper and wax, and I was to write out an order to my followers to bring the *Dauphin* hither. They left me in peace for one quarter of an hour, which gave me time to write three letters—one for Armand and the other two for Ffoulkes, and to hide them under the flooring of my cell. You see, dear, I knew that you would come and that I could give them to you then."

He paused, and that ghost of a smile once more hovered round his lips. He was thinking of that day when he had fooled Héron and Chauvelin into the belief that their devilry had succeeded, and that they had brought the reckless adventurer to his knees. He smiled at the recollection of their wrath when they knew that they had been tricked, and after a quarter of an hour's anxious waiting found a few sheets of paper scribbled over with incoherent words or satirical verse, and the prisoner having apparently snatched ten minutes' sleep, which seemingly had restored to him quite a modicum of his strength.

But of this he told Marguerite nothing, nor of the insults and the humiliation which he had had to bear in consequence of that trick. He did not tell her that directly afterwards the order went forth that the prisoner was to be kept on bread and water in the future, nor that Chauvelin had stood by laughing and jeering while—

No! he did not tell her all that; the recollection of it all had still the power to make him laugh; was it not all a part and parcel of that great gamble for human lives wherein he had held the winning cards himself for so long?

"It is your turn now," he had said even then to his bitter enemy.

"Yes!" Chauvelin had replied, "our turn at last. And you will not bend my fine English gentleman, we'll break you yet, never fear."

It was the thought of it all, of that hand to hand, will to will, spirit to spirit struggle that lighted up his haggard face even now, gave him a fresh zest for life, a desire to combat and to conquer in spite of all, in spite of the odds that had martyred his body but left the mind, the will, the power still unconquered.

He was pressing one of the papers into her hand, holding her fingers tightly in his, and compelling her gaze with the ardent excitement of his own.

"This first letter is for Ffoulkes," he said. "It relates to the final measures for the safety of the *Dauphin*. They are my instructions to those members of the League who are in or near Paris at the present moment. Ffoulkes, I know, must be with you—he was not likely, God bless his loyalty, to let you come to Paris alone. Then give this letter to him, dear heart, at once, tonight, and tell him that it is my express command that he and the others shall act in minute accordance with my instructions."

"But the *Dauphin* surely is safe now," she urged. "Ffoulkes and the others are here in order to help you."

"To help me, dear heart?" he interposed earnestly. "God alone can do that now, and such of my poor wits as these devils do not succeed in crushing out of me within the next ten days."

Ten days!

"I have waited a week, until this hour when I could place this packet in your hands; another ten days should see the *Dauphin* out of France—after that, we shall see."

"Percy," she exclaimed in an agony of horror, "you cannot endure this another day—and live!"

"Nay!" he said in a tone that was almost insolent in its proud defiance, "there is but little that a man cannot do an' he sets his mind to it. For the rest, 'tis in God's hands!" he added more gently. "Dear heart! you swore that you would be brave. The *Dauphin* is still in France, and until he is out of it he will not really be safe; his friends wanted to keep him inside the country. God only knows what they still hope; had I been free I should not have allowed him to remain so long; now those good people at Mantes will yield to my letter and to Ffoulkes' earnest appeal—they will allow one of our League to convey the child safely out of France, and I'll wait here until I know that he is safe. If I tried to get away now, and succeeded—why, Heaven help us! the hue and cry might turn against the child, and he might be captured before I could get to him. Dear heart! dear, dear heart! try to understand. The safety of that child is bound with mine honour, but I swear to you, my sweet love, that the day on which I feel that that safety is assured I will save mine own skin—what there is left of it—if I can!"

"Percy!" she cried with a sudden outburst of passionate revolt, "you speak as if the safety of that child were of more moment than your own. Ten days!—but, God in Heaven! have you thought how I shall live these ten days, whilst slowly, inch by inch, you give your dear, your precious life for a forlorn cause?

"I am very tough, m'dear," he said lightly; "'tis not a question of life. I shall only be spending a few more very uncomfortable days in this d—d hole; but what of that?"

Her eyes spoke the reply; her eyes veiled with tears, that wandered with heart-breaking anxiety from the hollow circles round his own to the lines of weariness about the firm lips and jaw. He laughed at her solicitude.

"I can last out longer than these brutes have any idea of," he said gaily.

"You cheat yourself, Percy," she rejoined with quiet earnestness. "Every day that you spend immured between these walls, with that ceaseless nerve-racking torment of sleeplessness which these devils have devised for the breaking of your will—every day thus spent diminishes your power of ultimately saving yourself. You see, I speak calmly—dispassionately—I do not even urge my claims upon your life. But what you must weigh in the balance is the claim of all those for whom in the past you have already staked your life, whose lives you have purchased by risking your own. What, in comparison with your noble life, is that of the puny descendant of a line of decadent kings? Why should it be sacrificed—ruthlessly, hopelessly sacrificed that a boy might live who is as nothing to the world, to his country—even to his own people?"

She had tried to speak calmly, never raising her voice beyond a whisper. Her hands still clutched that paper, which seemed to sear her fingers, the paper which she felt held writ upon its smooth surface the death-sentence of the man she loved.

But his look did not answer her firm appeal; it was fixed far away beyond the prison walls, on a lonely country road outside Paris, with the rain falling in a thin drizzle, and leaden clouds overhead chasing one another, driven by the gale.

"Poor mite," he murmured softly; "he walked so bravely by my side, until the little feet grew weary; then he nestled in my arms and slept until we met Ffoulkes waiting with the cart. He was no King of France just then, only a helpless innocent whom Heaven aided me to save."

Marguerite bowed her head in silence. There was nothing more that she could say, no plea that she could urge. Indeed, she had understood, as he had begged her to understand. She understood that long ago he had mapped out the course of his life, and now that that course happened to lead up a Calvary of humiliation and of suffering he was not likely to turn back, even though, on the summit, death already was waiting and beckoning with no uncertain hand; not until he could murmur, in the wake of the great and divine sacrifice itself, the sublime words:

"It is accomplished."

"But the *Dauphin* is safe enough now," was all that she said, after that one moment's silence when her heart, too, had offered up to God the supreme abnegation of self, and calmly faced a sorrow which threatened to break it at last.

"Yes!" he rejoined quietly, "safe enough for the moment. But he would be safer still if he were out of France. I had hoped to take him one day with me to England. But in this plan damnable Fate has interfered. His adherents wanted to get him to Vienna, and their wish had best be fulfilled now. In my instructions to Ffoulkes I have mapped out a simple way for accomplishing the journey. Tony will be the one best suited to lead the expedition, and I want him to make straight for Holland; the Northern frontiers are not so closely watched as are the Austrian ones. There is a faithful adherent of the Bourbon cause who lives at Delft, and who will give the shelter of his name and home to the fugitive King of France until he can be conveyed to Vienna. He is named Nauudorff. Once I feel that the child is safe in his hands I will look after myself, never fear."

He paused, for his strength, which was only factitious, born of the excitement that Marguerite's presence had called forth, was threatening to give way. His voice, though he had spoken in a whisper all along, was very hoarse, and his temples were throbbing with the sustained effort to speak.

"If those friends had only thought of denying me food instead of sleep," he murmured involuntarily, "I could have held out until—"

Then with characteristic swiftness his mood changed in a moment. His arms closed round Marguerite once more with a passion of self-reproach.

"Heaven forgive me for a selfish brute," he said, whilst the ghost of a smile once more lit up the whole of his face. "Dear soul, I must have forgotten your sweet presence, thus brooding over my own troubles, whilst your loving heart has a graver burden—God help me!—than it can possibly bear. Listen, my beloved, for I don't know how many minutes longer they intend to give us, and I have not yet spoken to you about Armand—"

"Armand!" she cried.

A twinge of remorse had gripped her. For fully ten minutes now she had relegated all thoughts of her brother to a distant cell of her memory.

"We have no news of Armand," she said. "Sir Andrew has searched all the prison registers. Oh! were not my heart atrophied by all that it has endured this past sennight it would feel a final throb of agonising pain at every thought of Armand."

A curious look, which even her loving eyes failed to interpret, passed like a shadow over her husband's face. But the shadow lifted in a moment, and it was with a reassuring smile that he said to her:

"Dear heart! Armand is comparatively safe for the moment. Tell Ffoulkes not to search the prison registers for him, rather to seek out Mademoiselle Lange. She will know where to find Armand."

"Jeanne Lange!" she exclaimed with a world of bitterness in the tone of her voice, "the girl whom Armand loved, it seems, with a passion greater than his loyalty. Oh! Sir Andrew tried to disguise my brother's folly, but I guessed what he did not choose to tell me. It was his disobedience, his want of trust, that brought this unspeakable misery on us all."

"Do not blame him overmuch, dear heart. Armand was in love, and love excuses every sin committed in its name. Jeanne Lange was arrested and Armand lost his reason temporarily. The very day on which I rescued the *Dauphin* from the Temple I had the good fortune to drag the little lady out of prison. I had given my promise to Armand that she should be safe, and I kept my word. But this Armand did not know—or else—"

He checked himself abruptly, and once more that strange, enigmatical look crept into his eyes.

"I took Jeanne Lange to a place of comparative safety," he said after a slight pause, "but since then she has been set entirely free."

"Free?"

"Yes. Chauvelin himself brought me the news," he replied with a quick, mirthless laugh, wholly unlike his usual light-hearted gaiety. "He had to ask me where to find Jeanne, for I alone knew where she was. As for Armand, they'll not worry about him whilst I am here. Another reason why I must bide a while longer. But in the meanwhile, dear, I pray you find Mademoiselle Lange; she lives at No. 5 Square du Roule. Through her I know that you can get to see Armand. This second letter," he added, pressing a smaller packet into her hand, "is for him. Give it to him, dear heart; it will, I hope, tend to cheer him. I fear me the poor lad frets; yet he only sinned because he loved, and to me he will always be your brother—the man who held your affection for all the years before I came into your life. Give him this letter, dear; they are my instructions to him, as the others are for Ffoulkes; but tell him to read them when he is all alone. You will do that, dear heart, will you not?"

"Yes, Percy," she said simply. "I promise."

Great joy, and the expression of intense relief, lit up his face, whilst his eyes spoke the gratitude which he felt.

"Then there is one thing more," he said. "There are others in this cruel city, dear heart, who have trusted me, and whom I must not fail—Marie de Marmontel and her brother, faithful servants of the late queen; they were on the eve of arrest when I succeeded in getting them to a place of comparative safety; and there are others there, too all of these poor victims have trusted me implicitly. They are waiting for me there, trusting in my promise to convey them safely to England. Sweetheart, you must redeem my promise to them. You will?—you will? Promise me that you will—"

"I promise, Percy," she said once more.

"Then go, dear, tomorrow, in the late afternoon, to No. 98, Rue de Charonne. It is a narrow house at the extreme end of that long street which abuts on the fortifications. The lower part of the house is occupied by a dealer in rags and old clothes. He and his wife and family are wretchedly poor, but they are kind, good souls, and for a consideration and a minimum of risk to themselves they will always render service to the English *milors*, whom they believe to be a band of inveterate smugglers. Ffoulkes and all the others know these people and know the house; Armand by the same token knows it too. Marie de Marmontel and her brother are there, and several others; the old Comte de Lézardière, the Abbé de Firmont; their names spell suffering, loyalty, and hopelessness. I was lucky enough to convey them safely to that hidden shelter. They trust me implicitly, dear heart. They are waiting for me there, trusting in my promise to them. Dear heart, you will go, will you not?"

"Yes, Percy," she replied. "I will go; I have promised."

"Ffoulkes has some certificates of safety by him, and the old clothes dealer will supply the necessary disguises; he has a covered cart which he uses for his business, and which you can borrow from him. Ffoulkes will drive the little party to Achard's farm in St. Germain, where other members of the League should be in waiting for the final journey to England. Ffoulkes will know how to arrange for everything; he was always my most able lieutenant. Once everything is organised he can appoint Hastings to lead the party. But you, dear heart, must do as you wish. Achard's farm would be a safe retreat for you and for Ffoulkes: if—I know—I know, dear," he added with infinite tenderness. "See I do not even suggest that you should leave me. Ffoulkes will be with you, and I know that neither he nor you would go even if I commanded. Either Achard's farm, or even the house in the Rue de Charonne, would be quite safe for you, dear, under Ffoulkes's protection, until the time when I myself can carry you back—you, my precious burden—to England in mine own arms, or until—Hush-sh-sh, dear heart," he entreated, smothering with a passionate kiss the low moan of pain which had escaped her lips; "it is all in God's hands now; I am in a tight corner—tighter than ever I have been before; but I am not dead yet, and those brutes have not yet paid the full price for my life. Tell me, dear heart, that you have understood—that you will do all that I asked. Tell me again, my dear, dear love; it is the very essence of life to hear your sweet lips murmur this promise now."

And for the third time she reiterated firmly:

"I have understood every word that you said to me, Percy, and I promise on your precious life to do what you ask."

He sighed a deep sigh of satisfaction, and even at that moment there came from the guard-room beyond the sound of a harsh voice, saying peremptorily:

"That half-hour is nearly over, sergeant; 'tis time you interfered."

"Three minutes more, citizen," was the curt reply.

"Three minutes, you devils," murmured Blakeney between set teeth, whilst a sudden light which even Marguerite's keen gaze failed to interpret leapt into his eyes. Then he pressed the third letter into her hand.

Once more his close, intent gaze compelled hers; their faces were close one to the other, so near to him did he draw her, so tightly did he hold her to him. The paper was in her hand and his fingers were pressed firmly on hers.

"Put this in your kerchief, my beloved," he whispered. "Let it rest on your exquisite bosom where I so love to pillow my head. Keep it there until the last hour when it seems to you that nothing more can come between me and shame—Hush-sh-sh, dear," he added with passionate tenderness, checking the hot protest that at the word "shame" had sprung to her lips, "I cannot explain more fully now. I do not know what may happen. I am only a man, and who knows what subtle devilry those brutes might not devise for bringing the untamed adventurer to his knees. For the next ten days the *Dauphin* will be on the high roads of France, on his way to safety. Every stage of his journey will be known to me. I can from between these four walls follow him and his escort step by step. Well, dear, I am but a man, already brought to shameful weakness by mere physical discomfort—the want of sleep—such a trifle after all; but in case my reason tottered—God knows what I might do—then give this packet to Ffoulkes—it contains my final instructions—and he will know how to act. Promise me, dear heart, that you will not open the packet unless—unless mine own dishonour seems to you imminent—unless I have yielded to these brutes in this prison and sent Ffoulkes or one of the others orders to exchange the *Dauphin's* life for mine; then, when mine own handwriting hath proclaimed me a coward, then and then only, give this packet to Ffoulkes. Promise me that, and also that when you and he have mastered its contents you will act exactly as I have commanded. Promise me that, dear, in your own sweet name, which may God bless, and in that of Ffoulkes, our loyal friend."

Through the sobs that well-nigh choked her she murmured the promise he desired.

His voice had grown hoarser and more spent with the inevitable reaction after the long and sustained effort, but the vigour of the spirit was untouched, the fervour, the enthusiasm.

"Dear heart," he murmured, "do not look on me with those dear, scared eyes of yours. If there is aught that puzzles you in what I said, try and trust me a while longer. Remember, I must save the *Dauphin* at all costs; mine honour is bound with his safety. What happens to me after that matters but little, yet I wish to live for your dear sake."

He drew a long breath which had naught of weariness in it. The haggard look had completely vanished from his face, the eyes were lighted up from within, the very soul of reckless daring and immortal gaiety illumined his whole personality.

"Do not look so sad, little woman," he said with a strange and sudden recrudescence of power; "those d—d murderers have not got me yet—even now."

Then he went down like a log.

The effort had been too prolonged—weakened nature reasserted her rights and he lost consciousness. Marguerite, helpless and almost distraught with grief, had yet the strength of mind not to call for assistance. She pillowed the loved one's head upon her breast, she kissed the dear, tired eyes, the poor throbbing temples. The unutterable pathos of seeing this man, who was always the personification of extreme vitality, energy, and boundless endurance and pluck, lying thus helpless, like a tired child, in her arms, was perhaps the saddest moment of this day of sorrow. But in her trust, she never wavered for one instant. Much that he had said had puzzled her; but the word "shame" coming from his own lips as a comment on himself never caused her the slightest pang of fear. She had quickly hidden the tiny packet in her kerchief. She would act point by point exactly as he had ordered her to do, and she knew that Ffoulkes would never waver either.

Her heart ached well-nigh to breaking point. That which she could not understand had increased her anguish tenfold. If she could only have given way to tears she could have borne this final agony more easily. But the solace of tears was not for her; when those loved eyes once more opened to consciousness they should see hers glowing with courage and determination.

There had been silence for a few minutes in the little cell. The soldiery outside, inured to their hideous duty, thought no doubt that the time had come for them to interfere. The iron bar was raised and thrown back with a loud crash, the butt-ends of muskets were grounded against the floor, and two soldiers made noisy irruption into the cell.

"*Holà*, citizen! Wake up," shouted one of the men; "you have not told us yet what you have done with Capet!"

Marguerite uttered a cry of horror. Instinctively her arms were interposed between the unconscious man and these inhuman creatures, with a beautiful gesture of protecting motherhood.

"He has fainted," she said, her voice quivering with indignation. "My God! are you devils that you have not one spark of manhood in you?"

The men shrugged their shoulders, and both laughed brutally. They had seen worse sights than these, since they served a Republic that ruled by bloodshed and by terror. They were own brothers in callousness and cruelty to those men who on this self-same spot a few months ago had watched the daily agony of a martyred queen, or to those who had rushed into the Abbaye prison on that awful day in September, and at a word from their infamous leaders had put eighty defenceless prisoners—men, women, and children—to the sword.

"Tell him to say what he has done with Capet," said one of the soldiers now, and this rough command was accompanied with a coarse jest that sent the blood flaring up into Marguerite's pale cheeks.

The brutal laugh, the coarse words which accompanied it, the insult flung at Marguerite, had penetrated to Blakeney's slowly returning consciousness. With sudden strength, that appeared almost supernatural, he jumped to his feet, and before any of the others could interfere he had with clenched fist struck the soldier a full blow on the mouth.

The man staggered back with a curse, the other shouted for help; in a moment the narrow place swarmed with soldiers; Marguerite was roughly torn away from the prisoner's side, and thrust into the far corner of the cell, from where she only saw a confused mass of blue coats and white belts, and—towering for one brief moment above what seemed to her fevered fancy like a veritable sea of heads—the pale face of her husband, with wide dilated eyes searching the gloom for hers.

"Remember!" he shouted, and his voice for that brief moment rang out clear and sharp above the din.

Then he disappeared behind the wall of glistening bayonets, of blue coats and uplifted arms; mercifully for her she remembered nothing more very clearly. She felt herself being dragged out of the cell, the iron bar being thrust down behind her with a loud clang. Then in a vague, dreamy state of semi-unconsciousness she saw the heavy bolts being drawn back from the outer door, heard the grating of the key in the monumental lock, and the next moment a breath of fresh air brought the sensation of renewed life into her.

CHAPTER 30

Afterwards

"I am sorry, Lady Blakeney," said a harsh, dry voice close to her; "the incident at the end of your visit was none of our making, remember."

She turned away, sickened with horror at thought of contact with this wretch. She had heard the heavy oaken door swing to behind her on its ponderous hinges, and the key once again turn in the lock. She felt as if she had suddenly been thrust into a coffin, and that clods of earth were being thrown upon her breast, oppressing her heart so that she could not breathe.

Had she looked for the last time on the man whom she loved beyond everything else on earth, whom she worshipped more ardently day by day? Was she even now carrying within the folds of her kerchief a message from a dying man to his comrades?

Mechanically she followed Chauvelin down the corridor and

along the passages which she had traversed a brief half-hour ago. From some distant church tower a clock tolled the hour of ten. It had then really only been little more than thirty brief minutes since first she had entered this grim building, which seemed less stony than the monsters who held authority within it; to her it seemed that centuries had gone over her head during that time. She felt like an old woman, unable to straighten her back or to steady her limbs; she could only dimly see some few paces ahead the trim figure of Chauvelin walking with measured steps, his hands held behind his back, his head thrown up with what looked like triumphant defiance.

At the door of the cubicle where she had been forced to submit to the indignity of being searched by a wardress, the latter was now standing, waiting with characteristic stolidity. In her hand she held the steel files, the dagger and the purse which, as Marguerite passed, she held out to her.

"Your property, citizeness," she said placidly.

She emptied the purse into her own hand, and solemnly counted out the twenty pieces of gold. She was about to replace them all into the purse, when Marguerite pressed one of them back into her wrinkled hand.

"Nineteen will be enough, citizeness," she said; "keep one for yourself, not only for me, but for all the poor women who come here with their heart full of hope and go hence with it full of despair."

The woman turned calm, lack-lustre eyes on her, and silently pocketed the gold piece with a grudgingly muttered word of thanks.

Chauvelin during this brief interlude, had walked thoughtlessly on ahead. Marguerite, peering down the length of the narrow corridor, spied his sable-clad figure some hundred metres further on as it crossed the dim circle of light thrown by one of the lamps.

She was about to follow, when it seemed to her as if someone was moving in the darkness close beside her. The wardress was even now in the act of closing the door of her cubicle, and there were a couple of soldiers who were disappearing from view round one end of the passage, whilst Chauvelin's retreating form was lost in the gloom at the other.

There was no light close to where she herself was standing, and the blackness around her was as impenetrable as a veil; the sound of a human creature moving and breathing close to her in this intense darkness acted weirdly on her overwrought nerves.

"*Qui va là?*" she called.

There was a more distinct movement among the shadows this time, as of a swift tread on the flagstones of the corridor. All else was silent round, and now she could plainly hear those footsteps running rapidly down the passage away from her. She strained her eyes to see more clearly, and anon in one of the dim circles of light on ahead she spied a man's figure—slender and darkly clad—walking quickly yet furtively like one pursued. As he crossed the light the man turned to look back. It was her brother Armand.

Her first instinct was to call to him; the second checked that call upon her lips.

Percy had said that Armand was in no danger; then why should he be sneaking along the dark corridors of this awful house of Justice if he was free and safe?

Certainly, even at a distance, her brother's movements suggested to Marguerite that he was in danger of being seen. He cowered in the darkness, tried to avoid the circles of light thrown by the lamps in the passage. At all costs Marguerite felt that she must warn him that the way he was going now would lead him straight into Chauvelin's arms, and she longed to let him know that she was close by.

Feeling sure that he would recognise her voice, she made pretence to turn back to the cubicle through the door of which the wardress had already disappeared, and called out as loudly as she dared:

"Goodnight, citizeness!"

But Armand—who surely must have heard—did not pause at the sound. Rather was he walking on now more rapidly than before. In less than a minute he would be reaching the spot where Chauvelin stood waiting for Marguerite. That end of the corridor, however, received no light from any of the lamps; strive how she might, Marguerite could see nothing now either of Chauvelin or of Armand.

Blindly, instinctively, she ran forward, thinking only to reach Armand, and to warn him to turn back before it was too late; before he found himself face to face with the most bitter enemy he and his nearest and dearest had ever had. But as she at last came to a halt at the end of the corridor, panting with the exertion of running and the fear for Armand, she almost fell up against Chauvelin, who was standing there alone and imperturbable, seemingly having waited patiently for her. She could only dimly distinguish his face, the sharp features and thin cruel mouth, but she felt—more than she actually saw—his cold steely eyes fixed with a strange expression of mockery upon her.

But of Armand there was no sign, and she—poor soul!—had difficulty in not betraying the anxiety which she felt for her brother. Had the flagstones swallowed him up? A door on the right was the only one that gave on the corridor at this point; it led to the *concierge's* lodge, and thence out into the courtyard. Had Chauvelin been dreaming, sleeping with his eyes open, whilst he stood waiting for her, and had Armand succeeded in slipping past him under cover of the darkness and through that door to safety that lay beyond these prison walls?

Marguerite, miserably agitated, not knowing what to think, looked somewhat wild-eyed on Chauvelin; he smiled, that inscrutable, mirthless smile of his, and said blandly:

"Is there aught else that I can do for you, citizeness? This is your nearest way out. No doubt Sir Andrew will be waiting to escort you home."

Then as she—not daring either to reply or to question—walked straight up to the door, he hurried forward, prepared to open it for her. But before he did so he turned to her once again:

"I trust that your visit has pleased you, Lady Blakeney," he said suavely. "At what hour do you desire to repeat it tomorrow?"

"Tomorrow?" she reiterated in a vague, absent manner, for she was still dazed with the strange incident of Armand's appearance and his flight.

"Yes. You would like to see Sir Percy again tomorrow, would you not? I myself would gladly pay him a visit from time to time, but he does not care for my company. My colleague, Citizen Héron, on the other hand, calls on him four times in every twenty-four hours; he does so a few moments before the changing of the guard, and stays chatting with Sir Percy until after the guard is changed, when he inspects the men and satisfies himself that no traitor has crept in among them. All the men are personally known to him, you see. These hours are at five in the morning and again at eleven, and then again at five and eleven in the evening. My friend Héron, as you see, is zealous and assiduous, and, strangely enough, Sir Percy does not seem to view his visit with any displeasure. Now at any other hour of the day, Lady Blakeney, I pray you command me and I will arrange that Citizen Héron grant you a second interview with the prisoner."

Marguerite had only listened to Chauvelin's lengthy speech with half an ear; her thoughts still dwelt on the past half-hour with its bitter joy and its agonising pain; and fighting through her thoughts of Percy there was the recollection of Armand which so disquieted her. But though she had only vaguely listened to what Chauvelin was saying, she caught the drift of it.

Madly she longed to accept his suggestion. The very thought of seeing Percy on the morrow was solace to her aching heart; it could feed on hope tonight instead of on its own bitter pain. But even during this brief moment of hesitancy, and while her whole being cried out for this joy that her enemy was holding out to her, even then in the gloom ahead of her she seemed to see a vision of a pale face raised above a crowd of swaying heads, and of the eyes of the dreamer searching for her own, whilst the last sublime cry of perfect self-devotion once more echoed in her ear:

"Remember!"

The promise which she had given him, that would she fulfil. The burden which he had laid on her shoulders she would try to bear as heroically as he was bearing his own. Aye, even at the cost of the supreme sorrow of never resting again in the haven of his arms.

But in spite of sorrow, in spite of anguish so terrible that she could not imagine Death itself to have a more cruel sting, she wished above all to safeguard that final, attenuated thread of hope which was wound round the packet that lay hidden on her breast.

She wanted, above all, not to arouse Chauvelin's suspicions by markedly refusing to visit the prisoner again—suspicions that might lead to her being searched once more and the precious packet filched from her. Therefore, she said to him earnestly now:

"I thank you, citizen, for your solicitude on my behalf, but you will understand, I think, that my visit to the prisoner has been almost more than I could bear. I cannot tell you at this moment whether tomorrow I should be in a fit state to repeat it."

"As you please," he replied urbanely. "But I pray you to remember one thing, and that is—"

He paused a moment while his restless eyes wandered rapidly over her face, trying, as it were, to get at the soul of this woman, at her innermost thoughts, which he felt were hidden from him.

"Yes, citizen," she said quietly; "what is it that I am to remember?"

"That it rests with you, Lady Blakeney, to put an end to the present situation."

"How?"

"Surely you can persuade Sir Percy's friends not to leave their chief in durance vile. They themselves could put an end to his troubles tomorrow."

"By giving up the *Dauphin* to you, you mean?" she retorted coldly.

"Precisely."

"And you hoped—you still hope that by placing before me the picture of your own fiendish cruelty against my husband you will induce me to act the part of a traitor towards him and a coward before his followers?"

"Oh!" he said deprecatingly, "the cruelty now is no longer mine. Sir Percy's release is in your hands, Lady Blakeney—in that of his followers. I should only be too willing to end the present intolerable situation. You and your friends are applying the last turn of the thumbscrew, not I—"

She smothered the cry of horror that had risen to her lips. The man's cold-blooded sophistry was threatening to make a breach in her armour of self-control.

She would no longer trust herself to speak but made a quick movement towards the door.

He shrugged his shoulders as if the matter were now entirely out of his control. Then he opened the door for her to pass out, and as her skirts brushed against him he bowed with studied deference, murmuring a cordial "Goodnight!"

"And remember, Lady Blakeney," he added politely, "that should you at any time desire to communicate with me at my rooms, 19, Rue Dupuy, I hold myself entirely at your service."

Then as her tall, graceful figure disappeared in the outside gloom he passed his thin hand over his mouth as if to wipe away the last lingering signs of triumphant irony:

"The second visit will work wonders, I think, my fine lady," he murmured under his breath.

CHAPTER 31

An Interlude

It was close on midnight now, and still they sat opposite one another, he the friend and she the wife, talking over that brief half-hour that had meant an eternity to her.

Marguerite had tried to tell Sir Andrew everything; bitter as it was to put into actual words the pathos and misery which she had witnessed, yet she would hide nothing from the devoted comrade whom she knew Percy would trust absolutely. To him she repeated every word that Percy had uttered, described every inflection of his voice, those enigmatical phrases which she had not understood, and together they cheated one another into the belief that hope lingered somewhere hidden in those words.

"I am not going to despair, Lady Blakeney," said Sir Andrew firmly; "and, moreover, we are not going to disobey. I would stake my life that even now Blakeney has some scheme in his mind which is embodied in the various letters which he has given you, and which—Heaven help us in that case!—we might thwart by disobedience. Tomorrow in the late afternoon I will escort you to the Rue de Charonne. It is a house that we all know well, and which Armand, of course, knows too. I had already inquired there two days ago to ascertain whether by chance St. Just was not in hiding there, but Lucas, the landlord and old-clothes dealer, knew nothing about him."

Marguerite told him about her swift vision of Armand in the dark corridor of the house of Justice.

"Can you understand it, Sir Andrew?" she asked, fixing her deep, luminous eyes inquiringly upon him.

"No, I cannot," he said, after an almost imperceptible moment of hesitancy; "but we shall see him tomorrow. I have no doubt that Mademoiselle Lange will know where to find him; and now that we know where she is, all our anxiety about him, at any rate, should soon be at an end."

He rose and made some allusion to the lateness of the hour. Somehow it seemed to her that her devoted friend was trying to hide his innermost thoughts from her. She watched him with an anxious, intent gaze.

"Can you understand it all, Sir Andrew?" she reiterated with a pathetic note of appeal.

"No, no!" he said firmly. "On my soul, Lady Blakeney, I know no more of Armand than you do yourself. But I am sure that Percy is right. The boy frets because remorse must have assailed him by now. Had he but obeyed implicitly that day, as we all did—"

But he could not frame the whole terrible proposition in words. Bitterly as he himself felt on the subject of Armand, he would not add yet another burden to this devoted woman's heavy load of misery.

"It was Fate, Lady Blakeney," he said after a while. "Fate! a damnable fate which did it all. Great God! to think of Blakeney in the hands of those brutes seems so horrible that at times I feel as if the whole thing were a nightmare, and that the next moment we shall both wake hearing his merry voice echoing through this room."

He tried to cheer her with words of hope that he knew were but chimeras. A heavy weight of despondency lay on his heart. The letter from his chief was hidden against his breast; he would study it anon in the privacy of his own apartment so as to commit every word to memory that related to the measures for the ultimate safety of the child-King. After that it would have to be destroyed, lest it fell into inimical hands.

Soon he bade Marguerite goodnight. She was tired out, body and soul, and he—her faithful friend—vaguely wondered how long she would be able to withstand the strain of so much sorrow, such unspeakable misery.

When at last she was alone Marguerite made brave efforts to compose her nerves so as to obtain a certain modicum of sleep this night. But, strive how she might, sleep would not come. How could it, when before her wearied brain there rose constantly that awful vision of Percy in the long, narrow cell, with weary head bent over his arm, and those friends shouting persistently in his ear:

"Wake up, citizen! Tell us, where is Capet?"

The fear obsessed her that his mind might give way; for the mental agony of such intense weariness must be well-nigh impossible to bear. In the dark, as she sat hour after hour at the open window, looking out in the direction where through the veil of snow the grey walls of the Châtelet prison towered silent and grim, she seemed to see his pale, drawn face with almost appalling reality; she could see every line of it, and could study it with the intensity born of a terrible fear.

How long would the ghostly glimmer of merriment still linger in the eyes? When would the hoarse, mirthless laugh rise to the lips, that awful laugh that proclaims madness? Oh! she could have screamed now with the awfulness of this haunting terror. Ghouls seemed to be mocking her out of the darkness, every flake of snow that fell silently on the window-sill became a grinning face that taunted and derided; every cry in the silence of the night, every footstep on the quay below turned to hideous jeers hurled at her by tormenting fiends.

She closed the window quickly, for she feared that she would go mad. For an hour after that she walked up and down the room making violent efforts to control her nerves, to find a glimmer of that courage which she promised Percy that she would have.

CHAPTER 32

Sisters

The morning found her fagged out, but more calm. Later on, she managed to drink some coffee, and having washed and dressed, she

413

prepared to go out.

Sir Andrew appeared in time to ascertain her wishes.

"I promised Percy to go to the Rue de Charonne in the late after-noon," she said. "I have some hours to spare and mean to employ them in trying to find speech with Mademoiselle Lange."

"Blakeney has told you where she lives?"

"Yes. In the Square du Roule. I know it well. I can be there in half an hour."

He, of course, begged to be allowed to accompany her, and *anon* they were walking together quickly up toward the Faubourg St. Honoré. The snow had ceased falling, but it was still very cold, but neither Marguerite nor Sir Andrew were conscious of the temperature or of any outward signs around them. They walked on silently until they reached the torn-down gates of the Square du Roule; there Sir Andrew parted from Marguerite after having appointed to meet her an hour later at a small eating-house he knew of where they could have some food together, before starting on their long expedition to the Rue de Charonne.

Five minutes later Marguerite Blakeney was shown in by worthy Madame Belhomme, into the quaint and pretty drawing-room with its soft-toned hangings and old-world air of faded grace. Mademoiselle Lange was sitting there, in a capacious armchair, which encircled her delicate figure with its frame-work of dull old gold.

She was ostensibly reading when Marguerite was announced, for an open book lay on a table beside her; but it seemed to the visitor that mayhap the young girl's thoughts had played truant from her work, for her pose was listless and apathetic, and there was a look of grave trouble upon the childlike face.

She rose when Marguerite entered, obviously puzzled at the un-expected visit, and somewhat awed at the appearance of this beautiful woman with the sad look in her eyes.

"I must crave your pardon, *mademoiselle*," said Lady Blakeney as soon as the door had once more closed on Madame Belhomme, and she found herself alone with the young girl. "This visit at such an early hour must seem to you an intrusion. But I am Marguerite St. Just, and—"

Her smile and outstretched hand completed the sentence.

"St. Just!" exclaimed Jeanne.

"Yes. Armand's sister!"

A swift blush rushed to the girl's pale cheeks; her brown eyes expressed unadulterated joy. Marguerite, who was studying her closely, was conscious that her poor aching heart went out to this exquisite child, the far-off innocent cause of so much misery.

Jeanne, a little shy, a little confused and nervous in her movements, was pulling a chair close to the fire, begging Marguerite to sit. Her words came out all the while in short jerky sentences, and from time to time she stole swift shy glances at Armand's sister.

"You will forgive me, *mademoiselle*," said Marguerite, whose simple and calm manner quickly tended to soothe Jeanne Lange's confusion; "but I was so anxious about my brother—I do not know where to find him."

"And so, you came to me, *Madame*?"

"Was I wrong?"

"Oh, no! But what made you think that—that I would know?"

"I guessed," said Marguerite with a smile. "You had heard about me then?"

"Oh, yes!"

"Through whom? Did Armand tell you about me?"

"No, alas! I have not seen him this past fortnight, since you, *mademoiselle*, came into his life; but many of Armand's friends are in Paris just now; one of them knew, and he told me."

The soft blush had now overspread the whole of the girl's face, even down to her graceful neck. She waited to see Marguerite comfortably installed in an armchair, then she resumed shyly:

"And it was Armand who told me all about you. He loves you so dearly."

"Armand and I were very young children when we lost our parents," said Marguerite softly, "and we were all in all to each other then. And until I married he was the man I loved best in all the world."

"He told me you were married—to an Englishman."

"Yes?"

"He loves England too. At first, he always talked of my going there with him as his wife, and of the happiness we should find there together."

"Why do you say 'at first'?"

"He talks less about England now."

"Perhaps he feels that now you know all about it, and that you understand each other with regard to the future."

"Perhaps."

Jeanne sat opposite to Marguerite on a low stool by the fire. Her elbows were resting on her knees, and her face just now was half-hidden by the wealth of her brown curls. She looked exquisitely pretty sitting like this, with just the suggestion of sadness in the listless pose. Marguerite had come here today prepared to hate this young girl, who in a few brief days had stolen not only Armand's heart, but his allegiance to his chief, and his trust in him. Since last night, when she had seen her brother sneak silently past her like a thief in the night, she had nurtured thoughts of ill-will and anger against Jeanne.

But hatred and anger had melted at the sight of this child. Marguerite, with the perfect understanding born of love itself, had soon realised the charm which a woman like Mademoiselle Lange must of necessity exercise over a chivalrous, enthusiastic nature like Armand's. The sense of protection—the strongest perhaps that exists in a good man's heart—would draw him irresistibly to this beautiful child, with the great, appealing eyes, and the look of pathos that pervaded the entire face. Marguerite, looking in silence on the dainty picture before her, found it in her heart to forgive Armand for disobeying his chief when those eyes beckoned to him in a contrary direction.

How could he, how could any chivalrous man endure the thought of this delicate, fresh flower lying crushed and drooping in the hands of monsters who respected neither courage nor purity? And Armand had been more than human, or mayhap less, if he had indeed consented to leave the fate of the girl whom he had sworn to love and protect in other hands than his own.

It seemed almost as if Jeanne was conscious of the fixity of Marguerite's gaze, for though she did not turn to look at her, the flush gradually deepened in her cheeks.

"Mademoiselle Lange," said Marguerite gently, "do you not feel that you can trust me?"

She held out her two hands to the girl, and Jeanne slowly turned to her. The next moment she was kneeling at Marguerite's feet and kissing the beautiful kind hands that had been stretched out to her with such sisterly love.

"Indeed, indeed, I do trust you," she said, and looked with tear-dimmed eyes in the pale face above her. "I have longed for someone in whom I could confide. I have been so lonely lately, and Armand—"

With an impatient little gesture, she brushed away the tears which had gathered in her eyes.

"What has Armand been doing?" asked Marguerite with an encouraging smile.

"Oh, nothing to grieve me!" replied the young girl eagerly, "for he is kind and good, and chivalrous and noble. Oh, I love him with all my heart! I loved him from the moment that I set eyes on him, and then he came to see me—perhaps you know! And he talked so beautiful about England, and so nobly about his leader the Scarlet Pimpernel—have you heard of him?"

"Yes," said Marguerite, smiling. "I have heard of him."

"It was that day that Citizen Héron came with his soldiers! Oh! you do not know Citizen Héron. He is the most cruel man in France. In Paris he is hated by everyone, and no one is safe from his spies. He came to arrest Armand, but I was able to fool him and to save Armand. And after that," she added with charming naivete, "I felt as if, having saved Armand's life, he belonged to me—and his love for me had made me his."

"Then I was arrested," she continued after a slight pause, and at the recollection of what she had endured then her fresh voice still trembled with horror.

"They dragged me to prison, and I spent two days in a dark cell, where—"

She hid her face in her hands, whilst a few sobs shook her whole frame; then she resumed more calmly:

"I had seen nothing of Armand. I wondered where he was, and I knew that he would be eating out his heart with anxiety for me. But God was watching over me. At first, I was transferred to the Temple prison, and there a kind creature—a sort of man-of-all work in the prison took compassion on me. I do not know how he contrived it, but one morning very early he brought me some filthy old rags which he told me to put on quickly, and when I had done that he bade me follow him. Oh! he was a very dirty, wretched man himself, but he must have had a kind heart. He took me by the hand and made me carry his broom and brushes. Nobody took much notice of us, the dawn was only just breaking, and the passages were very dark and deserted; only once some soldiers began to chaff him about me: '*C'est ma fille—quoi?*' he said roughly. I very nearly laughed then, only I had the good sense to restrain myself, for I knew that my freedom, and perhaps my life, depended on my not betraying myself. My grimy, tattered guide took me with him right through the interminable corridors of that awful building, whilst I prayed fervently to God for him and for myself. We got out by one of the service stairs and exit, and then he dragged me through some narrow streets until we came to a corner where a covered cart stood waiting. My kind friend told me to get into the cart, and then he bade the driver on the box take me straight to a house in the Rue St. Germain l'Auxerrois. Oh! I was infinitely grateful to the poor creature who had helped me to get out of that awful prison, and I would gladly have given him some money, for I am sure he was very poor; but I had none by me. He told me that I should be quite safe in the house in the Rue St. Germain l'Auxerrois, and begged me to wait there patiently for a few days until I heard from one who had my welfare at heart, and who would further arrange for my safety."

Marguerite had listened silently to this narrative so naively told by this child, who obviously had no idea to whom she owed her freedom and her life. While the girl talked, her mind could follow with unspeakable pride and happiness every phase of that scene in the early dawn, when that mysterious, ragged man-of-all-work, unbeknown even to the woman whom he was saving, risked his own noble life for the sake of her whom his friend and comrade loved.

"And did you never see again the kind man to whom you owe your life?" she asked.

"No!" replied Jeanne. "I never saw him since; but when I arrived at the Rue St. Germain l'Auxerrois I was told by the good people who took charge of me that the ragged man-of-all-work had been none other than the mysterious Englishman whom Armand reveres, he whom they call the Scarlet Pimpernel."

"But you did not stay very long in the Rue St. Germain l'Auxerrois, did you?"

"No. Only three days. The third day I received a communique from the Committee of General Security, together with an unconditional certificate of safety. It meant that I was free—quite free. Oh! I could scarcely believe it. I laughed and I cried until the people in the house thought that I had gone mad. The past few days had been such a horrible nightmare."

"And then you saw Armand again?"

"Yes. They told him that I was free. And he came here to see me. He often comes; he will be here *anon*."

"But are you not afraid on his account and your own? He is—he must be still—'suspect'; a well-known adherent of the Scarlet Pimpernel, he would be safer out of Paris."

"No! oh, no! Armand is in no danger. He, too, has an unconditional certificate of safety."

"An unconditional certificate of safety?" asked Marguerite, whilst a deep frown of grave puzzlement appeared between her brows. "What does that mean?"

"It means that he is free to come and go as he likes; that neither he nor I have anything to fear from Héron and his awful spies. Oh! but for that sad and careworn look on Armand's face we could be so happy; but he is so unlike himself. He is Armand and yet another; his look at times quite frightens me."

"Yet you know why he is so sad," said Marguerite in a strange, toneless voice which she seemed quite unable to control, for that tonelessness came from a terrible sense of suffocation, of a feeling as if her heart-strings were being gripped by huge, hard hands.

"Yes, I know," said Jeanne half hesitatingly, as if knowing, she was still unconvinced.

"His chief, his comrade, the friend of whom you speak, the Scarlet Pimpernel, who risked his life in order to save yours, *mademoiselle*, is a prisoner in the hands of those that hate him."

Marguerite had spoken with sudden vehemence. There was almost an appeal in her voice now, as if she were trying not to convince Jeanne only, but also herself, of something that was quite simple, quite straightforward, and yet which appeared to be receding from her, an intangible something, a spirit that was gradually yielding to a force as yet unborn, to a phantom that had not yet emerged from out chaos.

But Jeanne seemed unconscious of all this. Her mind was absorbed in Armand, the man whom she loved in her simple, whole-hearted way, and who had seemed so different of late.

"Oh, yes!" she said with a deep, sad sigh, whilst the ever-ready tears once more gathered in her eyes, "Armand is very unhappy because of him. The Scarlet Pimpernel was his friend; Armand loved and revered him. Did you know," added the girl, turning large, horror-filled eyes on Marguerite, "that they want some information from him about the *Dauphin*, and to force him to give it they—they—"

"Yes, I know," said Marguerite.

"Can you wonder, then, that Armand is unhappy. Oh! last night, after he went from me, I cried for hours, just because he had looked so sad. He no longer talks of happy England, of the cottage we were to have, and of the Kentish orchards in May. He has not ceased to love me, for at times his love seems so great that I tremble with a delicious sense of fear. But oh! his love for me no longer makes him happy."

Her head had gradually sunk lower and lower on her breast, her voice died down in a murmur broken by heartrending sighs. Every generous impulse in Marguerite's noble nature prompted her to take that sorrowing child in her arms, to comfort her if she could, to reassure her if she had the power. But a strange icy feeling had gradually invaded her heart, even whilst she listened to the simple unsophisticated talk of Jeanne Lange. Her hands felt numb and clammy, and instinctively she withdrew away from the near vicinity of the girl. She felt as if the room, the furniture in it, even the window before her were dancing a wild and curious dance, and that from everywhere around strange whistling sounds reached her ears, which caused her head to whirl and her brain to reel.

Jeanne had buried her head in her hands. She was crying—softly, almost humbly at first, as if half ashamed of her grief; then, suddenly it seemed, as if she could not contain herself any longer, a heavy sob escaped her throat and shook her whole delicate frame with its violence. Sorrow no longer would be gainsaid, it insisted on physical expression—that awful tearing of the heart-strings which leaves the body numb and panting with pain.

In a moment Marguerite had forgotten; the dark and shapeless phantom that had knocked at the gate of her soul was relegated back into chaos. It ceased to be, it was made to shrivel and to burn in the great seething cauldron of womanly sympathy. What part this child had played in the vast cataclysm of misery which had dragged a noble-hearted enthusiast into the dark torture-chamber, whence the only outlet led to the guillotine, she—Marguerite Blakeney—did not know; what part Armand, her brother, had played in it, that she would not dare to guess; all that she knew was that here was a loving heart that was filled with pain—a young, inexperienced soul that was having its first tussle with the grim realities of life—and every motherly instinct in Marguerite was aroused.

She rose and gently drew the young girl up from her knees, and then closer to her; she pillowed the grief-stricken head against her shoulder, and murmured gentle, comforting words into the tiny ear.

"I have news for Armand," she whispered, "that will comfort him, a message—a letter from his friend. You will see, dear, that when Armand reads it he will become a changed man; you see, Armand acted a little foolishly a few days ago. His chief had given him orders which he disregarded—he was so anxious about you—he should have obeyed; and now, mayhap, he feels that his disobedience may have been the—the innocent cause of much misery to others; that is, no doubt, the reason why he is so sad. The letter from his friend will cheer him, you will see."

"Do you really think so, *Madame?*" murmured Jeanne, in whose tear-stained eyes the indomitable hopefulness of youth was already striving to shine.

"I am sure of it," assented Marguerite.

And for the moment she was absolutely sincere. The phantom had entirely vanished. She would even, had he dared to re-appear, have mocked and derided him for his futile attempt at turning the sorrow in her heart to a veritable hell of bitterness.

CHAPTER 33

Little Mother

The two women, both so young still, but each of them with a mark of sorrow already indelibly graven in her heart, were clinging to one another, bound together by the strong bond of sympathy. And but for the sadness of it all it were difficult to conjure up a more beautiful picture than that which they presented as they stood side by side; Marguerite, tall and stately as an exquisite lily, with the crown of her ardent hair and the glory of her deep blue eyes, and Jeanne Lange, dainty and delicate, with the brown curls and the child-like droop of the soft, moist lips.

Thus, Armand saw them when, a moment or two later, he entered unannounced. He had pushed open the door and looked on the two women silently for a second or two; on the girl whom he loved so dearly, for whose sake he had committed the great, the unpardonable sin which would send him forever henceforth, Cain-like, a wanderer on the face of the earth; and the other, his sister, her whom a Judas act would condemn to lonely sorrow and widowhood.

He could have cried out in an agony of remorse, and it was the groan of acute soul anguish which escaped his lips that drew Marguerite's attention to his presence.

Even though many things that Jeanne Lange had said had prepared her for a change in her brother, she was immeasurably shocked by his appearance. He had always been slim and rather below the average in height, but now his usually upright and trim figure seemed to have shrunken within itself; his clothes hung baggy on his shoulders, his hands appeared waxen and emaciated, but the greatest change was in his face, in the wide circles round the eyes, that spoke of wakeful nights, in the hollow cheeks, and the mouth that had wholly forgotten how to smile.

421

Percy after a week's misery immured in a dark and miserable prison, deprived of food and rest, did not look such a physical wreck as did Armand St. Just, who was free.

Marguerite's heart reproached her for what she felt had been neglect, callousness on her part. Mutely, within herself, she craved his forgiveness for the appearance of that phantom which should never have come forth from out that chaotic hell which had engendered it.

"Armand!" she cried.

And the loving arms that had guided his baby footsteps long ago, the tender hands that had wiped his boyish tears, were stretched out with unalterable love toward him.

"I have a message for you, dear," she said gently—"a letter from him. Mademoiselle Jeanne allowed me to wait here for you until you came."

Silently, like a little shy mouse, Jeanne had slipped out of the room. Her pure love for Armand had ennobled every one of her thoughts, and her innate kindliness and refinement had already suggested that brother and sister would wish to be alone. At the door she had turned and met Armand's look. That look had satisfied her; she felt that in it she had read the expression of his love, and to it she had responded with a glance that spoke of hope for a future meeting.

As soon as the door had closed on Jeanne Lange, Armand, with an impulse that refused to be checked, threw himself into his sister's arms. The present, with all its sorrows, its remorse and its shame, had sunk away; only the past remained—the unforgettable past, when Marguerite was "little mother"—the soother, the comforter, the healer, the ever-willing receptacle wherein he had been wont to pour the burden of his childish griefs, of his boyish escapades.

Conscious that she could not know everything—not yet, at any rate—he gave himself over to the rapture of this pure embrace, the last time, mayhap, that those fond arms would close round him in unmixed tenderness, the last time that those fond lips would murmur words of affection and of comfort.

Tomorrow those same lips would, perhaps, curse the traitor, and the small hand be raised in wrath, pointing an avenging finger on the Judas.

"Little mother," he whispered, babbling like a child, "it is good to see you again."

"And I have brought you a message from Percy," she said, "a letter which he begged me to give you as soon as may be."

"You have seen him?" he asked.

She nodded silently, unable to speak. Not now, not when her nerves were strung to breaking pitch, would she trust herself to speak of that awful yesterday. She groped in the folds of her gown and took the packet which Percy had given her for Armand. It felt quite bulky in her hand.

"There is quite a good deal there for you to read, dear," she said. "Percy begged me to give you this, and then to let you read it when you were alone."

She pressed the packet into his hand. Armand's face was ashen pale. He clung to her with strange, nervous tenacity; the paper which he held in one hand seemed to sear his fingers as with a branding-iron.

"I will slip away now," she said, for strangely enough since Percy's message had been in Armand's hands she was once again conscious of that awful feeling of iciness round her heart, a sense of numbness that paralysed her very thoughts.

"You will make my excuses to Mademoiselle Lange," she said, trying to smile. "When you have read, you will wish to see her alone."

Gently she disengaged herself from Armand's grasp and made for the door. He appeared dazed, staring down at that paper which was scorching his fingers. Only when her hand was on the latch did he seem to realise that she was going.

"Little mother," came involuntarily to his lips.

She came straight back to him and took both his wrists in her small hands. She was taller than he, and his head was slightly bent forward. Thus, she towered over him, loving but strong, her great, earnest eyes searching his soul.

"When shall I see you again, little mother?" he asked.

"Read your letter, dear," she replied, "and when you have read it, if you care to impart its contents to me, come tonight to my lodgings, Quai de la Ferraille, above the saddler's shop. But if there is aught in it that you do not wish me to know, then do not come; I shall understand. Goodbye, dear."

She took his head between her two cold hands, and as it was still bowed she placed a tender kiss, as of a long farewell, upon his hair.

Then she went out of the room.

CHAPTER 34

The Letter

Armand sat in the armchair in front of the fire. His head rested against one hand; in the other he held the letter written by the friend whom he had betrayed.

Twice he had read it now, and already was every word of that minute, clear writing graven upon the innermost fibres of his body, upon the most secret cells of his brain.

Armand, I know. I knew even before Chauvelin came to me and stood there hoping to gloat over the soul-agony a man who finds that he has been betrayed by his dearest friend. But that d——d reprobate did not get that satisfaction, for I was prepared. Not only do I know, Armand, but I *understand*. I, who do not know what love is, have realised how small a thing is honour, loyalty, or friendship when weighed in the balance of a loved one's need.

To save Jeanne you sold me to Héron and his crowd. We are men, Armand, and the word forgiveness has only been spoken once these past two thousand years, and then it was spoken by Divine lips. But Marguerite loves you, and mayhap soon you will be all that is left her to love on this earth. Because of this she must never know—As for you, Armand—well, God help you! But meseems that the hell which you are enduring now is ten thousand times worse than mine. I have heard your furtive footsteps in the corridor outside the grated window of this cell and would not then have exchanged my hell for yours. Therefore, Armand, and because Marguerite loves you, I would wish to turn to you in the hour that I need help. I am in a tight corner, but the hour may come when a comrade's hand might mean life to me. I have thought of you, Armand partly because having taken more than my life, your own belongs to me, and partly because the plan which I have in my mind will carry with it grave risks for the man who stands by me.

I swore once that never would I risk a comrade's life to save mine own; but matters are so different now—we are both in hell, Armand, and I in striving to get out of mine will be showing you a way out of yours.

Will you retake possession of your lodgings in the Rue de la Croix Blanche? I should always know then where to find you in an emergency. But if at any time you receive another letter from me, be its contents what they may, act in accordance with the letter, and send a copy of it at once to Ffoulkes or to Marguerite. Keep in close touch with them both. Tell her I so far forgave your disobedience (there was nothing more) that I may yet trust my life and mine honour in your hands.

I shall have no means of ascertaining definitely whether you will do all that I ask; but somehow, Armand, I know that you will.

For the third time Armand read the letter through.

"But, Armand," he repeated, murmuring the words softly under his breath, "I know that you will."

Prompted by some indefinable instinct, moved by a force that compelled, he allowed himself to glide from the chair on to the floor, on to his knees.

All the pent-up bitterness, the humiliation, the shame of the past few days, surged up from his heart to his lips in one great cry of pain.

"My God!" he whispered, "give me the chance of giving my life for him."

Alone and unwatched, he gave himself over for a few moments to the almost voluptuous delight of giving free rein to his grief. The hot Latin blood in him, tempestuous in all its passions, was firing his heart and brain now with the glow of devotion and of self-sacrifice.

The calm, self-centred Anglo-Saxon temperament—the almost fatalistic acceptance of failure without reproach yet without despair, which Percy's letter to him had evidenced in so marked a manner— was, mayhap, somewhat beyond the comprehension of this young enthusiast, with pure Gallic blood in his veins, who was ever wont to allow his most elemental passions to sway his actions. But though he did not altogether understand, Armand St. Just could fully appreciate. All that was noble and loyal in him rose triumphant from beneath the devastating ashes of his own shame.

Soon his mood calmed down, his look grew less wan and haggard. Hearing Jeanne's discreet and mouselike steps in the next room, he rose quickly and hid the letter in the pocket of his coat.

She came in and inquired anxiously about Marguerite; a hurriedly expressed excuse from him, however, satisfied her easily enough. She wanted to be alone with Armand, happy to see that he held his head more erect today, and that the look as of a hunted creature had entirely gone from his eyes.

She ascribed this happy change to Marguerite, finding it in her heart to be grateful to the sister for having accomplished what the *fiancée* had failed to do.

For a while they remained together, sitting side by side, speaking at times, but mostly silent, seeming to savour the return of truant happiness. Armand felt like a sick man who has obtained a sudden surcease from pain. He looked round him with a kind of melancholy delight on this room which he had entered for the first time less than a fort-night ago, and which already was so full of memories.

Those first hours spent at the feet of Jeanne Lange, how exqui-site they had been, how fleeting in the perfection of their happiness! Now they seemed to belong to a far distant past, evanescent like the perfume of violets, swift in their flight like the winged steps of youth. Blakeney's letter had effectually taken the bitter sting from out his remorse, but it had increased his already over-heavy load of inconsol-able sorrow.

Later in the day he turned his footsteps in the direction of the river, to the house in the Quai de la Ferraille above the saddler's shop. Mar-guerite had returned alone from the expedition to the Rue de Cha-ronne. Whilst Sir Andrew took charge of the little party of fugitives and escorted them out of Paris, she came back to her lodgings in order to collect her belongings, preparatory to taking up her quarters in the house of Lucas, the old-clothes dealer. She returned also because she hoped to see Armand.

"If you care to impart the contents of the letter to me, come to my lodgings tonight," she had said.

All day a phantom had haunted her, the phantom of an agonising suspicion.

But now the phantom had vanished never to return. Armand was sitting close beside her, and he told her that the chief had selected him amongst all the others to stand by him inside the walls of Paris until the last.

"I shall mayhap," thus closed that precious document, "have no means of ascertaining definitely whether you will act in accordance with this letter. But somehow, Armand, I know that you will."

"I know that you will, Armand," reiterated Marguerite fervently.

She had only been too eager to be convinced; the dread and dark suspicion which had been like a hideous poisoned sting had only vaguely touched her soul; it had not gone in very deeply. How could it, when in its death-dealing passage it encountered the rampart of tender, almost motherly love?

Armand, trying to read his sister's thoughts in the depths of her blue eyes, found the look in them limpid and clear. Percy's message to Armand had reassured her just as he had intended that it should do. Fate had dealt over harshly with her as it was, and Blakeney's remorse for the sorrow which he had already caused her, was scarcely less keen than Armand's. He did not wish her to bear the intolerable burden of hatred against her brother; and by binding St. Just close to him at the supreme hour of danger he hoped to prove to the woman whom he loved so passionately that Armand was worthy of trust.

PART 3
CHAPTER 35
The Last Phase

"Well? How is it now?"

"The last phase, I think."

"He will yield?"

"He must."

"Bah! you have said it yourself often enough; those English are tough."

"It takes time to hack them to pieces, perhaps. In this case even you, Citizen Chauvelin, said that it would take time. Well, it has taken just seventeen days, and now the end is in sight."

It was close on midnight in the guard-room which gave on the innermost cell of the *Conciergerie*. Héron had just visited the prisoner as was his wont at this hour of the night. He had watched the changing of the guard, inspected the night-watch, questioned the sergeant in charge, and finally he had been on the point of retiring to his own new quarters in the house of Justice, in the near vicinity of the *Conciergerie*, when Citizen Chauvelin entered the guard-room unexpectedly and detained his colleague with the peremptory question:

"How is it now?"

"If you are so near the end, Citizen Héron," he now said, sinking his voice to a whisper, "why not make a final effort and end it tonight?"

"I wish I could; the anxiety is wearing me out more'n him," he added with a jerky movement of the head in direction of the inner cell.

"Shall I try?" rejoined Chauvelin grimly.

"Yes, an' you wish."

Citizen Héron's long limbs were sprawling on a guard-room chair. In this low narrow room, he looked like some giant whose body had been carelessly and loosely put together by a 'prentice hand in the art of manufacture. His broad shoulders were bent, probably under the weight of anxiety to which he had referred, and his head, with the lank, shaggy hair overshadowing the brow, was sunk deep down on his chest.

Chauvelin looked on his friend and associate with no small measure of contempt. He would no doubt have preferred to conclude the present difficult transaction entirely in his own way and alone; but equally there was no doubt that the Committee of Public Safety did not trust him quite so fully as it used to do before the *fiasco* at Calais and the blunders of Boulogne. Héron, on the other hand, enjoyed to its outermost the confidence of his colleagues; his ferocious cruelty and his callousness were well known, whilst physically, owing to his great height and bulky if loosely knit frame, he had a decided advantage over his trim and slender friend.

As far as the bringing of prisoners to trial was concerned, the chief agent of the Committee of General Security had been given a perfectly free hand by the decree of the 27th *Nivôse*. At first, therefore, he had experienced no difficulty when he desired to keep the Englishman in close confinement for a time without hurrying on that summary trial and condemnation which the populace had loudly demanded, and to which they felt that they were entitled to as a public holiday. The death of the Scarlet Pimpernel on the guillotine had been a spectacle promised by every demagogue who desired to purchase a few votes by holding out visions of pleasant doings to come; and during the first few days the mob of Paris was content to enjoy the delights of expectation.

But now seventeen days had gone by and still the Englishman was not being brought to trial. The pleasure-loving public was waxing impatient, and earlier this evening, when Citizen Héron had shown himself in the stalls of the national theatre, he was greeted by a crowded audience with decided expressions of disapproval and open mutterings of:

"What of the Scarlet Pimpernel?"

It almost looked as if he would have to bring that accursed Englishman to the guillotine without having wrested from him the secret which he would have given a fortune to possess. Chauvelin, who had also been present at the theatre, had heard the expressions of discontent; hence his visit to his colleague at this late hour of the night.

"Shall I try?" he had queried with some impatience, and a deep sigh of satisfaction escaped his thin lips when the chief agent, wearied and discouraged, had reluctantly agreed.

"Let the men make as much noise as they like," he added with an enigmatical smile. "The Englishman and I will want an accompaniment to our pleasant conversation."

Héron growled a surly assent, and without another word Chauvelin turned towards the inner cell. As he stepped in he allowed the iron bar to fall into its socket behind him. Then he went farther into the room until the distant recess was fully revealed to him. His tread had been furtive and almost noiseless. Now he paused, for he had caught sight of the prisoner. For a moment he stood quite still, with hands clasped behind his back in his wonted attitude—still save for a strange, involuntary twitching of his mouth, and the nervous clasping and interlocking of his fingers behind his back. He was savouring to its utmost fulsomeness the supremest joy which animal man can ever know—the joy of looking on a fallen enemy.

Blakeney sat at the table with one arm resting on it, the emaciated hand tightly clutched, the body leaning forward, the eyes looking into nothingness.

For the moment he was unconscious of Chauvelin's presence, and the latter could gaze on him to the full content of his heart.

Indeed, to all outward appearances there sat a man whom privations of every sort and kind, the want of fresh air, of proper food, above all, of rest, had worn down physically to a shadow. There was not a particle of colour in cheeks or lips, the skin was grey in hue, the eyes looked like deep caverns, wherein the glow of fever was all that was left of life.

Chauvelin looked on in silence, vaguely stirred by something that he could not define, something that right through his triumphant satisfaction, his hatred and final certainty of revenge, had roused in him a sense almost of admiration.

He gazed on the noiseless figure of the man who had endured so much for an ideal, and as he gazed it seemed to him as if the spirit no longer dwelt in the body, but hovered round in the dank, stuffy air of the narrow cell above the head of the lonely prisoner, crowning it with glory that was no longer of this earth.

Of this the looker-on was conscious despite himself, of that and of the fact that stare as he might, and with perception rendered doubly keen by hate, he could not, in spite of all, find the least trace of mental weakness in that far-seeing gaze which seemed to pierce the prison walls, nor could he see that bodily weakness had tended to subdue the ruling passions.

Sir Percy Blakeney—a prisoner since seventeen days in close, solitary confinement, half-starved, deprived of rest, and of that mental and physical activity which had been the very essence of life to him hitherto—might be outwardly but a shadow of his former brilliant self, but nevertheless he was still that same elegant English gentleman, that prince of dandies whom Chauvelin had first met eighteen months ago at the most courtly Court in Europe. His clothes, despite constant wear and the want of attention from a scrupulous valet, still betrayed the perfection of London tailoring; he had put them on with meticulous care, they were free from the slightest particle of dust, and the filmy folds of priceless Mechlin still half-veiled the delicate whiteness of his shapely hands.

And in the pale, haggard face, in the whole pose of body and of arm, there was still the expression of that indomitable strength of will, that reckless daring, that almost insolent challenge to Fate; it was there untamed, uncrushed. Chauvelin himself could not deny to himself its presence or its force. He felt that behind that smooth brow, which looked waxlike now, the mind was still alert, scheming, plotting, striving for freedom, for conquest and for power, and rendered even doubly keen and virile by the ardour of supreme self-sacrifice.

Chauvelin now made a slight movement and suddenly Blakeney became conscious of his presence, and swift as a flash a smile lit up his wan face.

"Why! if it is not my engaging friend Monsieur Chambertin," he said gaily.

He rose and stepped forward in the most approved fashion prescribed by the elaborate etiquette of the time. But Chauvelin smiled grimly and a look of almost animal lust gleamed in his pale eyes, for he had noted that as he rose Sir Percy had to seek the support of the table, even whilst a dull film appeared to gather over his eyes.

The gesture had been quick and cleverly disguised, but it had been there nevertheless—that and the livid hue that overspread the face as if consciousness was threatening to go. All of which was sufficient still further to assure the looker-on that that mighty physical strength was giving way at last, that strength which he had hated in his enemy almost as much as he had hated the thinly veiled insolence of his manner.

"And what procures me, sir, the honour of your visit?" continued Blakeney, who had—at any rate, outwardly soon recovered himself, and whose voice, though distinctly hoarse and spent, rang quite cheerfully across the dank narrow cell.

"My desire for your welfare, Sir Percy," replied Chauvelin with equal pleasantry.

"*La*, sir; but have you not gratified that desire already, to an extent which leaves no room for further solicitude? But I pray you, will you not sit down?" he continued, turning back toward the table. "I was about to partake of the lavish supper which your friends have provided for me. Will you not share it, sir? You are most royally welcome, and it will mayhap remind you of that supper we shared together in Calais, eh? when you, Monsieur Chambertin, were temporarily in holy orders."

He laughed, offering his enemy a chair, and pointed with inviting gesture to the hunk of brown bread and the mug of water which stood on the table.

"Such as it is, sir," he said with a pleasant smile, "it is yours to command."

Chauvelin sat down. He held his lower lip tightly between his teeth, so tightly that a few drops of blood appeared upon its narrow surface. He was making vigorous efforts to keep his temper under control, for he would not give his enemy the satisfaction of seeing him resent his insolence. He could afford to keep calm now that victory was at last in sight, now that he knew that he had but to raise a finger, and those smiling, impudent lips would be closed forever at last.

"Sir Percy," he resumed quietly, "no doubt it affords you a certain amount of pleasure to aim your sarcastic shafts at me. I will not begrudge you that pleasure; in your present position, sir, your shafts have little or no sting."

"And I shall have but few chances left to aim them at your charming self," interposed Blakeney, who had drawn another chair close to the table and was now sitting opposite his enemy, with the light of the lamp falling full on his own face, as if he wished his enemy to know that he had nothing to hide, no thought, no hope, no fear.

"Exactly," said Chauvelin dryly. "That being the case, Sir Percy, what say you to no longer wasting the few chances which are left to you for safety? The time is getting on. You are not, I imagine, quite as hopeful as you were even a week ago,—you have never been over-comfortable in this cell, why not end this unpleasant state of affairs now—once and for all? You'll not have cause to regret it. My word on it."

Sir Percy leaned back in his chair. He yawned loudly and ostentatiously.

"I pray you, sir, forgive me," he said. "Never have I been so d—d fatigued. I have not slept for more than a fortnight."

"Exactly, Sir Percy. A night's rest would do you a world of good."

"A night, sir?" exclaimed Blakeney with what seemed like an echo of his former inimitable laugh. "*La!* I should want a week."

"I am afraid we could not arrange for that, but one night would greatly refresh you."

"You are right, sir, you are right; but those d—d fellows in the next room make so much noise."

"I would give strict orders that perfect quietude reigned in the guard-room this night," said Chauvelin, murmuring softly, and there was a gentle purr in his voice, "and that you were left undisturbed for several hours. I would give orders that a comforting supper be served to you at once, and that everything be done to minister to your wants."

"That sounds d—d alluring, sir. Why did you not suggest this before?"

"You were so—what shall I say—so obstinate, Sir Percy?"

"Call it pig-headed, my dear Monsieur Chambertin," retorted Blakeney gaily, "truly you would oblige me."

"In any case you, sir, were acting in direct opposition to your own interests."

"Therefore, you came," concluded Blakeney airily, "like the good Samaritan to take compassion on me and my troubles, and to lead me straight away to comfort, a good supper and a downy bed."

"Admirably put, Sir Percy," said Chauvelin blandly; "that is exactly my mission."

"How will you set to work, Monsieur Chambertin?"

"Quite easily, if you, Sir Percy, will yield to the persuasion of my friend Citizen Héron."

"Ah!"

"Why, yes! He is anxious to know where little Capet is. A reasonable whim, you will own, considering that the disappearance of the child is causing him grave anxiety."

"And you, Monsieur Chambertin?" queried Sir Percy with that suspicion of insolence in his manner which had the power to irritate his enemy even now. "And yourself, sir; what are your wishes in the matter?"

"Mine, Sir Percy?" retorted Chauvelin. "Mine? Why, to tell you the truth, the fate of little Capet interests me but little. Let him rot in Austria or in our prisons, I care not which. He'll never trouble France overmuch, I imagine. The teachings of old Simon will not tend to make a leader or a king out of the puny brat whom you chose to drag out of our keeping. My wishes, sir, are the annihilation of your accursed League, and the lasting disgrace, if not the death, of its chief."

He had spoken more hotly than he had intended, but all the pent-up rage of the past eighteen months, the recollections of Calais and of Boulogne, had all surged up again in his mind, because despite the closeness of these prison walls, despite the grim shadow of starvation and of death that beckoned so close at hand, he still encountered a pair of mocking eyes, fixed with relentless insolence upon him.

Whilst he spoke Blakeney had once more leaned forward, resting his elbows upon the table. Now he drew nearer to him the wooden platter on which reposed that very uninviting piece of dry bread. With solemn intentness he proceeded to break the bread into pieces; then he offered the platter to Chauvelin.

"I am sorry," he said pleasantly, "that I cannot offer you more dainty fare, sir, but this is all that your friends have supplied me with today."

He crumbled some of the dry bread in his slender fingers, then started munching the crumbs with apparent relish. He poured out some water into the mug and drank it. Then he said with a light laugh:

"Even the vinegar which that ruffian Brogard served us at Calais was preferable to this, do you not imagine so, my good Monsieur Chambertin?"

Chauvelin made no reply. Like a feline creature on the prowl, he was watching the prey that had so nearly succumbed to his talons. Blakeney's face now was positively ghastly. The effort to speak, to laugh, to appear unconcerned, was apparently beyond his strength. His cheeks and lips were livid in hue, the skin clung like a thin layer of wax to the bones of cheek and jaw, and the heavy lids that fell over the eyes had purple patches on them like lead.

To a system in such an advanced state of exhaustion the stale water and dusty bread must have been terribly nauseating, and Chauvelin himself callous and thirsting for vengeance though he was, could hardly bear to look calmly on the martyrdom of this man whom he and his colleagues were torturing in order to gain their own ends.

An ashen hue, which seemed like the shadow of the hand of death, passed over the prisoner's face. Chauvelin felt compelled to avert his gaze. A feeling that was almost akin to remorse had stirred a hidden chord in his heart. The feeling did not last—the heart had been too long atrophied by the constantly recurring spectacles of cruelties, massacres, and wholesale hecatombs perpetrated in the past eighteen months in the name of liberty and fraternity to be capable of a sustained effort in the direction of gentleness or of pity. Any noble instinct in these revolutionaries had long ago been drowned in a whirlpool of exploits that would forever sully the records of humanity; and this keeping of a fellow-creature on the rack in order to wring from him a Judas-like betrayal was but a complement to a record of infamy that had ceased by its very magnitude to weigh upon their souls.

Chauvelin was in no way different from his colleagues; the crimes in which he had had no hand he had condoned by continuing to serve the government that had committed them, and his ferocity in the present case was increased a thousandfold by his personal hatred for the man who had so often fooled and baffled him.

When he looked round a second or two later that ephemeral fit of remorse did its final vanishing; he had once more encountered the pleasant smile, the laughing if ashen-pale face of his unconquered foe.

"Only a passing giddiness, my dear sir," said Sir Percy lightly. "As you were saying—"

At the airily-spoken words, at the smile that accompanied them, Chauvelin had jumped to his feet. There was something almost supernatural, weird, and impish about the present situation, about this dying man who, like an impudent schoolboy, seemed to be mocking Death with his tongue in his cheek, about his laugh that appeared to find its echo in a widely yawning grave.

"In the name of God, Sir Percy," he said roughly, as he brought his clenched fist crashing down upon the table, "this situation is intolerable. Bring it to an end tonight!"

"Why, sir?" retorted Blakeney, "methought you and your kind did not believe in God."

"No. But you English do."

"We do. But we do not care to hear His name on your lips."

"Then in the name of the wife whom you love—"

But even before the words had died upon his lips, Sir Percy, too, had risen to his feet.

"Have done, man—have done," he broke in hoarsely, and despite weakness, despite exhaustion and weariness, there was such a dangerous look in his hollow eyes as he leaned across the table that Chauvelin drew back a step or two, and—vaguely fearful—looked furtively towards the opening into the guard-room. "Have done," he reiterated for the third time; "do not name her, or by the living God whom you dared to invoke I'll find strength yet to smite you in the face."

But Chauvelin, after that first moment of almost superstitious fear, had quickly recovered his *sang-froid*.

"Little Capet, Sir Percy," he said, meeting the other's threatening glance with an imperturbable smile, "tell me where to find him, and you may yet live to savour the caresses of the most beautiful woman in England."

He had meant it as a taunt, the final turn of the thumb-screw applied to a dying man, and he had in that watchful, keen mind of his well weighed the full consequences of the taunt.

The next moment he had paid to the full the anticipated price. Sir Percy had picked up the pewter mug from the table—it was half-filled with brackish water—and with a hand that trembled but slightly he hurled it straight at his opponent's face.

The heavy mug did not hit Citizen Chauvelin; it went crashing against the stone wall opposite. But the water was trickling from the top of his head all down his eyes and cheeks. He shrugged his shoulders with a look of benign indulgence directed at his enemy, who had fallen back into his chair exhausted with the effort.

Then he took out his handkerchief and calmly wiped the water from his face.

"Not quite so straight a shot as you used to be, Sir Percy," he said mockingly.

"No, sir—apparently—not."

The words came out in gasps. He was like a man only partly conscious. The lips were parted, the eyes closed, the head leaning against the high back of the chair. For the space of one second Chauvelin feared that his zeal had outrun his prudence, that he had dealt a death-blow to a man in the last stage of exhaustion, where he had only wished to fan the flickering flame of life. Hastily—for the seconds seemed precious—he ran to the opening that led into the guard-room.

"Brandy—quick!" he cried.

Héron looked up, roused from the semi-somnolence in which he had lain for the past half-hour. He disentangled his long limbs from out the guard-room chair.

"Eh?" he queried. "What is it?"

"Brandy," reiterated Chauvelin impatiently; "the prisoner has fainted."

"Bah!" retorted the other with a callous shrug of the shoulders, "you are not going to revive him with brandy, I imagine."

"No. But you will, Citizen Héron," rejoined the other dryly, "for if you do not he'll be dead in an hour!"

"Devils in hell!" exclaimed Héron, "you have not killed him? You—you d—d fool!"

He was wide awake enough now; wide awake and shaking with fury. Almost foaming at the mouth and uttering volleys of the choicest oaths, he elbowed his way roughly through the groups of soldiers who were crowding round the centre table of the guard-room, smoking and throwing dice or playing cards. They made way for him as hurriedly as they could, for it was not safe to thwart the citizen agent when he was in a rage.

Héron walked across to the opening and lifted the iron bar. With scant ceremony he pushed his colleague aside and strode into the cell, whilst Chauvelin, seemingly not resenting the other's ruffianly manners and violent language, followed close upon his heel.

In the centre of the room both men paused, and Héron turned with a surly growl to his friend.

"You vowed he would be dead in an hour," he said reproachfully.

The other shrugged his shoulders.

"It does not look like it now certainly," he said dryly.

Blakeney was sitting—as was his wont—close to the table, with one arm leaning on it, the other, tightly clenched, resting upon his knee. A ghost of a smile hovered round his lips.

"Not in an hour, Citizen Héron," he said, and his voice flow was scarce above a whisper, "nor yet in two."

"You are a fool, man," said Héron roughly. "You have had seventeen days of this. Are you not sick of it?"

"Heartily, my dear friend," replied Blakeney a little more firmly.

"Seventeen days," reiterated the other, nodding his shaggy head; "you came here on the 2nd of *Pluviôse*, today is the 19th."

"The 19th *Pluviôse*?" interposed Sir Percy, and a strange gleam suddenly flashed in his eyes. "Demn it, sir, and in Christian parlance what may that day be?"

"The 7th of February at your service, Sir Percy," replied Chauvelin quietly.

"I thank you, sir. In this d—d hole I had lost count of time."

Chauvelin, unlike his rough and blundering colleague, had been watching the prisoner very closely for the last moment or two, conscious of a subtle, undefinable change that had come over the man during those few seconds while he, Chauvelin, had thought him dying. The pose was certainly the old familiar one, the head erect, the hand clenched, the eyes looking through and beyond the stone walls; but there was an air of listlessness in the stoop of the shoulders, and—except for that one brief gleam just now—a look of more complete weariness round the hollow eyes! To the keen watcher it appeared as if that sense of living power, of unconquered will and defiant mind was no longer there, and as if he himself need no longer fear that almost super-sensual thrill which had a while ago kindled in him a vague sense of admiration—almost of remorse.

Even as he gazed, Blakeney slowly turned his eyes full upon him. Chauvelin's heart gave a triumphant bound.

With a mocking smile he met the wearied look, the pitiable appeal. His turn had come at last—his turn to mock and to exult. He knew that what he was watching now was no longer the last phase of a long and noble martyrdom; it was the end—the inevitable end—that for which he had schemed and striven, for which he had schooled his heart to ferocity and callousness that were devilish in their intensity. It was the end indeed, the slow descent of a soul from the giddy heights of attempted self-sacrifice, where it had striven to soar for a time, until the body and the will both succumbed together and dragged it down with them into the abyss of submission and of irreparable shame.

Chapter 36

Submission

Silence reigned in the narrow cell for a few moments, whilst two human jackals stood motionless over their captured prey.

A savage triumph gleamed in Chauvelin's eyes, and even Héron, dull and brutal though he was, had become vaguely conscious of the great change that had come over the prisoner.

Blakeney, with a gesture and a sigh of hopeless exhaustion had once more rested both his elbows on the table; his head fell heavy and almost lifeless downward in his arms.

"Curse you, man!" cried Héron almost involuntarily. "Why in the name of hell did you wait so long?"

Then, as the prisoner made no reply, but only raised his head slightly, and looked on the other two men with dulled, wearied eyes, Chauvelin interposed calmly:

"More than a fortnight has been wasted in useless obstinacy, Sir Percy. Fortunately, it is not too late."

"Capet?" said Héron hoarsely, "tell us, where is Capet?"

He leaned across the table, his eyes were bloodshot with the keenness of his excitement, his voice shook with the passionate desire for the crowning triumph.

"If you'll only not worry me," murmured the prisoner; and the whisper came so laboriously and so low that both men were forced to bend their ears close to the scarcely moving lips; "if you will let me sleep and rest, and leave me in peace—"

"The peace of the grave, man," retorted Chauvelin roughly; "if you will only speak. Where is Capet?"

"I cannot tell you; the way is long, the road—intricate."

"Bah!"

"I'll lead you to him, if you will give me rest."

"We don't want you to lead us anywhere," growled Héron with a smothered curse; "tell us where Capet is; we'll find him right enough."

"I cannot explain; the way is intricate; the place off the beaten track, unknown except to me and my friends."

Once more that shadow, which was so like the passing of the hand of Death, overspread the prisoner's face; his head rolled back against the chair.

"He'll die before he can speak," muttered Chauvelin under his breath. "You usually are well provided with brandy, Citizen Héron."

The latter no longer demurred. He saw the danger as clearly as did his colleague. It had been hell's own luck if the prisoner were to die now when he seemed ready to give in. He produced a flask from the pocket of his coat, and this he held to Blakeney's lips.

"Beastly stuff," murmured the latter feebly. "I think I'd sooner faint—than drink."

"Capet? where is Capet?" reiterated Héron impatiently.

"One—two—three hundred leagues from here. I must let one of my friends know; he'll communicate with the others; they must be prepared," replied the prisoner slowly.

Héron uttered a blasphemous oath.

"Where is Capet? Tell us where Capet is, or—"

He was like a raging tiger that had thought to hold its prey and suddenly realised that it was being snatched from him. He raised his fist, and without doubt the next moment he would have silenced forever the lips that held the precious secret, but Chauvelin fortunately was quick enough to seize his wrist.

"Have a care, citizen," he said peremptorily; "have a care! You called me a fool just now when you thought I had killed the prisoner. It is his secret we want first; his death can follow afterwards."

"Yes, but not in this d—d hole," murmured Blakeney.

"On the guillotine if you'll speak," cried Héron, whose exasperation was getting the better of his self-interest, "but if you'll not speak then it shall be starvation in this hole—yes, starvation," he growled, showing a row of large and uneven teeth like those of some mongrel cur, "for I'll have that door walled in tonight, and not another living soul shall cross this threshold again until your flesh has rotted on your bones and the rats have had their fill of you."

The prisoner raised his head slowly, a shiver shook him as if caused by ague, and his eyes, that appeared almost sightless, now looked with a strange glance of horror on his enemy.

"I'll die in the open," he whispered, "not in this d—d hole."

"Then tell us where Capet is."

"I cannot; I wish to God I could. But I'll take you to him, I swear I will. I'll make my friends give him up to you. Do you think that I would not tell you now, if I could."

Héron, whose every instinct of tyranny revolted against this thwarting of his will, would have continued to heckle the prisoner even now, had not Chauvelin suddenly interposed with an authoritative gesture.

"You'll gain nothing this way, citizen," he said quietly; "the man's mind is wandering; he is probably quite unable to give you clear directions at this moment."

"What am I to do, then?" muttered the other roughly.

"He cannot live another twenty-four hours now and would only grow more and more helpless as time went on."

"Unless you relax your strict regime with him."

"And if I do we'll only prolong this situation indefinitely; and in the meanwhile, how do we know that the brat is not being spirited away out of the country?"

The prisoner, with his head once more buried in his arms, had fallen into a kind of torpor, the only kind of sleep that the exhausted system would allow. With a brutal gesture Héron shook him by the shoulder.

"He," he shouted, "none of that, you know. We have not settled the matter of young Capet yet."

Then, as the prisoner made no movement, and the chief agent indulged in one of his favourite volleys of oaths, Chauvelin placed a peremptory hand on his colleague's shoulder.

"I tell you, citizen, that this is no use," he said firmly. "Unless you are prepared to give up all thoughts of finding Capet, you must try and curb your temper, and try diplomacy where force is sure to fail."

"Diplomacy?" retorted the other with a sneer. "Bah! it served you well at Boulogne last autumn, did it not, Citizen Chauvelin?"

"It has served me better now," rejoined the other imperturbably. "You will own, citizen, that it is my diplomacy which has placed within your reach the ultimate hope of finding Capet."

"H'm!" muttered the other, "you advised us to starve the prisoner. Are we any nearer to knowing his secret?"

"Yes. By a fortnight of weariness, of exhaustion and of starvation, you are nearer to it by the weakness of the man whom in his full strength you could never hope to conquer."

"But if the cursed Englishman won't speak, and in the meanwhile dies on my hands—"

"He won't do that if you will accede to his wish. Give him some good food now and let him sleep till dawn."

"And at dawn he'll defy me again. I believe now that he has some scheme in his mind and means to play us a trick."

"That, I imagine, is more than likely," retorted Chauvelin dryly; "though," he added with a contemptuous nod of the head directed at the huddled-up figure of his once brilliant enemy, "neither mind nor body seem to me to be in a sufficiently active state just now for hatching plot or intrigue; but even if—vaguely floating through his clouded mind—there has sprung some little scheme for evasion, I give you my word, Citizen Héron, that you can thwart him completely, and gain all that you desire, if you will only follow my advice."

There had always been a great amount of persuasive power in Citizen Chauvelin, ex-envoy of the revolutionary Government of France at the Court of St. James, and that same persuasive eloquence did not fail now in its effect on the chief agent of the Committee of General Security. The latter was made of coarser stuff than his more brilliant colleague. Chauvelin was like a wily and sleek panther that is furtive in its movements, that will lure its prey, watch it, follow it with stealthy footsteps, and only pounce on it when it is least wary, whilst Héron was more like a raging bull that tosses its head in a blind, irresponsible fashion, rushes at an obstacle without gauging its resisting powers, and allows its victim to slip from beneath its weight through the very clumsiness and brutality of its assault.

Still Chauvelin had two heavy black marks against him—those of his failures at Calais and Boulogne. Héron, rendered cautious both by the deadly danger in which he stood and the sense of his own incompetence to deal with the present situation, tried to resist the other's authority as well as his persuasion.

"Your advice was not of great use to citizen Collot last autumn at Boulogne," he said, and spat on the ground by way of expressing both his independence and his contempt.

"Still, Citizen Héron," retorted Chauvelin with unruffled patience, "it is the best advice that you are likely to get in the present emergency. You have eyes to see, have you not? Look on your prisoner at this moment. Unless something is done, and at once, too, he will be past negotiating with in the next twenty-four hours; then what will follow?"

He put his thin hand once more on his colleague's grubby coat-sleeve, he drew him closer to himself away from the vicinity of that huddled figure, that captive lion, wrapped in a torpid somnolence that looked already so like the last long sleep.

"What will follow, Citizen Héron?" he reiterated, sinking his voice to a whisper; "sooner or later some meddlesome busybody who sits in the Assembly of the Convention will get wind that little Capet is no longer in the Temple prison, that a pauper child was substituted for him, and that you, Citizen Héron, together with the commissaries in charge, have thus been fooling the nation and its representatives for over a fortnight. What will follow then, think you?"

And he made an expressive gesture with his outstretched fingers across his throat.

Héron found no other answer but blasphemy.

"I'll make that cursed Englishman speak yet," he said with a fierce oath.

"You cannot," retorted Chauvelin decisively. "In his present state he is incapable of it, even if he would, which also is doubtful."

"Ah! then you do think that he still means to cheat us?"

"Yes, I do. But I also know that he is no longer in a physical state to do it. No doubt he thinks that he is. A man of that type is sure to overvalue his own strength; but look at him, Citizen Héron. Surely you must see that we have nothing to fear from him now."

Héron now was like a voracious creature that has two victims lying ready for his gluttonous jaws. He was loath to let either of them go. He hated the very thought of seeing the Englishman being led out of this narrow cell, where he had kept a watchful eye over him night and day for a fortnight, satisfied that with every day, every hour, the chances of escape became more improbable and more rare; at the same time there was the possibility of the recapture of little Capet, a possibility which made Héron's brain reel with the delightful vista of it, and which might never come about if the prisoner remained silent to the end.

"I wish I were quite sure," he said sullenly, "that you were body and soul in accord with me."

"I am in accord with you, Citizen Héron," rejoined the other earnestly—"body and soul in accord with you. Do you not believe that I hate this man—aye! hate him with a hatred ten thousand times more strong than yours? I want his death—Heaven or hell alone know how I long for that—but what I long for most is his lasting disgrace. For that I have worked, Citizen Héron—for that I advised and helped you. When first you captured this man, you wanted summarily to try him, to send him to the guillotine amidst the joy of the populace of Paris and crowned with a splendid halo of martyrdom. That man, Citizen Héron, would have baffled you, mocked you, and fooled you even on the steps of the scaffold. In the zenith of his strength and of insurmountable good luck you and all your myrmidons and all the assembled guard of Paris would have had no power over him. The day that you led him out of this cell in order to take him to trial or to the guillotine would have been that of your hopeless discomfiture. Having once walked out of this cell hale, hearty and alert, be the escort round him ever so strong, he never would have re-entered it again. Of that I am as convinced as that I am alive. I know the man; you don't. Mine are not the only fingers through which he has slipped. Ask citizen Collot d'Herbois, ask Sergeant Bibot at the barrier of Menilmontant, ask General Santerre and his guards. They all have a tale to tell. Did I believe in God or the devil, I should also believe that this man has supernatural powers and a host of demons at his beck and call."

"Yet you talk now of letting him walk out of this cell tomorrow?"

"He is a different man now, Citizen Héron. On my advice you placed him on a regime that has counteracted the supernatural power by simple physical exhaustion and driven to the four winds the host of demons who no doubt fled in the face of starvation."

"If only I thought that the recapture of Capet was as vital to you as it is to me," said Héron, still unconvinced.

"The capture of Capet is just as vital to me as it is to you," rejoined Chauvelin earnestly, "if it is brought about through the instrumentality of the Englishman."

442

He paused, looking intently on his colleague, whose shifty eyes encountered his own. Thus, eye to eye the two men at last understood one another.

"Ah!" said Héron with a snort, "I think I understand."

"I am sure that you do," responded Chauvelin dryly. "The disgrace of this cursed Scarlet Pimpernel and his League is as vital to me, and more, as the capture of Capet is to you. That is why I showed you the way how to bring that meddlesome adventurer to his knees; that is why I will help you now both to find Capet and with his aid and to wreak what reprisals you like on him in the end."

Héron before he spoke again cast one more look on the prisoner. The latter had not stirred; his face was hidden, but the hands, emaciated, nerveless and waxen, like those of the dead, told a more eloquent tale, mayhap, then than the eyes could do. The chief agent of the Committee of General Security walked deliberately round the table until he stood once more, close beside the man from whom he longed with passionate ardour to wrest an all-important secret. With brutal, grimy hand he raised the head that lay, sunken and inert, against the table; with callous eyes he gazed attentively on the face that was then revealed to him, he looked on the waxen flesh, the hollow eyes, the bloodless lips; then he shrugged his wide shoulders, and with a laugh that surely must have caused joy in hell, he allowed the wearied head to fall back against the outstretched arms, and turned once again to his colleague.

"I think you are right, Citizen Chauvelin," he said; "there is not much supernatural power here. Let me hear your advice."

CHAPTER 37

Chauvelin's Advice

Citizen Chauvelin had drawn his colleague with him to the end of the cell that was farthest away from the recess, and the table at which the prisoner was sitting.

Here the noise and hubbub that went on constantly in the guard room would effectually drown a whispered conversation. Chauvelin called to the sergeant to hand him a couple of chairs over the barrier. These he placed against the wall opposite the opening, and beckoning Héron to sit down, he did likewise, placing himself close to his colleague.

From where the two men now sat they could see both into the guard-room opposite them and into the recess at the furthermost end of the cell.

"First of all," began Chauvelin after a while, and sinking his voice to a whisper, "let me understand you thoroughly, Citizen Héron. Do you want the death of the Englishman, either today or tomorrow, either in this prison or on the guillotine? For that now is easy of accomplishment; or do you want, above all, to get hold of little Capet?"

"It is Capet I want," growled Héron savagely under his breath. "Capet! Capet! My own neck is dependent on my finding Capet. Curse you, have I not told you that clearly enough?"

"You have told it me very clearly, Citizen Héron; but I wished to make assurance doubly sure, and also make you understand that I, too, want the Englishman to betray little Capet into your hands. I want that more even than I do his death."

"Then in the name of hell, citizen, give me your advice."

"My advice to you, Citizen Héron, is this: Give your prisoner now just a sufficiency of food to revive him—he will have had a few moments' sleep—and when he has eaten, and, mayhap, drunk a glass of wine, he will, no doubt, feel a recrudescence of strength, then give him pen and ink and paper. He must, as he says, write to one of his followers, who, in his turn, I suppose, will communicate with the others, bidding them to be prepared to deliver up little Capet to us; the letter must make it clear to that crowd of English gentlemen that their beloved chief is giving up the uncrowned King of France to us in exchange for his own safety.

"But I think you will agree with me, Citizen Héron, that it would not be over-prudent on our part to allow that same gallant crowd to be forewarned too soon of the proposed doings of their chief. Therefore, I think, we'll explain to the prisoner that his follower, whom he will first apprise of his intentions, shall start with us tomorrow on our expedition, and accompany us until its last stage, when, if it is found necessary, he may be sent on ahead, strongly escorted of course, and with personal messages from the gallant Scarlet Pimpernel to the members of his League."

"What will be the good of that?" broke in Héron viciously. "Do you want one of his accursed followers to be ready to give him a helping hand on the way if he tries to slip through our fingers?"

"Patience, patience, my good Héron!" rejoined Chauvelin with a placid smile. "Hear me out to the end. Time is precious. You shall offer what criticism you will when I have finished, but not before."

"Go on, then. I listen."

"I am not only proposing that one member of the Scarlet Pimpernel League shall accompany us tomorrow," continued Chauvelin, "but I would also force the prisoner's wife—Marguerite Blakeney—to follow in our train."

"A woman? Bah! What for?"

"I will tell you the reason of this presently. In her case I should not let the prisoner know beforehand that she too will form a part of our expedition. Let this come as a pleasing surprise for him. She could join us on our way out of Paris."

"How will you get hold of her?"

"Easily enough. I know where to find her. I traced her myself a few days ago to a house in the Rue de Charonne, and she is not likely to have gone away from Paris while her husband was at the *Conciergerie*. But this is a digression, let me proceed more consecutively. The letter, as I have said, being written tonight by the prisoner to one of his followers, I will myself see that it is delivered into the right hands. You, Citizen Héron, will in the meanwhile make all arrangements for the journey. We ought to start at dawn, and we ought to be prepared, especially during the first fifty leagues of the way, against organised attack in case the Englishman leads us into an ambush."

"Yes. He might even do that, curse him!" muttered Héron.

"He might, but it is unlikely. Still it is best to be prepared. Take a strong escort, citizen, say twenty or thirty men, picked and trained soldiers who would make short work of civilians, however well-armed they might be. There are twenty members—including the chief—in that Scarlet Pimpernel League, and I do not quite see how from this cell the prisoner could organise an ambuscade against us at a given time. Anyhow, that is a matter for you to decide. I have still to place before you a scheme which is a measure of safety for ourselves and our men against ambush as well as against trickery, and which I feel sure you will pronounce quite adequate."

"Let me hear it, then!"

"The prisoner will have to travel by coach, of course. You can travel with him, if you like, and put him in irons, and thus avert all chances of his escaping on the road. But"—and here Chauvelin made a long pause, which had the effect of holding his colleague's attention still more closely—"remember that we shall have his wife and one of his friends with us. Before we finally leave Paris tomorrow we will explain to the prisoner that at the first attempt to escape on his part, at the slightest suspicion that he has tricked us for his own ends or is leading us into an ambush—at the slightest suspicion, I say—you, Citizen Héron, will order his friend first, and then Marguerite Blakeney herself, to be summarily shot before his eyes."

Héron gave a long, low whistle. Instinctively he threw a furtive, backward glance at the prisoner, then he raised his shifty eyes to his colleague.

There was unbounded admiration expressed in them. One blackguard had met another—a greater one than himself—and was proud to acknowledge him as his master.

"By Lucifer, Citizen Chauvelin," he said at last, "I should never have thought of such a thing myself."

Chauvelin put up his hand with a gesture of self-deprecation.

"I certainly think that measure ought to be adequate," he said with a gentle air of assumed modesty, "unless you would prefer to arrest the woman and lodge her here, keeping her here as an hostage."

"No, no!" said Héron with a gruff laugh; "that idea does not appeal to me nearly so much as the other. I should not feel so secure on the way—I should always be thinking that that cursed woman had been allowed to escape—No! no! I would rather keep her under my own eye—just as you suggest, Citizen Chauvelin—and under the prisoner's, too," he added with a coarse jest. "If he did not actually see her, he might be more ready to try and save himself at her expense. But, of course, he could not see her shot before his eyes. It is a perfect plan, citizen, and does you infinite credit; and if the Englishman tricked us," he concluded with a fierce and savage oath, "and we did not find Capet at the end of the journey, I would gladly strangle his wife and his friend with my own hands."

"A satisfaction which I would not begrudge you, citizen," said Chauvelin dryly. "Perhaps you are right—the woman had best be kept under your own eye—the prisoner will never risk her safety on that, I would stake my life. We'll deliver our final 'either—or' the moment that she has joined our party, and before we start further on our way. Now, Citizen Héron, you have heard my advice; are you prepared to follow it?"

"To the last letter," replied the other.

And their two hands met in a grasp of mutual understanding—two hands already indelibly stained with much innocent blood, more deeply stained now with seventeen past days of inhumanity and miserable treachery to come.

CHAPTER 38

Capitulation

What occurred within the inner cell of the *Conciergerie* prison within the next half-hour of that 16th day of *Pluviôse* in the year 2 of the Republic is, perhaps, too well known to history to need or bear overfull repetition.

Chroniclers intimate with the inner history of those infamous days have told us how the chief agent of the Committee of General Security gave orders one hour after midnight that hot soup, white bread and wine be served to the prisoner, who for close on fourteen days previously had been kept on short rations of black bread and water; the sergeant in charge of the guard-room watch for the night also received strict orders that that same prisoner was on no account to be disturbed until the hour of six in the morning, when he was to be served with anything in the way of breakfast that he might fancy.

All this we know, and also that Citizen Héron, having given all necessary orders for the morning's expedition, returned to the *Conciergerie*, and found his colleague Chauvelin waiting for him in the guard-room.

"Well?" he asked with febrile impatience—"the prisoner?"

"He seems better and stronger," replied Chauvelin.

"Not too well, I hope?"

"No, no, only just well enough."

"You have seen him—since his supper?"

"Only from the doorway. It seems he ate and drank hardly at all, and the sergeant had some difficulty in keeping him awake until you came."

"Well, now for the letter," concluded Héron with the same marked feverishness of manner which sat so curiously on his uncouth personality. "Pen, ink and paper, sergeant!" he commanded.

"On the table, in the prisoner's cell, citizen," replied the sergeant.

He preceded the two citizens across the guard-room to the doorway, and raised for them the iron bar, lowering it back after them.

The next moment Héron and Chauvelin were once more face to face with their prisoner.

Whether by accident or design the lamp had been so placed that as the two men approached its light fell full upon their faces, while that of the prisoner remained in shadow. He was leaning forward with both elbows on the table, his thin, tapering fingers toying with the pen and ink-horn which had been placed close to his hand.

"I trust that everything has been arranged for your comfort, Sir Percy?" Chauvelin asked with a sarcastic little smile.

"I thank you, sir," replied Blakeney politely.

"You feel refreshed, I hope?"

"Greatly so, I assure you. But I am still demmed sleepy; and if you would kindly be brief—"

"You have not changed your mind, sir?" queried Chauvelin, and a note of anxiety, which he vainly tried to conceal, quivered in his voice.

"No, my good M. Chambertin," replied Blakeney with the same urbane courtesy, "I have not changed my mind."

A sigh of relief escaped the lips of both the men. The prisoner certainly had spoken in a clearer and firmer voice; but whatever renewed strength wine and food had imparted to him he apparently did not mean to employ in renewed obstinacy. Chauvelin, after a moment's pause, resumed more calmly:

"You are prepared to direct us to the place where little Capet lies hidden?"

"I am prepared to do anything, sir, to get out of this d—d hole."

"Very well. My colleague, Citizen Héron, has arranged for an escort of twenty men picked from the best regiment of the *Garde de Paris* to accompany us—yourself, him and me—to wherever you will direct us. Is that clear?"

"Perfectly, sir."

"You must not imagine for a moment that we, on the other hand, guarantee to give you your life and freedom even if this expedition prove unsuccessful."

"I would not venture on suggesting such a wild proposition, sir," said Blakeney placidly.

Chauvelin looked keenly on him. There was something in the tone of that voice that he did not altogether like—something that reminded him of an evening at Calais, and yet again of a day at Boulogne. He could not read the expression in the eyes, so with a quick gesture he pulled the lamp forward so that its light now fell full on the face of the prisoner.

"Ah! that is certainly better, is it not, my dear M. Chambertin?" said Sir Percy, beaming on his adversary with a pleasant smile.

His face, though still of the same ashen hue, looked serene if hopelessly wearied; the eyes seemed to mock. But this Chauvelin decided in himself must have been a trick of his own overwrought fancy. After a brief moment's pause he resumed dryly:

"If, however, the expedition turns out successful in every way—if little Capet, without much trouble to our escort, falls safe and sound into our hands—if certain contingencies which I am about to tell you all fall out as we wish—then, Sir Percy, I see no reason why the government of this country should not exercise its prerogative of mercy towards you after all."

"An exercise, my dear M. Chambertin, which must have wearied through frequent repetition," retorted Blakeney with the same imperturbable smile.

"The contingency at present is somewhat remote; when the time comes we'll talk this matter over—I will make no promise—and, anyhow, we can discuss it later."

"At present we are but wasting our valuable time over so trifling a matter—If you'll excuse me, sir—I am so demmed fatigued—"

"Then you will be glad to have everything settled quickly, I am sure."

"Exactly, sir."

Héron was taking no part in the present conversation. He knew that his temper was not likely to remain within bounds, and though he had nothing but contempt for his colleague's courtly manners, yet vaguely in his stupid, blundering way he grudgingly admitted that mayhap it was better to allow Citizen Chauvelin to deal with the Englishman. There was always the danger that if his own violent temper got the better of him, he might even at this eleventh hour order this insolent prisoner to summary trial and the guillotine, and thus lose the final chance of the more important capture.

He was sprawling on a chair in his usual slouching manner with his big head sunk between his broad shoulders, his shifty, prominent eyes wandering restlessly from the face of his colleague to that of the other man.

But now he gave a grunt of impatience.

"We are wasting time, Citizen Chauvelin," he muttered. "I have still a great deal to see to if we are to start at dawn. Get the d—d letter written, and—"

The rest of the phrase was lost in an indistinct and surly murmur. Chauvelin, after a shrug of the shoulders, paid no further heed to him; he turned, bland and urbane, once more to the prisoner.

"I see with pleasure, Sir Percy," he said, "that we thoroughly understand one another. Having had a few hours' rest you will, I know, feel quite ready for the expedition. Will you kindly indicate to me the direction in which we will have to travel?"

"Northwards all the way."

"Towards the coast?"

"The place to which we must go is about seven leagues from the sea."

"Our first objective then will be Beauvais, Amiens, Abbeville, Crecy, and so on?"

"Precisely."

"As far as the forest of Boulogne, shall we say?"

"Where we shall come off the beaten track, and you will have to trust to my guidance."

"We might go there now, Sir Percy, and leave you here."

"You might. But you would not then find the child. Seven leagues is not far from the coast. He might slip through your fingers."

"And my colleague Héron, being disappointed, would inevitably send you to the guillotine."

"Quite so," rejoined the prisoner placidly. "Methought, sir, that we had decided that I should lead this little expedition? Surely," he added, "it is not so much the *Dauphin* whom you want as my share in this betrayal."

"You are right as usual, Sir Percy. Therefore, let us take that as settled. We go as far as Crecy, and thence place ourselves entirely in your hands."

"The journey should not take more than three days, sir."

"During which you will travel in a coach in the company of my friend Héron."

"I could have chosen pleasanter company, sir; still, it will serve."

"This being settled, Sir Percy. I understand that you desire to communicate with one of your followers."

"Someone must let the others know—those who have the *Dauphin* in their charge."

"Quite so. Therefore, I pray you write to one of your friends that you have decided to deliver the *Dauphin* into our hands in exchange for your own safety."

"You said just now that this you would not guarantee," interposed Blakeney quietly.

"If all turns out well," retorted Chauvelin with a show of contempt, "and if you will write the exact letter which I shall dictate, we might even give you that guarantee."

450

"The quality of your mercy, sir, passes belief."

"Then I pray you write. Which of your followers will have the honour of the communication?"

"My brother-in-law, Armand St. Just; he is still in Paris, I believe. He can let the others know."

Chauvelin made no immediate reply. He paused awhile, hesitating. Would Sir Percy Blakeney be ready—if his own safety demanded it—to sacrifice the man who had betrayed him? In the momentous "either—or" that was to be put to him, by-and-by, would he choose his own life and leave Armand St. Just to perish? It was not for Chauvelin—or any man of his stamp—to judge of what Blakeney would do under such circumstances, and had it been a question of St. Just alone, mayhap Chauvelin would have hesitated still more at the present juncture.

But the friend as hostage was only destined to be a minor leverage for the final breaking-up of the League of the Scarlet Pimpernel through the disgrace of its chief. There was the wife—Marguerite Blakeney—sister of St. Just, joint and far more important hostage, whose very close affection for her brother might prove an additional trump card in that handful which Chauvelin already held.

Blakeney paid no heed seemingly to the other's hesitation. He did not even look up at him, but quietly drew pen and paper towards him, and made ready to write.

"What do you wish me to say?" he asked simply.

"Will that young blackguard answer your purpose, Citizen Chauvelin?" queried Héron roughly.

Obviously, the same doubt had crossed his mind. Chauvelin quickly re-assured him.

"Better than anyone else," he said firmly. "Will you write at my dictation, Sir Percy?

"I am waiting to do so, my dear sir."

"Begin your letter as you wish, then; now continue."

And he began to dictate slowly, watching every word as it left Blakeney's pen.

"'I cannot stand my present position any longer. Citizen Héron, and also M. Chauvelin—'Yes, Sir Percy, Chauvelin, not Chambertin—C, H, A, U, V, E, L, I, N—That is quite right—'have made this prison a perfect hell for me.'"

Sir Percy looked up from his writing, smiling.

"You wrong yourself, my dear M. Chambertin!" he said; "I have really been most comfortable."

"I wish to place the matter before your friends in as indulgent a manner as I can," retorted Chauvelin dryly.

"I thank you, sir. Pray proceed."

"—'a perfect hell for me,'" resumed the other. "Have you that?—'and I have been forced to give way. Tomorrow we start from here at dawn; and I will guide Citizen Héron to the place where he can find the *Dauphin*. But the authorities demand that one of my followers, one who has once been a member of the League of the Scarlet Pimpernel, shall accompany me on this expedition. I therefore ask you'—or 'desire you' or 'beg you'—whichever you prefer, Sir Percy—"

"'Ask you' will do quite nicely. This is really very interesting, you know."

"—'to be prepared to join the expedition. We start at dawn, and you would be required to be at the main gate of the house of Justice at six o'clock precisely. I have an assurance from the authorities that your life should be in-violate, but if you refuse to accompany me, the guillotine will await me on the morrow.'"

"'The guillotine will await me on the morrow.' That sounds quite cheerful, does it not, M. Chambertin?" said the prisoner, who had not evinced the slightest surprise at the wording of the letter whilst he wrote at the other's dictation. "Do you know, I quite enjoyed writing this letter; it so reminded me of happy days in Boulogne."

Chauvelin pressed his lips together. Truly now he felt that a retort from him would have been undignified, more especially as just at this moment there came from the guard room the sound of men's voices talking and laughing, the occasional clang of steel, or of a heavy boot against the tiled floor, the rattling of dice, or a sudden burst of laughter—sounds, in fact, that betokened the presence of a number of soldiers close by.

Chauvelin contented himself with a nod in the direction of the guard-room.

"The conditions are somewhat different now," he said placidly, "from those that reigned in Boulogne. But will you not sign your letter, Sir Percy?"

"With pleasure, sir," responded Blakeney, as with an elaborate flourish of the pen he appended his name to the missive.

Chauvelin was watching him with eyes that would have shamed a lynx by their keenness. He took up the completed letter, read it through very carefully, as if to find some hidden meaning behind the very words which he himself had dictated; he studied the signature, and looked vainly for a mark or a sign that might convey a different sense to that which he had intended. Finally, finding none, he folded the letter up with his own hand, and at once slipped it in the pocket of his coat.

"Take care, M. Chambertin," said Blakeney lightly; "it will burn a hole in that elegant vest of yours."

"It will have no time to do that, Sir Percy," retorted Chauvelin blandly; "an' you will furnish me with citizen St. Just's present address, I will myself convey the letter to him at once."

"At this hour of the night? Poor old Armand, he'll be abed. But his address, sir, is No. 32, Rue de la Croix Blanche, on the first floor, the door on your right as you mount the stairs; you know the room well, Citizen Chauvelin; you have been in it before. And now," he added with a loud and ostentatious yawn, "shall we all to bed? We start at dawn, you said, and I am so d——d fatigued."

Frankly, he did not look it now. Chauvelin himself, despite his matured plans, despite all the precautions that he meant to take for the success of this gigantic scheme, felt a sudden strange sense of fear creeping into his bones. Half an hour ago he had seen a man in what looked like the last stage of utter physical exhaustion, a hunched up figure, listless and limp, hands that twitched nervously, the face as of a dying man. Now those outward symptoms were still there certainly; the face by the light of the lamp still looked livid, the lips bloodless, the hands emaciated and waxen, but the eyes!—they were still hollow, with heavy lids still purple, but in their depths there was a curious, mysterious light, a look that seemed to see something that was hidden to natural sight.

Citizen Chauvelin thought that Héron, too, must be conscious of this, but the Committee's agent was sprawling on a chair, sucking a short-stemmed pipe, and gazing with entire animal satisfaction on the prisoner.

"The most perfect piece of work we have ever accomplished, you and I, Citizen Chauvelin," he said complacently.

"You think that everything is quite satisfactory?" asked the other with anxious stress on his words.

"Everything, of course. Now you see to the letter. I will give final orders for tomorrow, but I shall sleep in the guard-room."

"And I on that inviting bed," interposed the prisoner lightly, as he rose to his feet. "Your servant, citizens!"

He bowed his head slightly and stood by the table whilst the two men prepared to go. Chauvelin took a final long look at the man whom he firmly believed he had at last brought down to abject disgrace.

Blakeney was standing erect, watching the two retreating figures— one slender hand was on the table. Chauvelin saw that it was leaning rather heavily, as if for support, and that even whilst a final mocking laugh sped him and his colleague on their way, the tall figure of the conquered lion swayed like a stalwart oak that is forced to bend to the mighty fury of an all-compelling wind.

With a sigh of content Chauvelin took his colleague by the arm, and together the two men walked out of the cell.

CHAPTER 39

Kill Him!

Two hours after midnight Armand St. Just was wakened from sleep by a peremptory pull at his bell. In these days in Paris but one meaning could as a rule be attached to such a summons at this hour of the night, and Armand, though possessed of an unconditional certificate of safety, sat up in bed, quite convinced that for some reason which would presently be explained to him he had once more been placed on the list of the "suspect," and that his trial and condemnation on a trumped-up charge would follow in due course.

Truth to tell, he felt no fear at the prospect, and only a very little sorrow. The sorrow was not for himself; he regretted neither life nor happiness. Life had become hateful to him since happiness had fled with it on the dark wings of dishonour; sorrow such as he felt was only for Jeanne! She was very young and would weep bitter tears. She would be unhappy, because she truly loved him, and because this would be the first cup of bitterness which life was holding out to her. But she was very young, and sorrow would not be eternal. It was better so. He, Armand St. Just, though he loved her with an intensity of passion that had been magnified and strengthened by his own overwhelming shame, had never really brought his beloved one single moment of unalloyed happiness.

From the very first day when he sat beside her in the tiny *boudoir* of the Square du Roule, and the heavy foot fall of Héron and his bloodhounds broke in on their first kiss, down to this hour which he believed struck his own death-knell, his love for her had brought more tears to her dear eyes than smiles to her exquisite mouth.

454

Her he had loved so dearly, that for her sweet sake he had sacrificed honour, friendship and truth; to free her, as he believed, from the hands of impious brutes he had done a deed that cried Cain-like for vengeance to the very throne of God. For her he had sinned, and because of that sin, even before it was committed, their love had been blighted, and happiness had never been theirs.

Now it was all over. He would pass out of her life, up the steps of the scaffold, tasting as he mounted them the most entire happiness that he had known since that awful day when he became a Judas.

The peremptory summons, once more repeated, roused him from his meditations. He lit a candle, and without troubling to slip any of his clothes on, he crossed the narrow ante-chamber, and opened the door that gave on the landing.

"In the name of the people!"

He had expected to hear not only those words, but also the grounding of arms and the brief command to halt. He had expected to see before him the white facings of the uniform of the Garde de Paris, and to feel himself roughly pushed back into his lodging preparatory to the search being made of all his effects and the placing of irons on his wrists.

Instead of this, it was a quiet, dry voice that said without undue harshness:

"In the name of the people!"

And instead of the uniforms, the bayonets and the scarlet caps with tricolour cockades, he was confronted by a slight, sable-clad figure, whose face, lit by the flickering light of the tallow candle, looked strangely pale and earnest.

"Citizen Chauvelin!" gasped Armand, more surprised than frightened at this unexpected apparition.

"Himself, citizen, at your service," replied Chauvelin with his quiet, ironical manner. "I am the bearer of a letter for you from Sir Percy Blakeney. Have I your permission to enter?"

Mechanically Armand stood aside, allowing the other man to pass in. He closed the door behind his nocturnal visitor, then, taper in hand, he preceded him into the inner room.

It was the same one in which a fortnight ago a fighting lion had been brought to his knees. Now it lay wrapped in gloom, the feeble light of the candle only lighting Armand's face and the white frill of his shirt. The young man put the taper down on the table and turned to his visitor.

"Shall I light the lamp?" he asked.

"Quite unnecessary," replied Chauvelin curtly. "I have only a letter to deliver, and after that to ask you one brief question."

From the pocket of his coat he drew the letter which Blakeney had written an hour ago.

"The prisoner wrote this in my presence," he said as he handed the letter over to Armand. "Will you read it?"

Armand took it from him and sat down close to the table; leaning forward he held the paper near the light and began to read. He read the letter through very slowly to the end, then once again from the beginning. He was trying to do that which Chauvelin had wished to do an hour ago; he was trying to find the inner meaning which he felt must inevitably lie behind these words which Percy had written with his own hand.

That these bare words were but a blind to deceive the enemy Armand never doubted for a moment. In this he was as loyal as Marguerite would have been herself. Never for a moment did the suspicion cross his mind that Blakeney was about to play the part of a coward, but he, Armand, felt that as a faithful friend and follower he ought by instinct to know exactly what his chief intended, what he meant him to do.

Swiftly his thoughts flew back to that other letter, the one which Marguerite had given him—the letter full of pity and of friendship which had brought him hope and a joy and peace which he had thought at one time that he would never know again. And suddenly one sentence in that letter stood out so clearly before his eyes that it blurred the actual, tangible ones on the paper which even now rustled in his hand.

But if at any time you receive another letter from me—be its contents what they may—act in accordance with the letter but send a copy of it at once to Ffoulkes or to Marguerite.

Now everything seemed at once quite clear; his duty, his next actions, every word that he would speak to Chauvelin. Those that Percy had written to him were already indelibly graven on his memory.

Chauvelin had waited with his usual patience, silent and imperturbable, while the young man read. Now when he saw that Armand had finished, he said quietly:

"Just one question, citizen, and I need not detain you longer. But first will you kindly give me back that letter? It is a precious document which will for ever remain in the archives of the nation."

But even while he spoke Armand, with one of those quick intuitions that come in moments of acute crisis, had done just that which he felt Blakeney would wish him to do. He had held the letter close to the candle. A corner of the thin crisp paper immediately caught fire, and before Chauvelin could utter a word of anger, or make a movement to prevent the conflagration, the flames had licked up fully one half of the letter, and Armand had only just time to throw the remainder on the floor and to stamp out the blaze with his foot.

"I am sorry, citizen," he said calmly; "an accident."

"A useless act of devotion," interposed Chauvelin, who already had smothered the oath that had risen to his lips. "The Scarlet Pimpernel's actions in the present matter will not lose their merited publicity through the foolish destruction of this document."

"I had no thought, citizen," retorted the young man, "of commenting on the actions of my chief, or of trying to deny them that publicity which you seem to desire for them almost as much as I do."

"More, citizen, a great deal more! The impeccable Scarlet Pimpernel, the noble and gallant English gentleman, has agreed to deliver into our hands the uncrowned King of France—in exchange for his own life and freedom. Methinks that even his worst enemy would not wish for a better ending to a career of adventure, and a reputation for bravery unequalled in Europe. But no more of this, time is pressing, I must help Citizen Héron with his final preparations for his journey. You, of course, citizen St. Just, will act in accordance with Sir Percy Blakeney's wishes?"

"Of course," replied Armand.

"You will present yourself at the main entrance of the house of Justice at six o'clock this morning."

"I will not fail you."

"A coach will be provided for you. You will follow the expedition as hostage for the good faith of your chief."

"I quite understand."

"H'm! That's brave! You have no fear, Citizen St. Just?"

"Fear of what, sir?"

"You will be a hostage in our hands, citizen; your life a guarantee that your chief has no thought of playing us false. Now I was thinking of—of certain events—which led to the arrest of Sir Percy Blakeney."

"Of my treachery, you mean," rejoined the young man calmly, even though his face had suddenly become pale as death. "Of the damnable lie wherewith, you cheated me into selling my honour, and made me what I am—a creature scarce fit to walk upon this earth."

"Oh!" protested Chauvelin blandly.

"The damnable lie," continued Armand more vehemently, "that hath made me one with Cain and the Iscariot. When you goaded me into the hellish act, Jeanne Lange was already free."

"Free—but not safe."

"A lie, man! A lie! For which you are thrice accursed. Great God, is it not you that should have cause for fear? Methinks were I to strangle you now I should suffer less of remorse."

"And would be rendering your ex-chief but a sorry service," interposed Chauvelin with quiet irony. "Sir Percy Blakeney is a dying man, Citizen St. Just; he'll be a dead man at dawn if I do not put in an appearance by six o'clock this morning. This is a private understanding between Citizen Héron and myself. We agreed to it before I came to see you."

"Oh, you take care of your own miserable skin well enough! But you need not be afraid of me—I take my orders from my chief, and he has not ordered me to kill you."

"That was kind of him. Then we may count on you? You are not afraid?"

"Afraid that the Scarlet Pimpernel would leave me in the lurch because of the immeasurable wrong I have done to him?" retorted Armand, proud and defiant in the name of his chief. "No, sir, I am not afraid of that; I have spent the last fortnight in praying to God that my life might yet be given for his."

"H'm! I think it most unlikely that your prayers will be granted, citizen; prayers, I imagine, so very seldom are; but I don't know, I never pray myself. In your case, now, I should say that you have not the slightest chance of the Deity interfering in so pleasant a manner. Even were Sir Percy Blakeney prepared to wreak personal revenge on you, he would scarcely be so foolish as to risk the other life which we shall also hold as hostage for his good faith."

"The other life?"

"Yes. Your sister, Lady Blakeney, will also join the expedition tomorrow. This Sir Percy does not yet know; but it will come as a pleasant surprise for him. At the slightest suspicion of false play on Sir Percy's part, at his slightest attempt at escape, your life and that of your sister are forfeit; you will both be summarily shot before his eyes. I do not think that I need be more precise, eh, citizen St. Just?"

The young man was quivering with passion. A terrible loathing for himself, for his crime which had been the precursor of this terrible situation, filled his soul to the verge of sheer physical nausea. A red film gathered before his eyes, and through it he saw the grinning face of the inhuman monster who had planned this hideous, abominable thing. It seemed to him as if in the silence and the hush of the night, above the feeble, flickering flame that threw weird shadows around, a group of devils were surrounding him, and were shouting, "Kill him! Kill him now! Rid the earth of this hellish brute!"

No doubt if Chauvelin had exhibited the slightest sign of fear, if he had moved an inch towards the door, Armand, blind with passion, driven to madness by agonising remorse more even than by rage, would have sprung at his enemy's throat and crushed the life out of him as he would out of a venomous beast. But the man's calm, his immobility, recalled St. Just to himself. Reason, that had almost yielded to passion again, found strength to drive the enemy back this time, to whisper a warning, an admonition, even a reminder. Enough harm, God knows, had been done by tempestuous passion already. And God alone knew what terrible consequences its triumph now might bring in its trial, and striking on Armand's buzzing ears Chauvelin's words came back as a triumphant and mocking echo:

"He'll be a dead man at dawn if I do not put in an appearance by six o'clock."

The red film lifted, the candle flickered low, the devils vanished, only the pale face of the Terrorist gazed with gentle irony out of the gloom.

"I think that I need not detain you any longer, citizen, St. Just," he said quietly; "you can get three or four hours' rest yet before you need make a start, and I still have a great many things to see to. I wish you goodnight, citizen."

"Goodnight," murmured Armand mechanically.

He took the candle and escorted his visitor back to the door. He waited on the landing, taper in hand, while Chauvelin descended the narrow, winding stairs.

There was a light in the *concierge's* lodge. No doubt the woman had struck it when the nocturnal visitor had first demanded admittance. His name and tricolour scarf of office had ensured him the full measure of her attention, and now she was evidently sitting up waiting to let him out.

St. Just, satisfied that Chauvelin had finally gone, now turned back to his own rooms.

CHAPTER 40

God Help Us All

He carefully locked the outer door. Then he lit the lamp, for the candle gave but a flickering light, and he had some important work to do.

Firstly, he picked up the charred fragment of the letter, and smoothed it out carefully and reverently as he would a relic. Tears had gathered in his eyes, but he was not ashamed of them, for no one saw them; but they eased his heart and helped to strengthen his resolve. It was a mere fragment that had been spared by the flame, but Armand knew every word of the letter by heart.

He had pen, ink and paper ready to his hand, and from memory wrote out a copy of it. To this he added a covering letter from himself to Marguerite:

"This—which I had from Percy through the hands of Chauvelin—I neither question nor understand—He wrote the letter, and I have no thought but to obey. In his previous letter to me he enjoined me, if ever he wrote to me again, to obey him implicitly, and to communicate with you. To both these commands do I submit with a glad heart. But of this must I give you warning, little mother—Chauvelin desires you also to accompany us tomorrow—Percy does not know this yet, else he would never start. But those fiends fear that his readiness is a blind—and that he has some plan in his head for his own escape and the continued safety of the *Dauphin*—This plan they hope to frustrate through holding you and me as hostages for his good faith. God only knows how gladly I would give my life for my chief—but your life, dear little mother—is sacred above all—I think that I do right in warning you. God help us all."

Having written the letter, he sealed it, together with the copy of Percy's letter which he had made. Then he took up the candle and went downstairs.

There was no longer any light in the *concierge's* lodge, and Armand had some difficulty in making himself heard. At last the woman came to the door. She was tired and cross after two interruptions of her night's rest, but she had a partiality for her young lodger, whose pleasant ways and easy liberality had been like a pale ray of sunshine through the squalor of every-day misery.

"It is a letter, *citoyenne*," said Armand, with earnest entreaty, "for my sister. She lives in the Rue de Charonne, near the fortifications, and must have it within an hour; it is a matter of life and death to her, to me, and to another who is very dear to us both."

The *concierge* threw up her hands in horror.

"Rue de Charonne, near the fortifications," she exclaimed, "and within an hour! By the Holy Virgin, citizen, that is impossible. Who will take it? There is no way."

"A way must be found, *citoyenne*," said Armand firmly, "and at once; it is not far, and there are five golden *louis* waiting for the messenger!"

Five golden *louis!* The poor, hardworking woman's eyes gleamed at the thought. Five *louis* meant food for at least two months if one was careful, and—

"Give me the letter, citizen," she said, "time to slip on a warm petticoat and a shawl, and I'll go myself. It's not fit for the boy to go at this hour."

"You will bring me back a line from my sister in reply to this," said Armand, whom circumstances had at last rendered cautious. "Bring it up to my rooms that I may give you the five *louis* in exchange."

He waited while the woman slipped back into her room. She heard him speaking to her boy; the same lad who a fortnight ago had taken the treacherous letter which had lured Blakeney to the house into the fatal ambuscade that had been prepared for him. Everything reminded Armand of that awful night, every hour that he had since spent in the house had been racking torture to him. Now at last he was to leave it, and on an errand, which might help to ease the load of remorse from his heart.

The woman was soon ready. Armand gave her final directions as to how to find the house; then she took the letter and promised to be very quick, and to bring back a reply from the lady.

Armand accompanied her to the door. The night was dark, a thin drizzle was falling; he stood and watched until the woman's rapidly walking figure was lost in the misty gloom.

Then with a heavy sigh he once more went within.

Chapter 41

When Hope Was Dead

In a small upstairs room in the Rue de Charonne, above the shop of Lucas the old-clothes dealer, Marguerite sat with Sir Andrew Ffoulkes. Armand's letter, with its message and its warning, lay open on the table between them, and she had in her hand the sealed packet which Percy had given her just ten days ago, and which she was only to open if

461

all hope seemed to be dead, if nothing appeared to stand any longer between that one dear life and irretrievable shame.

A small lamp placed on the table threw a feeble yellow light on the squalid, ill-furnished room, for it lacked still an hour or so before dawn. Armand's *concierge* had brought her lodger's letter, and Marguerite had quickly despatched a brief reply to him, a reply that held love and also encouragement.

Then she had summoned Sir Andrew. He never had a thought of leaving her during these days of dire trouble, and he had lodged all this while in a tiny room on the top-most floor of this house in the Rue de Charonne.

At her call he had come down very quickly, and now they sat together at the table, with the oil-lamp illuminating their pale, anxious faces; she the wife and he the friend holding a consultation together in this most miserable hour that preceded the cold wintry dawn.

Outside a thin, persistent rain mixed with snow pattered against the small window panes, and an icy wind found out all the crevices in the worm-eaten woodwork that would afford it ingress to the room. But neither Marguerite nor Ffoulkes was conscious of the cold. They had wrapped their cloaks round their shoulders and did not feel the chill currents of air that caused the lamp to flicker and to smoke.

"I can see now," said Marguerite in that calm voice which comes so naturally in moments of infinite despair—"I can see now exactly what Percy meant when he made me promise not to open this packet until it seemed to me—to me and to you, Sir Andrew—that he was about to play the part of a coward. A coward! Great God!" She checked the sob that had risen to her throat, and continued in the same calm manner and quiet, even voice:

"You do think with me, do you not, that the time has come, and that we must open this packet?"

"Without a doubt, Lady Blakeney," replied Ffoulkes with equal earnestness. "I would stake my life that already a fortnight ago Blakeney had that same plan in his mind which he has now matured. Escape from that awful *Conciergerie* prison with all the precautions so carefully taken against it was impossible. I knew that alas! from the first. But in the open all might yet be different. I'll not believe it that a man like Blakeney is destined to perish at the hands of those curs."

She looked on her loyal friend with tear-dimmed eyes through which shone boundless gratitude and heart-broken sorrow.

He had spoken of a fortnight! It was ten days since she had seen

Percy. It had then seemed as if death had already marked him with its grim sign. Since then she had tried to shut away from her mind the terrible visions which her anguish constantly conjured up before her of his growing weakness, of the gradual impairing of that brilliant intellect, the gradual exhaustion of that mighty physical strength.

"God bless you, Sir Andrew, for your enthusiasm and for your trust," she said with a sad little smile; "but for you I should long ago have lost all courage, and these last ten days—what a cycle of misery they represent—would have been maddening but for your help and your loyalty. God knows I would have courage for everything in life, for everything save one, but just that, his death; that would be beyond my strength—neither reason nor body could stand it. Therefore, I am so afraid, Sir Andrew," she added piteously.

"Of what, Lady Blakeney?"

"That when he knows that I too am to go as hostage, as Armand says in his letter, that my life is to be guarantee for his, I am afraid that he will draw back—that he will—my God!" she cried with sudden fervour, "tell me what to do!"

"Shall we open the packet?" asked Ffoulkes gently, "and then just make up our minds to act exactly as Blakeney has enjoined us to do, neither more nor less, but just word for word, deed for deed, and I believe that that will be right—whatever may betide—in the end."

Once more his quiet strength, his earnestness and his faith comforted her. She dried her eyes and broke open the seal. There were two separate letters in the packet, one unaddressed, obviously intended for her and Ffoulkes, the other was addressed to M. le baron Jean de Batz, 15, Rue St. Jean de Latran a Paris.

"A letter addressed to that awful Baron de Batz," said Marguerite, looking with puzzled eyes on the paper as she turned it over and over in her hand, "to that bombastic windbag! I know him and his ways well! What can Percy have to say to him?"

Sir Andrew too looked puzzled. But neither of them had the mind to waste time in useless speculations. Marguerite unfolded the letter which was intended for her, and after a final look on her friend, whose kind face was quivering with excitement, she began slowly to read aloud:

"I need not ask either of you two to trust me, knowing that you will. But I could not die inside this hole like a rat in a trap—I had to try and free myself, at the worst to die in the open beneath God's sky. You two will understand and understanding you will trust me to the end. Send the enclosed letter at once to its address. And you, Ffoulkes, my most sincere and most loyal friend, I beg with all my soul to see to the safety of Marguerite. Armand will stay by me—but you, Ffoulkes, do not leave her, stand by her. As soon as you read this letter—and you will not read it until both she and you have felt that hope has fled and I myself am about to throw up the sponge—try and persuade her to make for the coast as quickly as may be—At Calais you can open up communications with the *Daydream* in the usual way, and embark on her at once. Let no member of the League remain on French soil one hour longer after that.

"Then tell the skipper to make for Le Portel—the place which he knows—and there to keep a sharp outlook for another three nights. After that make straight for home, for it will be no use waiting any longer. I shall not come. These measures are for Marguerite's safety, and for you all who are in France at this moment. Comrade, I entreat you to look on these measures as on my dying wish. To de Batz I have given rendezvous at the Chapelle of the Holy Sepulchre, just outside the park of the Château d'Ourde. He will help me to save the *Dauphin*, and if by good luck he also helps me to save myself I shall be within seven leagues of Le Portel, and with the Liane frozen as she is I could reach the coast.

"But Marguerite's safety I leave in your hands, Ffoulkes. Would that I could look more clearly into the future and know that those devils will not drag her into danger. Beg her to start at once for Calais immediately you have both read this. I only beg, I do not command. I know that you, Ffoulkes, will stand by her whatever she may wish to do. God's blessing be for ever on you both."

Marguerite's voice died away in the silence that still lay over this deserted part of the great city and in this squalid house where she and Sir Andrew Ffoulkes had found shelter these last ten days. The agony of mind which they had here endured, never doubting, but scarcely ever hoping, had found its culmination at last in this final message, which almost seemed to come to them from the grave.

It had been written ten days ago. A plan had then apparently formed in Percy's mind which he had set forth during the brief half-hour's respite which those fiends had once given him. Since then they had never given him ten consecutive minutes' peace; since then ten days had gone by; how much power, how much vitality had gone by too on the leaden wings of all those terrible hours spent in solitude and in misery?

"We can but hope, Lady Blakeney," said Sir Andrew Ffoulkes after a while, "that you will be allowed out of Paris; but from what Armand says—"

"And Percy does not actually send me away," she rejoined with a pathetic little smile.

"No. He cannot compel you, Lady Blakeney. You are not a member of the League."

"Oh, yes, I am!" she retorted firmly; "and I have sworn obedience, just as all of you have done. I will go, just as he bids me, and you, Sir Andrew, you will obey him too?"

"My orders are to stand by you. That is an easy task."

"You know where this place is?" she asked—"the Château d'Ourde?"

"Oh, yes, we all know it! It is empty, and the park is a wreck; the owner fled from it at the very outbreak of the revolution; he left some kind of steward nominally in charge, a curious creature, half imbecile; the *château* and the chapel in the forest just outside the grounds have oft served Blakeney and all of us as a place of refuge on our way to the coast."

"But the *Dauphin* is not there?" she said.

"No. According to the first letter which you brought me from Blakeney ten days ago, and on which I acted, Tony, who has charge of the *Dauphin*, must have crossed into Holland with His Little Majesty today."

"I understand," she said simply. "But then—this letter to de Batz?"

"Ah, there I am completely at sea! But I'll deliver it, and at once too, only I don't like to leave you. Will you let me get you out of Paris first? I think just before dawn it could be done. We can get the cart from Lucas, and if we could reach St. Germain before noon, I could come straight back then and deliver the letter to de Batz. This, I feel, I ought to do myself; but at Achard's farm I would know that you were safe for a few hours."

"I will do whatever you think right, Sir Andrew," she said simply; "my will is bound up with Percy's dying wish. God knows I would rather follow him now, step by step,—as hostage, as prisoner—any way so long as I can see him, but—"

She rose and turned to go, almost impassive now in that great calm born of despair.

A stranger seeing her now had thought her indifferent. She was very pale, and deep circles round her eyes told of sleepless nights and

days of mental misery, but otherwise there was not the faintest outward symptom of that terrible anguish which was rending her heart-
strings. Her lips did not quiver, and the source of her tears had been
dried up ten days ago.

"Ten minutes and I'll be ready, Sir Andrew," she said. "I have but
few belongings. Will you the while see Lucas about the cart?"

He did as she desired. Her calm in no way deceived him; he knew
that she must be suffering keenly and would suffer more keenly still
while she would be trying to efface her own personal feelings all
through that coming dreary journey to Calais.

He went to see the landlord about the horse and cart, and a quarter
of an hour later Marguerite came downstairs ready to start. She found
Sir Andrew in close converse with an officer of the Garde de Paris,
whilst two soldiers of the same regiment were standing at the horse's
head.

When she appeared in the doorway Sir Andrew came at once up
to her.

"It is just as I feared, Lady Blakeney," he said; "this man has been
sent here to take charge of you. Of course, he knows nothing beyond
the fact that his orders are to convey you at once to the guard-house
of the Rue Ste. Anne, where he is to hand you over to Citizen Chauvelin of the Committee of Public Safety."

Sir Andrew could not fail to see the look of intense relief which,
in the midst of all her sorrow, seemed suddenly to have lighted up the
whole of Marguerite's wan face. The thought of wending her own
way to safety whilst Percy, mayhap, was fighting an uneven fight with
death had been well-nigh intolerable; but she had been ready to obey
without a murmur. Now Fate and the enemy himself had decided
otherwise. She felt as if a load had been lifted from her heart.

"I will at once go and find de Batz," Sir Andrew contrived to
whisper hurriedly. "As soon as Percy's letter is safely in his hands I will
make my way northwards and communicate with all the members of
the League, on whom the chief has so strictly enjoined to quit French
soil immediately. We will proceed to Calais first and open up communication with the *Daydream* in the usual way. The others had best
embark on board her, and the skipper shall then make for the known
spot of Le Portel, of which Percy speaks in his letter. I myself will go
by land to Le Portel, and thence, if I have no news of you or of the
expedition, I will slowly work southwards in the direction of the Château d'Ourde. That is all that I can do. If you can contrive to let Percy

or even Armand know my movements, do so by all means. I know that I shall be doing right, for, in a way, I shall be watching over you and arranging for your safety, as Blakeney begged me to do. God bless you, Lady Blakeney, and God save the Scarlet Pimpernel!"

He stooped and kissed her hand, and she intimated to the officer that she was ready. He had a hackney coach waiting for her lower down the street. To it she walked with a firm step, and as she entered it she waved a last farewell to Sir Andrew Ffoulkes.

CHAPTER 42

The Guard-House of the Rue Ste. Anne

The little *cortège* was turning out of the great gates of the house of Justice. It was intensely cold; a bitter north-easterly gale was blowing from across the heights of Montmartre, driving sleet and snow and half-frozen rain into the faces of the men, and finding its way up their sleeves, down their collars and round the knees of their threadbare breeches.

Armand, whose fingers were numb with the cold, could scarcely feel the reins in his hands. Chauvelin was riding close beside him, but the two men had not exchanged one word since the moment when the small troop of some twenty mounted soldiers had filed up inside the courtyard, and Chauvelin, with a curt word of command, had ordered one of the troopers to take Armand's horse on the lead.

A hackney coach brought up the rear of the *cortège*, with a man riding at either door and two more following at a distance of twenty paces. Héron's gaunt, ugly face, crowned with a battered, sugar-loaf hat, appeared from time to time at the window of the coach. He was no horseman, and, moreover, preferred to keep the prisoner closely under his own eye. The corporal had told Armand that the prisoner was with Citizen Héron inside the coach—in irons. Beyond that the soldiers could tell him nothing; they knew nothing of the object of this expedition. Vaguely they might have wondered in their dull minds why this particular prisoner was thus being escorted out of the *Conciergerie* prison with so much paraphernalia and such an air of mystery, when there were thousands of prisoners in the city and the provinces at the present moment who *anon* would be bundled up wholesale into carts to be dragged to the guillotine like a flock of sheep to the butchers.

But even if they wondered they made no remarks among themselves. Their faces, blue with the cold, were the perfect mirrors of their

467

own unconquerable stolidity.

The tower clock of Notre Dame struck seven when the small cavalcade finally moved slowly out of the monumental gates. In the east the wan light of a February morning slowly struggled out of the surrounding gloom. Now the towers of many churches loomed ghostlike against the dull grey sky, and down below, on the right, the frozen river, like a smooth sheet of steel, wound its graceful curves round the islands and past the facade of the Louvres palace, whose walls looked grim and silent, like the mausoleum of the dead giants of the past.

All around the great city gave signs of awakening; the business of the day renewed its course every twenty-four hours, despite the tragedies of death and of dishonour that walked with it hand in hand. From the *Place de La Révolution* the intermittent roll of drums came from time to time with its muffled sound striking the ear of the passer-by. Along the quay opposite an open-air camp was already astir; men, women, and children engaged in the great task of clothing and feeding the people of France, armed against tyranny, were bending to their task, even before the wintry dawn had spread its pale grey tints over the narrower streets of the city.

Armand shivered under his cloak. This silent ride beneath the leaden sky, through the veil of half-frozen rain and snow, seemed like a dream to him. And now, as the outriders of the little cavalcade turned to cross the Pont au Change, he saw spread out on his left what appeared like the living panorama of these three weeks that had just gone by. He could see the house of the Rue St. Germain l'Auxerrois where Percy had lodged before he carried through the rescue of the little *Dauphin*. Armand could even see the window at which the dreamer had stood, weaving noble dreams that his brilliant daring had turned into realities, until the hand of a traitor had brought him down to—to what? Armand would not have dared at this moment to look back at that hideous, vulgar hackney coach wherein that proud, reckless adventurer, who had defied Fate and mocked Death, sat, in chains, beside a loathsome creature whose very propinquity was an outrage.

Now they were passing under the very house on the *Quai de La Ferraille*, above the saddler's shop, the house where Marguerite had lodged ten days ago, whither Armand had come, trying to fool himself into the belief that the love of "little mother" could be deceived into blindness against his own crime. He had tried to draw a veil before those eyes which he had scarcely dared encounter, but he knew that that veil must lift one day, and then a curse would send him forth, outlawed and homeless, a wanderer on the face of the earth.

Soon as the little *cortège* wended its way northwards it filed out beneath the walls of the Temple prison; there was the main gate with its sentry standing at attention, there the archway with the *guichet* of the *concierge*, and beyond it the paved courtyard. Armand closed his eyes deliberately; he could not bear to look.

No wonder that he shivered and tried to draw his cloak closer around him. Every stone, every street corner was full of memories. The chill that struck to the very marrow of his bones came from no outward cause; it was the very hand of remorse that, as it passed over him, froze the blood in his veins and made the rattle of those wheels behind him sound like a hellish knell.

At last the more closely populated quarters of the city were left behind. On ahead the first section of the guard had turned into the Rue St. Anne. The houses became more sparse, intersected by narrow pieces of *terrains vagues*, or small weed-covered bits of kitchen garden.

Then a halt was called.

It was quite light now. As light as it would ever be beneath this leaden sky. Rain and snow still fell in gusts, driven by the blast.

Someone ordered Armand to dismount. It was probably Chauvelin. He did as he was told, and a trooper led him to the door of an irregular brick building that stood isolated on the right, extended on either side by a low wall, and surrounded by a patch of uncultivated land, which now looked like a sea of mud.

On ahead was the line of fortifications dimly outlined against the grey of the sky, and in between brown, sodden earth, with here and there a detached house, a cabbage patch, a couple of windmills deserted and desolate.

The loneliness of an unpopulated outlying quarter of the great mother city, a useless limb of her active body, an ostracised member of her vast family.

Mechanically Armand had followed the soldier to the door of the building. Here Chauvelin was standing and bade him follow. A smell of hot coffee hung in the dark narrow passage in front. Chauvelin led the way to a room on the left.

Still that smell of hot coffee. Ever after it was associated in Armand's mind with this awful morning in the guard-house of the Rue Ste. Anne, when the rain and snow beat against the windows, and he stood there in the low guard-room shivering and half-numbed with cold.

There was a table in the middle of the room, and on it stood cups of hot coffee. Chauvelin bade him drink, suggesting, not unkindly, that the warm beverage would do him good. Armand advanced further into the room and saw that there were wooden benches all round against the wall. On one of these sat his sister Marguerite.

When she saw him she made a sudden, instinctive movement to go to him, but Chauvelin interposed in his usual bland, quiet manner.

"Not just now, citizeness," he said.

She sat down again, and Armand noted how cold and stony seemed her eyes, as if life within her was at a stand-still, and a shadow that was almost like death had atrophied every emotion in her.

"I trust you have not suffered too much from the cold, Lady Blakeney," resumed Chauvelin politely; "we ought not to have kept you waiting here for so long, but delay at departure is sometimes inevitable."

She made no reply, only acknowledging his reiterated inquiry as to her comfort with an inclination of the head.

Armand had forced himself to swallow some coffee, and for the moment he felt less chilled. He held the cup between his two hands, and gradually some warmth crept into his bones.

"Little mother," he said in English, "try and drink some of this, it will do you good."

"Thank you, dear," she replied. "I have had some. I am not cold."

Then a door at the end of the room was pushed open, and Héron stalked in.

"Are we going to be all day in this confounded hole?" he queried roughly.

Armand, who was watching his sister very closely, saw that she started at the sight of the wretch, and seemed immediately to shrink still further within herself, whilst her eyes, suddenly luminous and dilated, rested on him like those of a captive bird upon an approaching cobra.

But Chauvelin was not to be shaken out of his suave manner.

"One moment, Citizen Héron," he said; "this coffee is very comforting. Is the prisoner with you?" he added lightly.

Héron nodded in the direction of the other room.

"In there," he said curtly.

"Then, perhaps, if you will be so good, citizen, to invite him thither, I could explain to him his future position and our own."

Héron muttered something between his fleshy lips, then he turned back towards the open door, solemnly spat twice on the threshold, and nodded his gaunt head once or twice in a manner which apparently was understood from within.

"No, sergeant, I don't want you," he said gruffly; "only the prisoner."

A second or two later Sir Percy Blakeney stood in the doorway; his hands were behind his back, obviously hand-cuffed, but he held himself very erect, though it was clear that this caused him a mighty effort. As soon as he had crossed the threshold his quick glance had swept right round the room.

He saw Armand, and his eyes lit up almost imperceptibly.

Then he caught sight of Marguerite, and his pale face took on suddenly a more ashen hue.

Chauvelin was watching him with those keen, light-coloured eyes of his. Blakeney, conscious of this, made no movement, only his lips tightened, and the heavy lids fell over the hollow eyes, completely hiding their glance.

But what even the most astute, most deadly enemy could not see was that subtle message of understanding that passed at once between Marguerite and the man she loved; it was a magnetic current, intangible, invisible to all save to her and to him. She was prepared to see him, prepared to see in him all that she had feared; the weakness, the mental exhaustion, the submission to the inevitable. Therefore, she had also schooled her glance to express to him all that she knew she would not be allowed to say—the reassurance that she had read his last letter, that she had obeyed it to the last word, save where Fate and her enemy had interfered with regard to herself.

With a slight, imperceptible movement—imperceptible to everyone save to him, she had seemed to handle a piece of paper in her kerchief, then she had nodded slowly, with her eyes—steadfast, reassuring—fixed upon him, and his glance gave answer that he had understood.

But Chauvelin and Héron had seen nothing of this. They were satisfied that there had been no communication between the prisoner and his wife and friend.

"You are no doubt surprised, Sir Percy," said Chauvelin after a while, "to see Lady Blakeney here. She, as well as citizen St. Just, will accompany our expedition to the place where you will lead us. We none of us know where that place is—Citizen Héron and myself are entirely in your hands—you might be leading us to certain death, or

471

again to a spot where your own escape would be an easy matter to yourself. You will not be surprised, therefore, that we have thought fit to take certain precautions both against any little ambuscade which you may have prepared for us, or against your making one of those daring attempts at escape for which the noted Scarlet Pimpernel is so justly famous."

He paused, and only Héron's low chuckle of satisfaction broke the momentary silence that followed. Blakeney made no reply. Obviously, he knew exactly what was coming. He knew Chauvelin and his ways, knew the kind of tortuous conception that would find origin in his brain; the moment that he saw Marguerite sitting there he must have guessed that Chauvelin once more desired to put her precious life in the balance of his intrigues.

"Citizen Héron is impatient, Sir Percy," resumed Chauvelin after a while, "so I must be brief. Lady Blakeney, as well as citizen St. Just, will accompany us on this expedition to whithersoever you may lead us. They will be the hostages which we will hold against your own good faith. At the slightest suspicion—a mere suspicion perhaps—that you have played us false, at a hint that you have led us into an ambush, or that the whole of this expedition has been but a trick on your part to effect your own escape, or if merely our hope of finding Capet at the end of our journey is frustrated, the lives of our two hostages belong to us, and your friend and your wife will be summarily shot before your eyes."

Outside the rain pattered against the window-panes, the gale whistled mournfully among the stunted trees, but within this room not a sound stirred the deadly stillness of the air, and yet at this moment hatred and love, savage lust and sublime self-abnegation—the most power full passions the heart of man can know—held three men here enchained; each a slave to his dominant passion, each ready to stake his all for the satisfaction of his master. Héron was the first to speak.

"Well!" he said with a fierce oath, "what are we waiting for? The prisoner knows how he stands. Now we can go."

"One moment, citizen," interposed Chauvelin, his quiet manner contrasting strangely with his colleague's savage mood. "You have quite understood, Sir Percy," he continued, directly addressing the prisoner, "the conditions under which we are all of us about to proceed on this journey?"

"All of us?" said Blakeney slowly. "Are you taking it for granted then that I accept your conditions and that I am prepared to proceed on the journey?"

"If you do not proceed on the journey," cried Héron with savage fury, "I'll strangle that woman with my own hands—now!"

Blakeney looked at him for a moment or two through half-closed lids, and it seemed then to those who knew him well, to those who loved him and to the man who hated him, that the mighty sinews almost cracked with the passionate desire to kill. Then the sunken eyes turned slowly to Marguerite, and she alone caught the look—it was a mere flash, of a humble appeal for pardon.

It was all over in a second; almost immediately the tension on the pale face relaxed, and into the eyes there came that look of acceptance—nearly akin to fatalism—an acceptance of which the strong alone are capable, for with them it only comes in the face of the inevitable.

Now he shrugged his broad shoulders, and once more turning to Héron he said quietly:

"You leave me no option in that case. As you have remarked before, Citizen Héron, why should we wait any longer? Surely we can now go."

CHAPTER 43

The Dreary Journey

Rain! Rain! Rain! Incessant, monotonous and dreary! The wind had changed round to the southwest. It blew now in great gusts that sent weird, sighing sounds through the trees, and drove the heavy showers into the faces of the men as they rode on, with heads bent forward against the gale.

The rain-sodden bridles slipped through their hands, bringing out sores and blisters on their palms; the horses were fidgety, tossing their heads with wearying persistence as the wet trickled into their ears, or the sharp, intermittent hailstones struck their sensitive noses.

Three days of this awful monotony, varied only by the halts at wayside inns, the changing of troops at one of the guard-houses on the way, the reiterated commands given to the fresh squad before starting on the next lap of this strange, momentous way; and all the while, audible above the clatter of horses' hoofs, the rumbling of coach-wheels—two closed carriages, each drawn by a pair of sturdy horses; which were changed at every halt. A soldier on each box urged them to a good pace to keep up with the troopers, who were allowed to go at an easy canter or light jog-trot, whatever might prove easiest and least fatiguing. And from time to time Héron's shaggy, gaunt head would appear at the window of one of the coaches, asking the way, the distance to the next city or to the nearest wayside inn; cursing the troopers, the coachman, his colleague and everyone concerned, blaspheming against the interminable length of the road, against the cold and against the wet.

Early in the evening on the second day of the journey he had met with an accident. The prisoner, who presumably was weak and weary, and not over steady on his feet, had fallen up against him as they were both about to re-enter the coach after a halt just outside Amiens, and Citizen Héron had lost his footing in the slippery mud of the road. His head came in violent contact with the step, and his right temple was severely cut. Since then he had been forced to wear a bandage across the top of his face, under his sugar-loaf hat, which had added nothing to his beauty, but a great deal to the violence of his temper. He wanted to push the men on, to force the pace, to shorten the halts; but Chauvelin knew better than to allow slackness and discontent to follow in the wake of over-fatigue.

The soldiers were always well rested and well fed, and though the delay caused by long and frequent halts must have been just as irksome to him as it was to Héron, yet he bore it imperturbably, for he would have had no use on this momentous journey for a handful of men whose enthusiasm and spirit had been blown away by the roughness of the gale, or drowned in the fury of the constant downpour of rain.

Of all this Marguerite had been conscious in a vague, dreamy kind of way. She seemed to herself like the spectator in a moving panoramic drama, unable to raise a finger or to do aught to stop that final, inevitable ending, the cataclysm of sorrow and misery that awaited her, when the dreary curtain would fall on the last act, and she and all the other spectators—Armand, Chauvelin, Héron, the soldiers—would slowly wend their way home, leaving the principal actor behind the fallen curtain, which never would be lifted again.

After that first halt in the guard-room of the Rue Ste. Anne she had been bidden to enter a second hackney coach, which, followed the other at a distance of fifty metres or so, and was, like that other, closely surrounded by a squad of mounted men.

Armand and Chauvelin rode in this carriage with her; all day she sat looking out on the endless monotony of the road, on the drops of rain that pattered against the window-glass and ran down from it like a perpetual stream of tears.

474

There were two halts called during the day—one for dinner and one, midway through the afternoon—when she and Armand would step out of the coach and be led—always with soldiers close around them—to some wayside inn, where some sort of a meal was served, where the atmosphere was close and stuffy and smelt of onion soup and of stale cheese.

Armand and Marguerite would in most cases have a room to themselves, with sentinels posted outside the door, and they would try and eat enough to keep body and soul together, for they would not allow their strength to fall away before the end of the journey was reached.

For the night halt—once at Beauvais and the second night at Abbeville—they were escorted to a house in the interior of the city, where they were accommodated with moderately clean lodgings. Sentinels, however, were always at their doors; they were prisoners in all but name, and had little or no privacy; for at night they were both so tired that they were glad to retire immediately, and to lie down on the hard beds that had been provided for them, even if sleep fled from their eyes, and their hearts and souls were flying through the city in search of him who filled their every thought.

Of Percy they saw little or nothing. In the daytime food was evidently brought to him in the carriage, for they did not see him get down, and on those two nights at Beauvais and Abbeville, when they caught sight of him stepping out of the coach outside the gates of the barracks, he was so surrounded by soldiers that they only saw the top of his head and his broad shoulders towering above those of the men.

Once Marguerite had put all her pride, all her dignity by, and asked Citizen Chauvelin for news of her husband.

"He is well and cheerful, Lady Blakeney," he had replied with his sarcastic smile. "Ah!" he added pleasantly, "those English are remarkable people. We, of Gallic breed, will never really understand them. Their fatalism is quite Oriental in its quiet resignation to the decree of Fate. Did you know, Lady Blakeney, that when Sir Percy was arrested he did not raise a hand. I thought, and so did my colleague, that he would have fought like a lion. And now, that he has no doubt realised that quiet submission will serve him best in the end, he is as calm on this journey as I am myself. In fact," he concluded complacently, "whenever I have succeeded in peeping into the coach I have invariably found Sir Percy Blakeney fast asleep."

"He—" she murmured, for it was so difficult to speak to this callous wretch, who was obviously mocking her in her misery—"he—

475

you—you are not keeping him in irons?"

"No! Oh no!" replied Chauvelin with perfect urbanity. "You see, now that we have you, Lady Blakeney, and citizen St. Just with us we have no reason to fear that that elusive Pimpernel will spirit himself away."

A hot retort had risen to Armand's lips. The warm Latin blood in him rebelled against this intolerable situation, the man's sneers in the face of Marguerite's anguish. But her restraining, gentle hand had already pressed his. What was the use of protesting, of insulting this brute, who cared nothing for the misery which he had caused so long as he gained his own ends?

And Armand held his tongue and tried to curb his temper, tried to cultivate a little of that fatalism which Chauvelin had said was characteristic of the English. He sat beside his sister, longing to comfort her, yet feeling that his very presence near her was an outrage and a sacrilege. She spoke so seldom to him, even when they were alone, that at times the awful thought which had more than once found birth in his weary brain became crystallised and more real. Did Marguerite guess? Had she the slightest suspicion that the awful cataclysm to which they were tending with every revolution of the creaking coach-wheels had been brought about by her brother's treacherous hand?

And when that thought had lodged itself quite snugly in his mind he began to wonder whether it would not be far more simple, far more easy, to end his miserable life in some manner that might suggest itself on the way. When the coach crossed one of those dilapidated, parapetless bridges, over abysses fifty metres deep, it might be so easy to throw open the carriage door and to take one final jump into eternity.

So easy—but so damnably cowardly.

Marguerite's near presence quickly brought him back to himself. His life was no longer his own to do with as he pleased; it belonged to the chief whom he had betrayed, to the sister whom he must endeavour to protect.

Of Jeanne now, he thought but little. He had put even the memory of her by—tenderly, like a sprig of lavender pressed between the faded leaves of his own happiness. His hand was no longer fit to hold that of any pure woman—his hand had on it a deep stain, immutable, like the brand of Cain.

Yet Marguerite beside him held his hand and together they looked out on that dreary, dreary road and listened to of the patter of the rain and the rumbling of the wheels of that other coach on ahead—and it was all so dismal and so horrible, the rain, the soughing of the wind in the stunted trees, this landscape of mud and desolation, this eternally grey sky.

CHAPTER 44

The Halt at Crecy

"Now, then, citizen, don't go to sleep; this is Crecy, our last halt!"

Armand woke up from his last dream. They had been moving steadily on since they left Abbeville soon after dawn; the rumble of the wheels, the swaying and rocking of the carriage, the interminable patter of the rain had lulled him into a kind of wakeful sleep.

Chauvelin had already alighted from the coach. He was helping Marguerite to descend. Armand shook the stiffness from his limbs and followed in the wake of his sister. Always those miserable soldiers round them, with their dank coats of rough blue cloth, and the red caps on their heads! Armand pulled Marguerite's hand through his arm and dragged her with him into the house.

The small city lay damp and grey before them; the rough pavement of the narrow street glistened with the wet, reflecting the dull, leaden sky overhead; the rain beat into the puddles; the slate-roofs shone in the cold wintry light.

This was Crecy! The last halt of the journey, so Chauvelin had said. The party had drawn rein in front of a small one-storeyed building that had a wooden verandah running the whole length of its front.

The usual low narrow room greeted Armand and Marguerite as they entered; the usual mildewed walls, with the colour wash flowing away in streaks from the unsympathetic beam above; the same device, "*Liberté, Egalité, Fraternité!*" scribbled in charcoal above the black iron stove; the usual musty, close atmosphere, the usual smell of onion and stale cheese, the usual hard straight benches and central table with its soiled and tattered cloth.

Marguerite seemed dazed and giddy; she had been five hours in that stuffy coach with nothing to distract her thoughts except the rain-sodden landscape, on which she had ceaselessly gazed since the early dawn.

Armand led her to the bench, and she sank down on it, numb and inert, resting her elbows on the table and her head in her hands.

"If it were only all over!" she sighed involuntarily. "Armand, at times now I feel as if I were not really sane—as if my reason had already given way! Tell me, do I seem mad to you at times?"

He sat down beside her and tried to chafe her little cold hands.

There was a knock at the door, and without waiting for permission Chauvelin entered the room.

"My humble apologies to you, Lady Blakeney," he said in his usual suave manner, "but our worthy host informs me that this is the only room in which he can serve a meal. Therefore, I am forced to intrude my presence upon you."

Though he spoke with outward politeness, his tone had become more peremptory, less bland, and he did not await Marguerite's reply before he sat down opposite to her and continued to talk airily.

"An ill-conditioned fellow, our host," he said—"quite reminds me of our friend Brogard at the Chat Gris in Calais. You remember him, Lady Blakeney?"

"My sister is giddy and over-tired," interposed Armand firmly. "I pray you, citizen, to have some regard for her."

"All regard in the world, Citizen St. Just," protested Chauvelin jovially. "Methought that those pleasant reminiscences would cheer her. Ah! here comes the soup," he added, as a man in blue blouse and breeches, with sabots on his feet, slouched into the room, carrying a tureen which he incontinently placed upon the table. "I feel sure that in England Lady Blakeney misses our excellent *croutes-au-pot*, the glory of our *bourgeois* cookery—Lady Blakeney, a little soup?"

"I thank you, sir," she murmured.

"Do try and eat something, little mother," Armand whispered in her ear; "try and keep up your strength for his sake, if not for mine."

She turned a wan, pale face to him, and tried to smile.

"I'll try, dear," she said.

"You have taken bread and meat to the citizens in the coach?" Chauvelin called out to the retreating figure of mine host.

"H'm!" grunted the latter in assent.

"And see that the citizen soldiers are well fed, or there will be trouble."

"H'm!" grunted the man again. After which he banged the door to behind him.

"Citizen Héron is loath to let the prisoner out of his sight," explained Chauvelin lightly, "now that we have reached the last, most important stage of our journey, so he is sharing Sir Percy's mid-day meal in the interior of the coach."

He ate his soup with a relish, ostentatiously paying many small attentions to Marguerite all the time. He ordered meat for her—bread, butter—asked if any dainties could be got. He was apparently in the best of tempers.

After he had eaten and drunk he rose and bowed ceremoniously to her.

"Your pardon, Lady Blakeney," he said, "but I must confer with the prisoner now, and take from him full directions for the continuance of our journey. After that I go to the guard-house, which is some distance from here, right at the other end of the city. We pick up a fresh squad here, twenty hardened troopers from a cavalry regiment usually stationed at Abbeville. They have had work to do in this town, which is a hot-bed of treachery. I must go inspect the men and the sergeant who will be in command. Citizen Héron leaves all these inspections to me; he likes to stay by his prisoner. In the meanwhile, you will be escorted back to your coach, where I pray you to await my arrival, when we change guard first, then proceed on our way."

Marguerite was longing to ask him many questions; once again she would have smothered her pride and begged for news of her husband, but Chauvelin did not wait. He hurried out of the room, and Armand and Marguerite could hear him ordering the soldiers to take them forthwith back to the coach.

As they came out of the inn they saw the other coach some fifty metres further up the street. The horses that had done duty since leaving Abbeville had been taken out, and two soldiers in ragged shirts, and with crimson caps set jauntily over their left ear, were leading the two fresh horses along. The troopers were still mounting guard round both the coaches; they would be relieved presently.

Marguerite would have given ten years of her life at this moment for the privilege of speaking to her husband, or even of seeing him—of seeing that he was well. A quick, wild plan sprang up in her mind that she would bribe the sergeant in command to grant her wish while Citizen Chauvelin was absent. The man had not an unkind face, and he must be very poor—people in France were very poor these days, though the rich had been robbed and luxurious homes devastated ostensibly to help the poor.

She was about to put this sudden thought into execution when Héron's hideous face, doubly hideous now with that bandage of doubtful cleanliness cutting across his brow, appeared at the carriage window.

He cursed violently and at the top of his voice.

"What are those d—d *aristos* doing out there?" he shouted.

"Just getting into the coach, citizen," replied the sergeant promptly.

And Armand and Marguerite were immediately ordered back into the coach.

Héron remained at the window for a few moments longer; he had a toothpick in his hand which he was using very freely.

"How much longer are we going to wait in this cursed hole?" he called out to the sergeant.

"Only a few moments longer, citizen. Citizen Chauvelin will be back soon with the guard."

A quarter of an hour later the clatter of cavalry horses on the rough, uneven pavement drew Marguerite's attention. She lowered the carriage window and looked out. Chauvelin had just returned with the new escort. He was on horseback; his horse's bridle, since he was but an indifferent horseman, was held by one of the troopers.

Outside the inn he dismounted; evidently, he had taken full command of the expedition, and scarcely referred to Héron, who spent most of his time cursing at the men or the weather when he was not lying half-asleep and partially drunk in the inside of the carriage.

The changing of the guard was now accomplished quietly and in perfect order. The new escort consisted of twenty mounted men, including a sergeant and a corporal, and of two drivers, one for each coach. The cortege now was filed up in marching order; ahead a small party of scouts, then the coach with Marguerite and Armand closely surrounded by mounted men, and at a short distance the second coach with Citizen Héron and the prisoner equally well guarded.

Chauvelin superintended all the arrangements himself. He spoke for some few moments with the sergeant, also with the driver of his own coach. He went to the window of the other carriage, probably in order to consult with Citizen Héron, or to take final directions from the prisoner, for Marguerite, who was watching him, saw him standing on the step and leaning well forward into the interior, whilst apparently, he was taking notes on a small tablet which he had in his hand.

A small knot of idlers had congregated in the narrow street; men in blouses and boys in ragged breeches lounged against the verandah of the inn and gazed with inexpressive, stolid eyes on the soldiers, the coaches, the citizen who wore the tricolour scarf. They had seen this sort of thing before now—*aristos* being conveyed to Paris under arrest, prisoners on their way to or from Amiens. They saw Marguerite's pale face at the carriage window. It was not the first woman's face they had seen under like circumstances, and there was no special interest about this *aristo*. They were smoking or spitting, or just lounging idly against the balustrade. Marguerite wondered if none of them had wife, sister, or mother, or child; if every sympathy, every kind of feeling in these poor wretches had been atrophied by misery or by fear.

At last everything was in order and the small party ready to start.

"Does anyone here know the Chapel of the Holy Sepulchre, close by the park of the Château d'Ourde?" asked Chauvelin, vaguely addressing the knot of gaffers that stood closest to him.

The men shook their heads. Some had dimly heard of the Château d'Ourde; it was some way in the interior of the forest of Boulogne, but no one knew about a chapel; people did not trouble about chapels nowadays. With the indifference so peculiar to local peasantry, these men knew no more of the surrounding country than the twelve or fifteen league circle that was within a walk of their sleepy little town.

One of the scouts on ahead turned in his saddle and spoke to Citizen Chauvelin:

"I think I know the way pretty well, Citizen Chauvelin," he said; "at any rate, I know it as far as the forest of Boulogne."

Chauvelin referred to his tablets.

"That's good," he said; "then when you reach the mile-stone that stands on this road at the confine of the forest, bear sharply to your right and skirt the wood until you see the hamlet of—Le—something. Le—Le—yes—Le Crocq—that's it in the valley below."

"I know Le Crocq, I think," said the trooper.

"Very well, then; at that point it seems that a wide road strikes at right angles into the interior of the forest; you follow that until a stone chapel with a colonnaded porch stands before you on your left, and the walls and gates of a park on your right. That is so, is it not, Sir Percy?" he added, once more turning towards the interior of the coach.

Apparently, the answer satisfied him, for he gave the quick word of command, "*En avant!*" then turned back towards his own coach and finally entered it.

"Do you know the Château d'Ourde, citizen St. Just?" he asked abruptly as soon as the carriage began to move.

Armand woke—as was habitual with him these days—from some gloomy reverie.

"Yes, citizen," he replied. "I know it."

"And the Chapel of the Holy Sepulchre?"

"Yes. I know it too."

Indeed, he knew the *château* well, and the little chapel in the forest, whither the fisher-folk from Portel and Boulogne came on a pilgrimage once a year to lay their nets on the miracle-working relic. The chapel was disused now. Since the owner of the *château* had fled no one had tended it, and the fisher-folk were afraid to wander out, lest their superstitious faith be counted against them by the authorities, who had abolished *le bon Dieu*.

But Armand had found refuge there eighteen months ago, on his way to Calais, when Percy had risked his life in order to save him—Armand—from death. He could have groaned aloud with the anguish of this recollection. But Marguerite's aching nerves had thrilled at the name.

The Château d'Ourde! The Chapel of the Holy Sepulchre! That was the place which Percy had mentioned in his letter, the place where he had given rendezvous to de Batz. Sir Andrew had said that the *Dauphin* could not possibly be there, yet Percy was leading his enemies thither, and had given the rendezvous there to de Batz. And this despite that whatever plans, whatever hopes, had been born in his mind when he was still immured in the *Conciergerie* prison must have been set at naught by the clever counter plot of Chauvelin and Héron.

"At the merest suspicion that you have played us false, at a hint that you have led us into an ambush, or if merely our hopes of finding Capet at the end of the journey are frustrated, the lives of your wife and of your friend are forfeit to us, and they will both be shot before your eyes."

With these words, with this precaution, those cunning fiends had effectually not only tied the schemer's hands but forced him either to deliver the child to them or to sacrifice his wife and his friend.

The impasse was so horrible that she could not face it even in her thoughts. A strange, fever-like heat coursed through her veins, yet left her hands icy-cold; she longed for, yet dreaded, the end of the journey—that awful grappling with the certainty of coming death. Perhaps, after all, Percy, too, had given up all hope. Long ago he had consecrated his life to the attainment of his own ideals; and there was a vein of fatalism in him; perhaps he had resigned himself to the inevitable, and his only desire now was to give up his life, as he had said, in the open, beneath God's sky, to draw his last breath with the storm-clouds tossed through infinity above him, and the murmur of the wind in the trees to sing him to rest.

Crecy was gradually fading into the distance, wrapped in a mantle of damp and mist. For a long while Marguerite could see the sloping slate roofs glimmering like steel in the grey afternoon light, and the quaint church tower with its beautiful lantern, through the pierced stonework of which shone patches of the leaden sky.

Then a sudden twist of the road hid the city from view; only the outlying churchyard remained in sight, with its white monuments and granite crosses, over which the dark yews, wet with the rain and shaken by the gale, sent showers of diamond-like sprays.

CHAPTER 45

The Forest of Boulogne

Progress was not easy, and very slow along the muddy road; the two coaches moved along laboriously, with wheels creaking and sinking deeply from time to time in the quagmire.

When the small party finally reached the edge of the wood the greyish light of this dismal day had changed in the west to a dull reddish glow—a glow that had neither brilliance nor incandescence in it; only a weird tint that hung over the horizon and turned the distance into lines of purple.

The nearness of the sea made itself already felt; there was a briny taste in the damp atmosphere, and the trees all turned their branches away in the same direction against the onslaught of the prevailing winds.

The road at this point formed a sharp fork, skirting the wood on either side, the forest lying like a black close mass of spruce and firs on the left, while the open expanse of country stretched out on the right. The south-westerly gale struck with full violence against the barrier of forest trees, bending the tall crests of the pines and causing their small dead branches to break and fall with a sharp, crisp sound like a cry of pain.

The squad had been fresh at starting; now the men had been four hours in the saddle under persistent rain and gusty wind; they were tired, and the atmosphere of the close, black forest so near the road was weighing upon their spirits.

Strange sounds came to them from out the dense network of trees—the screeching of night-birds, the weird call of the owls, the swift and furtive tread of wild beasts on the prowl. The cold winter and lack of food had lured the wolves from their fastnesses—hunger had emboldened them, and now, as gradually the grey light fled from the sky, dismal howls could be heard in the distance, and now and then a pair of eyes, bright with the reflection of the lurid western glow, would shine momentarily out of the darkness like tiny glow-worms, and as quickly vanish away.

The men shivered—more with vague superstitious fear than with cold. They would have urged their horses on, but the wheels of the coaches stuck persistently in the mud, and now and again a halt had to be called so that the spokes and axles might be cleared.

They rode on in silence. No one had a mind to speak, and the mournful soughing of the wind in the pine-trees seemed to check the words on every lip. The dull thud of hoofs in the soft road, the clang of steel bits and buckles, the snorting of the horses alone answered the wind, and also the monotonous creaking of the wheels ploughing through the ruts.

Soon the ruddy glow in the west faded into soft-toned purple and then into grey; finally, that too vanished. Darkness was drawing in on every side like a wide, black mantle pulled together closer and closer overhead by invisible giant hands.

The rain still fell in a thin drizzle that soaked through caps and coats, made the bridles slimy and the saddles slippery and damp. A veil of vapour hung over the horses' cruppers and was rendered fuller and thicker every moment with the breath that came from their nostrils. The wind no longer blew with gusty fury—its strength seemed to have been spent with the grey light of day—but now and then it would still come sweeping across the open country, and dash itself upon the wall of forest trees, lashing against the horses' ears, catching the corner of a mantle here, an ill-adjusted cap there, and wreaking its mischievous freak for a while, then with a sigh of satisfaction die, murmuring among the pines.

Suddenly there was a halt, much shouting, a volley of oaths from the drivers, and Citizen Chauvelin thrust his head out of the carriage window.

"What is it?" he asked.

"The scouts, citizen," replied the sergeant, who had been riding close to the coach door all this while; "they have returned."

"Tell one man to come straight to me and report."

Marguerite sat quite still. Indeed, she had almost ceased to live momentarily, for her spirit was absent from her body, which felt neither fatigue, nor cold, nor pain. But she heard the snorting of the horse close by as its rider pulled him up sharply beside the carriage door.

"Well?" said Chauvelin curtly.

"This is the cross-road, citizen," replied the man; "it strikes straight into the wood, and the hamlet of Le Crocq lies down in the valley on the right."

"Did you follow the road in the wood?"

"Yes, citizen. About two leagues from here there is a clearing with a small stone chapel, more like a large shrine, nestling among the trees. Opposite to it the angle of a high wall with large wrought-iron gates at the corner, and from these a wide drive leads through a park."

"Did you turn into the drive?"

"Only a little way, citizen. We thought we had best report first that all is safe."

"You saw no one?"

"No one."

"The *château*, then, lies some distance from the gates?"

"A league or more, citizen. Close to the gates there are outhouses and stabling, the disused buildings of the home farm, I should say."

"Good! We are on the right road, that is clear. Keep ahead with your men now, but only some two hundred metres or so. Stay!" he added, as if on second thoughts. "Ride down to the other coach and ask the prisoner if we are on the right track."

The rider turned his horse sharply round. Marguerite heard the clang of metal and the sound of retreating hoofs.

A few moments later the man returned.

"Yes, citizen," he reported, "the prisoner says it is quite right. The Château d'Ourde lies a full league from its gates. This is the nearest road to the chapel and the *château*. He says we should reach the former in half an hour. It will be very dark in there," he added with a significant nod in the direction of the wood.

Chauvelin made no reply, but quietly stepped out of the coach. Marguerite watched him, leaning out of the window, following his small trim figure as he pushed his way past the groups of mounted men, catching at a horse's bit now and then, or at a bridle, making a way for himself amongst the restless, champing animals, without the slightest hesitation or fear.

Soon his retreating figure lost its sharp outline silhouetted against the evening sky. It was enfolded in the veil of vapour which was blown out of the horses' nostrils or rising from their damp cruppers; it became more vague, almost ghost-like, through the mist and the fast-gathering gloom.

Presently a group of troopers hid him entirely from her view, but she could hear his thin, smooth voice quite clearly as he called to Citizen Héron.

"We are close to the end of our journey now, citizen," she heard him say. "If the prisoner has not played us false little Capet should be in our charge within the hour."

A growl not unlike those that came from out the mysterious depths of the forest answered him.

"If he is not," and Marguerite recognised the harsh tones of Citizen Héron—"if he is not, then two corpses will be rotting in this wood tomorrow for the wolves to feed on, and the prisoner will be on his way back to Paris with me."

Someone laughed. It might have been one of the troopers, more callous than his comrades, but to Marguerite the laugh had a strange, familiar ring in it, the echo of something long since past and gone.

Then Chauvelin's voice once more came clearly to her ear:

"My suggestion, citizen," he was saying, "is that the prisoner shall now give me an order—couched in whatever terms he may think necessary—but a distinct order to his friends to give up Capet to me without any resistance. I could then take some of the men with me, and ride as quickly as the light will allow up to the *château*, and take possession of it, of Capet, and of those who are with him. We could get along faster thus. One man can give up his horse to me and continue the journey on the box of your coach. The two carriages could then follow at foot pace. But I fear that if we stick together complete darkness will overtake us and we might find ourselves obliged to pass a very uncomfortable night in this wood."

"I won't spend another night in this suspense—it would kill me," growled Héron to the accompaniment of one of his choicest oaths. "You must do as you think right—you planned the whole of this affair—see to it that it works out well in the end."

"How many men shall I take with me? Our advance guard is here, of course."

"I couldn't spare you more than four more men—I shall want the others to guard the prisoners."

"Four men will be quite sufficient, with the four of the advance guard. That will leave you twelve men for guarding your prisoners, and you really only need to guard the woman—her life will answer for the others."

He had raised his voice when he said this, obviously intending that

Marguerite and Armand should hear.

"Then I'll ahead," he continued, apparently in answer to an assent from his colleague. "Sir Percy, will you be so kind as to scribble the necessary words on these tablets?"

There was a long pause, during which Marguerite heard plainly the long and dismal cry of a night bird that, mayhap, was seeking its mate. Then Chauvelin's voice was raised again.

"I thank you," he said; "this certainly should be quite effectual. And now, Citizen Héron, I do not think that under the circumstances we need fear an ambuscade or any kind of trickery—you hold the hostages. And if by any chance I and my men are attacked, or if we encounter armed resistance at the *château*, I will despatch a rider back straightway to you, and—well, you will know what to do."

His voice died away, merged in the soughing of the wind, drowned by the clang of metal, of horses snorting, of men living and breathing. Marguerite felt that beside her Armand had shuddered, and that in the darkness his trembling hand had sought and found hers.

She leaned well out of the window, trying to see. The gloom had gathered more closely in, and round her the veil of vapour from the horses' steaming cruppers hung heavily in the misty air. In front of her the straight lines of a few fir trees stood out dense and black against the greyness beyond, and between these lines purple tints of various tones and shades mingled one with the other, merging the horizon line with the sky. Here and there a more solid black patch indicated the tiny houses of the hamlet of Le Crocq far down in the valley below; from some of these houses small lights began to glimmer like blinking yellow eyes.

Marguerite's gaze, however, did not rest on the distant landscape—it tried to pierce the gloom that hid her immediate surroundings; the mounted men were all round the coach—more closely round her than the trees in the forest. But the horses were restless, moving all the time, and as they moved she caught glimpses of that other coach and of Chauvelin's ghostlike figure, walking rapidly through the mist. Just for one brief moment she saw the other coach, and Héron's head and shoulders leaning out of the window. His sugar-loaf hat was on his head, and the bandage across his brow looked like a sharp, pale streak below it.

"Do not doubt it, Citizen Chauvelin," he called out loudly in his harsh, raucous voice, "I shall know what to do; the wolves will have their meal tonight, and the guillotine will not be cheated either."

Armand put his arm round his sister's shoulders and gently drew her back into the carriage.

"Little mother," he said, "if you can think of a way whereby my life would redeem Percy's and yours, show me that way now."

But she replied quietly and firmly:

"There is no way, Armand. If there is, it is in the hands of God."

CHAPTER 46

Others in the Park

Chauvelin and his picked escort had in the meanwhile detached themselves from the main body of the squad. Soon the dull thud of their horses' hoofs treading the soft ground came more softly—then more softly still as they turned into the wood, and the purple shadows seemed to enfold every sound and finally to swallow them completely.

Armand and Marguerite from the depth of the carriage heard Héron's voice ordering his own driver now to take the lead. They sat quite still and watched, and presently the other coach passed them slowly on the road, its silhouette standing out ghostly and grim for a moment against the indigo tones of the distant country.

Héron's head, with its battered sugar-loaf hat, and the soiled bandage round the brow, was as usual out of the carriage window. He leered across at Marguerite when he saw the outline of her face framed by the window of the carriage.

"Say all the prayers you have ever known, citizeness," he said with a loud laugh, "that my friend Chauvelin may find Capet at the *château*, or else you may take a last look at the open country, for you will not see the sun rise on it tomorrow. It is one or the other, you know."

She tried not to look at him; the very sight of him filled her with horror—that blotched, gaunt face of his, the fleshy lips, that hideous bandage across his face that hid one of his eyes! She tried not to see him and not to hear him laugh.

Obviously, he too laboured under the stress of great excitement. So far everything had gone well; the prisoner had made no attempt at escape, and apparently did not mean to play a double game. But the crucial hour had come, and with it, darkness and the mysterious depths of the forest with their weird sounds and sudden flashes of ghostly lights. They naturally wrought on the nerves of men like Héron, whose conscience might have been dormant, but whose ears were nevertheless filled with the cries of innocent victims sacrificed to their own lustful ambitions and their blind, unreasoning hates.

He gave sharp orders to the men to close up round the carriages, and then gave the curt word of command:

"*En avant!*"

Marguerite could but strain her ears to listen. All her senses, all her faculties had merged into that of hearing, rendering it doubly keen. It seemed to her that she could distinguish the faint sound—that even as she listened grew fainter and fainter yet—of Chauvelin and his squad moving away rapidly into the thickness of the wood some distance already ahead.

Close to her there was the snorting of horses, the clanging and noise of moving mounted men. Héron's coach had taken the lead; she could hear the creaking of its wheels, the calls of the driver urging his beasts.

The diminished party was moving at foot-pace in the darkness that seemed to grow denser at every step, and through that silence which was so full of mysterious sounds.

The carriage rolled and rocked on its springs; Marguerite, giddy and overtired, lay back with closed eyes, her hand resting in that of Armand. Time, space and distance had ceased to be; only Death, the great Lord of all, had remained; he walked on ahead, scythe on skeleton shoulder, and beckoned patiently, but with a sure, grim hand.

There was another halt, the coach-wheels groaned and creaked on their axles, one or two horses reared with the sudden drawing up of the curb.

"What is it now?" came Héron's hoarse voice through the darkness.

"It is pitch-dark, citizen," was the response from ahead. "The drivers cannot see their horses' ears. They wait to know if they may light their lanthorns and then lead their horses."

"They can lead their horses," replied Héron roughly, "but I'll have no lanthorns lighted. We don't know what fools may be lurking behind trees, hoping to put a bullet through my head—or yours, sergeant—we don't want to make a lighted target of ourselves—what? But let the drivers lead their horses, and one or two of you who are riding greys might dismount too and lead the way—the greys would show up perhaps in this cursed blackness."

While his orders were being carried out, he called out once more:

"Are we far now from that confounded chapel?"

"We can't be far, citizen; the whole forest is not more than six leagues wide at any point, and we have gone two since we turned into it."

"Hush!" Héron's voice suddenly broke in hoarsely. "What was that? Silence, I say. Damn you—can't you hear?"

There was a hush—every ear straining to listen; but the horses were not still—they continued to champ their bits, to paw the ground, and to toss their heads, impatient to get on. Only now and again there would come a lull even through these sounds—a second or two, mayhap, of perfect, unbroken silence—and then it seemed as if right through the darkness a mysterious echo sent back those same sounds—the champing of bits, the pawing of soft ground, the tossing and snorting of animals, human life that breathed far out there among the trees.

"It is Citizen Chauvelin and his men," said the sergeant after a while, and speaking in a whisper.

"Silence—I want to hear," came the curt, hoarsely-whispered command.

Once more every one listened, the men hardly daring to breathe, clinging to their bridles and pulling on their horses' mouths, trying to keep them still, and again through the night there came like a faint echo which seemed to throw back those sounds that indicated the presence of men and of horses not very far away.

"Yes, it must be Citizen Chauvelin," said Héron at last; but the tone of his voice sounded as if he were anxious and only half convinced; "but I thought he would be at the *château* by now."

"He may have had to go at foot-pace; it is very dark, Citizen Héron," remarked the sergeant.

"*En avant*, then," quoth the other; "the sooner we come up with him the better."

And the squad of mounted men, the two coaches, the drivers and the advance section who were leading their horses slowly restarted on the way. The horses snorted, the bits and stirrups clanged, and the springs and wheels of the coaches creaked and groaned dismally as the ramshackle vehicles began once more to plough the carpet of pine-needles that lay thick upon the road.

But inside the carriage Armand and Marguerite held one another tightly by the hand.

"It is de Batz—with his friends," she whispered scarce above her breath.

"De Batz?" he asked vaguely and fearfully, for in the dark he could not see her face, and as he did not understand why she should suddenly be talking of de Batz he thought with horror that mayhap her prophecy anent herself had come true, and that her mind wearied and over-wrought—had become suddenly unhinged.

"Yes, de Batz," she replied. "Percy sent him a message, through me, to meet him—here. I am not mad, Armand," she added more calmly. "Sir Andrew took Percy's letter to de Batz the day that we started from Paris."

"Great God!" exclaimed Armand, and instinctively, with a sense of protection, he put his arms round his sister. "Then, if Chauvelin or the squad is attacked—if—"

"Yes," she said calmly; "if de Batz makes an attack on Chauvelin, or if he reaches the *château* first and tries to defend it, they will shoot us—Armand, and Percy."

"But is the *Dauphin* at the Château d'Ourde?"

"No, no! I think not."

"Then why should Percy have invoked the aid of de Batz? Now, when—"

"I don't know," she murmured helplessly. "Of course, when he wrote the letter he could not guess that they would hold us as hostages. He may have thought that under cover of darkness and of an unexpected attack he might have saved himself had he been alone; but now—now that you and I are here—Oh! it is all so horrible, and I cannot understand it all."

"Hark!" broke in Armand, suddenly gripping her arm more tightly.

"Halt!" rang the sergeant's voice through the night.

This time there was no mistaking the sound; already it came from no far distance. It was the sound of a man running and panting, and now and again calling out as he ran.

For a moment there was stillness in the very air, the wind itself was hushed between two gusts, even the rain had ceased its incessant pattering. Héron's harsh voice was raised in the stillness.

"What is it now?" he demanded.

"A runner, citizen," replied the sergeant, "coming through the wood from the right."

"From the right?" and the exclamation was accompanied by a volley of oaths; "the direction of the *château*? Chauvelin has been attacked; he is sending a messenger back to me. Sergeant—sergeant, close up round that coach; guard your prisoners as you value your life, and—"

The rest of his words were drowned in a yell of such violent fury that the horses, already over-nervous and fidgety, reared in mad terror, and the men had the greatest difficulty in holding them in. For a few minutes noisy confusion prevailed, until the men could quieten their quivering animals with soft words and gentle pattings.

Then the troopers obeyed, closing up round the coach wherein brother and sister sat huddled against one another.

One of the men said under his breath:

"Ah! but the citizen agent knows how to curse! One day he will break his gullet with the fury of his oaths."

In the meanwhile, the runner had come nearer, always at the same breathless speed.

The next moment he was challenged:

"*Qui va là?*"

"A friend!" he replied, panting and exhausted. "Where is Citizen Héron?"

"Here!" came the reply in a voice hoarse with passionate excitement. "Come up, damn you. Be quick!"

"A lanthorn, citizen," suggested one of the drivers.

"No—no—not now. Here! Where the devil are we?"

"We are close to the chapel on our left, citizen," said the sergeant.

The runner, whose eyes were no doubt accustomed to the gloom, had drawn nearer to the carriage.

"The gates of the *château*," he said, still somewhat breathlessly, "are just opposite here on the right, citizen. I have just come through them."

"Speak up, man!" and Héron's voice now sounded as if choked with passion. "Citizen Chauvelin sent you?"

"Yes. He bade me tell you that he has gained access to the *château*, and that Capet is not there."

A series of Citizen Héron's choicest oaths interrupted the man's speech. Then he was curtly ordered to proceed, and he resumed his report.

"Citizen Chauvelin rang at the door of the *château*; after a while he was admitted by an old servant, who appeared to be in charge, but the place seemed otherwise absolutely deserted—only—"

"Only what? Go on; what is it?"

"As we rode through the park it seemed to us as if we were being watched and followed. We heard distinctly the sound of horses behind and around us, but we could see nothing; and now, when I ran back, again I heard. There are others in the park tonight besides us, citizen."

There was silence after that. It seemed as if the flood of Héron's blasphemous eloquence had spent itself at last.

"Others in the park!" And now his voice was scarcely above a whisper, hoarse and trembling. "How many? Could you see?"

"No, citizen, we could not see; but there are horsemen lurking round the *château* now. Citizen Chauvelin took four men into the house with him and left the others on guard outside. He bade me tell you that it might be safer to send him a few more men if you could spare them. There are a number of disused farm buildings quite close to the gates, and he suggested that all the horses be put up there for the night, and that the men come up to the *château* on foot; it would be quicker and safer, for the darkness is intense."

Even while the man spoke the forest in the distance seemed to wake from its solemn silence, the wind on its wings brought sounds of life and movement different from the prowling of beasts or the screeching of night-birds. It was the furtive advance of men, the quick whispers of command, of encouragement, of the human animal preparing to attack his kind. But all in the distance still, all muffled, all furtive as yet.

"Sergeant!" It was Héron's voice, but it too was subdued, and almost calm now; "can you see the chapel?"

"More clearly, citizen," replied the sergeant. "It is on our left; quite a small building, I think."

"Then dismount and walk all round it. See that there are no windows or door in the rear."

There was a prolonged silence, during which those distant sounds of men moving, of furtive preparations for attack, struck distinctly through the night.

Marguerite and Armand, clinging to one another, not knowing what to think, nor yet what to fear, heard the sounds mingling with those immediately round them, and Marguerite murmured under her breath:

"It is de Batz and some of his friends; but what can they do? What can Percy hope for now?"

But of Percy she could hear and see nothing. The darkness and the silence had drawn their impenetrable veil between his unseen presence and her own consciousness. She could see the coach in which he was, but Héron's hideous personality, his head with its battered hat and soiled bandage, had seemed to obtrude itself always before her gaze, blotting out from her mind even the knowledge that Percy was there not fifty yards away from her.

So strong did this feeling grow in her that presently the awful dread seized upon her that he was no longer there; that he was dead, worn out with fatigue and illness brought on by terrible privations, or if not dead that he had swooned, that he was unconscious—his spirit absent from his body. She remembered that frightful yell of rage and hate which Héron had uttered a few minutes ago. Had the brute vented his fury on his helpless, weakened prisoner, and stilled forever those lips that, mayhap, had mocked him to the last?

Marguerite could not guess. She hardly knew what to hope. Vaguely, when the thought of Percy lying dead beside his enemy floated through her aching brain, she was almost conscious of a sense of relief at the thought that at least he would be spared the pain of the final, inevitable cataclysm.

Chapter 47

The Chapel of the Holy Sepulchre

The sergeant's voice broke in upon her misery.

The man had apparently done as the citizen agent had ordered and had closely examined the little building that stood on the left—a vague, black mass more dense than the surrounding gloom.

"It is all solid stone, citizen," he said; "iron gates in front, closed but not locked, rusty key in the lock, which turns quite easily; no windows or door in the rear."

"You are quite sure?"

"Quite certain, citizen; it is plain, solid stone at the back, and the only possible access to the interior is through the iron gate in front."

"Good."

Marguerite could only just hear Héron speaking to the sergeant. Darkness enveloped every form and deadened every sound. Even the harsh voice which she had learned to loathe and to dread sounded curiously subdued and unfamiliar. Héron no longer seemed inclined to storm, to rage, or to curse. The momentary danger, the thought of failure, the hope of revenge, had apparently cooled his temper, strengthened his determination, and forced his voice down to a little above a whisper. He gave his orders clearly and firmly, and the words came to Marguerite on the wings of the wind with strange distinctness, borne to her ears by the darkness itself, and the hush that lay over the wood.

"Take half a dozen men with you, sergeant," she heard him say, "and join Citizen Chauvelin at the *château*. You can stable your horses in the farm buildings close by, as he suggests and run to him on foot.

You and your men should quickly get the best of a handful of midnight prowlers; you are well armed and they only civilians. Tell Citizen Chauvelin that I in the meanwhile will take care of our prisoners. The Englishman I shall put in irons and lock up inside the chapel, with five men under the command of your corporal to guard him, the other two I will drive myself straight to Crecy with what is left of the escort. You understand?"

"Yes, citizen."

"We may not reach Crecy until two hours after midnight, but directly I arrive I will send Citizen Chauvelin further reinforcements, which, however, I hope may not necessary, but which will reach him in the early morning. Even if he is seriously attacked, he can, with fourteen men he will have with him, hold out inside the castle through the night. Tell him also that at dawn two prisoners who will be with me will be shot in the courtyard of the guard-house at Crecy, but that whether he has got hold of Capet or not he had best pick up the Englishman in the chapel in the morning and bring him straight to Crecy, where I shall be awaiting him ready to return to Paris. You understand?"

"Yes, citizen."

"Then repeat what I said."

"I am to take six men with me to reinforce Citizen Chauvelin now."

"Yes."

"And you, citizen, will drive straight back to Crecy, and will send us further reinforcements from there, which will reach us in the early morning."

"Yes."

"We are to hold the Citizen Chauvelin against those unknown marauders if necessary until the reinforcements come from Crecy. Having routed them, we return here, pick up the Englishman whom you will have locked up in the chapel under a strong guard commanded by Corporal Cassard, and join you forthwith at Crecy."

"This, whether Citizen Chauvelin has got hold of Capet or not."

"Yes, citizen, I understand," concluded the sergeant imperturbably; "and I am also to tell Citizen Chauvelin that the two prisoners will be shot at dawn in the courtyard of the guard-house at Crecy."

"Yes. That is all. Try to find the leader of the attacking party and bring him along to Crecy with the Englishman; but unless they are in very small numbers do not trouble about the others. Now *en avant*;

Citizen Chauvelin might be glad of your help. And—stay—order all the men to dismount and take the horses out of one of the coaches, then let the men you are taking with you each lead a horse, or even two, and stable them all in the farm buildings. I shall not need them and could not spare any of my men for the work later on. Remember that, above all, silence is the order. When you are ready to start, come back to me here."

The sergeant moved away, and Marguerite heard him transmitting the citizen agent's orders to the soldiers. The dismounting was carried on in wonderful silence—for silence had been one of the principal commands—only one or two words reached her ears.

"First section and first half of second section fall in, right wheel. First section each take two horses on the lead. Quietly now there; don't tug at his bridle—let him go."

And after that a simple report:

"All ready, citizen!"

"Good!" was the response. "Now detail your corporal and two men to come here to me, so that we may put the Englishman in irons, and take him at once to the chapel, and four men to stand guard at the doors of the other coach."

The necessary orders were given, and after that there came the curt command:

"*En avant!*"

The sergeant, with his squad and all the horses, was slowly moving away in the night. The horses' hoofs hardly made a noise on the soft carpet of pine-needles and of dead fallen leaves, but the champing of the bits was of course audible, and now and then the snorting of some poor, tired horse longing for its stable.

Somehow in Marguerite's fevered mind this departure of a squad of men seemed like the final flitting of her last hope; the slow agony of the familiar sounds, the retreating horses and soldiers moving away amongst the shadows, took on a weird significance. Héron had given his last orders. Percy, helpless and probably unconscious, would spend the night in that dank chapel, while she and Armand would be taken back to Crecy, driven to death like some insentient animals to the slaughter.

When the grey dawn would first begin to peep through the branches of the pines Percy would be led back to Paris and the guillotine, and she and Armand will have been sacrificed to the hatred and revenge of brutes.

The end had come, and there was nothing more to be done. Struggling, fighting, scheming, could be of no avail now; but she wanted to get to her husband; she wanted to be near him now that death was so imminent both for him and for her.

She tried to envisage it all, quite calmly, just as she knew that Percy would wish her to do. The inevitable end was there, and she would not give to these callous wretches here the gratuitous spectacle of a despairing woman fighting blindly against adverse Fate.

But she wanted to go to her husband. She felt that she could face death more easily on the morrow if she could but see him once, if she could but look once more into the eyes that had mirrored so much enthusiasm, such absolute vitality and whole-hearted self-sacrifice, and such an intensity of love and passion; if she could but kiss once more those lips that had smiled through life, and would smile, she knew, even in the face of death.

She tried to open the carriage door, but it was held from without, and a harsh voice cursed her, ordering her to sit still.

But she could lean out of the window and strain her eyes to see. They were by now accustomed to the gloom, the dilated pupils taking in pictures of vague forms moving like ghouls in the shadows. The other coach was not far, and she could hear Héron's voice, still subdued and calm, and the curses of the men. But not a sound from Percy.

"I think the prisoner is unconscious," she heard one of the men say.

"Lift him out of the carriage, then," was Héron's curt command; "and you go and throw open the chapel gates."

Marguerite saw it all. The movement, the crowd of men, two vague, black forms lifting another one, which appeared heavy and inert, out of the coach, and carrying it staggering up towards the chapel.

Then the forms disappeared, swallowed up by the more dense mass of the little building, merged in with it, immovable as the stone itself.

Only a few words reached her now.

"He is unconscious."

"Leave him there, then; he'll not move!"

"Now close the gates!"

There was a loud clang, and Marguerite gave a piercing scream. She tore at the handle of the carriage door.

"Armand, Armand, go to him!" she cried; and all her self-control, all her enforced calm, vanished in an outburst of wild, agonising passion. "Let me get to him, Armand! This is the end; get me to him, in the name of God!"

"Stop that woman screaming," came Héron's voice clearly through the night. "Put her and the other prisoner in irons—quick!"

But while Marguerite expended her feeble strength in a mad, pathetic effort to reach her husband, even now at this last hour, when all hope was dead and Death was so nigh, Armand had already wrenched the carriage door from the grasp of the soldier who was guarding it. He was of the South and knew the trick of charging an unsuspecting adversary with head thrust forward like a bull inside a ring. Thus, he knocked one of the soldiers down and made a quick rush for the chapel gates.

The men, attacked so suddenly and in such complete darkness, did not wait for orders. They closed in round Armand; one man drew his sabre and hacked away with it in aimless rage.

But for the moment he evaded them all, pushing his way through them, not heeding the blows that came on him from out the darkness. At last he reached the chapel. With one bound he was at the gate, his numb fingers fumbling for the lock, which he could not see.

It was a vigorous blow from Héron's fist that brought him at last to his knees, and even then, his hands did not relax their hold; they gripped the ornamental scroll of the gate, shook the gate itself in its rusty hinges, pushed and pulled with the unreasoning strength of despair. He had a sabre cut across his brow, and the blood flowed in a warm, trickling stream down his face. But of this he was unconscious; all that he wanted, all that he was striving for with agonising heartbeats and cracking sinews, was to get to his friend, who was lying in there unconscious, abandoned—dead, perhaps.

"Curse you," struck Héron's voice close to his ear. "Cannot some of you stop this raving maniac?"

Then it was that the heavy blow on his head caused him a sensation of sickness, and he fell on his knees, still gripping the ironwork.

Stronger hands than his were forcing him to loosen his hold; blows that hurt terribly rained on his numbed fingers; he felt himself dragged away, carried like an inert mass further and further from that gate which he would have given his lifeblood to force open.

And Marguerite heard all this from the inside of the coach where she was imprisoned as effectually as was Percy's unconscious body inside that dark chapel. She could hear the noise and scramble, and Héron's hoarse commands, the swift sabre strokes as they cut through the air.

Already a trooper had clapped irons on her wrists, two others held the carriage doors. Now Armand was lifted back into the coach, and she could not even help to make him comfortable, though as he was lifted in she heard him feebly moaning. Then the carriage doors were banged to again.

"Do not allow either of the prisoners out again, on peril of your lives!" came with a vigorous curse from Héron.

After which there was a moment's silence; whispered commands came spasmodically in deadened sound to her ear.

"Will the key turn?"

"Yes, citizen."

"All secure?"

"Yes, citizen. The prisoner is groaning."

"Let him groan."

"The empty coach, citizen? The horses have been taken out."

"Leave it standing where it is, then; Citizen Chauvelin will need it in the morning."

"Armand," whispered Marguerite inside the coach, "did you see Percy?"

"It was so dark," murmured Armand feebly; "but I saw him, just inside the gates, where they had laid him down. I heard him groaning. Oh, my God!"

"Hush, dear!" she said. "We can do nothing more, only die, as he lived, bravely and with a smile on our lips, in memory of him."

"Number 35 is wounded, citizen," said one of the men.

"Curse the fool who did the mischief," was the placid response. "Leave him here with the guard."

"How many of you are there left, then?" asked the same voice a moment later.

"Only two, citizen; if one whole section remains with me at the chapel door, and also the wounded man."

"Two are enough for me, and five are not too many at the chapel door." And Héron's coarse, cruel laugh echoed against the stone walls of the little chapel. "Now then, one of you get into the coach, and the other go to the horses' heads; and remember, Corporal Cassard, that you and your men who stay here to guard that chapel door are answerable to the whole nation with your lives for the safety of the Englishman."

The carriage door was thrown open, and a soldier stepped in and sat down opposite Marguerite and Armand. Héron in the meanwhile was apparently scrambling up the box. Marguerite could hear him muttering curses as he groped for the reins, and finally gathered them into his hand.

The springs of the coach creaked and groaned as the vehicle slowly swung round; the wheels ploughed deeply through the soft carpet of dead leaves.

Marguerite felt Armand's inert body leaning heavily against her shoulder.

"Are you in pain, dear?" she asked softly.

He made no reply, and she thought that he had fainted. It was better so; at least the next dreary hours would flit by for him in the blissful state of unconsciousness. Now at last the heavy carriage began to move more evenly. The soldier at the horses' heads was stepping along at a rapid pace.

Marguerite would have given much even now to look back once more at the dense black mass, blacker and denser than any shadow that had ever descended before on God's earth, which held between its cold, cruel walls all that she loved in the world.

But her wrists were fettered by the irons, which cut into her flesh when she moved. She could no longer lean out of the window, and she could not even hear. The whole forest was hushed, the wind was lulled to rest; wild beasts and night-birds were silent and still. And the wheels of the coach creaked in the ruts, bearing Marguerite with every turn further and further away from the man who lay helpless in the chapel of the Holy Sepulchre.

CHAPTER 48

The Waning Moon

Armand had wakened from his attack of faintness, and brother and sister sat close to one another, shoulder touching shoulder. That sense of nearness was the one tiny spark of comfort to both of them on this dreary, dreary way.

The coach had lumbered on unceasingly since all eternity—so it seemed to them both. Once there had been a brief halt, when Héron's rough voice had ordered the soldier at the horses' heads to climb on the box beside him, and once—it had been a very little while ago—a terrible cry of pain and terror had rung through the stillness of the night. Immediately after that the horses had been put at a more rapid pace, but it had seemed to Marguerite as if that one cry of pain had been repeated by several others which sounded more feeble and soon appeared to be dying away in the distance behind.

The soldier who sat opposite to them must have heard the cry too, for he jumped up, as if wakened from sleep, and put his head out of the window.

"Did you hear that cry, citizen?" he asked.

But only a curse answered him, and a peremptory command not to lose sight of the prisoners by poking his head out of the window.

"Did you hear the cry?" asked the soldier of Marguerite as he made haste to obey.

"Yes! What could it be?" she murmured.

"It seems dangerous to drive so fast in this darkness," muttered the soldier.

After which remark he, with the stolidity peculiar to his kind, figuratively shrugged his shoulders, detaching himself, as it were, of the whole affair.

"We should be out of the forest by now," he remarked in an undertone a little while later; "the way seemed shorter before."

Just then the coach gave an unexpected lurch to one side, and after much groaning and creaking of axles and springs it came to a standstill, and the citizen agent was heard cursing loudly and then scrambling down from the box.

The next moment the carriage-door was pulled open from without, and the harsh voice called out peremptorily:

"Citizen soldier, here—quick!—quick!—curse you!—we'll have one of the horses down if you don't hurry!"

The soldier struggled to his feet; it was never good to be slow in obeying the citizen agent's commands. He was half-asleep and no doubt numb with cold and long sitting still; to accelerate his movements he was suddenly gripped by the arm and dragged incontinently out of the coach.

Then the door was slammed to again, either by a rough hand or a sudden gust of wind, Marguerite could not tell; she heard a cry of rage and one of terror, and Héron's raucous curses. She cowered in the corner of the carriage with Armand's head against her shoulder and tried to close her ears to all those hideous sounds.

Then suddenly all the sounds were hushed and all around everything became perfectly calm and still—so still that at first the silence oppressed her with a vague, nameless dread. It was as if Nature herself had paused, that she might listen; and the silence became more and more absolute, until Marguerite could hear Armand's soft, regular breathing close to her ear.

The window nearest to her was open, and as she leaned forward with that paralysing sense of oppression a breath of pure air struck full upon her nostrils and brought with it a briny taste as if from the sea.

It was not quite so dark; and there was a sense as of open country stretching out to the limits of the horizon. Overhead a vague greyish light suffused the sky, and the wind swept the clouds in great rolling banks right across that light.

Marguerite gazed upward with a more calm feeling that was akin to gratitude. That pale light, though so wan and feeble, was thrice welcome after that inky blackness wherein shadows were less dark than the lights. She watched eagerly the bank of clouds driven by the dying gale.

The light grew brighter and faintly golden, now the banks of clouds—storm-tossed and fleecy—raced past one another, parted and reunited like veils of unseen giant dancers waved by hands that controlled infinite space—advanced and rushed and slackened speed again—united and finally torn asunder to reveal the waning moon, honey-coloured and mysterious, rising as if from an invisible ocean far away.

The wan pale light spread over the wide stretch of country, throwing over it as it spread dull tones of indigo and of blue. Here and there sparse, stunted trees with fringed gaunt arms bending to prevailing winds proclaimed the neighbourhood of the sea.

Marguerite gazed on the picture which the waning moon had so suddenly revealed; but she gazed with eyes that knew not what they saw. The moon had risen on her right—there lay the east—and the coach must have been travelling due north, whereas Crecy—

In the absolute silence that reigned she could perceive from far, very far away, the sound of a church clock striking the midnight hour; and now it seemed to her supersensitive senses that a firm footstep was treading the soft earth, a footstep that drew nearer—and then nearer still.

Nature did pause to listen. The wind was hushed, the night-birds in the forest had gone to rest. Marguerite's heart beat so fast that its throbbings choked her, and a dizziness clouded her consciousness.

But through this state of torpor she heard the opening of the carriage door, she felt the onrush of that pure, briny air, and she felt a long, burning kiss upon her hands.

She thought then that she was really dead, and that God in His infinite love had opened to her the outer gates of Paradise.

"My love!" she murmured.

She was leaning back in the carriage and her eyes were closed, but she felt that firm fingers removed the irons from her wrists, and that a pair of warm lips were pressed there in their stead.

"There, little woman, that's better so—is it not? Now let me get hold of poor old Armand!"

It was Heaven, of course, else how could earth hold such heavenly joy?

"Percy!" exclaimed Armand in an awed voice.

"Hush, dear!" murmured Marguerite feebly; "we are in Heaven you and I—"

Whereupon a ringing laugh woke the echoes of the silent night.

"In Heaven, dear heart!" And the voice had a delicious earthly ring in its whole-hearted merriment. "Please God, you'll both be at Portel with me before dawn."

Then she was indeed forced to believe. She put out her hands and groped for him, for it was dark inside the carriage; she groped, and felt his massive shoulders leaning across the body of the coach, while his fingers busied themselves with the irons on Armand's wrist.

"Don't touch that brute's filthy coat with your dainty fingers, dear heart," he said gaily. "Great Lord! I have worn that wretch's clothes for over two hours; I feel as if the dirt had penetrated to my bones."

Then with that gesture so habitual to him he took her head between his two hands and drawing her to him until the wan light from without lit up the face that he worshipped, he gazed his fill into her eyes.

She could only see the outline of his head silhouetted against the wind-tossed sky; she could not see his eyes, nor his lips, but she felt his nearness, and the happiness of that almost caused her to swoon.

"Come out into the open, my lady fair," he murmured, and though she could not see, she could feel that he smiled; "let God's pure air blow through your hair and round your dear head. Then, if you can walk so far, there's a small half-way house close by here. I have knocked up the none too amiable host. You and Armand could have half an hour's rest there before we go further on our way."

"But you, Percy?—are you safe?"

"Yes, m'dear, we are all of us safe until morning-time enough to reach Le Portel, and to be aboard the *Daydream* before mine amiable friend M. Chambertin has discovered his worthy colleague lying gagged and bound inside the chapel of the Holy Sepulchre. By Gad!

how old Héron will curse—the moment he can open his mouth!"

He half helped, half lifted her out of the carriage. The strong pure air suddenly rushing right through to her lungs made her feel faint, and she almost fell. But it was good to feel herself falling, when one pair of arms amongst the millions on the earth were there to receive her.

"Can you walk, dear heart?" he asked. "Lean well on me—it is not far, and the rest will do you good."

"But you, Percy—"

He laughed, and the most complete joy of living seemed to resound through that laugh. Her arm was in his, and for one moment he stood still while his eyes swept the far reaches of the country, the mellow distance still wrapped in its mantle of indigo, still untouched by the mysterious light of the waning moon.

He pressed her arm against his heart, but his right hand was stretched out towards the black wall of the forest behind him, towards the dark crests of the pines in which the dying wind sent its last mournful sighs.

"Dear heart," he said, and his voice quivered with the intensity of his excitement, "beyond the stretch of that wood, from far away over there, there are cries and moans of anguish that come to my ear even now. But for you, dear, I would cross that wood tonight and re-enter Paris tomorrow. But for you, dear—but for you," he reiterated earnestly as he pressed her closer to him, for a bitter cry had risen to her lips.

She went on in silence. Her happiness was great—as great as was her pain. She had found him again, the man whom she worshipped, the husband whom she thought never to see again on earth. She had found him, and not even now—not after those terrible weeks of misery and suffering unspeakable—could she feel that love had triumphed over the wild, adventurous spirit, the reckless enthusiasm, the ardour of self-sacrifice.

CHAPTER 49

The Land of Eldorado

It seems that in the pocket of Héron's coat there was a letter-case with some few hundred *francs*. It was amusing to think that the brute's money helped to bribe the ill-tempered keeper of the half-way house to receive guests at midnight, and to ply them well with food, drink, and the shelter of a stuffy coffee-room.

Marguerite sat silently beside her husband, her hand in his. Armand, opposite to them, had both elbows on the table. He looked pale and wan, with a bandage across his forehead, and his glowing eyes were resting on his chief.

"Yes! you demmed young idiot," said Blakeney merrily, "you nearly upset my plan in the end, with your yelling and screaming outside the chapel gates."

"I wanted to get to you, Percy. I thought those brutes had got you there inside that building."

"Not they!" he exclaimed. "It was my friend Héron whom they had trussed and gagged, and whom my amiable friend M. Chambertin will find in there tomorrow morning. By Gad! I would go back if only for the pleasure of hearing Héron curse when first the gag is taken from his mouth."

"But how was it all done, Percy? And there was de Batz——"

"De Batz was part of the scheme I had planned for mine own escape before I knew that those brutes meant to take Marguerite and you as hostages for my good behaviour. What I hoped then was that under cover of a tussle or a fight I could somehow or other contrive to slip through their fingers. It was a chance, and you know my belief in bald-headed Fortune, with the one solitary hair. Well, I meant to grab that hair; and at the worst I could but die in the open and not caged in that awful hole like some noxious vermin. I knew that de Batz would rise to the bait. I told him in my letter that the *Dauphin* would be at the Château d'Ourde this night, but that I feared the Revolutionary Government had got wind of this fact and were sending an armed escort to bring the lad away. This letter Ffoulkes took to him; I knew that he would make a vigorous effort to get the *Dauphin* into his hands, and that during the scuffle that one hair on Fortune's head would for one second only, mayhap, come within my reach. I had so planned the expedition that we were bound to arrive at the forest of Boulogne by nightfall, and night is always a useful ally. But at the guard-house of the Rue Ste. Anne I realised for the first time that those brutes had pressed me into a tighter corner than I had preconceived."

He paused, and once again that look of recklessness swept over his face, and his eyes—still hollow and circled—shone with the excitement of past memories.

"I was such a weak, miserable wretch, then," he said, in answer to Marguerite's appeal. "I had to try and build up some strength, when——

Heaven forgive me for the sacrilege—I had unwittingly risked your precious life, dear heart, in that blind endeavour to save mine own. By Gad! it was no easy task in that jolting vehicle with that noisome wretch beside me for sole company; yet I ate and I drank and I slept for three days and two nights, until the hour when in the darkness I struck Héron from behind, half-strangled him first, then gagged him, and finally slipped into his filthy coat and put that loathsome bandage across my head, and his battered hat above it all. The yell he gave when first I attacked him made every horse rear—you must remember it—the noise effectually drowned our last scuffle in the coach. Chauvelin was the only man who might have suspected what had occurred, but he had gone on ahead, and bald-headed Fortune had passed by me, and I had managed to grab its one hair. After that it was all quite easy. The sergeant and the soldiers had seen very little of Héron and nothing of me; it did not take a great effort to deceive them, and the darkness of the night was my most faithful friend. His raucous voice was not difficult to imitate, and darkness always muffles and changes every tone. Anyway, it was not likely that those loutish soldiers would even remotely suspect the trick that was being played on them. The citizen agent's orders were promptly and implicitly obeyed. The men never even thought to wonder that after insisting on an escort of twenty he should drive off with two prisoners and only two men to guard them. If they did wonder, it was not theirs to question. Those two troopers are spending an uncomfortable night somewhere in the forest of Boulogne, each tied to a tree, and some two leagues apart one from the other. And now," he added gaily, "*en voiture*, my fair lady; and you, too, Armand. 'Tis seven leagues to Le Portel, and we must be there before dawn."

"Sir Andrew's intention was to make for Calais first, there to open communication with the *Daydream* and then for Le Portel," said Marguerite; "after that he meant to strike back for the Chateau d'Ourde in search of me."

"Then we'll still find him at Le Portel—I shall know how to lay hands on him; but you two must get aboard the *Daydream* at once, for Ffoulkes and I can always look after ourselves."

It was one hour after midnight when—refreshed with food and rest—Marguerite, Armand and Sir Percy left the half-way house. Marguerite was standing in the doorway ready to go. Percy and Armand had gone ahead to bring the coach along.

"Percy," whispered Armand, "Marguerite does not know?"

"Of course, she does not, you young fool," retorted Percy lightly. "If you try and tell her I think I would smash your head."

"But you—" said the young man with sudden vehemence; "can you bear the sight of me? My God! when I think—"

"Don't think, my good Armand—not of that anyway. Only think of the woman for whose sake you committed a crime—if she is pure and good, woo her and win her—not just now, for it were foolish to go back to Paris after her, but *anon*, when she comes to England and all these past days are forgotten—then love her as much as you can, Armand. Learn your lesson of love better than I have learnt mine; do not cause Jeanne Lange those tears of anguish which my mad spirit brings to your sister's eyes. You were right, Armand, when you said that I do not know how to love!"

But on board the *Daydream*, when all danger was past, Marguerite felt that he did.

LEONAUR

ALSO FROM LEONAUR
AVAILABLE IN SOFTCOVER OR HARDCOVER WITH DUST JACKET

MR MUKERJI'S GHOSTS *by S. Mukerji*—Supernatural tales from the British Raj period by India's Ghost story collector.

KIPLINGS GHOSTS *by Rudyard Kipling*—Twelve stories of Ghosts, Hauntings, Curses, Werewolves & Magic.

THE COLLECTED SUPERNATURAL AND WEIRD FICTION OF WASHINGTON IRVING: VOLUME 1 *by Washington Irving*—Including one novel 'A History of New York', and nine short stories of the Strange and Unusual.

THE COLLECTED SUPERNATURAL AND WEIRD FICTION OF WASHINGTON IRVING: VOLUME 2 *by Washington Irving*—Including three novelettes 'The Legend of the Sleepy Hollow', 'Dolph Heyliger', 'The Adventure of the Black Fisherman' and thirty-two short stories of the Strange and Unusual.

THE COLLECTED SUPERNATURAL AND WEIRD FICTION OF JOHN KENDRICK BANGS: VOLUME 1 *by John Kendrick Bangs*—Including one novel 'Toppleton's Client or A Spirit in Exile', and ten short stories of the Strange and Unusual.

THE COLLECTED SUPERNATURAL AND WEIRD FICTION OF JOHN KENDRICK BANGS: VOLUME 2 *by John Kendrick Bangs*—Including four novellas 'A House-Boat on the Styx', 'The Pursuit of the House-Boat', 'The Enchanted Typewriter' and 'Mr. Munchausen' of the Strange and Unusual.

THE COLLECTED SUPERNATURAL AND WEIRD FICTION OF JOHN KENDRICK BANGS: VOLUME 3 *by John Kendrick Bangs*—Including twor novellas 'Olympian Nights', 'Roger Camerden: A Strange Story', and ten short stories of the Strange and Unusual.

THE COLLECTED SUPERNATURAL AND WEIRD FICTION OF MARY SHELLEY: VOLUME 1 *by Mary Shelley*—Including one novel 'Frankenstein or the Modern Prometheus', and fourteen short stories of the Strange and Unusual.

THE COLLECTED SUPERNATURAL AND WEIRD FICTION OF MARY SHELLEY: VOLUME 2 *by Mary Shelley*—Including one novel 'The Last Man', and three short stories of the Strange and Unusual.

THE COLLECTED SUPERNATURAL AND WEIRD FICTION OF AMELIA B. EDWARDS *by Amelia B. Edwards*—Contains two novelettes 'Monsieur Maurice', and 'The Discovery of the Treasure Isles', one ballad 'A Legend of Boisguilbert' and seventeen short stories to cill the blood.

LEONAUR

ALSO FROM LEONAUR

AVAILABLE IN SOFTCOVER OR HARDCOVER WITH DUST JACKET

THE COLLECTED SCIENCE FICTION AND FANTASY OF STANLEY G. WEINBAUM 1—INTERPLANETARY ODYSSEYS *by Stanley G. Weinbaum*—Classic Tales of Interplanetary Adventure Including: A Martian Odyssey, its Sequel Valley of Dreams, the Complete 'Ham' Hammond Stories and Others.

THE COLLECTED SCIENCE FICTION AND FANTASY OF STANLEY G. WEINBAUM 2—OTHER EARTHS *by Stanley G. Weinbaum*—Classic Futuristic Tales Including: *Dawn of Flame* & its Sequel The Black Flame, plus The Revolution of 1960 & Others.

THE COLLECTED SCIENCE FICTION AND FANTASY OF STANLEY G. WEINBAUM 3—STRANGE GENIUS *by Stanley G. Weinbaum*—Classic Tales of the Human Mind at Work Including the Complete Novel The New Adam, the 'van Manderpootz' Stories and Others.

THE COLLECTED SCIENCE FICTION AND FANTASY OF STANLEY G. WEINBAUM 4—THE BLACK HEART *by Stanley G. Weinbaum*—Classic Strange Tales Including: the Complete Novel The Dark Other, Plus Proteus Island and Others.

THE COLLECTED SCIENCE FICTION & FANTASY OF JACK LONDON 1—BEFORE ADAM & OTHER STORIES *by Jack London*—included in this Volume Before Adam The Scarlet Plague A Relic of the Pliocene When the World Was Young The Red One Planchette A Thousand Deaths Goliah A Curious Fragment The Rejuvenation of Major Rathbone.

THE COLLECTED SCIENCE FICTION & FANTASY OF JACK LONDON 2—THE IRON HEEL & OTHER STORIES *by Jack London*—included in this Volume The Iron Heel The Enemy of All the World The Shadow and the Flash The Strength of the Strong The Unparalleled Invasion The Dream of Debs.

THE COLLECTED SCIENCE FICTION & FANTASY OF JACK LONDON 3—THE STAR ROVER & OTHER STORIES *by Jack London*—included in this Volume The Star Rover The Minions of Midas The Eternity of Forms The Man With the Gash.

Printed in the USA
CPSIA information can be obtained
at www.ICGtesting.com
LVHW041328211023
761731LV00004B/10/J